EX LIBRIS

VINTAGE CLASSICS

ALSO BY ANDREY PLATONOV

The Foundation Pit

Soul

Happy Moscow

The Return and Other Stories

Fourteen Little Red Huts

ANDREY PLATONOV

Andrey Platonovich Platonov (1899–1951) began publishing poems and articles in 1918, while studying engineering. Between 1927 and 1932 he wrote his most politically controversial works, some of them first published in Russian only in the 1990s. After reading his story 'For Future Use', Stalin referred to Platonov as 'an agent of our enemies'. From September 1942, after being recommended to the chief editor of *Red Star* by his friend Vasily Grossman, Platonov worked as a war correspondent. He died in 1951, of tuberculosis caught from his son, who had spent three years in the Gulag. *Happy Moscow*, one of his finest novels, was first published in Russia only in 1991; letters, notebook entries and unfinished stories continue to appear.

ROBERT AND ELIZABETH CHANDLER

Robert Chandler's translations from Russian include works by Alexander Pushkin, Andrey Platonov, Vasily Grossman and Hamid Ismailov. He is the editor and main translator of *Russian Short Stories from Pushkin to Buida* and *Russian Magic Tales from Pushkin to Platonov*; together with Boris Dralyuk and Irina Mashinski, he has co-edited *The Penguin Book of Russian Poetry*. He first translated some sample extracts from *Chevengur* well over 40 years ago. His next publications will be another collection of Teffi and a selection of poems by Apollinaire and his Russian comtemporary Velimir Khlebnikov. He has run regular translation workshops in London and worked as a mentor for the British Centre for Literary Translation.

Elizabeth Chandler is a co-translator, with her husband, of Pushkin's *The Captain's Daughter* and of several works by Andrey Platonov and Vasily Grossman.

1 3 5 7 9 10 8 6 4 2

Vintage Classics is part of the Penguin Random House group of companies
Vintage, Penguin Random House UK,
One Embassy Gardens, 8 Viaduct Gardens, London SW11 7BW

Penguin Random House UK

First published by Harvill Secker in 2023
This edition published in Vintage Classics in 2025

penguin.co.uk/vintage-classics
global.penguinrandomhouse.com

A CIP catalogue record for this book is available from the British Library

ISBN 9781784879150

Printed and bound in Great Britain by Clays Ltd, Elcograf S.p.A.

The authorised representative in the EEA is Penguin Random House Ireland,
Morrison Chambers, 32 Nassau Street, Dublin D02 YH68

Penguin Random House is committed to a sustainable future for our business, our readers and our planet. This book is made from Forest Stewardship Council® certified paper.

FSC www.fsc.org MIX Paper | Supporting responsible forestry FSC® C018179

ANDREY PLATONOV

CHEVENGUR

TRANSLATED FROM THE RUSSIAN BY

Robert Chandler and Elizabeth Chandler

VINTAGE CLASSICS

CONTENTS

INTRODUCTION

I

THE SON of a railway worker who also gilded the cupolas of churches, the writer we now know as Andrey Platonov was born at the turn of a century—on September 1, 1899—and between town and country, on the edge of the Central Russian city of Voronezh. It seems fitting that Platonov should have been born so close to important boundaries in both time and space; in his mature work he seems to delight in eliding every conceivable boundary—between animal and human, between the animate and the inanimate, between souls and machines, between life and death. He writes about spiritual matters in material terms and about the material world in spiritual terms. He was not an Orthodox Christian, yet his work is full of biblical allusions and imbued with deep religious feeling. He was a passionate supporter of the 1917 October Revolution and remained sympathetic to the dream that gave birth to it, yet no one has written more searingly of its consequences. His status in the Soviet literary world was equally borderline. In 1929, *Chevengur* was typeset and a single copy was printed; the editors then decided against publication. In 1939 a selection of his literary criticism met with the same fate. Other stories were published during his lifetime, but many were immediately subjected to harsh official criticism.

The eldest of eleven children, he began work at age thirteen—in an office, then in a factory, then as an assistant engine driver. As a young writer, he adopted the pseudonym Platonov, a shortened form of his patronymic; his father's name was Platon Klimentov. He began publishing poems and articles in the local press in 1918. Whether he took part in active fighting during the Civil War is unclear; at one point he was attached to the Red Army as a journalist and propaganda worker and sent to the town of Novokhopiorsk, where he witnessed six changes of power in a single month. In 1921 he graduated from Voronezh Polytechnic. From 1922 to 1926 he worked in the province, first as an electrical engineer, then as a land-reclamation expert. In 1926 he and his wife and son moved to Moscow. Except for the war years, when he served as a correspondent for the army newspaper *Red Star*, he remained there until his death from tuberculosis in 1951.

In 1931, Platonov published "For Future Use"—a long story about collectivization and peasant life. This enraged Stalin, who notoriously wrote the word *Bastard* in the margin and severely reprimanded Alexander Fadeyev, the editor of the journal that had published the story. This left Platonov unable to publish for several years. In 1937, however, he published a small selection of stories titled *The River Potudan*. Between 1936 and 1940, he also published a number of unusual literary critical articles.

Between 1942 and 1946, he brought out seven small collections of war stories; with a few exceptions, these are weaker than his other mature work. In 1946, however, he published one of his very finest short stories, "The Return." This account of an army captain's troubled homecoming is tender, witty, and wise—and it probably accurately reflects the experience of millions of families. Nevertheless, since it lacked the then-obligatory tone of triumphant optimism, it evoked particularly vicious criticism. After that, Platonov was unable to publish any more of his own work, though the support of his influential friend Mikhail Sholokhov enabled him to publish two collections of adaptations of traditional folktales. The first—Bashkir folktales—is well written, but it does not greatly differ from other literary versions of similar folktales. The second—comprising seven Russian folktales—is another of Platonov's masterpieces. He makes few changes to the plots, and his stylistic changes are discrete—yet these versions are quintessential Platonov; they embody all his deepest concerns.

Platonov died of tuberculosis in 1951; he had caught the disease while nursing his son, who had been infected in the Gulag, after being convicted on a trumped-up charge of terrorism.

2

As a young man, between 1919 and 1921, Platonov published more than a hundred journalistic articles and one small volume of poetry. In 1921, however, shocked by the worst drought and famine for thirty years, he abandoned literature for more practical work. "Being someone technically qualified," he wrote, "I was unable to continue to engage in contemplative work such as literature."[1] During the mid-1920s he supervised the digging of no fewer than 763 ponds and 331 wells, as well as the draining of 2,400 acres of swamps and the building of three small rural power stations.[2]

Platonov's early work is clearly and boldly written. He believed that science and socialism were about to transform the world, and the evident sincerity and passion of his beliefs is touching. Nevertheless, these poems and articles would have been largely forgotten were it not for the stories and novels he wrote after his return to literature in late 1926. The suddenness with which Platonov turned into a major writer is astonishing. In a little over two years, while continuing to do other demanding jobs, he produced a body of work enough to establish him as one of Russia's greatest writers. He composed not only several of his best stories—"The Locks of Epifan" (January 1927), "The Town of Townsville" (March–May 1927), "The Innermost Man" (April–May 1927), and "Inhabitant of the State" (1927, month unknown)—but also his one completed long novel, *Chevengur* (summer 1927–May 1929). *Chevengur* is not only a remarkable novel in its own right, it also contains the seeds of many of Platonov's later works: the short novel *The Foundation Pit* (1930) develops the most confrontational of the exchanges in *Chevengur* between the Bolsheviks and anti-Soviet peasants; *Soul* (1935) is a much-expanded version of the chapters about the lost, orphaned, destitute people Platonov refers to in *Chevengur* as "others"; and *Happy Moscow* (1933–36) develops the chapter of *Chevengur* set in Moscow.

It is, of course, impossible to establish the deeper reasons for so extraordinary a burst of creativity. We can say a little, however, about some of the external triggers. First, in June 1926, Platonov was appointed deputy responsible secretary to the Central Bureau of Land Reclamation Specialists. This was an important position and it entitled him and his family to a Moscow residence permit and an apartment in the prestigious "House of Specialists," a large building providing accommodation for the Soviet cultural, political, and scientific elite. For a while, it seemed that Platonov's talent and his five years of dedicated work in land reclamation had been recognized. Within two months, however, he had been dismissed from his post and he and his family were threatened with eviction from their apartment. The cause of his conflict with the authorities is obscure; it may well have been his dogged independence of mind. All we know for sure, however, is that Platonov was in despair. He had no way of providing for his wife and young son. He was selling precious textbooks without which he feared he might be unable to work. At times, he contemplated suicide.

Fellow engineers from the Land Management Commissariat lent Platonov money, knowing he would be unable to return the loan, and eventually managed to find him work, in charge of land reclamation in the province of Tambov. He was aware, however, that he would not be welcomed in Tambov. The province had been a center of peasant resistance to the Soviet authorities and—unlike in his home city of Voronezh—he had few friends or allies in the town. Knowing he might be unable to stay long, he moved there alone in early December 1926, leaving his wife and son in Moscow. Life in Tambov proved as difficult as he feared. He felt deeply lonely and met with constant opposition in his work. He even received death threats.

Despite all this—or perhaps, because of it—he was miraculously successful in the creative work to which he suddenly and wholeheartedly returned. In a letter to his wife (January 5–6, 1927), he wrote, somewhat startlingly, "I'll stop now, my work on Peter's Volga–Don

Canal is waiting for me. There's very little historical material, really nothing at all. Once again I must lie on top of my 'muse.' She alone won't betray me. In 'Ethereal Tract' I raped 150 pages out of her. While I have a heart, a brain and this wild, dark will to create, my 'muse' will not betray me. She and I are one. Soulwise, my muse is my sex."[3] And a month later, on his return from ten days of travel, he wrote, "My journey around the province was difficult. In Kozlov I spent the night at the railway station. [...] I slept in Third Class, along with the unemployed. I learned much that is cruel and new from them. They have come from the Caucasus and are on their way to Siberia. In the morning I drank tea with them, treated them and listened to their unusual stories. Life is more difficult, my warm little crumb, than one can imagine. Wandering about these back-of-beyond parts, I've seen such sad things that I ceased to believe that luxurious Moscow, art, and suchlike still exist somewhere. But it seems to me that real art and real thought can only be born in such a back of beyond. [...] There are such sad places that even the least bit of happiness is shaming."[4]

Natalia Kornienko, the chief editor of the definitive edition of Platonov's work, has compared Platonov's three months in Tambov with Pushkin's famous "Boldino autumn," when he too was isolated for several months in the depths of provincial Russia. The comparison is just; Platonov did not write as many masterpieces in Tambov as Pushkin did in Boldino, but in one respect his "Tambov winter" was more important still. It was in Tambov that Platonov became a great writer; Pushkin, on the other hand, had achieved greatness long before his Boldino autumn.

Kornienko goes on to point out that Platonov consciously turned to Pushkin for inspiration during these months. In his letters to his wife, Platonov alludes several times to Pushkin's letters. On November 4, 1830, Pushkin wrote to his friend Anton Delvig, "I've written an abyss [*propast'*—in English we would more commonly say 'a mass' or 'a mountain'] of polemical articles"; on January 30, 1927, Platonov wrote, "I've written such an abyss [*propast'*] that my hand is now shaking."

Pushkin said that he had written his historical study *A History of the Pugachov Rebellion* "for himself." And in a letter to his friend Nikolay Pogodin, he wrote, "Literature was once a noble, aristocratic field. Now it is a louse-ridden marketplace."[5] Platonov, who at the time was also planning to write about the eighteenth-century Cossack rebel Yemelian Pugachov, alludes to both these remarks, writing, "In Pugachov I want to work *for myself,* not for the market—may it be damned!"[6]

Platonov's letters from Tambov include many other highly charged mentions of his writing. The most striking is this:

> Two days ago I experienced a great horror. I woke in the night—my bed is hard and uncomfortable. The night was weakly lit by a late moon, and there at the table beside the stove, just where I usually sit, I saw *myself.* This isn't some horror, Masha, this is something more serious. Lying in bed, I saw how I was also sitting at the table, half smiling, and writing swiftly. The I that was writing did not once look up and I couldn't see my tears on his face. When I wanted to jump up or shout, nothing in me would obey. I looked out through the window, but all I saw was the usual dim night sky. Looking again at the earlier place, I found I was not to be seen there.
>
> For the first time I have seen my living self—with an uncertain and ambiguous smile, in the colorless night gloom. I can't shake off this vision and there's no getting away from a terrifying presentiment... I once dreamed that I was speaking with Mikhail Kirpichnikov [from Platonov's story "Ethereal Tract"], and a day later I killed him off.[7]

It is hard to know what to make of this account—whether to understand it as a sign of some dangerous psychic split or as Platonov's discovery of his true vocation. It may, however, help us to grasp what so sharply distinguishes Platonov's mature work from his juvenilia. Irony entails the ability to see something from more than one point of view, and this nighttime "vision" shows Platonov looking at himself from outside. The early poems and articles entirely lack irony, whereas irony pervades almost every page of the mature work.

In *Chevengur* much of this irony is directed at Platonov's younger self. Sasha Dvanov, the novel's central figure, is clearly a self-portrait, and his surname is derived from the Russian *dva*, meaning "two." The duality suggested by this manifests itself in more than one way. Not only does Sasha have two "external" doubles—Proshka Dvanov, his hardheaded stepbrother, and Simon Serbinov, who represents the more skeptical Platonov of the late 1920s—but he also has two ways of interacting with the world. Sometimes he is an active, determined participant in events; sometimes he is a passive, mediumistic figure, with an insatiable need to enter into other things and beings—people, birds, animals, a locomotive, even a wooden fence—and merge with them.

Platonov's most extended discussion of this duality comes soon after an account of Sasha's narrow escape from being murdered by a band of anarchists:

> But inside every man there also lives a little onlooker—he takes no part in either his actions or suffering and is always dispassionate and always the same. His work is to see and to witness, but he has no say in a man's life and no one knows the reason for his solitary existence.[...]
>
> While Dvanov was a long way from himself and on the move, this onlooker saw everything within him, although he never warned or helped him. He lived parallel to Dvanov, but he was not Dvanov.
>
> He existed like a dead brother; everything human seemed to be present in him, but something slight and important was missing.[...]
>
> This onlooker is the eunuch of a man's soul. Here is what he witnessed.

The words about "the eunuch of a man's soul" are a far cry from "Soulwise, my muse is my sex." Nevertheless, they too relate to the act of writing. And the pages of *Chevengur* immediately following this passage can certainly be read as an account of what this eunuch witnessed, even if only in dream.

3

In March 1927 Platonov resigned from his position in Tambov and returned to Moscow, writing, "I preferred to be workless in Moscow than to fail in my Tambov work and so ruin my reputation. [...] Once again I was in Moscow without work and almost without hope."[8] As he had feared, he and his family were evicted from the House of Specialists and they had to rent a room privately. They also stayed for several months in a dacha belonging to Boris Pilniak, with whom Platonov collaborated for some time in 1927 and 1928.

Throughout the late 1920s, Platonov was publishing stories in Moscow journals and writing texts for the "radio newspaper" titled *Peasant Radio*. He also published three collections of stories. He was unable, however, to earn a living from writing alone, and in October 1927 he returned to work for the Land Management Commissariat. He also served as a correspondent for the newspaper *Socialist Agriculture*. No notebooks survive from the years 1927–29, but Platonov's earlier experience in land reclamation, together with these later assignments, evidently gave him a deep understanding of the reality of Russian village life.

Other writers who visited collective farms did so as members of Writers' Brigades—and were, of course, shown only a few model collective farms. Platonov, however, saw what was really happening and did not try to close his eyes to it. In August 1931 he was sent by the People's Commissariat of Agriculture to report on the progress of collectivization in the Central Volga and Northern Caucasus regions. The following notebook entry is one of many, all equally direct: "State Farm No. 22 'The Swineherd.' Building work—25% of the plan has been carried out. There are no nails, iron, timber [...] milkmaids have been running away, men have been sent after them on horseback and the women have been forced to work. This has led to cases of suicide . . . Loss of livestock—89–90%."[9] It is astonishing that Platonov dared to write so truthfully, even in a private notebook, when the official press was reporting only ever-greater success. This note was written two years after the completion of *Chevengur*, but many chapters of the novel are clearly informed by similar observations.

Platonov's journeys in the Central Russian steppe provided him with material not only for *Chevengur* but also for several other works: *The Foundation Pit*, the long stories "For Future Use" and "Sea of Youth," two film scripts, and two full-length plays. None of these was published in Platonov's lifetime except "For Future Use." To a reader unversed in Soviet history, these works may seem like the wildest of black fantasy—yet there is barely a page that does not directly relate to some real event from that time.

Some scholars have attended exclusively to Platonov's reflection of historical reality, often creating the impression that this is his only concern. Others have written about his stories' religious and mythological subtexts. Readers coming to Platonov's work for the first time often feel entranced but bewildered, unsure how to orient themselves in his shifting, unfamiliar world. Different layers of the texts flicker in and out of focus. One and the same chapter can at first seem to be a psychological vignette, then to resemble some ancient religious text and then to be evoking a political and historical reality so extraordinary as to be barely credible. The real and the surreal, the factual and the mythological, become hard to tell apart.

Chevengur is also unusually rich in sensory detail; Platonov's ability to evoke the smells, sounds, and atmosphere of a particular place and time is equal to that of D. H. Lawrence. This abundance of detail, along with Platonov's lack of interest in conventional plotting and character development, has led some critics to see the novel as lacking in structure. In terms of themes and symbolism, however, the novel is entirely coherent. Every incident or conversation relates to a few central concerns: the possibility of bringing about true communism, people's longing to overcome death, and a sense of orphanhood that is shared by almost all the characters.

Orphanhood—exile from home and family—is the most fundamental form of exile, and it is those without home or family, those with no stake in the world as it exists, who are most open to the seduction of utopian fantasies. The late critic and scholar Vitaly Shentalinksy once said to me that the true hero of *Chevengur* was the Russian people as a whole—as a collective orphan, deprived by the revolution of both their Mother Earth and their Father in Heaven. This at once brought to my mind a passage from *Chevengur*, a retort made by an angry peasant to one of the Bolsheviks: "All very clever. You give us the land, then confiscate every last grain we grow on it. Well, if that's the way it is, may you choke on that land. The only land left to us peasants now is the horizon. Who do you think you're fooling?" This peasant appears in only a single episode of *Chevengur*, but it is often minor characters who most clearly voice Platonov's own thoughts. There was indeed nothing left to the Russian people but the horizon—nothing but an ever-receding line of light, a shining *no-place* (the literal meaning of the word *utopia*), and the webs of delusion that can be spun from words.

4

Platonov's first plan for what would become *Chevengur* is titled "Maturing Star" and is dated 1927.[10] The first part is set in 1906–14, in a workers' settlement close to a locomotive works. Platonov writes:

> I shall try to show the complexity and depth of the working man, as a being with a muscular brain and a full-blooded heart. I shall oppose schematicness and oversimplification. I knew such workers personally—the so-called masses.
>
> The hero—the young son of a man employed in the locomotive works—is intelligent and impressionable. He reads a lot; he attempts suicide; he gets carried away by religion. For a while, he lives alone in a cave; then he joins a religious sect—"religious anarchists."

Shaken by news of his beloved father's death in an accident at the factory, the hero returns home, forgets religion, and looks for salvation elsewhere. He falls in love and, at the same time, is drawn into terrorist activities. In 1917 he joins the Bolsheviks. Within a few years he becomes an important engineer and throws himself into constructive work. "A new sense of life and the world. Love is transformed into sunny, combative feeling. Excavators are working and canals are being dug on the sites of the battles of the Civil War. The novel's last chapters carry a reborn mankind over a resonant, wise, maturing earth. A world that is almost fantastic. Yet there is nothing unfamiliar to us—it is our years, our earth, seen from a particular point of view."

Platonov incorporated several elements from this first plan into his final version of *Chevengur*. Sasha Dvanov has much in common with the hero of this plan; like him, he is a spiritual searcher and something of an engineer. Several major themes—suicide, anarchy, religious sectarianism, the accidental death of a father figure—remain important, though they are developed in different ways. Nevertheless, the tone of the final version is different. "Maturing Star" was to be written in a major key; *Chevengur* is written in a minor key. There is ambiguity about the ending, but it can certainly be seen as despairing. This is a pattern that Platonov would repeat many times in his career. He often appears to have planned to write upbeat works that would be accepted for publication—and then gone on to write something utterly unpublishable. He was, one might say, betrayed by his own talent, by his clear-minded and often ironic perception of Soviet reality.

The next stage in the composition of *Chevengur* was a draft, nearly two-thirds the length of the finished novel, titled "Builders of the Country." Many passages from this were incorporated verbatim into *Chevengur*. Two of the more obvious changes are that the earlier version is a first-person narrative and that the love story between the hero and his girlfriend, central to the draft, is almost omitted from the finished novel. Platonov was clearly feeling his way. In the course of revision, he omitted a great deal, often with the effect of making his authorial standpoint more ambiguous. The final version is a richly textured, multilayered patchwork. It is often uncertain whether a particular passage is being told by the narrator, or whether it is a rendition of the thoughts of an individual character. Because of the many flashbacks, it can also be difficult to determine the order of the events narrated. This may be an unintended effect of Platonov's changes of mind, but it is more likely that he consciously chose to imbue the latter chapters with something of the elusiveness of a dream.

The first part of the novel deals with the transition from an agricultural to an industrial society. Zakhar Pavlovich, the main character in these chapters, is a gifted craftsman modeled on Platonov's father. Like Platonov's father, Zakhar Pavlovich moves from traditional village life to the new world of factories and railways. For some time, he is in love with steam locomotives but is eventually disillusioned, realizing that machines do nothing to prevent human misery.

The second part is picaresque and satirical. Sasha Dvanov, Zakhar Pavlovich's adopted son, rides about the province along with Kopionkin, a reincarnation of Don Quixote. Kopionkin's name is derived from the Russian *kopio*, meaning "spear," and his Dulcinea is the German-Polish-Jewish revolutionary Rosa Luxemburg. Dvanov and Kopionkin visit villages and communes, hoping to find evidence of a spontaneous birth of true communism in the depth of the steppe.

The third part is set in Chevengur itself, a fictional town probably modeled on the real town of Boguchar, a center of Russian sectarianism where Platonov spent several months in the mid-1920s, building wells and a small power station. In this fictional steppe town, which appears to belong both to this world and to some other world of dream or legend, a group of fanatical Bolsheviks make a determined attempt to establish communism. They begin by exterminating first the bourgeoisie and then the half-bourgeoisie, believing that this will inevitably bring about communism, since nothing else will be left. They also repeatedly relocate all the town's buildings, so that property will become worn out and cease to oppress people. Eventually, however, Sasha Dvanov—in many respects, a Christ figure—arrives in Chevengur, and a more constructive and democratic communism is established under his guidance. This gentler regime, however, proves short lived. Chevengur is attacked and destroyed by a cavalry detachment; whether this is the White Guard or the Red Army is left unclear.

5

During the four decades between his death in 1951 and the collapse of the Soviet Union in 1991, a great deal of "intelligentsia folklore" sprang up around the image of Platonov. It was widely believed that he had been totally excluded from the literary world and had worked as a yardman. In reality, he remained a member of the Writers' Union until his death, and he and his family lived alongside other professional Soviet writers in an apartment of the Literary Institute. Being a naturally tidy person who enjoyed physical work, he sometimes *chose* to sweep the institute's yard.

There is no doubt that Platonov showed immense courage and determination in staying true to his creative vision, despite being unable to publish much of his best work. Nevertheless, the romantic image of Platonov as solitary hero has led people to underestimate the amount of help he received from more established figures. Not only did he benefit from the support of Vasily Grossman and Mikhail Sholokhov at critical moments during and after the war, but he also had generous mentors and backers at the beginning of his career. One of these was the journalist and editor Georgy Litvin-Molotov (1898–1972). Litvin-Molotov not only published Platonov's first book, the poetry collection *The Blue Depth* (1922), but also wrote a preface to it; and in 1927 and 1928, as chief editor of the monthly *Molodaia Gvardia* ("Young Guard"), he published two short collections of his prose, titled *The Locks of Epifan* and *The Innermost Man*.

Litvin-Molotov admired Platonov and the two men were friends. In a copy of *The Locks of Epifan* that he presented to Litvin-Molotov, Platonov wrote, "To Georgy Zakharovich Litvin-Molotov, to whom I am indebted for what is best and purest in my past and perhaps also in my future. With a deep love, that nothing will disturb."[11] And at some point, probably in mid-1927, Platonov gave Litvin-Molotov a draft copy of "Builders of the Country." Litvin-Molotov was clearly aware both of Platonov's gifts and of the danger to which these gifts exposed him; he responded with a long list of criticisms, but the sensitivity of these criticisms and the care with which he expresses them is moving. Litvin-Molotov begins by comparing the "healthy" feeling awoken in the reader by Platonov's earlier "Innermost Man" with the "generally negative" feeling awoken by "Builders of the Country." His central objections are that the criticisms of the revolution made by two anarchists are all too often proved right; that the Communists in the novel are portrayed as eccentric and ineffectual; and that "the author appears to have set himself the goal of demonstrating that the construction of socialism in one country is impossible. This—on the day after the Party has censured the opposition for putting forward exactly this view!" After making constructive suggestions for changes to each chapter, Litvin-Molotov ends, "If this were a bad work, I would not be writing all this. It is a good work, but for entirely comprehensible reasons it cannot be *acceptable* for publication in its present state. I want to warn you now, in order for you to correct it and erase the impression it creates—an impression that you yourself have said you did not in the least intend to evoke in the reader."[12]

In 1928 Platonov published two extracts from *Chevengur* in the literary journal *Krasnaia nov'* ("Red Virgin Soil"); in 1929 the first section, titled "Origin of a Master," came out, along with four other short works, as a small book. Platonov tried doggedly to publish *Chevengur* as a whole, but without success. In August 1929 he appealed to Maxim Gorky, the most authoritative literary figure of the time, writing:

> I ask you to read my manuscript. It is not being published (it has been refused by *Federatsia*). They say that the Revolution is incorrectly portrayed in the novel and that the work as a whole will be seen as counterrevolutionary. But I worked with

> very different feelings and now I don't know what to do. I am turning to you to ask you to read the manuscript and, if you agree, to say that the author is correct and that the novel constitutes an honest attempt to portray the beginning of a communist society.[13]

Like Litvin-Molotov, Gorky recognized Platonov's gifts. He replied in a similar tone:

> That you are talented is beyond doubt. It is also beyond doubt that you are a master of a very distinctive language. Your novel is extremely interesting. Its technical failings are its extreme prolixity, an excess of conversation and the fading away of the novel's "action." All this is especially noticeable in its second half.
>
> But, for all its indisputable worth, I do not think that your work will be published. Your anarchist frame of mind—evidently characteristic of your "spirit"—makes this difficult. Whatever you may have wished, you have portrayed reality in a lyrico-satirical light that is, of course, unacceptable to our censorship. For all the tenderness with which you relate to your characters, they are ironically colored and to the reader they seem simply "eccentrics" and "half-wits," rather than revolutionaries. I am not saying that this has been done intentionally, merely that this is the way it is. That is the reader's impression, i.e., my own impression. I may be mistaken.[14]

This is a thoughtful, sensitive, and evidently sincere response. Shortly afterward, Gorky wrote to Platonov again, suggesting that he adapt part of the novel for the theater: "This thought is inspired by your language. From the stage, from the lips of intelligent actors, it would sound brilliant. The presence in your work of humor—of lyrical humor—makes it clear that you could write a play. [...] In your psyche—as I see it—there is a kinship to Gogol. So: try your hand at comedy rather than more serious drama."[15] Platonov had in fact recently "tried his hand" at comedy. The previous year, in collaboration with Boris Pilniak, he had written a play titled *Fools on the Periphery.* That Gorky did not know this makes his suggestion all the more impressive.

Gorky continued to do what he could to help Platonov. In early 1934 he arranged for Platonov to be included in a "brigade" of writers to be sent to Central Asia with the aim of publishing a collective work in celebration of ten years of Soviet Turkmenistan. The collective work never appeared, but the assignment led to Platonov returning to Central Asia for several months in 1935 and to the composition of *Soul*, another masterpiece published only years after his death.

"Origin of a Master" was republished in several posthumous Soviet selections of Platonov's work, but *Chevengur* as a whole remained unpublished for many years. An incomplete Russian text was published in Paris in 1972; the first Soviet edition was published only in 1988. An initial English translation, marred by serious errors, was published in 1978. The first important Western cultural figure to give Platonov his due was probably the Italian poet and film director Pier Paolo Pasolini. Reviewing *Chevengur* in February 1973, he refers to the first eighty pages as "one of the most beautiful things [*una delle cose più belle*] in Russian literature." He sees Platonov as the equal of Mandelstam and Bulgakov and ends with special praise for the clarity of the narrative voice of this "entrancing poet" (*adorabile poeta*).[16]

—Robert Chandler

2022

CHRONOLOGY

All dates are New Style. That is, they are given in terms of the Gregorian calendar we use today.

1891	Opening of the Moscow–Voronezh–Kyiv railway line.
1891–92	A serious famine, which begins in the Volga valley and spreads as far as the Urals and the Black Sea, causes 375,000 to 400,000 deaths. The effects of a severe drought are compounded by government incompetence—above all, by a delay in banning the export of grain. Widespread public anger may contribute to a rebirth of Russian revolutionary movements.
1899	August 28. Birth of Andrey Platonovich Klimentov—now generally known by his pen name, Andrey Platonov—in Yamskaia Sloboda, on the outskirts of the city of Voronezh, about three hundred miles south of Moscow.
1913	Lavish official celebrations throughout the Russian empire of the tercentenary of the Romanov dynasty.
1914–18	First World War.
1917	March 8–16. The February Revolution—a spontaneous revolution that topples the Romanov monarchy.
1917	November 7. The October Revolution—the Bolshevik Party seizes power in a coup.
1917–22	November–October. Russian Civil War, accompanied by the draconian economic policies known as War Communism. Millions are killed before the Red Army, led by

Leon Trotsky, defeats the main White forces in 1920. Smaller battles continue for the next two years.

1921 After an uprising in March 1921 by sailors at the naval base of Kronstadt, Lenin makes a tactical retreat, introducing the somewhat more liberal New Economic Policy (NEP). Many of the more idealistic Communists see this as a shameful compromise with the forces of capitalism. The NEP, which continues until 1928, is not accompanied by any political liberalization.

This year also sees catastrophic drought and famine, worst of all in the Volga valley. Having published one collection of poems and at least two hundred social, political, and scientific articles, Platonov abandons literature for work as an engineer and land-reclamation expert, organizing the draining of swamps and the digging of ponds and wells.

1924 Death of Lenin. Petrograd is renamed Leningrad. Stalin begins to take over power.

1926 Platonov and his family move to Moscow. Platonov then moves to Tambov.

1929 Publication of Platonov's *Origin of a Master.*

1929–30 Winter. "Total Collectivization" of Soviet agriculture. Platonov evokes this tragic period in *The Foundation Pit*, a short novel first published only long after his death.

1938 May. Platonov's fifteen-year-old son, Platon, is arrested as a "terrorist" and "spy." He is sentenced to ten years in the Gulag, where he contracts tuberculosis.

1940 October. Platon is released from the Gulag.

1943 January. Platon dies of tuberculosis.

1951 January. Platonov dies of tuberculosis, having been infected by his son.

1972 First publication of *Chevengur* (Paris: YMCA Press).

1988 First Soviet publication of *Chevengur,* in the journal *Druzhba narodov.*

CHEVENGUR

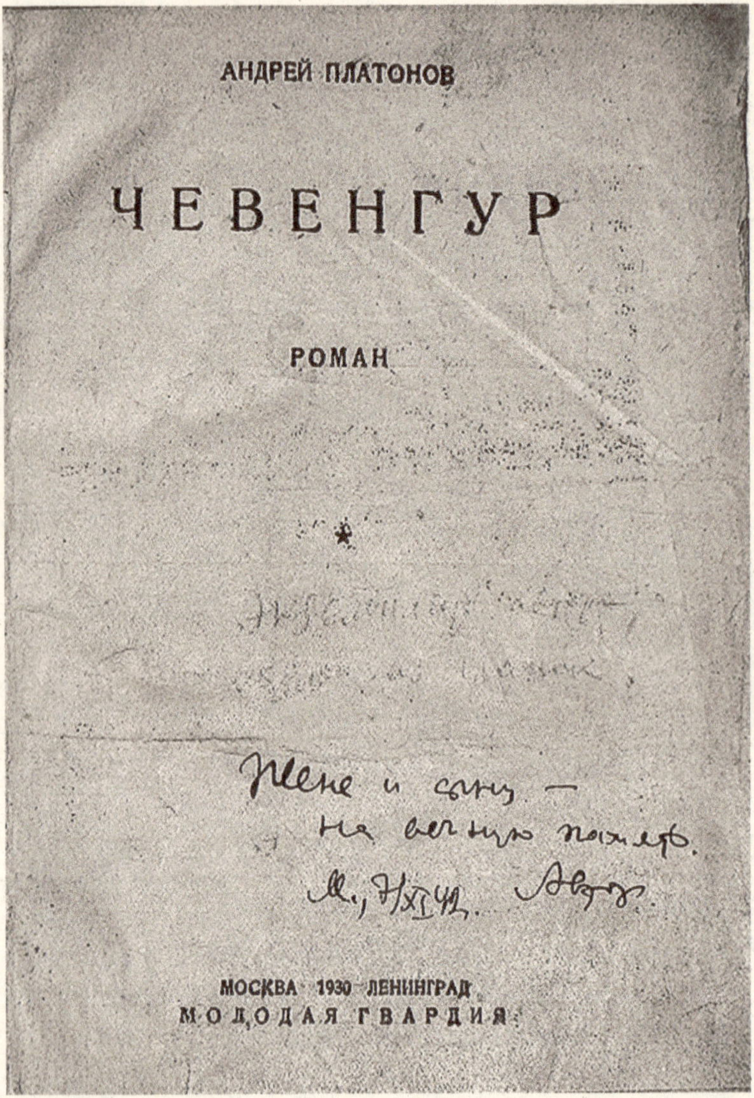

АНДРЕЙ ПЛАТОНОВ

ЧЕВЕНГУР

РОМАН

МОСКВА 1930 ЛЕНИНГРАД
МОЛОДАЯ ГВАРДИЯ

The title page of the 1930 edition of *Chevengur*, which was typeset but then canceled. A very few copies were even printed, and this one bears Platonov's dedication: "To my wife and son, to remember me by."

I

Old provincial towns have tumbledown outskirts, and people come straight from nature to live there. A man appears, with a keen-eyed face that has been worn to an extreme of sadness, a man who can fix up or equip anything but who has himself lived through life unequipped. There was not one artifact, from a frying pan to an alarm clock, that had not at some time passed through the hands of this man. Nor did he ever refuse to resole shoes, to cast shot for wolf hunting, or to turn out counterfeit medals for sale at old-time village fairs. But he had never made anything for himself—neither a family, nor a dwelling. In summer he simply lived out in nature, keeping his tools in a sack and using the sack as a pillow—more for the tools' safety than for softness. He protected himself from the early sun by placing a burdock leaf over his eyes when he lay down in the evening. In winter he lived on what remained from his summer's earnings, paying the verger for his lodging by ringing the hours through the night. He had no particular interest in people or nature, only in man-made artifacts of every kind. And so he treated people and fields with an indifferent tenderness, not infringing on their interests. During winter evenings he would sometimes make things for which there was no need: towers out of bits of wire, ships from pieces of roofing iron, airships out of paper and glue, and so on—all entirely for his own pleasure. Often he even delayed a chance commission; he might, say, have been asked to rehoop a barrel, but he would be busy fashioning a wooden clock, thinking it should work without a mechanism, from the earth's turning.

The verger didn't like these unpaid activities. "You'll be begging in your old age, Zakhar Pavlovich! That barrel's been sitting there for days, and you just keep stroking the ground with a bit of wood. Goodness knows what you're up to!"

Zakhar Pavlovich said nothing. To him the human word was like the noise of the forest to the forest's inhabitants—something you don't hear. The verger went on calmly watching and smoking—from frequent attendance at services he had lost his faith in God, but he knew for sure that Zakhar Pavlovich wouldn't get anywhere; people had been living in the world for a long time and they had already thought everything up. Zakhar Pavlovich, however, saw things differently: there were a great many things to be thought up, since there was still natural substance living untouched by human hands.

Every fifth year, half the village would go to the mines and cities, and the other half into the nearby forest: the harvest had failed. From time immemorial it has been known that, even in dry years, grasses, roots, and grains do well in forest clearings. The villagers who had stayed behind would rush out to these clearings—to save their vegetables from instant plundering by hordes of greedy wanderers. But this time there was a drought the following year too. The village bolted up its huts and set out onto the highway in two columns. One column set off to Kyiv to beg, the other to Luhans'k in search of work;[1] a few people turned off into the forest and overgrown gullies, where they took to eating raw grass, clay, and bark, and lived wild. The people who left were nearly all adults—the children had either taken care to die in advance or had run off to live as beggars. As for the unweaned babies, their mothers had let them gradually wither away, not allowing them to suck their fill.

There was one old woman, Ignatievna, who cured infants of hunger: she gave them an infusion of mushrooms mixed with sweet herbs, and the children fell peacefully silent with dry foam on their lips. A mother would kiss her child on its now aged, wizened forehead and whisper, "He's done with suffering, the dear. Praise the Lord!"[2]

Ignatievna was standing beside her. "He's passed on. He's at peace now—better off than the living. He's in paradise, listening to the silver winds."

The mother wondered at her child, believing its sad lot had been eased. "Take my old skirt, Ignatievna, I've nothing else to give you. Thank you!"

Ignatievna would hold the skirt up to the light and say, "You have a little cry, Mitrevna—that's right and proper. But your skirt's in tatters, you must throw in a kerchief too—or how about an iron?"

Zakhar Pavlovich was left alone in the village—he found he liked the absence of people. But he spent most of the time in the forest, sharing a dugout with an old loner and living on a brew of herbs whose uses the loner had studied beforehand.

Zakhar Pavlovich worked all the time, to forget his hunger, and he taught himself to make from wood everything he had previously made from metal. As for the loner—he had been doing nothing all his life, and now all the more so; until the age of fifty he had just looked around him, wondering what was what and waiting for something finally to emerge from the world's turmoil, so he could begin to act after a general calming and clarification; he was not in any way gripped by life and he couldn't bring himself to encroach on a woman in marriage or get up to any generally useful activity. He had felt surprised at birth and had remained surprised, his eyes light blue in his youthful face, until he was an old man. While Zakhar Pavlovich was making an oak frying pan, the loner would say in astonishment that he would never be able to fry anything in it. But Zakhar Pavlovich would pour water into the wooden frying pan and get the water to boil over a slow flame without the pan catching fire. The loner would stand stock-still with surprise. "That's mighty fine! But how, my friend, can a man ever figure out everything?"

These overwhelming universal mysteries made the loner lose heart. Nobody had ever explained to him the simplicity of events—or else the loner was entirely muddleheaded. And indeed, when Zakhar Pavlovich tried to tell him what makes the wind blow rather than stay in one place, the loner expressed still more surprise and was unable to understand a thing, although he sensed the origin of the wind with precision.

"I don't believe it! Say that again! From the rays of the sun, you say? What a story!"

Zakhar Pavlovich explained that the sun's rays were not a story, but simply heat.

"Heat?" the loner repeated in surprise. "E-e-e-h, the witch!"

The loner's surprise merely shifted from one object to another, changing nothing in his consciousness. What kept him going was not mind, but a sense of trustful respect.

By the end of the summer Zakhar Pavlovich had fashioned from wood every man-made artifact he had ever come across. The dugout and the adjacent space were filled with the products of his technical skills—a whole collection of agricultural tools, machines, instruments, arrangements, enterprises, and everyday appliances, all made entirely of wood. Strangely, there was not one object that repeated nature: a horse, for example, or a pumpkin.

One day in August the loner went into the shade, lay down on his stomach, and said, "Zakhar Pavlovich, I'm dying, yesterday I ate a lizard. I brought you two little mushrooms, but I fried myself a lizard. Wave a burdock leaf up above—I love the wind."

Zakhar Pavlovich waved a burdock leaf over him, fetched some water, and gave it to the dying man. "You're not really going to die. You just think you are."

"I will die, Zakhar Pavlovich, really and truly I will," said the loner, afraid to lie. "My innards don't hold anything, there's a huge worm living inside me, it's sucked up all my blood." The loner turned over onto his back. "What do you think—should I be afraid or not?"

"Don't be afraid," Zakhar Pavlovich answered positively. "I'd die myself, straightaway, but, you know, there's always artifacts keeping me busy…"

The loner was glad of this sympathy and he died toward evening without fear. At the time of his death Zakhar Pavlovich had gone to bathe in the stream and he found the loner already dead, suffocated by his own green vomit. The vomit was compact and dry, it had settled into a paste around the loner's mouth, and white small-caliber worms were at work in it.

During the night Zakhar Pavlovich woke up listening to rain—the second rain since April. "That would have given the loner a surprise," he thought. But the loner was soaking alone in the torrents pouring evenly down from the sky, and he was quietly swelling up.

Through the sleepy, windless rain something sang out sadly, in a muffled voice, from so far away that it was probably day where it was singing, and with no rain. Zakhar Pavlovich immediately forgot the loner, the rain, and his hunger. He got to his feet. It was the whistle of a distant machine, a living, working steam engine. Zakhar Pavlovich went outside and stood in the moisture of the warm rain that was quietly humming about a peaceful life, about the vastness of the long-lasting earth. The dark trees were dozing, their gnarled trunks embraced by the caress of the calm rain; their pleasure made them almost tremble, and they were rustling their branches without the least wind.

Zakhar Pavlovich paid no attention to the joy of nature; what excited him was the unknown, now-silent locomotive. "Even the rain acts," he said to himself as he lay down again, "while you just sleep and hide away in the forest to no purpose. The loner's died—and you'll die too. The loner never made a single artifact in all his life—all he ever did was watch, and try to get the hang of things. He was surprised by everything, he saw marvels in the simplest matters, and he never lifted a finger lest he encroach or do harm. All he did was pick mushrooms—not that he knew how to find them—and now he's died, without having ever harmed nature in any way."

In the morning there was a big sun and the forest sang with all the density of its voice, letting the morning wind pass beneath its underleaves. What Zakhar Pavlovich noticed was not so much morning as a change of shift. The rain had gone to sleep in the soil and the sun had taken its place; and now, because of the sun, the wind had begun to fuss about; the trees were bristling; bushes and grasses had begun to mutter; and even the rain itself, having hardly had any rest, was getting back onto its feet, aroused by the tickling warmth, and gathering its body into clouds.

Zakhar Pavlovich put his wooden artifacts into his sack—as many as there was room for—and set off into the distance, along the women's mushroom trail. He did not look at the loner: the dead are unprepossessing, although Zakhar Pavlovich had known one man, a fisherman from Lake Mutevo, who had questioned many people about death and whose curiosity had filled him with anguish.[3] This fisherman had loved fish not as food but as a special being that most probably knew the secret of death. He would show the eyes of dead fish to Zakhar Pavlovich and say, "Look—true wisdom! A fish stands between life and death, that's why it's mute and why it stares without expression. Even a calf thinks, but a fish doesn't—it knows everything already." Contemplating the lake for years on end, the fisherman had gone on thinking about one and the same thing: the interest of death. Zakhar Pavlovich had tried to talk him out of it: "It's nothing so very special—just somewhere a bit cramped." A year after that, the fisherman couldn't bear it any longer and threw himself into the lake from a boat, having bound his legs with a rope so as not to start swimming inadvertently. Secretly he simply didn't believe in death. What he really wanted was to have a look and see what was there; it might be a great deal more interesting than life in a village or on the shore of a lake. He saw death as another province, situated beneath the sky, as if at the bottom of the cool water, and it had an attractive pull.[4] A few of the men whom he had told about his intention to live for a while in death and then return had tried to dissuade him, but others had agreed. "Well, Dmitry Ivanich, nothing ventured, nothing gained. Go on, give it a try—then you can tell us about it." Dmitry Ivanich gave death a try; three days later he was dragged out of the lake and buried beside the fence in the village churchyard.

Now Zakhar Pavlovich was walking past the churchyard, and he began to look amid the thicket of crosses for the fisherman's grave. There was no cross standing over it; no lips had prayed for the fisherman, and his death had not distressed a single heart, since he had died not from some illness but because of his own inquisitive mind. The fisherman had not left a wife behind him—he was a widower, and he had a little son who had been living with other people. At the funeral, Zakhar Pavlovich had taken the boy by the hand. He was an affectionate, intelligent little boy—it was hard to say whether he took more after his mother or after his father. What had become of him? As an orphan, he had probably been among the first to die during these years of famine. The boy had followed his father's coffin with dignity and with no show of grief.

"Uncle Zakhar, did Father really mean to lie down like this?"

"No, it was a foolish whim. And he's not done you any favors, Sasha. It'll be a while before he catches any fish now."

"And why are the aunties all weeping?"

"Because they're humbugs."

When they placed the coffin beside the pit of the grave, no one wished to say goodbye to the dead man. Zakhar Pavlovich knelt down and touched the fisherman's fresh, bristly cheek, which had been washed clean at the bottom of the lake. Then he said to the boy, "Say goodbye to your father now. He's died forever and a day. Have a good look at him—you'll be remembering."

The boy pressed himself against his father's body, against his old shirt, which smelled of living, familiar sweat, because his shirt had been put on him specially for the coffin—it was not the shirt his father had drowned in. The boy felt his father's hands; they gave off a smell of fishy damp, and a tin wedding ring had been put on one finger, in honor of the forgotten mother. The little boy turned his head toward the other people, felt suddenly frightened of all these strangers, and began crying pathetically, gathering his father's shirt into folds as if to defend himself with it. His grief was wordless, lacking any consciousness of the rest of life and therefore inconsolable; the way he sorrowed for his dead father, the dead man might well have felt happy. And all the people by the coffin began crying too, out of pity for the boy and premature compassion for themselves, since each would have to die and be mourned in the same way.

For all his sorrow, Zakhar Pavlovich was able to think about the future. "That's enough of you and your wailing, Nikiforovna!" he said to one woman, who was sobbing and muttering hurried lamentations. "You're not howling with grief—you just want people to cry when you're dead and gone yourself. Take the boy in. You've got six mouths to feed as it is—you'll hardly notice one more."

Nikiforovna immediately recovered her peasant woman's reason, and her face was dry and fierce; she had been crying without tears, just with her wrinkles. "Hardly notice?" she replied. "I like that! The boy may not need much now, but wait till he starts growing. He'll be guzzling away, his trousers will always need darning... Nothing will be enough for him."

The boy was taken in by another of the women, Mavra Fetisovna Dvanova, who had seven children. The boy gave her his hand, and the woman wiped his face with her skirt, blew his nose, and took the orphan off to her hut.

The boy remembered the fishing rod his father had made for him; he had thrown the rod into the lake and forgotten about it. By now it must have caught a fish. He could go and eat the fish, so strangers wouldn't scold him for eating their food. "Auntie," he began, "I've caught a fish in the water. Let me go and look for it. I can eat it—then you won't have to feed me."

Mavra inadvertently puckered her face, blew her nose on the tip of her kerchief, and did not let go of the boy's hand.

Zakhar Pavlovich fell into thought and wanted to become a barefoot wanderer, but he remained in place. He felt deeply moved by grief and orphanhood. Some unknown conscience now apparent in his chest made him wish to walk over the earth without rest, to encounter grief in every village and weep over the coffins of strangers. But he was stopped by the artifacts that kept coming his way; the village elder gave him a clock to repair and the priest asked him to tune his grand piano. Zakhar Pavlovich had never heard real music; once, in the district town, he had seen a gramophone, but men had tormented it and it no longer played. It had stood in a tavern; people had broken the sides of its outer case in order to see through the trickery and find the man singing inside, and a darning needle had been stuck through the diaphragm. Zakhar Pavlovich spent an entire month tuning the piano, testing the plaintive sounds and examining the mechanism that came out with such tenderness. He would strike a key, and a sad singing would rise up and fly away; he would then look up and wait for the sound to return—it was too good to be squandered without trace. The priest got tired of waiting and said, "Don't waste time, my man, re-sounding tones. Just finish the job and stop trying to figure out what's none of your business." Zakhar Pavlovich took offense to the roots of his craftsman's being and inserted a hidden device that could be removed in one second but that was impossible to find without special knowledge. After that the priest had summoned Zakhar Pavlovich every week. "Come along, my friend, come along—the seraphic power of music has gone missing again." But Zakhar Pavlovich had not made this device for the sake of the priest, nor in order to go and delight in music more often himself. What had moved him was something very different: How, he wanted to know, had this artifact been constructed—an artifact that could touch any heart and make a man better and kinder? This was why he had inserted his secret device that was capable of interfering with euphony and drowning it with howls. After Zakhar Pavlovich had repaired the piano ten times and got to understand the structure of the quivering main board and the secret of the blending of sounds, he removed the device—and from then on sounds ceased to hold any interest for him.

Now, as he walked along, Zakhar Pavlovich recalled his past life and felt no regret. Over the years he had managed on his own to understand many different things and mechanisms, and he could reproduce them in his own artifacts as long as appropriate materials and instruments were to hand. He was walking through the village in order to meet the unknown machines and objects thrumming beyond the line where the mighty sky joined the peasants' unmoving strips of land. He was walking with the same heart as a peasant who makes the pilgrimage to Kyiv, when faith dries up and life becomes just a matter of keeping going to the end.

There was a charred smell on the village streets—from cinders, which were no longer being raked away by hens, because they had all been eaten. The huts stood full of childless silence. Burdocks that had long overgrown their norm were waiting for the huts' owners beside gates, on paths, and in all the familiar, well-trodden spots where not a single plant had been able to grow before; they were swaying like future trees. In the absence of people, the wattle fences had also begun to flower; hops and bindweed had wound around them, and some of the stakes and switches had taken root, promising to turn into thickets unless people came back. The wells in the yards had dried up; lizards climbed freely over the frames and ran down inside to rest and reproduce, away from the fierce heat. Zakhar Pavlovich was also somewhat surprised by the absurd fact that, even though the corn in the fields had all died long ago, there were green spikes of rye, oats, and millet, as well as rustling goosefoot, on the thatched roofs; they had sprouted from grains in the thatch. Yellowish-green birds from the fields had also moved into the huts and were even occupying the main rooms; dense clouds of sparrows flew up from under his feet, their busy, proprietorial songs carrying over the wind of their wings.

As he left the village, Zakhar Pavlovich caught sight of a bast sandal; it too had come to life without people and discovered its destiny—it had sent out a shoot of silver willow while making shade for the rootlet of the future bush by allowing the rest of its body to rot. The soil beneath the bast sandal must have been moister: a multitude of pale blades of grass were trying to edge their way through. There were no village objects that Zakhar Pavlovich loved more than bast sandals and horseshoes, and no structures he loved more than wells. A swallow was perched on the chimney of the last hut; at the sight of Zakhar Pavlovich it slipped into the chimney and there, in the dark of the flue, embraced its descendants with its wings.

He left the church behind and to his right; beyond it lay an open field, level and smooth, like a wind that has settled down. The small bell, the supporting voice, rang out—twelve times for midday. Bindweed had wrapped around the church and was doing its best to climb up to the cross. Beside the church walls the graves of the priests were covered by tall grass, and their low crosses were lost in its thickets. The verger, his task done, was still standing by the porch, observing the passage of summer; his alarm clock had gotten muddled during its many years of counting time, while the verger himself, on account of his age, had begun to sense time as keenly and precisely as grief or happiness. Whatever he was doing, even when he was asleep (although in old age life is stronger than sleep, ever vigilant and incessant), the verger would feel some kind of anxiety or longing whenever an hour had passed; he would then ring the hour and calm down again.

"So you're still alive, Grandad!" Zakhar Pavlovich said to the verger. "But who are you counting the hours for?"

The verger chose not to answer. During his seventy years of life he had become convinced that half of his actions had been carried out to no purpose and three-quarters of all his words had been spoken in vain; neither his wife nor his children had stayed alive as a result of his efforts, and his words had been forgotten like an extraneous noise. "I could speak to this man"—the verger took stock of himself—"but I'll be gone from his eternal memory before he's even walked a verst.[5] What am I to him? Neither helper nor protector."[6]

"You're working in vain," Zakhar Pavlovich reproached him.

To this stupidity the verger replied, "What do you mean? In my lifetime, our village has taken to the road ten times—and come back again later. And they'll come back this time too—there's no doing long without people."

"But what use is your ringing?"

The verger knew Zakhar Pavlovich as a man who allowed himself to be only too free with his hands but who did not know the value of time. "What use is my ringing? Huh! With the bell I shorten time and sing songs."[7]

"All right," said Zakhar Pavlovich, "keep on singing your songs." And he left the village.

On the edge of the village crouched a little hut, with no outbuildings; someone must have married in haste, quarreled with his father, and made a new home there. This hut was empty too; going inside was frightening. Only one thing cheered Zakhar Pavlovich as he left: a sunflower had grown up out of the chimney—it had already matured and was leaning its ripening head toward the rising sun.

The road was overgrown with dry grass, dilapidated by dust. When

Zakhar Pavlovich sat down for a smoke, he would see cozy little forests on the ground; each blade of grass was a tree. There was an entire little habitable world, with its own paths and its own warmth, equipped with everything necessary to satisfy the daily needs of small, preoccupied creatures. Zakhar Pavlovich gazed at the ants for some time and kept them in his head for another four versts of his journey before concluding, "Just give us the minds of ants or mosquitoes and we'll set our lives straight in no time at all! When it comes to communal life, these little creatures are master craftsmen. Man's nowhere near as skilled as an ant."

2

AND THEN Zakhar Pavlovich appeared on the outskirts of a city. He found himself somewhere to live—a shed beside the house of a carpenter, a widower with numerous children—then went outside and fell into thought: What should he turn his hand to now?

The carpenter came back from his work and sat down beside Zakhar Pavlovich.

"How much shall I pay you?" asked Zakhar Pavlovich.

The man wheezed with his throat, as if wanting to laugh. There was a hopelessness in his voice, and the particular, seasoned despair characteristic of those whom life has well and truly embittered.

"What do you do for a living? Nothing? Well, live here for free—until my boys rip your head off."

The man was not joking. That very night his sons—who were between ten and twenty years old—drenched the sleeping Zakhar Pavlovich with their urine and jammed the shed door shut with an oven fork. But Zakhar Pavlovich had never been interested in human beings and it was not easy to make him angry. He knew of the existence of machines, of complicated and powerful artifacts, and it was these machines, rather than acts of incidental loutishness, that were his measure of the nobility of man. And in the morning, as it happened, Zakhar Pavlovich noticed how deftly and seriously the eldest son set about making an ax handle; what was important about the boy, then, was not his urine but his skill with his hands.

After a week Zakhar Pavlovich was feeling so anguished from inactivity that he began, without asking, to put the carpenter's house in order. He repaired some shoddy joints on the roof, rebuilt the steps going up to the entrance room, and cleaned the soot from the chimney flues. In the evenings he fashioned stakes.

"What are you doing?" asked the carpenter, blotting his mustache with a crust of bread. He had just had a meal of potato and gherkins.

"Maybe they'll come in handy," Zakhar Pavlovich answered.

The carpenter chewed his crust and thought for a moment. "They'll do to fence off graves!" he said. "My lads' idea of a Lenten penance was to go and shit on every grave in the cemetery."

Zakhar Pavlovich's anguish was stronger than his sense of the uselessness of his labor, and he carried on cutting stakes until utter nighttime exhaustion. Unless he had a task in hand, the blood would flow from his fingertips into his head, and he would think so deeply about everything at once that his thoughts turned into a mad whirl, while his heart filled with aching fear. As he wandered about the sunlit yard during the day, he was unable to overcome the thought that man had descended from the worm, and that a worm was a simple and ghastly little tube with nothing inside it—just empty stinking darkness. As he observed the houses in the city, Zakhar Pavlovich discovered their precise resemblance to closed coffins, and he began to feel frightened of spending the night in the carpenter's home. His feral appetite for work, finding no outlet, was eating away at his soul; he was no longer in control of himself and he was tormented by all kinds of feelings that had never arisen in him when he was working. He began to have dreams; his father, a miner, was dying, and his mother was pouring milk from her breast over him to revive him, but his father said angrily, "Let me suffer freely, you bitch!" Then Father lay there for a long time, postponing his death. Mother stood over him and asked, "Well? How much longer will you be?" With the bitterness of a martyr, Father spat, turned onto his front, and reminded her, "Bury me in my old trousers. Give these ones to Zakhar."

The only thing that cheered Zakhar Pavlovich was to sit on the roof and look into the distance, at the place two versts from the city where impetuous railway trains sometimes passed by. The rotation of the locomotive's wheels and its fast breathing made Zakhar Pavlovich's body buzz with joy, and his sympathy with the engine made his eyes moisten with light tears.

The carpenter kept an eye on his tenant for a while and then began to feed him for free from his table. During the first meal the carpenter's sons put snot in Zakhar Pavlovich's bowl, but their father got up and, without a word, swung a punch that brought up a swelling on his eldest son's cheekbone.

"I'm a man like any other man," the carpenter pronounced calmly as he sat down again, "but I've produced such scum, you know, that one of these days they'll be the death of me. Look at Fedka—he's got the strength of the devil! And where that great mug of his comes from, I've no idea. They've been on cheap rations since the day they were born."

The first autumn rains began—at the wrong time and to no avail. The peasants had long since disappeared in distant lands; many had died on the roads, never reaching the mines or the southern wheat. Zakhar Pavlovich went with the carpenter to look for work at the railway station; the carpenter knew someone there who worked as an engine driver.

They found the driver in the staff room, where the train crews caught up on their sleep. He said there were a lot of people, and no work; the remnants of the nearby villages were all living at the station and doing what little work there was for low pay. The carpenter went out and came back with a ring of sausage and a bottle of vodka. After drinking the vodka, the driver told Zakhar Pavlovich and the carpenter about locomotive engines and Westinghouse brakes. "You know what momentum builds up on a downgrade—with a train of sixty axles!" he said, indignant at his listeners' ignorance and demonstrating the force of momentum with a supple gesture of his hands. "Yes! You turn the brake wheel, a blue flame shoots up from the brake shoes under the tender, you get it in the back of the neck from the trucks, the regulator's closed but the locomotive hurtles on—with the chimney roaring in protest! Oh to hell with it all! Give me more vodka! You should've bought some gherkins too—sausage is dense stuff. It packs your stomach."

Zakhar Pavlovich sat there in silence; it was clear he wouldn't be taken on—how, after all, could he go straight from wooden frying pans to working with locomotives? The engine driver's stories had made his passion for mechanical artifacts grow sadder and more repressed, like unrequited love.

"Why so down?" said the driver, noticing Zakhar Pavlovich's sorrow. "Come along to the depot tomorrow. I'll have a word with the foreman—maybe they'll take you on as an engine cleaner. You can't afford to hang back, you son of a bitch, if you want to earn your daily—" The engine driver stopped in midsentence; he had begun to belch. "Damn it," he went on, "your sausage has gone into reverse. You can't have paid more than a kopek a pound for it, you skinflint—I'd have done better to eat greasy rags with my vodka." The driver turned to Zakhar Pavlovich again and went on: "But a locomotive must be like a mirror—so spotless it won't spoil the finest of gloves. Not a speck of dust—locomotives don't like dust. An engine, my brother, is a maiden. Not a woman, no—one open hole too many and an engine won't budge."

The driver launched into abstract reflections about various women. Zakhar Pavlovich listened and listened, and understood nothing; he didn't know that you could love women in some special way and from a distance, but he did know that such a man should get married. Talk about the creation of the world or about unknown artifacts could be interesting; but talk about a woman, like talk about men, was boring and made no sense. Zakhar Pavlovich had once had a wife himself; she had loved him and he had not treated her badly, but she had not brought him any particular joy. People are endowed with many attributes; if you devote too much thought to such matters, you can end up hooting with joy just because you keep on breathing from second to second. But where does this get you? It's just a game, it's playing with your own body—not a serious existence outside yourself.

Never in his life had Zakhar Pavlovich had any respect for this kind of talk.

An hour later the driver remembered that it was now his shift. Zakhar Pavlovich and the carpenter accompanied him to his locomotive, which had just taken on coal and water. From a distance, the driver called out to his mate in a deep, authoritative voice, "Pressure?"

"Seven atmospheres," the man answered unsmilingly, leaning out of the window.

"Water level?"

"Normal."

"Firebox?"

"I've opened the blower."

"Excellent."

The following morning Zakhar Pavlovich came back to the depot. The foreman, a little old man without much faith in living people, scrutinized him for a long time. He loved locomotives so painfully and jealously that he felt horror whenever he saw them moving. Had it been up to him, he would have granted rest eternal to every locomotive, so that they would not be mutilated by the rough hands of the ignorant. In his view there were few machines but all too many people; people were alive and could stand up for themselves, whereas an engine was a tender, fragile, and defenseless being. To drive it properly, you needed to leave your wife, clear your head of every worry, and dip your bread in machine oil; only then—and after ten years of patient waiting—should a man be allowed near a locomotive![1]

The foreman went through agonies as he studied Zakhar Pavlovich. Where he ought to press with one finger, the brute would take a swing with a sledgehammer; when he should just be stroking the glass on the pressure gauge, he'd bear down so hard he'd snap off the whole apparatus—pipe and all. No, how could it be right to let a plowman approach a mechanism? "My God, my God!" the foreman raged with wordless but heartfelt passion, "where are you, you mechanics of old, you driver's mates, you firemen and engine cleaners? There was a time when men trembled beside a locomotive, but nowadays everyone thinks he's cleverer than a machine. Swine, sacrilegious bastards, scoundrels, lackeys of the devil! By rights, traffic along the railways ought to be brought to a halt immediately! What are today's mechanics? They're not people—they're a walking disaster! Tramps, circus riders, chancers. You can't trust them with so much as a bolt—and they've already got their hands on the regulator! In my day, if there was the least tapping in a locomotive, if the connecting rods began to sing, I'd sense it in the ends of my fingernails—and without even moving from the spot. I'd feel such distress I'd be trembling all over. I'd find out what was wrong at the very first stop. I'd find it with my lips, I'd lick it out, I'd suck it out, I'd grease it with my own blood—I'd never just drive on blindly! And this fella thinks he can come straight out of the rye and onto a locomotive!

"Run back home now—and wash your face before you go near a locomotive!" said the foreman.

The following day, having washed, Zakhar Pavlovich reappeared. The foreman was lying under a locomotive and cautiously touching the springs, lightly tapping them with a little hammer and pressing his ear to the ringing metal. "Motia," he called out to one of the workers, "tighten this nut a fraction!"

Using a monkey wrench, Motia tightened a nut half a turn. The foreman immediately got so upset that Zakhar Pavlovich began to feel sorry for him.

"Motiushka!" said the foreman with a quiet, oppressed sadness, though he was grinding his teeth. "What have you gone and done now, you bastard? What I said was—tighten the nut! Which nut? The main nut. And what do you do? You send me round the twist by twisting the locknut. And now you're forcing the locknut. And now you're touching the locknut again. What's to be done with you dumb animals? Get lost, cretin!"

"Let me, mister mechanic, loosen the locknut again by one half-turn, and then I'll tighten the main nut by a hair's breadth," said Zakhar Pavlovich.

Grateful that a bystander could recognize his rightness, the foreman replied in a peaceful, heartfelt voice, "Ah, you saw, did you? The man . . . the man's a lumberjack, not a mechanic! A nut—he doesn't even know the names of the different nuts! Huh? What can you do? He bashes a locomotive about as if it were a woman, as if it were some damned slut! Oh my God! All right then, come over here and adjust the nut like I said!"

Zakhar Pavlovich crawled beneath the locomotive and did everything precisely and delicately. The foreman then busied himself until evening with locomotives and arguments with their drivers. After the lights had been lit, Zakhar Pavlovich reminded the foreman that he was still there. The foreman stopped in front of him again, thinking his thoughts. "An engine's father is the lever, and its mother is the inclined plane," he said tenderly, remembering something close to his heart, which brought peace to him at night. "Tomorrow you can try cleaning fireboxes—mind you're on time! But I don't know, I'm not promising anything—we'll give it a try, we'll see how it goes. It's a serious matter. A firebox—understand? Not just anything, but a firebox! All right then, off you go, off you go."

Zakhar Pavlovich slept one more night in the carpenter's shed; at dawn, three hours before work began, he arrived at the depot. Polished rails stretched out before him; stationary freight trucks bore the names of distant lands: Trans-Caspian, Trans-Caucasian, Ussuriysk. Strange, special people were walking about over the tracks. They were intelligent and thoughtful—switchmen, engine drivers, rolling stock inspectors, and so on. All around were buildings, steam engines, devices, and artifacts.

Before Zakhar Pavlovich lay a new world of appealing ingenuity—a world he had loved for so long it seemed he had always known of it—and he resolved to stand his ground there forever.

3

A YEAR before the failed harvest Mavra Fetisovna had fallen pregnant for the seventeenth time. Her husband, Prokhor Abramovich Dvanov, felt less joy than is expected. As he observed fields, stars, and the vast, flowing air every day, he had often said to himself, "There's enough for everyone." And he had lived at peace in a hut swarming with the small people who were his offspring. His wife had given birth sixteen times; seven of the children had survived, and then there was an eighth, a fosterling—the son of the fisherman who had drowned of his own accord. When his wife had led the orphan in by the hand, Prokhor Abramovich had not objected. "Well, the more little ones swarming about, the more surely the old can die. Feed him, Mavrusha!"

The orphan ate some bread and milk, then turned away and screwed up his eyes against the strange people.

Mavra Fetisovna looked at him and sighed. "A fresh tribulation from the Lord. He'll die before he's grown any. I can see death in his eyes—it'll be a waste of good bread."

But two years later the boy was still alive and he hadn't fallen ill even once. He ate little, and Mavra Fetisovna had made her peace with the orphan. "Eat, my darling, eat!" she would say. "If you don't eat here, you won't eat anywhere else!"

Need and children had long ago subdued Prokhor Abramovich; he paid no deep attention to anything at all—to children being ill or new children being born, to a poor harvest or to a tolerable harvest—and so everyone thought of him as a kind man. Only his wife's almost yearly pregnancies brought him a little joy; the children were his only sense of the stability of his own life—with their soft little hands they made him plow, look after the household, and generally take care of things. He moved about, labored, and lived through life as if half-asleep, having no surplus energy for inner happiness and not knowing anything at all definitely. Prokhor Abramovich prayed to God, but with no heartfelt inclination toward him; the passions of youth—love for women, yearning for tasty food, and so on—had not endured, because his wife was plain and the food was monotonous and unnourishing year in, year out. The multiplication of children diminished Prokhor Abramovich's interest in himself; somehow it made him feel cooler and lighter. The farther Prokhor Abramovich lived, the more patient and unconscious he grew with regard to events in the village. If all Prokhor Abramovich's children had died in the course of a day, he would have gathered the same number of fosterlings the next day; and if the fosterlings had perished too, he would have immediately walked away from his smallholder's fate, set his wife free, and gone off barefoot who knows where—somewhere, perhaps, where a heart is no less sad but where feet, at least, know joy.

His wife's seventeenth pregnancy disturbed Prokhor Abramovich because of his concerns about the next year's harvest: that autumn fewer children had been born in the village than the year before, and, most important of all, Aunty Marya had not given birth. She had given birth every year for twenty years except during the years preceding a drought, and the whole village was aware of this; if Aunty Marya walked by empty, the men would say, "Marya's like a maiden again—it'll be a hungry summer."

This year too Marya was thin and free.

"Lying fallow, are you, Marya Matveyevna?" men would ask respectfully as they walked by.

"And what of it?" said Marya. Unused as she was to running idle, she felt ashamed.

"Never mind, you'll start a son soon—you're right good at that."

"Life's for living—why live in vain?" said Marya more boldly. "As long as there's bread."

"That's the trouble. A woman can give birth easily enough, but the wheat doesn't always keep up. You, though—you're a witch. You know your right time."

Prokhor Abramovich said to his wife that she'd chosen a bad time to fall pregnant.

"Ay, Prosha!"[1] she sighed. "It's me, not you, who gives birth to them, and it'll be me who goes out begging for them."

Prokhor Abramovich said no more.

Then it was December, and there was no snow—the winter wheat froze. Mavra Fetisovna gave birth to twins.

"She's laid two at once," Prokhor Abramovich said by her bedside. "Well, praise the Lord—what else can we do? Looks like these two will live—they've got wrinkled foreheads and they're making their little hands into fists."

The fosterling stood there and looked with a distorted, aged face at what he could not understand. In him arose a caustic warmth of shame on behalf of adults; he at once lost his love of them and sensed his loneliness—he wanted to run away and hide in some gully. He had felt just as lonely, bleak, and frightened after seeing two dogs coupling—he had not eaten for the next two days and had disliked all dogs ever since. The new mother's bed gave off a smell of raw meat and of moist, milky calf, but Mavra Fetisovna was too weak to sense anything herself and she felt stifled beneath the motley patchwork blanket. She bared one of her legs; it was plump, wrinkled with age and the fat of motherhood. On it Sasha could see the yellow spots of some kind of deadened sufferings and thick blue veins, full of stiffened blood, that had spread tight beneath her skin and were ready to split it open so as to make their way out. One treelike vein showed how somewhere or other her heart was beating away, forcefully driving her blood through bodily crevices that had collapsed and narrowed.

"Having a good look, are you?" Prokhor Abramovich asked the fosterling, whose strength was now failing him. "You've got two new brothers now, Sasha. Cut yourself a piece of bread and go and run about outside—it's brightened up a bit now."

Sasha went outside, without the bread. Mavra Fetisovna opened her white and watery eyes and called out to her husband, "Prosha! Counting the orphan, we've got ten now, and you and I make twelve."

Prokhor Abramovich had already worked this out for himself. "Let them live," he said. "An extra mouth brings extra bread."

"They say we're in for a famine—God forbid! Whatever will become of us—with little ones, and babes in arms?"

"There won't be a famine," Prokhor Abramovich decided for peace of mind. "If the winter wheat fails, then the spring wheat will make up for it."

The winter crops did indeed fail; after being nipped by autumn frosts, they suffocated in the spring beneath a crust of ice. The spring wheat brought now fear, now joy; in the end it ripened, but only after a fashion, yielding just a few times more grain than they'd sown. Prokhor Abramovich's eldest son was eleven, and the boy they'd taken in was about the same; one of the two had to go out alone and beg, to bring help to the family in the shape of dry rusks of bread. Prokhor Abramovich said nothing: he would have regretted sending his own son—and he felt ashamed to send out the orphan.

"Why are you sitting there without a word?" Mavra Fetisovna asked angrily. "Agapka's sent her seven-year-old out into the world, Mishka Duvakin's sending his little girl—while you sit there as if carved from stone, without a care in the world. There isn't enough millet to last till Christmas and we haven't seen bread since Bread Savior's Day."[2]

Prokhor Abramovich spent that evening making some old sackcloth into a bag that was roomy and comfortable. Twice he called Sasha over and measured the bag against his shoulders. "All right?" he asked. "Not pulling on you here?"

"It's all right," said Sasha.

Little Proshka was sitting beside his father and rethreading the needle for him each time the stiff thread slipped out, since his father couldn't see clearly.

"Papa, are you packing Sasha off to go begging tomorrow?" he asked.

"Why are you sitting there blathering?" the father snapped. "When you're a bit older, you'll be doing your share of begging too."

"I won't go begging," said Proshka. "I'll go thieving. Remember how you told us about Uncle Grisha's mare being pinched? The thieves did all right for themselves—and Uncle Grisha went and bought himself a gelding. When I grow up, I'll steal that gelding."

In the evening Mavra Fetisovna fed Sasha better than her own children—after they'd eaten, she fed him separately, giving him kasha with butter and all the milk he could drink. Prokhor Abramovich fetched a stick from the threshing barn and, when everyone was asleep, he made it into a little walking staff. But Sasha was not asleep, and he could hear Prokhor Abramovich shaping the stick with a bread knife. As for Proshka, he was quietly snuffling, shrinking away from a cockroach that was wandering across his neck. Sasha removed the cockroach, but he was afraid to kill it and he threw it down onto the floor.

"Still awake, Sasha?" asked Prokhor Abramovich. "Come on, get some sleep now!"

The children always woke early; they would begin fighting in the dark, while the roosters were still dozing. The old folk would have woken up and be scratching their bedsores, but only for the second time during the night. Not a bolt would be creaking in the village, nor were there any cheeps from the fields. It was at this hour that Prokhor Abramovich led the orphan out beyond the village bounds. The boy was half-asleep, trustfully clutching Prokhor Abramovich's hand. It was dank and chilly; the verger was ringing the hour and the bell's resonant sorrow disturbed the boy. Prokhor Abramovich bent down toward the orphan. "Look, Sasha, look over there. The track leaves the village and climbs up a hill, see? Just keep walking along it. After a while you'll see an enormous village and a fire-lookout tower, on a little hill. Don't be scared, just keep going. It's a city, that's all, and there'll be lots of grain in the granaries there. When your bag's full, come home and rest. Well, goodbye, my little son."

Sasha held Prokhor Abramovich's hand and looked into the gray morning bleakness of the steppe autumn.

"Have there been rains there?" Sasha asked, about this distant city.

"Heavy rains!" Prokhor Abramovich confirmed.

Then the boy left the hand he had been holding and, not looking at Prokhor Abramovich, quietly set off on his own, with stick and bag, keeping his eyes on the track where it climbed the hill, so as not to lose his direction. The boy disappeared behind the church and the graveyard and remained out of sight for a long time. Prokhor Abramovich stayed where he was and waited for the boy to reappear on the other side of the dip. Solitary early-morning sparrows were digging about on the road—they looked chilled. "They're orphans too," thought Prokhor Abramovich. "Who's going to throw *them* anything."

Sasha entered the graveyard, not knowing what he wanted. Now, for the first time, he thought about himself. He touched his chest: *This here is me*. Everywhere else, however, was alien and different from him. The home he had lived in, where he had loved Prokhor Abramovich, Mavra Fetisovna, and Proshka, had not been his home at all—he had been taken away from it and out onto a chilly morning road. Clenched in his half-childish sad soul, which had not been diluted by the calming water of consciousness, lay a hurt that was complete and pressing and that he could feel right up to his throat.

The graveyard was covered with dead leaves; their stillness at once made any feet quiet and tread more peacefully. There were peasant crosses everywhere, many without a name and with no memory of the one lying at peace. Sasha was interested in the most decrepit crosses, the ones that were also getting ready to fall down and die in the ground. Graves without crosses were better still—in their depths lay people now orphaned forever: their mothers too had died, and the fathers of some had drowned in rivers and lakes. The mound over the grave of Sasha's father had almost flattened—new coffins were carried deep into the cemetery along a path that led straight across it.

Patient and close by lay his father, not complaining how awful it was for him to be left alone all winter. What is there down there? It's bad there, it's quiet and cramped there; a boy with a stick and a beggar's bag can't be seen from down there.

"Father, they've driven me out to go begging. Soon I'll come down and be dead with you—you must be lonely there on your own, and I'm lonely too."

The boy placed his staff on the grave and heaped leaves over it, so it would keep safe and wait for him.

Sasha decided to hurry back from the city as soon as he had collected a full bag of rusks; then he would hollow out a dugout beside his father's grave and live there, since he had no home.

Prokhor Abramovich had gotten tired of waiting and was about to make his way back. But Sasha had crossed the dried-up streams in the gully and was now climbing the clay slope. His gait was slow and tired—though it was a joy to know that he would soon have a home and a father of his own. So what if his father was dead and not saying anything—he would always be lying close by, with warm sweat on his shirt and arms that had embraced Sasha during their shared sleep by the shore of the lake. His father might be dead, but he was whole and unchanging, always the same.

"What's happened to his stick?" wondered Prokhor Abramovich.

The morning had turned damp. The boy was struggling up the slippery slope, dropping now and then onto his hands and knees. The bag was swinging about, free and loose, like someone else's clothes that don't fit.

"A right mess I've made of that. It's not a beggar's bag, it's a bag for a greedy-guts," said Prokhor Abramovich, tardily reproaching himself. "How's he going to manage it when it's full of bread? But it's too late now… Goodness knows…"

High up, where the path turned toward the invisible other side of the steppe, the boy stopped. In the dawn of the day to come, on the line of the village horizon, he was standing above what seemed a deep chasm, on the shore of the sky's lake. Sasha looked fearfully into the emptiness of the steppe; the height, the distance, and the dead earth were damp and vast, and so everything seemed alien and terrible. But Sasha needed to stay whole and then return to the lowlands of the village and the cemetery—his father was there, it was cramped there, and everything was small, sad, and protected by earth and trees from the wind. And so he went on toward the town, to find rusks of bread.

Prokhor Abramovich began to pity the orphan, who was now disappearing over the top of the hill. "The wind will exhaust the boy's strength, he'll lie down in the boundary ditch and that'll be the end of him. The wide world is no wooden hut."

Prokhor Abramovich wanted to catch up with the orphan and bring him back so that they could all die in a heap and in peace—but he had children of his own back at home, along with a wife and the last remnants of the spring wheat.

"We're all of us good-for-nothing swine!" thought Prokhor Abramovich, this self-definition bringing him a degree of relief. All through the day, though, he was silently miserable in the hut, keeping himself busy with the useless activity of wood carving. At times of misfortune he always distracted himself by carving pines or imaginary trees—his knife was blunt and so his art had developed no further. Mavra Fetisovna wept intermittently over the adopted child who had left. Eight of her children had died—and she had sat by the stove and wept intermittently over each of them for three days. This was for her what wood carving was for her husband. He, for his part, already knew how much longer Mavra Fetisovna would weep while he himself carried on with his rough carvings: a day and a half.

Proshka watched and watched; in the end he began to feel jealous. "What are you two weeping about? Sasha will come back all right. And what you should be doing, Father, is making me some felt boots. Sasha's not your son—he's an orphan. All you're doing, old man, is sitting there blunting your knife."

"Heavens!" said Mavra Fetisovna. In her astonishment she had stopped crying. "He talks just like an adult. Only a little louse—and he's already scolding his father."

But Proshka was right: after two weeks the orphan came back. He brought so many rusks and dry buns that it seemed he could hardly have eaten anything himself. Nor did Sasha get a chance to eat anything back at home, because toward evening he lay down on the stove and couldn't get warm—all his warmth had been blown out of him by the winds of the road. In his delirium he mumbled about a stick hidden in the leaves and about his father: his father should take care of the stick and wait for Sasha to come to the lakeside dugout where crosses grow and fall.

Three weeks later, when the orphan had recovered, Prokhor Abramovich took his whip and walked to the city to stand in the market squares until he found work.

Twice Proshka followed Sasha to the cemetery. He saw that the orphan was digging himself a grave with his hands and that he couldn't dig deep. He brought the orphan his father's spade and said that it was easier to dig with a spade—that was how everyone dug.

"You'll be thrown out anyway," he informed Sasha. "Father hasn't sown anything since autumn, and come summer Mama will be laying again—let's hope it's not triplets. Yes, you'll be thrown out all right!"

Sasha kept trying to use the spade, but it was too big for him and the work soon exhausted him.

The occasional drops of sharp late rain chilled Proshka as he stood there and proffered advice: "Don't dig too wide—we can't afford a coffin, you'll be lying in the earth. And you'd better get on with it—Mama will be having her baby soon, we won't be wanting an extra mouth to feed."

"I'm digging a dugout," said Sasha. "I'm going to live here."

"Without any of our food?" inquired Proshka.

"Without anything at all. I'll pick chervil in the summer and live on that."

"All right then," said Proshka, now reassured. "But don't think you can come begging from us. We won't have anything to give away."

After earning enough for five forty-pound bags of flour, Prokhor Abramovich came back from the city on someone else's cart and lay down on the stove.

By the time they had eaten half of the flour, Proshka was wondering what they would do next. "Lazybones," he accused his father, who was looking down from his place on the stove at the identically screaming twins. "We'll get through the last of the flour—then starve to death. You brought us into the world—it's your job to feed us."

"A true splinter off the devil you are!" Prokhor Abramovich cursed from up above. "You try being father then, you little brat—take my place!"

Proshka sat there with perplexity on his face, wondering how to become Father. He already knew that children came out of Mother's belly—her belly was all scarred and wrinkled—but then where do orphans come from? Proshka had twice woken up in the night and seen that Mama's belly was being kneaded by Father—and then her belly had swollen and more hangers-on had been born, wanting more bread. He reminded his father about this: "Don't go lying on top of Mother, lie beside her and sleep. Look at Parashka. She hasn't got any little ones at all—Grandpa Fedot hasn't been kneading her belly."

Prokhor Abramovich got down from the stove, put on his felt boots, and looked around for something. There was nothing superfluous in the hut, so Prokhor Abramovich took a twig broom and struck Proshka across the face with it. Proshka didn't cry out—he simply lay facedown on the bench. Prokhor Abramovich silently began beating him, trying to accumulate rage inside himself.

"Doesn't hurt, doesn't hurt, still doesn't hurt," said Proshka, not showing his face.

After this beating, Proshka got up and said, without pausing for breath, "And send Sasha packing. We don't want any extra mouths here."

Prokhor Abramovich felt more beaten than Proshka and was sitting gloomily by the cradle with the now-silent twins. He had beaten Proshka because Proshka was right: Mavra Fetisovna was getting big again and there was no winter wheat to sow. Prokhor Abramovich's life was like the life of the grasses in the bottom of a hollow. In spring, floodwaters from melting snow rush down on them; in summer—downpours of rain; when it's windy—sand and dust; and in winter they're stifled by close, heavy snow. All the time, every minute, they live beneath blows and burdens—and this is why grasses in gullies grow hunchbacked, ready to bow down and let misfortune pass through them. What tumbled down on Prokhor Abramovich was children—they came more often than harvests and brought more trouble than being born oneself. Had the fields been as productive as his wife, and his wife in less of a hurry with her fertility, Prokhor Abramovich would long have been a well-fed and contented man. But all his life children had streamed down on him, and his soul had been buried, as a gully is buried by silt, beneath clayey accumulations of cares—which had led to Prokhor Abramovich having almost no sense of his own life and personal concerns. Those who were childless and free interpreted this state of oblivion as laziness.

"Proshka, Proshka, my boy!" called Prokhor Abramovich.

"What is it?" Proshka asked sullenly. "First you beat me, then you call me 'My boy.'"

"Proshka, run along to Auntie Marya and see what her belly's doing—is it big or small? Seems I haven't seen her for a long time. She isn't ill, is she?"

Proshka seldom felt resentful for long and he was businesslike when it came to family needs.

"I should be Father and you should be Proshka," he said in a matter-of-fact tone. "What's the good of looking at her belly? You haven't sown any winter wheat, so we'll be going hungry anyway."

Proshka put on his mother's jerkin, then went on grumbling away as if he were head of the household. "People talk a lot of nonsense. There were rains last summer, but Marya stayed empty. She could have given birth to another bread eater, but she missed her chance."

"The winter wheat froze," his father said quietly. "She was right."

"A baby sucks its mother, it doesn't eat bread," Proshka retorted. "And the mother can eat the spring wheat. I'm not running along to look at that Marya of yours. If her belly's big, then you'll just stay there on top of the stove. You'll say there'll be plenty of wheat and wild grains in the spring. But we lot don't want to starve—and it's you and Mama who brought us into this world."

Prokhor Abramovich said nothing. He and Sasha were similar, both speaking only when asked a question. In his dealings with Proshka, Prokhor Abramovich—though he was in his own house—was sometimes like an orphan himself. Nevertheless, he still didn't really know what to make of Sasha. Was he a good soul or not? Fear may have prompted him to go out begging, but there was no knowing what other thoughts went through his head. In reality, Sasha had few thoughts because he considered all adults and other children to be cleverer than him, and he was afraid of them. But he was less afraid of Prokhor Abramovich than of Proshka, who counted every crumb and who had no love for outsiders.

4

WALKING through the village, his bottom sticking out and his long, destructive hands brushing the grass, was a hunchbacked cripple: Piotr Fyodorovich Kondaev. It was a long time since he had had any pains in the small of his back—a sign that the weather was not going to change.

That year the sun had ripened early up in the sky; it was burning as fiercely by the end of April as it usually did deep in July. The men fell silent, their feet sensing dry soil and the rest of their bodies sensing a space of deathly heat that was now here to stay. The children observed the horizons, so as not to miss the appearance of a rain cloud. But from the dirt roads rose whirling columns of dust, and carts from other villages continued to pass through this dust.

Kondaev was now walking down the middle of the street toward the other end of the village—toward the home of fifteen-year-old Nastya, the wench who was his soul's constant concern. He loved her with a part of himself that was often painful and that was as sensitive as the heart of someone more upright—the place where his hump broke out from his lower back. To Kondaev the drought was a pleasure and he had high hopes of it. His hands were always all yellow and green—as he walked along, he destroyed grasses and rubbed them between his fingers. He was glad of the famine, which would drive every good-looking man far away in search of work—and many of them would die, freeing the women for Kondaev. Under the taut sun, which made the soil burn and smoke with dust, Kondaev smiled. Every morning he washed in the pond and caressed his hump with strong, sure hands that were fit for inexhaustible embraces of his future wife.

"All right," he said, content with himself. "The men will go away—and the women will stay. And once a woman's had a taste of me, she'll remember me all her life—I'm a mean lean bull of a man."

Kondaev clapped his long, thoroughbred hands and imagined he was holding Nastya in them. He even felt surprised: How was it that in Nastya, in such weakness of body, lived secret, mighty charm? The mere thought of her was enough to make him swell with blood and go hard. To free himself of the pull and palpability of his imagination, he would swim in the pond and take as much water inside him as if there were a cave in his body; he then sprayed it back out again together with the saliva of love's sweetness.

On his way home, Kondaev spoke to every man he encountered and advised them to leave the village and look for work. "The city's a fortress," he said. "There's plenty of everything there, while here the sun glares down point-blank and it will keep on like that. Think there'll be a harvest? You must be mad!"

"But what about you, Piotr Fyodorovich?" the man would reply, asking about another's fate in order to find a way out for himself too.

"I'm a cripple," Kondaev announced. "I'll be fine—I'll live off pity. But you'll soon be starving your woman to death, you great hump-head. You should go and look for work—you'll be needing to send her a few cartloads of flour."

"Yes, maybe I will," the man would sigh reluctantly, still hoping to get by one way or another without leaving home—living off the odd cabbage and berry, along with mushrooms and grasses. And after that—well, who knows?

Kondaev loved old wattle fences, the clefts of dead tree stumps, and every kind of decrepitude, sickliness, and submissive, barely living warmth. In these solitary places the quiet evil of his lust found its joy. He would have liked to wear the whole village down to a state of exhausted silence, so that nothing would hinder his embrace of powerless living beings. Kondaev lay in the silence of morning shadows and foresaw half-ruined villages, overgrown streets, and a thin, blackened Nastya, delirious from hunger, lying in prickly, dried-up straw.[1] The merest glimpse of life, whether in a blade of grass or a young girl, transported Kondaev into quiet jealous savagery. If it was grass, he would crush it to death in his merciless, amorous hands, which sensed any living thing as avidly and terribly as the virginity of a woman; if it was a woman or girl, he was filled in advance and forever with hatred for her father, her brothers, and her husband or future husband, and he wished they would die or else disappear in search of work. This second hungry year filled Kondaev with hope—soon he would be the only man left in the village and he would rage over the women to his heart's desire.

The intense heat was quickly aging not only plants, but also the village huts and the stakes in the wattle fences. Sasha had noticed the same thing the summer before. In the morning he would see peaceful, transparent dawns and recall his father and early childhood on the shore of Lake Mutevo. And then, as bells rang for the early liturgy, the sun would rise and quickly transform the whole earth and village into old age, into people's dry, congealing malice.

Proshka climbed onto the roof, wrinkling his troubled face as he kept watch on the sky. Every morning he asked his father the same questions: Was the small of his back aching? And when would the moon be washing?[2]

Kondaev liked walking up and down the village street at midday, delighting in the frenzy of buzzing insects. Once he noticed Proshka leaping out onto the street in only his shirt because he thought there'd been a drop from the sky.

The huts were almost singing from the terrible silence, a silence made incandescent by the sun, while the straw on the roofs had blackened and was giving off a slow smell of smoldering.

"Hey, Proshka!" called the hunchback. "Watching over the sky, are you? Not exactly cold today, is it?"

Proshka understood that there hadn't been any drop from the sky—he had only imagined it. "Go grope other people's hens, you broken cripple!" he said, more and more upset by his disappointment over the drop. "People are living their last hour of life—and the man's glad. Go grope Papa's cockerel!"

Inadvertently and precisely, Proshka had hit the mark. In answer,

Kondaev cried out in sharp pain and bent to the ground, looking for a stone. There was no stone, and so he threw a handful of dry dust at Proshka. But Proshka knew everything in advance and was already back in his hut. The hunchback ran into the yard, his hands trailing along the ground as he ran. There he came across Sasha. Kondaev swung at him and struck him with the bones of his lean fingers, and the bones in Sasha's head resounded. Sasha fell; the skin on his skull had burst and his hair was soaking in clean, cool blood.

Sasha regained consciousness but then half forgot himself again and saw his dream. Still remembering that it was hot, that it was a long, hungry day, and that he had been hit by the hunchback, Sasha saw his father out on the lake amid damp mist. Father was on a boat, disappearing into murky places and throwing mother's tin ring onto the shore. Sasha was picking the ring up from the damp grass and then the hunchback was loudly hitting him on the head with it. There was a crack as the sky split apart and black rain suddenly poured from its fissures. Everything went silent; the ringing of the white sun died away behind a mountain, on drowning meadows. On these meadows stood the hunchback, pissing on a small sun that was already fading of its own accord. But alongside the dream Sasha could see the present day, which was still continuing, and he could hear Proshka talking to Prokhor Abramovich.

Kondaev, meanwhile, was chasing someone else's hen from one threshing floor to another, making the most of the dearth of people and the general misery. He did not catch the hen—it flew up in fear into a tree beside the street. Kondaev wanted to shake the tree but he saw someone coming by on a cart and quietly set off back home—as if thinking about nothing in particular. Proshka had spoken the truth: Kondaev liked groping hens and sometimes went on groping them until the hen began to shit on his hand in pain and horror, although there were occasions when it prematurely laid a liquid egg; if there were no people around, Kondaev would suck up the immature egg from his cupped hand and tear off the hen's head.

In autumn, if there had been a good harvest, people still had a lot of strength left in them, and grown-ups and children alike would entertain themselves tormenting the hunchback: "Piotr Fyodorovich, for the love of God, come and feel our cockerel!"

These insults were more than Kondaev could endure, and he would chase after the offenders until he'd caught some youngster or other and inflicted some minor mutilation on them.

Now, once again, Sasha saw only the same old day. He had long seen heat in the guise of an old man, and night and cool in the guise of little boys and girls.

A window in the hut had been opened and Mavra Fetisovna was tossing about desperately beside the stove. For all her practice in giving birth, something was now getting too much for her.

"I'm feeling sick! This is getting hard, Prokhor Abramovich. Get the midwife."

Not until the bell for vespers, not until long, sad shadows, did Sasha get up from the grass. The windows in the hut were closed and the curtains drawn. The midwife carried a tub out into the yard and emptied it by the fence. A dog ran up and ate everything except the liquid.[3] Proshka was in the hut; he hadn't come out for a long time. The other children were running about in neighbors' yards. Sasha was afraid of getting up and going inside at the wrong time. The shadows of the grasses had joined together and the light, low wind that had been blowing through them all day had dropped. The midwife came out onto the porch in her headscarf, said a prayer toward the dark east, and left. Calm night began. A cricket in the little earth bank tried out its voice, then sang for a long time—and its song wrapped the yard, the grass, and the distant fence into a single children's birthland where life was better than anywhere else in the world. Sasha looked at the buildings—changed by darkness but now more familiar than ever—at the wattle fences and the shafts of sleighs overgrown by grass—and he felt sorry for them: they were just like him, but they were silent, they couldn't move, and one day they would die forever.

Sasha thought that if he left, it would be still more boring for them all to live in one place, and Sasha felt glad that he was needed here.

Inside the hut the new baby began to howl, and the cricket's steady song was drowned out by a voice unlike any word. The cricket fell silent—it too was probably listening to the frightening howl. Proshka came out, carrying Prokhor Abramovich's hat and the bag with which they'd sent Sasha out to beg in the autumn.

"Sasha!" Proshka shouted into the breathless night air. "Come here at once, you parasite!"

Sasha was close by. "What is it?" he asked.

"Here, take this—Father's giving you his hat. And here's your bag—go away and keep it with you. And whatever you collect, eat it yourself. Don't bring it back to us."

"And you're all going to carry on living here without me?" asked Sasha, unable to believe they had stopped loving him there.

"Sure—why wouldn't we? We've got one more bread eater here now—otherwise you could live here for free. But we don't want you around now. You're a burden. Mama didn't give birth to you—you got born on your own."

Sasha went off beyond the wicket gate. Proshka stood for a while on his own, then followed the orphan out, to remind him not to come back again. The orphan had not yet gone anywhere—he was looking at the small light in the windmill.

"Sasha," Proshka ordered, "don't go coming back here again! We've put bread in your bag, we've given you a hat—so get going! If you like, you can sleep in the barn, it'll be night soon. But don't come anywhere near the windows or Father might change his mind."

Sasha set off toward the cemetery. Proshka locked the gate, looked round their yard, and picked up a stray pole.

"Not a single damned drop of rain!" Proshka said in the voice of an old person, and spat through a gap in his front teeth. "Beat your head against the damned ground for all the good it'll do!"

Sasha made his way to his father's grave and lay down in the little cave he'd half dug. Walking among the crosses was frightening, but he fell asleep as peacefully beside his father as he had long ago, in their dugout on the shore of the lake.

Later two peasants came into the graveyard and quietly began breaking off crosses for firewood, but Sasha, carried away by sleep, heard nothing.

5

ZAKHAR Pavlovich lived without any need for anyone: he could sit for hours before the door of a locomotive firebox where a flame was burning.

This replaced for him the great pleasure of friendship and conversation with people. Observing a living flame, Zakhar Pavlovich would live too—his head thinking in him, his heart feeling, and his whole body quietly contented. Zakhar Pavlovich respected coal, wrought iron, sleeping raw materials, and half-manufactured items of all kinds, but he truly loved and sensed only the finished artifacts into which man had been transformed through labor and that would live on further with a life of their own. During lunch breaks Zakhar Pavlovich didn't take his eyes off the locomotive and silently suffered inside him the love he felt for it. He had amassed in his lodgings a large number of bolts, old valves, petcocks, and other mechanical articles. He had put them in a row and would spend hours gazing at them, never feeling bored or alone. And Zakhar Pavlovich certainly was not alone—to him machines were people, and they awoke feelings, thoughts, and wishes in him. The locomotive's front wheels—its pony truck—made Zakhar Pavlovich start to worry about the infinity of space. He went out at night just to look at the stars: Was there space in the world? Was there room enough in it for wheels to live and turn eternally? The stars shone with enthusiasm, but each one was alone. Zakhar Pavlovich wondered what the sky resembled. And he remembered the junction station, where he had sometimes been sent to collect wheel flanges. From the platform he had seen a sea of solitary signals; he had seen switches, semaphores, crossovers, warning lights, and the headlamps of speeding locomotives. The sky was no different, just more distant and better ordered as regards calm work. Then Zakhar Pavlovich tried to judge by eye how far it was to a deep blue, changing star; he held his hands apart to make a gauge, then mentally applied this gauge to space. The star was shining two hundred versts away. This disturbed him, although he had read that the world was infinite. He would have liked the world to be well and truly infinite so that wheels would always be necessary and be fashioned without interruption for the joy of all, but he found it impossible to sense infinity.

"It's a long way," said Zakhar Pavlovich. "Goodness knows how many versts. But somewhere or other the last little bit runs out and you find you've come to a dead end. If infinity really did exist, it would simply unravel in all that space and there would no longer be anything hard. Infinity—huh! There has to be a dead end somewhere."

For two whole days and nights Zakhar Pavlovich was troubled by the thought that there might, in the end, not be enough work for wheels, but then it occurred to him that the world could be stretched out when all the roads and tracks came to an end; space too, like strip iron, could be warmed up and made to go farther. After that, Zakhar Pavlovich gave no more thought to infinity.

The foreman was aware of Zakhar Pavlovich's loving work—he cleaned fireboxes till they shone and never damaged the metal—but he never said so much as a word of praise to him. The foreman knew very well that machines live and move more of their own accord than because of the mind and competence of people; people have nothing to do with it. On the contrary, the goodness of nature, of energy and metal, merely spoils people. Any idiot can light a fire in a firebox—but the locomotive will move forward by itself, and the idiot will be mere freight. And if technology goes on being so obliging, then people's doubtful successes will lead them to degenerate into rust—and there'll be nothing left but to have hardworking locomotives crush the lot of them and to give the machine the freedom of the world. The foreman, however, abused Zakhar Pavlovich less than he abused the others: Zakhar Pavlovich always used a hammer with sorrow rather than with crude force; he did not spit just anywhere when he was working on a locomotive, and he did not scratch the bodies of machines mercilessly with his tools.

"Mister Foreman!" Zakhar Pavlovich asked on one occasion, emboldened by his love for the cause. "Why is it that man's just so-so, neither bad nor good, while machines are all equally splendid?"

The foreman listened angrily. He was jealous of other people's regard for locomotives, considering his own feeling for them to be a personal privilege.

"Gray devil!" the foreman said to himself. "Who does he think he is—loving mechanisms! Dear God!"

Opposite the two men stood a locomotive that was being fired up for a night express. The foreman looked at the locomotive for a long time and was filled with his usual joyful sympathy. The locomotive stood huge and magnanimous, and there was warmth in the harmonious curves of its majestic tall body. The foreman concentrated, sensing inside him an unaccountable humming ecstasy. The gates of the depot opened into the evening space of summer—into a swarthy future, into a life that can repeat itself in the wind, in elemental speeds on the rails, and in the self-abandon of night, risk, and the tender thrum of a precise machine.

A surge of some kind of savage strength of inner life, similar to youth and a premonition of the thundering future, led the foreman to clench his hands into fists. He forgot Zakhar Pavlovich's lowly qualifications and answered, as if to a friend or an equal, "You've done a bit of work and it's done your mind some good. While people—pah! They lie around in their homes and are worthless. And as for birds . . ."

A locomotive let off steam, drowning all words. The foreman and Zakhar Pavlovich went out into the resonant evening air and began walking about between ranks of cold locomotives.

"Yes, take birds! They're very charming, but they don't work—and that means they leave nothing behind when they're gone. Have you seen birds labor? They don't. Granted, they fuss about a bit for food and shelter—but where are their technological artifacts? Where's their angle of application on their own lives? There's no such thing, and there never will be."

"But what's man got?" asked Zakhar Pavlovich, not understanding.

"Man has machines! Understand? Man is the starting point for every mechanism, while birds just end in themselves."

Zakhar Pavlovich thought the same as the foreman, and he lagged behind only in finding the necessary words—which was an irritating brake on his musings. To the two men nature untouched by man seemed charmless and dead—tree and beast alike. Neither beasts nor trees awoke in Zakhar Pavlovich and the foreman any fellow feeling, since no man had taken part in their production; there was no precision of craftsmanship in them, not a single conscious tap with a hammer. They lived independently, unseen by Zakhar Pavlovich's lowered eyes. Whereas any artifact, especially if made from metal, lived an enlivened existence and even—with regard to both structure and strength—seemed more interesting and mysterious than man. Zakhar Pavlovich took great delight in one constant thought: How was it that a strength hidden in man's blood had suddenly manifested itself in exciting machines that were greater than their makers in both size and significance?

And it really was just as the foreman said: in labor every man surpasses himself, crafting artifacts that are better and more durable than his own day-to-day significance. Moreover, Zakhar Pavlovich observed in locomotives the same hot excited human strength that in a working man remains speechless and without any outlet. Usually a metalworker only talks well when he's had a few drinks; inside a locomotive, however, man always feels he is big and terrible.

Once Zakhar Pavlovich was unable for a long time to find the bolt he needed to restore the thread of a damaged nut. He wandered about the depot, asking if anyone had a three-eighths bolt. He was told there was no such thing, although everyone in the depot had some. In reality the men were simply feeling bored, and they amused themselves through mutual complication of one another's tasks. Zakhar Pavlovich was not yet familiar with the sly, hidden merriment to be found in any workshop. This quiet jesting allowed the other workers to endure the length of the working day and the tedium of repetitive labor. In the name of amusing his neighbors, Zakhar Pavlovich had performed many unnecessary tasks. He went to get rags from the store when there were heaps of them lying in the office; he made wooden ladders and containers for oil when there were more than enough of them in the depot already. On one occasion he was even prompted, without authorization from a superior, to change the fusible plugs in a locomotive boiler; had he not been stopped in time by a chance stoker, he would have been dismissed without further ado.

Unable to find the necessary bolt, Zakhar Pavlovich began cutting a thread on a pintle, and he would have succeeded in this task, because his patience never ran out, but someone handed him a bolt and said, "Hey, Three-Eighths Bolt, here you are!"

From then on Zakhar Pavlovich was known as "Three-Eighths Bolt"; he was less often misled, however, when there was some tool he urgently needed.

Never, though, did anyone realize that Zakhar Pavlovich preferred the name Three-Eighths Bolt to his Christian name; it was like a crucial part of any and every machine and it somehow allowed Zakhar Pavlovich to share bodily in that true country where iron inches triumph over earthly versts.

6

WHEN Zakhar Pavlovich was young he had thought that when he was big he'd grow clever. But life passed by like a sheer enthusiasm, with no taking stock of anything and no stops. Not once did Zakhar Pavlovich sense time as some solid thing coming toward him; for him it existed only as a riddle in the mechanism of the alarm clock. But when Zakhar Pavlovich learned the secret of the pendulum, he saw that there was no such thing as time; there was only the evenly balanced taut force of the spring. But there was something quiet and sad in nature—some forces or other were clearly acting irrevocably. Zakhar Pavlovich observed rivers: nothing in them wavered, neither their speed nor the level of their water, and this constancy was a source of bitter anguish. There were, of course, floods, and suffocating downpours, and winds that knocked the breath out of you, but what operated most of the time was quiet, indifferent life—flows of water, the growth of grasses, and the changing seasons. Zakhar Pavlovich supposed that these evenly balanced forces kept the whole earth in stupor; to him they seemed proof that nothing changes for the better—as villages and people were, so they will remain. In the name of the preservation of the balance of forces in nature, human misfortune keeps being repeated. Four years ago the harvest had failed—men had left the village in search of work and children had lain down in early graves—but this fate had not gone away forever. It had returned, for the precision of movement of general life.[1]

No matter how long he lived, Zakhar Pavlovich saw with astonishment, he was neither changing nor growing cleverer; he stayed exactly the same as when he was ten or fifteen years old. A few of his former foresensings had now become everyday thoughts, but this had not brought about any change for the better. He had seen his future life as a deep and deep-blue expanse, so far away as to be almost deathless. Zakhar Pavlovich had thought that the farther he lived, the smaller this space of unlived life would become, while the dead, trampled-down path behind him would grow longer and longer. He had been mistaken; life went on growing and accumulating, yet the future in front of him also went on growing and stretching onward—more deeply and mysteriously than in his youth, as if Zakhar Pavlovich were moving away from the end of his own life or intensifying his hopes and faith in life.

Seeing his face in the glass of locomotive headlamps, he would say to himself, "Would you believe it! Soon I'll be dying, but I'm still the same as ever."

Toward the beginning of autumn, the number of holidays increased; one week, three consecutive days were holidays.[2] This made Zakhar Pavlovich feel bored, and he would walk far down the railway line in order to see trains moving at full speed. On the way he suddenly found himself wanting to go and visit the mining village where his mother was buried. He had an exact memory of the burial place and someone else's metal cross beside the meek and nameless grave of his mother. The cross still bore a rusty eternal inscription now almost wasted away—about the death of Ksenia Fyodorovna Iroshnikova in 1813, from the illness of cholera, at the age of eighteen years and three months. Also engraved there were the words SLEEP IN PEACE, BELOVED DAUGHTER, TILL THE DAY THE YOUNG MEET THEIR PARENTS AGAIN.

Zakhar Pavlovich felt a strong wish to dig up his mother's grave and have a look at her, at her bones and hair and all the last disappearing remnants of his childhood birthland. Even now he would not have minded having a living mother, because he didn't sense in himself any particular difference from childhood. Then too, in the light blue mist of his early days, he had loved nails on a fence, the smoke of roadside forges, and the wheels on a cart—because they turned.

Wherever little Zakhar Pavlovich went when he left home, he had known that he had a mother, eternally waiting for him, and he had been afraid of nothing.

The railway line was sheltered on both sides by bushes. Sometimes there were beggars sitting in the shade of the bushes, eating or changing their footwear. They saw triumphant locomotives pulling trains at high speeds. But not one beggar knew what made these locomotives move. Nor did any of them ever think about a simpler question: What kind of happiness were they living for? Nor did any of the almsgivers know what faith, hope, and love lent strength to the beggars' legs on the sandy roads. Sometimes Zakhar Pavlovich would drop two kopeks into an outstretched hand. Without giving any thought to it, he was paying for what he had been granted and they had been deprived of: an understanding of machines.

A tousle-headed boy was sitting beside the railway and sorting through rusks, putting the moldy ones to one side and the fresher ones into his bag. The boy was thin, but his face was lively and alert.

Zakhar Pavlovich stopped, drawing on his cigarette in the fresh air of early autumn. "Grading, eh?" he asked.

The boy didn't understand this technical term. "Give us a kopek, uncle," he said, "or let me finish your smoke for you."

Zakhar Pavlovich took out five kopeks. "Probably you're just a cheeky little bastard," he said, destroying the goodness of his act with coarse words, so as not to feel ashamed.

"No, I'm not a bastard, I'm a beggar," the boy replied, packing the rusks tight into his bag. "I've got a mother and father—only they've disappeared because of the hunger."

"Who's this great bag of food for then?"

"I'm going to see if there's anyone at home. Mother and the little ones might have come back. They'll need something to eat."

"Whose kid are you?"

"My father's—I'm no orphan. But it's the other beggars who're cheeky bastards—I've had sense whipped into me by my father."

"And who is your father?"

"My father came from my mother too—out of her belly. A man

kneads her belly and out come bread eaters, as if from nowhere. Just you try begging for that crowd!"

Dissatisfaction with his father made the boy sink into gloom. He'd long ago tucked the five kopeks away in the pouch that hung from his neck and that already held a fair number of other copper coins.

"You must be worn out by now," said Zakhar Pavlovich.

"Yes, I am," the boy agreed. "It's hard work, you know, getting money out of devils like you. I have to blag and blag till I'm famished. You've given me five kopeks—and I bet you wish you hadn't. You wouldn't catch me giving money away."

The boy took a moldy crust from the pile of spoiled bread; he was evidently taking the best bread back to the village—to his parents—and eating the bad bread himself. Zakhar Pavlovich liked this.

"I suppose your father must really love you?"

"He doesn't love anything—he's a lazybones. I love my mother more, blood comes out of her insides. Once I washed her shirt, when she was ill."

"What's your father's name?"

"Papa Proshka. But we're not from round here."

Zakhar Pavlovich inadvertently remembered a sunflower growing from the chimney of an abandoned hut, and thickets of tall grass on a village street. "So you're Proshka Dvanov, you son of a bitch!"

The boy expelled from his mouth a half-chewed green mess, but he didn't throw it away. He put it on top of his bag—to be finished later.

"Are you Uncle Zakhar then?"

"Yes."

Zakhar Pavlovich sat down. He had suddenly sensed time in another way: time was Proshka's journey from his mother into alien cities. Zakhar Pavlovich saw that time was the movement of grief and that it was as tangible an object as any substance, even if nothing could be fashioned from it.

Someone who looked like a novice discharged from his vows, instead of continuing on his way, sat down and stared at Zakhar Pavlovich and the boy. His lips were red, having kept the puffy charm of infancy; his eyes were meek, though without sharp intelligence. It was not the face of an ordinary vagrant—most vagrants are accustomed to having to pit their wits against constant misfortune.

Proshka was disturbed by this man, especially by his lips.

"What are you sticking out your lips for? Want to kiss my hand?"

This novice got to his feet and continued on his own particular way, with no precise idea where it led.

Proshka sensed this at once and called out after him, "Off he goes—but where he's going, he doesn't know. Turn him round—and back he'll come. Bread-eating devil!"

Zakhar Pavlovich was a little startled by Proshka's early quickness of mind—he himself had been slow to understand people's ways and had long thought them cleverer than himself.

"Proshka!" Zakhar Pavlovich began. "What happened to that little boy, the fisherman's orphan? Your mother took him in."

"You mean Sasha?" Proshka replied. "He left the village before any of us. He was a fiend—the bane of our lives. He stole our last loaf of bread and off he went into the night. I ran after him, I ran and ran. Then I gave up and went back home."

Zakhar Pavlovich believed and fell into thought.

"And where's your father?"

"Looking for work. And he told me to feed the whole family. I traveled far and wide begging for bread. Then I went back home and found no one there. No mother and no children. Nettles in the huts instead of people."

Zakhar Pavlovich gave Proshka fifty kopeks and told him to call round again when he next came to the city.

"Give me your cap—you don't care about anything anyway," said Proshka. "Otherwise, I'll be getting my head washed by the rain—I might catch cold."

Zakhar Pavlovich gave him his cap, first removing his railwayman's badge—which was dearer to him than any headgear.

A long-distance train went by and Proshka stood up, wanting to get away quickly, before Zakhar Pavlovich took back the money and cap. The cap fit ted Proshka's shaggy head perfectly—but he merely tried it on, took it off again, and stuffed it into his bag, along with the bread.

"Well, goodbye," said Zakhar Pavlovich. "God be with you!"

"Easy enough for you to say," said Proshka. "You've always got bread. We haven't."

Zakhar Pavlovich didn't know what more to say—he had no more money.

"The other day I saw Sasha in the city," said Proshka, sounding more and more serious. "The dumb idiot's not going to last long. He's too shy to beg properly, so nobody gives him anything. I gave him some bread and went hungry myself. It must have been you who first brought Sasha to mother—so you should give us some money for him!"

"See if you can bring him to me sometime," said Zakhar Pavlovich.

"How much will you give me?"

"Come payday, I'll give you a rouble."

"Very well," said Proshka. "In that case I'll bring him. But don't let him visit too often—or he'll walk all over you."

Proshka set off—but not on the road that led to his village. No doubt he had calculations and farseeing plans of his own with regard to the procurement of bread.

Zakhar Pavlovich watched for a while as Proshka went on his way. Somehow he began to doubt whether artifacts and machines truly were more precious than any human being.

The boy was moving farther and farther away, and with vast nature deposited all around him, his petty body seemed more and more pitiful. Proshka was walking along the railway line on foot, while others rode in trains; the railway line had nothing to do with Proshka and did not help him. He looked at bridges, rails, and locomotives as indifferently as he looked at the trees, winds, and sands beside the line. For Proshka, every artificial construction was merely another form of nature on land that belonged to others. By means of a live reasoning mind, he went on somehow or other tensely existing. Yet he could hardly be fully sensing his own mind; this was clear from the way he spoke unexpectedly, almost unconsciously, and was surprised at times by his own words, whose reason was higher than his childhood.

Proshka disappeared round a curve in the line—alone, small, and with no defense of any kind. Zakhar Pavlovich wanted to bring him back forever, but the boy was too far away.

The next morning Zakhar Pavlovich felt less than his usual desire to go to work. In the evening he felt a sense of anguish and went straight to bed. The bolts, petcocks, and pressure gauges that always stayed on the table could not dispel his boredom and emptiness—he looked at these things and felt he didn't belong with them. Something was boring through him; it was as if his heart were grinding away, having gone into reverse and not being used to this. Zakhar Pavlovich was unable to forget Proshka's thin little body wandering down the line into a distance where a vast, obstructive nature seemed to have collapsed all around him. Zakhar Pavlovich thought without clear thoughts, without the complexity of words—just with the heat of impressionable feelings—and this caused him great torment. He could see the pitifulness of Proshka, who didn't even realize how bleak things were for him; he could see the railway line working separately from Proshka and his sharp-witted life—and he was unable to understand what any of this was about; he simply felt sad and couldn't give a name to his sorrow.

The following day—two days after the meeting with Proshka—Zakhar Pavlovich did not go inside the depot. He took down his ticket in the workers' entrance but then hung it back up again. He spent the day in a gully, under the sun and spiderwebs of a Saint Martin's summer. He heard the whistles of locomotives and the noise of their speed but he didn't go and look, no longer respecting locomotives.

The fisherman had drowned in Lake Mutevo, the loner had died in the forest, and the empty village had been overgrown by tabernacles of grass, but the verger's clock kept going, and the trains kept going too, in accord with the timetable, and the correctness of these clocks and trains now made Zakhar Pavlovich feel dismal and ashamed.

"What if Proshka had *his* savvy and *my* years?" Zakhar Pavlovich considered. "He'd shake things up all right, the son of a bitch. Though little Sasha would still be begging even in Proshka's kingdom."

The warm mist of love for machines in which Zakhar Pavlovich had lived peacefully and securely had been scattered by a clean wind, and Zakhar Pavlovich saw before him the defenseless lonely life of people who live naked, without the self-deceit of faith in the help of machines.

The foreman gradually ceased to hold Zakhar Pavlovich in regard. "I really thought you might be a master, one of the old school," he said to himself, "but you're the same as the rest of them. Factory fodder, slag shit out by a woman."

Zakhar Pavlovich's confusion of soul really did bring about the loss of his diligent skill. It turned out to be difficult even to hit a nail correctly on the head just for the sake of payment with money. The foreman knew this better than anyone. Once a worker had lost the feeling that drew him toward machines, once labor had ceased to be a man's second nature and become mere monetary need, it would be the end of the world—or worse: after the last master had died, the last bastards would come to life, to devour the plants of the sun and spoil the artifacts of the masters.

7

THE SON of the inquisitive fisherman was so meek that he thought everything in life was for real. When no one gave him alms, he believed they were all no richer than he was. If he was still alive, it was only because one young metalworker had a wife who had fallen ill and there had been no one to leave her with when he went out to work. Alone in the room, his wife felt bored and frightened. And there was a charm about this boy—who was gray from exhaustion and who begged without the least attention to what anyone gave him—that appealed to the worker. He sat the boy down to watch over the sick woman, who remained dearer to him than anyone in the world.

For days on end Sasha sat on a stool beside the sick woman's feet, and the woman seemed as beautiful to him as his mother had been in his father's memories. And so he kept on living, helping the sick woman with the selflessness of a late childhood that no one before had accepted. The woman grew to love him and, unaccustomed to having a servant, always spoke to him respectfully, addressing him by his full name: Alexander.[1] But she soon recovered and her husband said to Sasha, "There you are, there's twenty kopeks for you—now go and find somewhere else!"

Sasha took the unfamiliar money, went out into the yard, and began to cry.

Beside the privy, sitting astride the garbage and rummaging about beneath him, was Proshka. He was gathering bones, rags, and tin. He was smoking, and his face had aged from the dust and ashes of garbage heaps.

"Weeping again, you snot-nosed devil?" asked Proshka, not interrupting his work. "Do a bit of digging about yourself. I'll go and get myself some tea—I ate something salty."

Proshka, however, went not to the tavern but to Zakhar Pavlovich. Zakhar Pavlovich, being only barely literate, was reading a book aloud to himself: "Count Victor put his hand to his brave and devoted heart and said, 'I love you, my darling.'"

At first Proshka was silent, thinking Zakhar Pavlovich was telling an old fairy tale, but then he lost interest and said, "Zakhar Pavlovich, give us a rouble. I'll bring you little Sasha the orphan."

"Eh?" exclaimed Zakhar Pavlovich in alarm, turning toward Proshka. His face looked sad and old, though his wife would still have loved it had she been alive.

Proshka once again named his price for Sasha, and Zakhar Pavlovich gave him a rouble; it would be good to have someone else around, even if it were only Sasha. The carpenter had left to work in a factory where they creosoted sleepers, and Zakhar Pavlovich had ended up with the emptiness of two rooms. During the preceding months, life with the carpenter's sons had been entertaining, though hardly peaceful. The lads had grown so big that they didn't know what to do with their own strength; they had set fire to the house several times but had always quenched these fires without letting them get out of hand. The father raged at them, but they just said, "Why are you so scared of a bit of fire, old man? What burns will never rot. We should burn you too, you old fool. Then you won't rot in the grave and make a stink."

Before they all left, the sons had flattened the privy and docked the yard dog's tail.

Proshka didn't go to fetch Sasha straightaway. First he bought a packet of Fellow Villager cigarettes and had a chat with the women in the stall. Then he went back to the garbage heap.

"Sasha," he said. "Come with me. I'm going to take you somewhere—to get you to stop pestering me once and for all."

8

DURING the following years Zakhar Pavlovich fell deeper and deeper into decline. So as not to die alone, he got himself a companion, a dreary woman by the name of Darya Stepanovna. Losing his sense of self made life easier for him: at the depot he was distracted by work, and at home he was nagged by this woman. This double shift of tedium brought no joy to Zakhar Pavlovich, but without it he would have wandered off and become a tramp. Machines and artifacts no longer held any passionate interest for him. First, however much he worked, people went on living poor and pitiful lives; second, the world had clouded over and become no more than an indifferent daydream—probably Zakhar Pavlovich was too worn-out and was indeed foresensing his own quiet death. So it often goes with craftsmen approaching old age; the hard substances they have been dealing with for whole decades secretly teach them the immutability of universal destructive fate. Before their very eyes, locomotives are taken out of service; they decay for years beneath the sun and are then broken up for scrap. On Sundays Zakhar Pavlovich would go to the river, to catch fish and think through his last thoughts.

At home his consolation was young Sasha, though his constantly dissatisfied wife prevented him from concentrating even on him. Maybe this was for the best: if Zakhar Pavlovich had been able to concentrate entirely on what moved him, he would probably have begun to cry.

Whole years passed by in this life of distraction. Sometimes, as he watched Sasha reading, Zakhar Pavlovich would ask from his bed, "Sasha, is anything troubling you?"

"No," Sasha would answer, accustomed as he was to the ways of his adoptive father.

"What do you think?" Zakhar Pavlovich would say, continuing his doubts. "Is it absolutely necessary for everyone to live, or not?"

"Yes, it certainly is," said Sasha, who had some understanding of his father's anguish.

"Have you ever read anything that says *why*?"

Sasha put his book down. "I've read that the further it goes, the better life gets."

"Ah!" said Zakhar Pavlovich trustingly. "Is that written in print?"

"Yes, it is."

Zakhar Pavlovich sighed. "All things are possible. Few can know."

Sasha had been working in the depot for a year as an apprentice, to qualify as a mechanic. He was attracted to machines and the mastering of new skills, though not in the same way as Zakhar Pavlovich; his attraction was not the curiosity that comes to an end with the discovery of a machine's secret. He was interested by machines in the same way as he was interested by everything active and living; what he wanted was less to know them than to feel them, to live their life. So, on his way back from work, Sasha would imagine he was a locomotive and would produce all the noises of a locomotive in motion. As he fell asleep, he would think that the village hens had all been asleep for a long time, and this sense of community with hens or a locomotive brought him satisfaction. Sasha was unable ever to act separately; first, he would look for something similar to his action, and then he would act—not out of his own need but out of sympathy for something or someone.

"Just like me," Sasha would often say. "I'm no different." Looking at an aged fence, he would say in a heartfelt voice, "Still standing!"—and then stand there a while for no reason. Sitting at home on autumn evenings, when the shutters creaked dismally and Sasha felt bored and dreary, he would listen to the shutters, sense how dreary it was for them—and give up feeling dreary himself.

When Sasha felt tired of going out to work, he would console himself by thinking about the wind, which blew day and night. Seeing it, he would say, "I'm no different. But I only work days. The wind works nights too. That's even worse."

Trains began to run more frequently—war had begun. The war meant nothing to the railway workers—they weren't sent off to fight and the war was as distant from their lives as the locomotives that the workers repaired and refueled only for them to haul carriages transporting unknown and idle people.

Sasha felt monotonously how the sun keeps moving, the seasons keep passing, and trains keep running, day after round day. He was already forgetting not only his fisherman father but also Proshka and the village; as he grew older, he was moving toward events and things he had yet to feel, yet to allow into his body. Sasha had no consciousness of himself as a solid and self-sustaining object—he was always imagining something or other with his heart, and this left no room for any representation of his own self. His life went its way persistently and at a deep level, as if in the cramped warmth of a mother's dream. He was under the sway of external visions—like a traveler under the sway of fresh countries. Though more than sixteen years old,[1] he had no aims of his own, but then he had no inner resistance to fellow feeling for another life—whether it was the frailty of the stunted grass out in the yard, or a chance nighttime passerby, coughing from lack of shelter in order to be heard and pitied. Sasha would hear and pity. He would be filled with the dark excitement of soul felt by a mature man during a one and only love for a woman. He would look out the window at the passerby and imagine whatever he could about him. The passerby would disappear into the deep dark, his feet scraping the small stones of the pavement, which were even more nameless than he was. Distant dogs let out scary and resonant barks, and tired stars fell now and again from the sky. Maybe, in the very deepest part of the night, amid cool, flat steppe, wanderers were now walking somewhere, and within them, as within Sasha, silence and dying stars were being transformed into the moods of personal life.

Zakhar Pavlovich never got in Sasha's way; he loved him with all the devotion of old age, with all the emotion of hopes that were unclear and unaccountable. Often he asked Sasha to read to him about the war, since he found it hard to make words out by lamplight.

Sasha read about battles, burnings of cities, and a terrible waste of metal, people, and property. For some time, Zakhar Pavlovich listened in silence. Then he said, "I've been thinking about all this. Is man really such a danger to man that power has to stand between them? War is the doing of power and governments. Yes, all my days I keep thinking that war's been thought up on purpose by governments. No ordinary person could have dreamed it up."

Sasha asked how things ought to be.

"Some other how," said Zakhar Pavlovich. "Why didn't they send someone like me along?" he continued, more and more agitated. "If they'd sent me to the German when this quarrel began, we'd have straightened things out in no time. It would have been cheaper than war. But they went and sent the cleverest people."[2]

Zakhar Pavlovich couldn't imagine there was anyone in the world with whom you can't talk to heart to heart. But then those up above—the tsar and those who served him—could hardly be fools. And that meant the war must be sport, a game they'd started on purpose. Here Zakhar Pavlovich was at a loss. Was it possible to talk heart to heart with a man who killed on purpose, or did you have to begin by taking away his harmful weapons, his wealth and importance?

The first time Sasha saw someone killed was there in the depot. It was during the last hour of the working day, just before the hooter. Sasha was packing piston glands when two engine drivers carried in the pale foreman; blood was oozing thickly from his head and dripping onto the oily ground. They took the foreman into the office and someone began telephoning the hospital. Sasha was surprised that the blood was so red and young, while the foreman himself was so gray and old; it was as if, within him, he were still a child.

"Damned fools!" the foreman exclaimed in a clear voice. "Wipe my head with oil. At least that'll stop the blood."

One of the firemen quickly brought a bucket of oil, plunged some rags into it, and wiped them across the foreman's head, which was greasy with blood. The head turned black, and everyone could see it giving off some kind of vapor.

"That's right, that's right!" said the foreman encouragingly. "I don't feel so bad now. And you thought I was going to die? Don't celebrate too soon, you bastards!"

The foreman gradually grew weaker and lost his consciousness. Sasha could make out pits in his head. Squashed down, forced deep into these pits were hairs that had died already. No one any longer remembered their grievances against the foreman, in spite of the fact that, even now, a bolt was more precious and of more use to him than a man.

Zakhar Pavlovich, who also happened to be standing there, was keeping his eyes open with difficulty, so that tears wouldn't fall from them for all to see and hear. No matter how unkind a man is, no matter how clever or brave, he is still sad and pitiful and he dies from weakness of strength.

The foreman opened his eyes and gazed penetratingly into the faces of his subordinates and comrades. Clear life still shone in his eyes, but some misty tension was wearing him out and his eyelids had gone pale and were pressing back, beneath his brows, against the top of his eye sockets.

"What's up with you all?" he asked, with a remnant of his usual irritation. No one was crying—except Zakhar Pavlovich, who had dirty, involuntary moisture running down from his staring eyes and across his cheeks. "Standing around crying! The hooter hasn't gone yet!"

The foreman closed his eyes and kept them for a while in tender darkness. He had no sense of any kind of death—his body's former warmth was still there with him; it was just that he had never sensed this warmth before, whereas now he seemed to be bathing in the hot exposed juices of his own insides. All this had already happened to him—but a very long time ago and there was no remembering where. When he opened his eyes again, the men around him seemed to be standing in rippling water. One of them was standing just above him, very low, as if he had no legs; he was covering his aggrieved face with a dirty work-damaged hand.

This made the foreman angry. Quickly, because the water above and around him was already darkening, he said, "Goodness knows what he's crying about. And that swine Geraska's gone and burned out another boiler... What's there to cry about? It's easy enough to make a new man."

Then the foreman recalled where he had seen this quiet, hot darkness; it was merely the cramped space inside his mother and once again he was pressing himself between her parted bones, but he couldn't get through because of having grown old and too big.

"Get on with it and make a new man," he said. "It's not so easy to make a damned nut—but you can make a man just like that."[3]

At this point the foreman took in a breath and began sucking something with his lips. It was clear that he was in a tight corner and feeling stifled; he was pushing with his shoulders and struggling to make room for himself forever.

"Push me a bit deeper into the pipe," he whispered with swollen, childish lips, clearly aware that he would be born again in nine months' time. "Ivan Sergeich, call Three-Eighths Bolt. Get the dear fellow to grip me with a locknut."

The stretcher arrived too late. There was no longer any point in taking the foreman to the hospital.

"Take the man home," the workers said to the doctor.

"Out of the question," the doctor replied. "He's required for our records."

The statement recorded later read:

> The senior foreman received mortal injuries while towing a cold locomotive coupled to a hot locomotive by means of a thirty-foot steel hawser. While crossing a switch, the hawser made contact with the upright of a trackside lamp which then collapsed, its bracket inflicting injury on the head of the foreman, who from the hot locomotive's tender was observing the

locomotive being towed. The incident occurred thanks to the negligence of the foreman, and also in consequence of a failure properly to observe the rules governing the movement and exploitation of locomotives.

Zakhar Pavlovich took Sasha by the hand and left the depot to go back home. At supper his wife said there was little bread for sale and no meat to be found anywhere.

"Then we're all goners, and that's that," Zakhar Pavlovich replied without sympathy. For him, the whole of everyday life had lost all important meaning.

For Sasha, at that time of his early life, each day had a nameless charm of its own that would never be repeated in the future; the image of the foreman disappeared for him into the dream of memories. But Zakhar Pavlovich had no such self-healing power of life; he was old, and old age is as tender and exposed to death as childhood, and he went on grieving for the foreman all the rest of his life.

9

NOTHING else during the following years moved Zakhar Pavlovich—except that sometimes, in the evenings, when he watched Sasha reading, he felt a surge of pity for him. Zakhar Pavlovich would have liked to say to Sasha, "Don't wear yourself out with your books. If there were anything serious there, everyone would have embraced one another long ago." But Zakhar Pavlovich said nothing; something as simple as joy constantly stirred in him, but mind prevented it from speaking out. He longed for some kind of abstracted and calming life on the shores of smooth lakes, with friendship replacing all words and enlightened true wisdom of the meaning of life.

Zakhar Pavlovich was unable to think everything through. All his life he had been distracted by chance interests like machines and artifacts, and only now had he remembered himself. His mother should have whispered something in his ear when she was feeding him from her breast—something as vital and necessary as her milk, whose taste he had now forgotten forever; but his mother hadn't whispered anything to him, and you can't comprehend the whole world on your own. And so Zakhar Pavlovich began to live with resignation, no longer counting on universal radical improvement. However many engines were made, neither Sasha nor Proshka nor he himself would ever be sitting in the carriages they pulled. Locomotives labored only for other people, or for soldiers—but then soldiers are transported against their wishes. Steam engines are meek creatures, with no will of their own. Zakhar Pavlovich now felt more pity for them than love, and sometimes, in the depot, he would talk to a locomotive face-to-face.

"About to set off, are you? All right, off you go! But look how hard you've been working your pistons—those damned passengers must be a fair weight."

The locomotive would remain silent, but Zakhar Pavlovich still heard it.

"It's poor-quality coal and the fire bars get blocked," the locomotive was saying sadly. "The uphill gradients are hard going. And there are a lot of women going to the front too, to their men, and they've each got a hundred pounds of buns with them. And then there's the mail vans—we used to have only one to pull, but now it's two. People are living apart, so they write letters."

"Hmm," murmured Zakhar Pavlovich, pensively carrying on the conversation and not knowing how he could help the locomotive when people were so overloading it with the weight of their separation. "Don't overdo it," he said. "Take it easy."

"That's not possible," the locomotive replied with the meekness of wise strength. "From up on an embankment I see a lot of villages. I see people crying—they're waiting for letters and wounded loved ones. But have a look at my piston gland—they've packed it too tight. Once we get going, I'll overheat the piston."

Zakhar Pavlovich went and loosened the bolts on the piston gland. "Phew, damned bloody tight. What were they playing at, the bastards?"

"What do you think you're doing?" asked the duty mechanic. "Did anyone especially ask you to tinker about with that gland? Yes—or no?"

"No," said Zakhar Pavlovich meekly. "It just seemed the bolts looked a little tight."

The mechanic was not angry. "If it just seemed, better to leave well alone! Anyway, it's a hopeless business. Steam ends up escaping whatever we do."

After this, the locomotive went on quietly grumbling to Zakhar Pavlovich, "Of course, tightening the bolts doesn't help. The rod's worn out in the middle. That's why steam keeps escaping. Do they think I do it on purpose?"

"Yes, I noticed the worn-out rod," sighed Zakhar Pavlovich. "But I'm only a cleaner, you know. Why would anyone listen to me?"

"I know," the locomotive sympathized in a deep voice—and sank further into the dark of its cooling strength.

"That's what *I* say!" Zakhar Pavlovich agreed.

When Sasha enrolled for evening classes, Zakhar Pavlovich felt secret delight. He had lived through his whole life on his own strength, without any help. No one had ever prompted him in any way—his own feeling had always got there first; Sasha, however, had books speaking other people's mind to him. "I've suffered—he reads. Simple as that!" Zakhar Pavlovich thought enviously.

After reading for a while, Sasha would begin to write. Zakhar Pavlovich's wife couldn't get to sleep because of the lamp. "He keeps writing," she would say. "But why?"

"Go to sleep," Zakhar Pavlovich advised her. "Close the lids over your eyes—and sleep."

His wife would close her eyes, but even through her eyelids she could see kerosene burning in vain. And she was not mistaken—it really was in vain that the lamp burned in the youth of Alexander Dvanov, lighting up the soul-irritating pages of books whose guidance he would in any case never follow. However much he read and thought, inside him there always remained some kind of empty place—and through this emptiness passed the unwritten and untold world, like an anxious wind. At the age of seventeen Sasha still had no armor over his heart—neither faith in God, nor any other peace of mind; he would not give a name not its own to the nameless life opening before him. But he didn't want the world to stay unnamed; he was merely waiting to hear its proper name from its own lips—rather than other people's contrived labels.

One night he was sitting there in his usual anguish. His heart, not closed by faith, was suffering inside him and wanting to be consoled. He lowered his head and imagined inside his body an emptiness that life, day after day, is constantly entering and leaving, neither lingering nor growing stronger, as even and steady as a distant hum in which you can't make out the words of a song.

Sasha felt cold, as if a real wind were blowing through him and into the spacious darkness behind him, while in front of him, where this wind was being born, was something transparent, weightless, and vast—mountains of living air that he must transform into his own breath and heartbeats. His heart missed a beat on account of this foreboding—and the emptiness inside his body opened out still further, ready to seize hold of future life.

"This—is me!" Sasha said loudly.

"Who?" asked Zakhar Pavlovich, who was not asleep.

Sasha immediately fell silent, overcome by sudden shame that carried away all the joy of his discovery. He had thought he was sitting alone, but Zakhar Pavlovich had been listening.

Zakhar Pavlovich noticed this and did away with his question by answering it with equanimity. "A reader—that's what you are. Why not go to bed? It's late."

Zakhar Pavlovich then yawned and said peacefully, "Don't torment yourself, Sasha. You're not that strong anyway." After that, he put his head under the blanket and said in a whisper, for himself, "This one will drown too. Curiosity will draw him into the water." And then, still in a whisper, "But one day I'll breathe my last too, here on this pillow. All the same in the end."

The night continued quietly—workers were coupling rolling stock at the station and their coughing could be heard from the entrance room. It was late February, last year's grass was now showing on the edges of ditches, and Sasha gazed at it as if it were the Creation. He felt for the dead grass and he studied it with a diligent attention that he never applied to himself.

He could sense another person's distant life so intensely that it warmed his blood, but he found it difficult to imagine his own life. When it came to himself, he had only thoughts, whereas what lay outside him imprinted itself into his being. He was unaware that it might be any different for other people.

Once Zakhar Pavlovich unburdened himself to Sasha, as if they were equals. "A boiler blew up yesterday on a series Shch. locomotive," he began.[1]

Sasha already knew this.

"So much for science!" said Zakhar Pavlovich, upset both by this and for some other reason. "The locomotive's fresh from the factory—and look at the rivets! Nobody knows anything serious anymore—life pushes back against mind."

Sasha didn't understand the difference between mind and body, and he said nothing. Zakhar Pavlovich seemed to be saying that mind was feebleminded, whereas machines were invented by the intuition of man's heart, independently of mind.

Now and again, from the station, came the hubbub of troop trains. Kettles clattered, and people spoke in strange tongues, like tribes of nomads.

"They're on the move," said Zakhar Pavlovich. "They'll arrive at something."

Disillusioned by old age and the wrong paths of his entire life, he was not in the least surprised by the February Revolution.[2]

"Revolution's easier than war," he explained to Sasha. "It must be easier—or people wouldn't go along with it. Something's not right."

It was now impossible to deceive Zakhar Pavlovich. To avoid all risk of getting things wrong again, he rejected the Revolution.

He told all the other workers that the cleverest people, once again, were safeguarding power—no good would come of it.

Up until October he went on mocking, sensing for the first time the pleasure of being someone clever. But one October night he heard shooting in the city, and all that night he stayed outside, going back in only when he needed to light a cigarette. All night long he was slamming doors, not letting his wife sleep.

"Calm down, you crazy heathen!" grumbled the old woman, tossing and turning in her solitary bed. "You'll wear your feet out. And you know what'll happen now—there'll be no bread anywhere, and no clothes. You'd think their hands would drop off from all that shooting—did they grow up without mothers?"

Zakhar Pavlovich was standing in the middle of the yard with a glowing cigarette, lending his support to the distant shooting.

"Who's to say?" Zakhar Pavlovich ruminated and went back in to light another cigarette.

"Lie down, you devil!" his wife advised him.

"Sasha, are you awake?" Zakhar Pavlovich asked excitedly. "Fools are taking hold of power out there. Who knows—maybe life will smarten up."

In the morning Sasha and Zakhar Pavlovich set off into the city. Zakhar Pavlovich was looking for the most serious party, in order to join it at once. All the political parties were housed in one government building, and each believed it was better than all the others.[3] Zakhar Pavlovich was gauging the parties against his reason—he was looking for the one that had no incomprehensible program and where everything they said was clear and true. Nowhere, however, did they tell him precisely how and when earthly bliss would dawn. Some replied that happiness was a complex artifact and that man's aim lay not in happiness but in the zealous fulfillment of historical laws. And others said that happiness was a matter of out-and-out struggle, which would last eternally.[4]

"Like that, is it?" said Zakhar Pavlovich, with sensible surprise. "Work with no wages, you mean. That's not a political party, that's exploitation. Let's go somewhere else, Sasha! At least religion had festivals. It had its yearly Triumph of Orthodoxy. People had a chance to celebrate!"[5]

From the next party they heard that man was such a magnificent and greedy being that it was strange even to think about sating him with happiness—that would be the end of the world.

"Just what we need!" said Zakhar Pavlovich.

Behind the end door in the corridor was the very last party, with the very longest name.[6] There was only one gloomy man sitting there; the others had gone off to exercise their power.

"What do you want?"

"We both want to join. Will it be the end of everything soon?"

"Socialism, you mean?" the man misunderstood. "A year from now. Today we're merely occupying institutions."

"Then put our names down," said Zakhar Pavlovich joyfully.

The man gave each of them a packet of small books and a sheet of paper half covered in printed words. "Program, statutes, resolution, questionnaire," he said. "Fill them in—and you need two references each."

Zakhar Pavlovich went all cold, foreseeing deception. "Can't we do it now, by word of mouth?" he asked.

"I can't register you by memory. The party will forget you."

"But we'll keep showing up."

"Impossible—how am I going to make out party cards for you? I can only do that from the questionnaire—and if you're approved by the meeting."

Zakhar Pavlovich noticed that the man was speaking clearly, precisely, fairly, and without the least trust. Probably he stood for the very cleverest of powers; within a year this power would either construct the whole world once and for all or else kick up a futility to exhaust even the heart of a child.

"You join up, Sasha," he said. "Give it a try. As for me, I'll wait for a year."

"No," said the party man. "We don't do trials. Either you're ours completely and forever—or else you can knock on other doors."

"Well then, join good and proper," Zakhar Pavlovich agreed.

"Now you're talking," said the man.

Sasha sat down to fill in the form. Zakhar Pavlovich began asking the man about the Revolution. His answers were offhand; his mind was on something more serious.

"The ammunition factory workers went on strike yesterday, and there's been a mutiny at the barracks—got that? And in Moscow the workers and poorest peasants have been in power for two weeks now."

"Huh?"

The party man then got distracted by his telephone. "No, I can't," he said into the mouthpiece. "I've got representatives of the masses here, someone has to take care of informing them." After that, he turned back to Zakhar Pavlovich. "What do you mean—*huh*? The party's sent representatives there to instill organization into the movement, and we seized the city's vital centers during the night."

Unable to understand this, Zakhar Pavlovich replied indignantly, "But it was the soldiers and workers who mutinied—you lot didn't do a thing. Why can't they simply keep going under their own power?"

"Comrade worker," the party member said calmly, "if we'd all taken that line, the bourgeoisie would be back on their feet by now, with rifles in their hands, and there'd be no Soviet power."

"Maybe there'd be something better," thought Zakhar Pavlovich, though what this might be was beyond him. He then doubted aloud, "But there aren't any of the poorest peasants in Moscow."

The gloomy party man frowned still more deeply; he imagined to himself all the great ignorance of the masses—and how much trouble the party would have with this ignorance in the future. He felt tired in advance and said nothing in reply. But Zakhar Pavlovich went on pestering him with direct questions; he wanted to know who was the town boss now, and was he someone the workers knew well?

This severe and direct supervision suddenly made the gloomy man turn merry and animated. He made a telephone call. Zakhar Pavlovich gazed at the telephone with forgotten enthusiasm. "That's something I overlooked," he said, remembering his various artifacts. "I never made one of them."

"Give me comrade Perekorov," the party man said down the line. "Perekorov? Listen now. We need to organize regular information for the newspaper. It would be a good idea to put out a bit more popular literature... Yes, I'm listening... Who are you then? A Red Army soldier? Get off the line then—you don't understand a thing."

Zakhar Pavlovich got angry again. "I was asking because my heart aches—and you think a newspaper will console me? No, my friend, all power is sovereign power—it's all monarchs and tsars, bishops and holy metropolitans. I've been thinking things through."

"What's to be done, then?" asked his perplexed interlocutor.

"Property must be humbled. And people left without supervision. Things will work out better like that—believe me!"

"But you're talking anarchy!"

"What do you mean—anarchy? I mean self-made life."

The party man shook his shaggy and insomniac head. "That's the petty bourgeois in you speaking. In six months' time you'll see for yourself that you're fundamentally mistaken."

"We can wait," said Zakhar Pavlovich. "If you need longer, we'll grant you an extension."

Sasha finished filling in his form.

"He can't be right," Zakhar Pavlovich said as they went back home. "Things can't be that clear and precise. Or perhaps they can."

In his old age Zakhar Pavlovich had come to feel angry and bitter. It was important to him now that the revolver should be in the hands of the right person—he was dreaming of a pair of calipers that would enable him to measure the worth of the Bolsheviks. Only during the last year had he understood how much he had lost in his life. He had expended everything—yet his many years of activity had not in any way changed the wide-open sky above him, nor had he won anything that might justify a now-weakened body in which some kind of central shining strength had beaten and struggled in vain. He had brought himself to the point of eternal separation from life without gaining possession of what was most essential in it. And now here he was, looking with sorrow at the wattle fences and trees, and at all the strangers to whom in the course of fifty years he had failed to bring any joy or protection and from whom he would soon have to part.

"Sasha," he said. "You're an orphan. You were given your life for free. Don't spare yourself, live what's true."

Sasha said nothing, respecting the hidden suffering of his adoptive father.

"Do you remember Fedka Bespalov?" Zakhar Pavlovich carried on. "He used to work with us, then he died. They'd tell him to go and measure something. He'd do it with his fingers and then off he'd go, holding his hands apart. By the time his hands had got back to us, a yard would have turned into a fathom. People would ask what the hell he thought he was doing. 'It's no skin off my nose,' he'd reply. 'I won't get sacked just for this.'"

Only the following day did Sasha understand what his father had been trying to tell him.

"These Bolsheviks may be fine people and great martyrs of Marxism, but you must keep your wits about you," Zakhar Pavlovich counseled him. "Remember. Your father drowned, we know nothing about your mother, and millions of people live without souls—this is something huge and important. A Bolshevik must have an empty heart, so that there's room in it for everything."[7]

Zakhar Pavlovich's own words were inflaming him, drawing him into ever deeper despair. "Otherwise . . . otherwise, it's into the firebox with you and there you are—smoke blown away by the wind! Smoke in the wind and slag shoveled onto the embankment. Do you understand me, or not?"

Zakhar Pavlovich's excitement of mind changed to a sense of heartfelt emotion. Shaken, he went off to the kitchen to light a cigarette. Then he came back and shyly embraced his adopted son. "Sasha, don't be upset with me. I'm an orphan too, neither of us has anyone to complain to."

Sasha was not upset. He sensed the need in Zakhar Pavlovich's heart, but he believed that the Revolution was the end of the world. In the world of the future Zakhar Pavlovich's anxiety would be instantly annihilated, and his own fisherman father would find what he had willfully drowned for. In the clarity of his feeling Sasha already possessed this new world—but it was something that could only be made; it couldn't be told in words.

Six months after this, Sasha entered the newly opened railway school; then he transferred to the polytechnic. In the evenings he read technical textbooks aloud to Zakhar Pavlovich, who was filled with delight simply by the incomprehensible sounds of science and the fact that his Sasha understood them.

But after a while Sasha's studies were curtailed, and for a long time. The party ordered him to the front line of the Civil War—to the steppe town of Urochev.

Zakhar Pavlovich sat at the station with Sasha for days on end, waiting for a troop train heading in the right direction, and he smoked his way through three pounds of *makhorka*,[8] so as not to get agitated. The two of them had already talked through everything except love. In an embarrassed voice Zakhar Pavlovich then spoke some words of warning about love, "You're a big lad now, Sasha, you don't need me to tell you anything. The main thing is not to get involved with any of that deliberately—it's a deceptive business. There's nothing there, but it's as if you're being dragged somewhere, you keep wanting something. Everyone has an entire imperialism encamped down below."

Sasha was unable to sense imperialism in his body, although he deliberately imagined himself naked.

When a troop train came in and Sasha managed to squeeze into a carriage, Zakhar Pavlovich said from the platform, "Write to me sometime, just to say you're alive and well. Just a few words."

"I'll write more than that," Sasha replied. Only then had he noticed how old and orphan-like Zakhar Pavlovich had become.

The station bell must have sounded five times—five triple rings—but the train was unable to get going. Strangers pushed Sasha farther into the carriage, away from the door, and he didn't appear again.

Zakhar Pavlovich was exhausted, and he set off back home. The walk took him a long time; he kept forgetting to light a cigarette and so suffered all the way from a feeling of petty irritation. Back home he sat at the little corner table where Sasha had always sat, and he began spelling out passages from Sasha's algebra book, understanding nothing but gradually finding consolation for himself.[9]

10

UROCHEV had been taken by the Cossacks while Dvanov was on his way there, but then the detachment of Nekhvoraiko the Teacher had managed to push them out of the town.[1] Urochev was surrounded by dry ground, except for the approach from the river, which was through bog; there the Cossacks had kept up only a feeble vigilance, counting on the ground being impassable. But Teacher Nekhvoraiko had shod his horses with bast shoes, so they wouldn't drown, and had captured the town during one desolate night, forcing the Cossacks out into the boggy valley, where they remained for a long time, since their horses were barefoot.

Dvanov called at the RevCom[2] and talked to the people there. There were complaints about the lack of calico for Red Army underwear, as a result of which the lice on the men were as thick as kasha—but the men were resolved to keep on fighting down to bare earth. In the words of the RevCom chairman, a mechanic at the depot, "Revolution means risk. Maybe we'll churn up the ground and leave only clay. If it doesn't go well for the workers, let those sons of bitches fend for themselves!"

Dvanov was given no particular task. All anyone said was, "Live here with us, that'll suit us all. Then we'll have a look and see what you ache for the most."

Men the same age as Dvanov were sitting in a club on the market square and diligently reading revolutionary literature. Around the readers hung Red slogans,[3] and the windows looked out onto a dangerous expanse of open country. Both readers and slogans were defenseless—it was possible, straight from the steppe, to shoot a bullet into the head of a young Communist bent over a book.

While Dvanov was getting accustomed to militant steppe revolution and beginning to love his comrades there, a letter came from the provincial capital ordering him to return. He set off from the town without a word and on foot. The station was four versts' walk, but he didn't know how he would go any farther; he had heard that the Cossacks had seized the railway. A band coming across the fields from the station was playing sad music—it turned out that the cold body of the now-dead Nekhvoraiko was being carried back to the town. He and his entire detachment had been bluntly wiped out by the prosperous inhabitants of a large village called Peski. Dvanov felt sorry for Nekhvoraiko, because he had only music to weep over him, not his mother and father, and there was no feeling on the faces of the men following behind, who were themselves braced for inevitable death in the daily routines of revolution.

As Dvanov looked back, the town was sinking beyond the reach of his eyes into its valley, and he felt sorry for the lonely town of Urochev, as if without him it had become still more defenseless.[4]

At the station, Dvanov felt the anxious call of space that was abandoned and forgotten. Like everyone, he was attracted by earth's far distance, as if everything distant and invisible missed him and were calling to him.[5]

Ten or more nameless people were sitting on the ground and hoping for a train to take them away to a better place. They were living through the torments of the Revolution without complaint, patiently wandering through steppe Russia in search of bread and salvation. Dvanov went outside, saw some kind of military train on track number 5, and walked over to it. The train was made up of eight open wagons carrying carts and artillery, followed by two coaches. Two more open wagons carrying coal had been coupled on behind the coaches.

After checking his documents, the unit commander allowed Dvanov into one of the coaches. "But we're only going as far as Razguliay

Junction, comrade!" he added. "We'll be stopping there, we'll be nearly at our position."

Dvanov accepted this; at least, he'd have less far to walk.

The Red Army gunners were nearly all asleep. They had been fighting near Balashov for two weeks and were badly tired. Two of them, however, had already slept their fill and were sitting by the window, singing a quiet song to relieve the boredom of war. The commander was lying down and reading *The Adventures of a Hermit, a Lover of the Beautiful,* published by Tieck,[6] while the political commissar had disappeared somewhere inside the telegraph office. The coach, probably, had carried many Red Army soldiers, who had felt lonely and homesick during long journeys and had scribbled all over the benches and inside walls with the indelible pencils soldiers always use when writing back home.

With heartfelt sorrow, Dvanov read these dictums—at home too, he had used to read each new calendar right to the end of the year.

"Our hope is anchored to the seabed," an unknown journeying soldier had written, giving the date and place of his meditation as Dzhankoy, September 18, 1918.[7]

Night fell and the train moved off, without a departing whistle. It was very warm in the coach and Dvanov began to doze; he woke in darkness. What had woken him was the grinding of brake blocks, and also some kind of continuous sound. The window then blazed with the light of a moment, and the air outside was made hot by a shell. It had exploded nearby, brightly illuminating the stubble and the quiet night fields. Dvanov got to his feet.

The train came to a timid stop. Dvanov and the commissar got out. It seemed the line was being fired on by Cossacks—their guns were flashing not far away, but they kept overshooting.

The night was chilly and sad, and it was a long walk to the locomotive. The boiler was hardly making any noise, and a small light, like an icon lamp, was shining over the pressure gauge.

"Why've we stopped?" asked the commissar.

"I'm worried about the line, comrade PolitCom. Cossacks are

shelling it and we've extinguished our lamps—there could be an accident," the driver answered quietly from up above.

"Nonsense. The shells are going over our heads," said the commissar. "Just get going again. Quick—and quiet as you can!"

"Well, all right then," said the driver. "But I've only got one mate, and that's not enough. Give me a soldier to help with the firebox."

Dvanov promptly climbed up into the cab. A shell exploded ahead of the locomotive and lit up the whole train. The engine driver went pale, moved the regulator handle, and shouted to Dvanov and the stoker, "Keep up steam!"

Dvanov diligently began thrusting wood into the firebox. The locomotive got going, with boiling speed. Ahead lay lifeless darkness—and within this darkness, perhaps, lay track that had been sabotaged. They swayed so wildly on the curves that Dvanov wondered if they would come off the rails. The engine was abruptly and repeatedly cutting off steam and they could sense a resonant flow of air from the friction of its hurtling body. Sometimes they heard beneath them the rumble of little bridges, while clouds up above flared with a mysterious light as they reflected the glow escaping from the open firebox. Dvanov was soon bathed in sweat, and he felt surprised that the driver was still keeping up such a speed—after all, they had cleared the Cossack battery long ago. But the frightened driver was endlessly demanding more steam; he was even helping to feed the firebox himself, and he didn't once move the regulator from its extreme position.

Dvanov looked out from the cab. Silence had long ago set in throughout the steppe; there was no disturbance other than the passage of the train itself. Speeding toward them were misty lights—probably a station.

"Why's he going so fast?" Dvanov asked the driver's mate.

"I don't know," the mate replied gloomily.

"There'll be an accident—and we'll be responsible," said Dvanov, not knowing what to do.

The locomotive was quivering with tension and swaying its entire body, searching for a chance to hurl itself down the embankment and escape the power and pent-up speed that were suffocating it. Sometimes Dvanov felt that the locomotive had already left the rails and the coaches were about to follow and he was dying in the quiet dust of soft soil—and he put his hands to his chest to keep his heart from terror.

When the train leaped over the switches and crossings of an unknown station, he saw the wheels strike flashes of fire.

Then the locomotive would sink once again into the dark depths of its future track and the fury of an engine at full speed. The curves nearly threw the locomotive crew off their feet while the coaches and wagons behind, going at too great a speed to beat out a rhythm, hurtled over the rail joints with a scream of wheels.

The driver's mate evidently felt this had gone on long enough. "Ivan Palych!" he said to the driver, "we're nearly at Shkarino. Why not stop there? We can take on water!"

The driver heard this but said nothing. Dvanov realized that exhaustion had made the driver forget to think, and so he carefully opened the lower stopcock on the tender; he intended to empty out the remaining water and so prevent the driver from continuing at this pointless speed. But the driver eased back the regulator anyway. He moved away from the window; his face looked calm now, and he was reaching for his tobacco. Dvanov calmed down too and closed the stopcock. The driver smiled and said to him, "What made you do that? Ever since Marino Junction there's been a White armored train behind us. I was trying to get away."

Dvanov didn't understand. "So where's that train now? And why didn't you reduce speed after we passed the battery—before we got to Marino?"

"The armored train's dropped back—we can afford to slow down now," the driver replied. "Climb up on top of our logs and have a look at the track behind us!"

Dvanov climbed up onto the stack of logs. They were still going fast, and the wind cooled his body. Behind them lay total darkness—nothing but the screech of hurrying coaches.

"But why were you going so fast before Marino?" Dvanov persisted.

"The battery had seen us—they might have adjusted their aim. We needed to get farther away."

Dvanov decided the man must simply have panicked.

At Shkarino the train stopped. The commissar came up to them and expressed surprise at the driver's story. Shkarino seemed empty, and it was the water tower's very last water that was slowly flowing into the locomotive. Then a man from the station appeared; his voice muffled by the night wind, he informed them that there were Cossack patrols around Povorino and that they wouldn't get through.

"But we're only going as far as Razguliay!" the commissar replied.

"Uh-huh!" the man said and went off into the dark station building. Dvanov followed him in. The main hall was empty and dreary; what greeted him in this dangerous house of the Civil War was abandonment, oblivion, and long anguish. The unknown solitary man who had just spoken to the commissar lay down in a corner on a surviving bench and began to cover himself with meager clothing. Who this man was and how he had come to be there was a matter of heartfelt interest to Dvanov. How many times had he already met and how many times would he yet meet these unknown outsiders, these drifters who lived according to their own solitary laws—but never did his heart prompt him to go and question them or attach himself to them and disappear along with them from the order of life. Dvanov might, perhaps, have done better to go up to that man in Shkarino station and lie down beside him—and then, come morning, go out and disappear in the steppe air.

"The engine driver's a coward. There was no armored train!" Dvanov said to the commissar a little later.

"Well, the bastard will get us there somehow or other," the commissar answered with calm exhaustion. Turning away, he walked off to his coach, muttering sadly, "Ah Dunya, my Dunya, how are you finding food for my children now?"

Dvanov also set off back to the coach, not yet understanding why men suffer so much—one lying in an empty station, another yearning for his wife.

Dvanov lay down to sleep, but he woke before dawn, sensing the chill of danger. The train had stopped in wet steppe; the soldiers were snoring, scratching their bodies as they slept. There was the sound of fingernails rasping with pleasure against calloused skin. The commissar was asleep too, his face all puckered—probably he had been tormenting himself with memories of his abandoned family and had fallen asleep with grief on his face. The steppe had grown cold now, the late grass was bent over in the persistent wind, and yesterday's rain had turned the earth into viscous mud. The commander[8] was lying opposite the commissar, and he was asleep too. His book was open at a page about Raphael; Dvanov had a quick look—Raphael was called a living god of the early and happy humanity born on the warm shores of the Mediterranean. But Dvanov could not imagine such a time; then too the wind must have been blowing, and peasants would have been plowing in the heat and little children would have had mothers who died.

The commissar opened his eyes. "So we've stopped, have we?"

"Yes."

"What the devil's going on? Twenty-four hours to cover a hundred versts!" the commissar said angrily.

Dvanov went with him again to the locomotive.

It was standing abandoned. No driver and no driver's mate. Ten yards ahead lay clumsily dismantled rails.

The commissar's face took on a more serious look. "The devil only knows," he said. "Did they just wander off? Or were they attacked? And how are we going to get going again now?"

"They just wandered off," said Dvanov. "No doubt about it."

The stationary locomotive was still hot, and Dvanov resolved to stand in as driver; he would not go too fast. The commissar agreed, gave him two Red Army men as assistants, and ordered the other soldiers to repair the track.

After about three hours they got going again. Dvanov kept an eye on everything—fuel, water, and track—but something was troubling him. The big locomotive was obedient, and Dvanov did not push it too hard. Gradually, however, he grew bolder and went faster, though he still braked carefully on curves and gradients. He told the soldiers what to do, and they did a good job of keeping up the correct steam pressure.

They passed a small, deserted station called Zavalishny. An old man was sitting beside the latrines and eating bread; he didn't even glance at the train. Dvanov went slowly, keeping an eye on the switches, and then picked up speed. The sun had begun to come out through the mists and was slowly warming the damp, chilled earth. Occasional birds flew up over empty places and immediately flew down again to their food—lost, stray seeds.

They came to a long downhill gradient. Dvanov closed off the steam and kept going, with increasing speed, just from momentum.

Far into the distance the line looked clear, up to the dip in the steppe where an uphill gradient began. Dvanov felt calmer now and he left his seat, to see how his assistants were getting on and have a chat with them. After about five minutes he went back to the window and looked out. In the distance he could see a signal—probably Razguliay. Beyond the signal he could make out the smoke of a locomotive, but this didn't surprise him: Razguliay was in Soviet hands—he'd been told that in Urochev. There was some kind of headquarters there, and it maintained regular communications with the large junction station of Liski.

The locomotive smoke at Razguliay turned into a thick cloud, and Dvanov could see the front of the locomotive and its chimney. "He's probably just come from Liski," he said to himself. But the locomotive was moving toward the signal—and toward their train. "He'll stop now, he's going into a siding," Dvanov thought, watching the locomotive. But the rapid puffs of smoke from the chimney told a different story: the locomotive was coming toward them at a fair speed. Dvanov leaned right out of the window and watched intently. The locomotive passed the signal—it was pulling a heavy military or freight train along single track, heading straight for Dvanov's locomotive. Dvanov was going downhill, the other locomotive was going downhill too, and they would meet where the gradient changed. Dvanov realized this was going to end badly and pulled on the double alarm; seeing the oncoming train, the two Red Army men took fright.

"I'll slow the train down. Then jump!" said Dvanov. The men were, in any case, of no use. The Westinghouse brakes weren't working—Dvanov had learned that the day before, from the previous driver. There was nothing left but reverse steam. The other train had seen them and was letting out a continuous alarm whistle. Dvanov hooked the whistle ring to a valve so the alarm signal wouldn't be interrupted and began to move the reverser.

His hands had gone cold and could barely move the stiff spindle. Then he opened full steam and leaned against the boiler out of wilting exhaustion; he had not seen the soldiers jump, but he felt glad they were gone. The train crept slowly backward; the locomotive's wheels were skidding and water was spurting into the chimney. Dvanov wanted to leave the locomotive but was afraid he had torn the cylinder covers by going into reverse so abruptly.

Then he saw steam coming out of the cylinders and understood that it was only the packing glands—not the cylinders themselves—that were broken. The oncoming locomotive was approaching at a fair pace; the friction of the brake blocks was causing blue smoke to rise from beneath its wheels, but the train's weight was too great for the locomotive alone to be able to stifle its momentum. The engine driver was giving quick and abrupt triple whistles, signaling to his crew to apply the hand brakes; Dvanov understood everything, watching as if he were a bystander. At that hour, his slow thinking was a help to him—he felt afraid to leave his locomotive because he would have been shot by the political commissar or excluded in due course from the party. On top of that, neither Zakhar Pavlovich nor Dvanov's father would ever have left an undamaged hot locomotive to perish without a driver—and this too was something Dvanov well understood.

Dvanov seized hold of the windowsill to brace himself against the impact and took a last look at his oncoming adversary. From this other train people were spilling out onto the ground any old how, mutilating and saving themselves. He also noticed someone crash down onto the escarpment from the locomotive; probably it was the driver or his assistant. Dvanov looked back at his own train; there was no sign of anyone—probably the men were all still asleep.

He screwed up his eyes, fearing the thunder of a crash. Then, in an instant, on legs come to life, he swung himself out of the cab and grabbed hold of the handrail, ready to jump. Only now did he sense his helping consciousness; the boiler was sure to explode from the impact and he would be crushed as an enemy of the locomotive. Running beneath him, close at hand, was the strong, firm earth, which was waiting for his life yet which, in a moment, would be abruptly orphaned. The earth was unattainable and was slipping away as if alive.[9] Dvanov remembered something he had seen and felt in childhood; his mother was slipping away to the market, and he was chasing after her on unaccustomed, dangerous legs, crying his own tears and thinking that his mother had gone away forever and ever.

A warm silence of darkness shielded Dvanov's vision.

"I've got more to say!" he exclaimed—and disappeared in the cramped space clustered around him.

He came to himself a long way away and alone; old, dry grass was tickling his neck, and the world seemed very noisy. Both locomotives had their whistles and safety valves on full blast: the collision had distorted their springs. Dvanov's locomotive stood correctly on the rails, except that its frame had buckled and turned blue from the instant heat and tension. The Razguliay locomotive was at an angle and its wheels had cut into the ballast. The front coach of Dvanov's train had been split open; the two following coaches had smashed through it like a wedge. Two coaches from the other train had been squeezed out and thrown onto the grass; their bogies were lying on top of the locomotive's tender.

The commissar came up to Dvanov: "Still alive?"

"I'm all right. But what happened?"

"Don't ask me! Their driver says that his brakes failed and he went through Razguliay without stopping. We've arrested the cretin. And what the devil were you thinking about?"

This alarmed Dvanov. "I'd gone into reverse. Summon a commission. Let them check what position the lever's in."

"What's the use of that? Forty men are lying dead—we've lost men from both trains. At that cost, we could have captured a whole White town. And they say there are Cossacks roaming around—there's going to be trouble."

A rescue train soon arrived from Razguliay, bringing workers and tools. Everyone forgot about Dvanov, and he set off toward Liski on foot.

But on his path lay a man overthrown. He was swelling up with such speed that the movement of his growing body was visible and his face was slowly darkening, as if the man were tumbling into the dark. Dvanov even turned his attention to the daylight: If a man could darken like this, was daylight functioning?

Soon the man had grown so much that Dvanov felt frightened: the man might burst and splatter out his liquid of life. Dvanov stepped back, but the man began to subside and grow brighter. Probably he had died long ago—this was merely dead substances getting restless inside him.

A Red Army soldier was squatting down and looking at his groin, from which blood was pressing out like dark wine. His face was growing paler as he tried to push himself up with one hand, addressing his blood with slowing words, "Stop, you bitch—I'll get weak!"

But the blood went on thickening until it became something one could taste; then it went black and stopped completely. The soldier slumped back and said quietly, with the sincerity of someone not expecting an answer, "It's all so dismal—there's no one with me."

Dvanov went right up to the soldier and the soldier said clear-mindedly, "Shut out my sight!" The soldier continued to look, not blinking, through eyes that were growing dry, without the least tremor of eyelids.

"Why?" asked Dvanov, troubled and ashamed.

"It hurts," the soldier explained—and he clenched his teeth so as to shut his eyes. But his eyes wouldn't shut; they went on losing their light and color, turning into cloudy mineral.

The soldier's eyes had died, the passing reflections of a cloudy sky could be seen in them—as if nature had come back into the man now that oncoming life no longer obstructed its way. So as not to suffer, the soldier accommodated himself to nature through death.

Avoiding Razguliay station in case anyone stopped him and checked his documents, Dvanov disappeared into unpeopled parts—where people live without help.[10]

Railwaymen's huts, with their thoughtful inhabitants, had always attracted Dvanov—he imagined railwaymen to be wise and calm in their solitude. Dvanov went into these huts to drink water; he saw poor children playing not with toys but with imagination alone, and he could have stayed with them forever, to share their lot in life.

Dvanov also spent the night in one of these huts, though only in the entrance room, since a woman was giving birth inside and she passed the night in loud anguish. Her husband was wandering about without sleep, stepping over Dvanov and saying to himself in astonishment, "At a time like this . . . a time like this . . ."

He was afraid that the child being born to him might quickly perish in the calamity of revolution. The mother's loud anguish kept waking a four-year-old boy, who drank water, went outside to pee, and looked at everything as if he were an outsider who happened to live there, understanding but not approving. In the end, Dvanov unexpectedly dropped off and awoke in the wan light of morning, with long dreary rain pattering on the roof.

The contented father appeared and immediately said, "It's a boy."

"That's good," said Dvanov—and got up from his bed on the floor. "A future human being!"

"A future cowherd!" the new father retorted. "There's more than enough of us people already."

Dvanov went out into the rain, so as to keep going farther. The four-year-old was sitting in the window and smearing his fingers across the glass, imagining something unlike his own life. Dvanov waved goodbye twice, but the boy took fright and climbed down from the window—and so Dvanov saw no more of him and would never see him again.

"Goodbye!" Dvanov said to the hut and to his sleeping place, and he set off again toward Liski.

After a verst, he met a cheery old woman with a bundle.

"She's given birth already," Dvanov said to her, so she wouldn't feel she had to hurry.

"Already?" the woman replied with quick surprise. "It's come early, it'll be sickly. Dear, oh dear! But what is it, what has the good Lord given them?"

"A boy," Dvanov said with satisfaction, as if he had taken part in the event.

"A boy! One more who won't honor his parents!" the old woman decided. "It's hard work giving birth, my good fellow! If a man were ever to give birth, he'd be bowing down at the very feet of his wife and his mother-in-law."

The old woman at once embarked on a long speech of no interest to Dvanov. He cut her short.

"All right, Grandma, goodbye! You and I won't be giving birth—so why should we quarrel?"

"Goodbye, my dear! Remember your mother—be sure to honor her!"

Dvanov promised to honor his parents, gladdening the old woman with his respect.

11

LONG INDEED was the journey home. Dvanov walked amid the gray sorrow of a cloudy day and looked at the autumn earth. Sometimes the sun unclothed itself in the sky, resting its light on the grass, sand, and dead clay, and exchanging feelings with them without the least consciousness. Dvanov liked the sun's wordless friendship, its encouragement of the earth through light.

In Liski he got onto a train. It was full of sailors and Chinese making their way to Tsaritsyn. The sailors delayed the train in order to beat up the man in charge of the station nourishment point for giving them soup with no meat in it; after this the train set off peacefully. The Chinese ate all the fish soup the Russian sailors had refused, then used bread to mop up all the nourishing moisture from the sides of the soup pails and said to the sailors, in reply to their questions about death, "We love death! We love it very much!"[1] Then the well-fed Chinese lay down to sleep. During the night sailor Kontsov, prevented by thought from sleeping, stuck the barrel of his rifle through a gap in the carriage door and shot at the passing lights of railwaymen's huts and signals; he was afraid that he was defending people and might die for them without good reason, and so he was acquiring in advance a sense of obligation to fight on behalf of those who had suffered at his hand. Once he was done with shooting, Kontsov immediately and contentedly fell asleep and stayed asleep for four hundred versts; Dvanov had left long before Kontsov awoke, on the morning of the second day.

Dvanov opened the wicket gate into his yard and was glad to see the old tree growing beside the entrance room. The tree was covered in cuts and wounds; people chopping firewood had rested their axes in its trunk, but the tree was still alive, cherishing the green passion of foliage on its sick branches.

"You back, Sasha?" asked Zakhar Pavlovich. "It's good you've come back—I've been here on my own. With you gone, I didn't feel like sleeping. I just lay there and listened. 'What was that? Could it be you?' I didn't even lock the door because of you—so you could come straight in."

During his first days at home, Sasha shivered and tried to get warm on the stove, while Zakhar Pavlovich sat beneath him and dozed.

"Sasha, is there anything you want?" Zakhar Pavlovich would ask from time to time.

"No, I don't want anything."

"I was thinking that perhaps you should have something to eat."

Soon Sasha could no longer hear Zakhar Pavlovich's questions or see him weeping at night and hiding his face in the recess in the stove where Sasha's long socks were drying. Sasha had caught typhus, which kept returning, not leaving his sick body for eight months and then developing into pneumonia.[2] He lay in forgetfulness of life and only occasionally in the winter nights did he hear locomotive whistles and recall what they were; sometimes the rumble of distant artillery reached his indifferent mind, and then it felt hot and noisy again in the cramped space of his body. During moments of consciousness he lay empty and dried up. All he could sense was his skin, and he pressed himself down against his bedding; he felt he might simply fly away, just as the dry, light little corpses of spiders fly away.

Before Easter, Zakhar Pavlovich made a coffin for his adopted son; it was sturdy and splendid, with bolts and flanges—a last gift from a master-craftsman father to his son.[3] Zakhar Pavlovich wanted a coffin like this to preserve Sasha—if not alive, then at least intact for memory and love; every ten years Zakhar Pavlovich intended to dig Sasha up from the grave, so as to see his son and sense himself together with him.

Sasha first went out when the summer was new. The air felt heavy like water, the sun seemed noisy from the burning of its fire, and the entire world seemed fresh, pungent, and intoxicating to his weakness. Life once again shone before Sasha—there was springiness in his body, and his thoughts were leavened with fantasy.

A girl he knew, Sonia Mandrova, was looking over the fence at him. She couldn't understand why, if there had been a coffin, Sasha hadn't died.

"You haven't died?" she asked.

"No," Sasha replied. "And you're alive too?"

"I'm alive too. Together we're going to live. Do you feel well now?"

"Yes, I do. And you?"

"I feel well too. But why are you so thin? Is it that death was inside you but you said no to it?"

"Did you want me to die?" asked Sasha.

"I don't know," answered Sonia. "It happens. Many people start dying, then remain."

Sasha asked her to come over. Sonia climbed the fence in her bare feet and gently touched Sasha, having forgotten him during the winter. Sasha told her what he had dreamed during his illness and how dreary it had been in the darkness of sleep. There had been no people anywhere and he now realized how few of them there are in the world. It had been the same when he was walking through open steppe not far from the war—people's dwellings had been few and far between.

"When I said 'I don't know,'" said Sonia, "the words came out by mistake. If you'd died, I'd have started to cry for a long time. I'd rather you'd gone a long way away—then I'd have thought you were alive in one piece."

Sasha looked at her with surprise. Sonia had grown during this past year, although she had eaten little. Her hair had darkened and her body had acquired carefulness; being close to her now felt shameful.

"Sasha, you don't yet know. I'm studying now, I'm going to courses."

"What do they teach you?"

"Everything we don't know. One teacher says we're stinking dough and he'll make us into a sweet pie. He can say what he likes—after all, we're going to learn politics from him, aren't we?"[4]

"You—stinking dough?"

"So he tells us. But soon I won't be, and nor will the others, because I'll become a teacher of children and they'll start getting clever from when they're only little. And no one will call them stinking dough."

Sasha touched one of her hands, so as to get used to her again—and Sonia gave him her other hand too.

"You'll get well more quickly like this," she said. "You're cold, but I'm warm. Can you feel?"

"Sonia, come round this evening," said Sasha. "I'm tired of being on my own."

Sonia came round in the evening, and Sasha drew something for her and she showed him how to draw better. Zakhar Pavlovich quietly carried out the coffin and chopped it up into firewood. "What we need now is a cradle," he thought. "Where can I find iron supple enough to make springs from? There's none at work—the only iron we've got there is for locomotives. And who knows? Maybe Sasha will have children from Sonia and it'll be me who looks after them. Sonia will be old enough soon—and yes, it's good she exists. She's an orphan too."

After Sonia had left, Sasha felt frightened and immediately lay down to sleep until morning, so as to see a new day and have no memory of the night. But he lay there and saw the night with open eyes; now it had been stirred up and strengthened, life didn't want to forget itself in him. Sasha pictured to himself the darkness over the tundra; people exiled from the earth's warm places had gone there to live. These people had made a local railway line, in order to carry logs for the construction of dwellings to replace their lost summer climate. Sasha imagined he was an engine driver on this line transporting timber to build new cities, and in his mind he did all the work of the driver—crossing sections of unpeopled wilderness, taking on water at stations, whistling in the middle of a blizzard, braking, talking to his assistant—before finally falling asleep at the last station, on the shore of the Arctic Ocean. In his sleep he saw large trees, growing out of poor soil; around them was airy, faintly oscillating space, and an empty track leading patiently into the distance.[5]

Sasha envied all this; he would have liked to take the trees, the air, and the track and place them inside himself, so they would protect him and leave him no time to die. And there was something else that Dvanov wanted to remember, but the effort was heavier than the memory, and his thought disappeared round a bend of consciousness in sleep, like a bird from a wheel beginning to turn.

12

IN THE night the wind rose and chilled the whole town. In many houses, the children tried to escape the cold by warming themselves against the hot bodies of typhic mothers. The wife of Provincial ExecComm[1] chairman Shumilin also had typhus, and her two children were pressing themselves against her from both sides, so as to sleep in the warm. Shumilin himself had lit a primus stove on the table for illumination, since there was no lamp and the electricity had gone out, and he was designing a wind motor that would drag a plow on a rope and so prepare the ground for the next sowing. Horselessness had set in; waiting for a new generation of horses to be born and enter the province's tractive force was out of the question, so it was necessary to seek a way out through science.

After finishing his design, Shumilin lay down on the sofa. So as to correspond to the general meagerness of the Soviet land, which lacked many indispensable things, he curled up beneath his coat and fell quietly asleep.

In the morning it occurred to Shumilin that the provincial masses had probably thought something up already and that socialism might inadvertently have come about somewhere or other, since there was nothing people could do with themselves except join together out of fear of troubles and the strengthening of need. His wife looked at her husband through pale eyes burned out by typhus, and Shumilin hid himself once again beneath his coat.

"It's essential," he whispered to himself for peace of mind. "It's essential that we start socialism quickly. Otherwise she's a goner."

The children woke too, but they chose not to leave the warmth of the bed and tried to go back to sleep, so they wouldn't want to eat.

Shumilin quietly got ready and left for work. He promised his wife he'd be back in good time, but he made this promise every day and never came back until night.

There were people walking past the ExecCom building. Their clothes were all clayey, as if they lived in villages at the bottom of gullies and were now setting off into the distance without having cleaned themselves up.

"Where are you going?" Shumilin asked these wanderers.

"Where are we going?" said one old man, who had begun to grow shorter from the hopelessness of life. "We're going any which way, till someone curbs us. Turn us around—and we'll come back again."

"Better to go forward!" said Shumilin.

In his office he remembered a passage he had once heard read from a scientific book: speed, apparently, reduces the power of gravity and the weight of body and life—and this is why people in unhappiness try to keep moving. This was why Russian pilgrims and wanderers were constantly on the move—through movement they were dispersing the weight of the nation's grieving soul. His office looked out onto unsown, threadbare fields; sometimes a solitary man would appear there and gaze fixedly toward the city, resting his chin on his staff; then he would disappear into some gully or other, where he lived in the twilight of his own hut and hoped for something.

Shumilin telephoned the committee secretary to voice his anxieties: people were wandering about, in both the countryside and the city, thinking and wishing for something, while the party committee issued guidance from inside a room. Shouldn't the committee be sending some ethical and scientific young fellow out into the villages to look around and see if socialist elements of life had appeared there? The masses had their wants too—they might have come up with some kind of self-made life of their own. After all, help was something they were not yet accustomed to. "Yes," Shumilin concluded, "we must locate the point of greatest need—and strike. No time to waste!"

"All right then," agreed the secretary. "I'll find you someone, and you can equip him with directives."

"I need him today," Shumilin replied. "Have him sent to my home."

The secretary passed these instructions down and gave no more thought to the matter. The OrgDept clerk was unable to pass the secretary's order any further into the depth of the committee apparatus and so began to think for himself: Who could they detail to inspect the province? There was no one—every party member was already active. The only man they had was some Dvanov or other—he'd been called back from Urochev to repair the town water supply, but according to a note in his personal file he had fallen ill. "If he hasn't died, I'll send him," the clerk decided—and went off to inform the secretary.

"As a party member, Dvanov has done nothing outstanding," he said, "but then there has been no occasion here for anyone to stand out. Once great things happen, comrade secretary, our men will show what they're made of."

"All right," said the secretary. "Let them think something up—and then they'll grow greater."

In the evening Dvanov received a written summons: he was to go at once to the Provincial ExecCom chairman to talk with him about the imminent self-generation of socialism among the masses. Dvanov stood up and set off on legs unused to walking. Sonia was on her way back from her classes with a notebook and a burdock; she had picked the burdock because its skin was white underneath—at night it was combed by the wind and lit by the moon. Sonia had looked out of the window at this burdock when youthfulness kept her from sleep, and she had gone out onto a patch of waste ground and picked it. She already had a lot of plants at home—and most of them were immortelles, which grow on soldiers' graves.

"Sasha," she said, "they're about to send us out to the villages, to teach childhood how to read and write, but I'd rather work in a flower shop."

Sasha answered, "Nearly everyone loves flowers anyway, but who loves other people's children? There's only their parents."

Sonia was unable to grasp this; she was still full of sensations of life that prevented her from thinking correctly. And she went on her way feeling hurt.

Dvanov didn't know precisely where Shumilin lived. First he went into the yard of the approximate building where Shumilin should have been living. There was a little shack—the home of the yardman; it was already getting dark and the yardman was lying with his wife on the sleeping shelf above the stove. Bread had been left out on a clean tablecloth in case of an unexpected guest. Dvanov stepped into the hut as if into a village. It smelled of straw and milk, of the sated and well-ordered warmth in which the entire Russian village nation had been conceived, and the yardman, no doubt, was whispering to his wife about his everyday tasks.

At this time a yardman was titled yard sanitary officer, so as not to belittle his worth. In response to Dvanov's question about Shumilin, the sanitary officer put on his greatcoat, over the top of his underwear, and got into his felt boots. "I'll go and cool down a bit on behalf of the state," he called out, "but don't you go to sleep yet, Polya!"

Shumilin turned out to be feeding his sick wife grated potatoes from a saucer. The woman was weakly chewing the food. And with one hand she was pitying a three-year-old son huddled against her body.

Dvanov said why he'd come.

"Wait till I've fed my wife," said Shumilin. When he'd finished, he said, "You can see only too well, comrade Dvanov, what it is that we need. I work all day and in the evening I feed my woman by hand. We really must learn how to live some other way."

"But this isn't so bad either," said Dvanov. "When I was ill and Zakhar Pavlovich fed me by hand, I liked it."

"What did you like?" asked Shumilin, not understanding.

"When people are fed hand to mouth."

This was beyond Shumilin. "All right," he replied. "Whatever you say." He then asked Dvanov to walk about the province on foot and see how people were living: the poorest peasants—in all probability—had already heaped themselves together of their own accord and organized themselves into socialism. "We work here in our offices," he said sadly, "but the masses are living. I'm afraid, comrade Dvanov, that they'll get to see communism before we do—they've got no defense except comradeship. So, go and look around."[2]

Dvanov recalled various people wandering about the fields and sleeping in the empty dwellings of the front line. Perhaps those people really had heaped themselves together in some gully hidden from the wind and the state and were living there content with their friendship. Dvanov agreed to go and look for communism amid the spontaneous initiative of the population.

"Sonia," he said the following morning, "I'm going away. Goodbye!"

The young woman climbed onto the fence; she had been out in her yard, washing herself. "I'm being sent away too, Sasha. Auntie Klusha's throwing me out again anyway. I'll be better off living on my own in a village."

Sasha knew that Sonia had no parents and was living with a woman she called Auntie Klusha. But why was she going to a village all on her own? It turned out that Sonia and her friends were being discharged from their course ahead of time. Apparently, armed bands were forming in the villages; most of these men were unable to read or write, and young women were being sent to these villages as teachers, along with units of the Red Army.

"We'll meet again after the Revolution," said Dvanov.

"Yes, we will!" said Sonia. "Kiss me on the cheek and I'll kiss your forehead. That's how people say goodbye—I've seen them—and there's no one else for me to say goodbye to."

Dvanov touched Sonia's cheek with his lips and felt the dry wreath of her own lips on his forehead. Sonia turned away and stroked the fence with a tormented, uncertain hand.

Dvanov wanted to help Sonia, but he just bent down toward her and sensed the smell of faded grass given off by her hair. Then the young woman turned round and came to life again.

Zakhar Pavlovich was standing on the threshold with an unfinished metal suitcase; he wasn't blinking, so as not to accumulate tears.

13

DVANOV walked about the province, keeping to byroads and cart tracks. He needed to stay close to where people lived, and so he followed the gullies and river valleys. When he came to high ground, there was not a village to be seen; nowhere was smoke rising from stove chimneys, and seldom was wheat being cultivated so high up. There was nothing but wild grass, which provided food and shelter to birds and insects.

From the uplands, Russia seemed uninhabited, but there were villages and hamlets living everywhere in the deep gullies and beside shallow watercourses; people existed in thrall to water—it was near traces of water that they settled. At first Dvanov felt there was nothing to see; the province appeared the same everywhere, like the vision of a scant imagination. One evening, however, he had nowhere to spend the night and he could find shelter only in the warm grasses high on a plateau.

He lay down and dug his fingers into the soil beneath him. The earth felt rich and fertile, but it wasn't being plowed. Dvanov remembered about the province's horselessness, then fell asleep. At dawn he was woken by the weight of another body, and he pulled out his revolver.

"Don't be frightened," said the man pressing up against him. "I got cold in my sleep and I saw you lying there. Let's hold one another for warmth and go back to sleep."

Dvanov hugged him and they both got warm. In the morning, without letting go of the man, Dvanov asked in a whisper, "Why doesn't anyone plow here? This is black earth! Is it because there aren't any horses?"

"Wait," said the now-warm foot-walker, in a rough *makhorka*-laden voice. "I'd tell you, but without bread I can't turn my mind to anything at all. Once we were people—but now we're just mouths. Understand?"

"No—but what's the matter?" Dvanov replied in confusion. "I kept you warm all night—and now you turn uppity!"

The foot-walker got to his feet. "The night was the night," he said, "you damned cant-head. But man's grief follows the course of the sun. It sinks down into a man in the evening, and in the morning it rises up and departs. I felt cold at night—but now it's morning."

Among the odds and ends in Dvanov's pocket was a little bread. "Here," he said. "Let your mind turn to stomach stuff. I don't need you—I can find out what I want anyway."

That noon Dvanov found a distant village in an active gully. He informed the village soviet that settlers from Moscow were to be settled high on the steppe.

"They can settle there if they wish," said the soviet chairman. "But it'll be the end of them. There's no water, and it's a long way from anywhere. We've barely touched that earth in our lives. But if there were water there, we'd have sweated blood—yes, we'd have done all we can with that there land."

Now Dvanov was walking still farther into remote parts of the province, and he didn't know where to stop. He was thinking about the day when water would be shining on the high, dry ground—that, he thought, would be socialism.[1]

Soon he saw before him the narrow valley of some ancient long-dried-up river. In this valley lay the village of Petropavlovka—a great herd of greedy homesteads, tightly clustered around a watering place.

On the village street Dvanov saw boulders once brought there by glaciers. Now these boulders lay beside peasant huts and served as seats for the elderly.

Dvanov remembered these stones a little later, as he sat in the Petropavlovka village soviet. He had gone in there to request a billet for the coming night, and to write a letter to Shumilin. He didn't know how letters usually began, and he informed Shumilin that nature had no particular creative gift. She got her way through patience; she had brought a boulder from Finland to Petropavlovka on the tongue of a glacier, across plains and a numbing length of time. It was essential to collect water from deep underground and from the few gullies and bring it to the high steppe, in order to establish socialism there. This was nearer than dragging a boulder from Finland.

While Dvanov wrote, a peasant stood by the table waiting for something; he had a willful face and a crazed, home-cut little beard.

"Still at it!" this peasant exclaimed, certain of the universality of delusion.

"Yes, we are!" said Dvanov, who had gotten the measure of this troublemaker. "And we need to expose people like you for what you are—yes, out in the open steppe."

The peasant scratched his beard voluptuously. "Well, I never! Now they're sending us real smart ones. Without your sort we'd have never worked out how to fill our bellies."

"That's right," Dvanov sighed with indifference.

"Hey! Clear off, you nutter!" the soviet chairman shouted from behind the other table. "You're God—you shouldn't be mixing with the likes of us!"

This peasant, it turned out, thought he was a god, and there was nothing he didn't know. On principle, he had given up plowing and taken to nourishing himself on straight soil: wheat came from the soil, and so the soil must have its own self-sufficient satiety. It was simply a matter of learning to stomach it. People had thought he would die, but he went on living and, in front of everyone, picked out the clay that got stuck between his teeth. This won him a degree of respect.

When Dvanov and the secretary left the building together, they found God shivering on the threshold. "God," said the secretary, "take this comrade to Kuzya Pogankin's and say he's been sent by the soviet. Tell Kuzya it's his turn now!"

Dvanov set off, along with God.

They came across a youngish peasant who said to God, "Good Day, Nikanorych! It's time you became Lenin—you've been God long enough!"

But God suffered this patiently. He did not acknowledge this greeting. Only after a while did he say with a sigh, "What a realm!"

"Why?" asked Dvanov. "Because it doesn't observe God?"

"Yes," God admitted straightforwardly. "With their eyes they see, with their hands they feel—yet they don't believe. But they acknowledge the sun—even though they've never got hold of it in person. May they grieve right down to their roots, down to bare bark."

Outside Pogankin's hut, God left Dvanov and started back without saying goodbye.

Dvanov didn't let him go. "Wait—what do you mean to do now?"

God looked somberly into the expanse of the village, where he was a lonely human being.

"One night I'll announce the appropriation of the earth. Then people will believe out of fear."

God concentrated his spirit and was silent for a moment.

"And the next night," he continued, "I'll give the earth back again and win the Bolshevik glory I deserve."

Dvanov followed God with his eyes without condemnation. God went away, not thinking where he was going, hatless and barefoot, in only a light jacket. His food was clay; his hope—a dream.[2]

Pogankin welcomed Dvanov without warmth; poverty had dulled him. Through years of hunger his children had aged; like adults, they thought only about obtaining bread. The two little girls were already like housewives; they gossiped, used hairpins, and wore their mother's long skirts and blouses. It was strange to see these clever and preoccupied small women, acting entirely purposefully but not yet possessing a sense of procreation. To Dvanov, this omission made the little girls somehow distressing and shameful.

When it was dark, twelve-year-old Varia skillfully made a gruel from potato skin and a spoonful of millet. "Papa, come down and eat," she called out. "Mama, call the kids in. What are the idiots doing, freezing themselves out in the yard?"

Dvanov felt embarrassed: What would become of this Varia in time?

"And you look the other way," Varia said to Dvanov. "We can't feed all you lot—there are enough of us as it is."

Varia tidied her hair and straightened her blouse and skirt—as if beneath them lay something indecent.

Two boys came in—snotty, accustomed to hunger, yet happy on account of childhood. They did not know that a revolution was happening and they thought of potato skins as eternal food.

"How many times must I tell you to come in earlier!" Varia shouted. "Heathen brats! And take your clothes off—they're all we've got."

The boys threw off their worn-out sheepskins, but they had nothing on underneath them—neither trousers nor shirts. Then they climbed onto the bench beside the table and squatted down on it, naked. It was evidently their sister who had accustomed them to this economy with clothing. Varia piled the ragged sheepskins together and handed out spoons.

"Watch your father—and only take a spoonful when he takes one himself!" After issuing these instructions, Varia sat down in a corner and rested her cheek on the palm of one hand; a housewife, after all, eats last.

The boys kept a close eye on their father. As he took his spoon out of the bowl, so they both thrust their spoons in—and gulped the liquid down straightaway. Then they were back on watch, waiting with their empty spoons.

"I'll learn you!" Varia said menacingly if her brothers tried to sneak their spoons in at the same time as their father.

"Varia, Father's snatching all the thick stuff. Tell him he shouldn't," said one of the boys, accustomed by his sister to unbending justice.

Father must have been scared of Varia too—he began spooning up less of the thick stuff.

Outside the window, in a sky unlike the earth, alluring stars were ripening. Dvanov found the Pole Star and thought about how long it has to endure its existence; he too still had a long time to keep going.

"Tomorrow, like as not, we'll be seeing brigands!" said Pogankin, still chewing. He thwacked one of the boys across the forehead with his spoon—he had sneakily helped himself to a large piece of potato.

"What makes you say that?" asked Dvanov.

"It's a starry night—the roads will be firmer. Round here, mud brings peace; when the roads dry out, it's back to war."

Pogankin put down his spoon and tried to belch, but nothing happened.

"All yours now!" he then said to the boys.

They quickly attacked what was left in the bowl.

"Thanks to this fare I haven't hiccupped for a whole year," Pogankin informed Dvanov in a serious tone. "There was a time when you'd eat lunch and then, right through until vespers, you'd be calling on your dead parents after each hiccup. Food had taste then!"

Dvanov lay down so as to go to sleep and reach tomorrow sooner. Tomorrow he would walk to the railway line, to return home.

"Life here's probably dreary for you," said Dvanov, already settling himself for sleep.

"Well, I can't say it's merry!" said Pogankin. "Villages are always dreary. That's why surplus people get propagated—because it's dreary. Do you think men would all be tormenting their women if they had anything better to do?"

"You could move to the rich lands higher up!" said Dvanov. "You'll prosper there—you'll be merrier!"

Pogankin thought for a moment. "How can I move anywhere with a gaggle like this? Hey, you lot, go and take a leak before you go to bed!"

"You'd better do something," said Dvanov. "Or else those lands will be appropriated back from you."

"What do you mean? Has there been a decree?"

"There certainly has," said Dvanov. "Why let the best land go to waste? A whole revolution happened because of the land. Those lands have been given you—and now they hardly bear fruit. Soon they'll be allocated to others. Settlers from outside will make them their own. They'll dig wells, they'll establish farms in the dry gullies—and the earth will be fruitful. But you people only go there as visitors."

Pogankin was all anxiety; Dvanov had hit on his fear.

"Those lands are damn good," said Pogankin, starting to envy his own property. "They'll grow you whatever you like. But are you really telling me that Soviet power judges according to a man's zeal?"

"Of course," said Dvanov, smiling in the darkness. "The settlers will be peasants themselves, same as you villagers. But since they can master the earth better, it'll be them that are given it. Soviet power loves a good harvest."

"You're right there," said Pogankin gloomily. "Makes it easier to requisition our grain."

"There'll soon be a ban on state requisitioning," Dvanov improvised. "When the war dies down, it'll be the end of requisitioning too."[3]

"Yes, men here are saying the same thing. After all, how can anyone endure suffering beyond all suffering? Nothing like this goes on in any other realm in the world... Or will we really live better in the high steppe?"

"Of course you will," Dvanov insisted. "Go. Find some companions—find ten men like yourself—and get going."

Afterward Pogankin talked all this over with Varia and his sick wife—Dvanov had given their souls a dream.

In the morning, as Dvanov was eating millet porridge in the village soviet, he saw God again. God didn't want any porridge. "What's the use?" he asked. "Even if I eat it, it still won't fill me up forever."

The soviet refused Dvanov a cart. God pointed out to him the way to the village of Kaverino; from there it was twenty versts to the railway.

"Mark my words!" said God, looking downcast. "We're parting forever now—and no one will understand how sad this is. Where once was a twosome, there'll be only a one and a one. But don't forget. What makes a man grow is another man's friendship, whereas I grow only out of the clay of my soul."

"Is that why you're God?" asked Dvanov.

God looked sadly at this man who refused to believe a fact.

Dvanov concluded that this God was clever, only he lived back to front. But then a Russian can go either way; he can live forward, and he can live back again, and either way he stays whole.

14

LONG RAIN set in, and only toward evening did Dvanov reach the road over the hills. Below him lay the twilit valley of a quiet steppe river. But it was clear that the river was dying; it was being choked by silt from the ravines and was not so much flowing along its course as spreading out sideways into bogs.[1] Over these bogs already hung the melancholy of night. Fish had sunk down to the riverbed, birds had flown away to the silent remoteness of nests, and insects had gone still in crevices of lifeless sedge. Living creatures love warmth and the sun's irritating light; their triumphant chiming had now shrunk into low holes and burrows and slowed into a whisper.

But in the air Dvanov could hear indistinct verses of summer song, and he wanted to put the words back into them. He knew the excitement of a life repeated and multiplied by a surrounding sympathy. But a weak wind was tearing and scattering the song's verses in space; they were blending with the twilight forces of nature and becoming soundless, like clay. The movement Dvanov heard was not like his sense of consciousness.

In this world now fading and setting, Dvanov conversed freely with himself. He liked to talk alone in open spaces, but if anyone overheard him he would feel as ashamed as a lover caught with his beloved in the darkness of love. It takes words to turn current feeling into thought, and that is why a thoughtful man talks. But conversing with oneself is art, whereas conversing with others is entertainment.

"That's why man enters into society, into entertainment—like water going downhill," Dvanov concluded.

He made a half turn with his head and surveyed half of the visible world. And he began talking again, in order to think. "But all the same, nature's a down-to-earth event. These streams and hillocks people sing about are not merely poetry. They make it possible to give water to the soil, to cows, and to people. They'll bring profit, and that's a good thing. It's from earth and water that people are nourished, and it's with people that I've got to live."

As he walked farther, Dvanov began to tire, feeling boredom inside his whole body. The dreariness of exhaustion was drying up his innards, and his body's friction increased without the moisture of mental fantasy.

In a ravine below him, as the smoke from Kaverino came into view, the air was thickening into darkness. What existed down there was some kind of spongy quagmire—and perhaps strange people, huddling together, who had abandoned life's multiplicity for the simplicity of contemplation.

God from the village of Petropavlovka had living likenesses in these parts.

From the depth of the ravine came the snorting of tired horses. There were people down there, and their horses were plodding heavily through the clay.

A young, intrepid voice sang out from the front of this cavalry unit, but both words and tune were of distant origin.

In a faraway land,
Beyond a faraway sea,
What we dream of now lies
In the hands of the enemy.

The horses were now treading more easily. The rest of the unit began to sing too, drowning out the first song with a song of their own:

Dress in gold, little apple,
Fate is cruel and fickle.
Hard is the Soviet hammer,
Sharp is the Soviet sickle.

The solitary singer carried on, at odds with his unit:

> At hand lie my sword and my soul,
> But my joy lies far, far away...

The unit drowned out the next two lines, singing:

> Dear little apple,
> Apple of the soul,
> Fall into Soviet hands—
> You'll rot in the bowl.
> You were born on a tree,
> And there you belong—
> But if you're requisitioned,
> That's the end of this song.

The men whistled in unison and finished their song at full tilt:

> Red apple, green apple,
> Take care where you fall.
> Tell both Tsar and Soviet
> You belong to us all.[2]

Dvanov stopped, curious about this procession down below.

"Hey, you up above!" a voice shouted. "Come and join us below. We're the ones without leaders!"

Dvanov didn't move.

"Get walking!" said a deep, resonant voice, probably that of the first singer. "Otherwise, count up to a half—and you're in my sights."

Dvanov thought that Sonia would hardly survive a life like this, and he resolved not to preserve himself. "You lot can climb up here, it's drier! Why exhaust your horses down there, you White kulaks?"

The unit halted.

"Nikita, make a hole or two in him!" ordered the deep voice.

Nikita raised his rifle but first unburdened his oppressed soul at the expense of God: "By the scrotum of Jesus Christ, by the rib of the Mother of God, and by the whole Christian generation—fire!"

Dvanov glimpsed a flash of tensed silent fire and rolled off the path and down the side of the ravine, as if smashed on the leg with a crowbar. He did not lose clear consciousness, and as the ears of his rolling head pressed against it in turn, he heard a terrible noise in the earth's inhabited substance. Dvanov knew he was wounded in the right leg—an iron bird had pierced deep into it and was moving the spiny barbs of its wings.

Down in the ravine Dvanov grasped the warm leg of a horse and, with this leg beside him, he no longer felt frightened. The leg was quietly trembling from tiredness and it smelled of sweat, the grass of the roads, and the silence of life.

"His clothes are all yours, Nikita. Insure him against life's living flame!"

Dvanov heard. He squeezed the leg with both hands, and the leg turned into the fragrant living body of the being he had not known and would never know but now she had become unexpectedly necessary to him. Dvanov understood the mystery of her hair, his heart rose up toward his throat and he cried out in the oblivion of his liberation and at once felt a soothing and satisfied peace. Nature had not failed to take from Dvanov what his mother, unconscious and without memory, had borne him for: the seed of generation, so that new people should become a family. It was the time before death—and in delusion Dvanov deeply possessed Sonia. During his last moments, embracing soil and horse, he knew for the first time life's resonant passion; inadvertently he felt astonished at the insignificance of thought before this bird of immortality that had touched him with a trembling and wind-beaten wing.

Nikita came up and laid a hand on Dvanov's forehead: Was it still warm? Nikita's hand felt big and hot. Dvanov didn't want this hand to be torn away from him soon, and so he placed his own affectionate hand on top of it. But Dvanov knew that Nikita was merely checking, and he helped him, "Shoot me in the head, Nikita. Go on, split my skull open!"

Nikita and his hand had nothing in common—as Dvanov learned when Nikita shouted, in a thin, nasty voice out of keeping with the peace of life preserved in his hand, "Alive, are you? No, I won't split you, I'll unstitch you. Why should you die straightaway—you're a human being, aren't you? Lie there a bit and suffer—you'll die more substantially if you take your time over it."

The legs of the leader's horse drew near. The leader's deep voice then laid into Nikita. "If you keep on jeering at people like this, you bastard, it'll be you who gets unstitched into the grave. How many times must I tell you? We're not brigands, we're a unit of anarchy!"[3]

"Mother of life, liberty, and order!" said the supine Dvanov. "What's your surname?"[4]

The leader laughed. "What does it matter to you now? Mrachinsky."[5]

Dvanov forgot about death. He had read Mrachinsky's "Adventures of a Contemporary Agasfer."[6] Was this rider the writer?

"You're a writer! I've read your book. It *doesn't* matter to me now—but I liked it."

"Let the man bare himself! Why should I have to fuss about with a carcass? It's always a struggle to roll them over," said Nikita, getting bored of waiting. "His clothes are tucked in round the waist, they'll get ripped—and I can kiss goodbye to all my profit."

Dvanov began to undress, so as not to inflict loss on Nikita: what he said was true—you can't take the clothes off a corpse without ruining them. Dvanov's right leg had gone stubborn; it didn't obey when he tried to bend it, but it had stopped hurting. Nikita noticed and helped in a comradely way.

"It's here, isn't it, that I touched you?" asked Nikita, taking the leg carefully in his hands.

"Yes," said Dvanov.

"It's nothing much. The bone's intact, and the wound will heal over with a little grease—you're still a mere youngster! Parents still alive?"

"Yes," said Dvanov.

"Let them stay alive. They'll pine for you a bit, then forget. What else can parents do nowadays? Communist, are you?"

"Yes."

"Up to you, I guess. We all have our dreams."

The leader observed silently. The other anarchists were having a smoke and looking after their horses, paying no attention to Dvanov and Nikita. The last light of dusk died out over the ravine—another night had set in. Dvanov regretted that the vision of Sonia would now never be repeated; he did not recall anything else of his life.

"So you liked my book?" asked the leader.

Dvanov was already without his coat and trousers. Nikita had put them straight into his bag.

"I've already told you," Dvanov confirmed, and looked at the oozing wound on his leg.

"But what do you feel about the book's central idea? Do you remember it?" the leader persisted. "There's a man living alone, right on the line of the horizon."

"No," said Dvanov. "I've forgotten the idea, but you think in an interesting way. Sometimes that happens. You look at man the way the monkey looked at Robinson Crusoe. You understand everything back to front—and that's what makes it a good read."[7]

In attentive astonishment, the leader rose up in the saddle. "This is intriguing. Nikita, we'll take the Communist to Limanny Farmstead. Then he'll be all yours."

"And his clothes?" Nikita asked with concern.

Dvanov and Nikita finally came to an agreement: Dvanov would carry on living in a naked capacity. The leader made no objection, merely ordering Nikita, "Take care he doesn't get spoiled in the wind. He's a Bolshevik intellectual—a rare breed!"

The unit set off. Dvanov held onto the stirrup of Nikita's horse and tried to walk on only his left leg. His right leg wasn't hurting unless he put weight on it—then it remembered the wound and the iron barbs deep inside.

The ravine was going up into the steppe, narrowing as it climbed. There was a night wind; the naked Dvanov was hopping diligently on one leg, which kept him warm.

Nikita, up on his saddle, was proprietorially going through Dvanov's clothes. "You pissed yourself, damn you!" he said without malice. "Look at you all—just like little children! Not one of you has stayed clean for me. You all piss and crap straightaway, even if we take you to the latrines first. There was just one fellow, a district commissar he was. 'Shoot, you little runt,' he called out. 'Goodbye, Party and children!' That one didn't soil his clothes—he was special!"

Dvanov pictured this special Bolshevik to himself and said to Nikita, "Soon you lot will be being shot too—but you'll stay in your clothes. We Bolsheviks don't dress off the backs of the dead."

Nikita didn't take offense. "Just keep on hopping—you can chat later. And I can tell you, my brother, I won't be spoiling my own drawers. No, you'll get nothing out of me."

"I won't be looking," Dvanov reassured Nikita. "But if I see anything, I won't think the worse of you."

"I don't think any the worse of you either," Nikita said peaceably. "These things happen. What's precious to me is the clothes."

It took them about two hours to reach Limanny Farmstead. While the anarchists went and talked to the men there, Dvanov trembled in the wind and pressed his chest up against the horse, to warm himself. Then the horses were led away and Dvanov was forgotten on his own. As Nikita took his horse away, he said, "Do what you want. You won't run far on one leg."

Dvanov wondered whether to hide, but he sat down on the ground from weakness of body and began to weep in the village darkness. The village had gone silent; the brigands had all gone off to their billets and lain down to sleep. Dvanov crawled into a barn and climbed onto some millet straw. All through the night he saw the kind of dreams you live through more deeply than life and for that reason cannot hold in your memory. He woke in the long silence of a night that had come to a standstill, the time when children are said to do their growing. There were tears in his eyes from weeping. He remembered that he would be dying that day and embraced the straw as if it were a living body.

With this consolation he went back to sleep. In the morning Nikita took a while to find him. At first he decided that Dvanov must be dead, since he was sleeping with a total and unmoving smile. But this was only because Dvanov's unsmiling eyes were closed. Nikita knew vaguely that a living person's face never laughs or smiles completely; something in it always remains sad—either the eyes or the mouth.

15

SONIA Mandrova traveled by cart to the village of Voloshino and began living in the school as a teacher. She was also called on to deliver babies, to attend village get-togethers, and to treat wounds, and she did all this as best she could and without causing offense to anyone. Everyone needed her in this small village on the edge of a gully, and consoling their griefs and illnesses made Sonia feel important and happy.[1] But at night she would be left waiting for a letter from Sasha. She had given her address to Zakhar Pavlovich and everyone she knew, so they wouldn't forget to tell him where she was living. Zakhar Pavlovich had promised to do this and had given her a photograph of Sasha.

"Anyway," he said, "you'll be bringing it back again when you become his wife and start living with me."

"Yes, of course," said Sonia.

She looked out the school window at the sky and saw stars above the silence of night. The quiet was such that there seemed to be nothing in the steppe except emptiness. There was not enough air to breathe; that must be why stars fell down. Sonia kept thinking about the letter: Could it be delivered safely across open country? The letter had become the nourishing idea of her life; whatever she was doing, she believed that somewhere the letter was making its way toward her. In a hidden guise, it preserved for her alone the necessity of further existence and glad hope—and so Sonia labored with still greater care and zeal to lessen the unhappiness of the villagers. She knew that the letter would make reparation for all this.

But at this time letters were read by all and everyone. Dvanov's letter to Shumilin had been read back in Petropavlovka. First to read it had been the postman, and then everyone he knew with an interest in reading: the teacher, the deacon, the shopkeeper's widow, the sexton's son, and one or two others. Libraries were not functioning, books were not being sold—and people were unhappy and their souls in need of comfort. And so the postman's hut became a library. Especially interesting letters made no progress at all toward their addressees but were retained for rereading and repeated pleasure.[2]

Official letters were sent on immediately—everyone already knew what they said. The letters people learned most from were those merely transiting through Petropavlovka; unknown people wrote sadly and interestingly.

Letters that everyone had read were glued back down and sent farther on their way.

Sonia didn't yet know any of this—otherwise she would have gone on foot round every village post office. Above the sounds of the stove in the corner she could hear the snoring sleep of the watchman, who worked in the school not for wages but to safeguard the eternity of property. He would have preferred children not to enter the school at all—they scratched desks and smeared walls. The watchman foresaw that the schoolmistress would die unless he looked after her, while the school itself would be ripped apart to meet the villagers' domestic needs. Sonia slept more easily when she could hear someone living not far away, and she carefully wiped her feet on the mat and lay down on bedclothes white with cold. Meanwhile, turning their muzzles to the dark of the steppe, faithful dogs were barking.

Sonia curled up, to sense her body and warm herself with it, and began to fall asleep. Her dark hair was spread mysteriously over the pillow, while her mouth had opened from attention to a dream. She saw dark wounds appearing on her body; on waking, she quickly and without memory checked her body with her hand.

A stick was knocking roughly at the school door. The caretaker had left his place of sleep and was already in the entrance room, busy with the lock and bolt. He was cursing the restless man outside, "Stop that bloody bashing! There's a woman resting in here—and it's a thin door. What are you after?"

"What is this place?" asked a calm voice from outside.

"This is a school," answered the caretaker. "What do you think it is—an inn?"

"So there's a schoolmistress living here, is there?"

"Where else would the schoolmistress live?" the caretaker replied in surprise. "And what do you want her for? Why'd I let a cocky bastard like you in to see her?"

"Show her to us . . ."

"If the schoolmistress so wishes . . ."

"Let him in—who is it?" Sonia shouted, and ran out into the entrance room.

Two men dismounted—Mrachinsky and Dvanov.

Sonia took a step back. Before her stood Sasha—unkempt, dirty, and sad.

Mrachinsky looked at Sofia Alexandrovna condescendingly; her pitiful body did not merit his attention and efforts.

"Is there anyone else with you?" asked Sonia, not yet sensing her happiness. "Call your comrades, Sasha. I've got sugar—you can all have some tea."

Dvanov went out onto the porch, called out, then came back. Nikita appeared, along with another man who was short and thin and whose eyes lacked attentiveness, although from the threshold he had seen a woman and immediately felt attracted to her—not for the sake of possession, but to defend the oppressed weakness of women. His name was Stepan Kopionkin.

Kopionkin greeted everyone, bowing his head with strained dignity, and he offered Sonia a barberry candy he had been carrying about in his pocket for the last two months without knowing why.

"Nikita," said Kopionkin in a threatening voice he seldom used. "Boil some water in the kitchen—Petrusha will assist you in this. And see if you've got any honey anywhere—after all, there's not much you haven't plundered. Yes, when we're safely back in the rear, you reptile, I'll have you sentenced."

"How do you know the caretaker's called Petrusha?" Sonia asked with timidity and surprise.

Out of sincere respect, Kopionkin half got to his feet. "Comrade, I personally arrested him in the Bushinsky estate for resistance to the revolutionary people during the time of the destruction of confoundicated property!"

Sonia was clearly frightened by these men. Dvanov turned to her and said, "Do you realize who this man is? He's the commander of the field Bolshevik units. He saved me from murder by him over there!" Dvanov pointed at Mrachinsky. "That fellow talks about anarchy—yet he was scared of a further continuation of my life."

Dvanov was laughing; he did not bear grudges.

"I tolerate bastards like him until the first battle," Kopionkin declared. "You see, I found Sasha Dvanov naked and wounded in a village where this idiot here and his detachment were stealing chickens. They want noughtocracy, they tell me. 'What?' I ask. 'Anarchy,' they explain. The devil take them! Nought for us—while they keep their rifles. A load of hogwash, if you ask me! I had five men and they had thirty—but we still got the better of them. They're no fighters—mere pilferers! I kept him and Nikita as prisoners, and I freed the others after they'd sworn eternal loyalty to labor. Now I'll see if Mrachinsky deals with anarchic brigands the way he dealt with Sasha. If he's too soft on them, I'll be sure to reckon with him."

Mrachinsky was cleaning his fingernails with a splinter of wood. He maintained the modesty of a man unjustly defeated.

"But where are the other members of comrade Kopionkin's forces?" Sonia asked Dvanov.

"Kopionkin's sent them back to their wives for two days. He believes that the main cause of military defeats is men's loss of their wives. He wants to establish family armies."[3]

Nikita brought in some honey in a beer bottle, and the caretaker brought a samovar. The honey smelled of kerosene, but they consumed all of it.

"Thieving shit of a town mechanic!" Kopionkin said crossly. "Pilfering honey straight into a bottle—most of it must have ended up on the ground. Couldn't you have found a proper crock?"

Then Kopionkin turned suddenly animated. Holding up his cup

of tea, he pronounced, "Comrades! Let us at last drink so we can gather our strength for the defense of every infant on earth and in memory of the beautiful young woman Rosa Luxemburg. I swear that my own hand will lay on her grave all her murderers and tormentors."[4]

"Excellent!" said Mrachinsky.

"We'll slaughter the lot of them!" Nikita agreed, and poured some tea from his glass into his saucer. "Wounding women to death is impermissible."

Sonia sat there in fear.

They finished their tea. Kopionkin turned his cup upside down and tapped on it with one finger. Then he noticed Mrachinsky again. Remembering that he didn't like him, he said, "You go out to the kitchen, my friend, and in an hour's time you can water the horses." After that, he called out to the caretaker, "Stand guard over the horses, Petrusha!" Lastly, he ordered Nikita, "You go out too! And don't go knocking back all the water we've boiled—we may need it yet. Heaven knows what's making you so thirsty."

Nikita at once swallowed down the water and stopped feeling thirsty. Kopionkin sank gloomily into thought. His internationalist face now expressed no clear feeling; more than that, it was impossible to determine his origin—whether his family were oppressed laborers or professors; all the traits of his personality had been erased by the Revolution. And yet in only an instant, his eyes would cloud over with wild animation; he could, with conviction, have burned all the property on earth, so that nothing should remain in a man but adoration for his comrade.

But memories were again preventing Kopionkin from moving. From time to time he would glance at Sonia and love Rosa Luxemburg all the more. Both had black hair and pitifulness of body; Kopionkin could see this, and his love kept going farther along the path of memories.

His feelings about Rosa Luxemburg so agitated and saddened Kopionkin that his eyes filled with sorrowful tears. He strode wildly up and down, uttering threats against bourgeois and brigands, against

England and Germany—against all those responsible for the murder of his beloved.[5] "Not in my poor heart does my love flash now, but in my rifle and on my saber!" he declared, and unsheathed his sword. "Enemies of Rosa, of women and the poor—I shall scythe them down like steppe grass!"

Nikita came in with a crock of milk. Kopionkin was waving his sword about.

"No provisions today—and the man's still frightening last year's flies!" Nikita complained quietly but with irritation. Then he announced more loudly, "Comrade Kopionkin, this evening there's only liquid rations. I'd have done better by you, but you'd have given me another earbashing. The village miller slaughtered a sheep yesterday—allow us to requisition a soldier's share! After all, we're due our campaign norm."

"Your campaign norm?" Kopionkin replied. "All right then. Three military rations—but weigh them on the scales! Not a gram over the norm!"

"Certainly not!" Nikita confirmed, with justice in his voice. "That would be counterrevolution! I know what's correct and proper—you won't see the likes of me taking bones."

"And don't wake the population," Kopionkin added. "You can do your requisitioning tomorrow."

"By then, comrade Kopionkin, they'll have hidden their supplies," Nikita predicted. But he didn't go anywhere, since Kopionkin did not brook discussion and was capable of sudden action.

It was already late time. Kopionkin bowed to Sonia, wishing her peaceful sleep, and the four men went through to join Petrusha in the kitchen and lie down there. All five of them then lay in a row on some straw, and Dvanov's face soon turned pale from sleep; he went still, his head on Kopionkin's belly, and Kopionkin, who was sleeping with his saber and in full military dress, laid a hand on him for defense.

After waiting until everyone was asleep, Nikita got to his feet. First, he had a good look at Kopionkin. "Well, he's no mean snorer—the devil! Still, he's a good 'un!"

And he went out to look for some chicken or other for breakfast. Dvanov began tossing about in anxiety—he was afraid, in his sleep, that his heart was about to stop. Then he sat bolt upright in awakening.

"But where's socialism?" he remembered, and in search of this thing of his he stared into the room's darkness. It seemed to him that he had found socialism but then lost it, sleeping among these strangers. In fear of future punishment, Dvanov went outside with no shoes or hat, saw the mute, dangerous night, and then ran through the village into a faraway distance of his own.

So he ran on, across an earth growing paler and grayer, until he saw morning and the smoke of a locomotive at a steppe station. A train was standing there, waiting to depart according to the timetable.

Still in his faraway world, deep in a crowd that was stifling him, Dvanov began to move across the platform. Behind him was a zealous man who also wanted to travel. This man was pushing his way forward with such force that the friction was ripping his clothes, but all those directly in front of him—Dvanov among them—inadvertently found themselves inside the brakeman's cabin of a freight wagon. It had been impossible for the man to get on board except by pushing everyone in front of him onto the train first. Now he was laughing from success and reading aloud a little poster on the wall: "Soviet Transport is the Path for the Locomotive of History."[6]

This reader fully agreed with the poster; he pictured to himself a fine locomotive with a star on its front, traveling who knows where along the rails and with no passengers or freight of any kind. It was worn-out locomotives, not locomotives of history, that transported cheap, everyday things; the poster bore no relation to those traveling now.

Dvanov closed his eyes, in order to separate himself from every spectacle and to live without mind until he came to whatever it was that he had either lost or forgotten to see during his previous journey.

After two days he recalled why he was living and where he had been sent. But inside every man there also lives a little onlooker—he takes no part either in his actions or in his suffering and is always dispassionate and always the same. His work is to see and to witness, but he has no say in a man's life and no one knows the reason for his solitary existence. This corner of a man's consciousness is lit up day and night, like the caretaker's room in a large building. For days on end this ever-vigilant caretaker sits by a man's front door; he knows all the tenants of his building, but not one ever asks him for advice. The tenants come and go; the onlooker-caretaker follows them with his eyes. The extent of his impotent knowledge sometimes makes him seem sad, but he is always polite. He is solitary, and he has a room of his own in another building. In the event of fire, the caretaker telephones the firemen and goes outside to observe further developments.

While Dvanov was a long way from himself and on the move, this onlooker saw everything within him, although he never warned or helped him. He lived parallel to Dvanov, but he was not Dvanov.

He existed like a dead brother; everything human seemed to be present in him, but something slight and important was missing. A man never remembers him yet always trusts him; in the same way, a man leaves his home and his wife but does not feel jealousy with regard to the caretaker.

This onlooker is the eunuch of a man's soul. Here is what he witnessed.[7]

16

DURING the first hour Dvanov traveled silently. Wherever there is a mass of people, there immediately appears a leader. By means of this leader the mass ensures its vain hopes, while the leader extracts from the mass and its hopes both practical benefit and the pleasure of power. The brakeman's cabin, which contained twenty people, recognized as its leader the man who had squeezed them all inside in order to board the train himself. This leader knew nothing, but he gave out information about everything. And people believed him—each wanted to obtain a sack of flour somewhere and so they needed to be sure in advance of their success, so as to have the strength to struggle. The leader would tell them that literally everyone at their destination was trading flour; he had already been there himself. He knew this rich village, where the men ate chickens and wheaten buns. Soon it would be the day of the village's patron saint and every trader was sure to be invited to the feast.[1]

"The huts are as warm as bathhouses," the leader went on encouragingly. "Stuff yourself on mutton fat—then sleep like a log! When I was there, I had a jug of buttermilk every morning—that's why I don't have even a single tapeworm inside me now. And for lunch—first it's borscht till you're sweating all over, then you stuff down some meat, then it's kasha, and then bliny. You eat and eat till your jaws start to ache! Well, by now you've got a column of food climbing right up to your gullet. So you take a spoonful of fatback, you seal the food so it doesn't pop out again—and all you can do then is sleep. Not bad, eh?"

Everyone listened, in the fear of dangerous joy.

"Lord, might the old days really come back again?" a thin old man exclaimed in near rapture; he sensed his undernourished state as painfully and passionately as a woman senses a child who is dying. "No, that which has once been can never return! Oh, if only I could have a drop now, just a little shot, I'd forgive the tsar every one of his sins!"

"So you really want a drink that badly?" asked the leader.

"How can you ask, my boy? What haven't I drunk in my life? Varnish, polish... And I've paid good money for cologne water. All in vain. No joy to the soul. But vodka—do you remember? Pure and sanitary—the bitch! Transparent, God's own air—not a speck of nothing, not so much as a whiff of... Like a woman's tear. The bottle all clean and correct, the label so neat—true artfulness! What a life! Knock back a hundred grams and there's equality and fraternity for you, in front of your very eyes!"

The listeners all sighed with sincere regret for what had left them once and for all. The country outside was lit by a morning sky, and nature's sad steppe vistas were asking to be let into your soul, but no soul was letting them in and they were being left behind unseen, squandered by the train's progress.

Those travelling on that forgotten morning were wrapped in complaints and dreams, and they did not notice a young man standing among them, apparently asleep on his feet. He was not carrying any kind of bag or sack; probably he had some other container for flour, or else he was simply a man on the run. The leader wanted to check his documents in the usual way and asked him where he was going. Dvanov was not truly asleep and he answered, "To the next station."

"We'll be there in a moment," the leader informed him. "You shouldn't have taken up space on the train for such a short distance. You'd have done better to walk."

The station was lit by a kerosene lantern, although day had already begun, and under this lantern stood the assistant stationmaster on duty. The passengers ran out with their kettles, taking fright at the faintest hiss from the locomotive in case they were left there forever, but they could have taken their time—the train remained at this station all day and spent the night there too.

Dvanov dozed all that day near the railway and went in the evening to a spacious hut near the station where you could stay the night in exchange for some kind of payment. Inside this refuge hut people were lying on the floor in tiers, in the light of flames from a potbelly stove. A man with a lifeless black beard was sitting beside this stove, tending to the flames. There was such a racket from all the sighing and snoring that you might have thought everyone was at work rather than asleep; life then was so troubled that even sleep seemed like labor. Behind a wooden partition was another, smaller, darker room with a Russian stove. Sitting on this stove were just two naked men, busily mending their clothes. Dvanov was delighted to see space on the stove and he climbed up. The naked men moved aside a little. But the heat there was so extreme that you could have baked potatoes.

"You won't be able to sleep here, young fellow," said one of the naked men. "All you can do here is dry your lice."

Dvanov lay down all the same. It seemed to him as if he were with another person; he could see the flophouse, and at the same time he could see himself lying on the stove. He moved back a little, to make room for this fellow traveler and, having embraced him, forgot himself in sleep.

The naked men finished mending their clothes. One of them said, "It's late—that fellow there's already asleep." And they both got down onto the floor to look for crevices between the sleeping bodies. The black-bearded man's stove had gone out. He stood up, stretched out his hands, and said, "Oh, my dismal sorrows!" Then he went out and didn't come back again.

It turned cold in the hut. A cat appeared and made her way across the sleeping people, patting unkempt beards with a merry paw.

Someone misunderstood the cat and said from out of his sleep, "Nothing doing, little girl. We're as hungry as you are."

All of a sudden, in the middle of the floor, a puffy-looking youth with tufts of early beard sat straight up. "Mama, Mama! The shotgun, you old witch! Give me the shotgun, I'm telling you. And put a saucepan over his head!"

The cat arched her back, anticipating danger from this youth.

A neighboring old man was asleep, but age allowed his mind to carry on functioning even in sleep. "Lie down," he said. "Lie down and don't fret. Why so fearful when there are people around? Sleep now—and God bless you!"

The youth collapsed back without consciousness.

Night's starry sky was sucking away from the earth the last warmth of day; it was the time before dawn when air is pulled up into the heights. Clumps of tall, dew-covered grass outside the window had been transformed into the groves of lunar valleys. In the distance an express train was tirelessly hooting—it was being squeezed between heavy spaces and was crying out as it sped through the mute cleft of a cutting.

There was an abrupt sound of someone's sleeping life, and Dvanov came to. He remembered about the plywood suitcase he was taking to Sonia; in it was a mass of substantial bread rolls. But he couldn't see it there on the stove. He got carefully down onto the floor and began to search for it. He was trembling all over from fear of losing the case; his yearning for it was consuming all the strength of his soul. Thinking they must have hidden the case beneath them, he began to crawl around the room, groping between the sleeping people. The sleepers tossed and turned, but beneath them lay only naked floor; nowhere could he see the case. Appalled by this loss, Dvanov began to cry. He crept once again over the sleepers, touched their bags, and even looked into the stove. He pushed legs aside, scratched cheeks with the sole of a foot, or shifted an entire human being from his place. Seven of the sleepers awoke and sat up.[2]

"What are you looking for?" a handsome-looking peasant asked with quiet fury. "What's got into you, you sleepless satanoid?"

"You're closer, Stepan. Clobber him one with your boot," suggested another man, who was sleeping with his hat on, his head on a brick.

"Have you seen my case anywhere?" Dvanov asked the men who were threatening him. "It was locked. Yesterday it was here, but now it's gone."

A man with poor eyesight—but who was therefore all the more alert—felt for his bag and said, "You sly rat! A case? What case? You showed up empty-handed—I was sitting here with my eyes wide open. And now you're after someone else's case!"

"Bash him, Stepan—you've got a better-fed fist than me," said the man with the hat. "The fact stands: the bastard's gone and woken every citizen here. Now what? Seems we just have to sit and wait till morning."

Dvanov stood in the middle of them all, lost and waiting for help.

From the other room, from on top of the stove, came a firm voice: "Throw this tramp out straightaway! Else I'll get up and throw out the lot of you. Let a Soviet man have some peace at least in the night!"

"You're right!" shouted a big-boned lad by the door. "No use just talking!" He jumped to his feet, grabbed Dvanov round the middle as if he were a fallen tree trunk, and lugged him outside. "Cool down out here!" he said—and returned to the warmth of the hut, slamming the door behind him.

Dvanov set off down the street. A formation of stars was carrying out its labor of vigilance up above him. The stars made the sky beyond our world a little brighter; down below, all remained cool and pure.

Once out of the village, Dvanov wanted to run, but he fell. He had forgotten about his wounded leg, but it was continuously oozing both blood and thick moisture; strength of body and consciousness was departing through the aperture of the wound, and he would have liked to go back to sleep. Instead, however, he splashed the wound with water from a puddle, turned the bandage inside out, and carefully walked on farther, aware of his weakness. Ahead of him a new, better day was dawning; the light from the east was like a frightened flock of white birds rushing turbulently across the sky into the murky heights.

To the right of his path, on a slumped and eroded burial mound, was the village graveyard. Poor crosses, worn thin by the action of winds and waters, stood there faithfully, reminding living passersby that the dead had lived in vain and wanted to rise again. Dvanov raised one hand, saluting the crosses so that they would convey his sympathy down to the dead in their graves.

17

NIKITA was sitting in the Voloshino school kitchen and eating the body of a chicken, while Kopionkin and the other fighting people slept on the floor. Sonia awoke before any of them; she went over to the door and called Dvanov. But Nikita said that there was no trace of Dvanov; probably he had set off ahead, on his business of a new life, since he was a Communist. Then Sonia went barefoot into Petrusha the caretaker's cubicle. "Why are you all sleeping?" she asked, "when Sasha's not here?"

Kopionkin opened one eye, opening the other only when he was on his feet and had put on his hat. "Petrusha," he said, "I'm going out now. Boil up your water for the others. I'll be back around noon." Then he turned to Sonia. "Why didn't you tell me during the night, comrade?" he reproached her. "He's young—he could easily just snuff it out there. And there's a wound on him. Goodness knows where he's going—and with the wind whipping tears out of his eyes and all down his face."

Kopionkin went out into the yard. His horse was massively built, better suited to carrying logs than a human being. Having gotten used to Kopionkin and the Civil War, the horse fed on young wattle fencing and roof straw, and was content with little. But in order well and truly to eat his fill he needed one-eighth of a plot of young forest, which he would wash down with a small pond from the steppe. Kopionkin respected his horse, valuing it in third place—after, first, Rosa Luxemburg, and second, the Revolution.[1]

"Hello there, Strength of the Proletariat!" Kopionkin called out to his horse, who was breathing laboriously from being oversated with coarse fodder. "Let's go to Rosa's grave!"

Kopionkin hoped and believed that all the tasks and roads of his life would lead inevitably to the grave of Rosa Luxemburg. This hope warmed his heart and evoked in him a need for daily revolutionary exploits. Each morning Kopionkin would order his horse to set off toward Rosa's grave; and the horse was so accustomed to the word *Rosa* that he heard it as a command to go forward. After the sounds of Rosa, the horse would at once begin to shift his legs—no matter what the terrain: bog, forest, or abysses of snowdrifts.

"Rosa, Rosa!" Kopionkin would mutter from time to time as they rode on, and the horse would tense his stout body.

"Rosa!" Kopionkin would sigh, and he would envy the clouds floating toward Germany; they would pass over Rosa's grave and the earth she had trodden with her own shoes. To Kopionkin every direction of road and wind led toward Germany, and if they didn't, then they would circle the earth and end up in Rosa's motherland just the same.

If the road was long, if no enemies appeared and there were no exploits to exhaust his solitary body, his agitation would deepen and a sense of burning anguish would accumulate inside him.

"Rosa!" Kopionkin would cry out pitifully, frightening the horse, and, in empty places, he would weep large, countless tears that would later dry up by themselves.

Strength of the Proletariat usually grew tired not from the road, but from the heaviness of his own weight. The horse had grown up in the meadows beside the river Bitiug, and memory of the sweet and varied grasses of his birthplace sometimes made him dribble juicy saliva.[2]

"Wanting something to chew?" Kopionkin would remark from the saddle. "Next year I'll grant you a month's leave in the steppe grass. Then we can ride straight to her grave."

The horse felt grateful and went on zealously compressing the grass of the road down into its earth base. Kopionkin did not particularly try to guide the horse if the road unexpectedly forked. Strength of the Proletariat would independently prefer one road to another and always found the way to wherever Kopionkin's armed hand was most needed. Kopionkin for his part was without any plan or route, preferring to act at random and according to the will of his horse; life in general, he thought, was smarter than his own head.[3]

Groshikov the brigand had been pursuing Kopionkin for a long time but had never managed to encounter him—precisely because Kopionkin was without any idea where he was going, and Groshikov still more so.

Four or five versts from Voloshino, Kopionkin came to a hamlet of five dwellings. He bared his saber and, with its tip, knocked at each hut in turn.

Out of the huts darted women, frightened out of their wits, who had readied themselves long ago to pass away into death. "What do you want, my darling?" said one of them. "The Whites have left us, and we haven't got any Reds tucked away here either."

"Out onto the street!" Kopionkin commanded in a deep voice. "You and all your family—at once!"

Eventually seven women and two old men appeared. They had left their children inside and packed their husbands away into sheds.

Kopionkin inspected the hamlet's population and ordered, "Disperse to your homes! Get down, each of you, to tasks of peaceful labor!"

Dvanov was definitely not in this hamlet.

"Off we go, toward Rosa!" Kopionkin once again addressed Strength of the Proletariat.

Strength of the Proletariat began putting more ground behind him.

"Rosa!"

Wanting to persuade his own soul, Kopionkin would suspiciously inspect some naked bush: Was it longing for Rosa as much as he was? If not, he would move his horse closer and slash through the bush with his saber: *If you don't need Rosa, then don't exist for anything else—nothing is more necessary than Rosa.*

Stitched inside Kopionkin's hat was a colored poster with a portrait of Rosa Luxemburg. She was portrayed so beautifully that no woman could be a match to her. Kopionkin believed in the poster's accuracy and, lest he be overcome with emotion, was afraid to unstitch it.

Kopionkin went on until evening, riding through empty places and inspecting hollows: Was an exhausted Dvanov sleeping there? But he found only a quiet absence of people. Toward evening he came to a long village called Maloye and began checking the population hut by hut, seeking for Dvanov among the members of one family after another. Night set in at the far end of the village; Kopionkin descended into a gully and halted Strength of the Proletariat. And both man and horse fell silent in peace throughout the night.

In the morning Kopionkin gave Strength of the Proletariat time to eat his fill, then set off again to pursue his goal. The path led through drifts of sand, but Kopionkin rode on for a long time without stopping.

Difficulty of movement made Strength of the Proletariat break out in beads of sweat. It was midday, and they were on the edge of a small village. Kopionkin rode into the village and decreed a rest for his steed.

A woman was creeping through the burdocks in a copious fur coat and a small shawl. Kopionkin stopped her.

"Who are you?" he asked.

"Me? I'm the midwife."

"Are you telling me people are still being born here?"

The midwife was used to being sociable and she liked talking to men.

"You can say that again! Hordes of men have returned from the war. They've been giving us women a hard time."

"Listen, woman. Somewhere round here there's a fellow without a hat. His wife's struggling. She just cannot give birth, so he's looking for you. Go round the huts and see if you can find him anywhere. Then come and tell me. All right?"

"A skinny young fellow? In a satinet shirt?" inquired the midwife.

Kopionkin did his best to remember but was unable to say. For him, all people possessed only two faces: *our* kind or the alien kind.

Our kind had light-blue eyes. The alien kind usually had black or brown eyes—the eyes of tsarist officers or brigands. This was all he had ever noticed.

"That's the man!" Kopionkin agreed. "Trousers and a satinet shirt."

"Then I'll bring him to you. He was at Feklusha's. She was cooking potatoes for him."

"Bring him to me, woman, and I'll say a proletarian thank-you!" said Kopionkin, and stroked Strength of the Proletariat. The horse stood there like a machine—huge, trembling, and tightly enveloped by knots of muscle. With such a horse one could only plow virgin soil or uproot trees.

The midwife went off to Feklusha's.

Feklusha was washing her widow's clothes; she had bared her plump, rosy arms.

The midwife crossed herself and asked, "Where's your lodger? There's a man on horseback asking for him."

"He's asleep," said Feklusha. "The fellow's barely alive as it is. I'm not going to wake him."

Dvanov's right arm was hanging down from on top of the stove. From it could be gauged the deep, slow rhythm of his breathing.

The midwife returned to Kopionkin, who then went to Feklusha's on foot.

"Wake your guest!" he commanded.

Feklusha tugged Dvanov's arm. In sleepy fright Dvanov was quick to speak and show his face.

"Let's go, comrade Dvanov!" said Kopionkin. "The schoolmistress wants you delivered back to her."

Dvanov awoke and remembered. "No, let me be. I'm staying here. Go back to Voloshino."

"Up to you," said Kopionkin. "At least you're alive—which is excellent!"

Kopionkin went on riding till late, though the path he took was a shorter one. It was already night when he caught sight of the mill and the school's illuminated windows.

Mrachinsky and Petrusha the caretaker were playing checkers in Sonia's room; the schoolteacher herself was sitting at the kitchen table, resting her grieving head on her palms.

"He doesn't want to come back," Kopionkin reported. "He's at a widow's, lying on her stove."

"Well then, let him lie there," Sonia renounced Dvanov. "He still takes me for a little girl—but sometimes I feel sad too."

Kopionkin went out to the horses. The other members of his unit had not yet returned from their wives. As for the two brigands, they were hanging about to no purpose, filling their faces with the people's victuals. "If we carry on like this, there'll soon be no food left in any of our villages," Kopionkin said to himself. "We'll have no rear supply base. How will I get to Rosa then?"

Mrachinsky and Nikita went on busying themselves uselessly, demonstrating to Kopionkin their readiness for any zeal. Mrachinsky was standing on a heap of dry manure, trampling it flat with his feet.

"Go inside," Kopionkin ordered them, slowly thinking things through. "And tomorrow I'll set you both free. What's the use of my dragging disarrayed brigands around with me? What kind of enemies do you think you are? You're just parasites! You know now that I exist—and that's enough."

18

HIS LIFE now on hold, Dvanov was sitting in the comfort of a home and watching a woman hanging out her washing on a row of strings beside the stove. Horse fat was burning in a crock, with flames like the tongues of hell on paintings in local churches; village people were walking down the street to abandoned places nearby. The Civil War was evident all around them, in shards and splinters of the nation's possessions: dead horses, carts, brigands' coats and pillows. For the brigands, pillows took the place of saddles. This was why, in brigand units, one heard the command: "Onto your pillows!" In response Red Army commanders would yell out, as their horses flew after the brigands, "Quick! After the pillagers!"

The inhabitants of Middle Boltay used to go out at night into the gullies and glades and wander over the traces of past battles, searching for items of everyday use. Many people ended up with one item or another; this trade of picking apart the Civil War was not unprofitable. The Military Commissariat's decrees about the return of lost military equipment hung in the village in vain: weapons of war were disassembled and transformed into mechanisms of peaceful activities. A water-cooled machine gun, attached to a cast-iron pot, became a system for the production of moonshine; field kitchens were cemented into village bathhouses; parts of a three-inch field gun proved ideal for fluffing up wool before spinning, while the firing locks of cannons were made into wallowers for watermills. In one yard Dvanov saw a woman's shirt sewn from an English flag. It was drying in the Russian wind and had already acquired holes and signs of having been worn by a woman.

Feklusha, the mistress of the hut, stopped work.

"Why so thoughtful, young man?" she asked. "Are you hungry? Or are you feeling lonely?"

"I'm all right," said Dvanov. "It's quiet in your hut, and I'm resting."

"Rest then. You've nowhere to hurry to. You're still young—there's plenty of life left for you." Feklusha yawned, covering her mouth with her large, worker's hand. "But as for me, I've lived out my days. My man was killed in the tsar's war. I've nothing to live for, and sleep's always a blessing."

Feklusha undressed in Dvanov's presence, knowing she was no longer of interest to men.

"Put out the light," she said. "Else there'll be none left to get us up in the morning."

Dvanov blew into the crock. The barefoot Feklusha climbed up onto the stove.

"You can come up too. You won't be wanting to look at my shame now."

Dvanov knew that, were this person not in the hut, he would immediately run back to Sonia again or else go searching for socialism in the distance. Feklusha's way of defending Dvanov was through accustoming him to her own simplicity, as if she were a sister of his late mother, whom he did not remember and could not love.

When Feklusha fell asleep, Dvanov found it difficult to be on his own. They had hardly spoken all day, but Dvanov had not felt loneliness; Feklusha, after all, was keeping him in her mind and Dvanov sensed her without interruption, which released him from the power of his distant dream. Now, however, he no longer existed in Feklusha's consciousness and he felt the burden of his own coming sleep, when he too would forget everyone; bodily warmth would force his reason somewhere outside, and there it would remain as a sad and isolated observer.

The old belief called this exiled weak consciousness a guardian angel. Dvanov could still remember this meaning, and he felt sorry for his guardian angel, which would soon be leaving the close darkness of a living person and going out into the cold.

Somewhere in his own weary silence, Dvanov was missing Sonia, and he didn't know what he should do; he would have liked to take her into his arms and go forward with her, fresh and free for other and better impressions. The light outside the window was ceasing and, without a through draft, the air in the hut had gone stale.

Outside, people were on their way back from their labor of disarming the war, rustling and scuffling; some were dragging heavy weights and plowing the grass right down to the soil.

Dvanov quietly got up onto the stove. Feklusha was scratching her armpits and stirring about a little.

"Lying down, are you?" she asked flatly, through sleep. "Well then—sleep well."

The stove's hot bricks made Dvanov still more agitated; only when he was lost in delirium and exhausted from the heat did he fall asleep. Small things—little boxes, crocks, felt boots, blouses—turned into weighty objects of huge volume and then piled on top of him; he had to allow them to enter inside him and they squeezed in with difficulty, stretching his skin till it seemed about to burst. What scared him most was not that these things had come to life and were suffocating him but that his skin would explode and he would choke on hot, dry boot-felt stuck in its seams.

Feklusha put a hand on Dvanov's face. Dvanov sensed the smell of faded grass; he remembered his parting beside a fence with a pitiful, barefoot almost-woman and he squeezed Feklusha's hand. This helped to calm him and relieve his anguish. Taking hold of Feklusha's arm higher up, he pressed up against her.

"What are you tossing about for?" she asked. "Stop thinking and go to sleep."

Dvanov did not reply. His heart began to knock, as if it were something hard, and rejoiced loudly at its own freedom within. His life's quiet watchman sat in his own little room, neither rejoicing nor grieving—simply performing a necessary service.

With experienced hands, Dvanov began to caress Feklusha as if this were something he had already learned. Then his hands froze in fear and astonishment.

"What is it?" Feklusha whispered in a very close, loud voice. "We're all the same down there."

"You're sisters," said Dvanov with the tenderness of clear recollection, with an absolute need to do Sonia good through her sister.

Dvanov sensed neither joy nor complete oblivion; he was listening all the time to the fine, precise work of his heart. But then his heart gave out, slowed, slammed shut, and closed down—already empty. It had opened too wide and inadvertently released its only bird. The watchman-observer watched the bird fly away, carrying off on saddened, outstretched wings a body so weightless as to be indistinct. And the watchman wept; only once in a person's life does this watchman weep, only once does he lose his own calm for the sake of regret.

To Dvanov, the even paleness of night in the hut began to seem turbid; his eyes were clouding over. Things were small now, and back in their places. There was nothing he now wanted, and he fell asleep healthy.

Not until morning was Dvanov able to get his fill of rest. He woke late, when Feklusha was lighting a fire beneath a trivet in the hearth, but he fell asleep again. He felt as worn out as if he had been dealt an exhausting wound.

Around noon, Strength of the Proletariat stopped outside the window. To find his friend, Kopionkin jumped down from the horse's back a second time.

Kopionkin knocked on the window with his scabbard. "Mistress, I need to speak to your guest!"

Feklusha went over to Dvanov and gave his head a shake. "Wake up, my boy, there's a horseman outside. He wants to speak to you."

Still half-asleep, Dvanov could see only a pale blue mist.

Into the hut came Kopionkin, carrying a cap and a jacket.

"Well, comrade Dvanov, have you really come to a stop here for all eternity? Here's something for you from the schoolmistress—the goods you wear next to your skin!"

"I'm staying here forever," said Dvanov.

Kopionkin bowed his head, having no thought in it that might help. "Then I'll leave. Goodbye, comrade Dvanov."

In the top half of the window, Dvanov saw Kopionkin ride off into the depth of the plain, into distant parts. Strength of the Proletariat was carrying the elderly warrior away to wherever communism's living enemy now lived, and Kopionkin—indigent, distant, and happy—was disappearing farther and farther from Dvanov.

Dvanov jumped down from the stove. Out on the street he remembered about his wounded leg—but chose to let it take care of itself for the time being.

"Why've you come running after me?" asked Kopionkin, who was still only going at a walk. "I'll be dying soon. Then it'll just be you and the horse."

And he lifted Dvanov up and sat him on Strength of the Proletariat's backside. "Put your arms round my belly. Together we'll ride on and exist."

19

RIGHT up until evening, Strength of the Proletariat strode on forward. Dvanov and Kopionkin then stopped for the night on the border of forest and steppe, in a forester's hut.

"Anyone been passing by?" Kopionkin asked the forester. "Anyone different?"

But many travelers passed the night in his hut, and the forester replied, "These days there's a lot of folk riding about in search of food—more than anyone can remember. I'm a publical person—do you expect every one of their mugs to stick in my mind?"

"But why's there a smell of burning outside?" asked Kopionkin. It was not the first time he'd smelled something like this.

The two men went out into the yard.

"Can you hear?" asked the forester. "The grass keeps ringing, even though there's no wind."

"Yes," said Kopionkin, listening.

"It's the White bourgeois, some passersby told me—it's the White bourgeois sending signals through their radios. See, there's a smell of burning again."[1]

"Are you sure?" asked Kopionkin, sniffing.

"You must have a blocked nose. It's their wireless signals, they're singeing the air."

"Brandish your stick," Kopionkin commanded on the instant. "Garble their noise—so they can't make the words out." He then bared his saber and began slashing the dangerous air, until he began to feel a cramp where his well-practiced arm was attached to his shoulder.

"Enough," Kopionkin countermanded. "Now we've confused things for them."

After this victory Kopionkin felt satisfied; he saw the Revolution as the last remnant of Rosa Luxemburg's body, and he guarded it even in the smallest of ways. The now-silent forester gave each of his guests a hunk of good bread and sat down at a distance. Kopionkin paid no attention to the taste of the bread; he always ate without relish, slept without fear of dreams, and lived by what was close at hand, not yielding to his own body.

"Why are you feeding us?" Dvanov asked the forester. "We might be dangerous."

"In that case," Kopionkin interjected, "you shouldn't be eating! But anyway, grain gives birth to itself in the earth—the peasant just tickles it with his plow, like a woman tickles a cow's udder. It's not proper labor. Isn't that so, mister?"

"You're surely right," assented the man who had fed them. "You're the bosses in power, you know best."

"Kulak cretin!" replied Kopionkin, with quick rage. "Our power isn't terror, it's the meditativeness of the masses."

The forester agreed that it was now a matter of meditativeness.

Before going to sleep, Dvanov and Kopionkin talked about the day to come. "What do you think?" Dvanov asked. "Will we soon be relocating villages Soviet style?"

The Revolution had convinced Kopionkin once and for all of the submissiveness of every enemy. "Yes—and in no time at all!" he replied. "We can tell them we'll be giving the land away to the Ukrainians otherwise. Or we can simply employ armed force for the fulfillment of transportation duties of huts and farm buildings. We've said that the land is socialism—and so be it!"

"First we must bring water to the uplands," said Dvanov. "As it is, everywhere in these parts is dry—these valleys are an offshoot of the Trans-Caspian desert."

"We'll lay a pipeline," said Kopionkin, quick to console his comrade. "We'll install pipes and fountains. Even in dry years we'll wet the earth. The women will be rearing geese. There'll be down and feathers enough for all—a general flourishing."

At this point Dvanov fell asleep. Kopionkin put some soft grass beneath his wounded leg and also quieted down until morning.

In the morning they left the hut on the edge of the forest and headed out into the steppe.

Along the well-worn track a man was coming toward them on foot. From time to time he lay down on the ground and rolled some way at full length. Then he went back to walking again with his legs.

"What are you doing, you leper?" said Kopionkin, halting the traveler as they got close to him.

"I'm rolling along, my good fellow," explained the oncomer. "My legs are damned tired. Like this, I can give them a rest—and still move on farther."

Something made Kopionkin doubtful. "You should walk normal and orderly."

"But I'm on my way from Batum. It's two years since I last saw my family. The moment I start to rest, anguish and longing come down on me. But if I keep rolling, even if it's only slowly, home seems closer."

"What's that village over there?" asked Kopionkin.

"Over there?" said the wanderer, looking back. His face was deathly pale; in the course of his life, without realizing it, he had covered the distance to the moon. "Could be Khans' Yards. But heaven knows—there are villages living all over the steppe."

Kopionkin tried to probe further: "So it seems you well and truly love your wife?"

Through eyes misted over by the long road, the man on foot looked at the two horsemen. "Of course, I honor her. When she was giving birth, grief sent me right up onto the roof."

There was a smell of food in Khans' Yards, but in fact it was moonshine being distilled from grain. An unkempt woman—evidently linked to this secret production process—was rushing down the street, dashing into every hut, and immediately dashing out again.

"The Front!" she was warning the men. "They're back again!" And she kept glancing in horror at the armed might of Kopionkin and Dvanov.

The men were pouring water onto their fires, and smoke was billowing out of the huts. The moonshine mash was hurriedly being carried out to the pigs' troughs—causing the pigs, after eating their fill, to charge about the village in delirium.[2]

"Where, my honest fellow, is the village soviet?" said Kopionkin, addressing a lame citizen.

Invested with an unknown sense of worth, the lame citizen was walking with a slow, important step.

"'Honest fellow,' you say. You do in my leg—and now you call me honest! There's no soviet in this village. But I'm the plenipotentiary of the district RevCom—the power and chastising might of the poorest peasants. No matter that I'm lame—I'm the smartest person here. I can do anything!"

"Listen to me, comrade plenipotentiary!" said Kopionkin, with threat in his voice.

"Here we have the provincial ExecCom's chief representative at large!" Dvanov got down from the horse and held his hand out to the plenipotentiary. "Yes, this man's doing socialism in the province, in battle formation of revolutionary conscience and transportation duties. What do you have to show us?"

The plenipotentiary was in no way intimidated. "We've got plenty of mind, but no grain."

"But the fog of moonshine is drifting over the land expropriated from the landowners," Dvanov retorted.

The plenipotentiary took serious offense: "Don't speak idle words, comrade! Yesterday I signed a decree. Today is a day of thanksgiving in celebration of the village's deliverance from tsarism. I've granted the people total self-will and freedom for twenty-four hours. All can do as they please. I'm strolling about without opposition, while the Revolution enjoys a day of rest. Get it?"

"But who's granted you such self-power and autocracy?" said Kopionkin, frowning.

"Can't you see? Here in the village I'm Lenin," said the lame man, stating the obvious. "Today the kulaks are feasting the village poor. I've handed out receipts and am checking the execution of this measure in person."

"Have you completed your check?"

"Hut by hut, and also at random. Everything's in order. As for strength, it's higher proof than our prewar stuff. The horseless peasants are entirely content."

"And that woman rushing about in panic?" asked Kopionkin.

At this, the lame man turned indignant. "There's still no Soviet consciousness. People are scared of welcoming comrade guests from elsewhere. They'd rather pour their good away into the burdocks and pass themselves off as state poor. I know all their hidden ways, I can see their whole sense and meaning of life."

The lame man was called Fyodor Dostoevsky. This was how he had reregistered himself in a special protocol stating that the district RevCom plenipotentiary Ignaty Moshonkov had considered an application from citizen Ignaty Moshonkov[3] to be renamed in honor of the memory of the famous writer Fyodor Dostoevsky and had decreed as follows: that the change of name take effect from the beginning of the next day and forever after, and that all citizens should be offered the opportunity to reconsider their names: Were they, or were they not, satisfactory? The need for some resemblance to any new name would, of course, need to be borne in mind. Fyodor Dostoevsky had conceived this campaign in the interests of the self-perfection of the village citizens: a man who chose to call himself Liebknecht had better live like him—otherwise this splendid name would have to be repossessed. So far, two citizens had undergone official reregistration: Stepan Checher had become Christopher Columbus and the well-digger Piotr Grudin had become Franz Mehring—or, as he was more commonly called, Merin.[4] Fyodor Dostoevsky had authorized these names provisionally and pending further inquiry; he had asked the district RevCom to ascertain whether Columbus and Mehring were people of sufficient worth for their names to be adopted as models of further life or whether these names were mute for the Revolution. The RevCom had yet to reply. Stepan Checher and Piotr Grudin were, for the time being, living almost anonymously.

"Now you've renamed yourselves," Dostoevsky would tell them, "you must do something outstanding."

"We will," they both replied. "Just give us an official confirmation and a certificate."

"You can rename yourselves orally, but on official documents I shall continue for now to designate you in the old way."

"All right," said the petitioners. "Oral will be better than nothing."

Kopionkin and Dvanov had arrived in the middle of a period of profound thought, on Dostoevsky's part, about future perfections of life. He was thinking about comradely marriage, about the Soviet meaning of life, about the possibility of destroying night for the sake of an increase in harvests, about the organization of daily laboring happiness, and about the nature of the soul. Was the soul a pitiful heart, or a mind inside a man's head? Tormented by these and many other questions, Dostoevsky was keeping his family awake at night.

Dostoevsky's home housed a library of books, but he already knew them by heart. They brought him no consolation and he now had to do his own personal thinking.

After eating millet porridge in Dostoevsky's hut, Dvanov and Kopionkin began a pressing conversation with him about the need to construct socialism the following summer. Dvanov said that the need for such haste had been indicated by Lenin himself. "Soviet Russia," he continued eloquently, "is like a young birch tree with the goat of capitalism tearing toward it." He even cited a slogan from the newspapers:

Help our young birch grow
To keep it safe from Europe's greedy goat.

Concentrated imagination of the inevitable danger of capitalism made Dostoevsky turn pale. In his mind's eye he saw White goats eating our young Soviet bark. Stripped naked, the whole Revolution would freeze to death.

"So what's stopping us, comrades?" Dostoevsky exclaimed with inspiration. "Let's get started straightaway—we can do socialism by the New Year! The White goats will come galloping along in the summer, but by then the bark on the Soviet birch will be good and hard."

Dvanov quickly realized that Dostoevsky thought of socialism simply as a society of good people, and that things and structures meant nothing to him. "No, comrade Dostoevsky," he replied. "Socialism is like the sun. Its time is summer. It must be built on the fat lands of the high steppe. How many households are there in your village?"

"It's a big village. Three hundred and forty huts, and another fifteen families living nearby."

"Very good," said Dvanov, thinking as he went along. "You must divide them into five or six collectives. Announce immediate labor duties. For the time being the men can dig wells in the fallow land. Come spring, they can start transporting the buildings by cart. Do you have any well-diggers?"

Dostoevsky was slowly taking Dvanov's words into his inner being and transforming them into visible circumstances. He had no gift for the invention of truth and he could understand it only when he had turned thoughts into events here in his own region, but for him this was a slow process; he needed to picture for himself some familiar part of the steppe, move each village family there by name and then observe how things had turned out.

"Yes, we do have well-diggers," said Dostoevsky. "Franz Mehring, for example. He can sense water with his feet. He wanders about the gullies, divines the depths of underground water tables, and says, 'Dig here, my lads. Six fathoms down!' And then water gushes out wholesale. Seems that's the way his mother and father made him..."

Dvanov helped Dostoevsky to imagine socialism in the form of small collective settlements on anonymous poor-peasant land—but from there too people would wander off to become tramps or fighters and man would become a rare being. Dostoevsky felt there was something missing, some kind of general joy rising from every barnyard, something that would help his imagination of the future turn into love and warmth and that would summon up conscience and impatience as an active force inside his body—since socialism was temporarily absent in the outside world.

Kopionkin listened and listened, then turned indignant. "What a wretched little nit you are! You've received orders from the provincial ExecCom: 'Get socialism finished by summer!' So: unsheathe the sword of communism, since we have iron discipline! What kind of Lenin do you think you are? You're no more than a Soviet watchman. All you're doing, you damned soul, is dragging out the tempo of disorder and ruination."

Dvanov encouraged Dostoevsky further. "Cultured plants will make the earth brighter and more clearly visible from other planets. And then, the circulation of moisture will increase. The sky will become bluer and more transparent!"

Dostoevsky now felt joy; once and for all, he had seen socialism. It was a light blue, slightly moist sky, nourished by the breath of fodder crops. The wind was collectively stirring the rich lakes of cultivated fields, and life was so happy as to be noiseless. All that remained was to determine life's Soviet meaning. Dostoevsky had been chosen unanimously for this task—and now here he was, sitting for forty days and nights without sleep, deep in selfless and self-oblivious thought. Beautiful and clean-fleshed young women were bringing him tasty food—borscht and roast pork—but they were taking it away again untouched; Dostoevsky was unable to surface from his deep place of duty.[5]

The young maidens were falling in love with Dostoevsky—but they were one and all party members, and party discipline did not allow them to confess their love. In the line of duty and political consciousness, they suffered in silence.

Dostoevsky scratched a fingernail across the table, as if dividing the epoch in two: "I'll make you socialism! Even before the rye has ripened, socialism will be ready! I was wondering what was bringing me such anguish. It's because I was longing for socialism!"

"That's right," said Kopionkin in confirmation. "Everyone wishes to love Rosa."

Dostoevsky tried to follow this, but he did not quite understand. He could only surmise that Rosa was an abbreviated designation for the Revolution, or a slogan he did not know.

"Absolutely correct, comrade!" said Dostoevsky with pleasure, since the foundation of happiness had now been revealed. "But all the same, see how thin I've become—that's from leadership of the Revolution in my district."

"I understand. You're a stopgap—you have to plug every current of events," said Kopionkin, upholding Dostoevsky's worth.

But Dostoevsky was unable to fall asleep calmly that night. He tossed and turned, muttering at length the small change of his own reflections.

"What's got into you?" asked Kopionkin, hearing Dostoevsky's sounds. "Why are you jawing away like that? Why not make yourself well and truly sad? Remember the Civil War, remember its dead."

During the night Dostoevsky awoke the others. Still half-asleep, Kopionkin seized his saber, to meet any suddenly attacking enemy.

"I touched you for the sake of Soviet power," Dostoevsky explained.

"In that case," Kopionkin asked severely, "why didn't you wake us earlier?"

"We've got no livestock," Dostoevsky began. During the first half of the night he had managed to think socialism all the way through, until it became real life. "What kind of citizen is going to go out into the rich steppe without any livestock? What's the good of him dragging buildings around like so much luggage? My anxieties are tormenting me."

Kopionkin scratched his thin and abrupt Adam's apple, as if wanting to disembowel his throat.

"Sasha!" he said to Dvanov. "Don't sleep idly. Explain to this element here that he doesn't know Soviet laws." Then Kopionkin looked darkly and intently at Dostoevsky and addressed him directly. "What a thing to be thinking about! You're a White auxiliary, not a district Lenin! Tomorrow you must herd all the livestock together, if anyone has any left, and then divide it up per head and according to your revolutionary sentiment. Simple as that!"[6]

Kopionkin at once went back to sleep. He did not understand doubt and had none himself, seeing any uncertainty of spirit as a betrayal of the Revolution. Rosa Luxemburg had thought everything through in advance, on behalf of everyone—and all that was required now was feats of arms, to destroy enemies visible and invisible.

In the morning Dostoevsky went round the whole of Khans' Yards, announcing to every household the joint decree of the district RevCom and the provincial ExecCom concerning the revolutionary division of livestock, without exemption.

And so the livestock were all driven out onto the square, in front of the church, to the wails of the entire possessing class. But the poorer peasants were suffering too, pained by the sight of pitiful old women and the animals' moaning owners, and even some of the entirely destitute were wailing, although their share of livestock awaited them.

The women kissed the cows, while the men held their horses especially loosely and tenderly, trying to instill heart into them as if they were sons going off to the war, while they themselves wondered whether to weep or try to make the best of things as they were.

One peasant, tall and thin but with a small, naked face and a girlish voice, brought his horse along not only without reproach but with words of consolation for his grieving fellow villagers.

"What's got into you, Uncle Mitry?" he said in his high voice to a distraught old man. "To hell with horses—anyone would think it's your life that's being taken from you! Call this sorrow? They're seizing your horse—and that's all! Damn your horse—there's more where it came from! Take your sorrows back into your heart!"

Dostoevsky knew this peasant: an old runaway of a deserter. In early childhood, he had shown up from somewhere or other without certificate or document—and he could not be conscripted for even a single war. He possessed no name or date of birth, and officially he did not exist at all; in order to designate him somehow or other, for everyday convenience, his neighbors called the deserter "Half-Baked," while in the register of the former village soviet he had not been included at all. There had been one secretary who had written at the bottom of the list of names: "*Others*—1; *Sex*—Doubtful." But the following secretary had been unable to make sense of this and had added one more head to the count of long-horned cattle, deleting "*Others*" right through. And so Half-Baked went on living, a leak from society, like millet spilled on the earth from a cart.

But not long ago Dostoevsky had entered him, in ink, into the citizens' register under the title of "Evasive middle peasant without a personally acquired surname,"[7] thus firmly reinforcing his existence. Dostoevsky had, you might say, given birth to Half-Baked, for Soviet use.[8]

In the past, steppe life had followed in the tracks of cattle, and people still retained a fear of dying of hunger if they had no cattle, and so they were weeping more out of prejudice than from fear of losses.

Dvanov and Kopionkin arrived as Dostoevsky was beginning the distribution of livestock among the poor peasants.

"No mistakes now!" said Kopionkin, to ensure his reliability. "Is your revolutionary feeling fully present in you?"

Proud with power, Dostoevsky indicated with his hand that revolutionary feeling filled him from belly to neck. The method of division he had thought up was simple and clear: the best horses and cows were going to the poorest peasants. But since there was so little livestock, hardly anything was left for the middle peasants—just a sheep apiece for a few of them.

As the allocation drew to a successful close, the same Half-Baked stepped forward and said in a rasping voice, "Fyodor Mikhailovich, comrade Dostoevsky, this concern of ours is, of course, foolish—but don't you go getting upset at what I'm about to say to you now. Please don't go getting upset."

"Speak, citizen Half-Baked. Speak honestly and without fear," Dostoevsky resolved, openly and respectfully.

Half-Baked turned toward the grieving people. Even the poorest peasants were now grieving, clasping their gift horses in fear; many were discreetly returning livestock to the possessor class.

"In that case, listen to me, the whole throng of you! I shall ask as a simple fool. What, I ask you, is Petka Ryzhov going to do with my trotter? The only fodder Petka's got is the straw on his roof. He doesn't have so much as a spare stake in his plot, and the same half potato's been stewing in his belly for over two days now. And secondly—now don't be upset, Fyodor Mikhailovich, your business is revolution, we do understand—what's going to happen later as regards the foals? We're the poor peasants now. Does that mean the new horse owners will be bearing foals to benefit the likes of us? You must ask them, Fyodor Mikhailovich. Will these poor-peasant horse owners want to feed calves and foals just for us?"

Such sound sense struck everyone dumb.

Half-Baked registered the silence and continued, "In five years' time, as I see it, no one will have any livestock higher than a chicken. Who's going to want his cow to bear calves for the sake of his neighbor? And anyway, today's livestock will be kicking the bucket ahead of time. My horse that's now Petka's will be the first to go. The man's barely ever set eyes on a horse, and the only fodder he can offer it is his fence posts. Give me comfort, Fyodor Mikhailovich—only please don't go nursing grievance against me!"

Dostoevsky offered him comfort straightaway: "You're right, Half-Baked. This livestock allocation is without sense!"

Amid the circle of people, Kopionkin broke through into purity. "What do you mean—'without sense'? Are you on the side of the brigands? You need a good thorough baking yourself!" Inspiring terror and trembling, he went on: "What this half-baked kulak just told you is nonsense. Socialism will arrive instantaneously and put an end to everything. There'll be no time for anything to be born before life turns excellent. Consequent upon the confiscation of the trotter from Petka Ryzhov, I propose that it be transferred to comrade Dvanov, the plenipotentiary of the provincial ExecCom. And now go your separate ways, poor-peasant comrades, to do battle against ruination and collapse!"

The poor peasants set off uncertainly with their cows and horses, having forgotten how to handle them.

Half-Baked, dumbfounded, was looking at Kopionkin. What was tormenting him now was not the loss of his trotter, but curiosity.

"May I ask a word, comrade from the committee?" he finally ventured in his child's voice.

Kopionkin took pity. "Since power has not been granted you, then ask away!"

Politely and carefully, Half-Baked asked, "But what is socialism? What will it be like there? And where will goods come from to augment it?"

Without effort, Kopionkin explained, "If you were a poor peasant, you'd already know—but since you're a kulak you won't understand anything anyway."

In the evening Dvanov and Kopionkin wanted to leave, but Dostoevsky begged them to stay on until morning, so that he could learn definitively how to start socialism in the steppe and how to finish it off.

The long halt was starting to bore Kopionkin and he resolved to leave during the night.

"We've already told you everything," he informed Dostoevsky. "You have livestock. The peasant and working-class masses are on their feet. Now you need only declare transportation duties, dig wells and ponds in the steppe and, come spring, relocate structures. And ensure that socialism's taller than the grass by summer. I'll be coming to check!"

"So it turns out that only the poor peasants will be working—they're the ones with the horses now—while the prosperous peasants will be living to no purpose!" Dostoevsky replied, again yielding to doubt.

"So what?" said Kopionkin, without surprise. "It's out of the pure hands of the poor that socialism must originate—and the kulaks will perish in the struggle."

"That's right," said Dostoevsky, now satisfied.

That night Dvanov and Kopionkin set off, having once again admonished Dostoevsky with regard to the schedule for the construction of socialism.

Half-Baked's trotter was walking beside Strength of the Proletariat. For both riders it was a relief to sense the road drawing them out of the tight crampedness of a populated place and into the distance. Even a day and a night of sedentary life allowed the force of anguish to accumulate in each of their hearts; and for this reason Dvanov and Kopionkin were afraid of the ceilings of huts and aspired to open roads, which sucked out the superfluous blood from their hearts.

The broad road from the district town came out to meet the two riders, who took their horses into a steppe trot.

Up above them was a high stand of night clouds, still half lit by a sun that had set long before; the air, emptied by the day's wind, was no longer stirring. The freshness and silence of this wilted space made Dvanov feel weak, and he was beginning to doze off on his trotter. "If we come to a hut," he said, "let's snatch a few hours' sleep. Till sunrise."

Kopionkin pointed to a nearby strip of forest lying on the spacious earth like a black and welcoming silence.

"There's sure to be a forest inspector's hut somewhere there."

20

BARELY had the travelers entered a grove of concentrated, sad trees when they heard the weary voices of guard dogs, watching in the dark over the isolated home of a human being.

The forester, who looked after the forests out of love for science, was at this moment studying some very old books. He was seeking in the past for some parallel to these Soviet days, in order to learn the further agonizing fate of the Revolution and to find a way out for the salvation of his own family.

His forester father had left him a library of cheap books by the least read, least important, and most forgotten of authors. He used to say to his son that life's decisive truths exist secretly in abandoned books.

Bad books, in his view, were like unborn children who perished inside their mothers because of the disparity between their too-tender bodies and the world's harshness, which penetrated even a mother's womb.

"If even ten such children survived, they would make man into a triumphant and sublime being," he had said to his son in testament. "But the only children to be born are the most clouded of mind and insensitive of heart, those who can endure the abrupt air of nature and the struggle to track down food."

Today the forester was reading a book by Nikolay Arsakov that had been published in 1868.[1] It was titled *Second-Rate People,* and through the boredom of the dry word the inspector was searching for what he needed. He considered that no books were boring or meaningless if the reader searched vigilantly in them for the meaning of life. Boring books had their origin in boring readers, since the active principle in a book was the reader's eager yearning, not the skill of the author.

"Where have you come from?" the forester wondered with regard to the Bolsheviks. "You've probably already existed before. Nothing comes into being without resemblance to something else, without thieving what has already existed."

His two small children and his plump wife were sleeping peacefully and without thought. Looking at them from time to time, the forester called on all his power of mind, asking it to stand guard over these three precious beings. He needed to discover the future, in order to find his way about it in good time and not allow his nearest and dearest to perish.

Arsakov had written that the only steady improvement comes from second-rate people. Excessive mind is of no use at all—it is like wheat or rye on rich soil that collapses before it is ripe and cannot be reaped. Life's acceleration at the hands of higher people exhausts it—and so life loses what it had once possessed.

"People," according to Arsakov, "begin to act much too early, having understood little. Insofar as this is possible, it is best to reduce one's actions and grant freedom to the contemplative half of the soul. Contemplation is self-instruction from events outside one. Let people study the circumstances of nature for as long as possible, in order to commence their actions late but dependably, free of error, and with the sword of mature experience in their right hand. It should not be forgotten that all the sins of social life stem from interference in it by men young in reason. It is sufficient to leave history in peace for fifty years, in order for all effortlessly to attain an intoxicating prosperity."

The dogs let out howls of alarm, and the inspector, taking his rifle, went out to meet these late guests.

He then led the two horses, along with Dvanov and Kopionkin, through ranks of devoted dogs and maturing puppies.

Half an hour later, the three men were standing around a lamp in a log hut filled with the breath of life. The forester brought his guests some bread and milk.

He was alert, ready for trouble of any possible kind from these night people. But he felt reassured by Dvanov's unremarkable face and the way his eyes kept going still.

After he had eaten, Kopionkin took the open book and, with effort, read what Arsakov had written.

"What do you think?" he asked, giving the book to Dvanov.

Dvanov read.

"Capitalist quietism. Keep your head down—and don't lift a finger."

"I feel the same!" said Kopionkin, dismissing the vicious book to one side. "So, what's to be done with this forest now we have socialism?" he asked, sighing with embittered thought.

"Tell me, comrade, how much income does a hectare of forest provide?" Dvanov asked the forester.

"It depends," the man struggled to reply. "It depends on the forest, on its age and condition. There are many circumstances to consider."

"But on average?"

"On average? I should say ten or fifteen roubles."

"That's all? Less than from rye, I imagine?"

The forester tried not to say the wrong thing; he was frightened. "Yes, rye gives you a bit more. From one hectare, a peasant will get twenty or thirty roubles of clear profit. At least."

Kopionkin's face took on the furious look of a man who has been deceived. "Then this forest must be razed immediately and the land put under the plow! All these trees do is take space away from winter wheat."

The forester fell silent, intently observing Kopionkin's growing agitation. Writing in pencil on the pages of Arsakov's book, Dvanov was calculating the losses occasioned by forestry. After asking about the size of the forest, he drew up a final balance.

"The peasants are losing about ten thousand a year because of this forest," he calmly announced. "Rye, it seems, will be more profitable."

"It certainly will!" exclaimed Kopionkin. "The man's said that himself. These thickets must be cleared to the ground and sown with rye. Write out a decree, comrade Dvanov."

Dvanov recalled that it was a long time since he had been in contact with Shumilin. Still, Shumilin could hardly censure him for taking direct action in accord with evident revolutionary benefit.

The forester ventured a tentative objection. "I wanted to say that there has already been a strong development recently of spontaneous tree-felling. There is no need to fell any more of such robust and resolute plants."

"Well, so much the better," Kopionkin responded sharply. "We don't walk ahead of the people, we follow them. Evidently the people has already sensed that rye is better than trees. Write a decree, Sasha, ordering the forest to be felled."

Dvanov wrote a decree-appeal addressed to all the peasant-indigents of the Upper Motnia District. This decree, in the name of the Provincial ExecCom, proposed certification of the condition of the poor peasants and the urgent felling of the Bitterman Forest. By means of these measures, two roads into socialism would be laid down simultaneously. First, the poor peasants would receive timber—for the construction of new Soviet cities on the high steppe; second, land would be released for the sowing of rye and other cultures more profitable than slow-growing trees.

Kopionkin read through the decree.

"Excellent!" he said. "Let me sign below, to make it more frightening. There are a lot of people round here who remember me—I am, after all, an armed man."

And he signed with his full title: "Commander of the Rosa Luxemburg Unit of Field Bolsheviks of the Upper Motnia District, Stepan Yefimovich Kopionkin."[2]

"You can take this on horseback tomorrow to the neighboring villages—and then the other villages will find out by themselves," Kopionkin added, handing the paper to the forester.

"And what am I to do after the forest?" the man replied.

"Same as everyone else!" Kopionkin instructed. "Plow the land and feed yourself. You must have received enough salary during the year to feed an entire hamlet. Now you can live like the masses."

It was already late. Deep revolutionary night lay over the doomed forest. Before the Revolution Kopionkin had not sensed anything attentively—forests, people, and windswept expanses had not agitated him, and he had not meddled with them. But now a change had set in. Kopionkin listened to the even hum of the winter night and wanted this night to pass smoothly over Soviet lands.

Love for the felled Rosa did not exist alone in Kopionkin's heart. It lay there in its own warm nest, but this nest was woven out of green sprigs of concern about Soviet citizens, out of a difficult pity for all who had aged and grown frail from poverty and from furious, ceaseless battling against all enemies of the poor.

Night was singing its last hours over the Bitterman Forest. Dvanov and Kopionkin were lying on the floor, stretching out in sleep legs tired from long hours on horseback.

Dvanov dreamed that he was a little boy. He was squeezing his mother's breast in childish joy as he had seen others do, but he was afraid—and unable—to look up at her face. He did not understand this clearly, but he was scared he might see another face on top of his mother's neck—no less beloved, but not kin.

Kopionkin dreamed nothing, because for him everything came true while he was awake.

At this hour, perhaps, happiness was itself looking for its own happy people. These happy people, for their part, were resting from the day's social concerns, forgetting their kinship with happiness.

21

WITH THE dawn light of the sun Dvanov and Kopionkin set off farther and they appeared soon after midday at a meeting of the management committee of the "Friendship of the Poor Peasant" commune that lived in the south of the Novosiolovo District.[1] The commune had taken over Kariakin's former estate and was now discussing how best to adapt the buildings to the needs of its members—seven households. Toward the end of the meeting the committee adopted a proposal of Kopionkin's: that the commune should retain only the barest essentials—one of the houses, the shed, and the threshing barn—while handing over all remaining outbuildings and the other two houses to be dismantled by the neighboring village, so that the commune's superfluous property should not oppress the surrounding peasants.

The commune's scribe then began writing out warrants for dinner, inscribing each one by hand with the slogan "Proletarians of All Countries, Unite!"

All the commune's adult members—seven men, five women, and four girls—had undertaken specific duties.

A list of names and duties hung on the wall. All the members, in accord with this list and the regulations laid down, were occupied throughout the day with service to the collective. As for their duties, these had been retitled so as to demonstrate greater respect for labor. One woman had been designated director of communal nutrition. There was a manager of live traction and a master ironsmith, who was also the superintendent of dead inventory and building materials

—evidently not only a blacksmith but also a carpenter and a few other things in one person. There was a director of communal security and inviolability, a director for the propagation of communism in villages yet to be organized, a communal tutor to the young generation—and yet more positions of service.

Kopionkin spent a long time reading this paper and thinking some thought of his own. Then he asked the chairman, who was signing the dinner warrants, "But what about plowing? How's that going?"

Not looking up from his warrants, the chairman replied, "This year we haven't done any."

"How come?"

"Infringement of our internal regulations was out of the question. It would have entailed removing everyone from their duties—and what would have been left of our commune then? It was difficult enough as things stood. And we still had stores of grain from the estate."

"Ah, well, in that case," said Kopionkin, leaving his doubts behind.

"Yes," said the chairman. "We registered the grain straightaway and requisitioned it, for general satiety."

"You did well, comrade."

"No doubt about it. Everything was registered, and designated for listed mouths. We called in a medical assistant to establish a food norm once and for all without prejudice. Great thought has been devoted to everything. The commune is a great undertaking. A complication of life!"

Kopionkin gave his approval to this too; he believed that, if no one hindered them, people would always find a way to work things out in a just manner. His own duty was to keep the road toward socialism clear and free, and it was to this end he applied his armed hand and weighty directives. Only one thing now troubled him—this mention of a complication of life. He turned to Dvanov for advice: Should they not liquidate this commune without delay, lest the complication of life rendered it impossible to ascertain who was oppressing whom? But Dvanov advised Kopionkin against this, telling him he should let the commune be—they were excited to be carrying out mental labor and were complicating life out of joy. In the past they had worked with their bare hands and with no meaning in their heads—now let them rejoice in their reason!

"All right," said Kopionkin, with understanding. "But in that case they should complicate a bit better. We must help in the fullest measure. Think something up for them, something well and truly obscure."

Dvanov and Kopionkin decided to stay in the commune for a day and a night, to give their horses time to nourish themselves with fodder enough for the long road ahead.

The morning of a fresh, sunny day saw the start of a routine general meeting of the commune. Meetings were held every other day, to keep track of current events in good time. The agenda always contained two items: "the current moment" and "current matters." Before the meeting Kopionkin asked for permission to speak. This was granted with joyful enthusiasm, and there was even a proposal to grant the speaker boundless time.

"Speak without bounds, evening's a long time away," the chairman said to Kopionkin. But Kopionkin was unable to speak fluently for more than two minutes, because unauthorized thoughts would slip into his mind and mutilate one another until they lost all meaning, at which point he would bring his words to a stop and listen with interest to the noise in his head.

Kopionkin began from the premise that the purpose of the "Friendship of the Poor Peasant" commune was the complication of life with the aim of creating general confusion and of repelling, through all manner of complication, the kulak now lying low. "When everything is confined, complicated, and incomprehensible," he went on, "then there will be work aplenty for the honest mind, while miscellaneous elements will be unable to squeeze through the narrow bottlenecks of complexity. And so"—Kopionkin ended in haste, so as not to forget his concrete proposal—"I propose that general meetings should be held not every other day, but daily and even twice daily: first, for the further complication of general life, and second, in order that current events should not be carried away somewhere or other without attention and to no end. After all, anything can happen in the course of twenty-four hours—and you'll remain here in oblivion, as if amid the tall grass of the steppe."

Kopionkin stopped in the dried-up stream of his speech, as if on a sandbank, and laid his hand on the hilt of his saber, having forgotten all words in an instant. Everyone looked at him with fear and respect.

"The presidium proposes that this be carried unanimously," the chairman concluded in his well-practiced voice.

"Excellent," said someone standing at the front of the meeting. This was the manager of live traction, who had faith in the minds of strangers. Everyone raised their hands, simultaneously and vertically, testifying to their disciplined habits.

"No good at all!" Kopionkin declared loudly.

"What's wrong?" the chairman asked anxiously.

Kopionkin gestured at the meeting in vexation. "Let's have at least one girl always opposing."

"Why, comrade Kopionkin?"

"What sillies you are! For the sake of complication, of course!"

"Yes, you're right!" the chairman said joyfully. And he proposed that the meeting delegate Malania Otvershkova, the poultry and rye director, for the task of constant voting in opposition to everyone.

Then Dvanov reported on the current moment, taking into consideration the mortal threat posed by wandering brigands to communes scattered about the hostile and unpeopled steppe. "These brigands," he said, "want to extinguish the dawn. But the dawn is not a candle—it is the great sky where on distant and secret stars lies hidden the noble and mighty future of humanity's descendants. For it is beyond doubt that, after the conquest of the terrestrial globe, an hour of destiny will come for the entire universe, the moment of mankind's last judgment over the universe as a whole."[2]

"He speaks colorfully," the manager of live traction said in praise of Dvanov.

"Comprehend in silence," the chairman quietly advised him.

"Your commune," Dvanov continued, "must outwit the brigands, so that they don't understand what you have here. You must arrange everything so cleverly and in so complicated a manner that there is no manifestation of communism, even though it is present in reality. Suppose a brigand rides into the grounds of the commune with a sawn-off shotgun, looking for something to pilfer and someone to do away with. But he is met by a secretary with a rations book who says to him, 'If there is something you need, citizen, you will be given a ticket and you can go to the store. If you are a poor peasant, you will receive your rations gratis. Should you be *other*, you will serve for twenty-four hours in the position, let us say, of wolf hunter.' I assure you all that not one brigand will raise a sudden hand against you, because they will not immediately understand you. Then you can either buy them off, if the brigands outnumber you, or you can take them captive little by little as they ride about the estate in surprise and bewilderment, with their weapons at rest. Are my words correct?"

"Yes, almost," agreed the same loquacious manager of live traction.

"Unanimous, then, with one against?" declared the chairman. But matters proved more complicated. Malania Otvershkova, of course, voted against, but the director of soil fertility—a red-haired member of the commune with the uniform face of the masses—chose to abstain.

"Why?" asked the perplexed chairman.

"I shall abstain for the sake of complication!" the man equivocated.

In accord with a proposal from the chairman, he was then assigned the role of constant abstainer.

In the evening Dvanov and Kopionkin wanted to ride on farther—to the valley of the Chornaya Kalitva River. Brigands were living openly in two of the settlements there, systematically murdering members of Soviet power throughout the district. But the chairman persuaded them to stay until the evening meeting, so as to think collectively about a monument to the Revolution. The secretary had suggested that this be erected in the middle of the yard, while Malania Otvershkova, to the contrary, was in favor of the garden. The soil fertility director, for his part, was abstaining and saying nothing.

"So you think we shouldn't be putting it anywhere?" the chairman asked the abstainer.

"I abstain from voicing my opinion," the fertility director replied, with consistency.

"But the majority is in favor," stated the chairman, with concern. "We must put up a monument. The main thing is to think up a symbol."

Dvanov drew a symbol on a sheet of paper.

He handed the chairman his representation and explained, "The recumbent figure eight denotes the eternity of time, while the upright double-ended arrow denotes the infinity of space."

The chairman showed this symbol to the whole meeting. "Here we have both eternity and infinity. You can't think up anything cleverer than that. I propose we accept."

The proposal was accepted with one contrary vote and one abstention. The monument was to be erected in the middle of the estate, on an old millstone that had been awaiting the Revolution for long years. It would be constructed from iron rods by the master ironsmith.

"We did some good organizing there," Dvanov said to Kopionkin the following morning. They were moving along a clay track, beneath midsummer clouds, toward the distant Chornaya Kalitva valley. "Complication will now intensify still further and you can be sure that next spring, for complication's sake, they'll stop eating the last remnants of the estate and start plowing the earth."

"What clear thinking!" said Kopionkin happily.

"Couldn't be clearer. Sometimes, if a man's pretending to be ill for the sake of complexity, you only need tell him he's not ill enough and encourage him to get iller—and he'll end up getting better all on his own."

"Yes, he'll see health as a fresh complication, a rarity he's overlooked," said Kopionkin, reasoning all this through. And he had a thought of his own about the word *complication*: how good and unclear a word it was. Like a current moment: a moment—yet it flowed. Unimaginable.

"What's the word for those thoughts that flow first this way, then that way?" Kopionkin asked modestly. "Dilemmas?"

"Dialectics," Dvanov replied, with concision. Deep in his soul he loved ignorance more than culture: ignorance was an open steppe where the plant of any kind of knowledge might yet grow, whereas culture was a field long overgrown, where the soil's salts had all been taken up by plants and nothing more could grow. For this reason Dvanov was content that in Russia the Revolution had clean rooted out the few thickets of culture, while the people for their part remained the same as ever—empty and fertile, not a cornfield but wide-open steppe. And Dvanov was in no hurry to sow anything; he considered that good soil could not endure long without spontaneously bearing something precious and unprecedented, as long as the wind of war did not bring with it the seeds of capitalist weeds from Western Europe.

Once, amid the flat uniformity of the steppe, he glimpsed a crowd of distant wanderers. The sight of their multitude filled him with the power of joy, as if he had been touching these unreachable people in shared contact.

Monotonous memory of Rosa Luxemburg was causing Kopionkin to slump in the saddle. Suddenly and in spite of himself, he caught a glimpse of his own inconsolability, but the delirium of continuing life at once wrapped its warmth around this moment of reason, and he knew once again that he would soon reach another country and kiss Rosa's soft dress, which was being kept safe by her kinsfolk, and he would dig Rosa up from her grave and take her home with him into the Revolution. Kopionkin could even sense the smell of Rosa's dress—the smell of dying grass, fused with the hidden warmth of the remains of her life. He did not know that, in Dvanov's memory, Sonia Mandrova smelled the same as Rosa Luxemburg.

Once Kopionkin had stood for a long time before a portrait of Rosa Luxemburg in a district RevCom. He had looked at Rosa's hair and imagined it as a mysterious garden; then he had looked more closely at her rosy cheeks and contemplated the ardent revolutionary blood washing those cheeks from below and the whole of a face that was full of thought yet tearing toward the future.

Kopionkin had stood before this portrait until his invisible agitation swirled up to the point of tears. That same night, with passion, he hacked to pieces a kulak at whose instigation the peasants, a month earlier, had slit open a grain-requisitioning official's stomach and stuffed it with millet. The official had then lain for a long time on the church square, until the hens had cleaned out his stomach, pecking up the millet grain by grain.

That was the first time Kopionkin had cut up a kulak with fury.[3] Usually, rather than killing with passion, the way he lived his life, he killed with cool indifference, finishing lives off as if driven by some force of calculation and thrifty economy. Kopionkin saw brigands and members of the White Guard as enemies of minor importance, unworthy of his personal fury, and he killed with the same scrupulous everyday diligence with which a peasant woman weeds her millet. He fought accurately but without wasting time, without stopping or dismounting, unconsciously preserving his own feelings for further hope and movement.

22

THE MODEST Great Russian sky shone over the Soviet land with as much habit and monotony as if the Soviets had existed since time immemorial and the sky were in perfect accord with them. Within Dvanov there had already taken shape an immaculate conviction: that before the Revolution, the sky and all other spaces had been different, less dear to people.

Like an end to the world rose a quiet, distant horizon where the sky touched the earth and man touched man. The mounted wanderers were riding into the remote depth of their motherland. Now and again the road wound round the top of a ravine and an unhappy village could be seen in a far-off hollow. Dvanov would feel pity for this unknown lonely settlement and he would want to turn off toward it, so as to instigate the happiness of mutual life there without delay, but Kopionkin would not agree to this. First, he would say, they had to deal with Chornaya Kalitva. After that, they could return.

The day continued, dismal and unpeopled. The armed riders did not happen upon a single brigand.

"They're lying low!" Kopionkin exclaimed—and he felt inside him a heavy, oppressive force. "For the security of all," he went on, "we would have struck them hard. The reptiles are hiding away in corners, guzzling meat."

Leading straight out onto the road was an avenue of birch trees. It was still standing, but the peasants had been thinning the trees out. Most likely, there was a manor house not far from the road.

At the entrance to the avenue stood two low stone pillars. On one hung a handwritten newspaper; on the other a tin signboard with an inscription now half washed away by atmospheric precipitation: COMRADE PASHINTSEV'S REVOLUTION MEMORIAL RESERVE IN THE NAME OF WORLD COMMUNISM. WELCOME TO FRIENDS AND DEATH TO ENEMIES.

Some enemy hand had torn away half of the newspaper, and what remained was gradually being stripped by the wind. Dvanov took hold of it and read it aloud and in full, so that Kopionkin could hear.

The newspaper was called *The Good of the Poor*, being the official organ of the Velikomesto Village Soviet and the Executive District RevCom for the Maintenance of Security in the southeastern zone of the Pososhansk Region.

All that remained in it was an article titled "Tasks of the World Revolution" and half of a note that began, "Preserve Snow on Fields—Increase the Productivity of the Harvest of Labor."[1] Halfway through, this note lost track of its meaning: "Plow the Snow—and there will be nothing to fear from thousands of Kronstadts that have overshot the mark."

What were these overshooting Kronstadts?[2] All this troubled Dvanov and set him thinking.

"All writing is carried out for the sake of fear, for oppression of the masses," said Kopionkin, who could make no sense of this. "The letters of the alphabet were also invented for the complication of life. The literate man practices witchcraft through mind—and the man without letters works for him with his hands."[3]

Dvanov smiled. "Nonsense, comrade Kopionkin. The Revolution is the ABC for the people."

"Don't you misform me, comrade Dvanov! With us everything is decided by the majority. And, since nearly everyone is illiterate, the day will come for the illiterate to decree that the literate should unlearn their letters—in the name of universal equality. All the more so, since getting a few to unlearn their letters will be a lot simpler than teaching everybody from the very beginning. That would be the devil's own job. Teach, teach, teach—and then it will all get forgotten."

"Let's pay comrade Pashintsev a visit," said Dvanov, after more thought. "I have to send a written report to the provincial committee. I don't know what's happening there—it's a long time since I heard anything."

"What's there to know? The Revolution's moving along at its own pace."

They rode about one and a half versts along the avenue. Then they caught sight of a solemn white manor house on a hill, now so unpeopled as to seem abandoned. The columns before the main building, in the form of lifelike women's legs, imposingly supported a crossbeam on which rested only the sky. The building itself stood several yards farther back and had a colonnade of its own, in the shape of giant figures bowed in motionless labor. Kopionkin did not understand the meaning of the isolated columns and saw them as a remnant of a revolutionary settling of accounts with private property.

One of these columns bore a brass plate with the name of the landowner-architect and an outline in profile of his face. Below all this, in relief, was a verse in Latin:

> The universe is a running woman.
> Her legs make the earth turn.
> Her body trembles in the ether;
> In her eyes are the beginnings of stars.

Dvanov sighed sadly amid the silence of feudalism and examined the columns once again: six shapely legs of three chaste women.[4] Peace and hope entered into him, as they always did at the sight of art, that faraway necessity.

His only regret was that these legs, so full of the tension of youth, were not a part of his life, but it was good that the young woman carried by these legs had turned her life into enchantment, not into reproduction. She had been nourished by life, but life for her had been only raw material, not meaning, and this raw material had been refashioned into some other thing, where what was living and without form had been turned into something splendid and without feeling.

Kopionkin also grew more serious; magnificence was acceptable to him if it was beautiful and made no sense. If there was meaning and purpose in something magnificent—as, for example, in a large machine—Kopionkin saw it as an instrument for oppression of the masses and despised it with cruelty of soul. Standing before something pointless, on the other hand, he felt pity for himself and hatred for tsarism. It was, after all, the fault of tsarism that he was not moved by these immense feminine legs and that, but for Dvanov's sad face, he would not even have realized that he too should be feeling sad.

"If only," said Dvanov, "if only we too could build something worldwide and remarkable, leaving everyday concerns to one side."

"Things like that don't get built in a day," doubted Kopionkin. "Still, the bourgeoisie's no longer blocking our light and walling us off from the whole world. We'll soon be putting up pillars that are still taller and more excellent, better than shameful great shanks."

Over to the left, like graves in a country churchyard, remnants of outbuildings and small houses were lost in thickets of grass and bushes. The columns were standing guard over an empty, buried world. Rising over this level ruin were the delicate torsos of noble, ornamental trees.

"But we'll do better still," said Dvanov, "and across the entire territory of the world, not just in remote corners." Dvanov gestured at all and everything, but from some depth inside him he heard the words, "Watch out!" Something incorruptible, that never spared itself, was warning him from within.

"Of course, we'll build," Kopionkin confirmed, from inspired hope. "Fact and slogan. Our cause is inexhaustible."

Kopionkin then happened on some huge prints, left by human feet, and set his horse to follow them. "What on earth has the inhabitant of this place got on his feet?" he wondered in surprise. And he bared his saber: What if some giant guardian of the old order were to appear? The old landowners, after all, had well-nourished stooges who could, without warning, land you a clout that would snap your tendons.

Kopionkin was fond of tendons; he saw them as power cables and was afraid of tearing them.

The horsemen rode up to a massive eternal door that led to the semibasement of the destroyed building. The inhuman tracks went that way; it was clear that the idol had stamped up and down here, tormenting the ground into nakedness.

"Who can it be?" Kopionkin asked in astonishment. "Someone wild and fierce, no doubt about it. Be prepared, comrade Dvanov—he'll pounce on us any moment!"

Somehow Kopionkin now felt more cheerful. It was the same agitated delight that children know at night in a forest: terror half and half with a curiosity soon to be satisfied.

"Comrade Pashintsev!" shouted Dvanov. "Anyone here?"

No one. And the grass, in the absence of wind, was silent. The day was fading.

"Comrade Pashintsev!"

"Huh!" came a vast and distant sound, echoing from the earth's damp entrails.

"Come out here, hermit fellow!" Kopionkin commanded loudly.

"Huh!" came the somber, resonant response from this cellar-womb.

But there was no hint in this sound either of fear or of any wish to come out to them. The responder could well have been lying on his back.

Kopionkin and Dvanov waited, then began to feel angry.

"Come outside!" Kopionkin thundered.

"I don't want to," the unknown man replied slowly. "Go to the central building. You'll find bread and moonshine in the kitchen."

Kopionkin dismounted and struck the door loudly with his saber.

"Come out—or I'll be throwing a grenade!"

The man said nothing, perhaps waiting with interest for the grenades and whatever might follow. But then he said, "Come on, you bastard—get on with it! I've got a whole store of grenades here. The detonation will send you flying—right back into your mother!"

And once again he fell silent. Kopionkin didn't have any grenades.

"Get on with it, reptile!" the unknown man requested from his depth, with peace in his voice. "Let me check my artillery. My bombs must have got damp and rusty. Nothing will make the buggers explode."

"So-o!" Kopionkin uttered in a strange voice. "Well, come out then and receive a missive from comrade Trotsky."

The man thought for a moment, then said, "How can he be a comrade to me if he takes command over everyone? Commandants of the Revolution are no comrades of mine. Better to just throw your bomb—then we'll know where we are!"

Kopionkin kicked free a brick that had sunk into the soil, then took a swing and hurled it against the door. The door let out an iron howl—and remained in peace.

"Heathen blockhead!" Kopionkin determined. "The substance inside it's gone numb."

"Mine have gone mute too," the unknown man replied gravely. "You did pull the pin, did you? What make is it? Let me come and look."

Then came a rhythmic sound of swaying metal; someone truly was approaching with an iron tread. Kopionkin waited with his saber sheathed, his curiosity overcoming his prudence. Dvanov remained on horseback.

By now the unknown man was rumbling close by, but he did not accelerate his gradual step, only with difficulty overcoming the weight of his own powers.

The door opened swiftly; it was not bolted.

Kopionkin took two steps back, silenced by the spectacle he now saw. He had been expecting either horror or some immediate understanding. Instead, a man had appeared—yet had preserved his mystery.

Through the gaping door stepped a short man, encased in a cuirass and an entire suit of armor, with a helmet and a weighty sword, wearing powerful metal boots and with gaiters—each made of three connected bronze pipes—that crushed the grass to death.

The man's face, and especially his chin and brow, was defended by the flaps of the helmet, while on top of everything lay a lowered visor. All this defended the knight against any blows from an opponent.

Yet the man was short and not especially terrifying.

"Where's your grenade?" the apparition asked in a thin, hoarse voice. Only from a distance, reflected by things of metal and in the emptiness of his dwelling, had his voice possessed resonance; left to itself, the sound was pitiful.

"You reptile!" exclaimed Kopionkin, without anger but also without respect, watching the knight with interest.

Dvanov laughed openly. He had understood at once whose excessive outfit this man had appropriated.[5] But what made him laugh was the sight of a Red Army star, bolted onto the ancient helmet and secured with a nut.

"So what's making you scum so happy?" the knight asked coolly, still looking for the defective grenade. He was constantly struggling with the weight of his armor. Bending down was impossible for him; all he could do was feebly stir the grass with his sword.

"Don't go seeking out trouble, you pest!" Kopionkin said with gravity, returning to his more standard feelings. "Show us where we can lie down for the night. Have you got some hay?"

The knight's dwelling was the semibasement of one of the manor's outbuildings. There he had one large room, lit by the half-black light of an oil lamp. In a far corner lay a mountain of cold steel and knightly armor; in another, more central, spot stood a pyramid of hand grenades. There was also a table in the room, with a stool beside it. On the table stood a bottle of some unknown drink, or maybe poison. Glued to this bottle by means of bread pulp was a paper on which was written, in indelible ink:

DEATH TO THE BOURGEOISIE!

"Free me for the night!" asked the knightly warrior.

Kopionkin spent a long time unharnessing him from his immortal garb, needing to give considerable thought to its cleverest bits. Finally the knight fell apart and from the bronze husk appeared an ordinary comrade Pashintsev—a brownish fellow about thirty-seven years old, lacking one intransigent eye, but with a remaining eye that was all the more attentive.[6]

"Let's all have a glass!" said Pashintsev.

But alcohol, even in the old days, had had no effect on Kopionkin.

He chose consciously not to drink it, considering it purposeless for one's feelings.

Dvanov too did not understand alcohol, and so Pashintsev drank alone. He took the bottle with the inscription DEATH TO THE BOURGEOISIE! and poured directly into his throat.

"Vicious stuff!" he said, emptying the bottle. And he sat down, now looking benign.

"Good?" asked Kopionkin.

"Beetroot moonshine," Pashintsev explained. "There's an unmarried girl here who makes it with her own pure hands. An immaculate drink, my good brother, true spirit!"

"But anyway, just who are you?" Kopionkin inquired with irritated interest.

"I'm my own person," Pashintsev informed Kopionkin. "I passed myself a resolution to the effect that 1919 marked the last betrayal of everything. Yet again—armies, authorities, and laws of all kinds. And as for ordinary people—'You lot, fall into rank and obey! From tomorrow!' Well I say, to hell with all that!"

Pashintsev concisely formulated the entire current moment with a single gesture.

Dvanov stopped thinking and listened slowly to the man reasoning aloud.

"Remember 1918 and 1919?" Pashintsev asked with tears of joy. Those days lost forever called up ferocious memories in him; by midstory he was hammering his fist against the table and endangering all around him. "Now we'll never see any of it again," Pashintsev said with hatred. He was eager to convince Kopionkin, who was continually blinking. "Everything's been betrayed. Law has got going again. Difference has come between people. It's as if some devil's been testing man, weighing him on scales. Take me, for example—can anyone ever know just what breathes here?" Pashintsev rapped himself on his low skull, where his brain must have been compressed to make room for all his thinking. "Yes, brother, there is room here for expanses of every kind. And it's the same for everyone. But people want to reign over me. Well, what do you think? Is that a lying swindle or not?"

"It's a lying swindle," Kopionkin agreed, with simplicity of soul.

"All too true!" Pashintsev concluded with satisfaction. "And now I burn separately, away from the general bonfire."

Sensing that Kopionkin was as much an orphan of the earthly globe as he himself, Pashintsev begged him with heartfelt words to stay forever.[7]

"What more do you want?" said Pashintsev, forgetting himself in his joy at sensing a friendly human being. "Live here. Eat and drink—I've marinated five barrels of apples and dried two sacks of *makhorka*. We'll live among the trees as friends, we'll sing songs on the grass. People come to me in their thousands—here in my commune every pauper and beggar rejoices. Where else can they find easy shelter? In the village the soviets keep them under observation, the commissars are like watchdogs, the requisitioning committee searches even their bellies for grain—but officialdom daren't show its face here."

"They're afraid of you," deduced Kopionkin. "You go about all covered in iron. You sleep on a bomb."

"They're definitely afraid," Pashintsev agreed. "They made out they wanted to be neighborly, to do an inventory of the domain, but I appeared before the commissar in full harness and brandished one of my bombs: *Long live the commune!* And then there was the time they came round to requisition grain. I say to their commissar, 'Eat, you son of a bitch, eat and drink—but if you take more than you should, there'll be nowt left of you but a vile stink.' The commissar drank a cup of moonshine. 'Thank you, comrade Pashintsev!'—and off he rode. I gave him a handful of sunflower seeds and a prod in the back with that there iron poker and sent him off—back to official regions."

"And now?" asked Kopionkin.

"Not so bad. I live without the least leadership—and the result is excellent. I declared this a Revolution Memorial Reserve so the authorities wouldn't look askance, and I preserve the Revolution in an intact and heroic category."[8]

Dvanov glimpsed a charcoal inscription on the wall, traced by a trembling hand unused to writing. Holding up an oil lamp, he read the wall annals of the Revolution Memorial Reserve.

"Read, read away!" said Pashintsev. "Sometimes I don't speak for a long time. So long I can't bear it. Then I start talking on the wall. Too long without people—and my mind goes all cloudy."

Dvanov read the verses on the wall:

No bourgeoisie—but labor's back again.
The yoke of labor bows the peasant's neck.
Believe me, plodding peasant laborer—
Flowers in the fields have plumper lives than you.
No need to sow and plow, to sow and reap—
Let all the soil now bear self-seeded fruit
While you yourself live full and merrily.
Remember you have one, not twenty, lives
To live—and so, with all our holy commune,
Take hold of other strong and honest hands
And sing both loud and clear, so all can hear:
Enough of poverty, enough of sorrow!
Time now to live and feast, to feast and live!
Enough of poor and plodding earthly labor!
The Earth herself will feed us now for free!

Someone knocked on the door with an even, proprietorial knock.

"Huh?" answered Pashintsev. Having exhaled the inspiration of moonshine, he fell silent.

"Maxim Stepanych!" came a voice from outside. "I need a long pole for a cart shaft. Let me look for one in the wood. Otherwise I'll be stuck here all winter—the old shaft snapped when I was halfway back home."

"Out of the question," retorted Pashintsev. "How long must I go on teaching you? I've posted a decree on the barn wall: 'The earth is self-made and therefore belongs to no one.' If you took without asking, then I'd gladly allow it."

Hoarse from joy, the man outside said, "Well then, thank you! I won't touch the pole now I've gone and asked for it. I'll gift myself something else."

"That's right, you slave psychology!" Pashintsev said freely. "Don't ask—just gift yourself! You were born for free. It wasn't your own strength gave birth to you—so live life unaccounted!"

"Certainly, Maxim Stepanych!" confirmed the petitioner outside, with absolute seriousness. "What we seize unlicensed is what keeps us alive. But for this estate, half our village would be dead by now. This is the fifth year we've been carting off goods—you Bolsheviks are fair and just! Thank you, Maxim Stepanych!"

This angered Pashintsev: "There you go again—'Thank you'! Don't go taking anything more from here, you gray devil!"

"What's gotten into you, Maxim Stepanych? Why did I sweat and bleed for three years, in combat on the front line? My mate and I came with a cart and two horses to pick up an iron tub—and now you forbid it!"

"What a country!" Pashintsev said to himself and to Kopionkin. Then he addressed the door again. "But didn't you say you were after a shaft? And now you tell me what you want is a tub!"

The petitioner showed no surprise. "Who cares? As long as I take something! Sometimes all I take is a chicken—and then I see an iron axle lying about on the road. I can't carry it on my own, so the damned thing goes on lying there. No wonder we have such ruination everywhere."

"If you've come with a cart," Pashintsev replied, "then take a woman's leg with you, from the white columns. It'll come in handy one way or another."

"All right," said the now-satisfied petitioner. "We can tow it back with us easily enough. Then we can hew tiles from it."

The petitioner went off to carry out a preliminary inspection—to ensure there were no hitches when he came back to pillage it.

As night began, Dvanov suggested to Pashintsev that, instead of carting the whole estate to the village, he should resettle the villagers in the estate. "It would be less labor," he argued. "And the estate's high up—the land's more productive."

Pashintsev could not agree to this. "Come spring, tramps and vagabonds gather here from all over the province. The very purest proletariat. Where would they all go? No, I cannot countenance kulak domination here."

Dvanov understood that there would indeed be conflicts between the peasants and the vagabonds. But rich earth was being wasted. The inhabitants of the Revolution Memorial Reserve were not sowing anything. They were living off the remains of an orchard and the self-seeding of nature; their soup, no doubt, was made from nettles and goosefoot. "I know what," he said, as a solution unexpectedly came to him. "You must just swap everything round. Give the estate to the peasants and set up your Memorial Reserve in the village. It'll be all the same to you—it's your proletariat that matters, not where they go. As things stand, the villagers are languishing in the gully—while you live alone up on your hill."

Pashintsev looked at Dvanov with happy astonishment.

"That's truly excellent! I'll do just that. Tomorrow I'll go and mobilize the peasants."

"Will they come?" asked Kopionkin.

"They'll all be here within a day and a night," Pashintsev exclaimed with fierce conviction, his whole body stirred by impatience. "No," he continued, "I'll go straightaway!" He was now coming to love Dvanov too. At first he hadn't entirely liked him and the way he sat there without saying anything. Dvanov, he had thought, was someone who knew every thesis, program, and decree by heart—and Pashintsev had no love for know-it-alls. He had seen in life that the stupid and unfortunate were kinder than the clever—and more capable of changing their lives toward freedom and happiness. Secretly from everyone, Pashintsev believed that the workers and peasants were, of course, stupider than the learned bourgeoisie. On the other hand, they had more heart and soul—which promised them an excellent destiny.

Kopionkin calmed Pashintsev, saying that there was no need to hurry—come what may, their victory was assured.

Pashintsev agreed and then spoke at length about weeds. In his ruined childhood time he had liked to watch pitiful, doomed weeds as they spread through the millet. He knew that one fine day the women would mercilessly uproot these misplaced wild plants: cornflowers, sweet clover, and windflowers. These plants were more beautiful than the plain cereal grasses. Their flowers were like the sad eyes of children close to death; they knew that they would soon be ripped out of the ground by sweating women. But such plants were more alive and more enduring than the feeble ears of millet and rye—after the women they would be reborn, in countless and immortal quantity.

"And the poor are no different," Pashintsev concluded, regretting that he had drunk all the Death to the Bourgeoisie. "We have more might, and more heart, than those other elements."

That night Pashintsev was unable to curb himself. After donning a coat of mail on top of his shirt, he went off to some corner of the estate. There he was gripped by the night cool, but this did not chill him. On the contrary, the starry sky and a consciousness of his own low height beneath this sky drew him on toward large feeling and some instantaneous exploit. The power of the vast night world put Pashintsev to shame and he wanted at once, without further thought, to elevate his own dignity.

In the main building lived a small number of the definitively homeless who had not been registered anywhere. Through four of the windows he could see the flickering light of an open fire—food was being cooked in the hearth. Pashintsev knocked at the window with his fist, not pitying the peace of the inhabitants.

Out came a shaggy young woman in tall felt boots.

"What do you want, Maxim Stepanych? Why this night alarm?"

Pashintsev went up to her, compensating for her evident inadequacies with the inspiration of excited closeness.

"Grunya," he said, "let me kiss you, my husbandless dove. My bombs have dried up and no longer explode. I wanted to bring down the columns with them, but they're no good. Let me embrace you as a comrade."

Grunya yielded. "Something's happened to you. You used to seem like a serious man. But get all that iron off you, you'll be scaring my soft bits."

But Pashintsev kissed her briefly on the dark, dry crusts of her lips and set off back to his cellar. He felt more at ease now and less vexed by the mighty overhang of the sky. Anything large in volume and exceptional in quality awoke in him not contemplative pleasure but a martial feeling—an aspiration to outdo it, both in power and in importance.

"You all right?" he asked his two visitors, to give vent to his feelings of satisfaction.

"Time to go to sleep," said Kopionkin, yawning. "You've taken note of our directive—you're settling the peasants on capacious land. What's the use of us staying here to no purpose?"

"I'll be fetching the peasants tomorrow—and there'll be no sabotage," Pashintsev determined. "But stay here as my guests, for reinforcement of bonds! Tomorrow Grunya will cook you a meal. What I have here... No, you won't find the like of it anywhere. I keep thinking about Lenin. Should I summon him here? Say what you will, he is our leader."

Kopionkin looked Pashintsev up and down: A man who thought he could summon Lenin! Then he said, "While you were out, I had a look at your bombs. They're all spoiled. How do you manage to hold sway?"

Pashintsev did not argue with this. "Of course the bombs are no good," he replied. "I disarmed them myself. But people don't know this. I walk about clad in iron, I sleep on bombs. That's my strategy—outwitting and outflanking the enemy, with minimal forces! But don't go blurting this out wherever you go!"

The oil lamp went out. Pashintsev explained how things stood: "Lie down anywhere—it doesn't matter. We can't see a thing and there's no bedding. People consider me a sad member."

"Wayward, not sad," Kopionkin corrected him, settling himself down somehow or other.

Not taking offense, Pashintsev replied, "This, brother, is a commune of new life, not some town. We have no feather beds."

Toward morning the world grew poorer in starry magnificence and exchanged flickering brilliance for gray light. Night went on its way, like gleaming cavalry; onto the earth marched the infantry of a difficult campaign day.

To Kopionkin's surprise, Pashintsev brought him some roast mutton. After which the two horsemen left the Revolution Memorial Reserve by the road to the south, toward the Chornaya Kalitva valley. Beneath the white colonnade, in his stiff, knightly gear, stood Pashintsev, watching his fellow-thinkers pass out of sight.

23

AND AGAIN the two horsemen were on their way, while the sun rose over the poverty of the land.

Dvanov let his head droop; his consciousness was diminishing as a result of monotonous movement through a flat place. As for his heart, what Dvanov then sensed as his heart was more like a dam, constantly trembling from the pressure of a rising lake of feelings. These feelings were raised high by his heart and then fell to its other side, transformed into a flow of cooling thought. But above the dam burned the constant duty light of the watchman who does not participate in a human being but merely dozes within him for a paltry salary. This light sometimes allowed Dvanov to see both spaces—the warm, swelling lake of his feelings and the long swiftness of thought, cooled by its own speed, on the far side of the dam. At such moments Dvanov could outstrip the work of his heart—which not only nourished but also held back his consciousness—and was able to be happy.

"Let's go at a trot, comrade Kopionkin!" said Dvanov, who was filled to overflowing with powerful impatience for a future that awaited him beyond this road. In him had arisen the childish joy of knocking nails into walls, turning chairs into ships, and dismantling alarm clocks to see what was inside them. Above his heart quivered the frightening momentary light that happens out in the fields on close summer nights. Maybe what lived in him was the abstract love of youth, transformed into a part of his body, or maybe it was the continuing vital force of birth. But it was thanks to this force that Dvanov was able to catch sudden additional glimpses of unclear phenomena tracelessly floating in the lake of his feelings. He looked attentively at Kopionkin, who was riding with a calm spirit and a steady faith in the summer country of socialism not far away, where the friendly powers of humanity would bring Rosa Luxemburg back to life and make her a living citizen.[1]

The road then went downhill for many versts. You need only get up speed, it seemed, and you would take off and begin to fly.

In the distance a premature twilight had quieted over a dark and sad valley.

"Kalitva!" said Kopionkin, pointing ahead. And he felt as overjoyed as if he had already ridden right up to the settlement. The two horsemen were already thirsty and the spittle they spat out was white and half-dry.

Dvanov gazed into the bleak landscape ahead of him. Both earth and sky were miserable to the point of exhaustion. People there lived separately from one another and without acting effectively, fading like logs not stacked together into a blaze.

"There it is—raw material for socialism!" said Dvanov, studying the country. "Not a single construction—only the anguish of orphaned nature."

In sight of the settlement of Chornaya Kalitva the horsemen came upon a man with a sack. He took off his hat and bowed to the men on horseback, in accord with the old belief that all men are brothers. In response, Dvanov and Kopionkin bowed too, and all three men felt good.

"Still more of these plundering comrades, to hell with them all!" the man with the sack decided for himself once he was at a safe distance.

On the outskirts of the settlement stood two peasant sentries. One was holding a sawed-off shotgun; the other a stake from a wattle fence.

"Which lot are you?" they duly asked as Dvanov and Kopionkin rode up.

Kopionkin halted his horse, struggling to assess the significance of this military outpost.

"We are international!" he replied, remembering the title given to Rosa Luxemburg: International Revolutionary.

The sentries thought for a while.

"Jews, you mean?"

Kopionkin coolly bared his saber, with such deliberateness that the peasant sentries failed to understand it as a threat.

"Words like that will be the end of you," he pronounced. "Know who I am? Here!"

Kopionkin felt in his pocket, but he never carried documents or papers of any kind with him. All he found was bread crumbs and other such debris.

"Regimental adjutant!" said Kopionkin, addressing Dvanov. "Show the patrol our passes!"

Dvanov took out an envelope—he had no idea what lay inside it, but he had been carrying it about with him for over two years—and threw it down. The peasant sentries seized hold of it avidly, glad of this rare opportunity to perform their duty of service.

Kopionkin leaned down and, with the deft freedom of a master, knocked the shotgun out of the sentry's hands with his saber, not wounding him in the least. Kopionkin possessed within him the talent of revolution.

The sentry stretched out his shaken arm. "What's got into you, you blockhead? We're no more Reds than you are."

At this, Kopionkin changed. "Do you have many troops? And who are you?"

The peasants thought first one way and then another, but answered honestly, "A hundred heads, but only about twenty rifles. We've got Timofey Plotnikov with us now, from Ispodny Khutor. Yesterday we forced a grain-requisitioning detachment to retreat from our village, with losses."[2]

Kopionkin pointed them up the road he had just ridden down.

"Quick march, up there! Come to a regiment—bring it this way. Where's Plotnikov's HQ?"

"In the elder's yard, close to the church." And the two men looked with sorrow at their native village, wanting to step away from events.

"Off with you!" ordered Kopionkin. "Quick!" He then struck his steed with his scabbard.

A woman was squatting behind a fence. What she had gone outside for had come to a stop. At the sight of Kopionkin, she thought she had only minutes to live.

"Taking a slash, Granny?" Kopionkin called out.

She was not an old granny but a good-looking middle-aged woman.

"Go slash yourself, you pagan blockhead!" The woman stood up, stretching her skirt out, furious to the root of her being.

Kopionkin's steed, losing all bulk and mass, at once tore off in a fierce gallop, throwing its front hooves high in the air.

"Keep me in sight, comrade Dvanov, and don't drop behind!" Kopionkin shouted, gleaming his ready saber.

Strength of the Proletariat was pounding the ground weightily; Dvanov could hear the tinkling of windows in huts. But there was no one outside. There were not even any dogs throwing themselves at the two horsemen.

Kopionkin advanced through the streets and crossroads of the vast village, heading determinedly for the church. But Kalitva had been spreading out in family thickets for four hundred years. Standing athwart some streets, blocking all movement, were unexpected huts; other streets were brought to a dead end by new homesteads or else turned into narrow summer passages leading into open country.

Kopionkin and Dvanov ended up in a twisting knot of back streets that had them wheeling around on the spot. Kopionkin then opened a gate and sped off on a detour through threshing grounds. At first the village dogs barked warily and in isolation but then they began to answer one another. Excited by their own numbers, they were soon howling in unison, from one end of the village to the other.

"Comrade Dvanov," Kopionkin shouted, "no stopping now!"

Dvanov thought they were to gallop the length of the village and break through into open steppe beyond. He proved wrong; after emerging onto a broad street, Kopionkin galloped straight into the depth of the village.

The smithies were all locked up; the huts were silent, as if abandoned.

There was only one old man mending something beside a fence, but he did not turn to look at them; most likely, he was only too used to trouble of every kind.

Dvanov could hear a faint hum, which he took to be the clapper of the church bell being swung very gently, barely touching the metal.

The street turned a corner—and showed them a crowd of people, standing around a dirty brick building that looked as if it had formerly housed state shops selling vodka.

This crowd of people had only a single, gravelly voice; all that reached Dvanov was a wordless hum.

His face now thin and clenched, Kopionkin turned toward Dvanov.

"Shoot, Dvanov! Quick! The village is ours now!"

Dvanov shot twice somewhere into the church and heard himself let out a shout—echoing Kopionkin, who was brandishing his saber for the sake of inspiration. The crowd of peasants swayed, like an even wave, brightened as faces turned to look behind them, and then began to release streams of running people. Some of the crowd took to stamping about on the spot, grabbing at neighbors for help. These stampers were more dangerous than the runners; they confined fear in a tight corner and made it impossible for the brave to move freely.

Dvanov breathed in the peaceful smell of a village—and this smell of rotting straw and warm milk made his stomach ache; at that moment he couldn't have eaten even a pinch of salt. He felt a sudden fear of perishing in the large warm hands of the village, of suffocating in the sheepskin air of timid people who overwhelmed their enemy not with fury but through mass alone.

But Kopionkin was for some reason delighted by this crowd—and already counting on victory.

All of a sudden—from the windows of a hut beside which people were rushing about in panic—came the flashes of a hurrying salvo. Each shot had its distinct sound—the rifles must have been of every caliber.

Kopionkin entered into that oblivion of self that shuts the sense of life into a dark place and does not allow it to interfere in mortal matters. Holding his revolver in his left hand, Kopionkin fired into the hut, shattering a pane of glass.

Dvanov found himself by the threshold. All he had to do now was get down from his steed and enter the building. He fired at the door. At the thud of the bullet, the door slowly opened and Dvanov rushed inside. The entrance room smelled of medicine and the sadness of some defenseless human being. Lying in a storeroom was a peasant wounded in previous combats. Paying no attention to him, Dvanov crossed the kitchen and burst into the main room. There he found a peasant with reddish hair, standing with his right, whole hand raised above his head and his left hand, still holding a revolver, hanging down by his side. Occasional drops of blood were falling from it, like drops of rain from leaves, dismally counting out this man's end.

The windowpane had been smashed, but there was no sign of Kopionkin.

"Drop your weapon!" said Dvanov.

The brigand whispered something in fear.

"All right!" said Dvanov, enraged. "Then I'll shoot it off you, along with your hand."

The peasant dropped his revolver into his own blood and looked down, regretting that he had sullied his weapon. If he'd handed it over clean and dry, these men would have been more ready to pardon him.

Dvanov did not know what further to do with his wounded prisoner or what had happened to Kopionkin. He got his breath back and sat down in a velvet kulak armchair. The man was standing in front of him, both arms now hanging limply down. Dvanov noted with surprise that he did not look like a brigand. On the contrary, he appeared to be an ordinary peasant and was unlikely to be rich.

"Sit down!" said Dvanov, but the man did not move. Then Dvanov asked, "Are you a kulak?"

"No, we're the least and lowest round here," the peasant responded with evident truth. "And kulaks don't need to fight. They've got grain to spare and they know no one will manage to seize all of it."

Dvanov believed him and felt frightened. In his imagination he pictured the villages he had passed through, and their sad, pale inhabitants. "You could have shot me with your right hand," he said. "It's only your left hand that's wounded."

The brigand looked at Dvanov and thought slowly, not trying to save himself but simply to recall the whole truth.

"I'm left-handed. I didn't have time to escape—but I'd heard a regiment was advancing. If I was going to die, I wanted to take someone with me."

This troubled Dvanov still more. He was able to think in any situation, and this peasant was prompting him to recognize some sorrow of the Revolution, some futility beyond the grasp of its young mind. Dvanov had already sensed the alarm of the poor villages, but he could not have written it down in words.[3]

"Nonsense!" Dvanov wavered in thought. "Once Kopionkin's here, this fellow should be shot. When grass grows, it destroys the soil. Revolution's no different. It's a violent matter and a force of nature..." And then, all of a sudden, his consciousness changed once more. Silently cursing himself as a mean bastard, Dvanov ordered the man to go home.

The peasant began to walk backward toward the door, looking at the revolver in Dvanov's hand with petrified, spellbound eyes. Dvanov understood and chose not to put down his revolver, so as not to frighten the man with movement.

"Stop!" Dvanov called.

The peasant meekly readied himself.

"Have you had White officers here? And who's Plotnikov?"

The brigand struggled to overcome his weakness.

"No, we've had no one at all," the peasant replied quietly. "I'm sorry, my friend. There's been no one at all. Plotnikov is just one of us, from a hamlet nearby."

Dvanov sensed that the brigand was too frightened to lie. "All right, don't be afraid now. Just go quietly back home."

The brigand went on his way, trusting Dvanov. There was a tinkling sound from the remnants of glass in the window; Strength of the Proletariat had approached at a steppe gallop.

"Where are you going? And who are you?" Dvanov heard Kopionkin say. Not waiting for an answer, Kopionkin installed the captive brigand in the storeroom.

"You know, comrade Dvanov, I almost caught that Plotnikov of theirs," said Kopionkin, chest heaving with excitement. "Two of the bastards galloped away—yes, they've got good horses. Mine's made for plowing, not for making war. Though being on its back brings me good fortune—the beast's blessed with true consciousness. Well, we must call a village meeting."

Kopionkin then climbed up into the church tower and sounded the bell. Dvanov went out onto the porch in expectation. Some distant children came running out into the middle of the street, looked in Dvanov's direction, and ran off again. No one answered Kopionkin's urgent and resonant summons.

The bell sang somberly over the large settlement, evenly alternating inbreath and exclamation. Dvanov listened intently, forgetting what this alarm signified. In the bell's chant he could hear anxiety, faith, and doubt. These passions were no less a force within the Revolution itself—people are driven not only by faith cast in bronze but also by the tinny, cracked sound of doubt.

A man in an apron, with black hair and no hat, came up to the porch. Probably he was a blacksmith.

"What are you doing, coming here and upsetting people?" he asked straightforwardly. "Ride on farther, friends and comrades. We've got a dozen fools here—that's the only support you'll find in this village."

Dvanov asked him with equal directness to say what he had against Soviet power.

"That's why you won't last long—you shoot first and ask questions later," the peasant replied furiously. "All very clever. You give us the land, then confiscate every last grain we grow on it. Well, if that's the way it is, may you choke on that land. The only land left to us peasants now is the horizon. Who do you think you're fooling?"

Dvanov explained that the requisitioned grain went into the bloodstream of the Revolution and would nourish its future powers.

"Pull the other one," the blacksmith retorted knowingly. "One in ten of our people are either fools or vagabonds, sons of bitches who've never done a day's real labor in their lives. They'll follow anyone. If there were still a tsar, he'd have his supporters here too—enough for a party cell. And its good-for-nothings like that who make up your Bolshevik Party. 'Grain for the Revolution!' You fool, who's your Revolution going to help if the entire people is dying? And the war's supposed to be over."

The blacksmith stopped talking, realizing that the man before him was as strange as every other Communist. On the face of it—a man like any other man, but he acted against the common people.

The blacksmith's words made Dvanov smile inadvertently. Around 10 percent of the nation were indeed crazies who were up for anything—from Revolution to praying to God in a forest hermitage.

Then Kopionkin appeared. He responded to the blacksmith's reproaches with clarity, "You're a swine, my good fellow. We all live equally now—but you want the workers to starve while you brew moonshine out of their grain!"

"Equal doesn't mean better!" the blacksmith retorted. "What the hell do you understand about living equally? I've been thinking about this since the day I got married. For some reason the ones who order us about have always been crazies. As for the people, when have they ever had any power? And do you know why, my friend? It's because they've got more serious work to do—like feeding all kinds of fools for free!"

The blacksmith laughed with intelligence and rolled himself a cigarette.

"And what if grain requisitioning were abolished?" asked Dvanov.

The blacksmith cheered up for an instant, but then frowned again. "Not likely! And you'd come up with something worse, something different. Better the devil we know... Anyway, people have learned to hide their grain."

"This swinehead don't care nowt about nothing," Kopionkin concluded.

Villagers began to appear; around eight men sat down a short distance away. Dvanov went over to them. They turned out to be the surviving members of the Kalitva party cell.

"Time for a speech!" mocked the blacksmith. "Bar one or two, all the crazies are present."

The blacksmith went silent for a moment, then eagerly began again, "Now you just listen! There are five thousand of us here, children and adults. Remember this. And now let me foretell you. Take one-tenth part of the adults—when you've got that many in your cell, it'll be the end of your Revolution."

"Why?" asked Dvanov, bewildered by these calculations.

With impassioned bias, the blacksmith explained, "'Cause the crazies will all go off to be in power and the people will be left to live lives of their own. Both sides satisfied!"

Kopionkin proposed to the meeting that they should pursue Plotnikov straightaway, not wasting a minute, so as to liquidate him before he recruited new, living brigands. Dvanov found out from the local Communists that Plotnikov had wanted to decree a general mobilization but that nothing had come of it. Then there had been two days of village assemblies during which Plotnikov had tried to persuade men to volunteer. There had been another such assembly this very day, and it had been in session when Dvanov and Kopionkin attacked. As for Plotnikov himself, he knew the peasantry to a tee; he was a crafty fellow, loyal to his fellow villagers and therefore hostile to the rest of the world. The peasants respected him in place of their late priest.[4]

During this last assembly a woman had rushed up and shouted, "Quick! The Reds are on the outskirts. There's a whole mounted regiment galloping this way!"

And so, when Kopionkin and Dvanov first appeared, everyone had taken them for a regiment.

"Let's go, Dvanov," said Kopionkin, now bored with listening. "Where does that road lead? Who'll come with us?"

This embarrassed the village Communists.

"That's the road to Chernovka. But comrades, we're all of us horseless."

Kopionkin gave up on them with a shrug of dismissal.

The blacksmith looked vigilantly at Kopionkin, then stepped

toward him, extended a spacious hand, and said, "Well then, my good man, fare thee well!"

"I shall indeed," said Kopionkin, extending his own hand. "But remember. If *you* hope to fare well, you'd better watch out. The least hint of trouble—I'll be straight back to finish you off."

The blacksmith was not frightened. "*You* remember *me*! My name is Sotykh.[5] There's no one else here with that name. When it comes to a reckoning, I'll be there on horseback with my poker. Yes, I'll find myself a horse all right. I won't be like your lot—horseless dolts!"

Kalitva village lived on the slope between the high steppe and the valley of the Chornaya Kalitva. The valley itself was an impassable thicket of boggy undergrowth.

While people beat one another down in their quarrels, nature had been continuing its agelong work. The river had grown old; the valley's virgin grass had been covered by a deadly bog fluid that only harsh sedges and reeds could force their way through.

The valley's dead fleece now listened only to the indifferent songs of the wind. At the end of every summer the enfeebled river was fighting a losing battle against sand deposits washed down from the gullies, their fine dandruff cutting the river off forever from the distant sea.

"There, comrade Dvanov, look to your left," said Kopionkin, pointing to the blue of the clogged valley. "As a boy, I used to come here with my father. I'll never forget it. There was a scent of tall grasses that carried a whole verst. Now even the water is rotting."

Dvanov had seldom encountered such long, mysterious valleys. Why is it that, as they die, rivers stop their flow and cover the grassy mantles beside their banks with impassable bogs? Probably the death of rivers impoverishes the entire valley country. Kopionkin told Dvanov how much cattle and poultry the peasants in these parts had once had, when the river was fresh and alive.

The evening road followed the edge of the now-perished valley. It was only six versts from Kalitva to Chernovka, but the riders first noticed Chernovka only when they happened upon someone's threshing floor. At that time Russia was expending herself on illuminating the path for all nations, leaving her own huts in darkness.

Kopionkin set off to find out who was in power there; Dvanov stayed on the outskirts with the horses.

Night was setting in—a murky and dismal night. It was the kind of night that children fear, after they have known sleep's nightmares for the first time. Then they don't fall asleep, and they keep an eye on their mother, so that she will stay awake too and keep away horror.

But adult people are orphans, and today Dvanov stood alone outside a hostile village, observing the thawed steppe night and, above him, the cool lake of the sky.

He wandered about, then came back, listening to the dark and counting the slow time.

"I almost lost you," said an invisible Kopionkin, from a distance. "Feeling lonely, were you? Well, I've brought you some milk."

Kopionkin had not found out anything at all; neither who was in power, nor whether Plotnikov was in the village. He had, however, managed to obtain a crock of milk somewhere, and a ration of necessary bread.

After they had eaten, Kopionkin and Dvanov rode to the village soviet. Kopionkin found a hut with a soviet sign, but it was empty and tumbledown and there was no ink in the inkpot—Kopionkin stuck a finger into it to determine whether or not the soviet was exercising its power.

In the morning four elderly men appeared and began complaining: There were no authorities at all in the village—every power had abandoned them. Life had become scary. "Doesn't matter who—but we must have somebody," they begged. "Otherwise here we are in the backwoods—soon someone will be strangling their neighbor. How can we manage with no one in power? The wind doesn't blow out of nowhere—yet here we are, living without cause."

There had been many regimes in Chernovka, but all had come to nothing. Soviet power too had collapsed of its own accord. The peasant elected as chairman had ceased to act; he was not, he complained, held in enough respect. People knew him too well—and without respect how can there be power and authority? And so he had ceased to attend village soviet meetings. Men from Chernovka had ridden over to Kalitva to find themselves a new chairman—someone whom nobody knew and who would therefore enjoy general respect. But this too had failed. The Kalitva authorities had told them they had no instructions for the relocation of chairmen; they should elect someone worthy from among themselves.

"But what if we haven't got anyone worthy?" the men lamented. "We're all equal and too much alike. One man's a thief, another's a layabout, and a third has a battle-ax of a wife who hides his trousers away. What can we do?"

"Are you bored of life?" Dvanov asked sympathetically.

"Bored to death. From what travelers tell us, culture's eclipsed the whole of Russia, but it's passed us by. We've been left in the dark."[6]

Wafting in through the windows was a smell of damp manure and plowland warmth, an ancient village smell that called up memories of peace and procreation, and everyone gradually fell silent. Dvanov went outside to check the horses. There he was delighted by the sight of a scraggy and indigent sparrow working away with its beak in nourishing horse dung. It was six months since Dvanov had last seen a sparrow and not once had he thought about where in the world they sheltered. Many good things slipped past Dvanov's poor and narrow mind; even his own life often flowed around it, like a stream around a rock. The sparrow flew up onto a wattle fence. The peasants who had been lamenting about power and authority went outside too. The sparrow took off from the fence, reciting its gray, poor-peasant song on the wing.

One of the peasants went up to Dvanov. He was pockmarked and emaciated, the kind of man who never comes out with a request straightaway but begins at a distance with middling subjects, intently assessing the character of the person to whom he is speaking: Will it, or will it not, be acceptable for him to ask for some relief or exemption? It's possible to spend an entire night talking to someone like this about how the Orthodox faith on earth is faltering, when what the man really wants is more timber. And he may even have already felled some trees in what had once been government forest—his questions are simply his oblique way of checking what price he'll have to pay for taking the law into his own hands.

In both appearance and bearing the peasant who had just come up to Dvanov was rather like the departed sparrow. Both saw their own life as a criminal activity and lived in constant expectation of chastisement from the powers that be.

Dvanov asked him to say straightaway and nakedly what he was after. But Kopionkin heard Dvanov through the window and warned him that, if he talked to the man like that, he'd never get him to speak at all. Dvanov would do better to take it step by step.

The peasants laughed. They understood that the two men before them were neither useful nor a danger.

The pockmarked man spoke first. He was a loner, without land or family, sentenced by society to honor the interests of others.

Little by little the conversation got as far as the Kalitva lands bordering those of Chernovka. After passing through some contested woodland, it settled on matters of power.

"Maybe we need power and authority, maybe we're better off without them," the pockmarked man explained from both points of view. "If you look from the middle, there's no seeing the ends, but if you start from one end there's a long way to go. Well, *you* see what sense you can make of it all!"

Dvanov hurried him on: "If you have enemies, then you need Soviet power."

But the man knew what was at issue. "Well, we may not have enemies, but there's space all around us. There's nowt to stop anyone galloping up. A thief cherishes another's kopek more than his own rouble ... Everything's as it always was—the grass goes on growing and the weather changes day by day, but at times we can't but feel jealous. Who knows what benefits we may have missed out on? Word goes there's to be no more requisitioning, but we're still afraid to sow."

Dvanov was shocked: No more requisitioning? Where had the pockmarked man heard this? But the man had no idea. Maybe he truly had heard it—or maybe he had inadvertently thought it up from his own heart. All he could say was that a deserter with no documents had passed through the village, eaten kasha with him, and informed him that requisitioning was now over. Peasants had gone to call on Lenin in his Kremlin tower; they had stayed three days and nights there and thought up a change of policy.[7]

This saddened Dvanov. He withdrew inside the building and did not reappear. The peasants all went back to their own huts, only too accustomed to news of senseless petitions.

"Listen to me, comrade Kopionkin!" Dvanov said agitatedly. There was nothing Kopionkin feared more than the unhappiness of others; as a boy, he had wept still more bitterly at the funeral of a man he didn't know than even his widow. He turned sad in anticipation and half opened his mouth to listen better. "Comrade Kopionkin!" said Dvanov. "You know what? I feel like making a trip into town. Wait for me here—I'll be back soon. Make yourself temporary chairman of the soviet, so it doesn't get too dreary for you here. The peasants will agree—you've seen them, you know what they're like."

"Yes, of course," Kopionkin replied joyfully. "Go on your way—I'll wait for you here even if I have to wait a whole year. And yes, I'll make myself chairman. I need to scratch around a bit and see what's going on round here."

24

IN THE evening Dvanov and Kopionkin kissed in the middle of the road and both felt senselessly ashamed. Dvanov then set off toward the railway.

Kopionkin stood there for a long time, although his friend was no longer in sight. Then he went back to the village soviet and began to weep in the empty building. All night long he lay in silence and without sleep, with helpless heart. The village round about seemed motionless, not making its presence felt through even a single living sound, as if forever renouncing its wearisome and vexatious fate. Only the naked white willows in the empty yard rustled now and again, letting time pass through them on its way toward spring.

Through the window Kopionkin observed the agitated darkness outside. Sometimes it was pierced by a pale, fading light that smelled of damp and the boredom of a new, unpeopled day. Perhaps morning was coming, or perhaps this was a dead, wandering moonbeam.

In the long silence of the night Kopionkin imperceptibly began to lose his tension of feeling, as if he were being cooled by solitude. A weak light of doubt and self-pity was slowly originating in his consciousness. In memory he turned toward Rosa Luxemburg, but he saw only an emaciated woman in a coffin, like a mother drained of life by childbirth. There was now no stirring in Kopionkin of the tender attraction that had formerly heartened him with a merry, transparent strength of hope.

Surprised and saddened, he lay enveloped by the sky's night and many years of tiredness. He could not see himself in his sleep—and if he could, he would have taken fright: asleep on the bench was an old, worn-out man, with an alien face covered by a martyr's deep wrinkles—a man who had never, in all his life, done himself any kindness. There is little real difference between clear consciousness and the vision of dreams—what happens in dream is the same life, only with its meaning laid bare. For a second time, Kopionkin was dreaming of his long-dead mother. The first time had been just before his wedding; his mother had been walking away from him down a dirty country track. Her greasy blouse gave off a smell of cabbage soup and babies, and her back was so thin that her ribs and vertebrae showed through. She was walking away, stooping, not reproaching her son in any way. Kopionkin knew that there was nothing waiting for her where she was going and he set off at a run, taking the roundabout path through the gully. Vegetable and melon growers used to spend the warmer months on the edge of the forest, and he wanted to build his mother a hut in a place somewhere she would find another father and a new son.

Now too his mother's face bore its usual look of grief. Using only the edge of her handkerchief so as to keep the rest of it clean, she was wiping her tear duct wrinkles. Small and withered beside her grown-up son, she was saying, "So you've found yourself another slut, Stepan—and left your mother to the mercy of strangers! God be with you!"

The mother was forgiving, because she had lost her motherly power over the son to whom she had given birth from her own blood and who had now moved so wickedly far from his mother.

Kopionkin loved his mother and Rosa equally, since for him they were the same first being, just as past and future both lived in his one life. He did not know how this could be, but he felt Rosa to be a continuation of his childhood and his mother—not an insult to his old mother.

That his mother was angry with Rosa made his heart sink. "Mama, she's dead, the same as you are," he said, regretting the helplessness of his mother's fury and spite.

The old woman moved her handkerchief away—she was not crying, after all.

"A likely story, my boy!" she snapped. "She'll talk, and she'll spin around on her heels—and it'll all look fine. But make her your wife—and you'll find you've no one to sleep with. Skin, bones, and a mug as ugly as sin. Look, here she comes—your sweetheart. The bitch has taken you for a ride!"

Rosa was coming down the street—small, alive, and real, with sad black eyes, like in the picture in the village soviet. Kopionkin forgot his mother and broke the windowpane—for better observation of Rosa. Outside the window lay a summer village street, as empty and boring as any other village street in the heat and drought, but there was no Rosa. A chicken flew out from an alley and started to run down a rut, its outspread wings stirring up the dust. After the chicken came people, looking cautiously around—and then more people, carrying one of the cheap, unpainted coffins provided from communal funds for unrecorded people who have forgotten their kin.[1]

In the coffin lay Rosa. Her face was covered in the yellow blotches of a woman unfortunate in childbirth. Unwomanly gray had settled in the black of her hair, and her eyes had been sucked beneath her brow in tired renunciation of everyone living. There was no one she needed, nor was she dear to those now carrying her. The bearers were laboring only because of social pressure, fulfilling the obligations that fell on each household.

Kopionkin observed intently and did not believe. This was not the same woman. The woman he'd known had had eyesight and eyelashes. The closer the men brought Rosa, the more darkness he saw in her ancient face—it was a face that had seen only the neighboring villages and poverty.

"You're burying my mother!" he shouted.

"No, this one's never had a husband," one of the bearers replied without the least sorrow, adjusting the towel on his shoulder. "But why here? Why couldn't she have pegged out in some other village? It's all the same to her now."

The man wanted payment. Kopionkin understood and was quick to reassure these men working under compulsion. "Come back once she's under the earth. I'll treat you."

"All right," the man replied. "A funeral with no farewell drink is a sin. She may be a handmaiden of the Lord now, but she's still a fair weight. Ouch—my shoulder!"

Kopionkin was still lying on the bench, waiting for the men to return from the graveyard. He could feel a cold draft. He got up to do something about the broken pane, but the window was intact. What he had felt was a morning breeze, and Strength of the Proletariat had long been neighing out in the yard, needing water. Kopionkin straightened his clothes, hiccupped, and went outside. The arm of the neighbors' well was moving down, lowering a bucket. A young woman behind the wattle fence was stroking a cow, so she would let herself be milked, and saying in a low, tender voice, "Masha, Mashenka, don't turn and don't sway. What's holy will stay, may all sins fall away."

Somewhere over to the left, a barefoot man was pissing from the threshold of his hut and shouting to an invisible son, "Vaska, go and water the mare!"

"I already have—so shut up!"

"Vaska, go and grind some millet—or I'll smash you over the head with a mortar!"

"Why always me? I did the millet yesterday. Go and grind it yourself!"

Sparrows were busying themselves about the huts and yards, as if they were domesticated and a part of the family—and indeed, swallows may look very splendid but they fly away every autumn to luxurious countries, while sparrows stay here, to share the cold and human want. The sparrow is a true proletarian bird, pecking its bitter grain. All tender creations on earth can perish from long and gloomy adversity, but such life-bearing creatures as peasants and sparrows will remain and endure until a warmer day.

Kopionkin smiled at the sparrow, which was able to find a huge promise in its tiny and unavailing life. What kept it warm on a chilly morning was clearly not seeds and grains but some dream unknown to human beings. Kopionkin also lived not by bread or general well-being, but by unaccountable hope.

"You're doing right," he said, not taking his eyes off the working sparrow. "You're no giant, but you seize what you need. If man were like you, the whole world would have come into blossom long ago."

Yesterday's pockmarked peasant came round early. Kopionkin drew him into conversation, then went to have breakfast with him in his hut. While they were sitting at the table, he asked all of a sudden, "Is there anyone in this village by the name of Plotnikov?"

The man looked at Kopionkin intently, wondering what lay behind this question.

"That's me—Plotnikov. But what are you after? There are only three family names in this village—Plotnikov, Ganushkin, and Tselnov. Which Plotnikov do you want?"

"The one with the chestnut stallion. A nippy, handsome stallion—looks like a joy to ride. Know who I mean now?"

"Ah, you mean Vanka! I'm Fyodor. He's from another family. And his stallion's been lame since the day before yesterday. So it's him you want, is it? I'll go and fetch him."

Pockmarked Fyodor went outside. Kopionkin took out his revolver and laid it on the table. Fyodor's sick wife looked numbly down at him. She was lying on the stove, hiccupping in fear, more and more violently.

"Seems someone's thinking of you," Kopionkin said with concern. "Any idea who?"[2]

The woman twisted her mouth into a smile, wanting to win her guest's sympathy but unable to speak.

Soon, Fyodor came back with Vanka Plotnikov. He turned out to be the man in bare feet who had earlier been yelling at his son. He was now wearing felt boots, and politely kneading between his hands a frail hat that must have dated back to his bachelor days. He had no distinguishing features; to tell him apart from others of his kind, you would need to live with him. Only the color of his eyes was unusual—the deep brown of thieving and secret designs. Kopionkin sullenly studied this brigand. The man was not bothered by this—or else he simply chose to put on a bold front.

"Why stare at me like that? Looking for comrades?"

Kopionkin stopped him in his tracks. "So, do you intend to make trouble? Are you going to incite people against Soviet power? Tell me straight. Yes or no?"

Getting a sense of Kopionkin's ways, Plotnikov puckered his brow and looked down at the floor, to show his obedience and voluntary regret with regard to his illegal actions.

"No, not anymore—and I mean what I say."

For the sake of severity, Kopionkin remained silent for a while. Then he concluded, "Well, keep me in mind. I'm retribution without trial. Yes, I'll rip you up by the roots just like that. I'll dig right down, far as your mother's mother—and coffin you on the spot. Go back home now—and keep my presence in mind!"

When Plotnikov left, the pockmarked peasant gasped and stammered in respect. "Now that's what I call justice. I can see you're the true power now."

Kopionkin at once came to like pockmarked Fyodor because of his homespun longing for true power and authority—all the more so since Sasha Dvanov liked to say that Soviet power was the reign of a multitude of ordinary, unimpressive people.

"What do you mean by power?" he replied. "We're a force of nature."

25

THE CITY buildings now seemed too large to Dvanov; his eyes had grown used to small huts and open steppe.

Summer was shining down on the city, and the birds that had already reproduced were singing amid the buildings and on telegraph poles. The city from which Dvanov had set out had been a stern fortress, that knew only disciplined service of the Revolution. It was for this alone that Red Army soldiers and factory and office workers had lived and endured; at night no one had existed but sentries, checking the documents of agitated midnight citizens. The city Dvanov saw now was utterly changed—not a place of unpeopled holiness but a festive settlement, illuminated by summer light.

At first he thought that the city had been taken by the Whites. There was a canteen in the railway station where wheaten loaves were being sold without ration cards and with no queue. Next to the station, beside the Provincial Provisions Committee building, hung a damp sign. On it was written concisely and crudely, in letters that had run because of the poor-quality paint:

EVERYTHING ON SALE TO ALL CITIZENS.
PREWAR BREAD, PREWAR FISH,
FRESH MEAT
OUR OWN SALTED VEGETABLES

In small letters beneath the sign was the company name: Arduliants, Romm, Kolesnikov, and Co.

Dvanov decided this must be a joke, and he went inside the shop. There he saw furnishings and equipment that he had glimpsed only in his youth and had long forgotten: counters under glass, shelves on the wall, proper scales instead of steelyards, polite shop assistants instead of Provisions Committee agents and supplies managers, a lively crowd of customers, and stocks of food products giving off a smell of satiety.

"A far cry from the rations distribution center!" a man declared with feeling, contemplating this picture of trade.

Dvanov looked at him with hatred. Rather than being troubled, the man smiled triumphantly—as if to say, "Stare all you like. What fills me with joy is now a legitimate fact!"

As well as the customers, there was a whole crowd of onlookers, all taking a lively interest in this joyous event. They outnumbered the customers, and they too were indirectly participating in the store's activities. Someone might go up to the bread, break off a small piece and put it into his mouth. The shop assistant would await further developments without protest. The lover of trade would chew on the bread for some time, steering it around his mouth with his tongue and seeming deep in thought. Finally, he would pronounce his verdict:

"Just the very slightest tang, I'd say. Is it made with yeast?"

"Sourdough."

"Ah, it shows. Still, it's good flour—not like what we got in our rations. And your baker knows his business—no doubt about it!"

Then the man went over to the meat, pinched it affectionately and gave it a long sniff.

"Well, shall I cut you a piece?" asked the assistant.

"I was looking to see if it's horsemeat," said the researcher. "But I can see it isn't. No tendons, no sign of foam. Otherwise, well, you know how it is—with horsemeat you get foam instead of fat. And my stomach doesn't like that—I'm not in good health."

Not letting his irritation show, the assistant took a firm hold of the meat. "Horsemeat! What's gotten into you? This is the best sirloin, Circassian White. Can't you smell the tenderness of it? It'll melt in your mouth. You can eat it raw, like curd cheese."

The satisfied man withdrew into the crowd of observers and reported his discoveries in detail.

Not leaving their posts, the onlookers began a sympathetic analysis of the shop's functioning, in all its aspects. Two of them, unable to restrain themselves, began to help the assistants—blowing dust off the counters, wiping the scales with a feather to ensure greater accuracy and arranging the counterweights in their correct order. One of these volunteers cut some paper into little slips, wrote down the name of each item on sale, attached the slips of paper to short bits of wire and then stuck these makeshift pins to the corresponding products. Each product now had a small sign over it, allowing the customer a clear understanding of what was what. Above the millet bin: "Grains of millet." Above the beef: "Fresh meat from the cow." And so on, all in accord with conventional norms.[1]

His friends admired his painstaking work. These people, ahead of their time, were the forefathers of the public services improvers of later years. Customers entered, read—and had all the more faith in the goods below the inscriptions.

One old woman came in and studied the establishment for a long time. Her head was trembling from age, along with hunger, and her inhibitory centers were failing her; involuntary moisture was oozing from her nose and eyes. She went up to the assistant and held out a rations card, its rips mended with stern, unbleached thread.

"You can put that away, Granny," the assistant declared. "There's no need for it now. Goodness knows what you found to eat, with your children all dying."

"Have we truly lived to see the day?" the old woman asked with feeling.

"We have. Lenin tooketh away—and now he giveth."

"Our kind father!" she whispered. And she began to weep as copiously as if she could count on another forty years of this good life.

Expiating the sins of War Communism, the assistant gave her a chunk of well-baked bread to take home with her.

Dvanov understood that this was not a joke, that the Revolution now had another look on its face. He did not see any more stores on his way back home, but doughnuts and *pirozhki* were being sold on every corner. People were buying food, eating food, and talking food. The city was feasting. Everyone now knew that it is difficult to grow grain, that the life of plants is as complex and tender as the life of human beings, and that the sun's rays make the earth sweat from exhausting labor. They had grown used to looking at the sky, to feeling for those working the land so that they would get the weather they needed—so that the snow would all melt in one go and the water left on the fields would not turn into an icy crust that would ruin the winter wheat. They had learned much they had not known before. Their responsibilities had broadened; their sense of life had become social. The doughnuts they savored not only added to their own satisfaction but also increased their respect for anonymous labor; their pleasure was doubled. And so, as they took in food, they would hold an open palm beneath their mouths—so as to catch any falling crumbs and eat them too.

There were large crowds on the boulevards, contemplating a life that was new to them. Many of them had eaten meat the previous day and were feeling an unaccustomed burst of strength. It was a Sunday, and so hot as to be almost stifling. The warmth of the summer sky was cooled only by a wandering wind from distant fields. Beside some of the buildings sat beggars, cursing Soviet power with conscious deliberation even though passersby saw their presence as a sign of the easing of life and were giving them money; during the previous four years both beggars and pigeons had entirely disappeared from the cities.

Dvanov crossed a public garden. Used as he was to the steppe and its airy freedom, he felt disorientated by the mass of people. For a while, a young woman who looked rather like Sonia was walking beside him. She had the same weak, gentle face and was screwing up her eyes a little at all the new impressions. Her eyes, though, were darker than Sonia's; they moved rather slowly, as if from some unresolved concern—and yet were half-closed, hiding their sorrow. "By the time socialism sets in, little Sonia will have become Sofia Alexandrovna," Dvanov said to himself. "Time will keep passing."

Zakhar Pavlovich was sitting in the entrance room, polishing Sasha's battered childhood shoes, to keep them intact longer for the sake of memory. He embraced Sasha and began to cry, since his love for his adopted son was constantly growing. And Dvanov, holding Zakhar Pavlovich's body, was thinking, "What will we do with our mothers and fathers in the communism to come?"

26

IN THE evening Dvanov went round to Shumilin. Many others were striding along the streets to be with their sweethearts. Now that they were getting better nourished, people had begun to sense their souls. Not everyone was drawn to the stars; many had grown tired of large ideas and infinite expanses. They had learned that stars could be reduced to a handful of rationed millet, while what kept ideals safe and sound was the typhus louse.

Shumilin was eating, so he asked Dvanov to join him at table.

An alarm clock was working away on the table and Shumilin secretly envied it; the clock never stopped laboring, while he himself had to interrupt his life in order to sleep. Dvanov, however, did not envy time—he sensed he had a reserve of life and knew he would be able to overtake the movement of the clock.

"No time to waste on digestion," said Shumilin. "Time to be off to the party meeting. Are you coming too? Or are you too smart now, cleverer than any of us?"[1]

Dvanov did not respond to this. Then, as they made their way to the district committee, he recounted as best he could what he had done in the province, but he could see that Shumilin was taking almost no interest.

"Yes, I've heard about all that," Shumilin replied. "But your mission, you wayward fool, was to go and have a look, to see what was going on. You, after all, have fresh eyes—while I only get to see documents, which don't tell me a damned thing. And then you go and make havoc. What made you incite the peasants to chop down the Bitterman Forest, you son of a bitch! You collected a band of wastrels and wandered about making trouble!"[2]

Dvanov went red in the face from hurt and conscience. "They're not wastrels, comrade Shumilin. If need be, they'll do another three revolutions just like that!"

Shumilin said no more; he put more trust in papers, it seemed, than in people. And so they walked on in silence, each feeling awkward before the other.

A powerful breeze, as if from a fan, was blowing through the doors of the hall in the city soviet building where the meeting was to be held. A mechanic by the name of Gopner was holding one palm up in the air and saying to comrade Fufaev that there must be two atmospheres of pressure within the hall. "If you could collect the whole party together here," he was reasoning, "we could set up an electricity-generating station. I'll be damned if we couldn't power it on the party's breath alone!"

Dismayed by the meeting's delayed start, Fufaev was despondently scrutinizing the electric lighting. Little Gopner was coming up with still more of his technical calculations, then telling Fufaev all about them. Probably, he had no one to talk to at home and was glad to be among so many people.

"You keep thinking away," Fufaev said quietly and to the point, letting out a deep sigh with his bony mound of a chest that had long ago ripped through every one of his shirts; they all now had darns in them. "But it's time we all shut our mouths and began working in broad earnest."

Gopner could not understand why Fufaev had twice been awarded the Order of the Red Banner.[3] Fufaev himself, preferring the future to the past, had never spoken about this; Fufaev looked on the past as a now-useless fact, something that had been destroyed once and for all, and he kept his medals in a trunk at home, not on his chest. Gopner had learned about the medals only from Fufaev's boastful wife, who knew every detail of her husband's life as precisely as if she had given birth to him herself.

There was only one little thing she didn't know—why it is that people receive medals and special rations. But her husband just said, "For service, Polya. Which is how it should be." This reassured Polya, who imagined her husband doing clerical service in a government office.

From a distance, Fufaev's face appeared fierce; from close by, however, his eyes looked peaceful and imaginative. His large head clearly indicated some kind of primal strength of silent mind, yearning within his skull. In spite of his forgotten wartime deeds, consolidated only in the records of disbanded divisions, Fufaev revered agriculture and quiet, productive labor in general. He was now in charge of the provincial department for the salvage and reuse of scrap material and was therefore obliged to be constantly thinking things up. This suited him; his most recent undertaking had been the establishment of a network of manure depots; upon presentation of a coupon, the horseless poor could obtain manure for the fertilization of their plots. But Fufaev did not rest on his laurels; at first light he was riding around the city in his small horse cab, looking at streets, going into backyards, and questioning beggars in the hope of discovering still more scrap for state use. It was also on the broad field of rubbish that he had first encountered Gopner. Fufaev asked everyone he met with equal seriousness, "Comrade, our state is not so very rich. Do you have anything you don't need—for salvage and scrap?"

"Such as, for example?" a comrade might ask.

Fufaev was always quick to reply. "Any kind of raw materials, or things that are going rusty, or a bast sponge, or anything dearer to me than to you."

"A bast sponge!" the comrade would repeat in surprise. "I only use twigs in the bathhouse. It's years since I've used anything else."[4]

But sometimes people gave Fufaev more practical advice. Prerevolutionary archives, for example, could be used to heat children's homes. Tall weeds on back streets and blind alleys could be systematically mowed to provide ready fodder for an extensive goats' milk industry, providing cheap milk to those without property and to wounded Civil War veterans.

At night Fufaev dreamed of scrap materials of every kind, in the guise of abstract mountains of anonymous old junk. He would wake in shock, appalled by his own position of responsibility, since he was an honorable man. Gopner once advised him not to worry beyond his powers. Better, he suggested, to send a circular instructing the citizens of the old world to keep a close guard on their clutter, in case it should ever be required by the Revolution. Not that it ever really would be required, since the new world would be constructed from eternal material never to be discarded.

After that, Fufaev had felt a little calmer. He was less often tormented by these dream mountains.

Shumilin knew both Fufaev and Gopner, while Dvanov knew only Gopner.

"Greetings, Fyodor Fyodorovich!" said Dvanov. "How's life going for you?"

"Regularly," Gopner replied. "Except that bread's now being sold freely, damn it."

Shumilin then spoke briefly to Fufaev. The Provincial Party Committee was preparing to appoint Fufaev chairman of a commission to assist sick and wounded Red Army soldiers. Fufaev agreed, already accustomed to such obscure positions. Many other former commanders also worked in trade unions and social security or insurance offices that played only a minor role in the Revolution's fate—except that now and then, after being criticized for crawling along at the tail end of the Revolution, these institutions managed to sit themselves on its neck.

Military figures, for some reason, looked on all service to the state with respect and, in the name of iron discipline, were willing to assume responsibility for a Red Corner,[5] even though in the past they had commanded a division.

Sensing the depth of Gopner's dissatisfaction, Shumilin said, "So you enjoyed your rations, did you—and you don't like free trade?"

"Certainly not," Gopner declared quickly and seriously. "Think food and Revolution can live together? Not in all my born days, damn it!"[6]

"But what kind of freedom does a hungry man have?" asked Shumilin, with a smile of intellectual disdain.

His voice still more elevated and inspired, Gopner replied, "We can be comrades, I tell you, only when we're up to our neck in the same trouble.[7] The moment there's bread and property, that's the end of any true human being. What kind of freedom can exist if we all have bread fermenting away in our gut and there's no room in our hearts to think about anything else? Thought loves grief, it loves lightness... Has there ever been a time when people with well-lined stomachs have lived in freedom?"

"You've read history?" Shumilin asked skeptically.

"I'm thinking for myself," Gopner replied with a wink.

"And what have you thought?"

"That we should let others consume bread and substances of all kinds—not accumulate them. If we can't do the very best by a man, then we can settle for giving him bread. But our aim was to give him the very best."

A bell rang in the hall—the meeting was about to begin.

"Time for a little serious thinking," Gopner said to Dvanov. "After all, you and I are subjects now, not objects, damn it.[8] Though just what that means, it's not so easy to grasp."

There was only one item on the agenda—the New Economic Policy.[9] Gopner pondered this. He had no love for politics or economics. Calculation, in his view, was all very well in a machine; real life was a matter of singular numbers and differences of one kind or another.

The committee secretary, a former railway engineer, had little respect for meetings—he saw them as a mere formality, since a workingman would never be able to think with the speed of speech. A proletarian's thought acts in his feelings, not beneath his bald patch. And so he usually curtailed the orators. "Tighter, comrade, tighter! Remember—grain is being requisitioned to fuel you and your twaddle!"

Sometimes, he would just address the meeting as a whole. "Comrades, has any one of you understood a single word? I haven't. We need to know," he rapped out ever more crossly, "what we should be doing when we walk out through these doors. And this fellow keeps lamenting about some kind of 'objective conditions.' What I say is that when there's a revolution, there are no objective conditions."

"Hear, hear!" shouted the meeting. "Quite right!" But even if the secretary had been quite wrong, there were so many people present that they'd have done things their own way anyway.

The secretary was looking sad. He was getting on in years and his secret wish was to be appointed director of some reading hut in a village, where he could build socialism by hand and make it into something everyone could see with their own eyes. Information bulletins, reports, summaries, and circulars were beginning to undermine his health. Sometimes he would take them home with him and fail to bring them back again, saying to the director, "Comrade Molelnikov, I'm afraid my little son burned them in the stove while I was asleep. I woke up—and found only ashes. Let's see if we can get by without sending out copies. Maybe it won't bring about counterrevolution, after all!" "All right," Molelnikov would reply. "It's clear enough that one can't get far just with documents. All anyone can put on paper is understandings. Keeping hold of a province through papers and documents is like holding a mare by the tail." Molelnikov came from peasant stock; he found his committee duties so tedious that he started a small vegetable garden in the yard and used to go out there now and again during working hours, to do a little real labor.

As for the secretary himself, he was now feeling relatively content. He understood the New Economic Policy as the Revolution being allowed to move forward under its own steam, according to the proletariat's own wishes. Until then, the Revolution had been hauled along by departments and institutions, as if the apparatus of State were a machine for the construction of socialism. It was with these thoughts that the secretary began his speech.

Dvanov was sitting between Gopner and Fufaev. In front of him some unknown man was muttering away without interruption, thinking something in his closed mind and unable to refrain from words. Those who had learned to think during the Revolution were constantly talking aloud, and no one was bothered by this.

Party people were not at all like one another. Each face had something self-made about it—as if this person had dug himself up from somewhere or other with only his own solitary strength. Open, a little mistrustful, darkened by constant tension, such a face stands out among a thousand others. The Whites in their day had unerringly seized on such self-made people and destroyed them with the same pathological frenzy with which normal children attack freaks and animals, with fear and voluptuous pleasure.

The gas of exhalations had already formed a kind of hazy local sky beneath the hall ceiling. The wan electric light was slightly pulsating—most likely there was not a single intact drive belt in the whole power station, and the seams in some old, worn belt were knocking against the pulley, affecting the dynamo's tension. A good half of those present understood this. The further the Revolution went, the more resistance it met from tired machines and artifacts that had long outworked their operational life and kept going only thanks to the mastery with which they were spurred on by mechanics and engineers.

The party member sitting in front of Dvanov went on muttering audibly onward, head bowed, not listening to the speaker.

Gopner was gazing abstractedly into the distance, carried by a current of double strength—the orator's speech and his own hurrying consciousness. Dvanov, for his part, always experienced a painful discomfort when he was unable to imagine a man closely and, however briefly, live his life a little. It was with some anxiety that he was now watching Gopner, a sinewy, elderly man all but eaten away by forty years of labor.

The skin on Gopner's nose, cheekbones, and earlobes was so taut that anyone looking at him felt a nervous itch. When Gopner undressed in the bathhouse, he probably looked like a mere boy, but he was, in fact, uncommonly strong, steady, and enduring. Long labor had greedily consumed his body. What was left was what remains even in the grave—hair and bones. Beyond all desires, made lean by the flatiron of labor, his life was now compressed into concentrated consciousness alone, lighting his eyes with the late passion of bare mind.

Dvanov recalled his previous meetings with Gopner. They had talked many times about installing locks on the Polny Aidar River, which passed through their city, and had smoked a lot of *makhorka* from Gopner's pouch. Their discussions had arisen not so much from the prospect of social good as from their own surplus enthusiasm, the value of which people had failed to appreciate.

The present speaker was using simple little words, every sound of which carried the movement of thought; in them could be sensed an invisible respect for others and a fear of their possible response, which made listeners feel that they too were intelligent.

One party member sitting near Dvanov announced to the hall with calm indifference, "We've got no rags left, so we're laying in a supply of burdock."

The electric light faded till it was only a red glow—evidently, the power station dynamo was now rotating only from its own momentum. Everyone looked up. Then the light quietly went out altogether.

"Yet again!" someone said in the dark.

In the silence they heard a cart pass loudly down the road and a baby crying in the distant room of the watchman.

Fufaev asked Dvanov what the secretary meant by "exchange of goods with the peasants within the limits of local circulation." Dvanov did not know. Nor did Gopner. "Wait!" he said. "If they manage to mend the drive belt at the power station, the secretary will explain."

The light came back on. The power station workers were used to sorting out problems on the go, with their machines still in operation.

"For Soviet power, free trade is fodder that's close to hand. It's a stopgap—so we can plaster over at least the most shameful spots of the general ruination."

"Get it?" Fufaev quietly asked Gopner. "The bourgeoisie are scrap material too. We must take them in hand and make good use of them."

"Right you are!" said Gopner, turning gray from some hidden weakness.

The speaker stopped in midflow. "What are you bellowing about, Gopner? Don't be in too much of a hurry to agree with me—there's lots I don't understand either. I'm not trying to persuade you, I'm asking for your advice. I'm no smarter than anyone else."

"You're no less smart," said Gopner, loudly but good-naturedly. "But if ever you get stupider than us, we'll have you replaced, damn you!"

The meeting laughed contentedly. In those days there was no defined cadre of famous people. On the contrary, everyone felt his own proper name and significance.

"String your words clearly together—and cut the thread short!" Gopner continued, not getting to his feet.

Dirt was dripping from the ceiling. Mucky water was coming down from some small ruination up in the attic. It was in vain, it now seemed to Fufaev, that his son had died from typhus and that antiprofiteering detachments had sealed off the cities, barring the peasants from taking bread to the markets and so allowing lice to grow fat and multiply.

Then Gopner's face went from gray to green. With the words, "Sasha, I feel sick," he got to his feet and walked toward the door, holding one hand to his mouth.

Dvanov followed. Once they were outside, Gopner stopped. He leaned his head against the cold brick wall.

"Go on a bit farther, Sasha," he said, seeming ashamed of something. "I'll be all right in a moment."

Dvanov stayed where he was. Gopner vomited up some undigested black food, though only a very little. He wiped his thin mustache with a red handkerchief.

"Year after year I lived with an empty belly," he explained in embarrassment. "And it did me no harm. And then today I ate three flatbreads one after the other. Seems I'm not used to it."

They sat down on the threshold. The window in the hall was wide open for air, and every word spoken inside was audible. Only the night kept silent, carefully carrying its blossoming stars over the earth's dark and empty places. The fire station stables were directly opposite the city soviet, but the watchtower had burned down two years earlier. The duty fireman now observed the city from the city soviet roof, walking backward and forward. This was boring, so he sang songs and clattered his boots over the sheet iron. Then Dvanov and Gopner both noticed that he had gone silent—probably he too could now hear what the secretary was saying in the hall.

The secretary was now talking about doomed comrades detailed to grain-requisitioning detachments. All too often our red banner had served as a drape for their coffins.

The fireman stopped listening and went back to singing his song.

> Striding bast shoes, no one inside them—
> Striding the steppe, with people beside them...

"What's that he's singing, damn it?" said Gopner. He fell silent and listened. "He sings about anything and everything—so he doesn't have time to think. Anyway, the water main's broken—what's the use of firemen?"

The fireman was at that moment looking at the city, illuminated only by stars, and wondering what would happen if it all went up in flames. The bare earth from beneath the city would become farmed fields. The fire brigade would become a village militia unit and his work would be calmer and easier.

27

BEHIND him Dvanov heard the slow steps of someone coming down a staircase. Unable to think in silence, this man was muttering his thoughts to himself. He could not think blindly—first he had to put his mental agitation into words. Only then, on hearing these words, could he feel anything clearly. Probably, he also read books aloud, to transform enigmatic dead signs into things of sound that he could sense.

"I ask you now!" The man was speaking to himself with conviction and listening attentively. "As if he were telling us something new. Trade, taxes, barter...That was all happening anyway. Trade went on in spite of everything, and grain requisitioning—after the villagers had hidden away half their grain—wasn't much different from these new taxes. Am I talking sense, or am I an idiot?"

Now and then, the man stopped for a moment on the stairs and voiced objections to his own thoughts, "Yes, you're an idiot. Do you really think that Lenin's dumber than you are? Come off it!"

The man was clearly in torment. The fireman on the roof began singing again, unaware of what was going on beneath him.

"Some new economic policy!" the man repeated in quiet astonishment. "Probably just a street name for communism. I get called by a nickname too—'the Japanese.' One just has to accept these things."

The man came over to Dvanov and Gopner. "Elemental communism's welling up inside me," he began. "Should I stopper it with a new policy, or not?"

"Better not," said Dvanov.

"That's it then—why go on doubting?" the man reassured himself, and took a pinch of snuff from his pocket. He was short, with a weak nose and a Japanese face. He was dressed in the uniform of a true Communist—a greatcoat off the shoulders of a deserter from the tsarist war.[1]

Dvanov realized that this was the party member who had been muttering in front of him during the meeting.

"Where are you from?" asked Gopner.

"From Communism," the visitor replied. "Heard of such a place?"

"Some village named in memory of the future?"

The man seemed delighted to have a story to tell. "What do you mean? Aren't you a party member? It's an inhabited point and locality, a whole district center. In the past it was called Chevengur. I was chairman of the RevCom there."

"Not far from Novosiolovsk?" asked Dvanov.

"Not far at all. But they're just ignorant loudmouths who have nothing to do with us. We've put an end to everything."

"An end to what?" Gopner asked mistrustfully.

"To all world history, of course. What good's it to us?"[2]

Neither Dvanov nor Gopner asked any further. The fireman clattered rhythmically over the slope of the roof, surveying the city through sleepy eyes. He stopped singing, then went silent—probably retiring into the attic to sleep. But that night his negligence did not go unnoticed. Someone in uniform stopped close to the three men talking on the street and shouted up at the roof, "Raspopov! Observer! This is the fire-brigade inspector. Anyone up there?"

Up above, there was only silence.

"Raspopov!"

The despairing inspector then went up onto the roof himself.

The night carried on with its quiet sounds—a breeze, young leaves and grass scrabbling its way through the soil. If Dvanov closed his eyes, he thought he could hear water letting out an even, sustained moan as it disappeared down a funnel into the earth. The chairman of the Chevengur District ExecComm took a pinch of snuff and kept trying to sneeze. The meeting had gone silent for some reason; probably they were all thinking.

"There are so many interesting stars up in the sky," Dvanov pronounced, "but we've got no lines of communication to them."

The inspector came back down from the roof, along with the duty fireman. His feet no longer warm from sleep, the latter was going along obediently, ready to meet his fate.

"That'll be a month of forced labor," the inspector said dispassionately.

"If I have to labor, I'll labor," said the guilty man. "What do I care? The rations are no different and the labor code is respected."

Gopner got to his feet, ready to go home. He now felt sick throughout his body. The Chevengur chairman sniffed his last pinch of snuff and declared openly and sincerely, "Oh, how I wish I were back in Chevengur!"

Dvanov suddenly began to miss Kopionkin, his distant comrade now keeping vigil somewhere in the dark of the steppe.

At that moment Kopionkin was standing on the porch of the Chernovka village soviet and quietly whispering verses about Rosa Luxemburg that he had composed in current days. Up above him hung stars, ready to drop onto his head, and beyond the last fence of the village boundary stretched the land of socialism, the motherland of unknown future nations. Strength of the Proletariat and Dvanov's trotter were evenly munching their hay, relying in all other respects on the courage and intelligence of mankind.

Dvanov got to his feet too, holding out his hand to the Chevengur chairman. "Tell me your name!"

Caught up in his own thoughts, the Chevengurian took a while to come back to himself. "Come and work with me, comrade!" he said. "Yes, things are good now in our Chevengur! The moon up in the sky and a vast laboring district beneath it—all deep in communism, like a fish in a lake.[3] All that we lack is recognition."

Gopner quickly put a stop to this boasting. "What moon, damn it! It reached its last quarter a week ago."

"I got carried away," the Chevengurian admitted. "But with no moon, things are better still. We've got lamps, with lampshades."

The three men set off down the street—to the accompaniment of troubled exclamations from some small birds in the front gardens, who were beginning to sense light in the east. Now and then it can be good to stay up whole nights without sleeping—on such nights the invisible half of the cool, windless world had sometimes revealed itself to Dvanov.

Dvanov liked the word *Chevengur.* It sounded like the enticing hum of an unknown country, although Dvanov had, in fact, already heard of this small district.[4] Learning that the Chevengurian would pass through Kalitva on his way back, Dvanov asked him to visit nearby Chernovka and tell Kopionkin not to wait for him any longer but to continue on his own way. Dvanov wanted to go back to his studies and complete his course at the polytechnical institute.

"That's no trouble," the Chevengurian agreed. "It's interesting, after communism, to see people living in separation."

"No end to the man's blathering!" said Gopner indignantly. "Ruination everywhere—and all he cares about is his light under a shade."

Dvanov wrote a brief note to Kopionkin, using a fence as his writing desk: "Dear comrade Kopionkin! There's nothing particular to say. The policy's different now, but it's correct. Give my trotter to any poor peasant. And go..."

Dvanov stopped. Where would it best for Kopionkin to go and settle himself for a long time?

"What's your family name?" Dvanov asked the Chevengurian.

"My name is Chepurny. But write, 'the Japanese.' That's the name the district's orientated on."[5]

Dvanov continued, "And go to the Japanese. He says they've got socialism there. If that's true, write and tell me. But I won't be coming back, even though I don't want to part from you. I still don't know what's best for me. I won't forget either you or Rosa Luxemburg.

"Your comrade-in-arms, Alexander Dvanov."

Chepurny took the sheet of paper from him and read it then and there. "A load of baloney," he said. "You have a weak feeling of mind."

They said goodbye and went their separate ways—Gopner and Dvanov to the edge of city, and the Japanese to an inn.

Zakhar Pavlovich was lying in bed when Sasha got back. "How was it?" he asked.

Sasha told him about the new economic policy.

"It's a lost cause," Zakhar Pavlovich concluded. "What doesn't ripen when it should was sown in vain. When they took power, they promised all kinds of good for the entire earthly sphere the very next day. And now they make out that objective conditions have got in the way. Nothing new there—Satan didn't make it easy for priests to get to heaven."

Once he was back in his room, Gopner's various pains disappeared.

"What is it I want?" he asked himself. "My father wanted to see God with his own eyes. But what I want, damn it, is some kind of empty place. So I can do everything from the beginning, depending on my own mind alone."

It was not joy that Gopner wanted, so much as precision.

28

THE JAPANESE, on the other hand, felt untroubled; in his town of Chevengur, the good things of life, the precision of truth, and the sorrows of existence all happened of themselves, as needed. Back at the inn, he fed some grass to his horse, then lay down in his cart to get some sleep.

"I'll put that trotter of Kopionkin's in harness too," he said to himself. "Why give it to some poor peasant when they get more than enough benefits already? I ask you now!"

In the morning, the inn yard was packed with the carts of peasants who'd come to the market. Each had brought only a small amount of produce—a *pood* of millet,[1] or five crocks of milk—so as not to be upset if it were confiscated. But there had been no antiprofiteering detachment at the city gate, so they were now expecting searches and raids within the city. For some reason, however, no search parties had appeared—and so the peasants were sitting on their goods in anguish.

"No confiscations today?" Chepurny inquired.

"Not a sign of them. We don't know whether to rejoice or grieve."

"How d'you mean?"

"What if they come up with something worse still? Better if they just took our stuff. This Soviet power's never going to let us live for free."

"Like that, is it?" thought Chepurny. "They should be branded as petty landowners. We should set the poor on them and liquidate this whole bourgeois, smallholding pestilence within twenty-four hours."

"Give me a smoke," said the same elderly peasant.

Chepurny looked at him askance, and as if from a distance. "You own land—and you beg from a man who has nothing."

The peasant understood but didn't show anger. "They've left us nothing, comrade. If it weren't for the requisitioning, I'd be filling my own pouch."

"Filling it?" doubted Chepurny. "Overfilling and then spilling, more likely!"

The peasant noticed a linchpin lying about on the ground, got down from his cart to pick it up, and tucked it behind the top of his boot.

"It all depends," he said calmly. "It says in the papers that comrade Lenin has come to love good accounting. If careless hands let grain spill, then it's right to fill your sack with them."

"Keep that sack with you all the time, do you?" Chepurny asked bluntly.

"Of course I do. And when I put food in my mouth, I don't let it fall out again. But you lot let grain spill to the ground—and don't bother to pick it up. We're honorable people here—what have you got against us?"

Chepurny, who in Chevengur had grown accustomed to breadth of thought, said nothing. He was chairman of the town's RevCom, but he never made use of this title. Back in the days when he'd sat in an office, he had entertained the pitiful thought that the villages were inhabited by people utterly identical to one another who didn't know how to continue their lives. It had seemed to him that, left to themselves, they would simply die out—which meant that his thoughtful care was essential to the entire district. Since he had begun to ride around the district, however, he had become convinced of the personal mind of each citizen and had long since abolished all administrative help to the population. And this elderly peasant had once again confirmed Chepurny's simple feeling that every living person gets to know his own fate while still inside his mother's belly and has no need of supervision.

As Chepurny was riding out of the yard, the innkeeper's henchman stopped him and demanded money for his night's lodging. Chepurny had no money and could not possibly have had any money. Chevengur had no budget, to the joy of the provincial authorities, who assumed that life in the town was proceeding on a sound, self-supporting foundation. In reality, however, the citizens of Chevengur had long ago decided that a happy life was preferable to any kind of labor, construction, and mutual accounting that required the sacrifice of man's comradely body, which lives only once.

Chepurny was unable to pay for his lodging.

"Take what you want," he said. "I'm a naked Communist."[2]

Hearing all this, the peasant who had just been arguing with the Chevengurian came up to the two men. "What does the law say he should pay?" he asked.

"One million if he didn't sleep indoors,"[3] said the man from the inn.

The peasant turned away and reached beneath his shirt for a small leather pouch hanging from his neck. "Take this, my friend, and let the man go," he said, and handed over the money.

"Work is work," the henchman excused himself. "My job is to knock the stuffing out of a man rather than let him leave this yard for free."

"Fair enough," the peasant calmly agreed. "This isn't open steppe. It's an establishment—a resting place for people and animals alike."

Once he had left the city, Chepurny felt freer and more intelligent. Before him, once again, lay calming space. This man from Chevengur did not like forests, hills, and buildings. What he liked was the earth's even belly, sloping against the sky, inhaling the wind and yielding a little beneath the weight of a foot-walker.

Listening to the RevCom secretary read out circulars, tables, questions necessary for the elaboration of plans, and other administrative material from the province RevCom, Chepurny had used to repeat the word *Po-li-ti-ka* and smile thoughtfully, secretly not understanding a word. After a while, the secretary had stopped reading to him, managing his entire workload without Chepurny's leadership.

Chepurny's cart was being pulled by a black horse with a white belly. Who it belonged to, he didn't know. He had first seen it on a city square, where it had been eating the newly planted saplings of a future park; he had brought the horse to the yard, put it in harness, and set off. That the horse had no owner made it all the more precious to the Chevengurian; there was no one to take care of it, except for any citizen at all. For this reason, all the animals in Chevengur District looked healthy and well fed, with rounded bodies.

The road drew Chepurny on for a long time. He sang all the songs he knew by heart. He wanted to think about something, but there was nothing to think about—everything was clear and the only thing left was action. Somehow he needed to move about and exhaust his happy life before it became too good, but it's difficult to exhaust oneself on a cart. He leaped down from the cart and began to run alongside his horse, which was panting with tired breath. After exhausting himself, he leaped up onto the horse's back, leaving the cart rattling along behind. He looked around at the cart—it seemed poorly constructed and was clearly heavy to pull.

"Whoa!" he said to the horse, then unhitched the cart. "Why expend the living life of a horse dragging a dead weight? I ask you now!" Abandoning the harness, he rode off on the liberated steed. The cart stood there, shafts resting on the ground, awaiting the mercy of the first peasant to ride by.

"Our blood's flowing now—both mine and the horse's!" Chepurny thought randomly, deprived of his own exertions as his horse galloped along. "No traces or harness now—I'll just have to keep Kopionkin's trotter on the rein."

Toward evening he reached some little steppe hamlet, as unpeopled as if everyone there had long ago laid down their bones. The evening sky seemed a continuation of the steppe—and the steed beneath the Chevengurian saw the infinite horizon as the terrible fate of its tired legs.

The Chevengurian knocked at someone's peaceful hut. An old man came out from the back door and looked at him from behind the fence.

"Unbolt your gate," said Chepurny. "You've got bread and hay here, haven't you?"

The old man remained fearlessly silent, studying the horseman with sensitive, accustomed eyes. Chepurny climbed over the fence and opened the gate himself. His now hungry horse moved toward the barn and at once began eating the grass outside, which had settled down for the night. The old man seemed confused by his guest's self-will. As if he himself were a stranger there, he sat down on a felled oak.

Chepurny found no one inside the hut. There was only the clean smell of dry old age, which no longer sweats or stains things with the traces of an excited body. On a shelf lay a chunk of bread baked from millet husks and minced grass. He left half of this for the old man and ate the rest himself, with effort.

The old man came back into the hut as night was falling. Chepurny was gathering the crumbs of snuff in his pocket, so as to enjoy a pinch and not feel dismal before sleep.

"Your horse won't stand still for one minute," said the old man. "I gave him a handful of hay. We've still got a little left. Why not let him have some, I said to myself."

The old man was speaking in an unthinking, abstracted voice, as if troubled by some burden of his own. Chepurny began to feel wary.

"Grandad, is it far from here to Kalitva?"

"Not so very far," said the old man. "Less far if you get back on your horse."

Chepurny cast a quick glance around the hut. Beside the stove was an oven fork. And he himself no longer carried a revolver, believing that the Revolution had already quieted down.

"What people are you here? Not brigands, are you?"

"To cheat death, two hares will devour a wolf, my good man. There are desperate fellows around, and the road's close by. Our village comes in handy if you're out to plunder and rob. And so our own men have taken to the thickets and gullies, along with their families. But a stranger who shows up here may find his life being forbidden."

Pushed low by night, blanketed by storm clouds, the sky offered no hope. Chepurny rode out of the village into the safety of the steppe dark. Finding its way by smell, his horse plodded on into the distance. The earth gave off dense clouds of lush warmth, and the Chevengurian breathed deep, then fell asleep, arms around his horse's neck.

29

THE MAN Chepurny was riding to meet was sitting that night at a table in the Chernovka village soviet. There was a lamp on the table, casting light on the vast dark beyond the window. Kopionkin was talking to three peasants, telling them that socialism meant water on the high steppe, where excellent land was going to waste.

"We've known that since we were children, Stepan Yefimych," they agreed, happy to be having a good talk, since they didn't feel like sleeping. "You're not from these parts, but you've understood all our needs just like that. How come—who told you these things? But what will we get in return? Preparing this socialism of yours for Soviet power will be a fair slog, don't you think?"

Kopionkin regretted that Dvanov was not there beside him. Dvanov would have demonstrated socialism to them through thought.

"What will you get in return?" Kopionkin tried to explain on his own. "First of all, peace in your hearts forever. What do you feel there now?"

"There inside me?" One of the men stopped and looked down at his chest, trying to make out what it contained. "All I have there, Stepan Yefimych, is sadness and a black place."

"Just as I thought," said Kopionkin.

"A year ago," the sad citizen continued, "I was burying my woman because of cholera. And this year the requisitions detachment ate our cow. We had soldiers billeted in the hut for two weeks on end—they drank the well dry. Us peasants remember these things."

"That's true!" the two witnesses confirmed.

Kopionkin's horse—Strength of the Proletariat—had grown fat

and swollen during these weeks of standstill. At night he would growl and snarl, from stagnant strength and long yearning for open steppe. During the day, men would come to the village soviet yard and walk around the horse several times. Strength of the Proletariat would look at his spectators grimly, lift up his head, and let out a sullen yawn. The men would step back respectfully from the grieving beast, then say to Kopionkin, "Quite a horse you have there, Stepan Yefimych. Beyond all price—a real Draban Ivanych!"[1]

Kopionkin had long known the worth of his steed. "He's a true proletarian beast," he would reply, "with more revolutionary consciousness than any of you."

Sometimes Strength of the Proletariat would start to tear down the barn where he was standing idle. Kopionkin would go out onto the porch and call out curtly, "Hey, cut it out, vagabond!"

The horse would then quiet down.

Proximity to Strength of the Proletariat had made Dvanov's trotter turn mangy. Its coat had grown long and shaggy and even the flight of a sudden swallow was enough to make it take fright.

"That trotter needs care," the visitors would say. "Else it will cover itself in shame."

Kopionkin had no direct responsibilities as committee chairman. Every day peasants would come along to the soviet to talk. Kopionkin would listen to what they said, but he hardly ever answered. It was only to prevent attacks by brigands that he continued to stand guard over the revolutionary village—though the brigands now seemed to have quieted down.[2]

At a village assembly, he declared once and for all, "Soviet power has given you a great good. Use it well, so there's nothing left over for our enemies. You're people and comrades, and I'm no smart-ass, so don't expect me to smooth over petty squabbles between neighbors. My role is concise: to chop through the roots of any and every subversion."

The peasants' respect for Kopionkin increased with each day; he never said a word about grain requisitions or compulsory cartage responsibilities and he simply stacked all the district RevCom missives to one side, for Dvanov to deal with on his return. Those who could read and write looked through these papers and advised Kopionkin to destroy them without further ado. Power could now be organized anywhere, they asserted, and he need fear no criticism.

"Have you read the new law, Stepan Yefimych?" they asked.

"No," Kopionkin replied. "Why do you ask?"

"'Cause Lenin's said it himself. He's declared that all power is now local—no longer somewhere high up above."[3]

"Then the district RevCom's invalid," Kopionkin concluded. "It's our lawful duty to throw out these papers."

"Couldn't be lawfuller," all present agreed. "And let's share them out for cigarette paper!"

Kopionkin liked this new law and began to wonder whether Soviet power could be established out in the open, with no structures at all.

"It could indeed," replied his thoughtful fellow-talkers. "As long as there are poor peasants close by, and the White Guard's some distance away."

Kopionkin felt reassured. That night the conversation came to an end at midnight; they had run out of fuel for the lamp.

"They don't send us enough kerosene," the peasants said sadly, leaving the building without having talked themselves out. "The state doesn't serve us well. See! They've sent us a whole bottle of ink—which we don't need at all. They should give us kerosene, or sunflower oil."

Kopionkin went outside to look at the night. He loved this element and always observed it before lying down to sleep. Strength of the Proletariat, sensing his friend, let out a quiet snuffle. Kopionkin heard this—and once again a small woman appeared to him in the guise of irrevocable regret.

She was now lying on her own somewhere, beneath the dark agitation of the spring night; her empty shoes—in which she had walked while she was warm and alive—lay abandoned on the floor of some storeroom.

"Rosa," said Kopionkin, in his second, small voice.

His steed whinnied in the barn, as if glimpsing the path ahead, and kicked at the crosspiece holding the bolt. He was ready to burst out onto the mud-drowned spring roads and rush headlong toward the German cemetery that was Kopionkin's best land; Kopionkin's stifled anxiety, which had long been hidden beneath the tasks of village soviet vigilance and comradely devotion toward Dvanov, now quietly laid itself bare. Knowing that Kopionkin was nearby, the steed began to rampage about, crashing the weight of his huge feelings against walls and bolts, as if it were he, rather than Kopionkin, who loved Rosa Luxemburg.

Kopionkin was seized with jealousy.

"Cut it out, vagabond!" he said to the horse, sensing within himself a warm wave of shame.

The steed grumbled and fell silent, having translated his passions into an inner screech of the chest.

Torn black clouds, the remnants of a distant downpour, were scudding frighteningly across the sky. Up above, probably, was a dark night whirlwind, while down below all was peaceful and quiet; the only sounds were the neighbors' hens stirring about and fences creaking from the movement of small, harmless reptiles.

Kopionkin leaned one arm against the clay wall. His heart sank inside him, losing its firm will.

"Rosa! Rosa, my Rosa!" he whispered, so that the horse wouldn't hear.

But his steed was looking with one eye through a chink, and his breath was so dry and hot on the boards that the wood began to crack. Seeing Kopionkin bowed and weak, the steed pressed his head and chest against the main upright and collapsed the whole edifice onto his hind end. From unexpected horror of nerves, Strength of the Proletariat then bellowed like a camel and, tossing the entire oppressive structure up and away with his hindquarters, shot out toward Kopionkin, ready to hurtle forward, to swallow air along with the foam of his mouth and to sense invisible roads.

Kopionkin's face dried straightaway, and a wind passed through his chest. Without saddling his steed, he leaped up onto him and felt joy. Strength of the Proletariat sped headlong out into the open; unable to jump because of heaviness of body, he flattened wattle fences and walls with his front legs, then stepped over them without deviating from his course. Kopionkin began to feel merry, as if his tryst with Rosa Luxemburg were now only a day's journey for him.

"A joy to be on the road!" Kopionkin said aloud, breathing in the dampness of the late night and sniffing the smells of grasses now pushing up through the earth.

The horse was hurrying into open space, scattering in his hoofprints the warmth of his strength. The speed made Kopionkin sense his heart diminish in weight and rise toward his throat. A little faster—and relieved happiness would have made Kopionkin begin to sing; but Strength of the Proletariat was too powerfully built to gallop for long and he soon returned to his usual capacious stride. Whether or not there was a path beneath the horse was unclear—but the earth's far edge had freshened with light and Strength of the Proletariat wanted to reach this edge as soon as possible, thinking it was where Kopionkin needed to go. Nowhere did the steppe come to an end; there was only a smooth, protracted slope toward a lowered sky—a slope no steed had yet fully overcome. From distant gullies to either side rose damp, cold mist, and quiet columns of smoke were climbing from the stoves of hungry villages. Kopionkin liked the mist, and the smoke, and these unknown, rested people.

"The joy of life!" he said to himself, while the cold crept down his neck, like irritating crumbs of bread.

Amid a strip of light, someone distant and distinct was scratching his head with one hand.

"A fine place for a scratch!" Kopionkin censured this man. "He must be up to something—standing in the middle of a field at dawn and not sleeping. I won't mess about, I'll ask for his documents straightaway and give the wretch a fright."

But Kopionkin was to be disappointed—the man scratching himself in the dawn light had not the least sign of a pocket or any kind of opening where indispensable documents might be kept. It took Kopionkin half an hour to ride up to him; by then sunlight was noising all over the sky. The man was sitting on a dry hillock, painstakingly extracting dirt from the crevices of his body, as if there were no water on earth to bathe with.

"Try organizing bastards like him!" Kopionkin said to himself—and decided not to ask the man for his documents, remembering that he too was paperless, apart from the portrait of Rosa Luxemburg sewn into his cap.

Far away, in the agitated mist from the sighing soil, stood a motionless horse. Its legs were so short that Kopionkin could not believe it was alive and real, but some small person was clinging without strength to its neck. With a zinging rapture of courage, Kopionkin shouted, "Rosa!"—and Strength of the Proletariat set off again, carrying his full body over the mud. The spot where the short-legged horse was standing turned out to be a now-vanished pond, once deep in water; the horse's legs had sunk into the silty sediment. The man on the horse's back was fast asleep, devotedly clasping the horse's neck, as if it were the body of a sensitive and devoted woman friend. The horse, indeed, was not asleep and was looking trustfully at Kopionkin, not expecting harm from him. The sleeping man was breathing unevenly and chuckling merrily deep in his throat; probably he was taking part in happy dreams of his own. Kopionkin looked the whole man over, from top to bottom, and was unable to sense him as an enemy; his greatcoat was too long and even in sleep his face was ready for revolutionary deeds and the tenderness of universal community. The sleeper's personality had no especial beauty—only the heartbeat in the veins of his thin neck indicated that this was someone kind, unpropertied, and compassionate. Kopionkin took the sleeper's cap off and looked inside; an ancient, sweat-stained tab read, G. G. BREYER, ŁÓDŹ.

Kopionkin put the cap back on the sleeping head, which did not know the name of the capitalist whose artifact it was wearing.

"Hey!" Kopionkin addressed the sleeping man, who had stopped smiling and turned more serious. "Why don't you change your bourgeois cap?"

The man was gradually waking up anyway, hurriedly concluding his captivating dreams of the gullies and ravines near his birthplace; people he knew, who had all died in the poverty of labor, were huddling together there in cramped happiness.

"Soon they'll be making you any hat you like in Chevengur, just like that," the man said, now fully awake. "Just find a piece of string and measure your head."

Kopionkin was long accustomed to the masses. "And who might you be?" he asked with cool indifference.

"Me? I live not far from here now. I'm a party member, the Japanese from Chevengur. I've come to see comrade Kopionkin, to collect a trotter from him, but I exhausted my horse and then dozed off myself."

"A likely party member you are!" retorted Kopionkin. "You don't want communism—just someone else's trotter."

"Not true, comrade, not true," said Chepurny, offended by this. "Would I dare take the trotter ahead of communism? We already have communism, but there aren't many trotters there."

Kopionkin looked at the rising sun. Such a huge, hot sphere and it floated up so easily toward its noon. Not everything in the world, then, was so very difficult and calamitous.

"So you've already organized communism there?"

"Indeed we have!" said the hurt Japanese. "I ask you now!"

"So it's only hats and horses you're short of—and you've got more than enough of everything else?"

Chepurny was unable to conceal his furious love for Chevengur. He took off his cap and threw it into the mud, then took out Dvanov's note about handing over the trotter and destroyed it into four parts.

"No, comrade," he said. "Chevengur doesn't collect property, it destroys it. Chevengur man is collective and outstanding. Chevengurians care for one another—not for chests full of clutter. As for the trotter, I've just been to the city. I picked up outmoded prejudice in the city soviet. It was the same in the inn—I picked up other people's lice there. Isn't that just the way things go, I ask you now!"

"Show me Chevengur then!" said Kopionkin. "Have you put up a memorial to comrade Rosa Luxemburg there? You lackeys probably haven't even thought about that, have you?"[4]

"Of course we have. It's made from virgin rock, in a rural settlement. And comrade Liebknecht's there too, speaking full height to the masses. The two of them didn't have to wait their turn—and if anyone else dies, they'll get their chance too!"

"But what do you think about comrade Liebknecht and Rosa yourself?" asked Kopionkin. "Was he what a man is for a woman with her—or is that just my imagination?"

"Just your imagination," the Chevengurian reassured Kopionkin. "They're conscious people! They don't have the time: when you think, you don't love. It's not as if they're like me and you... I ask you now!"

Rosa Luxemburg grew still dearer to Kopionkin, and his heart thudded with inexhaustible attraction toward socialism.

"Tell me what you've got in your Chevengur—socialism on uplands, or just transitional steps in that direction?" Kopionkin was now speaking in a different voice, like a son who, happening upon his brother after five years of silent separation, asks if his mother is still alive, though almost certain that the old woman is already dead.

Chepurny, living in socialism, had long gotten out of the habit of calamitous anxiety on behalf of everyone defenseless and beloved. In Chevengur he had demobilized society along with the tsar's army, since no one had wanted to expend their body for some general, invisible good; what they wanted was to see their own life returned to them from people who were close and comradely.

The Chevengurian calmly took some snuff and only then showed his indignation. "Why are you going on about uplands? Who do you think our gullies belong to now—the landlords? In Chevengur we have total socialism—every last hummock is international property. We have the highest supremacy of life!"

"And who owns the livestock?" asked Kopionkin, regretting with all his body's accumulated strength that the chance to bring about a bright world on the borders of the road leading to Rosa had been granted not to him and Dvanov, but to this stunted little man.

"We'll soon liberate the animals out into nature too," said Chepurny. "They're almost human themselves. They only lag behind us because of centuries of oppression. They want the same as us, they too want to be man!"

Kopionkin stroked Strength of the Proletariat, sensing the horse as his equal. He had already known this—it was just that he didn't have the same power of thought as the Chevengurian, which meant that many of his feelings remained unspoken and were transformed into mute yearning.

From behind a rise in the steppe, on the earth's skyline, appeared some carts, moving across Kopionkin's gaze as they carried small village people past the clouds. The carts were raising dust; evidently there had been no rain over there.

"Let's go to your Chevengur then. We can look at the facts."

"Yes," said Chepurny. "Let's go. I'm missing my Klavdiusha."

"Who's that? Your spouse?"

"We don't have spouses—only female comrades-in-arms."

30

UNDER the sun's sharp vision, mists were vanishing like dreams. And where at night it had been frightening, there now stretched only simple expanses, poor and illuminated. The earth lay exposed and in distress, like a mother whose blankets have slipped off her while she lies asleep. Murk was still quietly trembling over the steppe river that wanderers drank from, and goggle-eyed fish, anticipating light, were swimming close to the surface.

It was still another five versts to Chevengur, but airy views were already opening onto the district's unplowed fields, onto the damp of the small Chevengurka River, and onto all the sad, low places inhabited by the people of these parts. Walking along a damp gully was Firs the beggar;[1] in the huts and barns where he had spent the last few nights he had heard talk of a free place now laid bare in the steppe. Passing wanderers lived in this place and fed everyone with the crops they grew there.

All through his journeying, all through his life, Firs had walked beside water or over damp earth. He liked flowing water—it excited him and asked something of him. Firs did not know what the water needed or why it mattered to him. He simply chose places where the water was thickened with earth and dipped his bast shoes into this water; in the evening, he would spend a long time wringing out his footcloths, so he could try the water with his fingers and study its weakening flow once again. Near pools and waterfalls he would sit and listen to the living currents, feeling wholly calm and ready to lie down in the water himself and take part in this nameless stream. He had spent the previous night on the bank of a small river and listened all night long to the singing water. In the morning he had crawled down and nestled against the enticing moisture, achieving a peace of his own before reaching Chevengur.[2]

A little beyond Firs, amid the now-silent plain, a small town could be seen in the morning's piercing cleanness. Another elderly man was now looking at this town; the air's biting freshness and the low sun shining across at him were bringing tears to his kind eyes. Not only did this man have kind eyes—there was no less kindness in the whole of his soft, warm face, clean and chaste since the day of his birth. Aging as he was, he had a short, almost white beard, but this had never been a home to the nits that live in the beards of most old men. He was walking at a steady pace toward his life's useful goal. Anyone who had walked beside this man knew how touching and fragrant he was, how pleasant it was to carry on calm, honest conversations with him. His wife called him Father and spoke to him in a whisper; the meekness and delicacy of the first days of marriage still governed their lives. Perhaps for this reason, no children were born to them and there was an eternal, desiccated silence throughout their home. Only now and then did the wife call out peacefully, "Alexey Alexeyevich, come and eat the Lord's gifts, don't make me suffer."

Alexey Alexeyevich ate so very carefully that, even though he was nearly fifty, his teeth remained in good condition and his mouth did not smell of rot, only of warm breath. When he was young and his contemporaries were embracing girls or else—moved by the same sleepless strength of youth—going out at night and uprooting entire groves of trees on the outskirts of town, he had worked out through his own diligence that it was best to chew food for as long as possible. Since then, he had chewed every spoonful until it entirely dissolved in his mouth—which had taken up a quarter of his daytime life. Until the Revolution, he had been on the board of directors of a mutual credit association and a member of the town council of his small town, now on the border of the district of Chevengur.

Alexey Alexeyevich was now walking toward Chevengur, observing the district center from the surrounding heights. He was aware of the constant smell of freshly baked white bread wafting from the surface of his clean body, and his mouth was watering from the quiet joy of his presence in life.

In spite of the early hour, the old town was already in turmoil. People were wandering through the bushes and glades on the outskirts, alone or in pairs, but no one was carrying bundles or property of any kind. There was no ringing from any of Chevengur's ten bell towers; all that could be heard was the agitation of the inhabitants beneath the quiet sun of arable fields. Meanwhile, the buildings were slowly moving about—people invisible to Alexey Alexeyevich must have been dragging them somewhere. Before his eyes, a garden suddenly bent forward and set off gracefully into the distance; it too was being uprooted to a better place.

Just outside Chevengur, Alexey Alexeyevich squatted down, to tidy himself up before entering the town. He did not understand the science of Soviet life, but he was attracted by one of its branches—the co-operatives, which he had recently read about in the newspaper *Poverty*.[3] Until then he had lived in silence and, with no task to hold close to, he had lost his peace of mind. In fits of sudden irritation, he had sometimes extinguished the icon lamps in the Red Corner, causing his wife to lie down on her feather bed and let out loud sobs. But after reading about the co-operatives, Alexey Alexeyevich had gone over to the icon of Nikolay the Miracle Maker[4] and lit the lamp with his gentle wheaten hands. He had found his sacred task and a clean path of further life. He now sensed Lenin as he sensed his own dead father, who had once said to little Alexey, when he was scared and bewildered by a distant blaze, "Just come closer, Alyosha, hold me closer!" Alexey had held close to his father, who also smelled of fine wheaten bread; soon he had calmed down and begun to smile sleepily. "And there you were," his father had said to him, "all afraid for some reason." Then Alexey had fallen asleep, still not letting go of his father—and had woken in the morning to the sight of a fire in the stove, lit by his mother so she could bake cabbage pies.

After studying the article about co-operatives, Alexey Alexeyevich took Soviet power to his heart, accepting it as a warm and communal good. A high road of holiness had opened before him, leading to a divine kingdom of everyday contentment and fellowship. Until then, Alexey Alexeyevich had felt only fear of socialism—but now that socialism was called general co-operation, he fell sincerely in love with it. As a child, he had been afraid of Sabaoth, Lord God of Hosts;[5] for a long time he had not loved God. But when his mother said, "But where, my son, do you think I'll go when I die?"—then he began to love God too. Recognizing God as his father's deputy, he wanted him to defend his mother after her death.

Alexey Alexeyevich had come to Chevengur in search of the spirit of co-operation—people's salvation from poverty and mutual savagery of soul.

Alexey Alexeyevich could see from his nearby place that some unknown power of human reason was operating in Chevengur, but he forgave this rational power in advance, since it was acting in the name of people's co-operative unity and a practical, matter-of-fact love among them. Alexey Alexeyevich wanted to obtain a copy of the co-operative regulations and then go to the district ExecCom and have a brotherly chat with the chairman, comrade Chepurny, about the organization of a co-operative network.

Prior to this, however, Alexey Alexeyevich fell into thought, pondering the losses inflicted on Chevengur during the Revolution. Summer dust was rising from the hardworking earth into high places of intense heat. And the sky above the orchards, above the small district churches and the town's stationary property, lay buried in his mind as a touching recollection—even if the nature of this recollection was not something everyone could understand. Alexey Alexeyevich was now fully in possession of himself, feeling the sky's warmth as if it were his own childhood and his mother's skin; as in some distant time long passed into buried eternal memory, nourishment for all people was flowing from the sky's solar center, like a mother's blood along an umbilical cord.

For ages yet, this sun could have illuminated the well-being of Chevengur—its apple orchards, the iron roofs beneath which its inhabitants brought up their children, and the churches' hot, shining domes, timidly summoning mankind from the shade of the trees into the emptiness of round eternity.

Trees grew on almost every street, lending their branches as staffs to wanderers who passed through the town without staying the night. A multitude of grasses flourished in the yards of Chevengur, providing shelter, nourishment, and the meaning of life to whole hordes of insects in the atmosphere's lower reaches. Only partially did Chevengur belong to people; the density of these small and agitated beings was far greater, but this was not something that the old Chevengurians took into account.

What they did take into account were larger-scale events—such as winter storms, the summer heat, and the Second Coming of God.[6] During a hot summer, Chevengurians would warn their neighbors that there wasn't going to be any winter at all and that buildings would soon be catching fire of their own accord. Fathers would order adolescent sons to fetch water from the well and pour it over the outside walls of their houses, to postpone these blazes. After a hot day, it would often begin to rain during the night. "First it's too hot to breathe—and then rain!" people would marvel. "Never in all my born days!" If a blizzard blew up in winter, the Chevengurians knew in advance that they'd have to be clambering up their chimneys the following day—their houses were sure to be buried in snow, even though they all had spades at hand. "Think you'll be able to dig your way out of this with a spade?" an old man would say. "Listen to the wind out there—that's not how it should be in our parts! Uncle Nikanor's older than me. It's eighty years now since he first had a smoke—and even he can't remember such a pestilent winter. Who knows what we're in for now!"

During autumn gales, Chevengurians would lie down for the night on their floors, to rest more steadily and be closer to the earth and their graves. Secretly, every one of them believed that the gale or heat wave in question might turn into the Second Coming, but none of them wanted to leave their home prematurely or die before the fullness of their years—and so, after each gale, heat wave, or spell of extreme cold, they would get together and drink tea.

"It's all over now—the Lord be praised!" they would say, crossing themselves with a happy hand. "We were expecting the coming of Christ, but he's passed us by. May His holy will be done!"

If the old-timers lived without memory, then the rest of the inhabitants simply had no idea at all how to live when the Second Coming might set in any moment and they would all be labeled as either sheep or goats and turned into naked, destitute souls.

Alexey Alexeyevich had once lived for some time in Chevengur, and he was well aware of the precariousness of its spiritual lot. When Chepurny—after walking seventy versts from the railway station—had first assumed power over Chevengur and its district, he had thought that the whole town must be living by brigandry; it was clear that no one was doing any work at all, yet everyone ate bread and drank tea. And so he had sent out a questionnaire—a single question to which it was mandatory to reply: "To what purpose and on account of what production of substance do you live in the workers' state?"

Most of the population had given one and the same reply—first thought up by Lobochikhin, the church singer.[7] His neighbors had copied it out and then passed it on orally: "We live not for our own sake, but for the sake of the Lord."

Unable to imagine a godly life, Chepurny had set up a commission of forty to carry out a twenty-four-hour, household-by-household investigation. And he had studied the few clearer answers to his questionnaire. Among the occupations named were: key duties in town prison; expectation of the truth of life; impatience toward God; mortal venerability; reading aloud to wanderers and pilgrims; and fellowship with Soviet power. The complexity of civilian occupations was beginning to occasion him mental anguish, but, just in time, he recalled Lenin's slogan, "Directing a state is devilishly difficult."[8] This had brought him a sense of total calm. His forty men had appeared early the following morning, stopped in the entrance room for a drink of water after the long distance they had covered, and announced, "They're lying, comrade Chepurny. They do no work at all. They just lie there and sleep."

Chepurny was not stupid. "What's got into you all?" he had exclaimed. "It was nighttime. But what about their ideology? Can't you tell me anything about that!"

"They have no ideology," the commission's chairman had replied. "They're all just waiting for the end of the world."

"Did you tell them that ending the world now would be a counter-revolutionary measure?" Chepurny had asked. As a precaution, he was long accustomed to assessing every measure in relation to the revolutionary cause.

This had frightened the man. "No, comrade Chepurny! I thought that the Second Coming would suit them, and that it would be in our interests too."

"What do you mean?" Chepurny had asked sternly.

"No two ways about it," the man had replied. "As far as we're concerned, the Second Coming would be invalid. But as for the petty bourgeoisie, they'd be liable to elimination."

"You're right, you son of a bitch!" Chepurny had exclaimed, gripped by new understanding. "But how come I didn't work that out for myself? I'm meant to be smarter than you."

At this point, one of the forty had stepped modestly forward and said, "Comrade Chepurny, if I may—"

"And who are you?" Chepurny had never seen this man's face before, though he remembered everyone else's appearance by heart.

"Comrade Chepurny, my family name is Poliubezev and I am the chairman of the liquidation committee for the *zemstvo* affairs of the Chevengur District within its old boundaries.[9] I was nominated to this commission by that committee. I have with me a copy of the minutes of the committee meeting in question."

Alexey Alexeyevich Poliubezev had then bowed and stretched out a hand toward Chepurny.

"Does such a committee exist?" Chepurny asked in surprise, not acknowledging Alexey Alexeyevich's hand.

"Yes," came a reply from within the mass of the committee.

"Abolish it immediately, without further ado! Check whether there are any other surviving remnants of tsardom—and have them destroyed too!" After issuing these orders, Chepurny turned to Alexey Alexeyevich. "Please speak, citizen!"

Alexey Alexeyevich had then explained the town's production of substance with clarity and in scrupulous detail, thus further obscuring Chepurny's clear head. Chepurny's memory was vast but disordered. He absorbed life in bits and pieces. Fragments of the world he had seen and events he had encountered floated about inside his head as in a quiet lake, but these fragments, lacking any connections or living sense, never stuck together to form a single whole. He remembered wattle fences from Tambov Province, the faces and family names of beggars, and an artillery emplacement at the front. He knew Lenin's teachings to the letter. But these clear memories all floated about his mind elementally and did not amount to any useful understanding.

According to Alexey Alexeyevich, people had walked across the level steppe, seeking an existence for themselves somewhere distant. Their road was long, and they brought nothing from their homes other than their own bodies. And so they had exchanged their working flesh for nourishment—and Chevengur had gradually come into being, its population maturing. The migrant workers had then left, but the town had remained, relying on God.

"Did you too exchange your working body for a piffle of nourishment?" Chepurny had asked.

"No. I'm an office worker. My business is thought on paper."

"I just sensed a movement of talented feeling," Chepurny had continued. "Our first priority, I sense, must be to liquidate the flesh of nonlaboring elements. If only I had a secretary, someone to note me down straightaway."

Alexey Alexeyevich had not seen Chepurny since that day, and he did not know what had been happening in Chevengur. The *zemstvo* committee had, of course, been swiftly and forever abolished, its members dispersing to go and live with their relatives. Now, though, Alexey Alexeyevich had other matters to discuss with Chepurny. Thanks to the co-operative movement announced by Lenin, he now sensed something alive and sacred within socialism, and he wished

Soviet power well. Alexey Alexeyevich did not encounter a single person he knew—only some thin men wandering about and thinking about something to come. Close to the town boundary, twenty men were quietly relocating a wooden house. Two men on horseback were joyfully observing this work.

Recognizing one of these two horsemen, Alexey Alexeyevich called out, "Comrade Chepurny, may I invite you to join me for a brief discussion?"

"Alexey Alexeyevich!" replied Chepurny, who remembered everything real and concrete. "Please say whatever needs to be said."

"I want to speak briefly about co-operatives. Comrade Chepurny, have you read about the ethical path toward socialism outlined in the newspaper for the destitute titled *Poverty*?"

Chepurny had read nothing of the kind.

"What co-operatives? What pathway, when we've already reached our goal? What's got into you, dear citizen? You people were living for the sake of God, in the way of the workers. Now, my brother, the paths have all disappeared—everyone has arrived."

"Arrived where?" Alexey Alexeyevich asked meekly, losing the co-operative hope in his heart.

"Where do you think? The communism of life. Have you read Karl Marx?"

"No, comrade Chepurny."

"Well, you really should, dear comrade. History has ended—and you haven't even noticed."

Alexey Alexeyevich withdrew into unquestioning silence and set off into the distance, where old grasses were growing, former people lived, and where his old woman was waiting for her husband. Life might be sad and difficult there, but it was where Alexey Alexeyevich had been born and raised and had sometimes cried in his childhood and youth. He recalled his furniture, his rickety old hut, and his wife; he was glad that they too did not know Karl Marx and so would not wish to part from their husband and master.

31

KOPIONKIN had never found time to read Karl Marx. Confronted with Chepurny's erudition, he felt troubled.

"Is that really so?" he asked. "Does everyone here have to read Karl Marx?"

Chepurny allayed Kopionkin's anxiety. "No, I just wanted to scare the man. I haven't read him either, not in all my born days. I've just picked up a little at rallies and demonstrations—enough for agitation and propaganda. And there's really no need to read anything at all. In the old days, people read and wrote, but they didn't do any goddamn living. Yes, brother—all the swindlers ever did was seek out paths for others!"

Kopionkin looked around him. "Why are people moving houses about and carrying gardens around in their arms?" he asked.

"Today's a volunteer Saturday," Chepurny explained.[1] "People made the journey here on foot. And now they're eager to live in comradely closeness."

Like everyone else in the town, Chepurny had no defined place of residence. And so, Chepurny and Kopionkin went into a brick house that the participants in the volunteer Saturday had been unable to shift. Two men who looked like wanderers were sleeping in the kitchen on knapsacks, while a third was artfully frying some potatoes, using water from a cold kettle instead of oil.

"Comrade Piusia!"[2] Chepurny said to this man.

"What d'you want?"

"Any idea where I can find comrade Prokofy?"

Piusia took his time to answer this unimportant question. After struggling a little longer with his burnt potatoes, he said, "He's gone somewhere with your woman."

"You stay here," Chepurny said to Kopionkin. "I'll go and look for Klavdiusha. The woman's a real sweetheart."

Kopionkin unharnessed himself, spread his clothes out on the floor, and lay down half-naked, piling his inseparable weapons close beside him. It was warm in Chevengur and Kopionkin could smell the spirit of comradeship. Nevertheless, if only out of exhaustion, he felt sad and his heart longed to ride on somewhere farther. He had not yet seen in Chevengur any sign of clear, evident socialism—of a beauty amid nature so touching, so steadfast and edifying that it might be the birthplace of a second Rosa Luxemburg or a place for the scientific resurrection of the first, who had perished on German bourgeois soil. Kopionkin had already asked Chepurny what needed to be done in Chevengur. And Chepurny had replied, "Nothing. We don't have needs or tasks. You can live for yourself, internally! Life's good here in Chevengur—we've mobilized the sun for eternal work and disbanded society forever."[3]

Kopionkin saw that he was stupider than Chepurny and remained meekly silent. Before this, on the way to Chevengur, he had timidly asked Chepurny what Rosa Luxemburg would be doing if she were there with them now. All Chepurny had said in reply was, "Soon as we get to Chevengur, go and ask our Prokofy. He can express everything clearly—all I do is guide him with hunches of revolutionary foresight. Think I've been speaking words of my own? No, they're words I've been taught by Prokofy!"

After managing at last to fry his potatoes in water, Piusia woke the two sleeping wanderers. Kopionkin also got up to have something to eat—in order to fall asleep sooner, on a full stomach, and cease feeling sad.

"Is it true that people live well here in Chevengur?" he asked Piusia.

"They don't complain," Piusia answered slowly.

"But where can you see real socialism here?"

"Your eyes are fresh, you can see best," Piusia explained reluctantly. "Chepurny says that, after two years here, we're blinded by habit—and that stops us seeing freedom or other good things."

"Who lived here before you?"

"Bourgeoisie. Me and Chepurny organized a second coming for them."

"That's not possible. We have science now."

"So what?"

"Fill me in. Tell me the whole story."

"Think I'm some kind of storyteller? There was just an unexpected event, instigated by an ordinary committee."

"'Extra-ordinary,' you mean?"

"Yes, that's it. The Cheka."[4]

"Ah," said Kopionkin with confused understanding. "Then all's as it should be."

Strength of the Proletariat, tethered to the wattle fence outside, was snarling quietly at some men clustered around him. There were many people wanting to saddle this unknown, powerful horse and ride around Chevengur along the boundary road. But Strength of the Proletariat sullenly kept them at a distance, by means of his teeth, muzzle, and hooves.

"But you belong to the people now," one thin Chevengurian said gently. "Why act up?"

Hearing the mournful voice of his steed, Kopionkin went out to join him.

"Keep your distance," he said to these free people. "Can't you see, you goggling fools? The horse has a heart of his own."

"We can see all right," another Chevengurian replied with conviction. "We live in a comradely way, but your horse is a bourgeois."

Forgetting his respect for the oppressed before him, Kopionkin defended his steed's proletarian honor.

"You're lying, you vagabond. The Revolution's been riding my horse for five years now—and the Revolution's carried you a long way on its strong back!"

Kopionkin was unable to articulate his irritation further. He indistinctly sensed that these people were a great deal cleverer than himself, but such alien mind made him feel lonely. He remembered Dvanov, who always fulfilled whatever life brought him, ahead of reason and usefulness—and felt how deeply he missed him.

The blue heights standing over Chevengur filled Kopionkin with anguish; the road to his friend lay beyond the strength of his steed.

Gripped by sorrow, suspicion, and alarmed rage, Kopionkin decided there and then, on the spot and in the raw, to carry out an inspection of the Revolution in Chevengur. "Is this whole town simply a brigandry reserve?" he thought jealously. "I'll give these reptiles a taste of communism right now—I'll ram it right down their gullets."

Kopionkin drank some water in the kitchen and girded himself up. "The swine," he said to himself with growing indignation. "Even my horse has taken against them. They think communism's an empty piffle, just a matter of reason and material benefit. But what about the body of communism—where's that to be seen?"

Kopionkin's horse was always ready for urgent martial service. With the resonant passion of pent-up strength, he accepted Kopionkin onto his spacious, comradely back.

"Gallop ahead of me, show me the soviet!" Kopionkin called out threateningly to an unknown passerby on the street. The man tried to explain his position, but Kopionkin unsheathed his saber—and the man began to run, keeping pace with Strength of the Proletariat. Sometimes the man turned round and yelled out reproaches, saying that in Chevengur man neither labored nor ran, and that all taxes and obligations were now borne by the sun.

"Can everyone here be on convalescent leave?" Kopionkin doubted silently. "Or were field hospitals located here during the tsarist war?"

Then he called out again to the man on the run, "Are you telling me the sun should be running in front of my horse—while you lie flat on your back?"

The Chevengurian seized hold of a stirrup, to calm his rapid breathing and answer this question. "Here, comrade, man is allowed rest. It was only the bourgeoisie who were always hurrying. They needed to guzzle and oppress. But we eat calmly and are friends to one another...There now—there's your soviet."

Kopionkin slowly read an enormous crimson sign over the cemetery gate: SOVIET OF SOCIAL HUMANITY OF THE CHEVENGUR LIBERATED DISTRICT.

The soviet itself was located inside the church.[5] Kopionkin rode down a path through the cemetery to the church porch. In an arc over the main door were the words COME UNTO ME, ALL YE THAT LABOR AND ARE HEAVY LADEN, AND I WILL GIVE YOU REST.[6] And these words touched Kopionkin, though he had not forgotten whose slogan this was.

"But what about my own rest?" he thought—and saw exhaustion deep in his heart. "But no," he continued, addressing the slogan's author, "you'll never grant rest to anyone at all. You're not a class but an individual person! Today you'd be an SR, and I'd be writing you off."[7]

Without stooping, Strength of the Proletariat walked through into the central part of the cool church. His rider felt the surprise of a childhood suddenly returned to him, as if finding himself in his home village, in his grandmother's storeroom. It was not the first time Kopionkin had come across forgotten childhood places in these parts where he now lived, wandered, and battled. Long ago he had prayed in a village church just like this, but the place to which he had gone home afterward had been the cramped warmth of his mother—and it was possible that what constituted his childhood had been neither churches, nor the voices of the now-dead birds who had been his childhood companions, nor terrifying old men wandering in summer toward the holy mysteries of Kyiv. It may well be that what mattered most in Kopionkin's childhood had been the excitement of a small boy when he has a living mother and the summer air smells of the hem of her skirt. At that time of ascent, all old men truly do seem to be riddles, because their mothers have died—yet they still live on and don't cry.

At that time, when Kopionkin rode into the church, the Revolution was yet poorer than Faith and unable even to cover the icons with red cloth. A painted Lord Sabaoth looked down from the cupola onto the ambo, the raised platform where the RevCom met for its regular sessions.[8] At this moment, three people were sitting at a table painted a bold red. One was Chepurny, chairman of the district ExecCom; the second was a young man; and the third was a young woman with a cheerful, attentive face who could have been the Communist woman of the future. The young man, who had a copy of Yevtushevsky's arithmetic primer lying in front of him, was trying to prove to Chepurny that the sun was twelve times bigger than the Earth and that its powers were more than enough for everyone.[9]

"Stop thinking, Prokofy," Chepurny ordered. "It's for me to think—and for you to formulate."[10]

"You can feel this for yourself, comrade Chepurny," the young man went on without stopping. "What's the use of man fussing about if it's not scientific? You could gather everyone in the world together, for a single joint thrust—but even then they'd be as powerless against the sun as a smallholder against a commune. A waste of time—believe me!"

Chepurny half closed his eyes for the sake of greater concentration. "One moment you speak truth, the next you speak nonsense. Go along to the sanctuary and lie down with Klavdiusha—I need to feel out what you've said and check whether or not you're right."

Kopionkin reined in the weighty steps of his steed and declared his intention—to investigate the whole of Chevengur urgently and immediately. What if the town concealed a secret counterrevolutionary hotbed? "You're all very wise here," he concluded. "And smart minds are crafty—constantly thinking up ways to oppress the quiet ones."

Kopionkin had at once recognized the young man as a predator. His eyes were black and opaque. His whole face bore a bourgeois outlook, and there was something shameful about the flaring, snifferdog nose in its center. Honorable Communists have noses flat as bast shoes and eyes gray with trustfulness and fellow feeling.

"And you, my man, are a swindler," Kopionkin deduced. "Show me your documents."

"Here, brother!" the young man agreed good-humoredly.

Kopionkin took his papers. Before him, it appeared, was Prokofy Dvanov, a party member since August 1917.

"Do you know Sasha?" he asked, temporarily pardoning the man his oppressive face because of his family name.

"Yes, I knew him when I was little," the young man replied, smiling from superfluous mind.

"Chepurny must furnish me with a clean sheet of paper," Kopionkin ordered. "We shall call Sasha here. We must pit mind against mind, to ignite the sparks of communism."

"We've abolished the postal service, comrade," said Chepurny. "People live in a huddle and see one another in person. What do they want the post for, I ask you now! Here, my brother, proletarians are already bound tightly together."

Kopionkin felt no particular regret with regard to the post. During his life he had received just two letters and written only one. While fighting in the imperialist war, he had been informed that his wife had died; he had then needed to weep over her with the family, if only from a distance.

"Will anyone be going to the provincial capital on foot?" Kopionkin asked Chepurny.

"We have a foot-walker messenger," Chepurny remembered.

"Who's that, Chepurny?" asked the young woman held dear by both Chevengurians. She truly was very dear. Kopionkin even sensed that, were he still a young lad, he would embrace such a woman and hold her for a long time. From this woman emanated a slow, cool sense of peace.

"Mishka Luy, of course!" Chepurny reminded her. "His feet just eat up the road. Trouble is, you can send him to the provincial capital, but he'll end up in Moscow or Kharkiv—and you won't see him again till the next change of season. Not till the first snows are settling, or the first flowers are pushing up."

"I'll commission him," said Kopionkin. "Then he'll be back here in short order."

"Yes, he can go," Chepurny agreed. "To him, the road isn't labor—it's the development of life!"

"Chepurny," said the woman. "Give Luy some flour to barter. Then he can bring back a little shawl for me."

"Certainly, Klavdia Parfionovna," Prokofy reassured her. "We'll make the most of this opportunity."

In block letters, Kopionkin wrote a note for Dvanov:

SASHA, DEAR COMRADE AND FRIEND! HERE WE HAVE COMMUNISM AND BACK AGAIN. YOUR PRESENCE IS NEEDED, URGENTLY. NO ONE WORKS HERE—ONLY THE SUMMER SUN. PEOPLE MERELY BEFRIEND ONE ANOTHER WITHOUT LOVE. WOMEN EXTORT SHAWLS. THE WOMEN ARE SWEET, AND THEREFORE ALL THE MORE HARMFUL. I DO NOT MUCH LIKE YOUR BROTHER OR COUSIN. BUT THEN I'M NO SUBJECT, A MERE ABJECT BLOCKHEAD. I KEEP MY FEW THOUGHTS TO MYSELF, SINCE I AM FAR FROM RESPECTED HERE. THERE ARE NO EVENTS. THEY SAY IT'S SCIENCE AND HISTORY, BUT WHO KNOWS? WITH REVOLUTIONARY ESTEEM, KOPIONKIN. FOR THE SAKE OF OUR COMMON IDEALS, RIDE HERE AND JOIN US.

"Somehow I'm always thinking, seeing, and imagining things—it's hard on my heart," Chepurny confessed tormentedly into the dark air of the church. "Sometimes communism seems in good shape here, sometimes not. Perhaps I should go and see comrade Lenin, so he can formulate the whole truth for me in person!"

"Good idea, comrade Chepurny!" said Prokofy. "Comrade Lenin will give you a slogan—and you can bring it straight back to us. We can't go on like this, with my one head doing all the thinking. The vanguard tires too. Moreover, I don't receive any special benefits."

"And the work done by my heart?" replied Chepurny, upset by these words. "Doesn't that count for anything?"

Prokofy evidently valued his powers of reason and lost none of his dependable calm. "Feeling, comrade Chepurny, is elemental—a matter for the masses. Whereas thought is organization—and comrade Lenin tells us that nothing is of higher value to us than organization."

"So I must suffer, while you think thoughts. Which is worse?"

"Comrade Chepurny, I'll go to Moscow with you," the young woman announced. "I've never seen our central capital. I've heard it's quite something!"

"Whatever next!" snapped Kopionkin. "Take the creature straight to Lenin, Chepurny. 'Here you are,' you can say, 'a Chevengur woman, all primed for communism.' You're swindlers and swine, all of you."

"Are you saying something's wrong here?" Chepurny asked sharply.

"Very wrong!"

"But what would be right, comrade Kopionkin? My feelings have exhausted themselves."

"How would I know? My task is to see off enemy forces. When I've done that, what we need will come into being, all of itself."

Prokofy was smoking. He did not once interrupt Kopionkin. He was wondering how best to turn this unorganized armed force to the service of the Revolution.

"Klavdia Parfionovna, let's go out for a stroll and a little fun," Prokofy proposed with studied politeness. "Or you might start to feel weak."

As the couple went out toward the porch, Kopionkin gestured after them and said to Chepurny, "They're bourgeoisie. Keep that in mind."

"Really?"

"I mean what I say."

"What are we to do then? Subtract them from Chevengur?"

"Don't sow burdens of panic. Let communism be translated from idea into body—by means of an armed hand. Just wait till Sasha Dvanov appears—he'll show you what's what!"

"A smart fellow, is he?" Chepurny asked timidly.

"Comrade, he has blood thinking in his head, while your Prokofy has only bone." Kopionkin spoke with pride, articulating each syllable. "Understand?" Holding out his letter for Dvanov, he went on: "Here—set comrade Luy in motion!"

With all his tension of thought, Chepurny was unable to think up anything for himself—he could recall only useless, forgotten events that gave him no sense of truth. One moment, his mind saw Catholic churches in a forest they had marched through during the tsarist war.[11] Another moment, there was an orphan girl sitting beside a ditch and eating chervil—but when he had seen this little girl so uselessly preserved in his soul he would now never know. Nor was it even possible to say whether she was alive at all. For all he knew, Klavdiusha might be this very same girl—in which case she really was outstandingly beautiful and it would be sad to part with her.

"What are you gaping at?" asked Kopionkin. "Feeling ill?"

"My life's rushing past inside me," Chepurny replied, sounding tired and sad. "Like scraps of cloud in the wind."

"So that's what's weakening you," said Kopionkin, in sympathetic reproach. "Better if your life were like a real storm cloud! Let's go outside, somewhere fresh—this church smells of dank god."

"Yes, let's go—get your horse," Chepurny said with relief. "I'll be stronger out in the open."

As they went out, Kopionkin pointed to the words over the door of the RevCom church: COME UNTO ME, ALL YE THAT LABOR.

"Get that redone, Soviet style!"

"There's no one to think up the words, comrade Kopionkin."

"What about Prokofy?"

"That's beyond him—he's not so very deep. He can manage a subject, but predicates are beyond him.[12] I'll make your Dvanov my secretary—then Prokofy can play about all he likes. But tell me, why don't you like that sentence up there? It speaks totally against capitalism."

Kopionkin frowned fiercely.

"You reckon God's going to give peace to the masses all of his own accord? That's bourgeois thinking, comrade Chepurny. Once the masses rise up in revolution, they'll find peace and rest for themselves!"

Chepurny looked around him, at the town that constituted his ideal. The quiet evening now setting in was similar to Chepurny's aching doubt, to a premonition unable to exhaust itself through thought and so come to rest. Chepurny did not know that there is a universal truth and meaning of life—he had seen too many different people to think they might follow a single law. Prokofy had once proposed to Chepurny that they introduce science and enlightenment in Chevengur, but Chepurny had categorically vetoed any such attempt. "What's gotten into you?" he had replied. "Do you not realize what science is like? It'll be a returning point for the entire bourgeoisie. Every capitalist will suddenly make out he's a scientist and start salting organisms with some powder or other—and just you try arguing with them then! And after that science will keep on developing—and there's no knowing where it will end."

Chepurny had fallen seriously ill during the tsarist war and had learned medicine by heart. After recovering, he had qualified as a company field medic, but he still saw doctors as intellectual exploiters and oppressors.

"What do you think?" he asked Kopionkin. "This Dvanov of yours won't try to introduce science here in Chevengur, will he?"

"I've never heard him say anything about science. All that matters to him is communism."

"There are things that frighten me," Chepurny confessed. He then did his best to think. At the right moment, though, he remembered Prokofy, who had once found just the words he needed for his suspicion of science. "Under my supervision," Chepurny went on, "Prokofy formulated that a mind is no different from a house. Both are forms of property—and are therefore oppressors of the unscientific and all who have been enfeebled."

"Then you should arm the fools," Kopionkin replied, deftly resolving this problem. "That'll sort out the smart ones creeping about with their powders. Who do you take me for? I'm a fool too, brother—yet I live freer than free."

People were passing feebly by on the streets. Some had been moving houses about, others had been dragging gardens around in their arms. Now they were on their way to rest, talk, and live out the rest of the day amid their circle of comrades. There would be no labor or other occupations awaiting them the following day, since the sun—honored in Chevengur as the universal proletarian—now worked alone in the town on behalf of all and for the sake of all.[13] People were not obliged to carry out any work whatsoever. At Chepurny's instigation, Prokofy had come up with a particular interpretation of labor, declaring it once and for all to be a surviving remnant of bourgeois greed and animal-exploitative voluptuousness, since labor led to the creation of property, and property to oppression. The sun itself issued rations entirely adequate to support people, and any augmentation of these rations through deliberate human labor merely fed the bonfire of class warfare, since it led to the creation of superfluous harmful objects.

Having already come to some understanding of the solar system of Chevengur life, Kopionkin was surprised to discover that the Chevengurians worked every Saturday. Chepurny explained to him, "No, this isn't labor—these are voluntary Saturdays. Prokofy understood me perfectly. He came out with some grand words."

"Who is this Prokofy—your diviner, or something?" Kopionkin asked, with skepticism.

"No, not exactly. His narrow mind weakens my grand feelings. But he knows words, and without him I'd be living in mute torment. And there's no property production during these Saturdays—you don't think I'd permit such a thing, do you? Voluntary destruction of the petty-bourgeois inheritance, that's all that takes place on these days. And what oppression, I ask you now, can there be in that!"

"None whatsoever," Kopionkin agreed, with sincerity.

Chepurny and Kopionkin came to a shed that had been dragged out into the middle of a street.

"You should go and join your Klavdiusha," said Kopionkin. "You don't want to upset the woman!"

"Prokofy's taken her off to some unknown spot. Let him enjoy himself—we're all equal proletarians. He's explained to me that I'm no better a man than he is."

"But you said only just now that you have grand feelings—and that's the kind of man a woman needs."

Chepurny felt perplexed. Kopionkin's words were true. But his heart was aching and his mind was able to think.

"Comrade Kopionkin," he said, "my grand feelings ache in my chest—not down in my young parts."

"I see," said Kopionkin. "Well, in that case, stay here in the shed with me. My heart's in a bad way too."

Strength of the Proletariat chewed through all the grass that Kopionkin had scythed on the town square and, at midnight, he too lay down on the shed floor. The horse slept the way some children sleep, with half-open eyes. Through these eyes, and with a kind of sleepy meekness, he watched Kopionkin, who now lacked consciousness and was groaning from a sad, obscured sense of oblivion.

The communism of Chevengur was defenseless during these dark steppe hours, since people had temporarily curtailed their convictions, allowing the power of sleep to heal the exhaustion occasioned by their inner life of the previous day.

32

CHEVENGUR had taken to waking up late; its inhabitants were recovering from centuries of oppression and needed all the rest they could get. The Revolution had won dreams for the district of Chevengur, and the main profession there was now the soul.

Luy, the Chevengur foot-walker, was progressing at a full pace toward the provincial capital. On him he had the letter to Sasha Dvanov, and also some rusks and a birch bark water flask, now warming against his body. He had set off at an hour when only the ants and hens were up and about, and the sun had yet to bare the last corners of sky. Walking, and the intoxicating freshness of the air, had released Luy from doubts of thought and desire; the road was consuming him and freeing him from all excess of harmful life. Back in his youth he had figured out on his own how a stone can fly: because the joy of movement makes it lighter than air. Without knowing letters or books, Luy arrived at the conviction that communism must be the perpetual movement of people into the farthest parts of the earth. He had spoken about this to Chepurny many times, asking him to declare that communism meant journeying, and to liberate Chevengur from its eternity of stasis.

Anguished by the shortness of the town streets, Luy had said at a RevCom meeting, "Who does a man resemble—a horse or a tree? Tell me in all honesty!"

"He resembles something higher!" Prokofy parried. "He's like the open ocean, dear comrade. He's like the harmony of schemes and spheres!"

Luy had never seen any other water than that of rivers and lakes, and the only harmony he knew was that of the squeeze-box.

"I'd say a man was more like a horse," declared Chepurny, recalling horses he knew.

"I know what you mean," said Prokofy, continuing Chepurny's feelings. "A horse has a chest with a heart, and a noble face with eyes, but a tree doesn't."

"Exactly so, Prosha!" Chepurny said joyfully.

"That's why I said it!" Prokofy confirmed.

"Entirely true!" Chepurny approved in conclusion.

This satisfied Luy, and he proposed to the RevCom that they move Chevengur into the distance without delay. "A man needs to be bathed by the wind," he asserted. "Otherwise he'll go back to oppressing the weak in strength, or else he'll simply dry up of himself and start pining! But there's no getting away from friendship when you're on the road—and there'll be plenty for communism to do!"[1]

Chepurny made Prokofy take a precise note of Luy's proposal and it was duly discussed at a committee meeting. Although he sensed the fundamental truth of Luy's words, Chepurny did not give Prokofy any guiding intuitions, and so the meeting labored heavily on throughout that spring day. Finally Prokofy came up with a formal counterproposal: "In view of the impending epoch of wars and revolutions, the movement of people must be considered a most urgent indication of communism; more precisely, the district's whole population must launch itself against capitalism once the latter's crisis has well and truly come to a head, and from then on our victorious march must never halt, tempering people into a sense of comradeship on the roads of the entire terrestrial globe. In the meantime, however, it is appropriate to limit communism to the territory already wrested from the bourgeoisie, in order for us to have something to govern."[2]

"No, comrades," retorted Luy, rational as ever. "Communism cannot come to be in sedentary stasis. It would have neither enemy, nor joy."

Chepurny listened and Prokofy observed him attentively, unable to divine his vacillating feelings. "Comrade Chepurny," Prokofy tried to resolve the matter, "the liberation of the workers is the workers' own affair. Let Luy leave and liberate himself step by step. What business is it of ours?"

"Correct!" Chepurny concluded abruptly. "Keep walking, Luy. Movement is a matter for the masses—it's not for us to be tripping them up."

"Well then," said Luy, "thank you!" He bowed to the RevCom and went off in search of an imperative need to leave Chevengur for some other place.

A few days afterward Luy saw Kopionkin on his stout horse and at once felt ashamed that Kopionkin was going somewhere, whereas he, Luy, was living in a fixed place. Luy then wanted to get away even more, and still farther. Before his departure, however, he would have liked to make something of fellow feeling for Kopionkin—but what could he make it from? In Chevengur there were no things for presents. All he could do would be to water Kopionkin's horse, but Kopionkin strictly forbade strangers to approach his horse and always watered him in person. The world was full of houses and substances; the only ones lacking—Luy realized with regret—were those that signify the fellowship of people.

Luy resolved not to return to Chevengur from the provincial capital, but to make his way as far as Petrograd and then join the fleet and set off on a voyage, constantly observing the earth, the seas, and people—as total nourishment for his fraternal soul. When he came to a ridge high above the Chevengur valleys, Luy looked back at the town and the morning light: "Farewell, communism and comrades! If I live, I will recall each one of you!"

Kopionkin was exercising Strength of the Proletariat out beyond the town boundary, and he saw Luy on his high place.

"Looks as though the vagabond's turning off toward Kharkiv," Kopionkin said to himself. "While I'm stuck here in Chevengur—and the golden days of the Revolution are passing me by!" Kopionkin turned his horse back toward the town and set off at a steppe march, in order to investigate the whole of communism that very day, definitively, and to undertake his own measures.

Due to relocation of buildings, there were no longer any streets in Chevengur; the buildings all stood not in one place, but on the move. Strength of the Proletariat, accustomed to straight, even roads, grew agitated and broke into a sweat from the frequent turns.

Beside one lost and lopsided barn a young man and woman were lying under a single sheepskin; judging from her torso, the woman was Klavdiusha. Kopionkin carefully guided his horse around the sleepers; he felt embarrassed in the presence of youth, which he respected as the realm of the great future. It was for this same youthfulness, embellished by an indifference toward women, that he had come to love and respect Sasha Dvanov, his companion during the course of the Revolution.

From somewhere in the thick of the buildings came a protracted whistle. Kopionkin pricked up his ears. The whistling stopped.

"*Ko-pion-kin!* Comrade Kopionkin, let's go for a swim!" It was Chepurny, shouting somewhere nearby.

"Keep whistling! I'll head for your sound!" Kopionkin replied in a deep, deafening voice.

Chepurny began whistling vigorously, and Kopionkin continued to edge his way on horseback through the crevices of the jumbled town. Chepurny was standing just outside a shed, barefoot and with only a greatcoat over his naked body. Two of his fingers were in his mouth, for power of whistle, while his eyes were looking up into the solar height, where the sun's heat was now running wild.

After locking Strength of the Proletariat inside a shed, Kopionkin set off after the barefoot Chepurny, who on that day was happy, having once and for all become the brother of all men. On their way to the river they came across a multitude of now-awake Chevengurians—entirely ordinary people, except that they looked poor and were clearly not from these parts.

"A summer's day is long. What are they going to do with themselves?" asked Kopionkin.

"Are you asking about their zeal?" Chepurny responded, not quite understanding.

"Something like that."

"But a man's soul is his main profession. And its product is friendship and comradeship! What's wrong with that, I ask you now! Isn't that enough of an occupation for you?"

Kopionkin thought a little about the previous life of oppression. "Things are too damned good in your Chevengur," he said wistfully. "We may need to organize some grief. Communism needs to be caustic—a pinch of poison makes a dish tastier."

In his mouth Chepurny sensed the taste of fresh salt—and at once understood Kopionkin. "I think you're right. We must set about the deliberate organization of grief. Shall we start on that tomorrow, comrade Kopionkin?"

"No, I have other work. Wait till Sasha Dvanov comes. He'll understand everything for you."

"We could delegate it to Prokofy."

"Forget that Prokofy of yours. The lad just wants to reproduce with your Klavdiusha, but you keep trying to involve him!"

"Maybe you're right. We'll wait for your comrade-in-arms."

Inexhaustible water was rippling against the bank of the Chevengurka, and the air rising from it smelled of excitement and freedom; the two comrades began to bare themselves, to meet the water head-on. Chepurny threw off his greatcoat and at once looked naked and pitiful—yet his body gave off a warm smell of some kind of motherliness, long grown over and congealed, almost beyond Kopionkin's memory.

The sun then gave Chepurny its personal attention, lighting up his thin back and slipping inside all the sweaty fissures and flaws of his skin, in order to destroy with its heat the invisible creatures that make a body constantly itch. Kopionkin looked at the sun with respect; a few years earlier it had warmed Rosa Luxemburg and now it was helping the grass to live on her grave.

It was a long time since Kopionkin had been in a river, and he shivered for a while before getting used to the cold. But Chepurny swam boldly, opening his eyes under the water and bringing up from the bottom large pebbles, horses' heads, and bones of all kinds. From the middle of the river, which was farther than the clumsy Kopionkin could swim, Chepurny yelled out songs and became more and more loquacious. Kopionkin splashed about in the shallows, felt the water with his hands, and said to himself, "The river's like us—heading for some place where it'll feel good."

Chepurny swam back, bright and happy.

"You know, Kopionkin, when I'm in the water, I think I know the truth with utmost precision. But when I'm at the RevCom, it's all just thoughts and imaginings."

"Then you should work by the bank of the river."

"Theses from the provincial capital would get wet in the rain. You're a fool!"

Kopionkin did not know what a thesis was. He remembered the word from somewhere, but it carried no feelings with it. "It rains, and then the sun shines—so don't you worry about your theses," he said reassuringly. "The crops will come up anyway."

With effort Chepurny counted in his mind, helping his mind with his fingers. "So you're proclaiming three theses, are you?"

"We don't even need one," retorted Kopionkin. "It's only songs you have to write down to remember them."

"What do you mean? The sun's your first thesis, water's your second, and the soil's the third."

"What about the wind?"

"All right—four theses. Yes, you're right. Only you should know that if we don't answer these theses from the provincial capital and confirm that everything's fine here, they'll come and liquidate the whole of our communism."

"No way," Kopionkin thrust aside such a thought. "The people there are no different from us."

"No different from us, but they write what we can't understand and then, you know, they keep asking us to take better stock and to lead people more firmly. But what are we to take stock of, and what part of a body are we to lead people by?"

"What do they take us for?" Kopionkin asked in surprise. "Surely they don't think we'd let reptiles worm their way in? We have Lenin living behind us!"

Chepurny absentmindedly made his way through the rushes and picked some pale flowers; they were a feeble, nighttime color. He would give them to Klavdiusha; he possessed her little, but this only strengthened his attentive tenderness toward her.

After the flowers, Chepurny and Kopionkin got dressed and began to walk along the riverbank, over its moist mantle of grass. From there Chevengur seemed like some warm country—they could see barefoot people lit by the sun. Their heads were uncovered and they were enjoying the air and freedom.

"Things are good today," said Chepurny abstractedly. "All man's warmth is on the outside!" he said, pointing to the town and everyone in it. He then put two fingers in his mouth again, whistled, and in a delirium of ardent inner life made his way back into the water, without taking off his greatcoat. Driven by some black joy of abundant body, he flung himself through the rushes and into the clear river, to rid himself there of his obscure, yearning passions.

"The vagabond's full of joy—he thinks he's released the whole world into the freedom of communism!" Kopionkin said to himself crossly. "But I can't see that myself."

There was a boat in the rushes, and a naked man sitting in it in silence. He was gazing thoughtfully at the far bank, although he could have reached it in his boat. Kopionkin saw his weak, ribby body, and his ailing eye.

"You're Pashintsev, aren't you?" asked Kopionkin.

"Yes. Who else would I be?" the man answered at once.

"Then how come you've abandoned your post in the Revolution Reserve?"

Pashintsev sadly lowered his humbled head. "I have been basely exiled, comrade—cast down into the pit!"

"What about your grenades?"

"Seems I defused them too early. And so here I am now, wandering around without honor, like some tragical crackpot."

Kopionkin felt scorn for the faraway White thugs who had liquidated the RevReserve—and within him he felt an answering power of courage.[3] "Don't grieve, comrade Pashintsev. We'll finish off the

Whites without even leaving our saddles, and we'll replant your Reserve on fresh ground. What do you have left?"

From the bottom of his boat Pashintsev picked up a chainmail shirt.

"Not much," said Kopionkin. "All it defends is your chest."

"Who cares about heads?" said Pashintsev. "What's dearest to me is my heart. But I do have something to put on my head—and to hold in my hand." Pashintsev held up another small piece of armor—a visor for his forehead, with a red star screwed onto it for eternity—and a last empty grenade.

"Well, that'll be more than enough," said Kopionkin. "But tell me what happened to your Memorial Reserve! Don't say you grew so weak the peasants were free to kulakize it!"

Sorrow made Pashintsev barely able to speak. "There was talk of a far-reaching campaign to set up state farms in the area—but why this interrogation? You can see I've got nothing to hide."

Once again Kopionkin examined Pashintsev's naked body. "Get dressed then. Let's go and inspect Chevengur together. Here too we lack facts—and people see a dream."

But Pashintsev was unable to be Kopionkin's companion; apart from his visor, and his mail shirt, he turned out to have no clothes at all.

"Come along as you are!" Kopionkin encouraged him. "Think people have never seen a living body before? Yours isn't such a charm as all that—no different from what gets put in a coffin!"

"But you haven't grasped the root of this evil," said Pashintsev, fingering his metal clothes. "I was dismissed from the RevReserve in good order—alive and clothed, though branded a dangerous element. But then, when my own fellow villagers saw me—a man of the past and, what's more, defeated by an army—they reduced all my clothes off me. They just threw me my visor and mail shirt, to warm me in the small hours. As for the grenade—I kept a firm hold of that all the time."

"Was it really an entire army that advanced on you?" Kopionkin asked in surprise.

"It certainly was! A hundred men on horseback against one foot soldier. And they had field guns in reserve. Even then I held out for twenty-four hours—I frightened off a whole army with empty grenades. But then Grunka, one of the girls there, unmasked me—the bitch!"

"I see," said Kopionkin, with belief. "Well, let's get going. Give me your scrap iron—I can carry it for you in one hand."

Pashintsev got out of the boat and set off, following Kopionkin's dependable footprints in the riverside sand.

"Don't be afraid," said Kopionkin, trying to calm his naked comrade. "It's not you who exposed yourself. It's those semi-Whites—they've done you wrong."

Pashintsev understood that it was in the name of communism and the poor that he was now walking naked and barefoot, and so he was untroubled by the thought of women to come.

The first of these was Klavdiusha. After a brief inspection of Pashintsev's body, she covered her eyes with her scarf, like a Tatar woman. "What a dreadfully weedy man! And all covered in moles!" she said to herself. "Still, at least he's clean, and his skin's not all crusts and scabs." Out loud she said, "Citizens, this isn't the front line. Walking about naked is not entirely proper."

Kopionkin asked Pashintsev to pay no attention to a toad of this kind; she was a bourgeois and all she did was complain. First, she needed a shawl, then Moscow—and now she was pestering a naked proletarian. In spite of this, Pashintsev felt somewhat embarrassed and he put on his visor and mail shirt, leaving the greater part of his body apparent. "That's better," he declared. "They'll take this for the uniform of the new policy!"

"What more do you want?" said Kopionkin, after a quick glance. "You're almost clothed now. It'll just be a bit chilly from the iron."

"The iron will warm up from my body. After all, there's blood flowing inside me!"

"In me too!" sensed Kopionkin.

The iron turned out not to chill Pashintsev's body—Chevengur was too warm. People were sitting in rows in the narrow streets, between the displaced houses, and speaking quiet words to one another;

and they too—as well as the sun's rays—gave off warmth and breath. Pashintsev and Kopionkin made their way through the stifling, pervasive heat; the sun, the troubling smell of human beings, and the houses' cramped closeness made life seem like a dream beneath a padded quilt.

"Don't know why, but I feel sleepy," said Kopionkin. "What about you?"

"So, all in all," Pashintsev replied, not quite sure about himself.

Beside the permanent brick house where Kopionkin had stopped after first arriving in Chevengur was Piusia; he was sitting alone, staring at everything indefinitely.

"Listen, comrade Piusia!" Kopionkin began. "I'm required to carry out a reconnaissance of the whole of Chevengur. Take us on an inspection tour."

"That's possible," said Piusia, without getting to his feet.

Pashintsev went into the house and picked up an old, 1914-style soldier's greatcoat that was lying on the floor. It was a large size, and it straightaway brought peace to Pashintsev's whole body.

"Now you're dressed every bit like a citizen," pronounced Kopionkin. "Though it makes you less like yourself."

The three men set off into the distance, amid the warmth of the town's constructions. Withered orchards stood sadly in the middle of roads and in empty places; after being transplanted several times, and carried about on shoulders, they had lost their strength, in spite of the sun and rains.

"There's a fact for you!" said Kopionkin, pointing to the silenced trees. "These devils have constructed communism for themselves—but no such luck for the trees!"

The few stray children, whom they came across now and again in the clearings, had grown stout from air, freedom, and the absence of daily nurture. As for the adults—the nature of their lives in Chevengur remained unknown. Kopionkin did not detect any new feelings in them; from a distance they appeared as if on leave from imperialism, but there were no facts with regard to what lay inside and among them. Kopionkin considered good humor to be no more than a warm exhalation—not signifying communism—from the blood in a human body.

Close to the cemetery where the RevCom was located stretched a long depression where the soil had subsided. "Bourgeoisie are lying there," said Piusia. "And for good measure me and Chepurny knocked their souls out of them too."

With satisfaction Kopionkin tested the sunken earth of the grave with one foot. "Yes," he said, "I'm sure there was no other way."

"We recognized the necessity," said Piusia, in vindication of fact. "It's our turn to live."

Pashintsev, for his part, felt offended that the grave had not been properly filled in and packed down; it should have been made level, and an old orchard should have been moved there by hand—then the trees would have sucked the remains of capitalism out of the earth, economically transforming them into the green of socialism. In reality, however, Piusia had seen the proper leveling of the grave as a very serious matter. He had failed to carry out this important measure only because the provincial authorities had hurriedly removed him from his post as chairman of the Cheka—a decision at which Piusia had taken only very slight offense, since he was aware that Soviet institutions required people of education, not people like himself, and that bourgeoisie had their use there. Thanks to this awareness, Piusia had fallen silent in the mass of the Chevengur collective, recognizing once and for all that the Revolution was smarter than himself. Nothing scared him more than offices and written documents—at the sight of them he would instantly turn mute and feel weak and gloomy from head to toe, sensing the might of the black magic of thought and literacy. Back in Piusia's days the Chevengur Cheka had been located on the town meadow; instead of writing long reports on punitive measures against capital, Piusia had made these measures public and open, proposing that captured landlords be killed by their own laborers. This proposal had been put into effect. Now, however, since what they had in Chevengur was the definitive development of communism, the Cheka, in accord with a personal resolution of Chepurny's, had been closed down forever, and houses had been relocated on the meadow.

Kopionkin stood in thought over the common grave of the bourgeoisie, which was without trees, without a mound, and without memory. He felt confusedly that this was in order for Rosa Luxemburg's faraway grave to possess a tree, a mound, and eternal memory. He would, however, have preferred the grave of the bourgeoisie to have been properly packed down and leveled.

"You say you knocked the souls out of the bourgeoisie for good measure?" he said with doubt. "No, if you were dismissed, it was because you didn't finish off the bourgeoisie en masse, because you didn't fully kill them to death. You didn't even pack down the earth!"

Here Kopionkin was much mistaken. The Chevengur bourgeoisie had been slaughtered definitively and conscientiously. Not even life beyond the grave could bring them any joy: after their bodies, their souls had been executed too.

33

AFTER brief life in Chevengur,[1] Chepurny's heart had begun to ache from the dense presence in the town of petty bourgeoisie. The soil in Chevengur was too narrow for communism—it was infested with property and propertied people. It was imperative immediately to determine communism on a living base, but the living quarters had been occupied since time immemorial by strange people who smelled of candle wax. Chepurny had gone out specially into the fields and looked at fresh, open places: Was it there that communism should be begun? But he had decided against this, since Chevengur's tools and buildings, created by oppressed hands, would then have been lost to the proletariat and poor peasants. And he knew and saw how much the Chevengur bourgeoisie was haunted by expectation of the Second Coming—and he himself had nothing against such an event. And so, after about two months as chairman of the Revolutionary Committee, Chepurny's whole body had fallen into torment—the bourgeoisie were alive, there was no communism, and the path toward the future, according to reports from the provincial authorities, was a series of consistently progressing transitional steps in which Chepurny's intuition suspected a deception of the masses.

First, Chepurny had appointed a commission, and the commission had informed him of the necessity for a Second Coming. Initially, Chepurny had not responded; he was secretly intending to spare the bourgeois small fry, in order that the world revolution should have something to occupy itself with. But then Chepurny had felt the need to put an end to his torment and he summoned Piusia, the chairman of the Cheka. "Cleanse the town of the oppressive element!" he ordered.

"That can be done," said Piusia, preparing to kill all the inhabitants of Chevengur.[2]

Chepurny agreed to this with relief. "It's the kindest way," he said, continuing to argue his case. "Otherwise, brother, the entire people will end up dying on these transitional steps. And anyway bourgeoisie aren't really humans anymore. I've read that, as soon as he got himself born from the monkey, man turned round and killed them. So just remember—since we've now got a proletariat, what use is the bourgeoisie? It's vile!"

Piusia was personally acquainted with the bourgeoisie. He knew every street and could clearly visualize the face of every householder: Shchekotov, Komiagin, Pikhler, Znobilin, Shchapov, Zavyn-Duvailo, Perekrutchenko, Siusiukalov, and all their neighbors.[3] Moreover, Piusia knew their means of life and sustenance, and he was ready to kill any one of them by hand, even without use of a weapon. His soul had not known peace since the day he was appointed chairman of the Cheka; he had felt continually irritated that petty bourgeoisie were eating Soviet bread and living in his houses (Piusia had worked for twenty years as a stonemason), and that these reptiles remained quietly positioned athwart the Revolution. The most elderly and gap-toothed representatives of the bourgeoisie transformed the meek Piusia into a street fighter; during encounters with Shchapov, Znobilin, and Zavyn-Duvailo he had more than once laid into them with his fists. They had silently cleaned themselves up, enduring the insult and placing their hope in the future. The other bourgeois had kept out of Piusia's way, and he had no wish to seek them out in their homes—repeated irritation was stifling to his soul.

But Prokofy Dvanov, secretary of the district ExecCom, had not agreed to the wholesale and immediate extermination of the bourgeoisie. He said it had to be done more theoretically.

"All right then—formulate!" said Chepurny.

As he reflected, Prokofy shook back his meditative, Socialist

Revolutionary long hair. "On the basis of their own prejudice!" he began to formulate.

"I can feel something," said Chepurny. Not yet understanding, he was preparing to think.

"On the basis of the Second Coming!" Prokofy articulated with precision. "That's what they want—so let them have it! We won't be to blame."

Chepurny, however, saw things differently. "What do you mean? 'We won't be to blame?' We're the Revolution—we're to blame all round! If you just want to formulate for your own forgiveness, we can do without you."

Like every clever person, Prokofy did not lack composure. "It is essential, comrade Chepurny, to announce the Second Coming officially. And, on that basis, to cleanse the town for settlement of proletarian life."

"Yes, but will we have a part to play in all this?" asked Chepurny.

"In a general sense, yes! Only all domestic belongings will have to be distributed afterward, so they don't oppress us any longer."

"You can take the property for yourself!" said Chepurny. "The proletariat still has the use of its hands. But what, I ask you now, makes you hanker after bourgeois chests and cupboards at a time like this? Write out a decree."

Prokofy succinctly formulated the town bourgeoisie's future and handed Piusia a sheet of paper covered with writing. Piusia's role was to supply from memory the surnames of all property owners.

Chepurny then read that Soviet power was conceding to the bourgeoisie the entire infinite sky, equipped with stars and heavenly bodies, with the object of the organization there of eternal bliss; but as for the earth, foundational structures, and domestic inventory, these were to remain below—in exchange for the sky—and wholly in the hands of the proletariat and laboring peasantry.

The date for the Second Coming—which, in an organized and painless manner, would lead the bourgeoisie away to life beyond the grave—was given at the end of the decree.

The bourgeoisie were to present themselves in the church square at midnight on Wednesday—an hour scheduled in the light of a bulletin from the provincial meteorological bureau.

Prokofy had long been attracted by the obscure and impressive complexity of documents from the provincial capital, and it was with a smile of sensuality that he reproduced their style at a district level.

Piusia understood nothing of the decree, while Chepurny took a pinch of snuff and appeared interested in only one question: Why had Prokofy scheduled the Second Coming for Wednesday, in two days' time, rather than for that very evening?

"Wednesday's a fast day. They'll prepare themselves more calmly," Prokofy explained. "And it's expected to be overcast today and tomorrow—I've received bulletins about the weather."

"A needless reprieve," said Chepurny. He did not, however, particularly insist on bringing forward the Second Coming.

Prokofy for his part, together with Klavdiusha, visited all the homes of the propertied citizens, requisitioning in passing anything handy and not too cumbersome: bracelets, silk scarves, golden tsarist medals, powder for young ladies, and so on. Klavdiusha packed these items away in her trunk, while Prokofy issued the bourgeois an oral promise of a further extension of life in return for an increase to the republic's revenues; the bourgeois stood in the middle of the floor and expressed obedient gratitude. Right through until Wednesday evening Prokofy was unable to take a moment's break, and he wished he had scheduled the Second Coming for Friday night instead.

Chepurny was not worried that Prokofy had ended up with so many goods. These were not things that would adhere long to the proletariat; kerchiefs and powders would wear themselves out on heads and leave no trace in people's consciousness.

On Wednesday night the church square was taken over by the Chevengur bourgeoisie, who had been gathering there since early evening. Piusia had the area around the square cordoned off by Red Army men, and he infiltrated lean Chekists into the bourgeois crowd. Only three bourgeois from the list failed to appear—two had been crushed by their own houses, while the third had died of old age.

Piusia at once sent two Chekists to ascertain why the houses had fallen down, while he himself ordered the bourgeoisie to form up in a strict line. With them the bourgeois had brought bundles and small cases filled with soap, towels, underwear, white buns, and their small books listing family members to be remembered in prayer. Piusia checked the belongings of each person present, paying particular attention to the lists of family dead.

"Read!" he ordered one of his Chekists.

The man began to read, "For the repose of God's servants: Yevdokia, Marfa, Firs, Polikarp, Vasily, Konstantin, Makary, and every member of our family. For the health of Agrippina, Maria, Kosma, Ignaty, Piotr, Ioann, Anastasia with her progeny, and every member of our family, and the ailing Andrey."

"With her progidy?" Piusia repeated.

"That's right," confirmed the Chekist.

Standing behind the line of Red Army men were the bourgeois wives, weeping in the night air.

"Take these accomplices away," Piusia ordered. "We can do without progidies."

"We should finish them off too, comrade Piusia," said the Chekist.

"Why, blockhead? Their chief member's been docked."

The two Chekists returned from checking the collapsed houses and explained: the ceilings had fallen in because the lofts, packed with sacks of salt and flour, had been overburdened beyond all measure. The bourgeoisie had laid in reserves of salt and flour for nourishment during the passage of the Second Coming, so they could pass through it safely and then carry on with their lives.

"So it's like that, is it?" said Piusia. Not waiting for the hour of midnight, he lined up the Chekists. "All right, lads, let 'em have it!" he called out, and dispatched a bullet from his revolver into the skull of a neighboring bourgeois, Zavyn-Duvailo. Quiet steam came out of the bourgeois's head. Then a moist, maternal substance resembling candle wax began to show through his hair; but Duvailo did not fall—instead he sat down on his domestic bundle.

"Wrap a swaddling band round my throat, woman," Duvailo said patiently. "My soul's all flowing out of me there." And he fell from his bundle onto the earth, embracing the earth with outstretched arms and legs—as a master embraces his mistress.

The Chekists fired from their revolvers at the voiceless bourgeois, who had made their communion the day before—and the bourgeois fell awkwardly and askew, twisting their greasy necks to the point of damaging vertebrae. Each had lost the strength of his legs before any sense of a wound—so that the bullet would enter in a random place and living flesh would grow over it there.

Shchapov, a wounded merchant, was lying on the ground with diminished body, asking a Chekist who had bent down over him, "Let me breathe, good man, don't be too hard on me. Call my woman, so we can say goodbye. Or quick! Give me your hand! Don't go far—I'm scared on my own."

The Chekist tried to give him his hand. "Here you are—your time's up anyway."

Not waiting for the hand, Shchapov grasped a burdock leaf and clung to it for help, entrusting to it the life he had been unable to live out. He did not let go of it until the loss of his yearning for the woman to whom he'd wanted to say goodbye, and then his hands dropped down of their own accord, no longer needing friendship. The Chekist understood and felt agitated. With a bullet inside them the bourgeois, just like the proletariat, wanted comradeship; without a bullet, however, they loved only property.

Piusia, meanwhile, was bending down over Zavyn-Duvailo. "Where is it your soul's leaking out? From your throat? I'll knock it out of there right away!"

Piusia took hold of Duvailo's neck with his left hand, got a comfortable grip, and then pressed the muzzle of his revolver against it, just below the nape. But Duvailo's neck was itching, and he kept rubbing it against the cloth collar of his jacket.

"Stop fidgeting, you fool. Just a moment—and I'll scratch you good and proper!"

Duvailo was still living, and not afraid. "Take my head between your legs and squeeze till I scream out loud. My woman's nearby and I want her to hear me!"

Piusia smashed him on the cheek with his fist, so as to feel this bourgeois's body for the last time, and Duvailo cried out plaintively, "Mashenka, they're hurting me!"

Piusia waited until Duvailo had pronounced the last drawn-out syllables in full. After shooting him twice through the neck, he unclenched his gums, which had gone hot and dry.

Prokofy had observed this solitary murder from a distance, and he reproached Piusia. "Communists don't kill from behind, comrade Piusia!"

Upset by this, Piusia immediately found his mind. "Communists, comrade Dvanov, need communism—not officer-style heroics. So shut your mouth—or I'll send you up into the sky too! Nowadays every fucking whore wants to plug herself up with a red banner—as if that'll make her empty hole heal over with virtue! Well, no banner's going to hide you from my bullet!"

Chepurny appeared and put an end to this conversation: "What's going on here, I'd like to know! Bourgeois are still breathing on the earth—and you two are seeking communism in mere words!"

Chepurny and Piusia went off to make a personal inspection of the dead bourgeois. The dead were lying in clumps—in groups of three or five or still more—evidently trying to get close to one another, if only with a little of their bodies, during their last minutes of mutual parting.

Chepurny touched their throats with the back of his hand, the way a mechanic tests the temperature of a bearing, and it seemed to him that these bourgeois were still alive.

"I knocked the soul out of Duvailo's neck for good measure!" said Piusia.

"Quite right—the soul lives in the throat,"[4] Chepurny recalled. "Why do you think the Cadets string us up by the throat?[5] So the soul gets burned up by the rope—then you die good and proper! It's no good messing about—killing a man isn't easy!"

Piusia and Chepurny felt every one of the bourgeois and remained unconvinced of their definitive death. Some seemed to be sighing; while others had half closed their eyes and were shamming, in order to crawl away into the night and continue their lives at the expense of Piusia and the rest of the proletariat. Piusia and Chepurny then decided to further insure the bourgeois against any continuation of life. They loaded their revolvers and shot each prostrate property owner, one by one, through the glands in his neck.

"Now our cause is assured!" said Chepurny once they'd completed this task. "No proletarian in the world is poorer than a corpse."

"Things are on a firm footing now," Piusia said with satisfaction. "We should dismiss the Red Army men."

The Red Army men were dismissed, while the Chekists stayed to prepare a common grave for the former bourgeois population of Chevengur. By dawn, the Chekists had finished, and they threw all the dead into the pit, together with their bundles. Not daring to come up close, the wives of the murdered waited at a distance for the completion of the earthworks. But when the Chekists, to avoid leaving a mound, scattered the surplus earth on the empty, dawn-lit square and then plunged their spades into the ground and lit up their cigarettes, the wives of the dead began to advance on them from all the streets of Chevengur.

"Weep!" said the Chekists, and went off in exhaustion to sleep.

The wives lay down on the lumpy clay of the level, traceless grave and tried to mourn, but they had gotten chilled during the night, and their grief had already been suffered through, and now the wives of the dead were unable to weep.

34

AFTER learning how things had gone in Chevengur, Kopionkin decided not to punish anyone for the time being but to hold back until the arrival of Alexander Dvanov—all the more so, given that foot-walker Luy had now set off on his own way.

Luy had indeed covered a great deal of ground during these last days and he felt whole, sated, and happy. When he felt like eating, he would go into a hut and say to the mistress, "Woman, pluck me a chicken. I'm worn out." If the woman grudged him a chicken, then Luy would bid her farewell and continue on his way across the steppe, dining on chervil that had grown on account of the sun, not on account of someone's pitiful smallholding zeal. Luy never begged or stole. If no food came his way for a long time, he was sure to be eating his fill one day, and he did not suffer from hunger.

Luy had spent the night in the pit of a brick barn; there was now only forty versts of surfaced road to the provincial capital. To Luy this was an empty piffle, and he took things easy for a long time after sleeping. He lay there, wondering how best to have a smoke. He had tobacco, but no paper; he had smoked all his documents long ago—the only paper still left was Kopionkin's letter to Dvanov. Luy took the letter out, smoothed it over, read it twice through to commit it to memory, and then made it into ten empty cigarettes.

"I'll tell him the letter in my own voice—that'll make just as good sense." After reasoning this out, he confirmed his own words, "Yes, of course! No two ways about it!"

After his smoke, Luy went out onto the high road and set off along its soft verge. In the height and cloudy mist of the distance, on a ridge between two clean rivers, stood the old city—with its towers, balconies, and churches, and with the long buildings of offices, colleges, and law courts. Luy knew that people had lived there for a long time and hindered others from life. To one side of the city, on its outskirts, rose smoke from the four chimneys of a factory that made agricultural machinery to help the sun produce grain. Luy liked the distant smoke of the chimneys and the whistle of a locomotive as it sped through the remote depths of fields now bearing quiet grasses.

Luy would have left the city behind and not delivered Kopionkin's letter at all, except that the city lay on his direct path to Petrograd and the shores of the Baltic Sea. From there—from the cold of the empty plains of the Revolution—ships departed into the dark of the seas, to conquer in due course the warm bourgeois countries.

Gopner was at that same moment descending the hill from the city to the Polny Aidar River, and he could see the cobbled road stretching across the steppe toward the agricultural settlements. Luy—though far out of sight—was walking along the same road, imagining the Baltic fleet in the cold sea. Gopner crossed a bridge and sat down on the far bank to do some fishing. He threaded a live, suffering worm onto a hook, cast the line, and gazed into the quiet ripples of the passing river. The cool of the water and the smell of damp grass were stimulating breath and thought in him. He listened to the river's speech, thought about the peaceful life, the happiness beyond the earth's horizon, toward which every river floated but where they would never take him—and gradually lowered his dry head into the damp grasses, passing from calm of thought into sleep. A small fish—a silver bream—then got caught on his hook and struggled for four hours to escape into deep, free waters; the blood from its pierced lips mixed with the bloody juice of the worm. Then the bream grew tired of flinging itself about, swallowed a small piece of the worm for the sake of strength and once again began to tug at the hot, cutting iron, wanting to rid itself of the hook along with the cartilage of its lip.

*

From the height of the dyke, Luy caught sight of a thin, tired man asleep on the riverbank while a rod twitched about of its own accord by his feet. Luy walked over to him and pulled up the hooked bream. The bream went still in his hand, opened its gills, and started to die from frightened exhaustion.

"Comrade!" Luy said to the sleeper. "Asleep to the whole world! Look—a fish for you!"

Gopner opened his eyes, which had filled with nourishing blood, and considered this man who had appeared. The foot-walker sat down for a smoke and to have a look at the constructions of the opposing city.

"I dreamed I was looking at something for a long time," Gopner said to him, "and I hadn't quite finished. I woke up—and there you stand, like a fulfillment of wishes."

Gopner scratched his hungry, stubbly throat and felt downcast. His happy reflections had perished in sleep and not even the river could recall them to him. "To hell with you," he said crossly. "I'll be dismal again now you've woken me up."

"Winds blow, rivers flow, and fish swim," Luy began calmly and protractedly, "while you sit here rusting with grief. Try moving somewhere. The wind will breathe thought into you—and then you'll learn something!"

Gopner did not reply. Why should he reply to every passerby? What would this vagrant peasant know about communism?

"Do you happen to know where comrade Alexander Dvanov lives?" Luy asked, recalling his passing commission.

Gopner took the fish from Luy's hand and threw it back into the water. "Maybe it'll get its breath back," he explained.[1]

"It won't come back to life now," Luy doubted. "As for that comrade, he's someone I need to see face-to-face."

"What do you need to see him for, when I'll be seeing him myself?" Gopner said vaguely. "Someone you respect, is he?"

"No one wins respect just from his name, and I know nothing about what he does. Our comrades say he's urgently needed in Chevengur."

"What's going on there?"

"Communism and back again. So comrade Kopionkin writes."

Gopner looked searchingly at Luy, as if he were a machine requiring major overhaul. He understood what exhaustion of mind capitalism had brought about in such people.

"None of you have any qualifications or political consciousness. What kind of communism, damn it, can you bring about?"

"We have nothing at all," said Luy. "All we can possess is other people. That's why we now have comradeship."

Gopner felt an influx of well-rested strength. After brief thought, he spoke his mind. "That's clever, damn it, but it can't be relied on. No cross margin of safety. Get it? Or is communism something you're running away from?"

Luy knew that there was no communism outside Chevengur. Everywhere else, including the city on the hill, was no more than a transitional step.

"Where you live is a transitional step," he said. "And that makes you think I'm running away. But I'm just walking along. And when I get to the sea, I'll sail to the bourgeois states and start to ready them for the future. Communism's here in my body now—there's no getting away from it."

Gopner felt Luy's hand and examined it in the sunlight. It was large and sinewy, covered with the unhealing marks of former labor—those birthmarks of all the downtrodden. "Maybe his words are true," he said to himself. "Airplanes fly, damn it, even though they're heavier than air."

Luy returned to Kopionkin's word-of-mouth letter. Dvanov, he told Gopner, was to go to Chevengur without delay—otherwise communism might weaken there. Gopner reassured him and told him his own address.

"Say a word to my woman—she can give you something to eat and drink. As for me, I'll take off my shoes, wade out to the sandbar, and try to catch some chub on my line. Toward evening the damned critters will bite even beetles."

Luy was already used to parting quickly from people, since he was constantly meeting other—and better—people. And everywhere above him he saw the light of the sun's summer standstill, allowing the earth to accumulate plants for nourishment and bear people for comradeship.

After the foot-walker set off, Gopner decided that this man was similar to an orchard tree. Luy's body lacked unity of organization and construction. There was no coordination of the limbs and extremities, which grew out of him with the profligacy of branches and the sticky strength of timber.

Luy disappeared beyond the bridge, while Gopner lay down to rest a little longer. He was on leave, enjoying life as he did once every year. But he did not manage to catch any chub that day, because the wind soon got up, banks of storm clouds appeared behind the towers of the city, and he had to go back to his room. But sitting in a room with his wife was dreary, and he always longed to visit comrades—especially Sasha and Zakhar Pavlovich. And so, on his way home, he stopped at the familiar wooden house.

Zakhar Pavlovich was lying down. Sasha was reading a book, clasping above it his dry hands, which had grown unused to people.

"Have you heard?" said Gopner, to show that he hadn't come round for no reason. "In Chevengur they've organized full communism."

Zakhar Pavlovich's even snuffles came to a stop. He postponed his sleep and began to listen intently. Sasha said nothing, looking at Gopner with trustful excitement.

"Why gape at me like that?" said Gopner. "Airplanes are heavier than air, but somehow the damned things fly. Why shouldn't communism be able to get itself organized?"

"And that creature that's always gnawing away at the edges of the Revolution—that goat in a field of cabbages?" asked Zakhar Pavlovich. "How have they dealt with that?"

"My father's heard talk about 'objective conditions,'" Sasha explained. "And he's thinking of scapegoats."

"They've eaten that scapegoat," Gopner replied, as if this were something he had witnessed in person. "Now life's guilt will be on their own shoulders."

Behind the thin partition wall a man suddenly burst into tears, letting himself go more and more loudly. Beer mugs trembled as he beat his insulted head against a table. It was a Komsomol member who worked as a stoker at the railway depot and was making no progress toward any higher position. He sobbed a little, then blew his nose and fell silent.

"Any number of swine are careering about in cars and marrying plump actresses—while I just plod on the same as ever," he pronounced bitterly. "Tomorrow I'll speak to the district committee. I'll get them to transfer me to office work too. I know all the political literature, I could be directing on a mass scale. And they go and make me a stoker—and fourth grade, at that. They don't see the human being in me!"

Zakhar Pavlovich went out for some fresh air and to have a look at the rain: Was it from temporary clouds or had it set in? It had clearly set in—at least for the night, if not for the next twenty-four hours. The trees outside were being battered by the wind and rain, and guard dogs were barking away in other enclosed yards.

"Some weather!" Zakhar Pavlovich said to himself. "And soon I'll be losing my son again."

Back inside, Sasha was being summoned to Chevengur.

"We'll measure communism in its entirety," Gopner was saying. "We'll record a precise blueprint and bring it back with us to the Provincial PartCom. Once we've got a template from Chevengur, it'll be easy enough to make communism on one-sixth of the earth's circle."[2]

Dvanov thought silently about Kopionkin and his word-of-mouth letter: "Communism and back again."

Zakhar Pavlovich listened intently, then said, "All right—but the working man is a very weak fool, and communism is no paltry matter. What's needed in this Chevengur of yours is a whole relationship of people. Are you really telling me that's been sorted once and for all?"

"And why not?" Gopner replied with conviction. "Local power has inadvertently thought up something smart—and something's come of it, damn it. What's so surprising about that?"

Zakhar Pavlovich remained doubtful.

"That's all very well—but mankind's no light matter. We're not easy material to work with. A fool can't make a locomotive run, but we kept going even under the tsars. Understand?"

"I understand all right," said Gopner, "but I see something else when I look around me."

"Well, I don't," Zakhar Pavlovich said to the uncomprehending Gopner. "And I can tell you one thing for sure. I can make you anything you like out of iron, but there's no way I can make a Communist out of a man!"

"What d'you mean? No one's been *making* anyone into a Communist. People have made themselves, damn it, into themselves."

Here Zakhar Pavlovich was ready to agree. "Well, that's another story! What I wanted to say is that this local power of yours is neither here nor there. You can smarten up from working on artifacts, but power and government are another matter. The smartest people are in power already, so they no longer bother to use their minds. If people didn't put up with maltreatment, if they just cracked or split like cast iron, then we'd end up with the most excellent of governing powers."

"We'd end up with no power at all," said Sasha.

"Maybe," said Zakhar Pavlovich.

They could still hear the Komsomol member behind the wall. Still partially in the grip of his frenzy, he had fallen into a burdensome sleep. "Bastards," he sighed more resignedly—and then returned to his muttering, omitting crucial parts of the story. "Some sleep in couples on a real bed, while I lie alone on a brick shelf. Let me lie on something soft, comrade secretary, or hard labor will be the end of me. I've been paying my dues for years now—let me have my share. What's stopping you?"

Cold rain streamed down, filling the night with its noise. Sasha could hear heavy drops beating down on the streams and lakes in the streets. Only one thing comforted him in this shelterless weather—his memory of the old tale about the bubble, the straw, and the bast sandal who once managed, as a threesome, to overcome conditions no less undependable and impenetrable.

His comrade was only a bubble. *She* was a straw, not a woman, and he himself was the bast sandal. Yet they made their way in friendship through fields and puddles. So Sasha imagined, with childhood happiness, before admonishing himself, "I too have bubbles and straws as comrades, only somehow I abandoned them. I'm worse than the bast sandal."[3]

The night smelled of the steppe's faraway grasslands. On the other side of the street was a building where men were registered for military service during the day, though by evening this center had wearied of the tasks of the Revolution. Gopner took off his shoes, having decided to stay the night at Zakhar Pavlovich's, even though he knew he'd catch it from his wife when he got back home in the morning. "Found yourself a young lass have you?" she would yell, as she bashed him on the collarbone with a log. But then, what did nagging women know about comradeship? Left to themselves, they'd get out their little wooden saws and saw up all communism into petty-bourgeois pieces.

"Damn it all!" Gopner said, and sighed loudly. "It's not as if a man needs so very much. But there's no regular law and order."

"What are you grumbling about?" asked Zakhar Pavlovich.

"I'm talking about my home life. For every pound of living flesh on her, my wife's got five pounds of petty-bourgeois ideology. Quite a counterweight!"

The rain outside was coming to an end. The bubbles quieted and the earth gave off a smell of washed grass, the cleanness of cold water, and the freshness of open roads. Sasha lay down to sleep with a sense of regret. He felt he had lived that day in vain; he was ashamed of a sense of life's dreariness that had abruptly set in for him. He had felt better the day before, even though Sonia had returned from her village to her old room, bundled up what remained of her things, and gone off goodness knows where. She had knocked at Sasha's window and waved goodbye; he had gone out onto the street, but she was already out of sight. He had thought about her until evening—and that had sustained his existence. Now, though, he had forgotten what had kept him alive, and he was unable to sleep.

As for Gopner, he was already asleep—but his breathing was so weak and pitiful that Sasha was afraid life might come to an end in him. He went over to him, took his hand, which was hanging down to one side, and placed it on his chest. Once again, he listened to the sleeper's complex and tender life. He was clearly fragile, defenseless, and trusting—and yet, he too had probably been beaten, tormented, deceived, and hated. And now he was barely alive; in his sleep, his breathing had almost died away. Nobody ever looks at sleeping people, but they alone have faces that are real and beloved; when a man is awake, his face is distorted by memory, feeling, and need.

After calming Gopner's wide-flung arms, Sasha looked closely and with curiosity of tenderness at Zakhar Pavlovich, who had also deeply forgotten himself in sleep. Then he listened to the now-quieting wind and lay down too. His father lived soundly and sensibly in his sleep, much as in his daytime life, and so his face changed only a little at night. If he had dreams, they were useful dreams shortly before waking—not the kind that later make one feel dismal and ashamed.

Sasha curled up into a complete sense of his own body—and went still. Imperceptibly, like weariness being dispelled, Sasha's childhood day rose up before him, not in the depth of overgrown years but in the depth of his stilled, difficult, self-tormenting body. Through the twilit autumn evening, rain was falling like sparse tears onto the cemetery of his village birthland. The rope the caretaker had hung, so he could ring the night hours without having to climb the bell tower, was blowing about in the wind. Crumpled, emaciated clouds, with the look of village women who had just given birth, were passing low over the trees. Sasha himself, a little boy, was standing beneath the last leaves rustling over the grave of his birth father. The small clay mound had spread in the rains and then been flattened to nothing by passersby; the leaves falling on it were as dead as his buried father. Sasha had with him only an empty bag and the stick Prokhor Abramovich had given him for his long journey.

Unable to comprehend parting with his father, the boy touches the earth of the grave, just as he once felt his father's death shirt, and to him it seems that the rain smells of sweat and of his usual life, in his father's warm embrace on the shore of Lake Mutevo. That life, promised to him forever, will now never return—and he doesn't know whether this is all some kind of joke or whether he should cry. In place of himself, little Sasha leaves his father the stick; he buries it in the grave mound and covers it with newly dead leaves, so that his father will know how dismal it is for him to set off on his own—and that, for the sake of the stick and his father, he will always return from wherever he goes.

Sasha felt burdened, and he began to cry in his sleep, since he had still not taken the stick from his father. But his father was in a little dugout canoe, smiling at how his son had grown frightened at having to wait so long. This small death trap rocked and swayed at the slightest breath—a breath of wind or his father's breaths as he plied the oars—and his father's peculiar, always difficult face expressed a meek but avid pity toward half of the world. As for the remaining half of the world, that was something he didn't know, something he labored over in thought and perhaps even hated. His father got out of the boat, stroked the shallow water, took hold of the tip of a grass blade, not harming it in any way, embraced the little boy, and looked at the neighboring world as if it were his friend and fellow fighter in the struggle against his one and only enemy, who was invisible to all.

"Why cry, my lad?" he asked. "Your stick has grown into a tree. Look at it now! Think you'll be able to pull that up out of the ground?"

"But how will I get to Chevengur then?" the boy asked. "I'll be lonely without it."

His father sat down in the grass and looked silently at the far shore. This time he did not embrace his son.

"Don't be bored and lonely," he said. "It's the same for me too. I feel bored and lonely lying here. Go and do something in Chevengur. What's the good of us all lying dead?"

Sasha moved closer to his father and lay down in his lap, because he didn't want to go away to Chevengur. His father, too, began to weep, because they were parting. In his grief he clasped his son so close that the boy burst into tears, feeling himself alone forever. He went on holding on to his father's shirt for a long time. The sun had already risen above the forest, beyond which, in the distance, lived the alien Chevengur, and forest birds were already coming to the lake to drink, but his father continued to sit there, observing the lake and the superfluous rising day. The boy fell asleep. His father then turned the boy's face toward the sun, so that his tears would dry, but the light tickled the boy's closed vision and he awoke.

Gopner was putting on his tattered footcloths, while Zakhar Pavlovich was filling his tobacco pouch, about to go out to work. The sun was rising over the buildings, as it had over the trees, and its light was pressing down on Sasha's tear-stained face. Zakhar Pavlovich tied up his pouch, took a chunk of bread and two potatoes, and said, "Well, I'm off now. God be with you." Sasha looked at Zakhar Pavlovich's knees and at the flies, which were flying around like the forest birds.

"So," said Gopner. "Will you go to Chevengur?"

"Yes, I will. And you?"

"Think I'm a worse man than you, do you? I'm coming too."

"And your work? Will you get yourself discharged?"

"I'll just hand in my notice. Labor discipline, damn it, is not the be-all and end-all. Communism, today, is more precious. Or do you not think of me as a true Communist?"

Then Sasha asked Gopner about his wife. How would she manage for food? This made Gopner think, but not for long and not deeply.

"Oh, she'll keep going on sunflower seeds. She doesn't need much. Me and her don't have love—just the plain fact. Same with the proletariat. What gave birth to it wasn't love—just fact."

Gopner did not say what it was about the directive toward Chevengur that truly filled him with hope. It wasn't that he wanted his wife to have to live on seeds; what he wanted was to observe and measure, to obtain a template that would allow him to organize communism as soon as possible throughout the province. Communism would guarantee that his wife, along with other unnecessary people, would be well provided for in her old age; for the time being, however, she'd have to get by as best she could. If, on the other hand, people were simply to keep on working, neither would there be an end to their labors, nor would these labors lead to any improvement. Gopner had been working for twenty-five years without a break, and this had brought him no personal benefit in life. Things went on the same as ever, and time was wasted to no purpose. Neither food, nor clothing, nor happiness of heart—nothing increased and multiplied. It was clear, therefore, that what people needed was not labor but communism. In any case, his wife could always call on this same Zakhar Pavlovich—he was not someone to begrudge a proletarian woman a slice of bread. Submissive working people were also necessary; they continued to work without interruption at a time when communism was not yet of any practical benefit, even though it already required bread, disruption of families, and additional comforting of women.

35

Kopionkin spent twenty-four hours in Chevengur in a state of hope, but then grew tired of standing still in this town, not sensing communism there.

After the burial of the bourgeoisie, Chepurny—Kopionkin learned—had had no idea how to live for happiness, and he had gone off, for the sake of concentration, into distant meadows, to foresense communism in the living grass and in solitude. After two days and nights in unpeopled meadows, contemplating the counterrevolutionary goodness of nature, Chepurny felt a deep melancholy. In search of mind he turned to Karl Marx, thinking it was a huge book and that everything must have been written down there. He even felt surprised that, although the world was so sparse, with more open steppe than buildings and people, so many words about people and the world had already been thought up.

Nevertheless, Chepurny organized a reading of the book. Prokofy read aloud to him, and Chepurny laid down his head and listened with attentive mind, now and again pouring out kvas[1] for Prokofy, so that the reader's voice should not weaken. After the reading Chepurny understood nothing, but he felt lighter.

"Formulate, Prosha!" he said peacefully. "I can feel something."

Prokofy puffed up his mind and formulated with simplicity, "I suppose one thing, comrade Chepurny—"

"Don't keep on supposing. Just give me a resolution about the liquidation of the class of residual scum."

"I suppose one thing," Prokofy summarized thoughtfully. "Since nothing is said in Karl Marx about residual classes, then they can't exist."

"But they certainly do. Just go out onto the street—wherever you look, you find widows, shop assistants, or else dismissed overseers of the proletariat. What can we do about it, I ask you now!"

"I suppose that since, according to Karl Marx, they can't exist, then they should not exist."

"But they live and obliquely oppress us. How can that be?"

Now searching merely for an organizational model, Prokofy once again strained his accustomed head.

Chepurny warned him not to try to think in scientifical terms: science was not yet complete, it was only developing—you don't harvest rye till the ears are ripe.

"I think and suppose, comrade Chepurny, in systematic order," said Prokofy, finding a way out.

"Think a bit quicker—I'm getting agitated!"

"My premise is as follows: the remnants of the population should be removed as far as possible from Chevengur, so they get lost."

"Not clear enough. Shepherds will show them the way."

Prokofy went on with his discourse: "Everyone removed from the base of communism will be issued in advance with a week's rations—this will be the responsibility of the Liquidation Committee of the Evacuation Center."

"Ah, remind me about that—I'll dismiss the Liquidation Committee tomorrow."

"I'll note that down, comrade Chepurny. Next, the death penalty will be announced for the entire middle reserve remnant of the bourgeoisie—which will then be granted an immediate reprieve."

"What do you mean?"

"Their sentence will be commuted to eternal exile from Chevengur and from other bases of communism. Should these remnants reappear in Chevengur, they will be subject once again to the death penalty within twenty-four hours."

"That's entirely acceptable, Prosha! Please write the decree down the right-hand side of the paper."

Chepurny took a lengthy snort of snuff and protractedly savored its smell. He felt good now: The class of residual scum would be expelled beyond the district boundary and communism would come to be in Chevengur, since there was nothing else that could come into being. Chepurny took the work of Karl Marx into his hands and respectfully turned the densely printed pages. "The man wrote and wrote," he said with regret, "but we've done everything first and read about it afterward. He might as well not have written!"

Lest the book be read in vain, Chepurny left his written mark across the title: "Implemented in Chevengur up to the evacuation of the class of residual scum. Marx lacked the brains to write about them in his work. Future danger from them, however, is inevitable—and so we have taken our measures." Chepurny then carefully placed the book on the windowsill, sensing with satisfaction that its task had been achieved.

Prokofy wrote out the decree, and the two men parted. Prokofy went off to look for Klavdiusha, while Chepurny set off to inspect the town before the advent of communism. Around the houses—on the earth ledges around huts, on fallen oaks and other chance seats—alien people were sitting and warming themselves: old women, burly forty-year-old servants in blue caps whose employers had been shot, slight youths brought up on prejudices from the past, office workers exhausted from being laid off, and other supporters of a certain class. Seeing Chepurny wandering about, the sitters quietly got up and, without banging the gates, slowly disappeared inside their properties, trying to vanish without trace. There were crosses on every gate; they were chalked up every year on the eve of Epiphany, and this year there had been no strong, driving rain to wash them away. "I need to come by tomorrow with a camp cloth," Chepurny noted in his mind. "It's a disgrace."

The edge of town marked the beginning of deep, powerful steppe. A dense, vital air soothed and nourished the silent evening grass, and only far away, in the fading distance, was some restless man riding along in a cart and raising clouds of dust in the emptiness of the horizon. The sun had not yet set, but it was possible now to observe by eye its inexhaustible round heat: its red strength was surely enough for eternal communism and for a complete cessation of the internecine human folly entailed by the mortal need to eat—even though an entire heavenly body, without help from people, was working at the production of food. People should step back a little from one another, so as to fill this sunlit space between them with the stuff of friendship.

Chepurny wordlessly observed the sun, the steppe, and Chevengur, and keenly sensed the agitation of impending communism. He was afraid of his mounting emotions, whose dense force was plugging up the thoughts in his head and making inner experience difficult. Prokofy could have formulated something for him, and then everything would have felt more intelligible—but he didn't know where to look for Prokofy now.

"But communism's about to set in!" Chepurny quietly puzzled in the darkness of his agitation. "Why am I finding everything so hard?"

The sun went away, releasing moisture out of the air for the grass. Nature turned deep blue and peaceful, free now of the sun's noisy work on behalf of the general fellowship of exhausted life. A plant broken by Chepurny's foot laid its dying head on the leafy shoulder of a living neighbor. Chepurny moved his foot away and inhaled; from the remote, mute depths of the steppe came the smell of the sadness of distance, and of the sorrow of the absence of a human being.

Tall grass began just beyond Chevengur's last fences and continued, dense and without interruption, into the expanse of unmanaged steppe; Chepurny's feet felt comfortable in the warmth of the dusty burdocks growing fraternally among the other unauthorized plants. Tall vegetation surrounded the whole of Chevengur, serving as a close-knit defense against low-lying spaces in which Chepurny sensed an ingrained inhumanity. But for this vegetation, but for these patient, fraternal grasses that were like unhappy people, the steppe would have been unendurable; but the wind bore through the grass the seed of its multiplication—and a man, with pressure in his heart, was walking through it toward communism. Chepurny wanted to go away and rest from his feelings, but he waited instead for this man now approaching Chevengur from somewhere distant, through waist-high grass. It was immediately clear that he was not a remnant of scum, but one of the oppressed; he was advancing toward Chevengur as if against an enemy, muttering as he walked and with no expectation of shelter. The wanderer's gait was uneven, a lifetime of exhaustion was making his legs lurch apart, and Chepurny said to himself, "Here comes a comrade. I'll wait for him and embrace him in my sorrow. It's awful to be alone on the eve of communism!"

Chepurny touched a burdock. It too wanted communism: What were the steppe grasslands if not the friendship of living plants? Front gardens, flowers, and flowerbeds, on the other hand, were clearly the seedbeds of scum, and he must remember to mow them down and trample them to the ground forever: let plain grass be free to grow on the streets of Chevengur—like the proletariat, grass endured both the heat of life and the death of snows.

Not far from Chepurny the grass began to bend, rustling meekly, as if from the movement of some foreign body.

"I love you, Klavdiusha, and I want to eat you, but you always seem to be somewhere else!" came Prokofy's tormented voice. He had not expected Chepurny to pass that way.

Chepurny heard, but he was not upset: a man was coming toward him, and he didn't have a Klavdiusha either!

This man was already close, and he had a black beard, and eyes that were devoted to something or other. He was stepping through the clumps of vegetation with hot, dusty boots, which must have been giving off a smell of sweat.

Chepurny leaned pitifully against the fence; he realized with fear that this man with the black beard was very dear and precious to him. Had he not appeared, Chepurny would have begun to cry from grief in an empty, Lenten Chevengur; he had not quite believed that Klavdiusha could squat in the yard or have passion in her for reproduction—he had felt too much respect for her because of the comradely comfort she offered to all the lonely Communists of Chevengur; but now she had gone and joined Prokofy in the tall grass, at a time when the whole town was lying low in expectation of communism, and when he himself, in his sorrow, needed friendship. Had he been able to embrace Klavdiusha, he could calmly have waited another two or three days for communism; but as things were, with no one to bear the weight of his comradely feelings, it was impossible for him to continue any longer; even though no one was able to formulate the firm and eternal meaning of life, nevertheless you forget about this meaning when you live in friendship and the inseparable presence of comrades, when life's troubles are shared out equally and in small portions among martyrs who embrace one another.

The walker stopped in front of Chepurny.

"Are you waiting for comrades?"

"Yes," Chepurny said happily.

"You'll be waiting a long time—there are no comrades now! Or is it kinsfolk you're waiting for?"

"No—comrades."

"Good luck then," said the passerby, and began adjusting the pack of victuals on his back. "There are no comrades today. People who were just scraping by are now all too prosperous. I get about—and I've got eyes in my head."

Sotykh the blacksmith had grown used to disappointment. It was all the same to him whether he lived in the village of Kalitva or in some strange town, and so he had calmly abandoned his smithy for the summer and gone to hire himself out during the construction season as a fitter, since reinforcing-frames weren't so very different from fences and were therefore familiar to him.

"You see, comrades are good people," Sotykh continued, unaware how glad he was of this meeting, "but they're fools and they don't live long. Where can you find a comrade nowadays? The best—the ones who did their best for the poor—have been killed right into their graves. Those who endured are wandering about all lost. The parasite element lords the peace of power over everyone now. But if it's a comrade you're waiting for, you'll be waiting forever!"

Sotykh finally got his pack settled and took a step to go on his way, but Chepurny cautiously reached out to touch him and then began to weep from the agitation and shame of his defenseless friendship. Sotykh at first said nothing, testing Chepurny for lack of sincerity, but then he too let go of his guard against others, and all of him softened with relief.

"If you're crying, then you must be a comrade—one of those good, murdered comrades still with us! Give me a hug and then let's find somewhere to spend the night—we've got some long thinking to do. But don't waste your tears—people aren't songs. A song always makes me cry, I even cried at my own wedding!"

Chevengur closed its doors early, so as to sleep and not feel danger. And so no one, not even Chepurny, with his keen ears, knew that people were quietly conversing in some of the yards. Beside fences, in the shelter of burdocks, former shop assistants and dismissed office workers lay and whispered to one another about the Year of the Lord,[2] about the Thousand-Year Kingdom of Christ, about the future peace of a land refreshed by sufferings; without such conversations it would have been impossible for them to pass meekly along the hell bottom of communism.[3] Forgotten reserves, from centuries of the life of the soul, helped the old inhabitants of Chevengur to bear the remnants of their lives with full dignity of patience and hope. But for Chepurny and his scarce comrades it was harder—there were no books, no old tales, where communism had been written down, where it had been made into a song they could understand and call on for comfort in the hour of danger; Karl Marx looked down from the walls like an alien Sabaoth, and his terrifying books were unable to lead a man to any reassuring imagination of communism; posters from Moscow and the provincial capital depicted the hydra of counterrevolution and trains transporting cloth and calico to co-operative villages, but nowhere could Chepurny see a touching picture of the future in the name of which this hydra was to be beheaded and laden trains sent on their way. He had only the support of his own inspired heart, only its difficult strength with which to win this future, knocking out souls from the bourgeoisie's silenced bodies and embracing a blacksmith now legging it along the road.

Until the first purity of dawn Chepurny and Sotykh lay on the straw in an empty barn—in mental search of communism and its own life of the soul. Chepurny was glad to be with any proletarian—no matter what he said, right or wrong. It was good to stay awake and listen for a long time to a formulation for his own feelings, which had been stifled by their excessive strength; such formulation brings about inner peace and then you can sleep. Sotykh stayed awake too, though he fell silent many times and would start to doze; this, however, would restore his strength and he would wake, speak briefly, grow tired again, and slip back into semioblivion. Chepurny then straightened Sotykh's legs and folded his arms across his chest, so he would rest better.

"Don't stroke me—it's shaming," Sotykh would respond in the warm hush of the barn. "And somehow it's good here with you anyway."

As they were falling asleep, light began to shine through cracks in the barn door, and a smell of steaming manure came from the cool yard outside. Sotykh stood up for a moment and looked at the new day with eyes dazed from uneven sleep.

"What are you doing? Lie down on your right side and stop thinking," said Chepurny, regretting that time had passed by so quickly.

"But you don't let me sleep," Sotykh reproached him. "There are activists like you back in my village—they never leave a man in peace. You're an activist too—the devil take you!"

"But I can't sleep. What else can I do, I ask you now!"

Sotykh smoothed the hair on his head and untangled his beard, tidying himself up as if he might encounter death in his sleep. "If you can't sleep," he said, "it's because of acts of negligence—the Revolution's slowly losing its way. Lie down here beside me and go to sleep. Then, in the morning, gather what's left of the Reds—and strike! Or else you'll find your people have all just wandered off."

"I shall gather the Reds as a matter of urgency," Chepurny formulated to himself, and pressed himself against Sotykh's calm back, so as to recollect his strength more quickly in sleep. But Sotykh's sleep had been interrupted and he was unable to forget himself. "Already light," he thought, seeing the morning. "Time I was off. I'll have a rest later on, when it gets hot—I'll lie down in a gully. A right comrade we've got here! He wants communism—so end of story! Takes himself for the whole people."

Sotykh straightened Chepurny's head—which had lolled over to one side—covered his thin body with his greatcoat, and got up to leave forever.

"Goodbye, barn!" he said to his night lodging as he crossed the threshold. "Live long, don't burn down!"

A dog that had been sleeping in the depths of the barn went off somewhere in search of food, and her puppies began to wander about, yearning for their mother; one stout puppy pressed itself against Chepurny's neck for warmth and began licking it, just above the glands, with a greedy infant tongue. At first Chepurny just smiled—the puppy was tickling him—but then he began to wake up, thanks to the irritating chill of cooling saliva.

The passing comrade was no longer there, but Chepurny was rested now and he didn't grieve for him. "We must hurry up and finish off communism," Chepurny reassured himself. "Then that comrade will return to Chevengur too."

An hour later he called the Chevengur Bolsheviks—eleven men including himself—to the ExecCom building, and repeated words he had already said to them many times: "Come on, lads, we must make communism quickly—otherwise its historical moment will pass. Let Prokofy give us a formulation!"[4]

Prokofy, though in personal possession of all Karl Marx's works, always formulated everything about the Revolution exactly as he pleased—depending only on Klavdiusha's mood and objective circumstances.

Objective circumstances, the one brake on Prokofy's thinking, meant the obscure, but coherent and infallible, instinct of Chepurny. As soon as Prokofy began communicating by heart the work of Karl Marx, as proof of the Revolution's necessarily step-by-step progress and the long calm of Soviet power, Chepurny went taut from keen attention and radically rejected any postponement of communism.

"Prosha, don't try to think more powerfully than Karl Marx. He imagined the worst, because he was cautious—but if we can get communism going straightaway, then so much the better for Marx."

"I cannot deviate from Marx, comrade Chepurny," Prokofy would say with humble subordination of spirit. "If that's what his book says, then theory must be followed letter by letter."

Piusia sighed wordlessly beneath the weight of his own darkness. The other Bolsheviks never argued with Prokofy either; to them all words were the gibberish of a single man, not a matter for the masses.

"Everything you say, Prosha, is good and fair," Chepurny began gently and tactfully. "Only please say—don't you think this slow movement of the revolutionary spirit will be the death of all of us? I may be the first to go to the bad. I'll be worn down by power—no one can go on being better than everyone else forever!"

"As you wish, comrade Chepurny," Prokofy agreed with firm meekness.

Chepurny was quick to understand the feelings raging inside him. "No, comrade Dvanov, not as I wish, but as you all wish, as Lenin wishes, and as Marx kept thinking day and night! Let's get to work—we must cleanse Chevengur of all bourgeois remnants."

"Excellent," said Prokofy, "I've already prepared the draft of a binding resolution."

"Not a resolution, a decree," said Chepurny, for the sake of greater hardness of line. "We can resolve later. First we must lay down the law."

"We can have it published as a decree," Prokofy agreed once again. "Sign the resolution, comrade Chepurny."

"No," said Chepurny. "You heard me."

But the remnants of the Chevengur bourgeoisie did not obey this word-of-mouth decree pasted up with moistened flour on walls, fences, and shutters. The town's indigenous inhabitants felt certain that everything would come to an end any moment; things unheard of, that had never existed before, could hardly continue for long. And so, after waiting twenty-four hours for the remnants of the bourgeoisie to depart, Chepurny set off with Piusia to drive people out of their homes. Each time they entered a new house, Piusia found the most mature bourgeois present and silently smashed him on the cheekbone.

"Read the decree, have you?"

"Yes, comrade," the bourgeois would answer submissively. "Check my documents! I'm not a bourgeois—I'm a former Soviet employee. As soon as there's a need for administrative staff, I have the right to be taken on again."

Chepurny would take the scrap of paper:

> Issued to R. T. Prokopenko to confirm that he has on this day been released from the post of deputy commandant of the reserve bread and fodder stores of the Evacuation Center, and that it is evident from his Soviet standing and the movement of his modes of thoughts that he should be considered a revolutionarily dependable element.
>
> p.p. Director of the Evacuation Center, comrade P. Dvanov.

"Well?" asked Piusia.

Chepurny tore up the scrap of paper. "Expel him. We gave certificates like that to all the bourgeoisie."

"How can you do this, comrades?" Prokopenko pleaded. "You've seen my certificate—I'm a Soviet employee, I didn't even leave with the Whites when everyone else did."

"Where could you go? Your sort love your homes," said Piusia, getting to the bottom of Prokopenko's behavior and clapping him affectionately on the ear.

"Get down to work. All in all, I want the town empty!" After this definitive advice, Chepurny went on his way, so as not to suffer more agitation and to have time to prepare himself for communism.

The expulsion of the bourgeoisie, however, proved no easy task. At first Piusia worked alone—he beat up the remnants of the propertied class, he determined the quantity of food and belongings they would be allowed to take with them, and he packed these belongings into bundles; but by evening Piusia was so exhausted that, instead of hitting the inhabitants of each house, he simply packed their belongings in silence. "If I go on like this, I'll degenerate!" he thought in alarm and went off to find himself some Communist assistants.

But not even a whole detachment of Bolsheviks could have dealt with the residual bourgeoisie in twenty-four hours. Some of the capitalists asked if the Soviet regime would take them on as manual laborers, without wages or rations, while others begged to be allowed to live in the former churches and show fellow feeling with Soviet power, if only from a distance.

"No and no again!" replied Piusia. "You're no longer people, and all nature has changed."

Many of the half-bourgeoisie wept on the floor as they said farewell to their objects and remnants. Pillows lay on beds in warm heaps, capacious trunks stood there like inseparable relatives of the sobbing capitalists, and, as they made their way out, each half-bourgeois carried with them the perennial smell of their household—a smell that had long ago seeped through their lungs into their blood and been transformed into a part of their body. They did not all realize that this smell was the dust of their own belongings, but they had all, through their breathing, refreshed their blood with it. Piusia did not allow the half-bourgeoisie's grief to stagnate in one place. He would throw out onto the street a bundle containing the quota of minimal essentials and then—with the equanimity of a master craftsman grading humanity—seize a grieving person by the middle and sit them down on this bundle, as if on some island of last refuge. Out there in the wind, the half-bourgeois would cease grieving and start prodding the bundle instead: Had they been given their full entitlement? By late evening Piusia had evicted the entire class of residual scum, and he then sat down himself to have a smoke with his comrades. A fine, acrid rain set in—the wind grew silent in exhaustion and quietly lay down underneath this rain. The half-bourgeoisie were still sitting on their bundles in long, unbroken ranks, waiting for some appearance.

Chepurny appeared and, in his impatient voice, ordered them all to leave Chevengur at once and forever, since communism had no time to wait and the new class was standing idle as people waited for their common property and dwelling places. The remnants of capitalism heard Chepurny out but went on sitting there in the rain and silence.

"Comrade Piusia," said Chepurny with restraint. "What's gotten into these dreamers? Tell them to clear off before we kill them. With them around there's nowhere we can get the Revolution up and running!"

"Straightaway, comrade Chepurny!" replied Piusia, quickly taking out his revolver. "Clear off and get lost!" he then said to the nearest half-bourgeois.

The half-bourgeois hid his face in his dispossessed hands and began to weep protractedly, without any preliminary moans. Piusia sent a hot bullet into his bundle. Through the smoke the half-bourgeois got back up onto his legs, which had instantaneously regained their strength, while Piusia grabbed the bundle with his left hand and hurled it away.

"Off with you!" he determined. "The proletariat let you have your things as a present—you should've gone on your way with them. Now we're taking them back."

Piusia's subordinates hurriedly opened fire on the bundles and baskets of the town's former inhabitants—and the half-bourgeois slowly and without fear set off into the town's calm surroundings.

This left eleven people to live in the town; ten had fallen asleep, and the eleventh was wandering the lifeless streets in anguish. There was a twelfth, Klavdiusha, but she was considered the raw material of communal joy and therefore kept in a special house, away from the dangerous life of the masses.

Toward midnight the rain stopped, and the sky went still in exhaustion. A sad summer darkness lay over Chevengur, now quiet, empty, and terrible. With cautious heart, Chepurny closed the wide-open gates in front of the house of the former Zavyn-Duvailo and wondered what had happened to the town's dogs; in the yards there was nothing except immemorial burdock and kind goosefoot, and inside the houses, for the first time in long ages, no one was sighing in their sleep. Sometimes Chepurny would enter a room, sit in an armchair still preserved there, and take some snuff, just so as to move about a little and make a sound for himself. Sometimes he found piles of homemade buns in cupboards, and in one house there was a bottle of Vin Santo church wine.[5] Chepurny pressed the cork deeper into the bottle, so the wine wouldn't lose its taste before the arrival of the proletariat, and he threw a towel over the buns to keep off the dust. The beds everywhere were especially well equipped—the sheets lay fresh and cool and the pillows promised peace to any head; Chepurny tried out one of the beds, but he at once felt dismal and ashamed to be lying in such comfort, as if the bed had been given to him in exchange for his uncomfortable, revolutionary soul. In spite of these empty, well-furnished homes, not one of the ten other Chevengur Bolsheviks had chosen to spend the night in ease; instead, they were all lying together on the floor of a communal brick building requisitioned in 1917 for a revolution then without shelter. Chepurny likewise thought of that brick building as his only home—rather than the cozy warmth of these clean best rooms.

A defenseless sorrow lay over the whole of Chevengur—as in the yard of a father's house, when the mother has been carried out in a coffin and, along with the orphaned son, the fences and burdocks and the abandoned entrance room are all yearning for her. And the boy leans his head against the fence, strokes the rough boards with his hand and weeps in the darkness of an extinguished world, while the father wipes away his own tears and tells his son not to worry, saying everything will settle down and it'll all be all right in time. Chepurny was able to formulate his feelings only with the help of memories; he made his way into the future with a dark, expectant heart, sensing at least the edges of the Revolution and so managing to keep to the right course. But on this night there was not one memory to help Chepurny determine the situation of Chevengur. The houses stood there all dark—abandoned forever not only by the half-bourgeoisie, but also by the smaller animals. There were not even any cows anywhere; life had renounced this place and gone off to die in the tall steppe grass, relinquishing its dead fate to eleven men, ten of whom were sleeping while one was wandering about, with the sorrow of obscure danger.

Chepurny sat down on the ground by a wattle fence and softly, with two fingers, touched a burdock that was growing there; it too was alive—and was now going to live under communism. Somehow dawn was a long time coming, though surely it must have been time for a new day. Chepurny went still and began to feel afraid: Would the sun rise in the morning, would morning ever come—now that the old world was no longer?

The evening's storm clouds hung powerless and exhausted in a motionless place; all their moist fallen strength had been used by the steppe grass for growth and multiplication. Together with the rain, the wind had come down from above and had settled for a long time somewhere in the cramped space of the grass. Chepurny could remember empty nights in childhood that had come to a stop like this; it had felt just as cramped and dismal inside his body, and he hadn't wanted to go to sleep and had lain on the stove in the hut's stifling silence, a little boy with wide open eyes. Deep inside him, from his belly to his neck, he had sensed a kind of dry, narrow stream, constantly stirring his heart and carrying the sorrow of life into his child's mind; a piercing anxiety had made little Chepurny toss and turn on the stove, weeping and raging, as if a worm were tickling him right through the middle of his body. And this same dry, stifling anxiety was troubling Chepurny again, on a Chevengur night that might have extinguished the world forever.

"But things will be good tomorrow, if the sun rises," Chepurny reassured himself. "Why is communism making me grieve, as if I were a half-bourgeois?"

By now, the half-bourgeoisie were probably lying low in the steppe, or else walking away from Chevengur with heavy feet. Like all adults, they knew nothing of the anguish of uncertainty felt by children and party members; to them, the life to come was simply unhappy, but not dangerous or enigmatic, whereas Chepurny was sitting there in fear of the coming day, because on this first day everything would be somehow awkward and awful, as if what had long been virginity were now ripe for marriage and everyone would have to be wedded the following day.

Chepurny pressed his hands to his face in shame and did not move for a long time, enduring this senseless disgrace.

Somewhere in the middle of Chevengur a rooster crowed, and a dog, abandoning its master's yard, went quietly past Chepurny.

"Zhuchók, Zhuchók!" Chepurny called out joyfully. "Here—please!"

Zhuchók obediently came up and sniffed the outstretched human hand. The hand smelled of kindness and straw.

"You all right, Zhuchók? Can't say I am!"

There were burrs caught in Zhuchók's fur, and his behind was smeared with a mixture of dirt and horse-dung—he was a faithful small-town dog, guardian of Russian nights and winters, a typical resident of a middling property.

Chepurny led the dog into a house and fed him some white buns. The dog ate them with a quiver of alarm, since it was the first time in his life that such food had come his way. Chepurny noticed the dog's fright and found him a piece of homemade pie, with an egg filling, but the dog did not eat the pie—he just sniffed it and circled alertly around it, mistrusting life's gift. Chepurny waited for Zhuchók to calm down and eat the pie, but then he took it and swallowed it down himself—as evidence for the dog. Zhuchók rejoiced at being delivered from this poison and began sweeping the dusty floor with his tail.

"You must be a poor dog, not a bourgeois dog!" Chepurny said with affection. "Never in your life have you tasted fine flour—so here's to life in Chevengur!"

Two more roosters crowed outside. "That makes three fowl," Chepurny counted, "and one head of livestock."

The moment he left the best room and went out into the fresh air, Chepurny began to feel cold. He could now see another Chevengur: a cool and open town, lit by the gray light of a still far-away sun; its houses were not frightening to live in, and it was possible to walk along its streets, since the grass was growing just as before and the paths were still intact. The morning light was blossoming in space and eating away the frail, fading clouds.

"That means the sun will be ours!" said Chepurny, and pointed greedily to the east.

Two nameless birds flew by just above him and settled on a fence, shaking their small tails.

"You on our side too?" he said in greeting, throwing the birds a handful of crumbs and tobacco from his pocket. "Well then—have a bite to eat!"

Chepurny was now ready to sleep, and he no longer felt ashamed of anything. He was on his way toward the communal brick building where his ten comrades were lying, but he was met by four sparrows who, out of prejudice of caution, flew up onto a fence.

"I'd counted on you," he said. "You're kith and kin. And there's nothing to fear now. The bourgeoisie have gone. Well then—live free!"

A light was burning in the brick building. Two men were asleep, and the other eight were lying on their backs, gazing up into the high space above them; their faces were gloomy and closed off by obscure thought.

"Why aren't you asleep?" Chepurny asked them. "Today's our first day. The sun's already risen and birds are flying to join us—why lie here in fear?"

Chepurny lay down on the straw, wrapped his greatcoat around him, and fell silent in warmth and oblivion. Outside the window, dew was already rising to meet the naked sun, which had not betrayed the Chevengur Bolsheviks and was now rising above them. Piusia, who had not slept all night, got up with a rested heart and diligently washed and tidied himself in honor of the first day of communism. The lamp was burning with a yellow light from beyond the grave; Piusia extinguished it with pleasure of destruction and then remembered that nobody was guarding Chevengur—capitalists might move back in without warning, and once again it would be necessary to burn the lamp all night long, in order for the half-bourgeois to know that armed Communists were sitting there without sleep. Piusia climbed onto the roof and crouched against the metal, on account of the furious light from the dew now boiling in the sun. Then Piusia looked at the sun itself, with pride and proprietorial fellow feeling.

"Yes—shine down! Get things to grow—even from stones!" Piusia whispered with stifled excitement. He did not have enough words for a shout, since he did not trust his own knowledge. "Shine down!" he repeated, clenching his fists to help the light of the sun drive down into the clay, into the stones, and into Chevengur.

But the sun was pressing dryly and firmly into the earth anyway—and this first earth, in the weakness of exhaustion, had begun to stream with the juice of grasses and the moisture of loam, rippling and quivering all its far-flung, hairy steppe, while the sun simply went on getting hotter, turning stone-like from tense, dry patience.

The acrid sun made Piusia's gums start to itch. "It never used to rise like this," he noted with satisfaction. "Yes, my spine's prickling with courage, like when I hear a brass band."

Piusia looked into the distance—at the rest of the sun's path: Was there anything that might get in its way? He stepped back in outrage: yesterday's half-bourgeois had made an encampment on the outskirts of Chevengur; fires were burning, goats were grazing, and women were washing their clothes in puddles of rainwater. Dismissed clerks, and other half-bourgeois, were hard at work—probably digging dugouts—while three shop-assistants, working naked in the fresh air, were constructing a tent from underwear and sheets: anything to create property and a dwelling.

Piusia immediately started thinking: Where had the half-bourgeois got hold of so much fabric? He had issued it to them himself, according to a fairly stringent norm.

Piusia looked at the sun with mournful eyes, as if it had been snatched away from him. He scratched with his nails at his thin neck tendons and said into the air above him, with timidity of respect, "Wait—don't waste yourself on the class-alien!"

Having grown unused to wives and sisters, to cleanliness and substantial food, the Chevengur Bolsheviks led a self-made life. They washed with sand rather than soap; they dried themselves with their sleeves and with burdock leaves; they felt the hens and then searched for eggs in nooks and crannies. As for their main soup, they began cooking it in the morning, in an iron vat whose original purpose was unknown. Anyone who went past would throw in some nearby plants—nettles, dill, goosefoot, or any other edible green; a few hens would be tossed in, and the hindquarters of a calf, if one showed up at the right time—and the soup would go on cooking until late at night, when the Bolsheviks were done with revolution and ready to take in food, and when beetles, moths, and mosquitoes began to descend on the vat. The Bolsheviks would then eat—once every twenty-four hours—and sleep lightly.

Piusia went past the vat—where the soup was already boiling—and did not throw anything in.

He then opened the storeroom, took a heavy, dented bucket filled with machine-gun cartridge belts, and asked comrade Kirey, who was gulping down some raw eggs, to bring the machine gun along behind him. On peaceful days Kirey usually walked down to the lake and went hunting with this gun, nearly always bringing back a gull, or at least a heron; he had also tried to shoot the fish in the water but had seldom hit anything. Kirey did not ask Piusia where they were going; he was already looking forward to taking a potshot at whatever he came across—just as long as it wasn't live proletariat.

"Piusia, shall I knock you down a sparrow from up in the sky?" Kirey asked eagerly.

"I'd rather knock *you* down!" Piusia replied with feeling. "Was that you in the vegetable garden the other day—picking off hens?"

"But they end up in the pot anyway."

"Any way but not that way! You should strangle them by hand. Each bullet you squander—a surplus bourgeois lives longer."

"All right, Piusia, it won't happen again."

The fires in the encampment had already died down. The half-bourgeoisie's meal was ready; they wouldn't be going without hot food that day.

"See that bunch from yesterday?" said Piusia, pointing to the half-bourgeoisie, who were sitting round their extinguished fires in small collectives.

"Hah! They won't get away from me now!"

"And there you were wasting bullets on hens. Quick, train your machine on them point-blank! It'll pain Chepurny's soul if he wakes up to these remnants."

Kirey set up the machine gun with quick hands and got the cartridge belt moving there and then. As he maneuvered the bracket, Kirey managed now and again to take his hands away for a moment and slap them, to the bullets' staccato rhythm, against his cheeks, mouth, and knees—thus providing his own accompaniment. The bullets would then stray from the target and plow into the ground, throwing up earth and uprooting plants.

"Don't lose the adversary, keep him in your sights!" said Piusia, who was lying there with nothing to do. "Take your time, don't overheat the barrel!"

But Kirey needed to connect the machine gun's work with his own body, and it was impossible for him not to encourage the gun with his arms and legs.

On the floor of the brick house Chepurny began to toss and turn. He had not yet woken, but his heart had lost its accuracy of breath on account of the even pulsing of the nearby machine gun. His comrade Zheyev, asleep beside him, had also heard the sound, but had decided not to wake up since it was only Kirey somewhere nearby, shooting birds for their soup. Zheyev pulled up his greatcoat, covering both his own head and Chepurny's and so muting the sound of the gun. Because of the lack of air under the greatcoat, Chepurny then began to toss and turn even more, till in the end he threw off the coat completely, and having freed his breathing, awoke, since something was too quiet and dangerous.

The sun was already high in the sky. It was morning in Chevengur, and communism must have already set in.

Kirey came into the room and put a bucket of empty cartridge belts down on the floor.

"Take the bucket into the storeroom," said Piusia from outside, as he wheeled in the machine gun. "Why clatter about in there? You'll wake everyone."

"The bucket's a lot lighter now, comrade Piusia!" said Kirey, and took it to its standard place in the storeroom.

36

THE BUILDINGS in Chevengur were endowed with age-old stability, in keeping with the lives of the people there, who were so true to their own feelings and interests that they grew overexhausted from ministering to them and aged from the accumulation of property.[1]

It was hard for the proletarians to shift these solid, well-lived-in constructions, since the bottom rows of the houses' logs, laid without any foundation, had sent out roots into the deep soil. And so, after the relocation of buildings under Chepurny and socialism, the town square came to look like a plowed field; the proletarians had simply ripped the houses out of the ground, along with their roots, and dragged them about regardless. During those difficult voluntary Saturdays, Chepurny regretted having exiled the class of residual scum with destruction, since these scum could have manhandled the rooted buildings instead of the proletariat, who had endured more than enough already. But during those first days of socialism in Chevengur, Chepurny had not known that the proletariat would require auxiliary manual labor. On the very first day of socialism, Chepurny had woken so filled with hope by the sun, which had risen before him, and by the sight of all Chevengur lying ready and waiting, that he had asked Prokofy to go somewhere or other at once and summon the poor to Chevengur.[2]

"Go along, Prosha," Chepurny said quietly. "As it is, we're thin on the ground and without comradeship we'll soon be feeling bored and lonely."

Prokofy confirmed Chepurny's thinking. "Of course, comrade Chepurny. Socialism's a mass affair. Anyone else we should summon?"

"Call all the others you meet," Chepurny concluded. "Take Piusia with you and get moving. Any poor man you see, bring him here as a comrade."

"And these *others*?"

"Bring them too. Our socialism here is a fact."

"Without the support of the masses, comrade Chepurny, no fact possesses stability."

Chepurny did not doubt this. "That's why I said we'd soon be feeling bored and lonely—and that certainly wouldn't be socialism! Why try to prove things to me, when I've sensed them already?"

Prokofy made no objections and immediately went off to find transport, in order to go and fetch proletariat. Toward midday he found a horse wandering about the surrounding steppe and, with Piusia's mediation, he harnessed it to a phaeton.[3] And in the evening, after loading the carriage with two weeks' worth of supplies, he set off into the remaining country, beyond the Chevengur town boundary; he himself sat inside, perusing a century-old survey map, while Piusia attended to the horse, which was no longer accustomed to being in harness. Nine Bolsheviks walked behind the phaeton, to see how it moved, since this was its first journey under socialism and the wheels might not obey.

"Prosha!" Chepurny called out in farewell. "We'll hold the town—but mind you bring us the right and precise social element!"

"Huh!" said Prokofy, taking offense. "Think I've never seen proper proletariat in my life?"

Zheyev, an elderly Bolshevik who had grown stout thanks to the Civil War,[4] went up to the phaeton and kissed Prokofy on his chapped lips.

"Prosha," he said, "don't forget to find us some women too. We need women for tenderness, brother. Even if they're only beggar women. Otherwise . . . See—I start kissing you."

"That can be postponed," Chepurny replied. "You don't respect a woman as a comrade—all you notice is the elemental surroundings. And you, Prosha," he added, "must be guided by social indication, not by anyone's wishes. If a woman's a comrade, go ahead! But if she's back to front, send her packing!"

Zheyev did not reaffirm his wishes, since communism had been realized anyway and women were sure to appear in it, if only as secret comrades. But not even Chepurny was able to reach any further understanding of why woman posed such a danger for primary socialism, even if she were poor and a comrade. He knew only that in the past there had always been love for a woman and reproduction from her—and that this had been an alien and natural matter, not something human and Communist. For communal life in Chevengur, woman was acceptable in a drier and more human form but not in her full beauty, which did not constitute a part of communism, since the beauty of woman's nature had existed beforehand, under capitalism, as had mountains, stars, and other inhuman phenomena. These foresensings made Chepurny ready to welcome to Chevengur any woman whose face was darkened by the sorrow of poverty and the aging of labor. Such a woman would be fit only for comradeship and would not stand out within the oppressed mass and evoke the harmful curiosity of lonely Bolsheviks. For the time being, Chepurny acknowledged only class affection, not the womanly sort; he sensed class affection to be the close attraction a proletarian feels for a being of his own kind—whereas nature had gone its own way in creating the bourgeoisie and a woman's more womanly aspects, taking no account of the proletarian and the Bolshevik. For similar reasons, Chepurny, with his frugal concern for the preservation and integrity of Soviet Chevengur, saw benefit even in the tangential fact of Chevengur being located in flat, dreary steppe. The sky over Chevengur differed little from steppe; nowhere was there any sign of beautiful, natural forces that might distract people from communism and a comradely concern for one another.

In the evening of that same day, after Prokofy and Piusia had set off to fetch proletariat, Chepurny and Zheyev walked once around the town's boundary. They straightened stakes in the wattle fencing —since it was important now to take care even of fences—talked in the remoteness of night about Lenin's mind, and then decided that was enough. As he lay down to sleep, Zheyev told Chepurny that it would be good to place symbols of some kind around the town and also to wash the floors of the houses, to make everything proper for the approaching proletariat.

Chepurny agreed about the floors and said he would put up symbols on the taller trees. He was, in fact, glad of this task, since the coming of night was making him anxious. Probably the whole world and the entire bourgeois element knew of communism's appearance in Chevengur—and so the surrounding danger was now all the closer. The tread of White armies might be heard in the dark of the steppe, or the slow rustle of barefoot brigand detachments. Never again, then, would Chepurny see Chevengur's grasses and empty houses; nor would he see the comradely sun look down on this primary town as it prepared, with clean floors and freshened air, to greet the unknown, homeless proletariat now plodding along without the meaning of their own lives or the respect of others. One thing both calmed and inspired Chepurny: somewhere near Moscow or in the Valday Hills—as Prokofy had determined from the map—there was a distant, secret place called the Kremlin and Lenin was sitting there beside a lamp, thinking, writing, and not sleeping. But why was he writing now? Now, after all, there was Chevengur—and it was time for Lenin to stop writing, pour himself back into the proletariat, and live. Letting Zheyev go on ahead, Chepurny lay down in the comfortable grass of an impassable Chevengur street. He knew that Lenin was thinking about Chevengur and the Chevengur Bolsheviks, even though he did not know the names of these Chevengur comrades. Probably Lenin was writing a letter to Chepurny, telling him not to sleep, to guard communism in Chevengur, and to allow the feelings and life of all the nameless grassroots people to be drawn toward him. Lenin was telling Chepurny to have no fear of anything, since the long time of history had come to an end and poverty and grief had multiplied to such an extent that nothing else now remained. He was telling Chepurny and all his comrades to expect him as a guest in communism so that he, Lenin, could embrace in Chevengur all the earth's martyrs and put an end to the movement of unhappiness in life. And Lenin then sent his regards and decreed the firm establishment of communism in Chevengur forever.

At this point, Chepurny got to his feet, calm and rested, just slightly regretting the absence of some bourgeois or other, or even an unneeded fighter, whom he could have sent on foot to Lenin in his Kremlin, bearing dispatches from Chevengur.

"There, in the Kremlin, communism's probably reached a good age already," Chepurny thought enviously. "Lenin's there, after all. But what if they too call me 'the Jap'? It's the bourgeoisie who first gave me that name, and now there's no way I can send Lenin my real name."

A lamp was still burning in the brick house, and the eight Bolsheviks, anticipating some kind of danger, were unable to sleep. Chepurny went in and said, "Comrades, we need to do some thinking ourselves. There's no Prokofy for you now. The town stands wide open and there's no ideas written anywhere. Comrades passing by won't know who lives here and why. The same with the floors, they need a good wash. Zheyev said what a ruination we've got here—and he was right. We need to air the houses, to let the wind blow through them—otherwise it still stinks of bourgeoisie everywhere. We need to think, comrades. Otherwise, what are we here for, I ask you now!"

Each of the Chevengur Bolsheviks felt ashamed and did his best to think. Kirey listened to the noise in his head and waited for thoughts to come out, until his zeal and a rush of blood made the wax in his ears start to boil. Then he went up close to Chepurny and announced with quiet conscientiousness, "Comrade Chepurny, my mind is bringing pus out of my ears, but not a trace of a thought."

Instead of thought, Chepurny gave Kirey a more immediate task.

"Go for a walk around the town and see if you hear anything. Maybe you'll find someone wandering about, or perhaps standing still out of fear. Don't put an end to him straightaway. Bring him back here alive, so we can check him out."

"That I can do," Kirey agreed. "Otherwise, it's a vast night—the whole town could be dragged off into the steppe while we do our thinking."

"That could easily happen," Chepurny said anxiously. "And without the town you and I would have no life at all. Once again there'll be only our idea and war."

Kirey went out into the fresh air to guard communism, while the remaining Bolsheviks sat there, went on thinking, and listened to the lamp wick sucking up kerosene. And it was no less silent outside—so silent that Kirey's plodding, only slowly quieting footsteps rang out for a long time in the resonant emptiness of the night gloom and the town's newly won property.

Only Zheyev did not sit idle; he came up with a symbol he had once heard at a military political meeting in the wartime steppe. He told the others to bring him some clean cloth and he would write something on it to bring joy to passing proletarians and ensure that they did not pass the town by. Chepurny went to a bourgeois's former house and came back with some clean linen. Zheyev spread the linen out in the lamplight and gave his approval.

"It's a shame," he said. "So much diligence has gone into this, so much of the pure hands of women. It would be good if Bolshevik women can now learn to create stuff with such tenderness in it."

Zheyev lay down on his belly and began writing on the linen with coal from the stove. Everyone stood around him, sympathizing with him in his task of giving immediate expression to the Revolution, to bring relief to them all.

Hurried by the general air of expectation, Zheyev diligently tried to find a path through his memory. He then wrote out these words:

> COMRADES THE POOR. YOU HAVE MADE EVERY COMFORT AND THING IN THE WORLD. NOW YOU HAVE DESTROYED THEM AND WANT SOMETHING BETTER—ONE ANOTHER. TO THIS END, WE HERE IN CHEVENGUR SEEK TO ACQUIRE COMRADES FROM THE PASSING ROADS.

Chepurny was first to approve this symbol.

"Correct," he said. "I was feeling the same. Property is only of current benefit, while comrades are a necessity. Without them, you can't conquer anything—and you end up turning into a swine yourself."

And all eight men then carried the canvas through the empty town, to hang it on a pole near the beaten road where people might soon appear. Chepurny was in no hurry. He was afraid that, once they'd completed this task, the others would all lie down to sleep and he would be left alone, to endure the anxiety and anguish of this second Communist night. When he was among comrades, his soul was taken up with petty concerns—and this expenditure of his inner resources made life less frightening. But after they'd found two tall poles and prepared them, a midnight wind began to blow. This cheered Chepurny; if, in the bourgeoisie's absence, poles still swayed in the wind the same as ever, this was proof that the bourgeoisie was definitely not a force of nature.

Kirey was supposed to be walking around the town without interruption, but no one could hear him. The eight Bolsheviks stood there in the night wind, listening to noises out in the steppe and keeping close together, protecting one another from any acute nighttime danger that might suddenly sound from the disturbing darkness. Zheyev was incapable of awaiting an enemy for so long without killing him and so he set off alone into the steppe, on deep reconnaissance, while the other seven remained in reserve, not wanting to leave all the responsibility for the town on Kirey alone. These seven Bolsheviks lay down on the earth for warmth and listened to the surrounding night, which might be sheltering enemies with the comfort of its gloom.

Chepurny was first to make out some kind of quiet grinding, perhaps nearby, perhaps far away. Something was moving, threatening Chevengur, although the movement of this mysterious item was extremely slow, either because of its weight and strength or because it was damaged and exhausted. Chepurny got to his feet and the others followed. A compressed, exasperated flame momentarily illuminated an unknown expanse of cloud, like a glimmer of dawn extinguished over someone's dream—and, like a wind, the shock of this discharge rushed past over the bowing grasses. Chepurny and the other six ran forward in their usual line. The flash was not repeated. Chepurny kept running until his heart, having relived the war and the Revolution, had swelled right up to his throat. He then looked back at the town behind them. A light was burning there.

"Stop, comrades!" he shouted. "We've been outflanked. Zheyev, Kesha! Here, all of you! Piusia! Give it to them straight! Quick, where have you gone? Seems communism's made me go all weak."

The weight of his heart, now so full of blood that it took up his whole body, made Chepurny unable to get back onto his feet. Thin and sick, he lay on the ground with his revolver. Six Bolsheviks stood over him with their weapons, observing the steppe, Chevengur, and their fallen comrade.

"We must stick close together!" said Kesha. "We can carry the Jap back to Chevengur in our arms. That's the seat of our power, and we can't abandon a man with no family."

The Bolsheviks headed back toward Chevengur. They did not need to carry Chepurny long, since his heart soon subsided and returned to its own small place. A calm light was burning in someone's house and there was no longer any sound out in the steppe. The Bolsheviks advanced at their soldierly steppe pace, until they saw some tall grass lit by this window and the grass's shadow on the narrow path running down the center of a blocked street. Without a word of command, the Bolsheviks stood in line, their chests facing the enemy's luminous window. They raised their guns and fired a quick volley through the glass. The light went out—and out of the dark of the destroyed window appeared Kirey's bright face. He looked at the seven men, wondering who they could be. Who could be shooting in Chevengur when he himself was communism's night watchman?

After recovering his self-command, Chepurny said to Kirey, "The town's empty, brigands are running wild in the steppe—and here you are wasting kerosene! What's gotten into you? Leaving the town orphaned when the proletariat will come marching in tomorrow! Why, I ask you now!"

Kirey collected himself, then replied, "I was sleeping, comrade Chepurny—and I could see the whole of Chevengur in dream, as if from a treetop. Bare as can be, and the whole town deserted. But try walking about—and you can hardly see a thing. And there's the wind howling goodness knows what in your ear. Except that it's got no body, I'd have shot at that brigand wind."

"But why waste kerosene, you backward blockhead? Where will our proletariat find illumination when they appear? The proletariat loves reading. And what does a social scoundrel like you do? Burn up their kerosene!"

"Without music, comrade Chepurny, I can't fall asleep in the dark," Kirey confessed. "I like to sleep somewhere merry, where there's a fire or a light. Even a fly's better than nothing—as long as it buzzes."

"Well then, stop sleeping and get back to patrolling the town boundary," said Chepurny. "And we'll go and rescue Zheyev. We abandoned an entire comrade because of that signal of yours."

When they reached the end of Chevengur, the seven comrades lay down on the steppe and put their ears to the ground: Was anything still grinding in the distance? And was Zheyev making his way back or already lying dead until morning? A little later, Kirey joined them and said, "You lot are lying down, but a man is perishing out there. I'd run and look for him myself, but I'm guarding the town."

Kesha retorted that it was wrong to trade the entire proletariat for Zheyev alone. If they all rushed off to save a single personality, the town might be burned down by brigands.

"I'll extinguish the town," Kirey promised. "We've got wells. But they may have ended Zheyev's soul already. Why must we wait for proletariat? We don't have any proletariat, but we did have a Zheyev."

Chepurny and Kesha leaped to their feet and, with no pity for Chevengur, tore off into the continuing night of the steppe—and the five remaining Bolsheviks followed close at their heels.

Kirey went behind a fence, made some burdock leaves into a pillow, and lay down to listen out for the enemy until morning.

The clouds had dropped away a little toward the earth's edges, leaving the sky clear in the middle. Kirey was looking at a star, and the star at him, so that the night would not be boring. The Bolsheviks had all left Chevengur. Kirey lay there alone, surrounded by steppe as if by an empire, and thinking, "I live and live, but why? Probably, for life to go definitively well for me. The Revolution, after all, takes care of me. Like it or not, things will turn out pleasant. It's only now that they're bad. Proshka says it's because progress hasn't ended yet—that happiness will suddenly be revealed here in the emptiness. What's with that star? Shining and shining. Is there something it needs? If only it would fall—then I could have a look. But no, the star won't fall. What keeps it in place now is science, not God. If only morning would come. Here I lie, supporting all of communism. If I get up and leave, communism will leave Chevengur too—or maybe it'll remain somewhere or other. And what is this communism anyway? Is it a matter of buildings? Or of us Bolsheviks alone?"

Something wet dropped onto Kirey's neck but immediately dried up.

"Something dripping," he said to himself. "But how come, when there aren't any clouds? Something must be accumulating up there, then flying off at random . . . Well then, drop into my mouth." Kirey then opened his whole mouth and throat, but nothing more dropped in. "All right then, drop nearby," he said, showing the sky a burdock close beside him. "But leave me alone, give me some peace. Somehow, life's tired me out today."

Kirey knew that the enemy had to be somewhere, but he couldn't sense him in the poor, unplowed steppe—let alone in the purged, proletarian town—and so he fell asleep with the calm of a conclusive victor.

Chepurny, on the other hand, was afraid of sleep during these first proletarian nights and was glad to be sallying out against the enemy. It was not right to be feeling fear and shame now that communism was already present; it was better to be going into action alongside his comrades. And so, overcoming his heart's lack of awareness, he walked through the night steppe into the remoteness of alienated space, determined to fall upon the homeless, exhausted enemy and deprive his wind-chilled body of its last warmth.

"Silence all around, and then the bastards begin shooting," Chepurny muttered crossly. "They don't want us to get life started."

The Bolsheviks' eyes, accustomed during the Civil War to midnight dark, noticed somewhere in the distance a black body that must have come from elsewhere. Lying on the ground was what might have been a long piece of trimmed stone. The steppe in these parts was flat as the water of a lake and this foreign body did not belong to the local earth. Chepurny and the other marching Bolsheviks came to a halt, trying to determine the distance to this stationary alien object. But this proved impossible—the black body lay as if beyond an abyss; the tall grass transformed the darkness into a slow-moving wave, making it impossible to judge distance by eye. And so the Bolsheviks ran forward, their constant revolvers drawn.

There was a grinding sound from the black body. They could now hear that it was close by. Small, chalky stones were splitting apart and the earth's topmost crust was creaking. Halted by their curiosity, the Bolsheviks lowered their revolvers.

"A fallen star—no doubt about it," said Chepurny, unaware how his heart was burning after their long, hurried march. "We'll take it back to Chevengur and rough-hew it to five points. It's not an enemy—it's science, flying to join us in communism."

Chepurny sat down, overjoyed that even stars were drawn to communism. The body of the fallen star ceased grinding and came to a stop.

"There's no end to the good things that may come our way now," Chepurny explained to them all. "Now even stars will come flying to us, and comrades will step down from them, and birds will learn speech, like children come back to life. Communism's no joke—it's the end of the world!"

Chepurny lay down on the ground. He forgot about the night, the danger, and empty Chevengur, and recalled what he never recalled—his wife. What was lying beneath him, however, was empty steppe, not his wife—and he got back onto his feet.

"Maybe the International's sent us some kind of aid or machine," said Kesha. "Maybe it's some kind of iron roller, to crush the bourgeoisie with gravity. Since we're fighting here, the International must be thinking about us."[5]

Piotr Varfolomeyevich Vekovoy, the oldest of the Bolsheviks,[6] took off his straw hat and saw the unknown body clearly—only he couldn't remember what it was. The routines of a shepherd's life had endowed him with the ability to recognize a flying bird at night and to determine the species of a particular tree at a distance of several versts. It was as if his senses were located some way in front of him, allowing him to understand any phenomenon even without close proximity to it.

"It's got to be a barrel from the sugar refinery," he pronounced, not yet quite trusting himself. "Yes, that's what it is, and that's why the pebbles were cracking. The peasants from Krutevo must have gone off with it—and then found they couldn't get it all the way home. Weight outweighed greed. And they tried to drag it when they should have just rolled it!"

Once again the earth began to creak and crack. The barrel was now slowly turning, rolling toward the Bolsheviks. Deceived as he was, Chepurny was first to run up to the moving barrel. He fired at it from ten paces—and a cloud of rust showered onto his face. The barrel continued to advance on Chepurny and the other Bolsheviks, and they slowly began to give ground. There was no knowing what was causing the barrel to move; it was grinding its weight over the dry soil and preventing Chepurny from concentrating his thought on it, while night, now yielding to morning, had deprived the steppe of the last stray weakness of light previously emanating from the scarce stars high in the sky.

The barrel slowed down and began to rock about on the spot, unable to mount a small earth mound that was resisting its progress. Without thinking, Chepurny was about to speak, but before he had time for this, he heard a song, sung by the tired, sad voice of a woman:

> I dreamed of a fish in a lake
> And that fish turned out to be me.

Little as little can be,
I lived and swam to the sea...

Never did the song come to a conclusion, although the Bolsheviks would gladly have listened further, and they stood for a long time in greedy expectation of voice and song. The song did not continue and the barrel did not stir; most likely, the being they had heard singing inside the iron was exhausted and had lain down flat, forgetting both words and music.

"Listening, are you?" The voice was Zheyev's, from behind the barrel. He had not yet dared show himself, afraid he might be mistaken for a sudden enemy and killed.

"Yes," Chepurny replied. "Will she sing any more?"

"No," said Zheyev. "She's already sung three times. I've been on guard here for hours, like a shepherd. They push from inside and the barrel turns. I fired at it once, but to no avail."

"But who is it in there?" asked Kesha.

"I don't know," Zheyev explained. "Some half-wit bourgeois girl and her brother. Before you came, they were kissing. But then her brother went and died, and she started singing on her own."

"Seems she wants to become a fish," said Chepurny. "Must want to start life all over again. Why, I ask you now!"

"She does," said Zheyev. "That's for sure."

"What should we do with her?" asked Chepurny, now addressing all his comrades. "She's got a touching voice, and there's no art in Chevengur. Should we pull her out and return her to life?"

"No," said Zheyev. "She's too weak now, and half-witted into the bargain. And we've no food for her—she's a bourgeois. If she were a peasant woman, well and good... But she's just an outmoded throwback. We need fellow feeling, not art."[7]

"So what should we do?" Chepurny asked everyone once again.

No one said anything. Whether they took care of the bourgeois girl or left her made no useful difference.

"Into the gully with her then—and we can go back and wash

floors!" Chepurny decided. "Prokofy must have gone a long way by now. The proletariat may appear tomorrow."

The eight Bolsheviks set to work, rolling the barrel toward the spot, about a verst farther away from the town, where the ground began to slope down toward the edge of a ravine. Throughout this operation some kind of soft stuffing went on rolling about inside the barrel, but the Bolsheviks were in a hurry, doing their best to accelerate the barrel and not listening to the half-wit bourgeois girl, who had by then fallen silent. Soon the barrel was moving from its own momentum, heading down the slope toward the ravine—and the Bolsheviks were able to step back from their work.

"It's a boiler from the sugar refinery," said Vekovoy, wanting his memory to be correct. "But I kept wondering what kind of machine it could be."

"Yes," said Chepurny, "maybe you're right. But let it roll on its way. We can get by without it."

"I thought it was a round beam," said Kesha. "But you say it was a boiler."

"A boiler," said Vekovoy. "It's got rivets."

The boiler was still rolling down the slope. Not only was it not growing quieter with distance but it was grinding and humming more loudly than ever, since its acceleration was growing more swiftly than the space left behind. Chepurny squatted down, listening out for the boiler's end. The hum of its rotation suddenly ceased to be audible—it had passed over the cliff edge and was now flying through the air. Half a minute later it landed with a blunt, peaceful thump in the extinguished sand on the bed of the ravine, as if caught and held safe by someone's living hands.

The Chevengurians calmed down and began to make their way back through the steppe, which was already turning gray in the approaching light of the coming day.

Kirey was sleeping as before by the last fence of Chevengur, his head resting on a burdock leaf and his arms embracing his own neck, given the absence of a second person. The others went past Kirey, but he did not hear them, since sleep had turned him toward the deep places of his own life, and the warming light of childhood and peace was passing from them into his body.

Chepurny and Zheyev stopped in the first houses they came to and began to wash the floors with cold well water. The other six Chevengurians went on farther, so as to find better houses to tidy and clean. It was hard to work in the dark of the bourgeoisie's best rooms; the possessions there gave off some sleepy air of oblivion and cats had returned to many of the houses and were lying asleep on beds. The Bolsheviks threw out the cats and shook out the surprisingly complex bed linen—surely more than a tired person could need.

By midmorning, the Chevengurians had sorted out only eighteen houses, and there were many more still left. Then they sat down for a smoke but soon began to doze off, leaning against a bed or chest of drawers or else collapsing forward, shaggy heads touching newly washed floors. Never before had the Bolsheviks rested in the houses of the dead class enemy—but this did not seem to matter.

Kirey awoke alone, not knowing that his comrades had all returned to Chevengur during the night. Nor did he find anyone in the brick house. Either Chepurny must have ridden far away, in pursuit of brigands, or else, along with all his comrades-in-arms, he had died of his wounds somewhere or other in the unknown grass.

Kirey harnessed himself to the machine gun and dragged it to the spot on the outskirts of town where he had spent the night. The sun had already risen high in the sky, illuminating the entire empty steppe, where there was still no enemy to be seen. But Kirey understood that he had been entrusted with the task of preserving Chevengur intact, together with all its communism. And so he quickly set up the machine gun—to support proletarian power in the town—lay down beside it, and began to look around. He lay there as long as he could, but then he wanted to eat a chicken he had seen on the street the day before. Leaving the machine gun unguarded, however, was out of the question—that would have been equivalent to passing the armaments of communism straight into the hands of the White enemy—and so Kirey lay there a while longer, trying to think up some way of defending Chevengur that would allow him to hunt down the chicken.

"Why doesn't the chicken just come to me?" he wondered. "I'll be eating it anyway. Proshka's right—life's still totally unorganized. Although we have communism now. The chicken ought to just come to me."

Kirey looked down the street, to see if the chicken was coming, but all he could see was a wandering dog. The dog was bored and did not know whom to respect in the now-unpeopled town. People had thought it would guard their property—but they had left, and so the dog had left too, free of concerns but with no sense of happiness. Kirey called the dog over and picked the burrs out of its fur. The dog waited in silence for what would come next, looking at Kirey through mournful eyes. Kirey tethered the dog to his machine gun with a belt and calmly set off to hunt the chicken, since there were no sounds in Chevengur and he was sure to hear the dog's voice should an enemy or unknown person appear in the steppe. The dog sat down beside the gun and wagged its tail, in promise of vigilance and zeal.

Kirey searched for his chicken until noon, while the dog remained silent in the face of the empty steppe. At noon, Chepurny emerged from a neighboring house and took the dog's place by the machine gun, until Kirey returned with the chicken.

The Chevengurians went on washing floors for two more days, leaving doors and windows open, so that the floors would dry and the stagnant bourgeois air would be freshened by the steppe wind. On the third day, there appeared a neatly dressed old man with a staff—but for his age, Kirey would have killed him. This man turned to Chepurny and asked him who he was.

"A member of the Bolshevik Party," Chepurny informed him. "And what we have here is communism."

The man looked at Chepurny and said, "So I see. But I'm a poultry-breeding instructor from the Pochep Land Management Department. We want to breed Plymouth Rocks in the district, so I've come to ask the owners if they'll give us a rooster and a couple of hens as breeding stock.[8] I have here an official document stipulating cooperation in this task from all quarters. Without egg, our district will never get back on its feet."

Chepurny would have liked to give this man a rooster and two hens—it was, after all, Soviet power making this request—but he hadn't seen any such birds in Chevengur yards. He asked Kirey if there were any live hens in the town.

"Not any longer," said Kirey. "There was one around the other day, but I ate it all. If there were any, I'd be glad to help."

The man from Pochep thought for a moment. "Well, in that case, I apologize. But please certify on the back of this mandate that I've fulfilled my assignment—and that there are no hens in Chevengur."

Chepurny put the paper against a brick and spelled out his testimony: "This man came and went. We have no hens, since all have been expended as revolutionary detachment provisions. Chevengur RevCom Chairman *Chepurny*."

"Put the date," said the man on assignment. "Month and date. Without clear date of time, the document will be discredited."

But Chepurny did not know the month and date. He had forgotten to keep track of how long he had lived in Chevengur. He knew only that it was summer and the fifth day of communism. And so he wrote, "Summer. 5th com."

"That'll do," said the chicken breeder. "As long as there's some kind of sign. Thank you."

"Off you go then," said Chepurny. "Kirey, take him to the edge of town, so he doesn't hang about here."

Later, Chepurny sat down outside one of the houses to wait for the sunset. All the Chevengurians returned to the brick house, after preparing another forty houses for the arrival of the proletariat. To fill their stomachs, they ate the stale pies and sauerkraut that the town's bourgeoisie had stored in excess of their class needs, in hope of life without limit. Not far from Chepurny, a cricket, used to living in settled peace, began his grating song. Over the Chevengurka River rose the warmth of evening—as if the laboring earth were letting out a long sigh of exhaustion before the impending dark of rest.

"Very soon now the masses will be approaching," Chepurny quietly said to himself. "Chevengur will be alive with communism, and general mutuality will bring comfort to any unexpected soul."

That evening Zheyev kept wandering about the town's vegetable plots and meadows, looking at places beneath his feet, observing small trifles of life and regretting them. Before sleep, he liked to yearn a little for the interesting life of the future and to grieve for his parents, who had died long ago, too soon for their own happiness and the Revolution. The steppe disappeared from sight in the darkness; a point of flame burning in the brick house was now their only defense against the enemy and all doubts. Zheyev set off toward this flame, over grass that the darkness had made silent and weak. Sitting on the earth ridge outside one of the houses was Chepurny, still sleepless.

"Having a little sit?" said Zheyev. "Let me join you. I won't talk."

The other Chevengur Bolsheviks were already lying on straw on the floor, smiling and muttering in forgetful dreams. Only Kesha was on guard, patrolling the town. Sometimes they heard him coughing out in the steppe.

"When there's a war or revolution," said Zheyev, "people somehow always dream dreams. It's not like that in peacetime—then people sleep like logs."

Chepurny himself always had dreams and so he had no idea where they came from to agitate his mind. Prokofy could have explained, but this man Chepurny so needed was elsewhere.

"I've heard that, when it's molting, a bird sings in its sleep," Chepurny recalled. "It tucks its head under one wing and all you can see is down. And then out comes this gentle voice."

"But what *is* communism, comrade Chepurny?" asked Zheyev. "Kirey told me there was once communism on an island out in the sea.[9] But Kesha says it's something that clever people have thought up."

Chepurny wanted to think about communism, but he chose not to, deciding to ask Prokofy when he came back. But then he remembered that communism was already present in Chevengur, and he said, "Once the proletariat's living its own life, then communism appears of itself. But why, I ask you now, do you keep needing to *know*? You need to *feel* communism, to discover it on the ground! Communism is the reciprocal feeling of the masses. Soon Prokofy will be back, bringing the poor. Our communism will strengthen at once—then you'll recognize it straightaway!"

"But you still can't tell me for sure what it is?" Zheyev persisted.

"Who do you take me for?" Chepurny retorted crossly. "Not even Lenin's obligated to be able to tell you for sure. Communism's a matter for the entire proletarian mass, not for one man to think up all on his own. Outsmarting the proletariat's not so easy."

Kesha was no longer coughing out in the steppe. In the distance he had heard a deep hum of voices and he was lying low in the tall grass, to ascertain these passersby more precisely. But soon the hum died down, leaving only the barely audible disturbance of people simply standing about. There was no sound of footsteps; it was as if these people had soft, bare feet. Kesha began to walk on farther—through the tall Chevengur grass, where wheat, goosefoot, and nettles all grew in fraternal closeness—but then he turned back, deciding to wait for the light of day. The tall grass gave off the damp breath of the life of grains and grasses—ears of rye and small tabernacles of goosefoot lived there without harm to one another, embracing closely and keeping one another safe. Nobody had sown them and no one was bothering them, but, come autumn, the proletariat would put nettles in their soup and harvest rye, wheat, and goosefoot for nourishment through the winter. Still farther out in the steppe were millet, buckwheat, and sunflowers, all growing of their own accord, while back in the town's kitchen gardens were potatoes and vegetables of every kind. The Chevengur bourgeoisie had not sown or planted anything for three years, counting on the imminent end of the world, but the plants had gone on multiplying from their parents, observing a particular equation: three nettle roots to a single ear of wheat. Pondering the overgrown steppe, Chepurny had always said that it too was an International of cereals and flowers, guaranteeing plentiful nourishment to all the poor without the interference of labor and exploitation. The Chevengurians thus understood that nature refused to oppress man with labor, choosing instead to grant the destitute all necessary nourishment for free. The Chevengur

RevCom had, in its day, noted the obedience of conquered nature and resolved to erect a monument to her in the future—in the shape of a tree growing out of wild soil and, with two gnarled arms, embracing a man beneath the sun they shared.

Kesha plucked an ear of wheat and began sucking the damp pulp of its meager, unripe grains. Then, forgetting the taste of food, he spat it out of his mouth; he could hear the soft sounds of a cart moving slowly along the Chevengur high road. Piusia's voice was giving commands to the horse, while Proshka's was singing a song:

> Waves sound on the lake,
> A fisherman lies below.
> An orphan in a dream
> Wanders high and low...[10]

Kesha set off at a run. But when he reached the phaeton, he saw that Prokofy and Piusia were traveling empty—without the least proletariat.

Chepurny had immediately gotten all the sleeping Bolsheviks to their feet, so as to give the proletariat a solemn welcome and organize a Communist demonstration, but Prokofy told him that the proletariat was exhausted and had lain down to sleep until dawn, on the lee side of a burial mound in the steppe.

"Have they come with an orchestra and their own leader?" asked Chepurny. "Or just as they are?"

"Tomorrow, comrade Chepurny, you'll see everything for yourself," said Prokofy. "But don't bother me now. Piusia and I have traveled a thousand versts. We saw a steppe sea and we ate sturgeon. I'll report fully and formulate in due course."

"All right, Prosha, you go and sleep—but I'll go out to the proletariat," Chepurny said timidly.

But Prokofy did not agree. "Don't touch them. They're worn out as it is. The sun will rise soon and they'll make their way down into Chevengur."

37

CHEPURNY sat through the rest of the night in sleepless anticipation. He extinguished the lantern so as not to disturb those now asleep on the burial mound by expending their kerosene. He retrieved the Chevengur RevCom banner from a shed. After that, he cleaned the star on his headgear and set in motion the thriftless wall clock that had come to a stop long ago. Having fully prepared himself, he laid his head on his arms and ceased to think, so that nighttime would pass more quickly. And time did indeed pass quickly, since time is mind, not feeling, and Chepurny was not thinking anything in his mind. The straw on which the Chevengurians were lying grew slightly moist from the cool dew; morning was unfolding. Chepurny took the banner and set off toward the part of town opposite the mound where the pedestrian proletariat was now sleeping.

For about two hours Chepurny stood with his banner by the boundary fence, waiting for dawn and the awakening of the proletariat. He watched the sun eat through the misty dark over the earth and cast its light on the windblown, rainswept mound with its dreary, naked soil—and as he watched, he remembered a forgotten spectacle similar to this poor mound that had been gnawed away at by nature because it jutted out over the plain. What he saw now, lying on the slope of this mound, was a nation warming its bones in the first sun—and these people were themselves like decrepit black bones from the crumbling skeleton of someone's vast, perished life. Some of the proletarians were sitting; others were lying, pressing relatives or neighbors close against them so as to warm themselves more quickly. A thin old man wearing only trousers was standing there, scratching his ribs, while a boy sat by his feet and observed Chevengur without moving, not believing that a home had been prepared for him where he could shelter forever. Two brown men were checking each other's heads; they were like women searching each other's hair for lice, except that they were doing this not by eye, but by feel. Not one proletarian was hurrying down into Chevengur, probably not realizing that communism had been prepared for them there, along with rest and communal property. Half of the people were dressed only as far as their waists, while the other half wore only a greatcoat or long sackcloth cloak, with nothing beneath it but a dry, well-worn body, accustomed to weather, wandering, and need of all kinds.

With calm indifference, the proletariat stayed put on that Chevengur burial mound, not looking down at the man standing alone at the edge of the town with a banner of brotherhood in his hands. Yesterday's exhausted sun was rising over the deserted shelterlessness of the steppe and its light was empty—as if it were rising over an alien and forgotten country, inhabited only by these abandoned people on the burial mound, huddling together not out of kinship and love but because of their lack of clothing. Expecting neither help nor friendship, anticipating torment in this unknown town, the proletariat did not get to its feet; weakened strength, in fact, rendered them barely able to move. The scarce children were leaning against the sleepers, sitting amid the proletariat like mature men and women—they alone went on thinking when everyone else was asleep or ill. The old man stopped scratching his ribs and lay down again on his back, holding the boy close to his side, so that the chilled wind wouldn't blow against his skin and bones. Chepurny noticed that only one man was eating, tipping something from his palm into his mouth, chewing it, then knocking his head with a clenched fist, as if trying to cure some ache.

"Where have I seen all this before?" Chepurny tried to recall. Then too, long ago, the sun had been rising through the sleep of mist while a steppe wind blew against a burial mound slowly being destroyed by the elements. And on this mound he had seen indifferent, nonexisting people whom it was essential to help because they were the proletariat but whom it had been impossible to help, because they were satisfied with a single small consolation—the aimless sense of mutual attachment thanks to which these proletarians were able to walk the earth and sleep in whole detachments on the open steppe. In the past, Chepurny too had wandered about with other people in search of temporary work and had slept in sheds and barns, surrounded by comrades and insured by their fellow feeling against inescapable troubles—but he had failed to grasp that such a mutually inseparable life was to his own benefit. Now he saw with his own eyes the steppe and the sun, and people located on this mound between the earth and the sun but who possessed neither of them—and he sensed for the first time how in place of the steppe, the homes, the food, and the clothes that the bourgeoisie had acquired for themselves, the proletarians on the mound possessed one another, since everyone needs to possess something. When property lies between people, they calmly expend their powers on concerns about that property, but when there is nothing between people, then they choose not to part from one another and to preserve one another from cold in their sleep.

In a much earlier time of his life—though he could not remember whether this was last year or when he was a child—Chepurny had seen this same burial mound, the same unexpected appearance of the class poor and the same cool sun, doing no real work on behalf of the sparsely inhabited steppe. So it had once been, but he was unable, in his weak mind, to ascertain when. It was conceivable that Prokofy might have been able to divine Chepurny's memory, but even that was unlikely, since all that Chepurny was now seeing had been known to him long ago—although this was impossible, given that the Revolution had begun only recently. And so, in place of Prokofy, Chepurny tried to formulate this memory for himself. The sight of the proletariat clinging to the burial mound filled him with alarm and agitation. Gradually, however, he came to think that this present day would pass. It had already happened once before and it had passed then—which meant that there was no reason to grieve now; this present day would end, just as that previous day had been lived through and come to an end. "But if it weren't for the Revolution, you'd never glimpse a burial mound like this, let alone with proletariat on foot," Chepurny said to himself. "Though it's true that I also buried my mother twice. I walked behind her coffin, wept, and remembered that I'd already walked behind this same coffin, kissed these same deadened lips—and lived through the day whole and hale. And that meant I'd be able to live through this second day too. One and the same grief is easier to bear, it seems, the second time around. What in the world am I saying, I ask you now!

"You think you're remembering, but it never really happened!" Thanks to Prokofy's absence, Chepurny was able to formulate with good sense. "When I'm struggling, this devout element helps me out. 'You've been through this once,' it tells me, 'so don't worry. It won't be the end of you this time either. Just follow your own footsteps.' But then there are no footsteps to follow—and there never can be. Man lives his life forward, with only darkness ahead of him. Still, how come I'm the only one here? Where's the rest of our organization? Maybe that's why the proletariat isn't getting up off that mound. It's waiting to be shown more respect!"

Kirey came out of the brick house. Chepurny called to him, telling him to summon the entire organization, since the masses had appeared and the time had now come. In response to Kirey's demand, the organization duly awoke and came out to join Chepurny.

"Who is it you've brought us?" Chepurny asked Prokofy. "If it's the proletariat up there on that mound, then why—I ask you now—don't they come down and claim their town?"

"I've brought the proletariat and *others*," Prokofy replied.

This disturbed Chepurny. "What *others*? Not the class of residual scum again!"

"Who do you take me for?" Prokofy retorted crossly. "A snake—or a party member?! These *others* are simply others. Worse than proletariat—no one and nobody."[1]

"But who are they, I ask you now! Did they each have a class father? You found them in a social place, I take it, not in a wilderness?"

"They're fatherlessness," Prokofy explained. "They were living nowhere. They wander."

"Where to?" Chepurny asked respectfully. Everything dangerous and unknown, he felt, should be treated with dignity. "Where are they wandering to? Maybe we ought to curb them."

Prokofy was surprised by Chepurny's lack of political consciousness. "'Where are they wandering to'? To communism, of course. We can curb them right here."

"Go and call them down then! Tell them the town is theirs. All cleaned up and in order. And that the vanguard standing here by the fence wishes the proletariat all happiness and—yes—all the world, since it belongs to them anyway."

"What if they refuse the world?" asked Prokofy, who liked to keep ahead of things. "Maybe Chevengur alone will be more than enough for them?"

"But then, who'll end up with the world?" asked Chepurny, now entangled in theory.

"We will, as our base."

"You're a swine. We're the vanguard—and we belong to them, not them to us. The vanguard isn't a human being—it's a dead shield on a living body. It's the proletariat that's the true human being. So get going now—you semi-snake!"

Prokofy quickly managed to organize the proletarians and *others* up on the mound. There turned out to be many more people than Chepurny had been able to see. A good hundred of them—maybe two hundred. All distinct in appearance—though no different in need, since they were proletariat through and through.

People began to come down from the bare mound into Chevengur. Chepurny had always had a tender sense of the proletariat and known that it existed in the world as an inexhaustible concerted force, helping the sun to feed the cadres of the bourgeoisie, since the sun was enough for nourishment but not for greed. He had half understood that the noise in an empty place—the hum filling his ears in night shelters out in the steppe—was the sound of the oppressed labor of the world's working class as it moved forward, day and night, to secure food, property, and rest for its personal enemies, whom these substances of proletarian labor enabled to multiply. Thanks to Prokofy,

Chepurny held within him a convincing theory about the workers being the heroes of the future, wild and determined with regard to unorganized nature—but he had also discovered for himself a reassuring secret: that, rather than gazing at nature with admiration, the proletariat destroys it through labor. The bourgeois lives for nature—and makes children; the working man, on the other hand, lives for his comrades—and makes revolution. Only one thing was unclear: Was labor still necessary under socialism—or would nature, left to follow its own course, provide enough nourishment anyway? Here Chepurny was inclined to agree with Prokofy, who held that, in the absence of capitalism, the solar system alone would give communism the power of life, since work and zeal of all kinds had been invented by the exploiters, for the acquisition of abnormal surplus value, above and beyond the products of the sun.

Chepurny had been expecting close ranks of heroes of the future. What he saw, however, were people not marching but plodding along at their own pace; he saw comrades the like of whom he had never encountered—entirely without revolutionary worth or notable class characteristics. These people were anonymous *others*, living without the least significance, without pride, and without connection to the impending worldwide triumph. Even their age was hard to determine; all that could be seen was that they were poor, alien to all, and that they had no possessions except bodies that had grown by no will of their own. And so these *others* walked close together, looking more at one another than at Chevengur and its party vanguard.

One *other* caught a fly on the bare back of an old man in front of him, cruelly killed the fly against the ground, then stroked this man's back so as not to leave any mark or scratch on it. This brought about a vague change in Chepurny's feelings of surprise with regard to these *others*. Maybe these proletarians and *others* served as one another's only possessions, their only property of life—and perhaps this was why they watched one another with such concern, barely noticing Chevengur and carefully guarding their comrades from flies, just as the bourgeoisie guarded their homes and livestock.

Those first to descend from the mound were already approaching

Chevengur. Chepurny, not knowing how to formulate his thoughts with expression, asked Prokofy to do this on his behalf—and Prokofy gladly began:

"Comrade unpropertied citizens! The town of Chevengur is being given to you—not for predatoriness of the destitute—but so that you can put to use all property won from the bourgeoisie and organize a broad brotherly family for the sake of the town's integrity. Now we are inescapably brothers and family, in that our economy is socially united in a single household. So: live here honorably, at the head of the RevCom!"

Chepurny asked Zheyev how he had thought up the inscription on the canvas hung as a symbol on the far side of the town.

"I didn't think," said Zheyev. "It's from memory, it's not something I came up with myself. I must have heard it somewhere. You know how it is, there's no knowing what sticks in your head."

"Stop!" Chepurny said to Prokofy. He then turned to the pedestrian poor now massed around the Chevengurians.

"Comrades! Prokofy called you brothers and family, but that is an outright lie. Every brother has a father, while many of us have been utter and absolute fatherlessness from our first days. We are not brothers—we are comrades. For one another, we are both goods and the only good of true value, since we have no other property reserve of any kind, movable or unmovable. Also, it's a shame you didn't enter Chevengur from the other side. There you would have seen our symbol, along with inscribed words. Who came up with the words we don't know, but that doesn't matter, and anyway these words say what we wish to say: 'Best to destroy the entire well-ordered world and acquire one another in bare necessity—and so, proletarians of all lands, unite first of all!'[2] Now I've finished and I convey greetings to you from the Chevengur RevCom."

The proletariat and *others* from the burial mound then moved off into the depth of the town, not coming out with anything themselves and not making use of Chepurny's speech to develop their own consciousness; their strength was enough only for life in the current moment; they lived without any surplus, because there had been no reasons in time or nature for either their birth or their happiness—on the contrary, the mother of each of them had been first to weep, after inadvertently being made pregnant by a passerby father who then disappeared. After their birth they had found themselves to be mistaken. They were *others* in the world and nothing had been prepared for them there—less than for a blade of grass, which has its own little rootlet, its place and its gift of nourishment in shared soil.

These *others* had been born with no possibility of any gift: there could be no mind or generosity of feelings in them, because their parents had conceived them not through surplus of body but through nighttime anguish and weakness of sad strength. It had been the mutual oblivion of two people who had hidden away and were living secretly in the world—had they lived too happily and evidently, they would have been annihilated by those who are real, those who count in the state's population and who sleep in their own houses. Mind should not exist in these *others*—mind and enlivened feeling could exist only in people who possessed a free reserve of body and the warmth of peace over their heads, while the *others*' parents had only the remnants of a body exhausted by labor and etched by caustic grief, and such higher qualities as mind and plaintiveness of heart and feeling had disappeared due to a lack of rest and tenderly nourishing substances. And the *others* had emerged from their mothers' depths into the very deepest misfortune, because each mother had disappeared as soon as her legs could carry her after the weakness of childbirth—so as not to see her child and inadvertently start to love it forever. Left behind, the little *other* had to make himself into a future person, relying on no one, sensing only the faint warmth of his own innards; round about was the outside world, and the child-other lay in the middle of it and cried, thus resisting a first grief—the eternally lost warmth of his mother—that would remain unforgotten for the whole of life.

State people, sound, settled people—living in the comfort of class solidarity and bodily habits, in an accumulation of tranquility—create around themselves a likeness of their mother's womb and so are able to continue growing and bettering themselves, as in the childhood now far behind them; these *others*, however, had their first sense of the world in cold, in grass made moist by traces of their mother, and in aloneness—due to the absence of any continuing motherly strength to protect them. Their early life—as well as the expanses of earth they had crossed and that corresponded to the life they had lived through and gotten the better of—was remembered by these others as something alien to the vanished mother and that had caused her to suffer. But what had their life been? And what *were* the thinly populated roads in the image of which the world continued to exist in their consciousness?

Not one of the *others* had seen their father, and their only memory of a mother was their body's troubled longing for a lost peace—a longing transformed at the age of maturity into a depleting sadness. After being born, a child demands nothing from its mother—the child loves her, and even orphan-*others* never felt resentment toward the mothers who had forsaken them immediately and irrevocably. But, as a child grows, he expects a father; he has already taken in all he requires of the mother's natural forces and feelings. Even a child abandoned immediately after leaving the womb turns an inquisitive face toward the world; he wants to exchange nature for people, and it is the father who appears as a first friend and comrade after the mother's insistent warmth, when life is no longer constrained by her affectionate hands.

Not one *other*, as a little boy, had found his father and helper. If a mother had given birth to him, there had been no father to greet him on the road once he was born and living; and so the father had turned into an enemy and hater of the mother—absent everywhere, constantly dooming his powerless son to the risk of a life without help and therefore without success.

And so the life of the *others* was fatherlessness—a life that continued on an empty earth without that first comrade who might have taken them by the hand and led them toward people, so as to leave them an inheritance of people, ready to replace him when he died. Amid the wide world the others lacked nothing more than a father—and later, in Chevengur, the old man scratching his ribs up on the burial mound was heard singing a song that both moved and disturbed him:

Who's going to let me in:
Some animal, some bird?
Of parent, of father,
I have no word.

Almost all those whose advent was greeted by the Chevengur Bolshevik Organization had made themselves into human beings through their own personal strength; these were well and truly self-made people, each of whom had been surrounded by the frenzy of those with possessions and by the death of poverty. Grass is unsurprising in a meadow, where it is plentiful and where it lives in dense self-defense and with moisture beneath it. In these conditions it stays alive and keeps growing even without especial passion or need, but it is strange and rare for seeds of anonymous steppe grass uprooted by a storm to take root in bare clay or wandering sand—and what springs from such seeds is a life of loneliness, surrounded by empty countries of light, and able to find nourishment even in minerals.

Some people had entire armaments for the strengthening and development of their own precious life, but these *others* had only one weapon with which to hold their ground in the world: a remnant of parental warmth in an infant body. Even this, however, was enough to enable a nameless *other* to remain whole, to grow into manhood and live on toward a future of his own. The strength of these newcomers to Chevengur had been consumed by their past life, and to Chepurny they seemed like powerless and unproletarian elements, as if they had been warmed and illuminated all through their lives not by the sun but by the moon. But, having expended all their strength on maintaining within them this primeval parental warmth—in the face of the oncoming uprooting wind of an alien and hostile life—and having magnified this warmth by laboring for people who were real and endowed with names—these *others* had fashioned themselves into self-made people of unknown designation; moreover, this exercise in endurance and inner resources of body had created in them not only a mind full of curiosity and doubt but also a quickness of feeling ready to trade eternal bliss for a comrade of their own kind, since this comrade had no father or property yet was able to make one forget about both—and within them the *others* still bore hope, a hope that was fortunate and confident yet melancholy as loss. This hope had a certain precision: if the main thing—staying alive and whole—were successfully accomplished, then they hoped also to accomplish everything remaining, even if it were necessary to reduce the world to its last grave. If, however, they achieved and experienced this main thing without discovering what they needed still more—not happiness, but their own necessity—then they would never, in what remained of their lives, find what had once been lost, or else they would find that this lost thing had completely vanished from the earth: many *others*, after all, had traveled every road, whether open or impassable, and found nothing.

The apparent feebleness of the *others* sprang from the equanimity of their strength, and too much labor and torment of life had made their faces un-Russian. Chepurny noticed this before the other Chevengurians, who were more concerned by the scantiness of the *others'* clothing—as if they had no fear either of the night cold or of oncoming women. And so, once the newly arrived class had dispersed among the houses of Chevengur, Chepurny began to voice his doubts.

"Call this proletariat? Where on earth did you find them?" he said to Prokofy. "They're nothing but doubt—and they're not Russian."

Prokofy took the banner from Chepurny's hands and silently read the words of Karl Marx.

"Not proper proletariat!" he said. "They're class all right—first-class working class. Lead them forward and they'll march anywhere for you without a squeak of protest. This is true international proletariat. Look—they're not Russian, they're not Armenian, they're not Tatars—they're no one! I bring you live International—and what do you do? Pull a long face!"

Chepurny felt something thoughtfully and quietly said, "We need the iron tread of proletarian battalions.[3] The provincial committee sent us a circular to that effect—and you've herded along a crowd of *others*! How can the barefoot have an iron tread?"

"It's all right," Prokofy reassured Chepurny. "Let them walk barefoot—they've worked their heels so hard you can insert metal screws into them. Come the World Revolution, they'll march barefoot to the end of the world for you!"

The last of the proletarians and *others* disappeared into the houses and resumed their former lives. Chepurny decided to seek out the thin old man and invite him to an extraordinary meeting of the RevCom; organizational matters had been accumulating for some time. Prokofy fully agreed. He went to the brick house and began drafting projects of resolutions.

The thin old man was lying on the newly scrubbed floor of Shchapov's home. Sitting close to him was another man, anywhere between twenty and sixty years old, who was letting out a pair of child's trousers, so he could get into them himself.

"Comrade," Chepurny began, "could you come along to the brick house. That's where the RevCom meets, and we need you there."

"I will," said the old man. "The moment I get to my feet, I'll come straight along. But my innards are aching. Once they quiet down, you'll be seeing me."

By then, Prokofy was already perusing revolutionary documents from the provincial capital, a lamp burning beside him even though it was bright day. This lamp was always lit before the start of a RevCom meeting and it stayed lit until every last question had been resolved. Prokofy saw this as a symbol for their times, signifying that the light of solar life on earth must be replaced by the artificial light of the human mind.

The whole of Chevengur's central Bolshevik organization attended this ceremonial meeting of the RevCom, and some of the newly arrived *others* were also present, in a standing capacity and without voting rights. Chepurny was sitting next to Prokofy and all in all he felt satisfied; the RevCom had succeeded in holding the town until its settlement by the proletarian mass, and communism was now firmly consolidated in Chevengur forever. Only the old man—probably the most experienced of the proletarians—was missing; his insides must still have been aching. Chepurny sent Zheyev to go and fetch him. First, though, Zheyev should find some kind of soothing herbal infusion in the storeroom and give it to the old man to drink—only then should he carefully bring him along to join them.

Half an hour later, Zheyev came back with the old man, now greatly invigorated by a burdock infusion and the thorough massage Zheyev had just given to his back and stomach.

"Sit down, comrade," said Prokofy. "See the scope of our social concern for you? You're all right now—you won't be dying any time soon under communism."

"Let's get on with it," Chepurny determined. "Now that communism's already set in, why distract the proletariat with mere talk? Read us the circulars. And then our own formulations—so we can meet these circulars head-on!"

"On the provision of combined reports," Prokofy began, "in accord with the special form attached to our circular No. 438101, letters A, S, and also V; about the development of NEP throughout the district; about the tempo, extent, and manifestation of activity unleashed by oppositional classes in relation to NEP; about measures taken against these classes; and also about the strict confinement of NEP policies within a narrow channel."

"And our reply?" asked Chepurny.

"I'll draw up a little table for them, with a clear summary."

"Anyway, we haven't unleashed any unauthorized classes here. With communism, all such classes have disappeared," Chepurny retorted. Turning to the old man, he asked "What do *you* think—I ask you now!"

"Like that, things won't be too bad," the old man concluded.

"Get that formulated," Chepurny ordered Prokofy. "'Without such classes, things won't be too bad.' And let's move on to more important questions."

Prokofy then read a directive about the urgent need to establish consumers' co-operatives, rather than allowing private trade to strengthen, since the co-operative can be considered the masses' voluntary open road to socialism and beyond.

"That doesn't concern us, it's for districts that have fallen behind," said Chepurny, since he possessed within him a constant and central belief that communism had already been achieved in Chevengur. Then he addressed the old man again, with the words, "But how would *you* formulate this?"

"Not too bad," the old man formulated.

Prokofy, however, had other ideas.

"Maybe we should put in a request for supplies of provisions for a co-operative of that kind? After all, the proletariat has moved in on us. We need to stock up on food for it."

This surprised Chepurny. "But there's food of all kinds growing out in the steppe," he protested. "There's chervil and wheat—just help yourself. Pick it and eat it! The sun shines, the soil breathes, and the rains fall—what more do you need? Are you wanting to whip up the proletariat again, to drive them into yet more pointless zeal? We've gone beyond socialism—what we've got here is better still."

"I fully agree with you," said Prokofy. "For a moment I purposely forgot that we have already established communism here. I've just come back from traveling around other parts. They're still a long way from socialism—and that's why they need to suffer their way through the torments of co-operatives. Next on the agenda is trade unions and the importance of prompt payment of party membership dues."

"To whom?" asked Zheyev.

"To them," said Kirey, without thought.

"What them?" asked Chepurny.

"Doesn't say," Prokofy replied, after looking again at the circular.

"Write that they should tell us who the dues go to and why," said Chepurny, now getting used to formulating on his own behalf. "Maybe what you're reading is a nonparty document. Maybe lucrative positions are established with the help of these dues. And positions and titles, my brother, are as bad as property. We'd end up having to battle with the residual scum all over again. Why—when the whole of communism is already present in every soul here, and everyone wants to guard it?"

"There's a lack of class clarity here," Prokofy determined. "For now I'll note this question down in my mind."

"Yes, you do just that!" said Zheyev. "There's always a remainder left in the mind. And never enough of what lives, because what lives gets expended."

"Excellent," said Prokofy, and went on further. "Next comes a proposal to create a planning commission to compile a list of figures and dates for all income and expenditure of lives and property, until the end—"

"End of what?" inquired Chepurny. "Of the world? Or of the bourgeoisie alone?"

"No indication. It says, 'Requirements, expenses, potentials, and subsidies for the entire period of reconstruction, until the end.' And then a further proposal: 'To this purpose, to organize a plan drawing together all preconditional, coordinatory, and political-regulationary work, in order to transform the elemental cacophony of the capitalist economy into the harmony of a symphony uniting highest principle with the distinctive features of reason.' All clear and to the point, since this is a prescribed task."

At that, the members of the Chevengur RevCom bowed their heads as one man. Emanating from this document was the elemental power of higher mind—and this sapped the will of the Chevengurians, who were more accustomed to living things through than to preliminary deliberation.

After a pinch of snuff to restore his strength, Chepurny said meekly, "Proshka, give us something a bit simpler."

Before Prokofy could reply, the old man gave the saddened inhabitants of Chevengur a long, suffering look and muttered dejectedly to himself, saying nothing to help.

"I have a draft of a resolution already prepared," said Prokofy. "There's too much here for a simple note." And he began digging about in his vast pile of papers, where all that the Chevengur Bolsheviks had forgotten was articulated.

"But who needs all this? Is it for us here, or for *them*?" asked the old man. "All this reading of papers. Who's it all for? For us, or for *them* at the center?"

"For us, I assure you," Prokofy explained. "And they're sent to us not for reading aloud but to be executed."

Chepurny had recovered from his exhaustion and was now holding his head high; decisive sense had ripened inside it. "You see, comrade, they want the very cleverest people to figure out the current of life once and for all and forever, and before we're all lying under the ground. Until they do that, the rest of us must just keep on enduring and drifting along."

"But who *needs* all this?" the old man asked again. Apathetically, he closed his eyes, which had been harmed by the impression of the world he had passed through.

"We do," Chepurny replied agitatedly. "Who else, I ask you now, could it be for?"

"But we know best how to live our own lives," the old man explained. "This missive's not for us, it's for the rich man. When there were rich people, it was us who took care of them, but there was no one to grieve for your poor man—he grew up in an empty place and without the least reason. Still, it's the poor man who knows what's what in his life. Without even meaning to, he's made a whole world for other people to play with—and he can take care of himself even in sleep. He may not matter to himself, but he knows he's precious to someone."

"Your words, old fellow, aren't bad at all," Chepurny concluded. "So, Prokofy, formulate: The proletariat and others within its ranks have themselves organized the entire habitable world through their own concern and attention. It's a disgrace and a crying shame, then, to think that the world's first organizers need be organized by others. No one in Chevengur, therefore, wishes to be nominated as one of the very clever." Turning to the old man, Chepurny added, "All right, old fellow? Is that what you were saying?"

"Not bad at all," judged the old man.

"The scribe does not build a hut for the carpenter," said Zheyev.

"The cowherd knows best when to drink milk," said Kirey, wanting to have his say too.

"For every blockhead—a gram of lead in the head," said Piusia, with his usual gravity.

"Passed almost unanimously," Prokofy determined. "And now for current matters. In eight days' time, a party conference will be held in the provincial capital. We're to send a delegate—the chairman of our local organ of power."

"You go, Chepurny!" said Zheyev. "No need for discussion."

"Of course," decreed Prokofy. "This is an order."

Infringing the agenda, the elderly *other* squatted down and asked vaguely, "And just who are you lot?"

"We are the RevCom, the supreme district-level revolutionary organ," Prokofy replied. "Within the bounds of our revolutionary conscience, the revolutionary people has granted us particular competencies."

"So you lot are very clever too?" said the old man, thinking aloud. "Dying to write everlasting decrees?"

"You could put it like that," Prokofy confirmed, with the dignity of his competency.

"Ah, now I see!" the old man said gratefully. "And there I was, thinking you were doing all this of your own free will, because no one's given you any more serious work."

"Far from it," said Prokofy. "Our task is to lead the whole town and district uninterruptedly forward. All concern about safeguarding the Revolution falls on our shoulders. Do you realize, old fellow, how and why you've become a citizen here in Chevengur? It's because of us."

"Because of you? In that case, we all thank you."

"Not at all," Prokofy said modestly. "The Revolution is our duty and service. Only follow our instructions—you'll live, and everything will be excellent for you."

"Not so fast, comrade Dvanov," Chepurny said gravely. "It's not for you to usurp my position. Our elderly comrade has pointed out that those in power should feel shame, but you are obscuring him... Speak, comrade *other*!"

For a while, the old man said nothing. What first took place in him and his fellow *others* was not thought but a certain pressure of dark warmth. Then, one way or another, thought would speak its way out, cooling as it escaped.

"What I see as I look around," said the old man, "is that your work's not real. But you speak high and mighty—as if you're up on a mound and we're down below in a gully. It should be sick people working here, men who've lived through their last days and keep going from memory alone. It's soft and easy here, you're like night watchmen. But you're still hardy men—you should be doing something harder!"

"What do you want?" Prokofy asked straight out. "Are you after becoming chairman yourself?"

"God forbid!" exclaimed the appalled old man. "Never in all my days have I worked as a guard or watchman. Power, as I see it, is a mindless nonsense. It's where we should put good-for-nothings who aren't fit for anything better. As for you lot, you should be doing something real!"

"What should the fit and good-for-something be doing?" Prokofy led the old man on, hoping to trap him in dialectics.

"The fit-for-life should be living. What else is there?"

"Living for what?" asked Prokofy.

"For what?" Unable to think quickly, the old man came to a stop. After a pause, he said, "So that their skin and nails keep growing."

"And what use are nails?" asked Prokofy, still trying to corner the old man in some dialectical trap.

"Nails are dead," said the old man, evading Prokofy's maneuver. "They grow out from within, so that what's dead doesn't get stuck inside a man. Skin and nails wrap right round a man and protect him."

"Protect him from what?" asked Prokofy, not relenting.

"From the bourgeoisie, of course," Chepurny joined in, with understanding. "A man's skin and nails are Soviet power. How come you can't formulate that for yourself?"

"And his hair?" asked Kirey, with curiosity.

"No different from wool," said the old man. "Cut it with a knife—it won't hurt the sheep."

"Well, I think that, come winter, the sheep will get cold and die," said Kirey. "Once, when I was a boy, I shaved a kitten and buried it in the snow. I didn't understand whether or not it was human. And then the kitten caught a fever and died."

"None of this can be formulated in a resolution," said Prokofy. "We're an important organ—and this old fellow shows up from uninhabited parts. He knows nothing about nothing, tells us we're low qualification and no more than night watchmen and that only nobodies should be appointed to our position. He says that real people should be wandering about empty districts and steppe burial mounds. It's not even possible to write this resolution down on paper, since paper is only produced thanks to the correct leadership of Soviet power."

"Don't be too quick to take offense," said the old man. "We all have lives to live. But some work in need and poverty, while you sit and think in a room—as if you know all about other people and none of them have feelings of their own in their heads."

"So that's what you're getting at!" Prokofy exclaimed. "But do you not understand the necessity for the organization and cohesion of fractured and fragmented forces in a single clearly defined channel? We don't sit here merely in order to think—we sit here for the sake of the collection and compact organization of all proletarian forces."

The elderly proletarian remained skeptical. "If you're collecting them, then they must want to be together anyway. And that's what I'm saying to you. Your cause is certain—and that means it could be done by anyone, no matter how feeble they are. Even at night, no one's going to steal your work."

"Are you saying we should do our work at night?" asked Chepurny, now troubled.

"Maybe," said the elderly *other*, "if you're up for it. In daytime, some foot-walker might come by. He'll be walking his own road and he won't need anything from you, but the sight of him will make you ashamed. 'Here we are,' you'll say to yourselves, 'thinking how people should live their lives when they can decide that better themselves.' And then a living person passes by and maybe never comes back again."

Chepurny hung his head and felt burning shame. "Why did I think my position made me smarter than the whole proletariat?" he asked himself in confused anguish. "Seems I fear the proletariat and feel only shame before them."

After a general silence, Chepurny spoke: "Formulate as follows, comrade Dvanov. All future RevCom meetings are to be held at night. The brick building to be liberated for the proletariat."

"On what grounds?" asked Prokofy, trying to find a way out. "I need to record our motives."

"Motives? All right then. Our crying shame and disgrace in the face of the proletariat and *others*, who live out their lives in the daytime. Say that what is unimportant, like what is unseemly, is more fittingly carried out at an invisible time."

"Clear enough," said Prokofy. "And one receives more concentration at night. But where will we put the RevCom?"

"Any old barn or shed," Chepurny determined. "The worse, the better."

"I myself, comrade Chepurny, would suggest the church," said Prokofy. "That'll expose more contradiction—and the building is, in any case, improper for the proletariat."

"An appropriate formulation," Chepurny concluded. "Firm it up. What else have you got there in your papers? Let's finish soon!"

Prokofy put aside all remaining matters for his own personal decision and reported only the least important of all, which would take up the least time.

"There's also the question of the organization of mass productive labor in the form of voluntary Saturdays, so as to liquidate the general ruination and working-class poverty and thus inspire the masses forward and signify a great beginning."[4]

"Beginning of what?" asked Zheyev.

"Of communism, of course!" Chepurny explained. "Backward regions are instigating communism from every corner, but we've brought it to an end already."

"If we've ended it, do we need a beginning?" asked Kirey.

"Kirey!" said Prokofy, "you were merely co-opted, so sit there quietly."

The elderly *other* had been looking for some time at the heap of papers on the desk. It was evidently the work of a great many people. Words are composed of letters, and each letter requires mind and time. No one working alone could spoil so many sheets of paper. Were it a single man thinking and writing for everyone else, it would be easy to do away with him—but since there was a whole gang of such men, perhaps it was best to humor them for the time being and buy them off cheaply.

"We'll do the work for free," the old man said crossly. "We can contract to do that all right. Only let's have no more discussion—where does it get us?"

"Comrade Chepurny, here on hand," Prokofy concluded, "we have the will of the proletariat."

"What kind of sense does that make?" Chepurny asked in astonishment. "The sun gets by without any Bolsheviks—and a correct attitude to the sun is a part of our consciousness. But as for labor, we simply don't need it. First, we must reason the need."

"We can find something to do," promised the old man. "You've got a lot of buildings here, but few people. Maybe we should pack the buildings tighter together—then we can all live closer to one another."

"And we could drag the orchards along too," said Kirey. "They're lighter. Orchards make the air thicker, and they provide nourishment too."

Prokofy quickly found evidence in his papers to back up the old man's proposals. Everything, it appeared, had been thought up in advance by the very cleverest of people; everyone else need only live out their lives in accord with a meaning these men with illegible signatures had already determined.

"We have here a memorandum," Prokofy began, still looking through his papers, "according to which Chevengur is required to undergo total replanning and municipal improvement. Consequently, there can be no doubt of the necessity for the relocation of buildings and the provision of a constant flow of fresh air by means of orchards."

"No harm in improvement," the old man agreed.

At this point the whole Chevengur RevCom seemed to come to a stop. Often, the Chevengurians didn't know what to think further; they would sit there in expectation, while life drifted on inside them.

"Where there's a beginning, comrades, there's also an end," said Chepurny, not knowing what he would say next. "The enemy used to come at us head-on, but we fought back from our RevCom. Now we've got the proletariat instead. Either we must fight it too—or else accept that the RevCom's had its day."

In the Chevengur RevCom, words were pronounced without any direction toward other people, as if they were the orator's personal and natural necessity, and often speeches contained neither questions nor proposals but only surprised doubt. Rather than providing material for resolutions, this served only to express whatever those present might be living through at the time.

"Who are we?" said Chepurny, asking this question aloud for the first time. "We are comrades! Comrades to the oppressed of the countries of the world. And we shouldn't tear ourselves away from the warm onward current of the entire class or distance ourselves at a standstill. Like it or not, the working class made the whole world—so why, I ask you now, should we be struggling to think on its behalf? To the class, that's an insult—they'll categorize us as residual scum just like that. And here we must close the meeting, since everything is clear now and we all feel calm at heart."

The elderly *other* suffered now and then from wind and the runs, brought about by irregular nourishment. Sometimes he had gone without food for a long time—and then he had to make the most of any opportunity to fill himself up. This, however, had exhausted his stomach and often caused him to belch and vomit. During these episodes he would go somewhere deserted, to separate himself from people. In Chevengur he had eaten greedily and so had barely been able to sit through the whole of the RevCom meeting. The moment it finished, he went off into the tall grass of the steppe, lay down on his belly, and began to suffer, forgetting everything that was near and dear to him at an ordinary time.

In the evening, Chepurny set off toward the provincial capital,[5] with the same horse that Prokofy had used to fetch the proletariat. He set off alone as night was falling, into the darkness of a world he had long ago forgotten about in Chevengur. But he had barely passed beyond the town boundary when he heard the sounds of the old man's illness and felt obliged to track him down, to ascertain the reason for such unexpected signals out in the steppe. Having done this, Chepurny rode on farther, convinced that a sick person was a lukewarm counterrevolutionary. And there were also, he realized, still greater problems—it was necessary to determine what to do, under communism, with all those still suffering. But then Chepurny recalled that it was now up to the whole proletariat to do his thinking for him—and so, liberated from tyranny of mind, assured of the truth to come, he fell asleep in the lone, rumbling cart, with only a light sense of his own life and a faint sense of longing for the proletariat that must have just fallen asleep back in Chevengur. "And what are we to do about the horses, and the cows, and the sparrows?" he asked himself through sleep, but then he put these problems aside; he could rely instead on the strength of mind of an entire class—a class that had thought up not only all the world's property and artifacts but also the bourgeoisie to protect that property, and that had thought up not only the Revolution but also the party, to preserve the Revolution until communism.

The tall steppe grass continued to pass by, as if on its way back to Chevengur, while the man went on riding forward, half-asleep, not seeing the stars shining down from their dense height, from a future that was eternal but already attainable, from the ordered quiet where these stars moved as comrades—remaining close enough to remember one another, and staying far enough apart not to lose their differences and pointless mutual attraction.

38

As if into a dream, Kopionkin began to sink into Chevengur. He sensed its quiet communism as a warm peace throughout his body—though it was not the personal higher ideal he had secluded away in a small, anxious part of his chest. This made him want to carry out a thorough check of the town's communism, so that it might immediately awake passion in him, since Rosa Luxemburg had loved communism and he respected Rosa.

"Comrade Luxemburg is a woman," Kopionkin explained to Pashintsev. "But here you see men sprawled out all over the place. Threadbare clothes—and their bellies showing through. Some of them with an earring. I don't think this would be right for comrade Luxemburg. She'd feel doubt and shame, much like I do. Can't you see?"

Pashintsev, however, was not in any way checking Chevengur. He already knew the whole reason behind it.

"Why would she feel shame?" he asked. "She was a woman who knew what to do with a revolver. What we have here is a Revolution Memorial Reserve, like I had, like you saw when you spent the night there."

Kopionkin recalled Pashintsev's small village, the silent and barefoot wanderers who used to spend the night in the manor house, and Sasha Dvanov, the friend and comrade together with whom he had searched for communism amid the simple and best people.

"Your reserve was merely a shelter for those who had lost their way in a world of exploitation," he said. "What you had there was not communism. But what's brought it into being here is neglect and desolation. People were wandering around with no life. They found their way here and now they live without movement."

None of this troubled Pashintsev. He liked Chevengur and was living there to accumulate strength and recruit a fighting unit in order to strike at his Revolutionary Memorial Reserve and seize back the Revolution from the universal organizers seconded there. Most of all, he lay out in the open, inhaled the fresh air, and listened to the scarce sounds from the forgotten Chevengur steppe.

Kopionkin walked about Chevengur on his own, examining the proletarians and *others* at length, to ascertain whether Rosa Luxemburg was even the least bit precious to them, but none of them had heard of her at all. It was as if she had died in vain and not on their behalf.

On coming to Chevengur, the proletarians and *others* had quickly eaten up the bourgeoisie's remains of nourishment; by the time of Kopionkin's arrival they were living entirely on plants obtained from the steppe. During Chepurny's absence, Prokofy had organized regular Saturday volunteer labor, assigning to the proletariat the task of reconstructing the town and its orchards. The proletariat, however, had moved the buildings and lugged the orchards about not for the sake of labor but in order to pay for rest and shelter in Chevengur and to buy off Proshka and all power and authority. On his return from the provincial capital, Chepurny had left Prokofy's decree to the proletariat's discretion, hoping that they might come to see the buildings as traces of their oppression, dismantle them into useless pieces, and go on to live in the world without any covering at all, warming one another with only their own living bodies. Moreover, there was no knowing whether there would be winter under communism or whether there would always be the warmth of summer, since the sun had risen on the first day of communism and all nature therefore was fully on the side of Chevengur.

The Chevengur summer continued and time went on hopelessly passing, counter to life, yet Chepurny, along with the proletariat and *others*, had stopped amid time, summer, and all agitating elements and was living in the peace of his own joy, justly expecting life's final happiness to develop in a proletariat no longer troubled by anyone. This happiness of life already existed on earth, only it lay hidden within miscellaneous *others*. But even so, this happiness remained a substance, a fact and necessity.

Kopionkin alone walked about Chevengur without happiness and without calm hope. Had he not been waiting for Alexander Dvanov's general assessment of Chevengur, he would long ago have infringed the town's regime with an armed hand. But the further his time of patience extended, the more deeply his lonely feeling was touched by the Chevengur class. Sometimes it seemed to Kopionkin that the Chevengur proletariat was worse off than him, but that they were, nevertheless, more accepting, perhaps because they were secretly stronger. Kopionkin found comfort in Rosa Luxemburg, while the new Chevengurians had no joy ahead of them and no expectation of joy, contenting themselves with what enables all the dispossessed to keep living—a shared life with others the same as them, companions and comrades of the roads they have traveled.

Once Kopionkin remembered his older brother, who used to go out every evening to visit his sweetheart, leaving his younger brothers alone in the hut, feeling dismal without him. He himself had then tried to comfort his brothers, and they had gradually begun to comfort one another too, since this was necessary for them. Now, though, it was he who wanted to leave the house; lukewarm in his feelings for Chevengur, he wanted to go and join his sweetheart, Rosa Luxemburg—but the Chevengurians had no sweetheart and they would have to remain on their own and comfort one another.

As if already knowing that they would be left on their own in Chevengur, the *others* asked nothing either of Kopionkin or of the RevCom. The latter had their ideas and directives, while they themselves possessed only the necessity of existence. During the day, they wandered about the steppe, picking plants, digging up roots, and sating themselves on the raw products of nature; in the evenings, they lay down in the grass on the streets and went silently to sleep. Kopionkin too would lie down among them, to still his sense of anguish and allow time to pass more quickly. Sometimes he chatted to the thin old man, Yakov Titych, who turned out to know everything that other people only thought about or didn't even know how to think about. Kopionkin, for his part, knew nothing with any precision, since he lived through his life as it came, not guarding it with a vigilant and remembering consciousness.

Yakov Titych liked to lie in the grass in the evening, seeing the stars and humbling himself by thinking about distant luminaries where an unpeopled, unexperienced life—a life not accessible to him or intended for him—was running its course. He would turn his head from side to side, see other people falling asleep, and think sadly, "You've not been given a chance to live either." Then he would sit up for a moment and congratulate them all loudly, "And what of it? Me or a star—it's the same substance. Man is no lout. If he takes, it's from need, not greed."

Sometimes Kopionkin would be lying there too, and he would overhear similar discussions between Yakov Titych and his soul. "You're always feeling sorry for others," Yakov once informed himself. "You look at someone's sad body and you feel sorry for it. That body will suffer torment and die, and soon you'll be saying goodbye to it. But you never feel sorry for yourself. The moment you remember that you'll die and people will weep over you, then you feel sad about leaving them to weep on their own."

"Where, old fellow, do your troubled words come from?" Kopionkin asked him. "Class man means nothing to you, but you lie there and keep mouthing away."

The old man said nothing, and it was silent in Chevengur too.

People were lying on their backs, while a difficult, troubled night slowly unfolded above them, so quiet that it seemed as if words were sometimes being uttered up there and the sleepers were sighing in reply.

"Why are you silent, like the dark?" Kopionkin asked again. "Upset about the stars, are you? Why? They're silver and gold—not coins for the likes of us!"

But Yakov Titych was not ashamed of his words. "I wasn't talking,

I was thinking," he said. "Till you come out with words, you don't become clever. There's no cleverness in silence, only torment of feeling."

"Seems you must be clever," said Kopionkin. "You sound like a political meeting."

"That's not how I became clever."

"How then?" asked Kopionkin. "Be my comrade and teach me."

"I became clever because I made a man out of myself on my own, without parents or anyone else. All the life stuff and other stuff I had to obtain for myself—and then expend it all... Think it through in your mind, out loud!"

"Probably far too much stuff," Kopionkin thought out loud.

Yakov Titych sighed from hidden conscience, then spoke more openly. "Far too much, for sure. When you're old, you lie there and think, How, after me, can people and the earth still be whole? All the things I did, all the food I ate, all the thoughts I thought and hardships I lived through—as if I'd squandered the whole world and left nothing for others except stuff I'd already chewed. But then I realized that others are no different from me, that they too bear their difficult bodies from infancy, and somehow they all endure."

"Why from infancy?" asked Kopionkin. "Were you orphaned, or did your father renounce you?"

"I had no father," said the old man. "I had to get used to strangers and grow myself up alone, without comfort."

"If you had no father, how come you think people are worth no more than stars?" Kopionkin asked with surprise. "People should be more precious to you. Your home's here among them—there's nowhere else you can shelter. If you were a true Bolshevik, I wouldn't need to tell you all this—but you're just an orphaned old man."

Somewhere in the middle of the town, the moans of a child emerged from the primordial silence. Everyone not asleep could hear it—so quiet was night's presence on earth, while the earth herself, beneath this night, was as if absent. After the suffering child came two more voices—the child's mother and Strength of the Proletariat, neighing in alarm. Kopionkin at once got to his feet, no longer in the least sleepy. The old man, accustomed to suffering, said, "Could be a little boy, could be a little girl."

"Little ones weep—while old folk sleep," Kopionkin said accusingly—and went off to water his horse and comfort the crying child.

A wandering beggar woman who had come to Chevengur independently of the *others* was sitting in a dark entrance room, holding her child in her lap and quickly breathing warmth onto it from her mouth, to help it with her own strength. The child lay there meekly, not afraid of the torments of illness now clamping it into somewhere hot, cramped, and solitary. It was just moaning from time to time, not so much in complaint as in quiet sorrow.

"What is it, my darling? What is it?" the mother kept asking. "Say where it hurts and I'll warm you there. I'll kiss you there."

The little boy said nothing, looking at his mother with half-closed eyes that had forgotten her. His heart, isolated in the dark of his body, was beating so insistently, with such hope and fury, that it seemed a being apart, a friend to the child, drying the streams of festering death with the speed of its own ardent life. And his mother was stroking his chest, wanting to help his hidden and lonely heart and so relax the string on which her child's delicate life was now sounding and which she feared might fall silent. At this moment, she was not only tender and sensitive but also smart and calculating; she was afraid of forgetting something, of being too slow with the help that she knew and was able to give.

She was vigilantly recalling all of life—both her own life and what she had seen of the life of others—in order to extract from it everything she now needed to bring relief to her child. And so, without people, utensils, medicine, or linen, in this town she didn't know the name of and had come to by chance, this indigent mother was able to help her child not only with tenderness but also with healing; in the evening she had warmed his body with poultices, sluiced out his bottom with warm water, nourished him with sugared water, and resolved not to fall asleep as long as her child was alive.

But he was still in torment and his mother's hands were sweating from her child's warming body. He was now wrinkling his face and moaning, upset that he was suffering and his mother was sitting there and not giving him anything. His mother then gave him her breast to suck even though he was already in his fifth year. He greedily began to suck thin, scant milk from a breast that had long ago sagged.

"Please, say something," she begged. "Say what you want."

The child opened his pale, aged eyes, waited till he'd finished sucking, and then answered as best he could, "I want to sleep and float in the water. I've been ill and now I'm worn out. Wake me tomorrow, so I don't die. Else, I'll forget and die."

"No, you won't," said the mother. "I'll always be guarding you, and tomorrow I'll beg some meat for you."

"Keep holding me, so beggar women don't steal me," said the boy, who was growing weaker. "No one gives them anything, so they steal. It's so boring with you. It would be better if you got lost somewhere."

The mother looked at her child, now deep in oblivion, and felt pity. "My darling, if you're not meant to live in the world," she whispered, "it would be better to die in your sleep. Only you mustn't suffer, I don't want you to suffer, I want everything to be cool and easy for you."

For a while the boy forgot himself in the cool of peaceful sleep, but all of a sudden he screamed, opened his eyes, and saw his mother pulling him by the head out of a bag where he had been lying amid warm, soft bread. From illness and sweat his weak body had become covered in fur and pieces of it were flaking and crumbling away. Now his mother was handing out these little bits of him to naked beggar women.

"Mother," he said to her, "you're a fool of a beggar woman. Who's going to feed you when you get old? I'm thin enough as it is—and now you're giving me away to other people."[1]

But his mother didn't hear this. She was looking into his eyes, already like dead river pebbles. Forgetting that her boy was now suffering less, she was wailing in a voice so dismal that it sounded indifferent. "I nursed him, I cared for him, I'm not to blame," she was saying, to protect herself from years of anguish to come.

Chepurny and Kopionkin were the first of the Chevengurians to appear.

"What's up?" Chepurny asked the woman.

"I want him to live one more minute."

Kopionkin bent over and touched the boy. He loved the dead, since Rosa Luxemburg too was among them.

"What good will that be?" said Kopionkin. "The minute will pass, and he'll die again, and you'll be howling once more."

"No," the mother promised. "I won't cry again. But I didn't have time to memorize him—how he was when he was alive."

"All right," said Chepurny. "We can do that for you. I was ill for a long time myself. By the end of the capitalist slaughter, I'd become a medical assistant."

"But he's done for," said Kopionkin. "Why bother him?"

"What's so difficult, I ask you now!" said Chepurny, with stern dependability.

"He can manage to live another minute, if that's what his mother wants. He lived and lived—and then what? He just forgot how to do it! If he were frozen stiff, or if the worms were already at him, it would be another story—but this boy here's still hot. Inside him, he's still alive—it's only on the outside he's a goner."

While Chepurny was helping the boy to live one more minute, Kopionkin grasped that there was no communism whatsoever in Chevengur. This woman had only just brought her child here—and he was already dead.

"Stop messing about—you'll never organize him now," said Kopionkin. "If you can't sense his heart, then he's gone."

Chepurny, however, determinedly went on applying his medical knowledge. He caressed the boy's chest, touched his throat, high up and close to the ear, sucked air from the boy's mouth, and expected the deceased to live. "His heart?" he asked, forgetting his diligence and medical faith. "What's his heart got to do with it, I ask you now! The soul's in the throat, as I've proved to you."

"Maybe it is," Kopionkin agreed. "But the soul's still only an idea and it doesn't protect your life—it expends it! As for you, you live here in Chevengur, you don't work, and that makes you think the heart's got nothing to do with it. But the heart's a landless peasant.

It's a working man, laboring nonstop for the whole of a human being. And every one of you Chevengurians is an exploiter—and what you have here isn't communism!"

The mother brought some hot water to help Chepurny in his healing.

"Don't go getting upset," Chepurny said to her. "All Chevengur will be feeling for him now. You don't need to grieve much—only the very littlest bit."

"But when will he breathe?" asked the mother, listening intently.

Chepurny picked the child up, drew him close, placed him on his lap, and got him to stand, as when he was alive.

"Why are you doing all this without mind?" the mother asked bitterly.

Prokofy, Zheyev, and Yakov Titych appeared in the entrance room. They stood to one side and didn't ask anything, so as not to interfere.

"My mind's not a part of all this," Chepurny explained. "I'm acting from memory. Even without me, he must live through your minute. Communism's at work here, along with all nature. Anywhere else, he'd have died on you during the night. He's lived an extra day, I'm telling you—because of Chevengur!"

"Could well be," thought Kopionkin. "Yes, it's not impossible." And he wondered if there might be any sympathy for the dead child to be sensed in the air, in Chevengur or in the heavens above. But the weather was changing and he could hear the wind in the long grass. As for the proletarians, the ground was growing colder and they were getting to their feet to go and spend the night indoors.

"No," Kopionkin said to himself, and he looked out into the yard. "Nothing's changed. It's all the same as under imperialism. The weather's as agitated as ever and there's no sign of communism. But maybe there'll be an inadvertent breath from the child—who knows?"

"Don't torment him any longer," the mother said to Chepurny, who had just poured four drops of sunflower oil between the boy's obedient lips. "Let him rest now. I want him to be left alone. He told me he was worn out."

Chepurny untangled the dead boy's matted hair, which was already darkening, since his early childhood had ended. Quick, calming rain fell on the roof, but a sudden wind, letting itself go in the open steppe, tore the rain away from the earth and carried it off into the distant dark. Once again it was quiet, with only the smell of damp and clay.

"In a moment he'll breathe and look up at us," said Chepurny.

The five Chevengurians bent down over the child's alienated body, to take note immediately of his repeated life in Chevengur, since it would be all too short. The boy sat silently on Chepurny's lap, while his mother took off his warm socks and sniffed the sweat of his feet. A minute passed by—the minute the boy might have lived while his mother memorized him and took comfort, before he died once again. But the boy did not want to go through the agony of death twice and he stayed dead as before, resting in Chepurny's arms.

"I don't want him to live even just one more minute," said his mother, with understanding. "He'd have to suffer and go through death yet again. Let him be."

"What kind of communism's this?" Kopionkin said to himself, his doubts now conclusive. He went out into the yard, which was covered by the damp night. "No, it couldn't help the child take a single breath. A human being appeared, then died. It's not communism—it's a plague! It's time you left this town, comrade Kopionkin. Time you went somewhere far distant."[2]

Within him, Kopionkin sensed vigor, the companion of distance and hope. He now looked at Chevengur almost with sadness, since he would soon be parting with the town forever. Kopionkin always forgave the people he encountered and the towns and villages he left behind; his unrealized hopes were redeemed by parting. At night, though, he often lost patience. Darkness and people's defenseless sleep would entice him to venture deep into some central bourgeois state and carry out reconnaissance there while the capitalists lay naked and unconscious; he could finish them off straightaway and declare communism before dawn.

Kopionkin went to his horse. He looked him over and felt him, to ensure that he could ride away at any necessary moment. He could indeed; Strength of the Proletariat was as sturdy as ever, as willing to ride into the distance and future as when he had paced the roads of the past.

Somewhere on the outskirts of Chevengur an accordion began to play. One of the *others* couldn't sleep and was comforting his sleepless solitude. Kopionkin had never heard such music before. It was almost speaking, only just failing to come up with actual words, leaving them as unrealized melancholy.

"Whatever it has to say, it would be better if the music said it straight out," thought Kopionkin. The music unsettled him. "It sounds as if it's calling to me, but it wouldn't stop playing even if I went over there."

Nevertheless, Kopionkin set off toward the nighttime music. He wanted to take a last, thorough look at the people of Chevengur and discover in them the communism that nothing could make him feel. Even in open steppe, where organization of any kind was impossible, he had felt better than in Chevengur. Then he had been riding beside Sasha Dvanov. When he began to feel sad, Sasha had felt sad too—and their sadnesses had reached out to each other, met, and stopped halfway. In Chevengur, though, there was no comrade to meet his anguish, and it continued out into the steppe, into the emptiness of the dark air, and came to an end only in some lonely beyond. "The man goes on playing," thought Kopionkin. "There's no communism here and his sorrow keeps him from sleeping. Under communism, he would finish speaking his music. The music would come to an end and the man would come over and join me. But as it is, he leaves things unsaid—out of shame."

It was difficult to enter Chevengur and difficult to find your way out. The houses were without streets, cramped together and higgledy-piggledy, as if the inhabitants were huddling together by means of their dwellings—while between the houses grew steppe grass that people were unable to trample down, because they were barefoot.

Four heads appeared from out of the tall grass and said to Kopionkin, "Wait a little longer." It was Chepurny and those who had been with him around the child who had died.

"Wait," begged Chepurny. "Maybe he'll come back to life quicker without us."

Kopionkin squatted down in the grass too. The music stopped; instead there was the sound of winds and fluids gurgling about in Yakov Titych's belly. Yakov, for his part, merely sighed and endured further.

"What made him die?" asked Kopionkin. "He was born after the Revolution, wasn't he?"

"Yes, you're right. So what made him die, Prosha?" asked Chepurny, repeating this question in surprise.

Prokofy knew. "Everyone, comrades, is born, lives, and dies because of social conditions—and for no other reason."

Kopionkin got to his feet. Everything was now definite to him. Chepurny got to his feet too. He didn't yet know what was wrong, but he felt sad and ashamed in advance.

"So the child died from your communism, did he?" Kopionkin said sternly. "But you think communism's a mere social condition—and that's why there's no such thing as communism here! You'll have to answer to me for all this! You snatched the whole town away from the road of revolution, capital soul that you are!" Addressing the streets around him, he called out, "Pashintsev!"

"Yeah!" Pashintsev replied from a remote place of his own.

"Where are you?"

"Here!"

"Come *here* then! In full readiness!"

"Coming—I'm always ready!"

Chepurny was not afraid. His conscience tormented him; the smallest child in Chevengur had died from communism and he was unable to formulate any justification to himself.

"Prosha, is Kopionkin right?"

"Yes, comrade Chepurny, he is," Prokofy replied.

"What are we to do? Is it true? Have we really got capitalism here? Maybe the child's already lived through his minute? What's happened, where's communism gone? I saw it myself, we cleared a space for it."

"You need to make your way, at night, all the way to the bourgeoisie," Kopionkin advised. "And overcome them in their sleep, during darkness."

"Electric current is burning there, comrade Kopionkin," said the knowledgeable Prokofy. "The bourgeoisie live in shifts, day and night, night and day. They're in a hurry."

Chepurny went back to the wandering woman, in case social conditions were bringing the late boy back to life. The woman had placed the boy on a bed in the best room, lain down beside him, embraced him, and fallen asleep. Chepurny stood over them both and sensed his doubt. Should he wake the woman or not? Prokofy had once told him that in the presence of grief in one's heart one should either sleep or eat something tasty. There was nothing tasty in Chevengur, and so the woman had chosen to console herself with sleep.

"You asleep?" Chepurny quietly asked the woman. "Do you want us to find you something tasty? There's still food in the cellars, left from the bourgeoisie."

The woman went on sleeping silently. Her boy had rolled up against her. His jaw had dropped open, as if his nose were blocked and he could breathe only through his mouth. Looking more closely, Chepurny saw that the boy was already gap-toothed. He had gotten through his milk teeth and been slow to bring out his permanent teeth.

"Still asleep?" said Chepurny. "Why are you sleeping and sleeping?"

"No," said the transient woman, opening her eyes. "I lay down and dozed off."

"From grief? Or just like that?"

"Just like that," the woman said sleepily and listlessly. She had her right arm under her boy and wasn't looking at him, because out of habit she still sensed him to be warm and sleeping. Then the beggar woman sat up and covered her bared legs, which held a reserve of plumpness in case of the birth of future children. "Seems she's a good woman," Chepurny realized. "Someone must have ached for her."

The boy had left his mother's embrace and now lay there like one of the fallen in civil battle—flat on his back, with a face so sad that it seemed aged and full of consciousness, and clothed only in the single poor shirt of a class accustomed to wandering the earth in search of a life to be had for free. The mother knew that her child had fully sensed death, and her knowledge of this tormented her more than her own grief or the fact of separation. The boy, however, was not complaining to anyone; he lay there alone, patient and peaceful, ready for long frozen winters in the grave. Meanwhile, the unknown man still stood by their bed, wanting something from her for himself.

"He didn't breathe at all? I don't believe it! Things are different here—it's not like the old days."

"No," the mother replied. "I dreamed of him. In my dream he was alive and we were walking hand in hand through open steppe. It was warm and we'd had plenty to eat. I wanted to take him in my arms, but he said, 'No, Mama, I'll get there quicker on my own feet. And you and I must think—otherwise we'll stay beggars.' But we had nowhere to go. We sat down in a pit and both began to cry."

"You shouldn't have," Chepurny consoled her. "We could have given your boy Chevengur as his inheritance, but he refused it and died."

"We sat there and cried. Why were we living, if life wasn't for us? And then my boy says, 'Mama, it's better if I just die—I'm tired of walking this long road with you. Everything's the same, everything's one and the same.' And I say, 'All right, die. Maybe I'll forget myself too.' Then he lies down close beside me. He closes his eyes, but he's still breathing. He's alive, he just can't . . . 'No, Mama,' he says, 'I can't die.' 'Well,' I say. 'If you can't, then don't. We can walk on a bit farther. Maybe we'll find somewhere to stop for a while.'"

"He was alive with you, just now? Here on this bed?"

"Yes, he was lying on my lap and breathing. He couldn't die."

Chepurny felt some relief. "Yes, of course! How could he die in Chevengur, I ask you now! We've won him the right conditions here. I knew he'd breathe a little, only you shouldn't have gone on sleeping."

The mother looked at Chepurny with lonely eyes. "It seems, my good fellow, that you're after something else. My boy's dead, and that's the end of him."

"I'm not after anything," Chepurny was quick to reply. "Even your dream is precious to me. It means your boy lived a little longer in you and in Chevengur."

The woman fell silent, from grief and her own reflections.

"No," she said. "My child isn't precious to you. What matters to you is some thought of your own. Go away and leave me—I'm used to being left on my own. I've still got a long time to lie with him until morning—don't waste my last hours with him."

Chepurny left the beggar woman's house, content that—even if only in dream, only in his mother's mind—the boy had lived on with a remnant of his soul and not died in Chevengur immediately and forever. Communism, then, did exist in Chevengur and it operated independently of people. But where was it located? As he left the transient woman's family, Chepurny was unable to see or sense communism clearly in nighttime Chevengur, even though it now existed officially. "But there's no end to the ways people live unofficially!" he said to himself in surprise. "They lie in the dark with the deceased—and that makes them feel good. How come?"

"Well?" asked Chepurny's comrades, still out on the street. "What's happening?"

"He breathed. In dream he breathed, but really he wanted to die. When he was out in the steppe, he couldn't."

"That's it. He died when he got here," said Zheyev, with understanding. "Here in Chevengur, he found freedom. Life, death—whatever seemed best!"

"Couldn't be clearer," Prokofy determined. "If he'd wanted to die but couldn't, what kind of freedom is that?"

"What indeed, I ask you now!" said Chepurny, sweeping aside all doubts. At first he had struggled to grasp what his comrades were thinking. Now, though, seeing the general satisfaction with what had happened to the child, he too felt delighted. Only Kopionkin remained without hope.

"Why didn't the woman come out and join you?" he asked, in criticism of all the Chevengurians. "Why did she hide away with her child? She must have felt better in that room than inside your communism."

Yakov Titych was used to living silently, mulling over thoughts in the quiet of feeling, but he too could find the right words when he was upset. And so he did: "If she stayed with her little one, it's because all they have is their shared blood and this communism of yours. If she'd left the dead child, you'd have no ground to stand on."

Kopionkin began to respect this elderly *other* and further confirmed his correct words. "The only communism in Chevengur is in a dark place, with a little boy and one woman. But why do you think communism moves forward in me? Because Rosa and I have profound work to do—even if she is one hundred percent dead."

Prokofy saw this incident with death as a detail of only minor significance and was telling Zheyev how many women he had known with higher, lower, and middle education, giving numbers for each group. Zheyev was listening with envy; he had known only illiterate, uncultured, and submissive women.

"She was enchanting," said Prokofy, coming to the end of some story of his. "She possessed a particular art of personality. She was, you know, truly a woman, not just some peasant. Something, you know, along the lines of—"

"Along the lines of communism?" Zheyev ventured timidly.

"Something like that. I wanted her, but the cost would have been too great. She wanted payment in bread and cloth—it had been a year of all-round hunger. I was taking a little food and other stuff back to my family—my mother and father and all my brothers were stuck in their village—and I said to myself, 'No, to hell with you! My mother brought me into this world—and now you want to finish me off.' And so I went calmly back home. I missed her, but I did right by my family."

"What kind of education did she have?" asked Zheyev.

"The very highest. She showed me her documents. Seven years studying pedagogy alone. She schooled the minds of the children of civil servants."

Kopionkin heard the rumble of a cart out in the steppe. Could it be Sasha Dvanov?

"Chepurny," he said, "when Sasha arrives, send Proshka packing. He's a reptile through and through."

Chepurny agreed, as he had before. "Whatever you say. I'm always ready to exchange good for better!"

The cart rumbled on its way to somewhere nearby, without passing through Chevengur. Evidently, there were people living elsewhere, apart from communism, and they were even traveling about.

Within an hour, even the most tireless and vigilant Chevengurians had given themselves over to rest, until a new, fresh morning. The first to awake was Kirey, who had been asleep since the previous noon, and he saw a woman leaving Chevengur with the burden of a child in her arms. He would have liked to leave Chevengur too, because it was boring to live without war, with only completed conquest. If there were no war, then a man should live with his relatives—and Kirey's family lived a long way away, in the far east, on the shore of the Pacific Ocean, almost at the end of the earth and the beginning of a sky that covered capitalism and communism alike with total indifference. Kirey had walked from Vladivostok to Petrograd on foot, cleansing the earth for Soviet power and its idea, and now he had come to Chevengur, meaning to sleep there until he felt rested and began to get bored. At night, Kirey would look at the sky, which seemed to him like the Pacific Ocean. As for the stars, they were like the lights of ships, sailing past his birthplace on their way to the far west. Yakov Titych had also fallen silent. Here in Chevengur he had found some felt boots and used them to resole a pair of bast shoes,[3] and he would sing mournful songs in a rough voice. He intended these songs for his own soul, as a substitute for movement into the distance, but this had not stopped him from working on the bast shoes—songs, after all, were not enough for life.

Kirey would listen to the old man's songs and ask him what he was feeling so sad about. Hadn't he already had his fair share of life?

Yakov Titych forswore his old age. He considered himself twenty-five years old, rather than fifty, since throughout half his years he had been either ill or asleep. This, therefore, counted as loss, rather than gain.

"Where will you go, old man?" Kirey would ask. "You're bored here, but you won't find it easy out there. You've been cramped into a corner."

"I'll slip out, I'll hit the main road, and my soul will be free from me. There I'll be, a stranger to all, and I won't need *me*. And my life can disappear back to wherever it first came to me from."

"But life's good in Chevengur too!"

"The town's empty. All right for a wanderer wanting a rest. But the houses stand without need, there's no steadiness in the sun, and the people are pitiless. A man comes, a man goes—but there's no care for people, since food and property are cheap."

Kirey wasn't listening, since he could see the old man was lying. "Chepurny respects people," he said, "and he loves all comrades."

"He loves because of excess feeling, not out of need. Tomorrow I must go on my way."

Kirey himself had no idea what place was best for him. Chevengur, with its peace and empty freedom—or some distant and more difficult other town.

The following days were all sunny, as at the very beginning of communism, and a new moon was growing from night to night. Nobody, however, noticed this moon or took it into account; only Chepurny rejoiced at it, as if the moon too were essential to communism. In the mornings, Chepurny would go for a swim; later in the day, sitting in the middle of the street, on a tree that someone had lost, he would contemplate the town and its people as the dawn of the future, as an object of universal desire and his own liberation from the power of mind. It was a pity that Chepurny was unable to express himself.

Proletarians and *others* wandered around and within Chevengur, looking for ready nourishment in nature and the bourgeoisie's former plots of land—and they were finding it, since they remained alive to this day. Sometimes, an *other* would go up to Chepurny and ask, "What are we to do?"

This would astonish Chepurny. "Why ask *me*? Meaning must find its own way to come out of you. What we have here is communism, not tsardom."

The *other* would stand there and think about what he should do.

"Nothing's coming out of me. I've pushed all I can."

"Keep living and accumulating yourself," said Chepurny. "Then something will come out of you."

"There's nowhere what's inside me can disappear to," the *other* promised submissively. "But why isn't there anything here on the outside for us? Can't you order us some task?"

A second *other* came over to ask about the Soviet star: Why was a man's main mark now a star, not a cross or a circle? Chepurny sent him to Prokofy, who explained that the red star signified the earth's five continents, united under a single leadership and colored with the blood of life. The *other* listened, then returned to Chepurny to check the accuracy of this statement. Chepurny held the star in his hands and saw at once that dry old continents were neither here nor there; the star was a man, spreading his arms and legs wide apart to embrace another man. The *other* didn't understand why human beings should want to embrace. Chepurny's lucid reply was that it wasn't our fault; it was simply that our bodies were constructed for embraces, since otherwise we had nowhere to put our arms and legs. "The cross is a man too," the *other* recalled, "but why does he only have one leg when we stand on two?" This too Chepurny was able to answer. "At first people only wanted to hold one another with their arms, but after a while they lost their grip. And so they split their legs apart and used them as well." This satisfied the *other*. "Could well be," he replied, and went off to live.[4]

39

THAT EVENING the new moon had begun to wash herself and so it rained and darkness from the clouds set in early. Chepurny went into a house and lay down in the gloom, to rest and concentrate. After a while, some *other* appeared and told him that there was a general wish for songs to be rung on the church bells. The man with the town's only accordion had disappeared with it. No one knew where he'd gone and they had now grown accustomed to music and were unable to wait. Chepurny replied that this was up to the musicians; it was nothing to do with him. Soon after this, church bells sang out over Chevengur; the sound was softened by the pouring rain and resembled a human voice, singing without breath. To the accompaniment of the bells and the rain, another man appeared, indistinguishable in the silence of the early dark.

"What's up?" Chepurny asked sleepily.

"Is it you who's thought up communism here?" asked an old voice. "Show it to us in view."

"Go and call for Prokofy Dvanov, or anyone else. Anyone here can show you communism!"

The old man left. And Chepurny fell asleep; he now slept well in Chevengur.

"He told me to go and look for that Prosha of yours. Apparently, he knows everything," the old man said to his comrade, who was waiting outside, head bared to the rain.

"Let's go and look for him, then. It's twenty years since I last saw him—he'll be big now."

The elderly man took a dozen steps, then thought better of it. "We can leave that till tomorrow, Sasha. First, let's find some food and somewhere to spend the night."

"All right, comrade Gopner," said Sasha.

But when they began to look for food and shelter, they did not find any; there was, it turned out, no need to look. Gopner and Sasha Dvanov found themselves in communism and Chevengur, where every door was open because every house was empty and where everyone rejoiced to see people new to them, since the Chevengurians—instead of property—could only acquire friends.

The bell-ringer played the Easter Vigil on the bells of the Chevengur church; he was unable to play the "Internationale," even though he was a proletarian by birth and a bell-ringer only by one of his former professions. The rain had all fallen, the air was now silent, and the earth smelled of the wearisome life accumulated within it. The music of the bells, like the night air, challenged Chevengur man to renounce his present condition and go on forward—and since, in place of property and ideals, this man had only an empty body and there was nothing ahead of him but the Revolution, even the song of the bells called him to passions and alarm, not to peace and mercy. Chevengur had no art, although at one time Chepurny had longed for it; any melodic sound, however, even if directed toward the height of the unresponsive stars, freely transformed itself into a reminder of the Revolution, into a sense of conscience with regard to your own—and the class's—still unrealized triumph.

The bell-ringer grew weary and lay down to sleep on the floor of the belltower. In Kopionkin, however, feelings could linger for a long time, even whole years. He was unable to convey anything of these feelings to others and he could expend the life that happened within him only in longing, which he would quench through righteous deeds. After the bell music, Kopionkin did not wait for anything more; instead, he mounted Strength of the Proletariat and occupied the Chevengur RevCom, meeting no opposition. The RevCom was located in the church where the bells had been ringing, which was so much the better. Kopionkin waited there until dawn, then confiscated the committee's records. To that end, he tied all the files and papers into a single bundle and wrote on the top page, "All further action to be ceased. Convey to newly arrived proletarian people, for perusal. *Kopionkin.*"

Nobody appeared at the RevCom until noon. Kopionkin's horse was neighing from thirst, but Kopionkin made it suffer, for the sake of the seizure of Chevengur. Then Prokofy appeared. He took his briefcase out from under his belt as he crossed the porch, then walked through the establishment in order to work in the sanctuary. Kopionkin was waiting for him, standing on the ambo.[1]

"So you've come, have you?" he said. "Stop right there. Wait for me."

Prokofy obeyed. He knew that there was no correct government in Chevengur and that reasonable elements had to live within the more backward class, only gradually subjecting it to their leadership.

Kopionkin confiscated Prokofy's briefcase and his two lady's revolvers, then led him into the sacristy, to place him under arrest.

"Comrade Kopionkin, can you really make a revolution?" asked Prokofy.

"Yes. That's what I'm doing. As you can see."

"Have you paid your membership dues? Show me your party card."

"No. You were given power but you didn't provide the poor with communism. Sit and wait in the sanctuary."

Kopionkin's horse then began to snarl from thirst. Prokofy withdrew to the sacristy. Kopionkin looked in the cupboard where the communion wafers were kept, found a dish of *kutia*,[2] and held it out to Prokofy, so that he would have nourishment. He then locked Prokofy up with the help of a cross, inserting it between the handles of the sacristy doors.

Prokofy looked at Kopionkin through the grillwork and did not speak for some time. Then he said, "Sasha's arrived. He's wandering about the town, looking for you."

Kopionkin's joy made him want to eat. With effort, he maintained his calm in the face of the enemy.

"If Sasha's here, then I can release you. He'll know what to do with the likes of you. You're no longer a danger."

Kopionkin removed the cross from the sacristy door, mounted

Strength of the Proletariat, and rode through the narthex and porch and out into Chevengur.

Sasha Dvanov was walking down the street, not yet understanding anything but seeing that life was good in Chevengur. The sun, the only flower amid the fruitless sky, was shining down over the town and the steppe, and the irritated pressure of its overripe strength was forcing the bright heat of its flowering into the earth. Chepurny walked beside Sasha, trying to explain communism to him, but without success. Finally, noticing the sun, he pointed at it.

"There's our power base. It burns, yet never burns out."

"*Where's* your base?" asked Sasha, looking at the sky.

"Up there. We don't torment people. Instead, we live off the sun's surplus power."

"Why surplus?"

"Because if it weren't, the sun wouldn't release it to us—and it would turn black. But since it *is* surplus, the sun gives it to us—and we occupy ourselves simply with life! Get it?"

"I want to see for myself," said Sasha. Tired and trusting, he wanted to see Chevengur not in order to test it but in order better to sense the local brotherhood that had come into being there.

The Revolution had passed, like the day. Throughout Russia—in district towns, in steppes, and throughout remote parts—the shooting had fallen silent for a long time, and the roads of armies, horses, and the whole Bolshevik footsoldiery had gradually been taken over by grass. Expanses of field and plain lay in silence and emptiness, giving off a smell of new-mown hay, breathing their last while in the heights over Chevengur a late sun now languished alone. No one now appeared in the steppe on a warhorse. Some had been killed—their corpse never found and their name forgotten; others had curbed their horses and were back in their home villages, leading the poor forward not into open steppe but into a better future. And if anyone did appear in the steppe, no one looked twice at him, since he was sure to be someone harmless and at peace, going about routine tasks of his own. When he and Gopner arrived in Chevengur, Sasha had noticed that there was no longer the same alarm in nature, nor had there been the same sense of danger and calamity in the villages along their road. The Revolution had passed these places by, allowing peaceful longing to settle over the fields while it disappeared somewhere unknown, as if worn out by the paths it had traveled and now hiding away in man's inner darkness. There was a kind of evening in the world, and Sasha sensed that it was now evening in him too—a time of maturity, of happiness or regret. On a similar evening, the evening of his own life, Sasha's father had disappeared forever into the depths of Lake Mutevo, wanting ahead of time to see the future morning. Now another evening was beginning—maybe the end of the day whose morning the fisherman from Lake Mutevo had so wanted to see—and it was the turn of the fisherman's son to live through life's evening. Sasha was not so full of love for himself as to wish to achieve communism for his own personal life, but he went forward with everyone else because that was what they were doing and it was frightening to remain alone; having no father or family of his own, he wanted to be with others. Chepurny, on the other hand, was tormented by communism, just as Sasha's father had been tormented by the mystery of life after death. Unable to bear the mystery of time, Chepurny had cut short the duration of history through the urgent construction of communism in Chevengur, just as fisherman Dvanov had been unable to bear his own life and had transformed it into death, in order to experience at once the beauty of the beyond. But it was not his father's curiosity that made him precious to Sasha, nor did Sasha love Chepurny on account of his passion for immediate communism; Sasha had needed his father simply for being the man he was—and as his first lost friend—and he needed Chepurny because he too was a kinless comrade whom people would never take to themselves without communism. Sasha loved his father; and he loved Kopionkin, Chepurny, and many others because, like his father, they would perish from their lack of patience of life, leaving him alone among strangers.

Sasha recalled Zakhar Pavlovich, aged and barely alive. "Sasha," he would say, "do something in the world. You can see, people are living and perishing. We don't need anything much, only some little something."

And so Sasha had resolved to go to Chevengur, in order to know communism there and return to Zakhar Pavlovich to help him and many others now barely alive. But communism was not present in Chevengur on the outside—probably it lay hidden inside people. The surrounding steppe was unpeopled and lonely, while the *others* sitting drowsily outside the houses were few and far between. "My youth is coming to an end," Sasha thought. "It's quiet inside me and evening is passing by in all of history." The Russia where Sasha lived and wandered was empty and exhausted; the Revolution had gone past, its harvest had been gathered, and now people were silently eating the ripe grains, in order for communism to become the constant flesh of their bodies.

"History is sad, because history is time and it knows that it will be forgotten," Sasha said to Chepurny.

"You're right," said Chepurny in surprise. "But how come I failed to notice? That's why birds don't sing in the evening—only crickets. And that's hardly singing. It's the same here in Chevengur—the constant sound of crickets, and few birds. Because history's come to an end here! Why, I ask you, didn't we recognize the signs?"

Kopionkin came up on Sasha from behind. He gazed at him with the greed of his friendship and forgot to get off his horse. Strength of the Proletariat whinnied at Sasha, and only then did Kopionkin dismount. Sasha was looking sullen; he was ashamed of his excessive feeling for Kopionkin and afraid to express it and be mistaken.

Kopionkin's conscience, too, was troubled by secret relations between comrades, but he was emboldened by the merry whinnying of his horse.

"You're here, Sasha!" said Kopionkin. "Let me kiss you a little. Like that, I'll calm down sooner."

After kissing Sasha, Kopionkin turned to his horse and began quietly talking to him. Strength of the Proletariat responded with a look of sly mistrust, aware that the man did not truly want to be talking to him just then.

"Don't look at me," Kopionkin conversed quietly. "You can see how moved I am." But the horse did not turn away, his gaze as serious as ever. "You may be a horse," Kopionkin went on, "but you're a fool. And I know you want to drink—what makes you so silent?"

The horse let out a sigh. "Now I truly am a lost cause," Kopionkin said to himself. "I've even upset this dumb beast."

"Sasha," he then began. "How many years is it since the death of comrade Luxemburg? I'm thinking about her now. She's been dead a long time."

"Yes," Sasha replied, so quietly that Kopionkin could hardly hear him. Kopionkin turned around in fright. Sasha was silently crying, not putting his hands to his face, his tears dropping slowly onto the ground. There was nowhere he could turn his face away from both Chepurny and Kopionkin.

"A horse can be forgiven," Kopionkin said to Chepurny. "But you're a human being. Couldn't you have gone elsewhere?"

Kopionkin should not have said this. Chepurny had been standing there guiltily, trying to think how he could help these two people. "How come we have communism and they're still grieving?" he said to himself. "Is communism really not enough for them?"

"So you're just going to go on standing there?" said Kopionkin. "I seized and occupied your RevCom today—and all you do is observe me!"

"The RevCom's yours," Chepurny replied respectfully. "I was meaning to close it anyway. With people like we have here, what do we want with power?"

Fyodor Fyodorovich Gopner had slept well, got up, walked all around Chevengur, and—thanks to the absence of streets—lost his way in this district town. None of the inhabitants knew the address of RevCom chairman Chepurny, but they all knew where he was at that moment. Gopner was taken to join Chepurny and Sasha Dvanov.

"Sasha," he said, "there's no sign here of anyone doing any work. This is no place for a working man to live."

At first Chepurny felt upset and bewildered by this. Then, remembering what people were meant to live by in Chevengur, he attempted to reassure Gopner. "Here, comrade Gopner, people have only one profession—the soul. And we've decreed life itself to take the place of work. What do you think—does that seem all right to you?"

"I call it a disgrace," Kopionkin replied immediately.

"It may well be all right," said Gopner. "Only it's not clear what will hold people together. How are you doing that? Are you gluing them with spittle? Or molding them together through dictatorship alone?"

Being an honest man, Chepurny had already begun to doubt the completeness of Chevengur communism, although it should have been correct, since he had done everything not only according to his own mind but also in agreement with the collective sense of all the Chevengurians.

"Don't sup with a fool," Kopionkin said to Gopner. "Instead of good, this man organized glory. A child has died here from his general social conditions."

"Who's your working class here?" asked Gopner.

"The sun shines above us, comrade Gopner," Chepurny quietly informed him. "In the past, exploitation obstructed it and stood in its light, but not now. Now the sun labors on our behalf."

"So you really think communism's got going here?" Gopner asked a second time.

"Apart from communism, we have nothing, comrade Gopner," Chepurny explained sadly, thinking intensively so as not to make any mistake.

"I don't feel it yet," said Gopner.

Sasha had been watching Chepurny with such fellow feeling that he felt pain in his body during the latter's sad, labored replies. "Things are difficult and unclear for him," Sasha said to himself, "but he's going the right way, as best he can."

Then Sasha turned to Gopner. "We none of us know communism," he said aloud, "so we can't expect to recognize it here straightaway. And we shouldn't be interrogating comrade Chepurny. We don't know anything any better than he does."

Yakov Titych came up and joined them. Everyone looked at him and fell distractedly silent, afraid he might be hurt that they were talking without him. Yakov Titych stood there for a while, then said, "People can't even make themselves kasha, there's no buckwheat anywhere. But I used to be a blacksmith. Let me lug the smithy out onto the highway. I can work for the passersby. Maybe I'll earn enough for some grain."

"Deeper out in the steppe, there's buckwheat growing wild," said Chepurny. "You can help yourself!"

"By the time a man's walked all that way and found enough grain, he'll be still hungrier," Yakov Titych doubted. "Easier to do some work in the smithy."

"Let him do as he wants with the smithy," Gopner advised Chepurny. "Don't hinder the man."

Yakov Titych made his way between the buildings and into the smithy. A burdock had long ago taken root in the furnace, and beneath it was a hen's egg. Probably, the last hen had hidden here from Kirey, in order to lay, and the last rooster had died from male yearning in the dark of a shed.

The sun was already low in the sky and there was a charred smell coming off the earth. The melancholy of evening had set in, making every lonely man want to visit a friend or else simply go out into the steppe, to think and walk among the now-silent grasses, thus calming a life violated during the day. But the Chevengur *others* had no one to visit and no one likely to call on them. They lived inseparably from one another; during the day they had been wandering around the surrounding steppe in search of nourishing plants, and there was nowhere for any of them to spend time alone. As for Yakov Titych, the smithy made him feel weary and oppressed. The roof had gotten very hot and there were cobwebs everywhere; many of the spiders had already died and he could see their light little corpses, which eventually fell to the ground and turned into unrecognizable dust. Yakov Titych loved picking up little scraps and particles from the streets and backyards, looking at them and imagining what they had once been. Whose feelings, he wondered, had preserved and adored them? Maybe they were little bits of people, or of these same spiders, or of some nameless gnats—but nothing of them remained intact; all these creatures that had once lived and been loved by their children were now destroyed into dissimilar parts. There was not even anything that those left behind for life and further suffering could weep over. "I wouldn't mind everything dying," Yakov Titych said to himself, "if only a dead body remained whole, if only there were something to hold and remember. But as it is, the winds blow, water flows, and everything perishes and separates into dust. I call it torment, not life. And those who died, died for nothing—and now there's no finding anyone who lived back then. Sheer loss—each and every one of them."

In the evening the proletarians and *others* gathered together to cheer and entertain one another before lying down for the night. None of the *others* had a family, because they had all lived with such labor and concentration of energies as to leave no bodily surplus for reproduction. For a family, one needs seed and the strength of ownership, but these people had been exhausted from maintaining life in their bodies alone, and they had expended in sleep the time needed for love. In Chevengur, on the other hand, they sensed peace and sufficient food—and yet their comrades now brought them not contentment but melancholy. In the past, comrades had been made precious to them by grief; comrades had been necessary for warmth during sleep and the steppe cold, and for mutual insurance with regard to food—if one man came back empty-handed, another would bring something. Above all, it is good to have someone who is always present beside you if you have no wife or property and no one with whom to satisfy and expend the constant accumulations of your soul. In Chevengur there was property, there was wild grain out in the steppe, and in the kitchen gardens there were vegetables self-seeded from remnants of the previous year's crops; and as a result, without grief of food or the torment of sleeping on bare ground, the *others* had come to feel bored. They were scanty for one another; they looked at one another without interest. They were useless to themselves, and there was now no substance of use and benefit between them. One of them, Karpy by name, said to everyone that evening, "I want a family. Any number of swine live without a care, with their own seed to sustain them, but I live all inadvertently and without support. Why do I feel such a gulf beneath me?"

Agapka, an old beggar woman, also began to lament. "Take me, Karpy! I can bear your children. I can wash your clothes and make soup for you. It's strange being a wife, but it's good. What with all your worries clinging to you like burrs, there's no time for grief. Yes, you slip out of your own sight. But living the life we live now, there's no getting away from yourself."

"You're a low slut," Karpy replied, rejecting her offer. "I love high-minded, distant women."[3]

"Seems you've forgotten how I once kept you warm," said Agapka. "I wasn't distant for you then, when you came close inside where it hurts!"

Rather than denying the truth, Karpy merely clarified the date. "That was before the Revolution."

Yakov Titych said that communism was now present in Chevengur and that bliss had been given to all. In the past, simple people had possessed nothing inside their torsos, but now they were eating everything that grows on the earth—what more could anyone want? It was time to live and give real thought to something. Out in the steppe, many Red Army soldiers had died from the war. They had agreed to die in order that future people should be better than they themselves. "But those future people," Yakov Titych continued, "are *us*—and we've turned out to be good for nothing. Here we are, already wanting women and feeling bored. It's time we began craft and labor in Chevengur. Tomorrow we must lug the smithy out onto the highway—otherwise, travelers just pass us by."

The *others* did not listen and wandered off disjointedly, each sensing that he wanted something but not knowing what. A few of the newly arrived Chevengurians had been temporarily married in the past and they remembered this, saying that families are very pleasant, because with a family you no longer want anything and you feel less troubled in your soul; you want only peace for yourself and happiness in the future, for your children. Moreover, you feel sorry for your children and that makes you kinder, more patient, and more indifferent to the life going on around you.

The sun became huge and red and then hid beyond the earth's border, leaving in the air its already cooling heat; many of these *others* had believed in childhood that the sun was their father, going somewhere far away and baking potatoes for supper on a large bonfire. Chevengur's one and only laborer—the luminary of warmth, comradeship, and communism—settled down for the night; the moon—luminary of the lonely, luminary of wanderers who wander in vain—gradually began to shine in its place. Illuminated only by timid moonlight, the steppe and its expanses seemed to lie in the world beyond, where life is pale, thoughtful, and without feeling and where the flickering silence makes a man's shadow rustle the grass. Several people went off into the depth of the new night, away from communism and into the unknown; they had come to Chevengur together but were now going their separate ways. Some were going to look for wives, meaning to return to live life in Chevengur; some had grown thin on the town's vegetable fare and were setting off elsewhere to eat meat, while one boy left because he wanted, somewhere in the world, to find his parents.

Yakov Titych noticed how many people had silently disappeared from Chevengur, and he went to speak to Prokofy. "Go and fetch some wives," he said. "People want them now. You brought us here—now you must bring us some women. People have rested, and they say they can't get by any longer without them."

Prokofy wanted to say that women were working people too, that there was no ban on them living in Chevengur and therefore nothing to stop proletarians going and bringing back wives for themselves from other inhabited places—but then he remembered that Chepurny wanted thin and exhausted women who would not distract people from mutual communism. And so he replied, "Once you start families here, you'll soon be breeding petty bourgeoisie."

"Why does that frighten you?" asked Yakov Titych, with slight surprise. "'Petty' means *puny*."

Kopionkin and Sasha came in and joined them. Gopner and Chepurny remained outside. Gopner wanted to study the town, to learn what it was made from and what was located in it.

"Sasha!" said Prokofy. He wanted to feel joy but couldn't manage this straightaway. "Come to live with us, have you? I remembered you for a long time, but then I began to forget. I'd start to remember, but then I'd think, 'No, he must have died,' and I'd forget you again."

"I remembered you," Sasha replied. "The more I lived, the more I remembered you. And I remember Prokhor Abramovich, and Piotr Fyodorovich Kondaev and everyone in the village. Are they still whole and hale?"

Prokofy had loved his family, but now they had all died and there was no one else for him to love. He bowed his head, which worked on behalf of many people but was loved by almost no one.

"They're all dead, Sasha. The future will be setting in soon."

Sasha took Prokofy's sweaty, feverish hand and, sensing his shame over their childhood past, kissed him on his dry, embittered lips.

"We'll live together, Prosha. Don't worry. Here's Kopionkin—and Gopner and Chepurny will be back soon. Life must be good here. Quiet, a long way from anywhere, grass on all the streets... I've never been here before."

Kopionkin sighed quietly, not knowing what he should think or say. Yakov Titych, an outsider in this conversation, reminded everyone of their common concern. "So, what do you think? Are people to seek out their own wives, or will you go and fetch them en masse? Some people have already gone looking."

"Go and collect people together," said Prokofy. "I'll come along too and do some thinking there."

Yakov Titych went outside. Kopionkin realized what he wanted to say. "You don't need to think on behalf of the proletariat. It can think too."

"Sasha will come with me," said Prokofy.

"In that case, go along and think," Kopionkin agreed. "I thought you were going to think on your own."

It was light outside. Amid the sky's waste spaces, over the steppe emptiness of the earth, the moon was shining its forsaken, soulful light that almost sang from dream and silence. This otherworldly light slipped through the doors of the smithy—through rickety cracks lined with soot that had settled there in more industrious times. People were now walking toward the smithy. Tall and grieving, Yakov Titych had gathered them all together and was striding along behind them, as if herding cattle. When he looked up at the sky, he sensed his breath grow weaker, as if the weightless and illuminated heights above him were sucking the air out of his chest, so that he'd be lighter and able to fly there. "It must be good to be an angel," he thought, "if only they existed. Sometimes it gets boring with only people."[4]

The smithy doors opened and some of the people went in, although many remained outside.

"Sasha," Prokofy said quietly, "I don't have a home of my own in our village. I want to stay in Chevengur. But here you have to live alongside everyone else or you're expelled from the party, so please support me now. You don't have anywhere to live either. Let's organize everyone into a single obedient family, let's make the whole town a single home."

Sasha could see that Prokofy was troubled, and he promised to help him.

"Bring us wives!" many of the *others* shouted at Prokofy. "You brought us here—and then you left us all on our own! Fetch us some women, or do you think we're not people? It's awful being here alone—instead of living, we think! You talk about comradeship, but women are our truest comrades. What stops you settling some here in the town?"

Prokofy looked at Sasha and began to say that communism was not his concern alone but the concern of every proletarian in existence; proletarians now had to have minds of their own, as had been decreed during the last meeting of the Chevengur RevCom. If there were no one but proletarians in Chevengur, communism would happen of itself. It was all there could be.

And Chepurny, standing some distance away, was entirely content with Prokofy's words. They were a precise formulation of his own feelings.

"What use is mind?" one *other* called out. "We want to live as we wish."

"Please do!" Chepurny agreed immediately. "Prokofy, go and collect some women tomorrow!"

Prokofy said a little more about communism: That in the end communism was sure to set in completely, and so it would be better, and less painful, to organize it in advance. Whereas if women appeared in the town, they'd set up separate households instead of just the one Chevengur, where everyone now lived as a single orphan family, where people wandered about, slept in different places, and grew accustomed to one another from inseparability.

"You tell us that communism will come to be in the very endmost end," Yakov Titych pronounced slowly. "That means we won't enjoy it for long—if you're nearing the end, there's little time left. So what's the good of us desiring communism with every cell of our being if the great span of our lives must pass by without it? If the mistake's long and the truth's short, we'd do better to live the mistake! We're human beings—and you need to take that into account!"

From lonely Chevengur up to the deepest height stretched lunar oblivion and there was nothing there at all, which was why the moonlight was so full of yearning in the emptiness. Sasha looked that way and wanted to close his eyes at once, so as not to open them again until the following day, when the sun had risen and the world had become cramped and warm again.

"True proletarian thinking!" said Chepurny, in sudden assessment of Yakov Titych's words. He was glad that the proletariat was now thinking with its own head and that he no longer need worry about it or think on its behalf.

"Sasha!" Prokofy said in bewilderment. Everyone listened intently. "The old man's spoken well. Remember how you and I used to go begging? You just begged, and no one gave you anything. I lied and cajoled and always got good, tasty food and a few cigarettes."

Prokofy almost came to a stop because of his habitual caution, but he noticed that the *others* were open-mouthed from sincere attention and so he went on, overriding his fear of Chepurny. "How come we still feel uncomfortable, even though everything's so good here? Because—as one comrade has just correctly put it—every truth must come only a little and only at the endmost end, but we've organized the whole of communism here and now and it's not entirely to our liking. How come everything's correct here, with no bourgeoisie, with nothing but justice and solidarity—and yet the proletariat feels bored and lonely and longs for wives?"

At this point, Prokofy fell silent, afraid of developing his thoughts further. Sasha continued on his behalf: "You want to advise us all to sacrifice truth, since it won't come till the very end and won't live long anyway? You think we should go for some other happiness, which will live for a long time, until the very truest truth of all?"

"Yes, you know..." Prokofy began sadly. In sudden agitation, he went on: "You know how I loved my home and family back in our village. Love for my home made me chase you out to die, as if you were a bourgeois, but now I want to get used to living here. I want to make something for the poor, as if they were my family, and live quietly among them. But I just can't..."

Gopner was listening, but he didn't understand a thing. He asked Kopionkin, but he too didn't know who needed what, other than wives. "You see," Gopner concluded. "When people don't act, they end up with superfluous mind, which is worse than stupidity."

"I'll go and get a horse ready for you," Chepurny assured Prosha. "You must set out tomorrow at dawn—the proletariat wants love. Seems it wants to subjugate all the forces of nature. Excellent!"

The *others* went their separate ways; they did not have much longer to wait for their wives. Sasha and Prokofy went off together, beyond the town boundary. Above them, as if in the world beyond, the moon moved slowly toward its setting place, dragging itself incorporeally along. Its existence was useless; it did not make plants grow, and people slept beneath it in silence. The faraway sunlight which illuminated the earth's nighttime sister possessed substance that was hot, troubled, and alive, but this light reached the moon only after it was filtered through a dead length of space; everything alive and troubled was lost during the journey, and the light that remained was true and dead. Sasha and Prokofy had walked a long way and were speaking quietly; their voices were barely audible. Kopionkin had been watching them; he would have joined them, except that they sounded sad and he would have felt ashamed.

The path under Sasha's and Prokofy's feet was hidden by tall, peaceful grass, which had seized all the land around Chevengur not from greed but from life necessity. The two men were walking apart from one another, along the ruts of what had once been a well-trodden dirt road. Each wanted to sense the other, in order to help his own unclear, wandering life, but they had grown unused to each other. They felt awkward and were unable at first to talk freely. Prokofy was reluctant to yield Chevengur into the hands of wives, proletarians, and *others*; the only person to whom he did not regret giving gifts was Klavdiusha—though he didn't know why. He doubted the need to squander the whole town and all the property in it—to let everything fall into decay and ruin—simply to allow a disadvantageous truth to set in for some brief period at the very end of days. Might it not be better to keep all of communism and its happiness in careful reserve, in order to release it to the masses now and again in fractional portions and according to class need, thus safeguarding the inexhaustibility of both property and happiness?

"They'll be content enough," Prokofy said with conviction and something close to joy. "They're used to grief and can bear it easily. We should give them things a little at a time—then they'll love us. If we act like Chepurny and give them everything straightaway, they'll squander it all and soon be wanting more—and we'll have nothing to give them. And they'll depose us and kill us. Anyway, they don't know how much of anything the Revolution now possesses. I'm the only man with a complete inventory of the town. Chepurny wants everything done immediately. He wants nothing to be left and the end to set in, as long as that end is communism. But we'll never allow things to get to the end, we'll give them happiness a little at a time.

Then we can accumulate more—so we never run out of it.[5] What do you think, Sasha? Aren't I right?"

Sasha did not yet know to what extent Prokofy was right. What he wanted was fully to sense Prokofy's wishes, to imagine himself with Prokofy's body and life and so come to understand what made Prokofy think he was right. Sasha reached over to touch Prokofy and said, "Say more. I want to live here too."

Prokofy surveyed the bright but lifeless steppe and Chevengur itself. Its windowpanes glittered in the moonlight—and behind these windows slept solitary *others*, and in each of them lay a life that now demanded his thought and concern, lest it emerge from the cramped space of a body and be transformed into extraneous action. Sasha, however, did not know what each man's body contained within it, whereas Prokofy knew almost exactly—he was deeply suspicious of silent people.

Sasha was recalling many towns and villages and many people he had seen there. Prokofy, meanwhile, was pointing out that in Russian villages grief was a habit rather than a torment and that a son who has already received his share of the family legacy never returns to visit his father and does not in any way miss him. What bound father and son, therefore, was not feelings but property. And it was only the occasional unusual woman who had not smothered at least one of her newborn babies—and not necessarily on account of poverty, but in order to live more freely and enjoy love with her man.

"You can see for yourself, Sasha," Prokofy went on eloquently. "The satisfaction of desires leads them to be repeated, and people even start wanting something new. And every citizen wants to fulfill their feelings in a hurry, because pain and longing make them sense their own selves. But how can we organize everything people want? Give a man property today and he'll want a wife tomorrow—and next he'll be wanting round-the-clock happiness. It's more than history can ever manage. We'd do better to gradually diminish people. They can get used to that—and they're going to know suffering whatever we do."[6]

"But what is it you want to do, Prosha?"

"I want to organize the *others*. I've noticed that where there's organization, there's never more than one person who thinks. The others are empty boxcars, trailing behind the one in front. Organization's the very smartest thing; everyone knows himself, but no one possesses himself. And everyone feels good. Only the first person has it bad, because he thinks. With organization one can subtract much of what's superfluous from a man."

"But why, Prosha? All this will be difficult for you. You'll be the unhappiest person of all. It will be frightening for you to live alone and separate, above everyone else.[7] The proletariat live for one another. But what about you—what are you going to live by?"

Prokofy looked at Sasha with hard-headed condescension. A man like him, he thought, existed in vain. Sasha wasn't a Bolshevik, he was a beggar with an empty sack—just one more *other*. Better to talk to Yakov Titych—he at least understood that man can endure anything as long as he is given new, previously unknown sufferings. These don't hurt him at all—man feels grief only out of social habit, he doesn't just come up with it on his own. Yakov Titych would have understood that Prokofy's way of going about things was safe and secure. Sasha, on the other hand, felt another man to excess but was unable to measure him with any accuracy.

Out in the vast lunar steppe, the voices of the two men faded into silence. Kopionkin waited for Sasha a long time, but then he lay down in exhaustion and fell asleep in the tall grass on the outskirts of town.

At dawn, he was woken by the rattling of a cart. The general silence of Chevengur transformed every sound into thunder and alarm, but it turned out to be only Chepurny. He had got the cart ready and was about to go out into the steppe to look for Prokofy, to send him on his way in search of women. Prokofy, however, was close by; he and Sasha had come back to the town long ago.

"What kind of women do you want?" Prokofy asked, as he got into the cart.

"Nothing special," Chepurny replied. "Women, of course, but only just. You know... Just as long as you can see they're not men. Just the rawest of raw material. Nothing with any allure."

"All right," said Prokofy, and he prodded the horse forward.

"Can you manage that?" asked Chepurny.

Prokofy looked back, his face as intelligent and dependable as always. "Easy enough!" he said. "I'll herd along whoever you want. And no one will be left to sorrow alone—I'll lump them all into a single mass."

And Chepurny calmed down, knowing that the proletariat would soon be comforted. But then he rushed after Prokofy, grabbed hold of the back of the cart, and called out, "Bring one for me too, Prosha! I need some charm as well. I forgot that I'm a proletarian too. And there's no sign of Klavdiusha."

"She's gone to visit her aunt," Prokofy informed him. "I'll pick her up on my way back."

"I didn't know that," Chepurny replied, and put a pinch of snuff up his nose, so as to sense tobacco instead of the pain of separation from Klavdiusha.

40

FYODOR Fyodorovich Gopner had slept well, climbed the bell tower of the Chevengur church, and was observing the whole of the town where he had heard that future time had arrived and communism been achieved once and for all, so that all that remained was for people to live and be present there. Once, as a young man, working on repairs to the main Anglo-Indian Telegraph, he had spent time in parts similar to the Chevengur steppe.[1] That had been long ago, and he could never have imagined then that he would live to see communism, in an audacious town that he might even have passed through on his way back from the telegraph but which had left no trace in his memory. That was a shame; it would have been better if he had just stayed in Chevengur. Still, there was no knowing. People said that simple folk had a good life in Chevengur, but Gopner had not yet sensed this.

Sasha and Kopionkin were walking past below him, looking for somewhere to have a rest. They sat down by the cemetery fence.

"Sasha!" Gopner shouted from up above. "All this makes me think of the Anglo-Indian Telegraph. Nothing but open space and you can see far into the distance."

"Anglo-Indian?" Sasha repeated, imagining the distance and mystery the telegraph passed through.

"It hangs from iron uprights, Sasha, and each of them has a stamp. And the cable just goes on its way—across steppe, over mountains, and through lands of blazing heat."

Sasha felt a pain in his stomach. This always happened to him when he thought about faraway, unreachable lands with appealing and melodious names: India, Oceania, Tahiti—and the Solitude Islands, alone amid the blue ocean, resting on its coral depths.[2]

Yakov Titych was also strolling about nearby. He used to visit the cemetery every day; it was the nearest thing in Chevengur to a forest, and he loved listening to the dismal sound of a tree suffering in the wind. Gopner at once took a liking to Yakov Titych: a thin old man, the skin on whose ears had gone blue from tension, like on his own ears.

"Do you have a good life here?" asked Gopner, who had come down from the bell tower and was now sitting beside the fence, in a throng of people. "Or just so-so?"

"Not too bad," Yakov Titych replied.

"Nothing you need?"

"I can get by."

A fresh, sunny day was beginning, and like all Chevengur days, it was long. This length made life more noticeable, and Chepurny supposed that the Revolution had won more time for the *others*.

"What should we do now?" Gopner asked.

Everyone was a little troubled by this question; only Yakov Titych remained calm. "There's nothing we can do but wait," he said. "Work takes your mind off things, but there's none to be found here."

Yakov Titych went off to a small glade and lay down opposite the sun to warm up. He had slept the last few nights in the house of the former Ziuzin, having come to love this house because it was the home of a solitary cockroach he had taken to feeding. This cockroach led an obscure existence, without the least hope, but it lived patiently and steadily, not making a show of its sufferings, and so Yakov Titych cherished it and even secretly likened himself to it.[3] The house's roof and ceiling, however, had grown old and rickety. The night dew dripped through them onto Yakov Titych's body and this had chilled him, but he was unable to change his place of shelter because he pitied the cockroach as much as himself. Previously, he had lived in bare places where there had been nothing for him to become accustomed or attached to except another man like himself, a companion of the road. It was essential, though, for him to feel attachment to some living thing—so as to find his own patience of life through caring and attending to something, and so as to learn from observation how to live better and more lightly. Moreover, contemplation of someone else's life allowed Yakov Titych's own life to be expended out of sympathy; otherwise, his life had nowhere to go, since he existed only as a leftover, surplus to the world's population. On coming to Chevengur, the *others* had lost their sense of comradeship; instead, they had acquired property, along with a mass of domestic inventory that they would often reach out to and touch in bewilderment, wondering where all this could have come from; it was, after all, too expensive to have been given to them as a present. The *others* would touch these things timidly, as if they were the numb, sacrificed life of their perished fathers or of brothers now lost in other expanses of steppe. The new Chevengurians had once built huts and dug wells, but only far away, in colonized parts of Siberia, where their circular path of existence had once taken them.

And so, here in Chevengur, Yakov Titych remained almost as alone as after his birth. Having previously grown accustomed to people, he now had a cockroach. Living for the sake of this cockroach in a tumbledown house, he would be woken at night by the freshness of dew dripping down on him through the roof.

Amid the entire mass of *others*, Yakov Titych had made a particular impression on Gopner. Gopner saw him as the saddest and most derelict of men, continuing his further life only from the momentum of birth, but Yakov's inner sadness had, in fact, already gone numb. He no longer sensed it as a discomfort, and he lived on in order to forget himself one way or another. Before Chevengur, he had wandered about with other people and had come up with various thoughts. He had thought, for example, that his mother and father were alive and he was quietly moving toward them—and when he found them, everything would be good. Or he would choose another thought, that the foot-walker beside him was his own special person, holding within him everything most important that he himself still lacked; this meant that there was no need to worry—he could walk on farther with firm strength. And now, in Chevengur, Yakov Titych was living by means of the cockroach. Gopner, however, had no idea what to do in Chevengur. During his first two days he had wandered about and looked. The voluntary Saturdays, he had observed, had swept the town into a single heap, but life itself had decomposed into little pieces and not one of these pieces knew what it should join up with in order to stand its ground. And Gopner was unable to work out what needed to be fitted to what, and where, in order for life and progress to get underway in Chevengur once again.

"Sasha, it's time we began to set things straight."

"Set what straight?" asked Sasha.

"Communism in all its components, of course! Why else did we come here?"

Sasha took his time to reply. "What we have here, Fyodor Fyodorovich, is not some mechanism. It's people's lives. And you can't set people straight just like that—they need to order their own lives. I used to think that the Revolution was a locomotive, but now I can see that it isn't."[4]

Gopner at once wanted to picture all this precisely. He scratched his ear—from which the blue had disappeared now that he was properly rested—and suggested that, since there was no locomotive, everyone needed to have their own little steam engine of life. "But why is that?" he then asked, with something close to surprise.

"Probably, for the sake of more power," Sasha replied after a long pause. "Otherwise, how would anything ever get started?"

A dark blue leaf from a tree fell lightly to the ground near Sasha. It had already yellowed at the edges; it had lived its life, died, and was returning to the peace of the earth. Summer was ending, yielding place to autumn, the time of dense dews and desolate steppe roads. Sasha and Gopner looked up above them—the sky seemed higher now that it was being deprived of the sun's troubling power, which had made it hazy and low. Sasha felt a sense of loss and longing with regard to past time; time constantly comes into being and vanishes, while man with his hope for the future stays in one place. And Sasha understood why Chepurny and the Chevengur Bolsheviks so desired communism. It was the end of history, the end of time. Time moves only in nature—while man can't escape melancholy.

A barefoot, excited *other* ran past Sasha. Then Kirey dashed past, carrying a small dog in his arms because it was unable to keep up with him. A little farther behind came five more *others* who did not yet know where they were running. All five were getting on in years, but they hurtled forward with the happiness of childhood, while their long matted hair—shedding burdock spines and other litter from where they had slept—blew about in the oncoming wind. Last of all was Kopionkin, galloping resonantly by on Strength of the Proletariat, who had been standing idle too long; Kopionkin was waving at Sasha, then gesturing toward the steppe. Walking along the steppe horizon, as if up on a mountain, was a tall, distant man; his entire torso was surrounded by air, only the soles of his feet barely touching the earth's boundary line. It was toward this distant man that the Chevengurians were running—but he kept on walking and began to disappear on the far side of visibility. After rushing across half the steppe, the Chevengurians started back, alone as before.

Chepurny appeared somewhat later, also at a run. He was alarmed and overwrought.

"What's up—I ask you now!" he said to the *others* as they wandered sadly by.

"There was a man out there," they replied. "We thought he was on his way toward us, but he disappeared."[5]

Chepurny could not see the need for one distant man when there were many people and comrades close at hand. And he expressed his bewilderment to Kopionkin, when the latter rode up.

"How would I know!" Kopionkin replied from the height of his steed. "I was chasing after them, yelling, 'Citizens, comrades, fools, where are you galloping? Stop!' But they just ran on. Seems they're like me—they want the International. What's one town to them when there's a whole world beyond?"

Kopionkin waited a little, so Chepurny could think, then added, "I'll soon be on my way too. That man was going somewhere, but you just sit around and exist. If only your communism truly had come to be—but there's not a damned sign of it here! Ask Sasha—he's as upset as I am."

At this point Chepurny clearly sensed that the Chevengur proletariat desired the International—the distant, the foreign, the heterogeneous—so as to unite with them, so that all earth's motley life could grow together as a single bush. In the old days, gypsies, blackamoors, and outsiders of one kind or another had used to pass through Chevengur. Were they to appear anywhere, they could surely be enticed to stay in the town, but there had been no sign of any such people for a long time. After delivering the women, Prokofy would evidently have to travel to southern slave countries in order to resettle their downtrodden in Chevengur. As for those proletarians too aged and infirm to walk as far as Chevengur, aid could be dispatched to them in the form of property. The entire town could even be delivered to them wholesale, if that was what the International required. The Chevengurians themselves could then live in dugouts and warm gullies.

After coming back into the town, the *others* took to climbing up onto the roofs and looking out over the steppe, wondering if some man might be walking toward them from out there, or if Proshka might be bringing their wives, or if anything might have happened far away. But above the tall grass stood only quiet, empty air—and the wind was blowing homeless tumbleweed, that solitary pilgrim plant, down the overgrown dirt road toward the town. Yakov Titych's house had been relocated directly across the former highway and the southeasterly wind had driven an entire snowdrift of tumbleweed close up against it. From time to time Yakov Titych would clear away the heaps of plants, so that light could come through the windows and he could count the passing days. Except for that task, Yakov Titych did not go outside at all in daytime, though he went out into the steppe at night to gather nourishing plants. He was suffering again from wind and the runs, and he still lived alone with the cockroach. Every morning the cockroach used to climb up to the windowpane and gaze at the brightly lit warm steppe, his whiskers trembling from excitement and solitude. Out there he could see hot soil and rich mountains of food, around which petty little creatures were feasting, each lacking any sense of itself because it was one of so many.

Once Chepurny came by. There was still no sign of Prokofy, and Chepurny was already grieving for his lost, necessary friend, not knowing what to do with himself during this long time of waiting. The cockroach was sitting near the window as before. The day was great and warm over the expanse of steppe, but the air had become thinner and lighter—a ghost of itself. The cockroach looked out and yearned.

"Titych!" said Chepurny, "let him out into the sun! Maybe he's longing for communism too—but he thinks it's a long way away."

"What will I do without him?" asked Yakov Titych.

"You can go and be with people. Like I've come to be with you."

"I can't be with people. I'm a diseased man. And my disease makes itself heard all around."

Chepurny could never condemn a man of his own class, since they had too much in common. He was unable to sense further. "What's gotten into you—I ask you now! A diseased man? Communism itself came out of the disease of capital, and something will come of your suffering too. But what's happened to Prokofy? He's vanished without a trace."

"He'll show up again," Yakov Titych replied. Weakened by the pain he was enduring inside, he lay down on his belly. "He's been away six days now—but women love time, and they're wary."

Chepurny left Yakov Titych and went on to the smithy, in search of some kind of light food for the sick man. There, sitting on the anvil stone once used for shaping wheel rims, he found Gopner. Sasha was lying facedown nearby, taking an afternoon nap. Gopner was holding a potato, which he was pressing and squeezing from all angles, as if studying its construction. In reality, he was feeling dispirited and hopeless, and at such times he would always pick up the first objects that came to hand and expend his attention on them, to forget about whatever necessary thing he was lacking. Chepurny told

Gopner about Yakov Titych, saying he was ill and suffering on his own with a cockroach.

"Why've you left him alone then?" asked Gopner. "We should boil him up some kind of broth. In a moment, damn it, I'll go and find him!"

Chepurny also wanted to cook something, but he discovered that they'd run out of matches in Chevengur and so he didn't know what to do. But Gopner had an answer to this: they should start up the wooden pump over the shallow well in one of the displaced gardens, but without letting any water into it. In the past, the pump had brought up water to moisten the soil beneath the apple trees, and it was powered by a windmill. Gopner had noticed this system and he now assigned the water pump to the procurement of fire, by means of its piston's dry friction. Gopner told Chepurny to wrap straw around the wooden cylinder of the pump and set the windmill in motion. Then he should wait for the cylinder to begin to smolder and the straw to catch fire.

Cheered by this, Chepurny went on his way. Gopner woke Sasha.

"Sasha! Quick, get up! We need to busy ourselves a little. The thin old man's close to dying and the town needs fire. Sasha! Everything's so dismal—and all you do is sleep."

Sasha stirred in effort and pronounced as if from a distance—from his sleep, "I'll wake up soon, Papa—sleeping is dismal too. I want to live outside, it's cramped in here."

Gopner turned Sasha onto his back, so that he would draw his breath from the air rather than from the earth, and checked his heart, to see how it was beating in his dream. It turned out to be beating deeply, rapidly, and precisely; Gopner worried that it might be overwhelmed by its own speed and precision and then cease to function as a cutoff valve for the life now passing through Sasha—a life almost silent in sleep. Gopner contemplated the sleeping man: What was the peaceful, sustaining force now sounding in his heart? It was as if his lost father had charged Dvanov's heart, forever or for a long time, with his own hope, but this hope could never be realized and so kept on beating within the man. If this hope were realized, the man would die; if it were not realized, the man would remain but endure much suffering, his heart continuing to beat in its interminable place in the man's center. "Better that he should go on living," thought Gopner, looking at Dvanov's breathing. "We won't let him suffer." Dvanov was lying in the Chevengur grass and, wherever his life might aspire, its aims had to be amid homesteads and people, because farther away lay only grass that had wilted in the unpeopled steppe and a sky that, through its indifference, signified the isolated orphanhood of people on earth. Perhaps that was why a heart kept on beating—because it is afraid of being left alone in a world that is wide open and the same all over; through its beating, the heart is linked to the depth of the human race, which has charged it with life and meaning. This meaning, however, could not be distant and incomprehensible; for a heart to be able to beat, it had to lie close at hand, not far from the chest. Otherwise, the heart would lose all feeling and stop dead.

With parsimonious eyes, Gopner surveyed Chevengur. Even if it were no good, even if its houses stood in an impenetrable heap and its people were silent, he would still rather live there than in some distant and empty place.

Dvanov stretched out his body, now warm from sleep and rest, and opened his eyes. Gopner looked at him with serious concern. He seldom smiled, and moments of sympathy made him appear still more sullen; he was afraid of losing someone he cared about, and this fear of his looked like sullenness.

Meanwhile, Chepurny had gotten the mill and the pump going. The piston, running up and down inside the dry wooden cylinder, let out terrible screeches that could be heard all over Chevengur. Still, it was procuring a flame for Yakov Titych. With the utilitarian sensuality of labor, Gopner listened to the struggling machine. Soon they would be cooking hot, nourishing food for Yakov Titych's stomach; Gopner's sense of the benefit this would bring the old man caused saliva to accumulate in his own mouth.

Chevengur had known whole months of total silence. This was the first time anyone had heard the racket of a laboring machine.

All the Chevengurians had gathered around the machine and

were contemplating its industrious zeal on behalf of a weak old man. The trouble it was taking over a single sufferer was astonishing.

"Fine warriors you are!" said Kopionkin, the first to come and inspect the alarming sound. "A proletarian conceived and erected this! And for another proletarian! Nothing to give to a comrade—so you set up a wind-flapper and this here self-sucker!"

"Ah!" said the *others*. "Now we understand!"

Chepurny stayed close beside the pump, constantly checking its heat. The cylinder was getting hotter and hotter, but only slowly. Then Chepurny ordered the Chevengurians to lie down all around the machine, so that no cool air could blow on it from any direction. And they lay there until evening, when the wind died down completely and the cylinder cooled off, having failed to generate the least spark of fire.

"It never even got too hot to touch," Chepurny said of the pump. "Maybe there'll be a gale tomorrow. Then we'll pump up some heat in no time."

That evening Kopionkin sought out Sasha. He had been wanting for a long time to ask him about Chevengur: What was it they had in Chevengur? Communism—or back again? Should he stay, or was it all right to leave? Now, at last, he asked.

"Yes," Sasha replied. "It's communism."

"But how come I don't see it anywhere? Or is it still just thin on the ground? I ought to be feeling joy and sorrow—my heart gives way easily. I'm even scared of music. Someone only has to play a few notes on an accordion and I'm full of anguish and tears."

"You're a Communist yourself," Sasha replied. "Communism originates from Communists and exists among them. Why do you keep searching for it, comrade Kopionkin, when it's already stored inside you? Here in Chevengur there's nothing to hinder communism, so it comes into being of itself."

Kopionkin went over to his horse and turned it loose, to graze all night in the steppe. Usually he kept his steed close at hand day and night, no matter what.

The day came to an end—like someone leaving the room without finishing a conversation—and Sasha's feet began to feel cold. He stood there alone, amid wasteland, expecting to see someone. But there was no one to be seen—the *others* had taken to lying down to sleep early. Waiting for their wives was not easy for them, and they wanted to exhaust the hours in sleep. Sasha wandered off beyond the town boundary, where the stars shone farther away and more quietly, being located not over the town but over expanses already being laid waste by autumn. In the very last house, however, he heard people talking. Loose grass had piled up against all one side of this house as if, along with the sun, the wind too were now working on behalf of Chevengur, driving grass against the buildings to protect them from winter and create sheltered warmth inside them.

Sasha went inside. Yakov Titych was lying belly down on the floor, suffering his illness. Gopner was sitting on a stool, apologizing that the wind had been weak that day and they had been unable to procure fire; tomorrow, though, they could expect a gale—the sun had disappeared into distant clouds now being lit by flashes from the summer's last thunderstorm. And Chepurny was standing in silent anxiety.

Yakov Titych was not so much suffering as longing for life. Life no longer felt precious to him, but he knew in his mind that it was precious and so he quietly pined for it. The presence of visitors filled him with shame, since he was unable at that moment to sense his goodwill toward them; it would not matter to him if they were to disappear from the world. And his cockroach had left the window and found somewhere to live in the rooms of objects; he preferred oblivion in the crush of warm things to the sun-warmed but overly spacious, terrifying land beyond the glass.

"You really shouldn't love that cockroach so much, Yakov Titych," said Chepurny. "That's why you've fallen ill. If you'd stayed within human bounds, communism's social conditions would have acted on you—but on your own you're not strong enough. You've had to confront a whole onslaught of microbic filth. If you'd been with others, the microbes would have attacked them too, and you'd have been largely spared."

"Why, comrade Chepurny, is it wrong to love a cockroach?" Sasha asked hesitantly. "Maybe it's all right. Maybe if you don't want a cockroach, you're never going to want a comrade either."

Chepurny at once fell deep into thought. It was as if all his feelings had come to a stop; still more now did he understand nothing. "All right then, let the man be close to a cockroach," he said, reassuring himself through Sasha's authority. "After all, his cockroach too has chosen to make a life for itself in Chevengur."

Some membrane in Yakov Titych's stomach tightened so tight that he let out a groan in advance, afraid that it was about to snap—but then the membrane relaxed again. Yakov Titych let out a sigh; he felt sorry for his own body and for everyone present around him. He could see that people were standing nearby, each with innards of their own, and none of them knew what to do with their body while Yakov lay alone on the floor during his time of grief. Chepurny felt even more ashamed than the others, since he was accustomed to thinking that property had lost its value in Chevengur and that the proletariat, therefore, was now firmly united. But their inner beings, it seemed, still lived separately and were helplessly afflicted by suffering. People, then, could not be truly united—and this was why Gopner and Kopionkin could not detect the presence of communism; it had not yet become an intermediary substance between the inner beings of proletarians. At this point, Chepurny sighed too. Why, he wondered, did Sasha not do more to help? Sasha was present in Chevengur, but he remained silent. And as for the proletariat—what stopped it from entering into its full strength, now that it had only itself to rely on?

The light outside had faded and night had begun to deepen. Yakov Titych lay there in expectation; any moment now, everyone would go away for the night and he would be left to suffer alone.

But Sasha was unable to leave this thin, exhausted old man. He wanted to lie down beside him and stay there all night, all through his illness—just as, in long-ago childhood, he had lain with his father. But he did not do this; it would have been awkward and he knew how ashamed he himself would have felt if another person had lain down beside him, to share his illness and lonely night. The more

Sasha thought about what he should do, the less remained of his wish to stay with Yakov throughout the night—as if his mind were swallowing his feeling life.

"Yakov Titych, you live in a disorganized manner," said Chepurny, as if this were the cause of the man's illness.

"Don't talk nonsense to me!" Yakov Titych replied, hurt by this. "If that's what you think, then please organize these innards of mine. All you've done here is move buildings and furniture. But inner beings go on suffering, same as before. Go away and lie down for the night. It won't be long before the dew starts to drip."

"Damn the dew and its dripping!" said Gopner morosely. He then went outside and climbed up onto the roof, to inspect the holes that allowed drops of dew to chill the ailing Yakov Titych.

Sasha too had gotten up onto the roof and was holding on to the chimney. The moon was already glittering with cold; desolate dew was shining on damp roofs; and the steppe, for anyone left on their own there, was gloomy and frightening. Then Gopner found a hammer in a shed, fetched some plate shears and two sheets of old iron from the smithy, and began to repair the roof. Sasha was now down below, shearing the iron, straightening the nails, and then passing everything up to Gopner, who was sitting on the roof, hammering away for all Chevengur to hear. This was the first time, since the coming of communism, that hammer blows had rung out in the town, and that man himself had begun to labor, in addition to the sun. Chepurny had gone off into the steppe to listen out for Prokofy, but the sound of the hammer brought him quickly back. The other Chevengurians had also found it impossible to stay as they were and had come to watch in astonishment, wondering how and why men were suddenly working.

"Please don't be afraid," Chepurny said to them all. "He's not hammering for the sake of riches or material good. He had nothing to give as a present to Yakov Titych, so he began patching the roof over his head. And that's no bad thing to be doing!"

"Certainly not," people replied. They then stood there until midnight, until Gopner came down from the roof and said, "There'll be no dripping now!" And the *others* all sighed with satisfaction, knowing that nothing would now drip through onto Yakov Titych and that he could lie ill in peace. The Chevengurians at once felt a jealous parsimoniousness toward Yakov Titych, since it had been necessary to patch a whole roof for him to remain whole.

During the rest of the night the Chevengurians slept. Their sleep was calm and full of consolation—at the end of town stood a house snowed under by drifts of tumbleweed and in it lay a man who had now again become precious to them, and they missed him in their sleep. A toy can be similarly precious to a child, when he sleeps and waits for morning, when he will wake up and once again be with the toy that has fastened him to the happiness of life.

That night, there were only two men who did not sleep—Kirey and Chepurny. Both were thinking greedily about the following day, when everyone would get up, Gopner would procure fire from the pump, smokers would be smoking crushed burdock, and life would be good once more. Deprived as they were of families and labor, Kirey, Chepurny, and all the sleeping Chevengurians had no choice but to lend their souls to people and objects nearby, in order to multiply and thus lighten the accumulating life compressed in their bodies. Now their thoughts were with Yakov Titych—and this brought relief to all of them; their parsimonious fellow feeling for him allowed them to fall peacefully asleep, as if from exhaustion. Toward the end of the night, Kirey too quietly forgot himself in sleep. Chepurny whispered to himself, "Yakov Titych is asleep now, but I'm not," and then he too laid his weakened head to the ground.

The following day began with drizzle. The sun did not appear over Chevengur; people woke up but did not leave their houses. Autumn unease had set in, and the soil was falling into long sleep beneath the patient, incessant rain.

Gopner made a box around the water pump to protect it from the petty drizzle and so be able to procure fire all the same. Four of the *others* stood around Gopner and imagined they were taking part in his work.

In the meantime, Kopionkin had unstitched the portrait of Rosa

Luxemburg from his cap and sat down to copy it. He had suddenly felt like giving Sasha a picture of Rosa—maybe he too would then start to love her. He found some cardboard and began to draw on it with charcoal from the stove. Sitting at the kitchen table, poking out his gently moving tongue, he felt a peace and delight that he had never known in his past life. He accompanied each glance at the portrait of Rosa with an excited whisper—"My dear comrade woman"—and in the silence of Chevengur communism he would let out a deep sigh. Drops of rain moved down the windowpane; sometimes a gust of wind quickly dried the glass; the nearby wattle fence was a dismal sight—and Kopionkin sighed on further, moistened his palm with his tongue for the sake of artistry, and began to outline Rosa's mouth. By the time he got to her eyes, he was overwhelmed. Nevertheless, the grief he felt was not tormenting; it was merely the weakness of a still-hopeful heart—and this weakness had come about because all his strength was going into the painstaking art of drawing. He could not at this moment have leaped onto Strength of the Proletariat and galloped across the steppe mud to Germany and the grave of Rosa Luxemburg, so as to glimpse her earthen mound before it was washed away by the autumn rains. Kopionkin's eyes were tired from the wind of war and the open steppe, and all he could do was to wipe them now and again with the sleeve of his greatcoat. He was expending his sorrow in the zeal of labor; he wanted quietly to draw Sasha's attention to the beauty of Rosa Luxemburg and so make happiness for him, since it would have felt shameful to embrace and love Sasha immediately.

Along with Pashintsev, two of the *others* were chopping the sharp-leaf willow that grew in the sandy soil on the outskirts of town. In spite of the rain, they kept on working and had already accumulated a substantial heap of the trembling branches. Even from a distance, this alien activity caught Chepurny's attention, all the more so since people were getting wet and chilled for the sake of this brushwood. He went over to investigate.

"What are you doing?" he asked. "Why are you destroying plants and freezing yourselves?"

The three laborers, absorbed in themselves, went on greedily chopping short the impoverished life of the scrub.

Chepurny sat down on the damp sand. "Why?" he said to Pashintsev. "Cutting and chopping, cutting and chopping—why, I ask you now!"

"For firewood," Pashintsev replied. "We need to prepare in good time for winter."

"Prepare in good time for winter?" Chepurny repeated. "And what about snow? Have you considered that in winter we get snow?"

"When it falls, we certainly do," Pashintsev agreed.

"And when does it *not* snow?" asked Chepurny. Then he came to the point. "Chevengur will be covered by snow and living beneath the snow will be warm. Why do you need kindling and firewood, I ask you now!"

"This isn't for ourselves," Pashintsev reassured him. "We're chopping wood for whoever needs it. As for me, I've never in all my days needed heat. I'll heap up snow all around a hut—and that hut's where you'll find me."

"For whoever needs it?" Chepurny repeated doubtfully—but then he felt satisfied. "In that case, chop away! I thought you were chopping for yourselves—but if it's for someone else, that's another matter. It's not labor, it's a gift of help. Chop away! Only, why are you barefoot? You'll catch a chill. Let me at least give you my boots!"

"Me, catch a chill!" Pashintsev exclaimed, taking offense. "If it were cold enough to make *me* ill, *you'd* have met your death long ago."

Chepurny was not supposed to be wandering about and observing; this had been a mistake on his part. He often forgot that there was no longer a RevCom in Chevengur and that he was not its chairman. Now Chepurny recalled that he was not Soviet power and he walked away in shame, afraid that Pashintsev and the two *others* were now saying to themselves, "Thinks he's ever so good and clever, wants to be the wealthy director of all the poor of communism!" And he sat down behind a fence, so that they'd forget him at once and not have time to think anything about him at all.

From a nearby shed he heard quick little blows on stone; he pulled out a stake from the fence and walked that way, stake in hand, wanting to help whoever was laboring there. Inside the shed, he found Kirey and Zheyev, sitting on a millstone and chiseling small furrows across its face. It turned out that they wanted to start the windmill and grind various ripe grains into a fine flour so that they could bake tender little flatbreads for the ailing Yakov Titych. After each furrow, the two men would fall into thought, uncertain whether or not to score the stone further; failing to get to the end of this thought, they returned to their work. They were both troubled by the same doubt: the millstone would require a millrhynd[6]—and the only person in Chevengur who could fashion a millrhynd was Yakov Titych, who in the old days had worked as a blacksmith. But Yakov Titych would be able to make a millrhynd only when he had recovered and would no longer need flatbreads. It seemed then that, rather than scoring the stone now, they should wait for Yakov Titych to get back on his feet. On the other hand, if he did get better, mill, millrhynd, and flatbreads would all be unnecessary. And so, from time to time, Kirey and Zheyev would stop for the sake of doubt—but then return to work just in case, to feel within them the satisfaction of their concern over Yakov Titych.

Chepurny watched for a long time. He too began to doubt. "You're working in vain," he said tentatively. "What you sense now is stone, not your comrades. Soon Prokofy will return and he'll read aloud to everyone about how labor, like capitalism, gives birth to the bitch of contradiction... It's raining outside, the steppe's all dismal and dank, and the man still isn't back. I can't stop thinking about him."

Kirey was swayed by this. "Working in vain," he repeated. "Maybe. Yakov will get better anyway—communism has more power than flatbreads. I'd do better to give comrade Gopner some of the powder from my cartridges. Then he'll make fire more quickly."

"He doesn't need your powder," retorted Chepurny. "The power of nature's enough for everything. Entire luminaries are burning above us. How can straw not catch fire? But the moment the sun goes behind the clouds, you start laboring in its place. Capital's gone now—you should live more fittingly!"

But Kirey and Zheyev had no clear idea why they had been laboring. And so, when they got to their feet, leaving their concern over Yakov Titych scored on the stone, they felt only dreariness in the world.

Sasha and Piusia also didn't at first know why they had set off toward the Chevengurka River. The rain over the steppe and the valley was creating a particular yearning silence in nature, as if the damp, lonely fields wanted to draw closer to the people in Chevengur. Sasha thought with wordless happiness about Kopionkin, Chepurny, Yakov Titych, and all the *others* now living their lives in Chevengur. He saw these people as parts of a single socialism, surrounded by rain, steppe, and the gray light of an entire alien world.

"Piusia, are you thinking anything?" he asked.

"Yes," Piusia replied quickly. He felt a little embarrassed. He often forgot to think, and just then he had not been thinking anything at all.

"I'm thinking too," Sasha told him with satisfaction.

What Sasha meant by thinking was not the consideration of ideas but the constant imagination of beloved objects—and his main beloved objects now were the people of Chevengur. He saw their pathetic naked torsos as the essence of the socialism that he and Kopionkin had searched for in the steppe and now found. Sasha felt complete satisfaction of soul; he had not wanted to eat since the previous morning, nor had any thought of food even entered his mind. He was afraid now of losing his inner calm and sufficiency, and he wished to find another, secondary idea—something he could live by and expend, while keeping his main idea as an untouched reserve, returning to it only occasionally for the sake of happiness.

"Piusia," Sasha began. "It's true, isn't it, that Chevengur is the property of our souls? That we should cherish it in tight hearts and not keep fingering it every minute?"

"Yes, indeed!" Piusia confirmed with clarity. "If I see anyone lay a finger on it, I'll smash their heart out of their body!"

"There are people in Chevengur. They need to live and feed themselves," Sasha went on thinking, now still more reassured.

"Of course they do," Piusia agreed. "Even with the communism we've got here, they're just skin and bone. How can there be room for communism in the body of someone as skinny as Yakov Titych? There's barely enough space for the man himself."

They came to a thickly turfed, long-overgrown gully that opened onto the floodplain of the Chevengurka and then lost itself in the valley. Spreading across the gully's broad bed was a festering stream, fed by a living spring somewhere at the top of this gully. Water could be relied on even during the driest years, and there was always fresh grass growing beside the stream. What Sasha now wanted more than anything was to guarantee food for everyone in Chevengur, so that they would live long and without harm to themselves and, through their presence in the world, provide his mind and soul with the peace of inviolable happiness; it was necessary for each body in Chevengur to live steadfastly, because it was only in such a body that communism was alive as a substantial feeling. At this point Sasha stopped, in thought and concern.

"Piusia," he said, "let's put a dam across this stream. Why let water flow past people to no avail?"

"All right," Piusia agreed. "But who'll drink the water?"

"The earth, in summer," Sasha explained. He had decided to construct an irrigation system in the valley. The following summer, in accord with drought and need, he would cover the valley with moisture and so aid the growth of nourishing grains and grasses.

"Vegetable plots will do well here," said Piusia. "These are rich lands. Every spring black earth washes down from the high steppe, though by summer there's just gaping cracks and dry spiders."

An hour later, Sasha and Piusia came back to this spot with spades and began digging a canal to divert water from the stream, so that they could build their dam on dry ground. The rain did not let up, and cutting through the dense, sodden turf proved hard work.[7]

"But after this, people will always be well fed," said Sasha, working his spade with the zeal of greed.

"And how!" Piusia replied. "Liquid is a mighty matter."

Now Sasha no longer feared the loss or impairment of his main thought—about the safekeeping of the people in Chevengur. He had found a second, additional idea—that of irrigating the valley—which would serve both as a distraction and to help preserve within him the integrity of his first idea. He was still wary of making use of the people of communism; all he wanted for now was to live quietly and to conserve communism, without loss, in the form of its very first people.

At noon Gopner procured fire through his water pump. The hubbub of joy could be heard all over Chevengur, and Sasha and Piusia ran over to join Gopner and Chepurny. Chepurny had started a fire and was now boiling a pot of soup for Yakov Titych. This success filled him with a sense of triumphant pride: from the raw and damp, the proletariat had made fire.

Sasha told Gopner about his plan to build an irrigation dam across the stream, to help the growth of cereals and vegetables. Gopner said that the dam would require proper foundations; they'd need dry timber to make into strong piles. He and Sasha spent the rest of the day searching for timber, until they came to the old bourgeois cemetery, which was now—thanks to the town's compression due to the relocation of buildings during voluntary Saturdays—located outside the town boundary. Wealthy families had put up tall oak crosses in memory of departed relatives, and these crosses—the wooden immortality of the dead—had stood over the graves for decades. Gopner thought that these crosses would make good piles; they needed only to remove the crossbars and the little heads of Jesus Christ.

Late in the evening Gopner, Sasha, Piusia, and five of the *others* began rooting out crosses. Chepurny came along a little later, after feeding Yakov Titych. Wanting to help those already laboring for the sake of the town's future plenty, he joined in the work of uprooting.

Their footsteps inaudible amid the sounds of labor, two gypsy women came into the cemetery from out of the steppe. No one noticed them until they went over to Chepurny and stopped in front of him. Chepurny was digging up the root of a cross when he sensed a warm, damp smell that the wind had long ago banished from Chevengur. He stopped digging and went still and silent, hoping for this phenomenon to do more to reveal itself—but it gave off no sounds, only this smell.

"What's brought you here?" he asked. Barely looking at the women, he jumped to his feet.

"We were sent here by some young fellow we met," said one of the women. "We've come to hire ourselves out as wives."

"Prosha, I suppose!" said Chepurny, catching on. "Where is he now?"

"Over thataway," the woman replied. "He felt us over for diseases, then sent us along. So here we are—and it seems you need us. People are being put in the ground and you've no young women to bear you more."

Chepurny looked in confusion at these sudden women. One was young and seemingly taciturn; her small black eyes expressed the endurance of a painful life, and the rest of her face was covered by frail, exhausted skin. She had a Red Army greatcoat on her body, along with a cavalryman's peaked cap on her head. Her fresh black hair showed that she was still young and could have been pretty—but the time of her life had passed in hardship and to no avail. The other woman was old and gap-toothed, but she looked the more cheerful of the two; many years of customary grief made it seem to her that her life was getting easier and happier. Repeated grief no longer felt to this woman like grief; repetition turned it into relief.

Chepurny was moved by the tender appearance of the half-forgotten women. He looked at Sasha, wanting him to talk to the new arrivals, but there were tears of emotion in Sasha's eyes and he looked almost frightened.

"You're in Chevengur now," said Chepurny. The touching look of these women made him tense and unsure of himself. "Look around you. We have communism here—will you be able to cope with it?"

"Don't try to scare us, my handsome!" retorted the older woman, evidently versed in dealing with strangers. "We've seen worse than anything you've got here—yet we're none the worse for it. Whatever should be in a woman, we've brought it along for you. But what are you asking about? That young fellow of yours said any live woman can be a bride here—and now you ask if we'll be able to cope! Have no fear, my dear—you can't put us through worse than what we've been through already!"

Chepurny heard her out, then formulated an apology. "Of course, you can cope with life here! I was only testing you. If you've been scarred by capitalism, why would you be scared of communism!"

Gopner was still indefatigably digging up crosses, as if these two women had not appeared at all, and Sasha too was bent to his work, not wanting Gopner to think he was taking an interest in the women.

"Go on," Chepurny said to the women. "Go into the population. Cherish people with your care. You can see how we're struggling on their behalf!"

The gypsy women went on into Chevengur, to find husbands.

The *others* were sitting about—in houses, in sheds, beside thresholds—working with their hands at whatever they could. Some were planing wood; others, with new peace of heart, were darning sacks in order to gather wild grains out in the steppe; still others were going from house to house, asking, "Any gaps?"—then searching for bedbugs in the cavities of stoves and walls and crushing them there. Each *other* was working not for himself, but for someone else; each had seen Gopner mend the roof over Yakov Titych. Wishing comfort for his own life, each now looked on some other Chevengurian as his own best good—and so he began gathering grain for him, or cleaning up boards; from these boards he might then knock up some gift or other. Those now crushing bedbugs had not yet found in any single person the good that brings peace of heart and the wish to labor to protect their chosen one from the disasters of need. They were working simply because expenditure of strength made their tired body feel fresher. Nevertheless, they also drew some comfort from the knowledge that people would no longer be bitten by bedbugs. After all, the water pump had worked eagerly to make fire for Yakov Titych, even though the wind and the machine were not people.

An *other* by the name of Karchuk completed a long box and lay down to sleep in total satisfaction. It didn't matter that he had no idea what use this box might be to Kirey, whom Karchuk now felt to be a vital necessity to his soul.

As for Kirey, after finishing work on the millstone, he had gone out to crush a few bedbugs and then lain down for a rest. Life, he had decided, was now much better for the poor, since parasites would no longer be draining their thin bodies. Kirey had also noticed that the *others* often looked at the sun, admiring it because it nourished them, and today all the Chevengurians had clustered around the water pump, admiring both the pump itself and the wind that powered it. This had prompted in him a jealous question: Why, under communism, did people love nature and the sun but not notice Kirey himself? And so, in the evening, Kirey had gone back out to crush bedbugs, in order to labor no worse than nature and a wooden machine.

Karchuk was still thinking about his box, his thoughts not reaching any conclusion, when he drifted off to sleep. Just then, however, the two gypsy women walked in. Karchuk opened his eyes, too startled to speak.

"Good evening, husband!" said the older gypsy. "Feed us, then put us to bed. Fair shares of bread—and shared love too!"[8]

"What?" asked Karchuk, who was half-deaf. "I can do without all that. I'm all right as things are. I'm thinking about my comrade."

"What do you want with a comrade?" retorted the older gypsy, while the younger one stood there in silent embarrassment. "You'll share your body with me, you won't begrudge me your things, and you'll forget your comrade—I tell you verily!"[9]

She took off her kerchief and was about to sit down on the box prepared for Kirey.

"Don't touch that box!" yelled Karchuk, scared it would be damaged. "I didn't make it for *you*!"

The woman snatched up her scarf and took womanly offense.

"A sweet welcome you give us! If you can't pucker your mouth, then don't wish for cranberries!"[10]

The two women went out and lay down in a shed without conjugal warmth.

41

SIMON Serbinov was riding across Moscow in a tram. He was a tired, unhappy man, with a quick, compliant heart and a cynical mind. He had not bought a tram ticket and he had almost no desire to exist; evidently he was truly and deeply degenerating. Although he belonged to an iron yet optimistic party, he was incapable of feeling himself to be a happy son of the era. He did not feel generally liked and admired; he felt only the energy of the sadness of his own individuality. He loved women and the future and had no love for positions of responsibility that would allow him to bury his snout in the feeding trough of power. Not long before this, he had returned from an inspection of socialist construction in the distant open plains of the Soviet land. For four months he had traveled slowly through the deep, native silence of remote parts. During meetings of district party committees he had helped local Bolsheviks to prize peasant life from its smallholding roots, and in village reading huts he had read aloud stories by Gleb Uspensky.[1] The peasants had lived on silently, while Serbinov had ridden farther into the depths of the soviets, to obtain from laboring life an exact truth for the party. Like some other worn-out revolutionaries, Serbinov did not love the individual peasant or working man—he preferred them en masse, not separately.[2] And so, with the happiness of a man of culture, he was now again enjoying the city where he had been born, doing the rounds of his favorite haunts, examining elegant items in shopwindows, listening to the silent running of precious cars and inhaling their exhaust fumes as if they were an exciting perfume.

To Serbinov, it was as if Moscow were a ballroom where a lady was waiting for him—only this lady is lost in the distance, among warm, young crowds, and cannot see her interested cavalier, and the cavalier cannot find his way to her, because he has an objective heart and keeps meeting other deserving women so full of tenderness and inaccessibility that it becomes hard to understand how children ever get to be born in the world. Nevertheless, the more women he encountered—and the more artifacts he saw that could have been fashioned only by a master who had distanced himself from everything base and impure in his body—the more Serbinov's anguish deepened. Feminine youth brought him no joy, even though he was young himself, for he believed in advance that the happiness he so needed was unattainable. The previous evening, Serbinov had gone to a symphony concert; the music had sung about a beautiful human being and told of opportunities lost, and during intermissions he had gone to the toilet to give way to his emotions and dry his eyes out of sight of others.

While Serbinov was thinking, he saw nothing and rode along mechanically. Once he had stopped thinking, he noticed an entirely young woman standing near him and looking into his face. Serbinov did not find it difficult to meet her gaze, since she was observing him through eyes so touching, and so straightforward, that anyone could have borne it without embarrassment.

She was wearing a good summer coat and a clean woolen dress; all this covered the unknown comfortable life of her body—probably a working body, since she possessed no luxurious, plump curves. She was elegant, and entirely lacking in the usual voluptuous attractions. What touched Serbinov most was her evident happiness; she was looking at him and all around her with eyes of welcome and sympathy. This at once made Serbinov frown. The happy were alien to him; he did not like them and was afraid of them. "Either I'm degenerating," Serbinov said to himself, groping toward self-understanding, "or the happy are of no use to the unhappy."

The strangely happy woman got off at Theatre Square. She seemed like a lone, sturdy plant in a foreign land, too trusting to realize that it was alone.

Without this woman, the tram at once felt dismal. The conductress, her clothes besmeared by repeated contact with the garments of passengers, was noting down the numbers of tickets; people on short visits from distant parts were heading for the Kazan Station, chewing food in preparation for the long journey; and the electric motor moaned indifferently under the floor, locked without a female companion in cramped narrows of metal and couplings. Serbinov jumped down from the tram, afraid that the woman had disappeared from him forever in this crowded city where one can live alone and without meeting anyone for years on end. But the happy take their time about life; the woman was standing by the Maly Theatre, cupping her hand while a newspaper seller slowly counted out kopeks of change.

Serbinov went up to her, emboldened by fear of loneliness. "And there I was, thinking I'd already lost you," he said. "I was walking around looking for you."

"You didn't have to look long," she replied, checking the correctness of the kopeks. Serbinov liked this; he himself never checked his change, having no respect for the labor—neither his own, nor that of others—with which money is obtained. This woman's orderliness was something new and unknown to him.

"Do you want to go for a little walk with me?" the woman then asked.

"That's what *I've* just asked *you*," Serbinov replied, without grounds.

Not taking offense, the trustingly happy woman smiled and said, "Sometimes you meet someone and they suddenly seem good. You lose them as you go about your life. Then you miss them for a while and then you forget them. You thought I was good, right?"

"That's true," Serbinov entirely agreed. "If I'd lost you straightaway, I'd have missed you for a long time."

"But I didn't disappear straightaway, so you won't have to miss me for a long time!"

This woman's whole way of being—her gait and everything about her—was imbued with a rare pride of open calm, with no hint of servile nervousness or need for self-preservation in the presence of another person. She walked, laughed, and talked or fell silent as she wished. She did not keep a watchful eye on her life, or know how to adapt herself to the likes and dislikes of her companion. Serbinov tried to find ways to be pleasing to her, but nothing came of this—she did not change toward him. Then Serbinov gave up hope and thought with submissive sorrow about time—how it was now hurrying by, bringing closer his eternal parting from this happy woman who was endowed with some kind of refreshing life. It was impossible to love her, but parting from her would be all too sad. Serbinov remembered how often he had lived through an eternal parting, without recognizing it for what it was. Only too often he had lightheartedly pronounced the words "See you soon!" to a comrade or to someone he loved—and then never again set eyes on them in the world, or had any chance of being able to see them again. Serbinov did not know what he could do to satisfy his feelings of respect for this woman; had he known, he would have found it easier to say goodbye.

"Friendship's desires can never be slaked to the point of indifference, even only temporarily," he said. "Friendship is not marriage."

"You can work for your comrades," his companion replied. "It can be easier when you're exhausted—you can even live alone. And your comrades are left with the benefits of your labor. But as for me, I don't want to give myself away, I want to remain whole."

Serbinov sensed in his short-term friend a kind of unshakable structure—something so independent that it was as if she were invulnerable to people or were the end product of some unknown, deceased social class whose strength no longer operated in the world. He then pictured her as a remnant of an aristocratic breed; had all aristocrats been like her, then history would never have produced anything to follow them—on the contrary, they would have made from history whatever fate they required. All of Russia—Serbinov had noticed long ago—was inhabited by people who were either perishing or else struggling toward some kind of salvation. Many Russians were bent on destroying their own gifts and talents of life. Some drank vodka; others, their minds half-dead, frittered away their lives among a dozen of their own children; still others retired into the fields and imagined something or other in fantasy and to no purpose. But this woman, instead of ruining herself, had made herself.

And this, perhaps, was why she so moved Serbinov, since he was unable to make himself and was perishing, while still glimpsing the beautiful human being promised by the music. Or was all this merely his own melancholy, his sense that his own most vital necessity lay out of reach and that nothing could change this? That even if this woman became his lover, he'd tire of her before a week had gone by? But in that case, where had it come from—this touching face here in front of him, defended by its own pride, and this reserve of a completed soul, capable of understanding and unerringly helping another but never demanding help for itself?

There was no sense in walking any farther—this would only demonstrate Serbinov's weakness in relation to the woman—and so he said goodbye to her, wishing her to preserve a good memory of him. She said goodbye too, then added, "But if you feel very bored, then come round—and we can see each other!"

"Do *you* ever feel bored and lonely?" Serbinov replied, regretting having said goodbye to her.

"Of course I do, now and then. But I understand why I'm bored, so it doesn't trouble me."

She told Serbinov where she lived, and he began to make his way back. The street was dense with people and this made him feel calmer, as if the closeness of these strangers somehow protected him. He went to the cinema and then, once again, to a concert hall, to listen to music. He understood why he felt so sad—and this upset him. His mind was not helping him in any way; he was clearly degenerating. That night Serbinov lay in the quiet of his cool hotel room and silently attended to the action of his mind. It surprised him that, degenerate though he was, his mind was still able to determine the truth—and he did not trouble his mind with longing thoughts about the woman he had just met. Before him, with the unbroken flow of a journey, passed the whole of Soviet Russia—his indigent motherland, merciless to itself and a little similar to today's aristocratic woman. Serbinov's sad, ironic mind slowly recalled poor, unadapted people, trying in foolish ways to adapt socialism to the empty places of plains and ravines.

Something was already being established on the dreary fields of a

Russia that was being forgotten: people unwilling to plow the land to grow rye for their family were now, with patient suffering, establishing a garden of history for eternity and for their own future inseparability. But gardeners, like painters and singers, do not have sturdy, practical minds. All of a sudden, something agitates their weak hearts—and doubt then leads them to uproot plants that had barely begun to blossom and to sow instead the petty grasses of bureaucracy. A garden requires care and a long wait for the first fruits, but grasses ripen quickly and their cultivation requires neither labor nor the expenditure of the soul in patience. And after the garden of the Revolution was chopped down, its meadows had been given over to self-seeding grasses so that everyone could be fed without the torment of labor. Serbinov had indeed seen how little most people worked, since these seed-bearing grasses fed everyone for free. And so it would continue for a long time, until the grasses had eaten up all the soil and people were left with only clay and stone, or until the now-rested gardeners once again planted a cool garden on impoverished land that had been dried by a bleak wind.

Serbinov fell asleep in his usual sadness, his heart cramped and muted. In the morning he went to the party committee and was ordered to travel to a distant province to investigate the reported fact of a 20 percent reduction in the area of cultivated land; he was to set off the following day.[3] He spent the whole afternoon sitting on a boulevard and waiting for evening. This wait proved an exhausting labor, although Serbinov's heart was beating calmly, without the least hope of the good fortune of a woman of his own.

His intention was to call on his new young acquaintance. And he set off on foot, so as to expend the unneeded time and have a rest from the long wait.

Her address must have been inaccurate. Serbinov came to what had once been a large property—now a mixture of old and new buildings—and began to look for her. He climbed up many staircases. Sometimes, from fourth floors, he glimpsed the nearby Moscow River, where the water smelled of soap, but whose banks, frequented in that district by the naked poor, were like the approaches to an outhouse.

Serbinov rang at unknown apartments, where elderly people opened the door to him. These people felt that what they needed more than anything was peace—and they expressed surprise at Serbinov's desire to see someone who did not live there and was not registered there. Then Serbinov went back outside and, lacking the strength to get through the evening on his own, embarked upon a systematic search of all the living accommodations in the area. The following day, he believed, would be less difficult—he would be traveling to the missing land, which by now, in principle, must have been taken over by steppe grass. Serbinov happened upon his young acquaintance entirely by chance—she was coming down some stairs as he was making his way up. But for that, he would have had to make the round of another twenty responsible tenants. The young woman showed Serbinov into her room and then disappeared for a while. The room was empty, as if someone were not living there but only contemplating. Three empty crates from co-operative goods served as a bed, the windowsill served as a table, and clothes hung from nails on the wall, behind a threadbare curtain. Through the window Serbinov could see the same degraded Moscow River. The same naked torsos he remembered from his time on the bleak staircases of nearby buildings were still sitting meditatively on its banks. There was a closed door between this and the neighboring room. There, by means of measured reading aloud, a workers' faculty student[4] was absorbing political science into his memory. Earlier, probably, a seminary student would have lived there and studied the doctrines of the Ecumenical Councils, so as to arrive in due course, according to the laws of the dialectical development of the soul, at the stage of blasphemy.

The woman came back with something for her new acquaintance to eat and drink: pastries, sweets, a piece of cake, and half a bottle of Vin Santo church wine. Could she really be this naive!

Serbinov slowly began to eat these sweet feminine delicacies, his mouth touching the places where this woman's hands had held the food. Little by little, Serbinov ate everything and was satisfied, while the woman talked and laughed, as if happy to have sacrificed food instead of herself. Here, though, she was mistaken—Serbinov had only been admiring her and feeling the sorrow of a dismal human being in the world; he could no longer live peacefully, remain alone, and be independently content with life. This woman aroused longing and shame in him; had he gone outside, into the excited Moscow air, he would have felt better. For the first time in his life, Serbinov was not in possession of his own assessment of an opposite person; he was unable to smile down at this woman in order to become free and go on his way, the same lonely being as ever.

The moon was now shining over the houses, over the Moscow River and all the neighboring decrepitude. Rustling about beneath this moon, as if beneath an extinguished sun, were women and girls—the vagrant love of human beings. Everything had been arranged and equipped in advance; love came in the guise of a fact, in the guise of a definite, limited substance—so that it could be accomplished and come to an end. Serbinov denied the presence in love not only of any idea but even of any feeling; he considered it to be nothing more than a rounded body. It was impossible even to think about love, because the body of a beloved was created for the oblivion of thoughts and feelings, for the wordless labor of love and the mortal exhaustion that is the only consolation in love. All Serbinov now felt was that brief happiness of life that cannot be used since it is constantly decreasing. And so he did not try to enjoy anything; he saw world history as a useless bureaucratic institution, where the weight and meaning of existence is taken away from a human being with painstaking precision. Aware of his general defeat in life, Serbinov looked down at his hostess's feet. She was not wearing stockings. Her bare pink legs were filled with the warmth of blood and a light skirt covered the remaining fullness of her body, which was already burning with the tension of a mature, restrained life. "Who's going to extinguish your flame?" thought Serbinov. "Not me, that's for sure. I'm not worthy of you. My soul's like some back-of-beyond village, benighted and full of fear." He looked once more at her ascending legs and was unable to understand anything at all clearly. There was a path of some kind from these fresh, feminine legs to the necessity of trustful devotion to his usual, revolutionary cause, but that path was too long, and Serbinov yawned in advance from exhaustion of mind.

"How is your life going?" asked Serbinov. "And what's your name?"

"Sonia. In full, Sofia Alexandrovna. I live very well—either I'm working, or I'm waiting for someone."

"Meetings bring brief joys," said Serbinov, to remind himself of this. "You sigh when you're back out on the street, doing up the last button on your coat. It's sad to feel that everything has passed by in vain and you have to be absorbed in yourself again."

"But waiting for people is also a joy," said Sonia, "and if you sometimes meet them too, the joy can last long. There's nothing I love more than waiting for someone—I'm almost always waiting."

She put her hands on the table, then moved them to her strong knees, unaware of these unnecessary movements. Her life was like a noise, resounding around her. Serbinov even closed his eyes so as not to lose himself in this strange room filled with noise and smells that had nothing to do with him. Against the rest of her body, Sofia Alexandrovna's hands looked thin and old, and her fingers were wrinkled like a washerwoman's. And these maimed hands were of some comfort to Serbinov, lessening his jealousy of the man who would win her.

The food and drink on the table was all gone; Serbinov regretted having eaten hurriedly—now he would have to leave. But he was unable to leave; he was afraid that there were people better than him, and this was why he had come to Sofia Alexandrovna. Even on the tram, Serbinov had sensed in her an excessive talent of life that excited and irritated him.

"Sofia Alexandrovna," he began. "I wanted to tell you that I'm leaving tomorrow."

"You'll be all right!" said Sofia Alexandrovna, surprised by his tone. It was clear to him that she did not miss other people. She could get nourishment enough from her own life, which he had never been able to do himself. If she needed others, it was not because she wanted from them anything she herself lacked; it was, rather, that she needed to expend her own superfluous strength. Serbinov did not yet know anything about her, but he thought she was probably the unfortunate daughter of wealthy parents. In this, however, he turned out to be mistaken: Sofia Alexandrovna had no sooner been born than her mother had abandoned her at her place of birth.[5] She now worked as a machine cleaner at the Trekhgornaya textile factory. Serbinov then wondered aloud if she had ever loved someone and given birth to children herself.

"I've loved, but I haven't had children," Sofia Alexandrovna replied. "There are enough people in the world anyway. But if a flower could grow out of me, I'd gladly give birth to it."

"You're really saying you love flowers most of all? I don't call that love—it sounds more like hurt. Because you're no longer growing, no longer giving birth to yourself."

"Doesn't matter. When I have flowers, I don't go out anywhere and I'm not waiting for anyone. When I'm with flowers, I wish I could give birth to them. Otherwise, nothing at all really comes of any kind of love."

"Nothing at all," Simon repeated. And he began to hope for a relief to his jealousy, imagining that in the end Sofia Alexandrovna would turn out to be like himself—unhappy and lifeless in the midst of life. He did not like happy or successful people, because they are always departing for fresh, distant places of life and abandoning those near and dear to them. Serbinov had already been orphaned by many of his friends. Fearful of being left behind by everyone, he had coupled himself to the Bolsheviks—but this had not helped.[6] His friends went on fully expending themselves as if he weren't there and, before Serbinov had managed to save up anything from their feelings for himself, they had left him and moved on into their futures. Serbinov had laughed at them, bad-mouthed the poverty of their ambitions, and said that history had come to an end long ago—all that was happening now was a process of general leveling down. But back in his own room, destroyed by the grief of separation, not knowing where there was anyone who loved him and was waiting for him, he would lock the door and sit on the bed, his back to the wall. He would listen to the splendid clanging of trams as they carried people past the warm summer boulevards in order to visit one another. Tears of self-pity would slowly come to him; he would feel them dissolving the dirt on his cheeks as he continued to sit there in silence, not switching on the electric light.

Later, when the streets were growing quieter and friends and lovers were asleep, Serbinov would calm down: by then, many people were alone—some asleep, others lying on their own because they were tired from conversation or love—and so Serbinov was willing to be alone too. Sometimes he took out his diary and noted down thoughts and curses, in a numbered list: "Man is not meaning but a body full of passionate sinews, gorges of blood, hills, openings, delights, and oblivion"; "'I am bowed down greatly, For my loins are filled with a vile disease' means 'I am cowed, For my lions are filled with death and wily fleas'";[7] "History was set in motion by a base loser who invented the future so as to exploit the present—he thrust everyone out of their dwellings, then remained behind, where it was warm, habitable, and settled"; "I am a byproduct of my mother, along with her menstruation, and so I am unable to respect anything. I fear good people, since I am bad and they will abandon me. I fear the chill of being left on my own. I curse the fluid population, among whom I wish for society and membership"; "And in society I shall be not a member, but a freezing extremity."

Serbinov kept a jealous and suspicious eye on everyone he encountered: Was this person better than him? If so, then they must be stopped. Otherwise they would get ahead of him and never be an equal friend. Sofia Alexandrovna also seemed to him better than he himself, and therefore lost to him—and Serbinov wanted to save people up, as if they were money and a means of life. He had even started a diligent inventory of acquaintances, constantly adding to a special list of profits and losses in his household accounts book.

Sofia Alexandrovna would have to be recorded as a loss. But Serbinov wanted to mitigate this loss; there was a method he had not previously employed in his human economy, and this was why he always ended up with a deficit. What if he embraced this Sofia Alexandrovna, making himself into the image of a tenderly demented man wanting to marry her and no one else? Then Simon could develop passion within him, overcome this stubborn body of a higher human being, leave a trace of himself inside this body, realize at least momentarily his enduring bond with others—and go on his way, calm and with new hope, toward further predatory success among people. Somewhere nearby, trams were racing along with a nervous creaking and grating, full of people heading into the distance, away from Serbinov. He went over to Sofia Alexandrovna, put his hands under her shoulders, and raised her up, so that she stood in front of him at her full height. In the course of this, he discovered that she was a heavy woman.

"What are you doing?" she asked without fear, but with attentive tension.

Serbinov's heart missed a beat from the closeness of her foreign body, warmed as it was by an inaccessible oncoming life. At that moment, someone could have hacked at him with an ax—and he would not have felt pain. He was gasping for breath and there was a gurgling in his throat. All he could sense was a faint smell of sweat from Sofia Alexandrovna's armpits. He wanted to put his mouth to those hard, sweat-stiffened hairs and suck on them.

"I want to hold you a little," said Simon. "Please allow me—then I'll be off."

Feeling ashamed before this suffering man, Sofia Alexandrovna slightly raised her arms, to make it easier for him to support her in his weak embrace.

"Does this really help you?" she asked, her raised arms beginning to ache.

"And you?" asked Serbinov, listening to the distracting voice of a steam locomotive, singing about labor and tranquility amid a summer world.

"It's all the same to me."

Serbinov let go of her. "It's time I left," he said with equanimity. "Where's your toilet—I haven't washed today."

"Where you came in—and to the right. There's soap, but no towel. I put it in the laundry. I'm using a sheet instead."

"Give me the sheet then," said Serbinov.

The sheet smelled of her, of Sofia Alexandrovna. It was clear that she used it to give herself a thorough wipe in the morning, refreshing her body when it was parched from sleep. Serbinov moistened his tired, burning eyes—always the first part of his body to tire—but he did not wash his face. He quickly rolled the sheet into a convenient ball, then tucked this ball into the side pocket of his coat, which was hanging in the corridor opposite the toilet. Losing a human being, Serbinov wanted to preserve an incontrovertible document about them.

"I hung the sheet on the radiator to dry," he said. "I made it all wet. Goodbye. I'll be on my way now."

"Goodbye," Sofia Alexandrovna answered cordially. Unable to let a guest leave without more attention, she then asked, "Where are you going? You said you were going on a journey."

Serbinov told her about the province where 20 percent of the cultivated area had disappeared, and that he was going there to look for it.

"I've lived all my life in that province," Sofia Alexandrovna replied. "I had a splendid comrade there. If you come across him, give him my greetings."

"What's this man like?"

Serbinov thought about how he would go back to his room and sit down to record Sofia Alexandrovna as a loss incurred by his soul, in the column of irrecoverable property. Late night would rise over Moscow, and the many he loved would go to bed and dream of the silence of socialism. He would note them down with the happiness of complete forgiveness and enter minus signs against the names of lost friends.

Sofia Alexandrovna took out a small photograph from a little book.

"He wasn't my husband," she said of the man in this photograph, "and I didn't love him. But without him I started to feel bored. When we lived in the same city, I felt calmer. I always live in one city but love another."

"While I don't love any city," said Serbinov. "I just like to be where there are always lots of people out on the streets."

Sofia Alexandrovna looked at the photograph. It showed a man of about twenty-five. His eyes were sunken, as if dead, and they resembled tired watchmen. As for the rest of his face, it was impossible to remember it when you looked away. It seemed to Serbinov that this person was thinking two thoughts at once and finding no comfort in either. This meant that the face had no stopping place in repose and was hard to remember.

"He's not at all striking," she said, noticing Serbinov's indifference. "But then it's so easy to be with him! He feels his faith, and so people feel calmer in his presence. If there were many such men in the world, women would rarely get married."

"But where am I going to meet him?" asked Serbinov. "Maybe he's already dead? And what do you mean? Why wouldn't women marry?"

"There'd be no point. Marriage is embraces, jealousy, blood... I was married for one month. But you know all this anyway. With someone like him, though, there's probably no need for anything. Merely leaning against him is enough to make things all right."

"If I meet someone like that, I'll send you a postcard," Serbinov promised—and he hurried out to put on his coat, so he could slip away with the sheet.

From the landings on the staircase Serbinov caught glimpses of the Moscow night; there was now no one on the riverbank and the water flowed by like dead substance. He whispered to himself in passing that, were he to maim Sofia Alexandrovna, then she would take him in and he would come to love this staircase. Every day he would wait happily for the evening. There would be somewhere for him to make good on his own overdue life; another person would be sitting opposite him and this would allow him to forget himself.

Sofia Alexandrovna was left on her own—to sleep in dreary sleep until her morning work. At six o'clock in the morning, a newspaper boy came and pushed *The Workers Gazette* under her door.[8] Just in case, he knocked and called out, "Sonia, time you were up! Today makes ten days—you owe me thirty kopeks. Get up now, read the facts!"

In the evening, after her shift, Sofia Alexandrovna washed again, but this time she wiped herself dry with a pillowcase and then opened the window to the city's fading warmth. At this hour she was always waiting for someone, but no one ever came; some were busy with meetings, while others found it boring to sit with a woman and not kiss her. As it grew dark, she lay down prone on the windowsill to doze through her wait. Carts and cars went by below her and, from some hidden spot, the bells of an orphaned little church quietly proclaimed their good news. Many people had also passed by on foot and she had watched each of them expectantly, but no one had stopped at the outer door of her building. Then someone stood there for a while, threw a lit cigarette onto the pavement, and went inside. "No, not for me," Sonia decided. She went quiet. Somewhere, in the depth of the many floors, a man was walking about uncertainly, frequently stopping for thought or to catch his breath. Close to her door, the footsteps came to a stop. "No, keep going," Sonia whispered. But the man knocked. Forgetting her way from the window and down the little corridor, Sofia Alexandrovna opened the door. Serbinov came in.

"I couldn't leave," he said. "I've been missing you deep within me."

Simon was smiling as before, only more sadly. He already understood that no happiness awaited him here, while behind him lay only an echoing hotel room and his ledger of lost comrades. "Take your sheet back," he said. "It's in my coat pocket. It's dry now, and it no longer smells of you. Please excuse me—I slept on it."

Sofia Alexandrovna understood that Serbinov was tired. Without a word, not imagining that she herself might be of interest to her guest, she put together something for him to eat, from her own supper. Serbinov consumed this as his due—and then felt the grief of his own loneliness still more. He had a great deal of strength, but it had no direction and was crushing his heart to no purpose.

"What stopped you leaving?" she asked. "Are you feeling lonelier than you were yesterday?"

"I'm supposed to be going to look for steppe grass. A few years ago it was lice that threatened socialism.[9] Now it's steppe grass. Come with me!"

"No," said Sofia Alexandrovna. "I can't go anywhere."

Serbinov would have liked to lie down and go to sleep there and then; nowhere else would he have slept in such peace. He touched his back and his left side—for several months something once soft and tolerant had been turning into something hard and aching; probably this was the cartilage of youth, which had had its day and was now dying into permanent bone. That morning his forgotten mother had died. Simon had not quite known where she lived—probably in the next-to-last house of Moscow, where open country began. At the hour when Serbinov was eating ham or conscientiously brushing his teeth, freeing his mouth from rot and decay for the sake of kisses—his mother had died. Now he did not know what to live for. The last person for whom Serbinov's own death would have remained forever beyond consolation—this last person had died. Among those who still remained alive for Serbinov, there was no one similar to his mother. He could fail to love her, he had lost her address, but he had lived because his mother had shielded him for many years, walling him off with her need for him from the many other people who did not need him at all. Now this protective wall had collapsed—somewhere on the very edge of Moscow, almost in the country, an old woman who had taken better care of her son than of herself was lying in a coffin, and there was more life in the fresh boards of this coffin than in her dried-up body. And Serbinov felt the freedom and lightness of the life that was left to him. No one would lament his death now; no one would die of grief, as his mother had once promised to do—and as she would have done had she outlived him. It turned out that Simon had been able to go on living because he sensed his mother's love and safeguarded her peace by remaining whole in the world. His mother had served him as a defense, as a blind against everyone alien to him; thanks to his mother he had imagined the world to be in sympathy with him. And now his mother had disappeared, and without her everything had been laid bare. It was no longer obligatory to live, since there was no one alive for whom his existence was a mortal necessity. And so Serbinov had come to Sofia Alexandrovna to be with a woman, since his mother too had been a woman.

After sitting there for a while, Serbinov realized that Sofia Alexandrovna wanted to sleep, and he said goodbye to her. He did not say anything about the death of his mother. He wanted to reserve this for later, as a sound reason for paying Sofia another visit. He went back home on foot—a distance of six versts. Twice it began to drizzle, though not for long. On one boulevard, he felt he was about to cry; in expectation of tears, he sat on a bench, leaned forward, and adapted his face, yet he was unable to cry. He cried later, in a night beer hall, where there was music and dancing, though his tears were occasioned not by his mother but by the multitude of actresses and people beyond his reach.

Serbinov paid a third visit to Sofia Alexandrovna on Sunday. She was still asleep, and Simon waited in the corridor while she dressed. Through the door Serbinov said that his mother had been buried the day before and that he had come round so that they could go to the cemetery together, to see where his mother would now remain until the end of the world. Still not fully dressed, Sofia Alexandrovna let him in—and straightaway, without washing, set off with him to the cemetery. Autumn was already beginning; dead leaves were falling onto the graves of those buried there. Half-hidden among tall grasses and tabernacles of foliage, the crosses of eternal memory looked like people stretching their arms out in vain for embrace of the dead. One of the crosses neighboring the path bore the words of a silent complaint:

> I live and weep, while she
> is dead and without words.

The graves were crowded closely together and Simon's mother's grave, covered with fresh dust of the earth, stood out among frail, ancient mounds. Serbinov and Sofia Alexandrovna were standing under an old tree; its leaves rustled evenly in the flow of a constant wind, as if time had become audible in its passage and was being carried past up above them. From time to time people moved around in the distance, visiting dead relatives, but there was no one nearby. Sofia Alexandrovna was breathing steadily, close beside Simon, looking at the grave and unable to understand death, since she had no one close to her who might die. She wanted to grieve and feel pity for Serbinov, but she merely felt a little dismal from the long noise of the unceasing wind and the sight of the abandoned crosses. Serbinov stood before her, himself like a helpless cross, and she did not know how to help him in his senseless anguish, so he would feel better.

Serbinov, for his part, stood in terror before the thousands of graves. In them lay deceased people who had lived because they believed in eternal memory and the grief others would feel after their death, but they had all been forgotten—the cemetery seemed deserted and wooden crosses had taken the places of the living who should come there, to grieve and remember. So it would be with him, Simon; the one remaining person who would have visited him when he lay dead and beneath a cross was now lying in a coffin beneath his feet.

Serbinov touched Sofia Alexandrovna's shoulder with his hand so that she would recall him some time or other after their parting. She did not respond in any way. Then Simon embraced her from behind and laid his head on her neck.

"We'll be seen here," she said. "Let's go somewhere else."

They turned onto a side path and walked into the depth of the cemetery. There were few people, but there was no getting away from them. They encountered sharp-eyed old women. Gravediggers with spades unexpectedly emerged from the silence of thickets, and the bell-ringer leaned down from his tower to watch them. Sometimes they happened upon more comfortable, overgrown places, and there Serbinov would lean Sofia Alexandrovna against a tree or simply hold her close, lifting her almost off the ground. She would look at him reluctantly, but then they would hear a cough or the crunch of gravel—and Serbinov would once again lead Sofia Alexandrovna away.

Gradually, they traced a large circle around the whole of the cemetery, finding no refuge, and then returned to the grave of Simon's mother. They were both exhausted; Simon felt how his heart had grown weak from waiting and how he needed to pass on his grief and loneliness to another, friendly body and, perhaps, take from Sofia Alexandrovna what was precious to her, so that she would always regret her loss—hidden within Serbinov—and therefore remember him.

"Why do you need this now?" Sofia Alexandrovna asked. "Let's talk instead."

They sat on a huge tree root sticking up out of the ground and put their feet on his mother's grave mound. Simon said nothing; he did not know how to share his grief with Sofia Alexandrovna, unless he first shared himself with her. Even family property is considered shared only after the mutual love of husband and wife; all his life Serbinov had been aware that exchange of blood and body brings about the exchange of other everyday things and that it's never the other way round, since only what is valuable can make one cease to begrudge what is cheap. Nevertheless, Serbinov also accepted that his mind thought like this only because it was degenerate.

"What can I say?" he replied. "It's not easy for me now. Grief lives inside me, like a substance, and our words will remain separate from it."

Sofia Alexandrovna turned her suddenly saddened face toward Simon, as if afraid of suffering; either she understood or she had no idea at all. Simon cheerlessly embraced her and lifted her from the hard tree root to the soft mound of his mother's grave, with her legs in the grass farther down. He forgot whether there were still others in the cemetery, or if they had all left already, and Sofia Alexandrovna silently turned her face away from him, into lumps of earth containing the petty dust—carried on spades from deep in the ground—of other people's coffins.

After a while, Serbinov found in the forsaken depths of his pockets a small street photograph of a thin old woman. He hid it in the grave, where the ground had been softened by Sofia Alexandrovna's head—so that he need not remember his mother or suffer on her account.[10]

42

In Chevengur Gopner had made an orangery for Yakov Titych. The old man respected captive flowers; they allowed him to feel the silence of his own life. But what now shone over the whole world, and over Chevengur, was the slightly frowning, eventide sun of midautumn—and Yakov Titych's steppe flowers had lost nearly all their scent as their breath weakened. Yakov Titych had summoned thirteen-year-old Yegory, the youngest of the *others*, and was sitting with him under a glass roof amid the flowers' weak aroma. He was sorry to be dying in Chevengur, but he now had no choice, since his stomach had ceased to love food and had begun to turn even liquids into tormenting gas. Nevertheless, what made Yakov Titych wish to die was not illness but loss of patience with himself; his body had come to seem like a second person, an alien with whom he had lived through sixty tedious years and against whom he now felt indefatigable anger. At this moment Yakov Titych was looking out onto a field that Strength of the Proletariat was plowing, with Kopionkin following behind—and this made Yakov Titych wish all the more to forget himself, to escape from the anguish of inseparable presence with himself alone. He wanted to become a horse, or Kopionkin, or any capable object—anything to allow his mind to let go of his own life, which he had suffered to the very end and that had stuck to him like the scab of a wound. He reached out to feel Yegory, and this brought him relief. A boy, after all, is the best life, and if you can't live such a life yourself, you can at least have it near you and be thinking about it.

Barefoot Kopionkin was using the power of his warhorse to turn over the field, which had already reverted to virgin land. He was plowing not for his own nourishment, but for the future happiness of another person—Sasha Dvanov. Noticing that Sasha had grown emaciated in Chevengur, Kopionkin had gone around storerooms gathering handfuls of rye that had survived intact from the old world; he had then harnessed Strength of the Proletariat to a scratch plow, in order to turn over the soil and sow winter rye for his friend. Sasha, however, had not grown thin from real hunger. It was, rather, that he seldom felt like eating in Chevengur—thanks both to his own happiness and to practical concerns.

Sasha had the constant impression that something was troubling the Chevengurians and unsettling their shared lives. And this led him to share his body with them through labor. To help Kopionkin feel at home in Chevengur, he wrote down for him every day a chapter from the life story of Rosa Luxemburg, drawing on his imagination; and for Kirey—who now cared for Sasha with the anguish of warm friendship and who kept an eye on him at night lest he suddenly disappear from Chevengur—he dragged up from the riverbed a small black tree trunk that Kirey wanted to carve into a wooden weapon.

Chepurny, for his part, was continually chopping brushwood, along with Pashintsev; he had remembered that sometimes there were winters with very little snow—and that, should there be no snow to warm the houses, the entire population of communism might catch cold and be dead by the spring. Nor was Chepurny able to rest at night; he lay on the ground in the middle of Chevengur, so that he could put branches on an inextinguishable bonfire and fire would not disappear from the town. Gopner and Sasha had promised to make electricity soon, but they were constantly exhausted from their other demanding tasks. In the meantime, as they waited for electricity,[1] Chepurny lay under the raw sky of the autumn dark and, with dozing mind, guarded warmth and light for the sleeping *others*. The *others* would wake while it was still dark, and their awakening was a time of joy for Chepurny. The sound of creaking doors and banging gates could be heard all over the quiet town; bare, rested feet walked between houses in search of food and a meeting with comrades;

water buckets clattered and light dawned everywhere. At this point, Chepurny would fall asleep with satisfaction, while the *others* took over responsibility for the common fire.

Each of the *others* went out into the steppe or to the river; there they picked ears of grain or dug tubers, or used a hat on a stick to catch fish fry. The *others* ate only occasionally; they foraged in order to treat one another, but food was already growing scarce, and they now wandered through the steppe grass until evening in the anguish of both their own and other people's hunger.

As darkness fell, the *others* gathered in an open grassy place and prepared to eat. Karchuk got to his feet—he had worn himself out with labor all day, and in the evenings he liked to be among the common people.

"Friends and citizens," he said in his contented voice. "Yushka has a cough and a chest affliction. He needs light food. I've picked thousands of handfuls of grass for him and soaked them in the milk from flower stems. He can eat now without fear."

Yushka was sitting on some burdock leaves, with four potatoes. "I too, Karchuk, have a principle to hold up to you," he replied. "Ever since morning, I've felt the desire to surprise you with baked potatoes. I want you to lie down for the night on a full stomach!"

All around was night's rising terror. The unpeopled sky was growing sullenly colder, not allowing the stars to look out, and there was nothing anywhere to bring joy. The *others* ate and felt good. Amid this alienness of nature, ahead of the long autumn nights, each had provided himself with at least one comrade and now looked on this man as his very own—and, moreover, as that mysterious good on which someone may rely only in his imagination yet be healed in body; the mere existence of another necessary person—their presence safe and sound in the world—is enough to make them into a source of heartfelt peace and endurance, the *other's* highest substance and the wealth of his indigence. And so, through the presence of someone else who belonged to them, Chevengur and the raw damp of the night became entirely habitable and comfortable conditions for each of the lonely others. "Let him eat," Karchuk said to himself, as he watched

Yushka taking nourishment. "Then digestion will add to the blood in him and his sleep will be more interesting. And tomorrow he'll wake full and warm in body. What more could you ask for?"

As for Yushka, he swallowed down the last liquid of his food and then got to his feet amid the circle of people. "Comrades, we now live here as a population, in possession of our own principle of existence. And although we are the lowest of masses and deepest of dregs, we are missing someone and waiting for him!"

The *others* said nothing. Out of weariness from the day's cares about food and one another they laid their heads on their lower bodies.

"We're deficient in Proshka," Chepurny said sadly. "The good fellow's disappeared. He's not here amid Chevengur."

"It's time we organized the fire a bit stronger," said Kirey. "Proshka might appear at night—and Chevengur's an obscure place!"

"And how are we going to do that?" asked Karchuk. "A fire needs to blaze with splendor! How do you organize that with nothing but small-caliber brushwood? The only thing that'll ever organize for you is smoke!"

But by then the *others* were beginning to breathe softly from the onset of unconscious sleep, and they no longer heard Karchuk. Only Kopionkin had no wish for rest. "Nonsense!" he thought with regard to everything—and went off to see to his horse. Sasha and Pashintsev lay down back-to-back and, warming each other, did not sense their loss of mind until morning.

It was two days after this that the gypsy women had appeared and spent the night to no avail in Karchuk's shed. They had also tried to join up with the Chevengurians during the following day, but they were all working in different parts of the town or out amid the steppe grass; enjoying the company of women, instead of carrying on with their labor, would have made them feel ashamed before their comrades. Kirey had already managed to catch all the bedbugs in Chevengur and had made a saber from Sasha's black wood; when the gypsies appeared, he was digging up a stump to obtain materials for a pipe to give Gopner. The gypsy women went past him and disappeared in the shadowy distance; Kirey felt bodily weakness from sadness, as if he had glimpsed the end of his own life, but he gradually overcame this burden through expenditure of body in digging the earth. An hour later, the gypsy women reappeared—now on the high steppe horizon—but at once disappeared again, like the tail of a retreating train of carts.

"Life's beauties," Piusia remarked of the gypsies. He had been sorting through the *others'* newly washed rags, hanging them out to dry on wattle fences.

"Substantial stuff," said Zheyev.

"Only there's not a trace of revolution to be seen in their bodies," Kopionkin informed them. He needed a horseshoe, and for the last two days he had been searching in dense thickets of grass and every horsey place, but he had found only such trifles as baptismal crosses, bast shoes, sinews of one kind or another, and other litter of bourgeois life. "Without consciousness, there can be no beauty of face," he added, finding a bowl that had served before communism to collect capital for the furnishing of churches. "A woman without revolution is a mere half woman, the kind I can do without. She can help you get to sleep quicker, but that's the end of it. She's no fighting thing, she weighs less than my heart."

Sasha was in a neighboring entrance room, pulling out nails from chests and trunks, since nails were now required for wooden constructions of every kind. Through the doorway, he had seen the unfortunate gypsies going on their way and had pitied them. In Chevengur they could have become wives and mothers; people squeezing together in friendship, clustering in urgent work so as not to scatter apart over the terrible, kinless land—these people could have been still further strengthened by an exchange of bodies, by the sacrificial endurance of deep blood. Sasha gazed at the houses and wattle fences—marveling at all the warmth of working hands now hidden in them, at the number of lives that had grown cold in vain, never reaching an oncoming person, and which were now present in these walls, beams, and roofs. And for a while Sasha stopped looking for nails; he wanted to save himself and these *others* from being squandered in labor; he wanted everyone's best powers to remain within them for Kopionkin,

Gopner, and for all those who, like these two gypsy women, had left the industrious zeal of Chevengur for poverty and the open steppe. "I'd rather long for someone than do diligent work and forget about people," Sasha said to himself with certainty. "Everyone here has forgotten himself in work. That makes life easier for them, but it means happiness keeps being deferred."[2]

The autumn's transparent heat illuminated Chevengur's silent surroundings with a half-dead glittering light, as if there were no air above the ground, and now and then a dreary spider's web stuck to Sasha's face, but the grasses had already stooped toward the earth's mortal dust and were no longer accepting light and warmth; it was clear that they lived not only by the sun, but also in accord with a time of their own. Birds rose from the steppe horizon, then flew down again to more copious spots; Sasha watched these birds with the same yearning with which he had once watched flies living beneath the ceiling during his childhood with Zakhar Pavlovich. But then the birds flew up again and a slow dust hid them from sight; a troika and a carriage appeared, heading for Chevengur at a country trot. Sasha climbed up onto the fence, astonished by the sight of a traveling stranger. Then, from somewhere nearby, came a powerful sound of hooves. Kopionkin and Strength of the Proletariat had broken away from the outskirts of Chevengur and were tearing toward the distant carriage—to greet a friend or strike an enemy. Sasha walked out to the town boundary too, to help Kopionkin, if needed. But Kopionkin had already managed single-handedly. The coachman was leading the horses quietly along by the bridle, and the phaeton was empty. At a distance, the passenger followed on foot, with Kopionkin riding along behind him. In one hand, Kopionkin was holding his saber; in the other, the handle of a briefcase and a lady's revolver, which he was pressing against the briefcase with a long, unwashed finger.

The man who had been riding in the carriage was now on foot and disarmed, but his face bore no sign of the terror of waiting for death—only a smile of curiosity.

"Who are you? What's brought you to Chevengur?" Sasha asked.

"I've come from the capital to look for steppe grass. I didn't expect to find any, but it's growing in sound supply," replied Simon Serbinov. "And who are you two?"

The two men were standing almost point-blank against each other. Kopionkin was observing Serbinov vigilantly, enjoying the danger. The coachman stood by the carriage, letting out cross sighs and whispers; he was counting on these vagabonds to make off with his horses.

"Here we have communism," Kopionkin explained from his mount. "And we are all comrades here, because we used to live without any means of life. But what kind of a blockhead are you?"

"I'm a Communist too," Serbinov informed him. Sasha's face seemed familiar, and Serbinov was trying to remember where they might have met.

"Come to play at communism, have you?" Kopionkin replied, disappointed to have been deprived of danger. He then tossed the briefcase, along with the pocket revolver, into the steppe grass. "Women's weapons are no use to us here. You'd have done better to bring us a cannon—that would have been precious to us. And we'd have known you're a true Bolshevik. But you show up with a hefty briefcase and a tiny revolver—you're a pen-pusher, not a party member... Come on, Sasha, let's go back home!"

Sasha jumped onto Strength of the Proletariat's spacious rump, and he and Kopionkin rode off together.

Serbinov's coachman turned his horses around, to face the steppe, and climbed up onto his seat, eager to save himself. Serbinov walked a short distance toward Chevengur in thought, then stopped. Before him, old burdocks were peacefully living out the last of their warm summer life; in the distance—in the center of town—someone was tapping on wood with steady zeal; and the smell of some kind of potato food was wafting from a dwelling on the outskirts. Here too, evidently, people lived and nourished themselves on their daily joys and sorrows. But what did he, Serbinov, need? He did not know. And so he walked on toward Chevengur, an unknown place. As for the coachman, he noticed Serbinov's lack of interest in him, put the horses to a preliminary quiet walk, and then tore off, away from the town and into the purity of the steppe.

In Chevengur, Serbinov was immediately surrounded by *others*, all of whom took a vital interest in this unknown, fully clothed stranger. They looked at Serbinov and admired him; it was as if they'd been gifted an automobile and were expecting a pleasure ride. Kirey extracted a fountain pen from Serbinov's pocket and pulled off its top to make into a cigarette holder for Gopner. Karchuk gifted Serbinov's spectacles to Kirey.

"You'll see more now, and farther," he said.

"I shouldn't have gotten rid of that leather casebrief of his," said Kopionkin, now upset with himself. "I should have used it to make a Bolshevik cap for Sasha. Or perhaps not. Let it lie there—I'll gift Sasha my own cap."

Serbinov's shoes went to the feet of Yakov Titych, who needed something light in order to walk about his room, and the Chevengurians used Serbinov's coat to make trousers for Pashintsev, who had lived trouserless since the Revolution Memorial Reserve. After a few minutes, Serbinov sat down on a chair in the street, barefoot and wearing only a vest. Piusia then thought to bring him two baked potatoes, while *others* silently began to deliver whatever seemed best to them. One person gave him a sheepskin jacket, another some felt boots, and Kirey gave him a bag of writing equipment.

"Have this," he said. "You look like a smart type. You'll need this—and it's no use to us."

Serbinov accepted all this. Later he found his briefcase and revolver in the grass, which was beginning to wither; he removed from the briefcase its stuffing of papers and directives and threw away the leather skin. Among the papers was his accounts book of people he had wanted to possess as property; Simon would have regretted losing this, and in the evening he sat in his sheepskin jacket and felt boots—amid the silence of the exhausted town—and began to study this record. There was light from a candle stub, obtained from the bourgeoisie's stores by Kirey, and the house smelled of the greasy body of some alien person who had once lived there. Solitude and a new place always depressed Serbinov and gave him a stomachache. He was unable to write anything in his book; all he could do was read through it and see that his entire past had been an unmitigated loss. Not one person had remained with him throughout his life; no one's friendship had turned into dependable kinship. Serbinov was now alone. Only the secretary of his institution remembered him. This secretary knew that Serbinov was away on a mission but expected back—and the secretary required his return in order for the office to observe proper procedures. "He needs me," Serbinov imagined with a sense of affection for the secretary, "and he'll wait for me. I won't betray his memory of me."

Sasha Dvanov came round to check on Serbinov, who was already half-happy that a secretary somewhere was thinking of him—which meant that he, Simon, had a comrade. This was Serbinov's only thought and only source of comfort in nighttime Chevengur; there was no other idea he was able to sense, and only what he sensed could calm him.

"What are you after in Chevengur?" asked Sasha. "Let me tell you straight out. You'll never accomplish your mission here."

Serbinov hadn't even been thinking about his mission. Once again, he was trying to remember Sasha's familiar face. But he couldn't—and this disturbed him.

"Is it true that the area of land under cultivation here has decreased?" Serbinov asked in order to satisfy the secretary; he himself had little interest in crops.

"No," Sasha explained, "it's increased. Even the town is overgrown with grass."

"That's good," said Serbinov. He now considered his mission accomplished. In due course, he could state in his report that the area under cultivation had even grown by 1 percent, but had not in any respect decreased. Nowhere had he seen bare soil—the plants were, in fact, so closely packed as to be cramped.

Somewhere in the dank night air they heard a cough. This was Kopionkin, an aging man unable to sleep and wandering about on his own.

Sasha had approached Serbinov with suspicion, with the intention of removing the man from Chevengur. Once he was with him, however, he had no idea what further to say. Initially, Sasha was always afraid of a person, since he had no convictions so certain as to allow him to feel superior. On the contrary, another person's presence always evoked feelings in Sasha rather than convictions, and he would start to feel an excessive respect for this person.

Serbinov did not yet know where he was. The provincial silence, the replete air from the surrounding grass, made him yearn for Moscow. He wanted to go back there, and he resolved to leave Chevengur on foot the next day.

"What have you got here?" Serbinov asked Sasha. "Revolution?"

"We have communism. Hear that man coughing out there? It's comrade Kopionkin, he's a true Communist."

Serbinov was not greatly surprised; he had always considered the Revolution better than himself. All he could now see was his own pitifulness in this town, and he thought that he was like a stone in a river. The Revolution was passing over him, and he remained on the riverbed, weighed down by his attachment to his own self.

"But do you have grief or sadness in Chevengur?" he asked.

And Sasha said that they did. Grief and sadness—they too were part of man's body.

Sasha leaned forward, resting his forehead against the table. By evening he was always agonizingly tired—not so much from his activities of the day as from the care and fear with which he continuously watched over the people of Chevengur.

Serbinov opened a window to the outside air. Everything was quiet and dark; there was only a long midnight sound from the steppe, too peaceful to disturb the night calm. Sasha went to bed and fell asleep on his back. Hurrying after the guttering candle, Serbinov wrote a letter to Sofia Alexandrovna. Wandering proletarians, he informed her, had gathered together in a single place and brought about communism, and among them was a semi-intellectual type by the name of Dvanov, who probably no longer remembered what had first brought him to this town. Serbinov glanced at the sleeping Dvanov, at his face—now changed because of his closed eyes—and at his legs, stretched out in dead stillness. He looks, Serbinov went on, like that photograph of your early beloved, but it's hard to imagine that he ever loved you. Serbinov added that he always got stomachache when he was on a mission and that he'd find it only too easy, like this semi-intellectual, to forget what had brought him to Chevengur and remain here to exist.

The candle went out, and Serbinov lay down on a trunk, afraid he might not fall asleep for some time. But he fell asleep at once, and a new day set in for him instantaneously, as for a happy person.

By then, many different artifacts had accumulated in Chevengur. Serbinov saw these artifacts as he wandered about, but he did not understand their use.

That morning, he noticed a spruce wood frying pan on a table, and an iron flag, embedded in a roof—in a special perforation—but unable to yield to the wind. The town was now so tightly cramped that Serbinov wondered if it was, in fact, at the expense of living space that the area of cultivated land had increased. Wherever he looked, the Chevengurians were laboring diligently—sitting in the grass, standing in sheds or outside houses, each working at whatever was necessary. Two were hewing a tree trunk; someone was cutting and bending the iron removed from a roof to compensate for the shortage of construction materials; four other men were leaning against a fence and weaving bast shoes—for whoever took it into his head to become a wanderer.

Sasha had woken up before Serbinov and hurried off to find Gopner. The two had met in the smithy, and this was where Serbinov found them. Sasha had come up with an invention that would turn sunlight into electricity. For this, Gopner had taken all the mirrors in Chevengur out of their frames and also collected all the glass of any thickness. From these materials, Sasha and Gopner had made complex prisms and reflectors so that the light of the sun would be changed as it passed through them and become an electric current when it reached the far end of the apparatus. The apparatus had been ready two days before this, but no electricity had originated from it. *Others* kept coming to inspect Sasha's light machine and, although it was unable to work, they nevertheless concluded as seemed best to them: that this machine was correct and necessary, since it had been invented and prepared by the bodily labor of two comrades.[3]

Not far from the smithy stood a tower executed from clay and straw. At night, one of the *others* would climb the tower and light a bonfire so that wanderers out in the steppe could see where a haven had been prepared for them, but either the steppes had grown empty or the nights were unpeopled—no one had yet appeared in response to the light from the clay lighthouse.

While Sasha and Gopner sought to improve their solar mechanism, Serbinov set off toward the center of town. Walking between the houses had been narrow, but the town center was entirely impassable—the *others* had brought their latest artifacts there for completion and finishing touches. Among them were wooden wheels two fathoms across, iron buttons, clay statues depicting likenesses of beloved comrades, including Sasha Dvanov;[4] a self-turning machine made from broken alarm clocks; and a self-heating oven, filled with the stuffing from all Chevengur's pillows and quilts, but with room for only one person, the most chilled of all, to temporarily warm himself. And there were also objects whose use Serbinov could not figure out at all.

"Where is your ExecCom?" Serbinov asked Karchuk, who had other things on his mind.

"There was one, but it's gone now. It's already executed everything," Karchuk explained. "Ask Chepurny. Can't you see? I'm making a sword for comrade Pashintsev from the bone of a bull."

"And why's your town all cramped together when there's open space all around it?" Serbinov asked further.

Karchuk declined to answer. "Ask who you like, but not me. Can you really not see? I'm laboring—and that means my thoughts are not about you, but about Pashintsev, who I'm making this sword for."

And so Serbinov asked someone else—a man with a Mongolian face who had just returned from one of the gullies with a sack of clay for making statues.

"Because we live among ourselves without pause," Chepurny explained.

Serbinov laughed at Chepurny and at the two-fathom wooden wheels, and at the iron buttons. Serbinov felt ashamed of his laughter, but Chepurny stood there opposite him, looked at him, and did not take offense.

"You work laboriously," said Serbinov, to keep from smiling. "But I've seen your labors, and they're useless."

Chepurny looked at Serbinov seriously and vigilantly, seeing in him a man who had fallen behind the masses.

"But we're not working for use. We're working for one another."

Serbinov was no longer laughing—he could not understand. "What do you mean?" he asked.

"What I've just said," Chepurny confirmed. "What else could we be doing, I ask you now! But it seems you're not a party member, so let me explain. It was the bourgeoisie wanted labor to be of use, but that didn't work out. No one can endure constant torment of body for the sake of some object." He then noticed Serbinov's dispirited look and smiled. "Don't worry—you'll get used to things here, you won't come to harm."

Serbinov went on his way, bewildered. He was able to think up many things, but he was unable to understand what stood before his vision.

At lunchtime, Serbinov was called to a glade and served nettle soup followed by a kasha of mashed vegetables. After this, he felt completely nourished. He already wanted to leave Chevengur for Moscow, but Chepurny and Sasha asked him to stay until the following day. By then they'd have made Serbinov something to take on the road with him, and as a keepsake.

Serbinov agreed to stay, having decided not to go to the provincial capital in person but to send in a written report. That afternoon he wrote to the provincial party committee, informing them that there was no ExecCom in Chevengur. Instead, there were only a great many happy but useless things. It was unlikely that the area under cultivation had decreased; on the contrary, it had increased at the expense of the replanned, now closely cramped town, but there was no one who could sit down and provide information about such matters, since there was not a single sensible clerical worker to be found among the town's population. It seemed probable—Serbinov went on to suggest—that Chevengur had been seized by some unknown minor nation or by passing vagabonds. These people, in any case, were strangers to the art of information and their only way of signaling to the world was a clay beacon, on the top of which they burned straw or some other dry substance at night. Among these vagabonds there was one intellectual and one qualified craftsman, but both had entirely forgotten themselves. As for any practical conclusions to be drawn from these observations—Serbinov concluded—that was for the provincial center to determine.

Simon reread what he had written. His words had turned out clever, ambiguous, hostile, and mocking, in relation both to Chevengur and to the provincial center. This was Serbinov's usual way of writing about those whom he could not hope to acquire as comrades.[5] On his arrival in Chevengur, he had at once understood that everyone in the town had already adopted one another and that there was no one left over for him—and so it was impossible for him to forget the responsibilities of his mission.

After they had eaten, Chepurny went back to transporting clay. Serbinov asked him what he should do with his two letters: Where was the town post office? Chepurny took both letters from him and said, "Missing friends and family, are you? We can send someone on foot to the postal place. I'm missing my friend Prokofy too, but I don't know his location."

Karchuk had finished making the bone sword for Pashintsev; he'd have welcomed some further distraction from boredom, but there was no one else for him to think about or on whose behalf he could labor. Instead, he was scratching at the ground with one fingernail, sensing no vital idea of life.

"Karchuk," said Chepurny, "you've shown your respect for Pashintsev, and now you're sorrowing without a comrade. Please take comrade Serbinov's letters to the mail car. You can think about him as you make your way there."

Karchuk looked Serbinov mournfully up and down. "Maybe tomorrow," he said. "I don't yet have any feeling for him. Or maybe I'll set off this evening, if I feel drawn to this newcomer."

In the evening, it turned misty and the soil grew damp. Chepurny lit a straw fire on the clay tower so that the missing Proshka would notice it from a distance. Serbinov lay in an empty house, covered with some kind of bedding; he wanted to sleep and find calm in the provincial silence. He felt as if he were separated from Moscow not only by space but also by time—and he curled his body tight under the bedding, feeling his own legs and chest as a second and no less pitiful person whom he was warming and caressing.

Karchuk entered without asking, like some hermitage or remote monastery dweller.

"I'm setting off," he said. "Give me your letters."

Serbinov gave him the letters and said, "Sit with me a little. After all, for my sake you'll be walking all through the night anyway."

"No," Karchuk declined. "I'll think of you on my own."

Afraid of losing the letters, Karchuk took one in each hand, squeezed them into his fists, and set off.

43

Up above the earth's mist the sky was clear. The moon had climbed high, but its meek light weakened in the moist gloom, making the earth below seem like the bed of a river or lake.[1] The last people were quietly walking around Chevengur, and someone on the clay tower began a song; rather than rely on the light from the bonfire alone, he wanted to be heard in the steppe. Serbinov closed off his face with one hand, in order to sleep and not see, but he opened his eyes beneath his hand and was still less able to sleep. In the distance, an accordion struck up some merry battle song. The tune was similar to "Little Apple," but it was considerably more artful and affecting, perhaps a kind of Bolshevik foxtrot that Serbinov had not heard before.[2] Amid the music he could hear the creaking of some carriage or cart—someone must have been driving toward the town—and from somewhere far away came the sound of two equine voices. Strength of the Proletariat was whinnying from Chevengur and a mare out in the steppe was responding to him.

Simon went outside. Up on the clay lighthouse, a heap of straw and old wattle fencing burst into triumphant flame. As for the accordion, finding itself in trusty hands, it too did not slacken its sounds, but forced them out faster and faster, calling the population to life in one place.

The phaeton was being drawn by a skinny, whinnying horse. Seated in it were Prokofy and a naked musician—the man who had once left Chevengur on foot to find himself a wife. Walking in pairs behind the phaeton were ten or more barefoot women; Klavdiusha was one of the leading pair.

The Chevengurians met their future wives in silence. They stood beneath the lighthouse fire but did not take a step toward their wives or utter a word of greeting; these new arrivals were people and comrades, but they were, at the same time, women. Kopionkin was overwhelmed by both shame and esteem. Moreover, he was afraid to observe women—out of conscience before Rosa Luxemburg—and so he went off to appease Strength of the Proletariat, who was now bellowing.

The phaeton came to a stop. *Others* instantly unharnessed the horse and took the phaeton into their own hands, into the depth of Chevengur.

Prokofy curtailed the music and gestured to the procession of women not to hurry anywhere else.

"Comrades of communism!" Prokofy addressed the silence of a small nation. "Your measures have been executed. Before you stand your future spouses, conveyed to Chevengur in marching order—and for Zheyev I've allured a special beggar woman."

"How did you allure her?" asked Zheyev.

"It happens," Prokofy explained. "Musician, turn to the spouses together with your musical tool and play them a fanfare in order for them to fare well in Chevengur and love the Bolsheviks."

The musician played.

"Excellent," Prokofy pronounced. "Klavdiusha, lead the women to their resting places. Tomorrow we'll schedule a review and a celebration march past the town organization. The lighthouse fire offers no presentation of faces."

Klavdiusha led the half-asleep women into the dark of the empty town.

Chepurny embraced Prokofy around his chest and said to him alone, "Prosha, our need for women's no longer so very urgent. What matters is that you've appeared. Shall I make something for you and gift it to you tomorrow?"

"Gift me Klavdiusha!"

"I'd be only too glad, Prosha, but you've already gifted her to yourself. Have something else too!"

"I'll think it over," said Prokofy. "Somehow I feel a lack of demand now and there's no appetite in me." Then he called out, "Hello, Sasha!"

"Hello, Prosha!" Sasha replied. "Did you see any other people anywhere? And what keeps them alive out there?"

"What keeps them alive is endurance," Prokofy formulated for general reassurance. "They don't nourish themselves with revolution. People have been organizing counterrevolution. Hostile whirlwinds are already blowing across the steppe.[3] We alone remain with honor."

"Careful what you say, comrade!" said Serbinov. "I'm from out there myself, and I'm a revolutionary too."

"Which must have made life hard for you there," Prokofy concluded.

Serbinov could not answer.

The fire on the tower had gone out, and it had not been relit. "Prosha," Chepurny asked in the dark, "who was it, I ask you now, gifted you the music?"

"A passing bourgeois. I discounted the man's life, then gifted myself his music. There's no pleasure in Chevengur except for the bell—but that's religion."

"No, Prosha, we do have pleasure in Chevengur now, even without the bell or such intercessions."

Prokofy crawled into the lower part of the tower and lay down in exhaustion to sleep. Chepurny lay down close to him.

"Breathe more, warm up the air," said Prokofy. "I've gotten chilled, somehow, in empty places."

Chepurny raised himself up onto his elbows. He did rapid breathing for a long time, then took off his greatcoat, wrapped it around Prokofy, lay down close against him, and forgot himself in alienation of life.

Morning brought fine weather. The musician was first to get up. He played a preliminary march on his accordion, stirring up the *others*, who were by then rested.

The wives sat ready, now shod and dressed by Klavdiusha in what she had found in Chevengur's cupboards and storerooms.

The *others* arrived later and, out of embarrassment, avoided looking at those whom they had been assigned to love. Also present were

Gopner, Serbinov, and Sasha Dvanov, along with those who had first won Chevengur. Serbinov had come to request that a carriage be fitted out for his departure, but Kopionkin refused to allow him the use of Strength of the Proletariat. "I can give you my greatcoat," he said, "and I'll put myself at your disposal for twenty-four hours. Take whatever you want, but don't ask for my horse! Don't make me angry! How would I get to Germany then?" At that, Serbinov turned to Chepurny and asked for the other horse, the one that had brought Prokofy back the previous day. Chepurny told Serbinov that there was no need for him to leave—maybe he'd get used to life in Chevengur. After all, there was communism in the town and soon everyone would appear there. Why should Serbinov go off to join them if they'd all be heading the opposite way?

Serbinov walked away. "Why am I so eager to go back?" he was saying to himself. "That hot part of my body that left me for Sofia Alexandrovna has already been digested in her and destroyed like any other traceless food."

Chepurny began to speak his mind in a loud voice. Wanting to listen to an unknown word, Serbinov decided to stay where he was.

"Prokofy has gone to great pains," Chepurny pronounced in the midst of the people, "to combat the burdens of the proletariat. Here now he has delivered women to us, in appropriate quantity, even if on the low side in what truly counts. Let me turn then to the female contingent, to sound out to them a word of joy and expectation! Can someone tell me, I ask you now, why we respect the conditions of nature? Because these conditions are what we eat! And why have we reached out and beckoned women to us? Because we respect nature for food, and women for love. Here I declare our gratitude to the women who have entered Chevengur as comrades of a special build, and may they live as one with us and nourish themselves with peace and come to the possession of happiness through their comrade-people in Chevengur."

The women immediately took fright: previous men had always begun with them right at the end, but these ones were taking their time and pronouncing speeches. And so the women pulled their coats—the men's coats and greatcoats in which Klavdiusha had just dressed them—right up to their noses, covering the openings of their mouths. They were not afraid of love, since they had never loved; they were afraid that their bodies would be tortured, almost destroyed by these dry, patient men in soldiers' greatcoats, with faces streaked and blotched by life's hardships. These women did not possess youth or any other clear age. They had given away their body, their place of age and blossoming, in exchange for food, and since procurement of food had always entailed loss, their bodies had been expended before death—even long before death. For this reason they looked like little girls or old women—like worn-out mothers or younger, undernourished sisters. The caresses of husbands would be painful and frightening to them. In the course of the journey Prokofy had tried to hold them tight, taking them into the phaeton for testing, but they had cried out from his love, as from some illness of their own.

Now the women were sitting opposite the gaze of the Chevengurians and stroking under their clothes the wrinkles of excess skin on their worn bones. Among these new Chevengur parishioners, only Klavdiusha appeared comfortable and plump, but Prokofy already had feelings for her.

Yakov Titych was the most thoughtful of the Chevengurians observing the women. One seemed particularly sad, and she was now freezing beneath an old greatcoat. There had been times in the past when he had been ready to give up half of his life, while he still had plenty of life left to him, in order to find true kinship among strangers and *others*. *Others* had been comrades to him everywhere, but only through shared sorrow and cramped life—not by origin from the same womb. Now Yakov Titych had only a last scrap of remaining life—yet for true kinship, for the sake of a blood relative, he would have given up bread and freedom in Chevengur and set off once more on the unknown road of wandering and need.

Yakov Titych went up to the woman he had chosen and touched her face. On the outside, he thought, she resembled him.

"Whose are you?" he asked. "What keeps you alive in the world?"

The woman bowed her head, away from him. Yakov Titych glimpsed the nape of her neck. It was deeply sunken, the dirt of homelessness had gathered there, and her entire head—when the woman looked up again—clung on timidly, as if her neck were a stalk that was drying up and withering.

"Whose are you, so very scanty?"

"No one's," the woman replied. Alienated from Yakov Titych, she frowned and fiddled with her fingers.

"Let's go back home. I'll clean up your neck for you—I'll scrape off the dirt and scabs," Yakov Titych began again.

"I don't want that," the woman declined. "Just give me a little something, then I'll get back on my feet."

On the way, Prokofy had promised her marriage, but she, like her friends, had little idea what that meant. She had guessed only that her body would be tormented by one man rather than many, so she asked for a gift in advance of this torment. No one, after all, ever gives you anything afterward—they just throw you out. She shrank still more under her large greatcoat, guarding beneath it her naked body, which served her both for life and livelihood, and also as her one unrealized hope. An alien world—for this woman—began just above the outermost layer of her skin, and she had been unable to acquire anything from that world, not even clothes for warmth and preservation of the body that provided food for herself and happiness for others.

"What kind of wives do you call these, Prosha?" Chepurny questioned in doubt. "They're runts without substance. They can only have had eight months in the womb."

"What's that to you?" retorted Prokofy. "Let communism be their ninth month."

"Well said!" Chepurny exclaimed happily. "Chevengur will be a warm belly for them. In it they'll ripen quickly—and be born to completion."

"Right you are! And all the more so since a proletarian *other* has no need for any particular plumpness. All he needs is to rid himself of life's yearning. Anyway, what more do you want? You can't say they're not women. They've got emptiness, there's a space inside them."

"No," said Sasha. "Women like these don't make wives. But I've seen mothers looking like this, not that many of us still have living mothers."

"Or little sisters," Pashintsev determined. "I had one such rusty little sister. She ate badly and died from her own self."

Chepurny listened to everyone and out of habit was about to decree a judgment, but then he remembered his low mind and fell into doubt.

"Which do we have more of—husbands or orphans?" he asked, not trying to answer this question. "Let me formulate as follows. First, let every comrade kiss each of these pitiful women once—then it will be clearer what we can make of them. Comrade musician, please give your music to Piusia. Let him play to us from his musical sheets!"

Piusia struck up a march with a sense of the movement of troops; he had no respect for waltzes and songs of loneliness and would have felt ashamed to play them.

It fell to Sasha to go first. As he kissed each woman, he opened his mouth and pressed her lips between his own with greed of tenderness, while gently putting his left arm around the woman so that she would stand her ground and not incline away from him until he had finished touching her.

Serbinov also had to kiss all the future wives. He went last, but that did not make him any the less content. The presence of a second person—even if this were a stranger—always brought calm to Simon, and after kissing someone he would live with satisfaction for a whole day and night. Now he no longer much wanted to leave. He clasped his hands together from pleasure and smiled, unseen amid the movement of people and the tempo of the musical march.

"Well, comrade Dvanov, what do you think?" asked Chepurny, wiping his mouth and curious about further developments. "Are they wives, or will they be best as mothers? Piusia, give us silence for conversation!"

Sasha was unable to answer; he had never seen his mother, nor had he ever felt a wife. He recalled the dry frailty of the women's bodies he had just now supported during kisses, and how one woman, weak as a twig, had clung to him, hiding downward her sorrow-accustomed face. Memory had made him linger beside her. She smelled of milk and a sweaty shirt and he kissed her once more—on the front of her shirt, as in infancy he had kissed both body and sweat of his dead father.

"They'll be best as mothers," he replied.

"Whoever here is an orphan," Chepurny then declared, "should now choose for himself a mother."

Everyone there was an orphan—and there were ten women. No one moved forward in order to be first to receive his mother; each ceded her in advance to a more needy comrade. Then Sasha realized that the women were all orphans too. It would be better if they, first of all, chose brothers or fathers from among the Chevengurians—and let their say be final.

The women immediately all chose the very oldest of the *others*; there were even two who wanted to live with Yakov Titych, and he accepted both. Not one woman believed in the Chevengurians' fatherhood or brotherhood, so they all wanted a husband whose only need was sleep in a warm place. One of them, however, approached Serbinov. She was swarthy, part little girl and part woman.

"What do you want?" he asked fearfully.

"I want a little warm lump to be born out of me, and all that comes with that!"

"I can't, I'm leaving forever."

She exchanged Serbinov for Kirey.

"You'll do as a woman," Kirey said to her. "I'll gift you whatever you want! When your warm lump is born, I won't let it go cold."

Prokofy took Klavdiusha by the arm. "Well, and what are *we* going to do, citizen Klavdia?"

"Well, Prosha, we must act with consciousness."

"True enough," Prokofy determined. He picked up a piece of dismal clay and flung it somewhere into loneliness. "Somehow there's always something weighing on me. Is it time to organize a family? Or is it better to wait it out until the end of communism? And what about funds? How much have you accumulated for me?"

"How much? For what I've just sold, Prosha, I got real money. That's two fur coats and the silver. For everything else—only a pittance."

"All right. You can show me the accounts this evening. I believe you, but I worry all the same. And you're still keeping the money at your aunt's?"

"Where else, Prosha? That's where it's safest. And when will you take me to the city? You promised to show me the provincial capital—and then you bring me back here to this philistinism. What am I meant to do in this place—alone with these beggar women? With no one to try on a new dress with! And no one to show myself to? Call this country society? I call it a flophouse for peasant pilgrims. Why torture me with these people?"

Prokofy sighed: What can you do with such a personage, if her mind doesn't live up to her womanly charm?

"Klavdiusha, go and look after these women—and leave me to think. One mind is good, but two is too many."

The Bolsheviks and *others* had already left their former place, going their separate ways to work on artifacts for those comrades whom they sensed as an embodiment of their personal idea. Only Kopionkin was not working. Instead, he morosely groomed and caressed his horse, then smeared his weapon with goose fat from his emergency supply. After that, he went to look for Pashintsev, who was grinding and polishing stones.

"Maxim,"[4] he said "why are you sitting and wasting yourself? We've got women here now. And—that what's his name—Semyon Serbov with all his damned cases and briefs. What's up with you—how can you live and forget? The bourgeoisie are sure to strike soon. Where are your bombs, comrade Pashintsev? Where is your Revolution—and the memorial reserve you preserved?"

Pashintsev picked some dried muck out of his injured eye and, by means of the strength of one fingernail, thrust it into the fence.

"I sense all this too, Stepan, and I salute you! That's why I'm destroying my strength into this stone—otherwise I'd be weeping in anguish into the burdocks! But where's Piusia? Why's his music hanging up on a hook?"

Piusia was gathering sorrel in the back places of former homesteads.

"Wanting sounds again, are you?" he asked from behind a shed. "Feeling bored without heroism?"

"Piusia, play 'Little Apple' for me and Kopionkin. Give us a mood of life!"

"All right, in a moment!"

Piusia fetched his chromatic instrument and, with the serious face of a professional artiste, played "Little Apple" to the two comrades. Kopionkin and Pashintsev wept from emotion, while Piusia worked without a word in front of them. He was not living now, but laboring.

"Stop, don't overwhelm me!" said Pashintsev. "Give us some gloom now!"

"All right," said Piusia, and began a protracted melody. Pashintsev's face dried. He took in the mournful sounds and soon began to sing, following the music:

Ride on, comrade, and sing a song.
Sing, comrade, and ride ahead.
Our turn to die came long ago—
Shameful to live, yet sad to be dead.

Ride on, comrade, don't lose heart!
Two mothers promised life ahead—
But then my mama said to me, "First
Make sure your enemy's good and dead—
And only then lay down your head."

Kopionkin was sitting there without activity. "Enough of your wheezing!" he called out, halting the singer. "You didn't get a woman, so you want to encircle her with a song. Look—here's one of these witches already."

Kirey's future wife came up to them, swarthy as the daughter of a Pecheneg.[5]

"What are you after?" asked Kopionkin.

"Nothing much. I want to listen—music makes my heart ache."

"Pah! Reptile!" And Kopionkin got to his feet to move away.

Kirey then appeared, to reclaim his wife.

"What's up, Grusha? Where are you running off to? I picked some millet for you. Let's go and grind it—then we can have pancakes this evening. Something a bit floury's just what I need."

And they set off toward the storeroom where, until then, Kirey had occasionally spent the night, but that he had now made into a more permanent shelter for himself and Grusha.

Kopionkin made his way the length of Chevengur. He wanted a glimpse of steppe; imperceptibly, he had grown accustomed to Chevengur's cramped bustle and it was a long time since he had ridden out into the open. Strength of the Proletariat had been resting in the remote depths of a barn; hearing Kopionkin's footsteps, he whinnied toward his friend with a yearning maw. Kopionkin led him out onto the street and the horse began to caper about beside him, in anticipation of open steppe. When they reached the outskirts of town, Kopionkin jumped onto his steed's back and drew his saber. With all the power of a chest that has been quiet too long, he yelled out an indignant cry and set off at a resonant gallop, as if over granite, into the steppe's autumn silence. No one but Pashintsev witnessed this wild gallop across the steppe, followed by the disappearance of horse and rider into a distant gloom similar to the birth of night. Pashintsev had just climbed onto a roof from which he liked to observe the steppe's empty expanses and the flow of air above them. "He won't be back soon," he thought. "Now it's my turn to conquer Chevengur, to bring joy to Kopionkin."

Three days later, Kopionkin returned. He entered the town at a walk, on a horse grown thinner; he himself was dozing.

"Protect Chevengur," he said to Sasha and two *others* who were standing on his path. "Give the horse some grass—but leave it to me to water him when I get up." And Kopionkin freed his horse and fell asleep in a well-trodden, barefoot spot.

Sasha went off with the horse, thinking about the construction of a cheap proletarian cannon for the protection of Chevengur. There was grass close by. Sasha turned Strength of the Proletariat loose and stayed where he was, in the thick of the vegetation. He was not thinking about anything at all, and the elderly watchman of his mind was dutifully protecting his treasure from any disturbance; he was ready to admit only one visitor at a time, only one wandering thought from outside. Outside in the world, however, there was no thought at all. There was only the earth, going to seed as it stretched out into emptiness, while the waning sun worked in the sky like some boring artificial object and the Chevengurians thought not about cannons but about one another. Then the watchman opened the back door of memories, and Sasha again felt in his head the warmth of consciousness. He is a little boy, walking into the village at night; his father is leading him by the hand—and Sasha is closing his eyes, falling asleep on his feet and then waking up again. "What's up, Sasha? Is it the long day that's made you so weak? Come into my arms then, you can sleep on my shoulder." And his father lifts him up, onto his own body, and Sasha falls asleep with his head on his father's neck. Father is on his way to the village to sell some fish, and his bag of silver bream gives off a smell of damp and grass. There has just been a downpour and the road is all heavy mud, water, and icy cold. Suddenly Sasha wakes up and screams—something cold and heavy is creeping across his little face and his father is cursing a peasant who has just overtaken them, his iron cartwheels spattering both father and son with mud. "Papa, why does mud fly off a wheel?" "The wheel keeps turning, Sasha. The mud gets restless and its own weight makes it hurtle away."

"We need a wheel," Sasha then determined aloud. "A wooden disk with an iron rim. Then we can hurl bricks and stones at the enemy. Or any old debris, since we've got no shells. We can use horse power to turn the wheel and help with our hands—we can even hurl dust and sand... Oh, Gopner's back up on the dam—there must be a leak."

"Am I disturbing you?" asked Serbinov, who had slowly come up to him.

"No, but why do you ask? I wasn't taken up with my own self."

Serbinov was finishing the last of his Moscow cigarettes and was fearful with regard to further supplies.

"I think you used to know Sofia Alexandrovna?"

"I did," Sasha replied. "Did you know her too?"

"Yes."

Kopionkin was sleeping not far from the footpath. He stirred, raised himself up off the ground a little, let out a brief, wild yell, and then started snoring again, rustling the dead blades of grass with air from his nose.

Sasha looked at Kopionkin, reassured to see him asleep.

"I used to remember her before Chevengur, but here I've forgotten her," he then said to Serbinov. "Where does she live now and how come she told you about me?"

"She's in Moscow, working in a factory there. She remembers you. I've noticed that here in Chevengur people are like ideas for one another. And for her, *you* are an idea. Peace of soul still comes to her from you. You're an active warmth."

"You haven't understood us quite correctly. Still, I'm glad she's alive. Now I'll think about her too."

"Do. The way you see it, that means a great deal. To think means to possess or to love. It's worth thinking about her. She's alone now and looking at Moscow. Trams are clanging there and there are a great many people, but not everyone wants to acquire them."

Sasha had never seen Moscow, so all he could imagine of it was Sofia Alexandrovna. And his heart filled with shame and the viscous burden of memory. There had been a time when warmth of life had come to him from Sonia. He might have confined himself until death in the cramped space of a single person—and only now did he understand that terrible unrealized life in which he might have remained forever, as in a building that has collapsed. A sparrow sped past with the wind and settled on a fence, exclaiming in horror. Kopionkin raised his head a little and, gazing wild-eyed around the forgotten world, wept sincere tears; his hands pushed feebly into the dust to support his torso, which was weak from agitated sleep. "Sasha, my Sasha! Why did you never tell me that she's in torment in the grave and that her wound is hurting? Why am I living here, abandoning her to lonely suffering in the grave?" Kopionkin uttered the words with a wail of complaint at the hurt being done to him, at the unbearable force of grief now howling inside his body. Shaggy and aging, sobbing, he tried to leap to his feet in order to gallop away. "Where's my horse, you bastards? Where is my Strength of the Proletariat? You poisoned her in your shed, you deceived me with communism, you'll be the death of me." And Kopionkin collapsed back, returning to sleep.

Serbinov looked into the distance; Moscow was a thousand versts away, and his mother too was now lying in the orphanhood of the grave, suffering in the earth. Sasha went over to Kopionkin. He laid the sleeping man's head on his hat and noticed his half-open eyes, darting about in dream. "Why reproach me?" he whispered. "What about my father? Isn't he suffering at the bottom of the lake? Isn't he still waiting for me? I remember too."

Strength of the Proletariat stopped eating grass and cautiously made his way over to Kopionkin, not stamping his hooves. The horse bent his head to Kopionkin's face and sniffed the man's breath, then touched his loosely closed eyelids with his tongue. Kopionkin calmed down, fully closed his eyes, and slipped into the stillness of continuing sleep. Sasha tethered the horse to a fence, close to Kopionkin, and set off to join Gopner at the dam, along with Serbinov. Serbinov's stomach was no longer aching and he had forgotten that this town was the alien location of a weeklong mission—his body had gotten used to the town's smell and to the thin steppe air. Beside a hut on the outskirts he found a clay monument to Prokofy, protected by burdock leaves from the rain. Shortly before this, Chepurny had been thinking about Prokofy; he had then made him a monument, and this fully satisfied and concluded his feelings for Prokofy. Now Chepurny was missing Karchuk, who had left with Serbinov's letters, and he was preparing the materials for another clay monument—to this comrade who had disappeared.

The statue bore only a faint likeness to Prokofy, but then it immediately and unmistakably brought to mind not only Prokofy but also Chepurny. The artist had sculpted this monument to his chosen dear comrade with an inspired tenderness and the roughness of unskilled labor—and the result had been a cohabitation, a symbiosis that revealed the honesty of Chepurny's art.

Serbinov had not understood the value of a different art. He had appeared stupid in Moscow conversations amid society, because he sat and enjoyed the sight of people, not understanding or listening to what they were saying. He stopped in front of the monument—as did Sasha. "It should have been made from stone, not clay," he said. "As it stands, time and weather will melt it away. This isn't art. This marks the end of the worldwide prerevolutionary abuse of both art and labor. It's the first time I see something without falsehood and exploitation."[6]

Sasha said nothing. He didn't know how else things could be. And they continued on their way to the river valley.

Gopner was not working on the dam. He was sitting on the bank, making a winter window frame out of a small tree. This was for Yakov Titych, who was afraid that his two women—his two daughters—would get chilled in the winter. Sasha and Serbinov waited for Gopner to finish, so that they could all three work together on the wooden disk for hurling stones and bricks at Chevengur's enemies. As he sat there, Sasha noticed how quiet it had grown in the town; those who had received a mother or daughter now seldom emerged from their dwellings, trying instead to labor under one roof with this family member, working on unknown things. But could they truly be happier inside their homes than out in the open air?

It was impossible to tell, and the sadness of not knowing impelled Sasha to superfluous movement. He got to his feet, did some thinking, then went to look for materials from which to construct the shooting disk. Until evening, he wandered about the snug little world of Chevengur's backyards and sheds. Here too, in this stagnation, in the remote depths of small forests of wormwood, it would somehow be possible to exist selflessly in patient abandonment, for the good of faraway people. Sasha unearthed a variety of dead things—worn-out shoes, wooden barrels that had contained tar, deceased sparrows, and much else. Sasha picked these objects up, voiced his regret at their demise and oblivion, and then returned them to their former places, so that everything in Chevengur would remain whole—until a better day of redemption in communism. In the midst of dense goosefoot, Sasha stumbled against something and was barely able to fight his way free—he had fallen between the spokes of a cannon wheel that had lain there forgotten since the war. In both strength and diameter, it was just what they needed for the manufacture of a machine catapult. But the wheel was difficult to roll, since it was heavier than he himself, and so Sasha called out for help to Prokofy, who was enjoying the fresh air with Klavdiusha. Together they got the wheel to the forge, where Gopner checked its condition manually, gave his approval, and said he would stay the night in the forge, beside the wheel, to think through the work in peace.

Prokofy had chosen as his dwelling the brick Bolshevik house where previously everyone had lived and slept without separation. The house was now in good order, thanks to Klavdiusha's womanly care, and the stove was lit every other day to ensure the air's dryness. Flies lived on the ceiling; sturdy walls guarded Prokofy's family peace; and the floor was always scrubbed, as if before a Sunday. Prokofy liked to stretch out on the bed and watch the flies moving on foot over the warm ceiling—just as they had wandered about the ceiling of his parents' hut in his village childhood. Lying there, he would feel calmer, and he would think up ideas for the procurement of funds for his family's further life and security. Now he had brought Sasha back with him, to treat him to tea and jam and some of Klavdiusha's buns.

"See the flies on the ceiling, Sasha?" he said. "Flies used to live in our home too. Do you remember, or have you lost sight of them?"

"I remember them," Sasha replied. "But I remember the birds in the sky even better. They flew about the sky like flies beneath the ceiling—and now they fly over Chevengur, as if over a room."

"That's it. You lived by a lake, not in a hut. The sky was your only covering. For you, the birds up in the sky were like our family flies."

After the tea and jam, Prokofy and Klavdiusha went to bed, warmed each other, and fell quiet, while Sasha slept on a wooden bench. In the morning, Sasha showed Prokofy the birds flying over Chevengur, in the lower air; Prokofy said they were like quick-moving flies in nature's morning room. And Chepurny, walking barefoot and not far away, with only a greatcoat over his naked body, looked like Prokofy's father when he returned from the imperialist war. Here and there smoke was rising from chimneys, and there was the same smell as long ago, as their mother prepared their morning meal.

Prokofy felt concerned. "Soon it will be winter," he said. "We should be preparing fodder for communism."

"Yes, Prosha, we should start soon," Sasha agreed. "Only why did you bring jam for yourself—and not for anyone else? Kopionkin hasn't drunk anything but cold water for years."

"What d'you mean? Didn't I treat you to jam yesterday? Or did you put so little in the glass you couldn't taste it? Shall I bring you a spoonful right now?"

Sasha didn't want jam. He was in a hurry to find Kopionkin, to be with him during his sad time.

"Sasha!" Prokofy shouted after him. "Look at the sparrows tearing about—they're like great fat flies!"

Sasha didn't hear and Prokofy went back to his family room. Flies were still flying about there—and through the window he could see the birds over Chevengur. "No difference between them," he decided. "I'll drive to the bourgeoisie again and bring back two barrels of jam for the whole of communism. Then the *others* can drink tea and lie under the birds' sky—as if they're in the best room of a hut."

After looking over the heavens again, Prokofy calculated that the sky covers much more property than a ceiling. The whole of Chevengur lay under the sky like the furniture of a best room in a family of *others*. What if the *others* were to set off once more on their wanderings? What if Chepurny then died and Sasha were to inherit Chevengur? Prokofy realized that he had misjudged. It was essential that he immediately classify Chevengur as a family room and name himself as the elder brother with a right to all the furniture under the clear sky.[7] It was enough just to look at the sparrows—they were fatter than flies and more densely packed. Prokofy examined his living quarters once more, with an appraising eye, and decided that it would be to his advantage to exchange them for the town as a whole.

"Klavdiusha! Klavdiusha!" he called to his wife. "I feel I'd like to gift you all our furniture!"

"All right," said Klavdiusha. "Why not? I could take it to my aunt straightaway, before the autumn mud!"

"Yes," Prokofy agreed. "Get that done straightaway. And then stay with your aunt till I've received Chevengur in full."

Klavdiusha understood her own need for these things, but she did not understand why Prokofy needed to remain alone to acquire Chevengur, when it all but belonged to him anyway. She asked him to explain.

"You lack political grounding," Prokofy replied. "If you're here when I first receive the town, then everyone will understand that I'll be gifting it to you alone."

"Gift me the town, Prosha! I'll go to the city and come back with carts to transport it!"

"You're tearing ahead without warrant! Why would I gift you the town? Because I sleep with you, people will think. 'He's hardly likely to begrudge her the town,' they'll say, 'if he shares his body with her.' But with you out of the way, it'll be another story. No one will think I'm acquiring the town for myself."

"What do you mean?" Klavdiusha exclaimed in hurt. "Who else will you gift the town to?"

"Blessed bureau of life! Listen to my formulations! What would I want with a town—they'll all think—if I have no dependents and my entire body's whole and hale? But the day the town's mine, I'll evacuate all the goods to some other inhabited point—and summon you there! Get yourself ready to leave now, and I'll take an inventory of the town."

Prokofy took a sheet of headed RevCom notepaper from a chest and went off to record his future property.

Zealous as ever, the sun was working in the sky for the sake of earthly warmth, but less labor was now being carried out in Chevengur itself. Kirey was lying on a heap of grass just inside his house, holding his wife, Grusha, in sleepy embrace.

"Why aren't you gifting anything away into communism, comrade?" Prokofy asked Kirey, when he came to inventory the household.

Kirey woke up. Grusha, on the other hand, closed her eyes from the shame of marriage.

"What's communism to me? I've got Grusha now as a comrade and I can't keep up with my tasks for her. I can't even keep up with procuring food—my life outlay's too much for me."

Once Prokofy was gone, Kirey leaned over Grusha and sniffed the life held just below her throat and the faint smell of deep warmth there. At any moment of desire for happiness, Kirey could take into his inner being both Grusha's warmth and her accumulation of body—and then sense the peace of the meaning of life. Who else could have given him what Grusha did not begrudge him? And how could he now begrudge her anything? On the contrary, he was constantly tormented by conscientious concerns: that he was not giving Grusha enough food and that he was being slow to equip her with clothes. Kirey no longer looked on himself as someone of value, because the very best, most hidden, and tender parts of his body had passed into Grusha. When he went out into the steppe for food, Kirey noticed that the sky above him had grown paler than before, and the calls of the few birds were more muted, while in his chest he felt weakness of spirit. After gathering fruits and cereals, Kirey would return to Grusha in exhaustion, determined from then on to give thought to her alone, to look on her as his Communist idea and let that bring peace and happiness to him. But the time of rest and equanimity would pass—and Kirey would start to feel unhappiness, and life's meaninglessness without the substance of love. The world would blossom around him, the sky would turn into a blue silence, the air would become audible, and the birds over the steppe would be singing about their own imminent disappearance, and all this would seem to Kirey to be a creation higher than his own life—yet after renewed kinship with Grusha, the world would again seem hazy and pitiful, and Kirey would cease to envy it.

The remaining *others*, who were many years younger, saw the women as mothers and merely warmed themselves with them, since the air in Chevengur had turned cold from autumn. And this existence with mothers was now all they needed; no longer was anyone devoting his body to his surrounding comrades by means of labor at the manufacture of gifts. In the evenings, the *others* took the women to distant places of the river and washed them there, since the women were so thin that they were ashamed to visit the bathhouse—even though Chevengur possessed a bathhouse and the stove there could have been lit.

Prokofy did the rounds of the inhabitants currently present and compiled all the town's dead things into his premature inventory. Toward the end of this task, he came to the smithy on the outskirts of town. Gopner and Sasha were working there, and they watched as Prokofy recorded the building on his list. Kopionkin then approached from somewhere far off, bearing a log on his shoulder. Serbinov was walking behind him; as a member of the intelligentsia, he was clumsily supporting an eighth of the log's weight.[8]

"Get out of here!" Kopionkin said to Prokofy, who was standing in the entrance to the smithy. "Some bear burdens, while you just hold papers."

Prokofy moved out of his way, but he noted down the log and left with satisfaction.

Kopionkin dropped the log to the ground and sat down to catch his breath.

"Sasha, when will Proshka ever feel grief? Grief to make him stop in the middle of somewhere and weep?"

Sasha looked at Kopionkin, exhaustion and curiosity brightening his eyes.

"But wouldn't you want to protect him from grief? After all, no one's ever drawn him close to them. And so he's forgotten to need people and taken to collecting property, instead of comrades."

At this, Kopionkin's thoughts changed; he had once seen an unneeded man weeping in the wartime steppe. The man had been sitting on a stone, a wind of autumn weather blowing in his face, and not even the Red Army transport train would accept him, because he had lost all his documents—and the man himself had a wound in his groin and it was unclear whether he was weeping on account of being left behind or because his groin had become empty while his life and head had been preserved in full.

"Yes, I would protect him, Sasha. I can't control myself before a man in grief and bitterness. I'd have taken him up on my horse with me and carried him away into life's distance."

"Don't wish grief on him then—or you'll end up pitying your enemy."

"All right, Sasha," said Kopionkin, "I won't. Let the man find himself in the midst of communism. Then he'll join up with humanity of his own accord."

That evening it began to rain in the steppe, but the rain passed by the edge of Chevengur, leaving the town dry. This phenomenon did not surprise Chepurny; he was aware that nature had long known about communism in the town and did not wet it at the wrong time. A whole group of *others*, however, set off into the steppe, accompanied by Chepurny and Piusia, to inspect the wet place and convince themselves. Kopionkin believed in the rain and did not go anywhere, preferring to stay with Sasha and rest by the fence near the smithy. Kopionkin had little sense of the usefulness of conversation and was now telling Sasha that air and water are cheap things, but necessary—and that much the same can be said about stones; they too are needed for something. Kopionkin's words served not to express meaning but to convey his feelings toward Sasha; silence was something he found troubling.

"Comrade Kopionkin," asked Sasha, "which is dearer to you—Chevengur or Rosa Luxemburg?"

"Rosa, comrade Dvanov," Kopionkin replied in alarm. "There was more communism in her than in all Chevengur. That's why the bourgeoisie killed her—while this town's still in one piece, even with elemental nature all around it."

Sasha possessed no reserve of fixed love. He lived by Chevengur alone—and he was afraid of expending the town. He existed only by means of his everyday people—Kopionkin, Gopner, Pashintsev, and the *others*—but he constantly worried that they might all disappear somewhere one morning or else die off gradually. Sasha bent down, plucked a blade of grass, and examined its timid body: when no one was left, this grass was something he could preserve.

44

Kopionkin stood up. Running toward them from somewhere out in the steppe was Chepurny. Without a word and without stopping, he would have sped by into the depth of the town. Kopionkin seized hold of his greatcoat to halt him.

"Where are you hurtling when there's been no alarm?"

"Cossacks! Cadets on horseback! Comrade Kopionkin! Ride out and fight, I beg you! I'm going back for my rifle."[1]

"Sasha, go and wait in the smithy," said Kopionkin. "I'll deal with them on my own. But mind you stay inside—I won't be long!"

Four of the *others* who had set off with Chepurny came running back, but Piusia was lying low in some crevice. His shot rang out with fire in the darkening silence. Sasha—revolver drawn—ran toward this shot. After a short time, Kopionkin galloped heavily past him on Strength of the Proletariat. Following these first fighters, a sheer armed force of Bolsheviks and *others* emerged from the outskirts of town; those without firearms bore a poker or a stake from a wattle fence. The women were there too, alongside everyone else. Serbinov came running behind Yakov Titych with his lady's Browning, looking for someone to shoot at. Chepurny was riding the horse that had earlier drawn Prokofy's carriage. As for Prokofy, he was running just behind Chepurny, advising him first to appoint a commanding officer and organize a proper staff—otherwise doom would begin.

At a gallop, Chepurny discharged an entire cartridge clip into the distance. He tried to catch up with Kopionkin but couldn't. Kopionkin leaped on his horse over the prone Piusia. Rather than shoot at an opponent, he unsheathed his saber, preferring to relate to the enemy more closely.

The enemy were riding along the former road. They held their rifles across their chests, not preparing to fire, and were urging their horses forward. Being in strict formation and under clear command, they faced the first shots from Chevengur calmly and without fear. Quick to see their advantage, Sasha braced his feet against a small hollow and picked off the detachment commander with the fourth bullet from his revolver. Again, however, the enemy did not fall into disarray. With no loss of impetus, they transferred the commander deep inside the formation and brought their horses to a full trot. Their calm advance was imbued with the mechanical strength of victory, but the Chevengurians possessed the elemental power of self-defending life—and communism, moreover, existed on Chevengur's side. Chepurny well understood this; he stopped his horse, raised his rifle, and felled three enemy to the ground. Piusia, meanwhile, managed to cripple the legs of two horses with bullets fired from his place in the grass; the horses fell behind the detachment, trying to creep forward on their bellies and digging the dust of the earth with their muzzles. Pashintsev hurtled past Sasha in his visor and coat of mail. In his outstretched right hand he held the shell of a hand bomb, aiming to overpower the enemy by mental fear alone, since the bomb had no filling and Pashintsev was carrying no other weapon.

As if of its own accord, as abruptly as if it comprised only two horsemen, the enemy detachment stopped. These soldiers unknown to Chevengur then raised their rifles at some inaudible command, pointed them toward the Bolsheviks and approaching *others* and, without a shot, continued their advance on the town.

The evening stood motionless above people, and night was not darkening over them. The machinelike enemy thundered its hooves over the virgin land, blocking the *others* from the open steppe, from their road into future countries of light, and from any exodus out of Chevengur. Pashintsev called on the bourgeoisie to surrender and pulled the pin of his empty bomb. Again, the advancing detachment received an inaudible command—rifles flashed and went dull. Pashintsev and seven *others* fell to the ground. Four more Chevengurians, enduring their burning wounds, ran on to attack the enemy by hand.

Kopionkin had already reached the detachment. He commanded Strength of the Proletariat to rear up, meaning to destroy these brigands with his saber and the weight of his steed. Strength of the Proletariat lowered his hooves onto the torso of an oncoming horse, which sank to the ground with shattered ribs, and Kopionkin swept his saber through the air, helping it with all his body's live strength in order to slash the rider apart before the man's face entered his memory. With a jarring crack that echoed up Kopionkin's arm, the saber plunged into the alien warrior's saddle. Kopionkin grabbed the man's young, ginger-haired head with his left hand, let go for a moment while he took a swing, smashed him on the crown of the head with this same hand, and overthrew his enemy onto the ground. Next, an alien saber blinded Kopionkin's eyes; taken aback, he seized the saber with one hand while cutting off the attacker's forearm—along with this saber—with his other hand. After tossing aside both saber and burdensome limb, lopped off at the elbow, he glimpsed Gopner, who was battling in the thick of the horses, holding his revolver by the muzzle and using it as a cudgel. From tension and thinness of face, or from being slashed, the skin had split on Gopner's cheekbones and beside his ears. Blood was gushing out in waves, and Gopner was doing his best to wipe it away, so that it wouldn't tickle his neck and hinder his fighting. Kopionkin gave the cavalryman to his right a kick in the stomach, since this man was positioned between him and Gopner—and just managed to nudge his horse into a quick jump. Otherwise, Strength of the Proletariat would have trampled on Gopner, who by then had been hacked to death.

Kopionkin broke free from alien encirclement, while Chepurny charged into the other flank of the mounted enemy patrol and sped on his poor nag through their swift-moving formation, trying to kill with the weight of his rifle, for which he now had no cartridges. The fury of one wild swing with this empty rifle sent Chepurny flying to the ground, since his blow did not land on the intended enemy.

Chepurny was then lost to sight, in a dense thicket of trampling hooves. Kopionkin took advantage of a brief respite to suck his bloody hand, with which he had seized the blade of the saber, and then tore forward to kill all and everyone. He penetrated without harm through the entire enemy detachment, remembering nothing, and then turned the now snarling Strength of the Proletariat in order to record everything in his memory—otherwise the battle would not yield consolation and victory would lack all sense of tired labor over the death of the enemy. Five horsemen broke away from the main patrol and began to slash at *others* fighting in the distance, but the *others* knew how to defend themselves with patience and tenacity—this was not the first time that enemies had tried to block them from life. They flung bricks at the troops and lit straw bonfires on the outskirts of town, from which they snatched small embers to fling at the muzzles of the skittish cavalry horses. Yakov Titych struck one horse on the rump with a smoldering piece of wood; the sweat from under the horse's tail made the wood splutter and hiss—and the desperate, screeching mare carried her warrior a good two versts from Chevengur.

"What are you doing, using fire as a weapon?" asked another soldier, who had just ridden up to Yakov Titych. "I'll kill you!"

"All right," said Yakov Titych. "Kill me. We've got no iron or steel, and we can't defeat you with our bodies alone."

"I'll take you at a gallop—so you don't notice your death."

"Do as you like. Any number of people have died already, but no one takes death into account."

The soldier rode some distance away, took his horse into a gallop, and cut Yakov Titych down to the ground. Serbinov was dashing about with his last bullet, which he was keeping for himself. Then he stopped and anxiously checked his revolver: Was the bullet still there?

"I said I'd chop him down—and that's what I did," the cavalryman said to Serbinov, wiping his saber against his horse's hide. "That'll teach him to fight with fire!"

The cavalryman was in no hurry to return to the fight. He was looking around him, wondering who else to kill and who was to blame. Serbinov raised his revolver against him.

"What's gotten into you?" the soldier exclaimed in surprise. "I'm not harming you!"

Serbinov took the man at his word and put away his revolver. But the cavalryman turned his horse and charged at Serbinov. Simon fell, struck in the stomach by a hoof; he sensed his heart recede into the distance and then struggle to beat its way back into life. He was aware what his heart was up to and did not particularly wish it to succeed. Sofia Alexandrovna, after all, was still alive—and she could preserve within her a trace of his body and thus continue his existence. The soldier bent down and, without taking a swing, cut open Serbinov's stomach. Nothing emerged from it—neither blood, nor entrails.

"It's you who was so eager to shoot," said the cavalryman. "If you hadn't been in such a hurry, you'd still be with us."

Sasha was on the run, holding two revolvers; he had taken the second from the dead commander. He was being chased by three horsemen, but Kirey and Zheyev intercepted them and drew them away.

The soldier who had killed Serbinov then stopped Sasha. "And where are you off to?" he asked. Sasha, without replying, shot him down with both his revolvers and rushed to the aid of Kopionkin, who was in peril somewhere or other. Nearby, it was now quiet—the fighting had moved on into the center of Chevengur, and that was where the drumming of hooves now sounded.

"Grusha!" Kirey called out in the silence that had set in. He was lying in the steppe with his chest split open and weakened life.

"What is it?" Sasha called out as he ran up to him.

Kirey was unable to speak his word.

"Well, goodbye," said Sasha, bending down over him. "Let's kiss, to make it easier."

Kirey opened his mouth in anticipation, and Sasha embraced his lips with his own.

"Is Grusha alive, or not?" Kirey managed to get out.

"She's dead," Sasha replied, to ease Kirey's worries.

"I'll die too. It's bleak," said Kirey, again overcoming his weakness. At that point, he died, his iced-over eyes still open to the outside.

"There's nothing more for you to look at," Sasha whispered. He lowered Kirey's eyelids over his gaze, then stroked his burning head. "Farewell!"

Kopionkin had broken free from the tight crush of Chevengur. He had no saber and was covered in blood, but he was alive and battling. Four cavalrymen were pursuing him on exhausted horses. Two stopped and fired at him. Kopionkin wheeled Strength of the Proletariat round and galloped unarmed at the enemy, wanting to fight point-blank. But Sasha noticed this move toward death and, dropping onto one knee for precision of aim, began to fell the cavalrymen, shooting with each revolver in turn. By the time Kopionkin reached them, they had fallen beneath the stirrups of their agitated horses. Two sank to the ground, but the other two were unable to free their legs. Dangling beneath their wounded horses, their corpses were carried out into the steppe.

"Are you alive, Sasha?" Kopionkin called out. "There are alien forces in the town—and our people are all dead. Hold on... Something's starting to hurt..."

Kopionkin laid his head on Strength of the Proletariat's mane.

"Help me down, Sasha, so I can lie on the ground."

Sasha took him down onto the ground. The blood from his first wounds had already dried on Kopionkin's torn and slashed greatcoat, and the fresh, liquid blood had not yet seeped through to it.

Kopionkin lay on his back to rest.

"Turn away from me, Sasha. You can see. I'm unable to exist."

Sasha turned away.

"Don't look at me anymore. I'm ashamed to be deceased in front of you. I stayed too long in Chevengur and so now I'm ending, and Rosa will suffer in the ground alone."

All of a sudden Kopionkin sat up. Recovering his battle voice, he thundered out, "They're waiting for us, comrade Dvanov!" Then he collapsed, dead face to the ground, and all of him went hot.

Strength of the Proletariat picked up Kopionkin's body by his greatcoat and carried it off toward some dear place in the forgotten freedom of the steppe. Sasha followed the horse until the last nooses of the greatcoat tore and Kopionkin turned out to be half-naked, pitted by wounds more than he was covered by clothes. The horse sniffed the dead man all over and eagerly began to lick the blood and fluid from the gaping wounds, to share in his fallen companion's last possessions and diminish the pus of death. Sasha then mounted Strength of the Proletariat and set off into the open steppe night. He rode until morning, not hurrying the horse. Sometimes Strength of the Proletariat stopped, looked back, and listened, but Kopionkin lay silent in the darkness behind them—and the horse would step forward again of his own accord.

45

IN THE afternoon, Sasha recognized an old road that he had seen in childhood, and he guided Strength of the Proletariat along it. The road went through a village and then within a verst of Lake Mutevo. And in this village, as the horse strode on, Sasha passed his birthland. The huts and sheds looked newer, smoke was rising from chimneys, the time must have been about midday, and the steppe grass had long since been scythed from roofs covered by earth. The verger began ringing the hour, and Sasha heard the familiar bell as the time of childhood.[1] He stopped the horse by the well, to let him rest and drink from the trough there. On the earth ledge around a nearby hut sat a hunchbacked old man—Piotr Fyodorovich Kondaev. He did not recognize Sasha, and Sasha did not say who he was. Piotr Fyodorovich was catching flies in the warmth of the sun and eviscerating them in his hands with the happiness of the satisfaction of his life, too oblivious to give thought to the alien horseman.

Sasha had no feelings for his birthplace and he rode on. He passed quiet fields, now harvested and deserted. The lower earth smelled of the sadness of decrepit grass, and from it began a hopeless sky that made the whole world into an empty place.

The water in Lake Mutevo was slightly agitated, ruffled by a noon wind that had already died down in the distance. Sasha Dvanov rode to the water's edge; in his early life Sasha had bathed in this water and fed from it; its depths had once brought peace to his father—and this last kin and comrade of Sasha's had been longing for him throughout lonely decades cramped in the earth. Strength of the Proletariat bowed his head and stamped one hoof—something was bothering him. Sasha looked down and saw a fishing rod, dragged from higher up the shore by the horse's leg. Caught on the hook was a dried, broken skeleton of a little fish—and Sasha recognized that it was his own rod, forgotten there in childhood.[2] He looked around at the silent, unchanging lake and went taut and alert. His father still remained—his bones, his body's once living substance, what was left of his sweat-soaked shirt, a whole birthland of life and warm friendship. And so for Sasha there existed a cramped, inseparable place that expected the return through eternal friendship of the blood long ago apportioned him in his father's body. Sasha urged Strength of the Proletariat forward, until the water came up to the horse's chest. Without farewell, continuing his own life, Sasha got down from the saddle and into the water—in search of the path along which his father had once passed in inquisitiveness of death, though Sasha was now moved by a sense of the shamefulness of life before a weak, forgotten body, the remains of which had exhausted themselves in the grave. Sasha, after all, was one and the same with that still-not-destroyed, flickering trace of his father's existence.[3]

Strength of the Proletariat could hear the rustle of the grass and weeds underwater, and muck from the lake had risen up to his head, but the horse pushed the patch of unclean water away with his mouth, drank a little from a bright place in the middle, returned to dry land, and set off back home to Chevengur, at a conservative pace.

The horse appeared in the town only on the third day after Sasha's departure, since he had lain and slept for a long time in a steppe hollow. After that, he forgot the way and wandered about open steppe until he heard Karchuk calling out to him. Karchuk was also heading for Chevengur, together with an old man he had happened across. The old man was Zakhar Pavlovich; unable to wait any longer for Sasha to return to him, he had set off himself, to find Sasha and bring him back home.

Karchuk and Zakhar Pavlovich found none of their people in Chevengur. The town was empty and dismal; there was just one spot, near the brick house, where Proshka was sitting and crying amid all the property that had come his way.

"Why are you crying, Prosha," said Zakhar Pavlovich, "and not complaining to anyone? Want me to give you a rouble again? Go and find Sasha."

"No," said Prokofy. "I'll bring him for free." And he set off in search of Sasha Dvanov.

Summer 1927–May 1929

TRANSLATOR'S ACKNOWLEDGMENTS

Excerpts from early drafts of this translation have been published in Asymptote, Chteniya, e-flux journal, The Portable Platonov, *and* Pretexts. *My thanks to all the editors concerned.*

I FIRST tried to translate Platonov nearly fifty years ago. I eventually realized that I needed all the help I could get. Over the decades, many people have helped me in many ways. Co-translating *Soul* and *The Foundation Pit* with Olga Meerson deepened my understanding of Platonov immeasurably. Among the other scholars, writers, and translators from whom I have learned are Anna Aizman, Rad Borislavov, Maria Bloshteyn, Nadya Bourova, Maria Chehonadskih, Ben Dhooge, Maria Dmitrovskaya, Boris Dralyuk, Natalia Duzhina, Leonid Elyon, Caryl Emerson, Carl Foster, Robert Hodel, Elena Kolesnikova, Natalia Kornienko, Angela Livingstone, Nina Malygina, Irina Mashinski, Mikhail Mikheev, Veronica Muskheli, Eric Naiman, Alexander Nakhimovsky, Elena Ostrovskaya, Natasha Perova, Natalia Poltavtseva, Aai Prins, Valery Vyugin, and Evgeny Yablokov. Translating can be lonely work; sharing the task has been a joy. And I believe that Platonov would have liked the thought of these translations being the product of collective labor. I also thank countless other people who have helped me with specific questions—many of them through the email forum SEELANGS. I am deeply grateful to the members of the SEELANGS community for their generosity, tolerance, and general willingness to help.

The work of a dedicated and conscientious group of scholars at the Institute of World Literature (IMLI), a branch of the Russian

Academy of Sciences, deserves a special mention. Under the guidance of Natalia Vasilievna Kornienko, this group has been researching Platonov's typescripts and manuscripts since the early 1990s, painstakingly establishing reliable texts; written in pencil, with many changes, Platonov's manuscripts are not easy to read. A "dynamic transcription" of the text of *Chevengur*, indicating all Platonov's deletions and changes, was published in 2019 (*Arkhiv A. P. Platonova, kn. 2*). This "archive" version forms the basis of the text included in the third volume (2022) of the excellent scholarly edition of Platonov's complete works that this group is publishing, volume by volume, over the decades. It is this text that we have translated. We have also incorporated a great deal of material from the extensive notes.

Vladimir Sharov's "Platonov's People" (*Narod Andreya Platonova*) was first published in *Literaturnaya matritsa, XX vek: uchebnik, napisannyi pisatelyami* (Literary Matrix, 20C: A textbook written by writers), ed. V. Levental', S. V. Drugoveiko-Dolzhanskaya, and P. Krusanov (Saint Petersburg: Limbus Press, 2011), 2:579–609. Oliver Ready thanks Caryl Emerson for her suggestions and improvements.

—R. C.

THE HISTORY OF CHEVENGUR

An Excerpt from an Early Draft of Chevengur

CHEVENGUR existed apart from iron roads and highways. People were born in these plains, then emerged from them, but there was no beaten track passing through the town. Around Chevengur lived villages—a birthland of destitution—from which superfluous people had for an entire age set off for temporary work in the mines and cities. Chevengur itself lay on the path between these multiplying naked villages and the countries of earnings—Moscow and the Donbas. It was at this point on their journey that superfluous people coming from distant homesteads found that they had exhausted their pedestrian strength and their provisions from home, and so they would stop there in order to earn enough to move on farther. For low wages or—more often—simply for food, these transient workers had during the previous sixty years built an entire town. But for the journeying hardships of shelterless, wandering people, Chevengur would not have come into being; until the war and the Revolution, the Chevengur bourgeoisie had benefited from their labor.

All year round, people had come here at a slow walk from the depth of their village homesteads. On the outskirts of Chevengur, they had lain down in the grass and slept for whole days and nights, plastered with flies, not sensing the heat of the sun, with a blue tinge to their open lips. After their sleep, they had felt hungry, eaten up any last crumbs of bread in their knapsacks, and then gone the rounds of the Chevengur households to hire themselves out.

A hundred or a hundred and fifty versts to the east of Chevengur were high, dry steppes, where the villages were large but a long way apart. There was plenty of land, but each new child forced either the father or eldest son to leave the village in search of employment, since the family's land was distant, waterless, and beyond their strength to work. Only the strongest peasants, with property and equipment they could depend on, were able to settle this high, waterless steppe, taking refuge by building isolated homesteads. More ordinary people, on the other hand, remained in the villages, split up their holdings among their sons, and divided the land into ever-thinner strips located so far away that they ended up, in effect, as wasteland. Men would visit these parcels of land once a year, to check that the land remained intact and to grieve over it. During years of drought, mothers and children would leave the villages too, to work or beg in Chevengur. There was nowhere else nearby, and the children were not strong enough to walk far. In these villages every mother was widowed, and every child lived the life of an orphan, since their husbands and fathers had all gone far from their birthland, in search of bread.

Every journeying peasant knew that in Chevengur he would procure his allowance of victuals—and so he would rest beforehand just outside the town.

A Chevengur householder would come out onto his porch and address the barefoot men outside: "How come there are so many of you now? Don't tell me your land has narrowed and you've been left with no room."

The peasants would remain silent. They were seeking wages, not answers to questions. "What skills do you have?" a settled Chevengurian would ask skeptically. "I need a barn to store grain. Good logs, with joints like they fashioned in the old days—but you lot are no craftsmen!"

The passing workers, however, would stay there to build the barn, trimming the logs neatly, since need makes it possible to trim logs however is required. They would turn out to be unexpectedly deft with their hands, since foot-walkers are used to hard-won bread and would put their hearts into any work that came their way. If one of them was at a loss, he would remember his wife and children, the only people who loved and desired him, and he would resolve the difficulty, turning grief into craftsmanship and the sturdy construction of a stranger's barn. But the settled Chevengurians would be watching all the time from their porches, checking that no leftover wood was being pilfered and never praising the work of these peasants. "Call that work!" a householder would say in apparent surprise. "You should have been trimming the logs, not just hacking at them. Now take my grandfather, he was a true carpenter! A hundred and one years he lived, yes, he was on his feet till the year of the tsar's coronation. I've heard that a tsar too is honored with a hundred and one gunshots. And as for my grandad's work—a householder would gladly swap his own home for one of my grandad's barns. That old man left nothing to chance. Where others would have put a mere pole, he placed a beam. Where there was no need for any support at all, he'd slip in a tie piece. A true craftsman he was—someone you could depend on, the kind of man they don't make anymore! And over the years he built only four buildings. But *your* work is in vain—all you've done is spoil good materials. If ever I find some true, old-style craftsmen, we'll have to dismantle it."

Astonished by the seriousness of town labor, the seasonal workers would stand there and breathe, guilty ahead of time. The Chevengurian would retire inside his home for a grumble. He would let time pass, wearying his soul with regret over the ruined timber while the worker-peasants waited outside, frightened by the town's mental life and noisy streets. The householder and his wife would agonize over what to do with these peasants who had just built them a barn. "Let them at least dig round the trees in the orchard," the wife would order. "What's gotten into you—giving them bread for free!"

The workers would dig over the orchard, sweep the yard, and fetch buckets of water. Then the householder would give each of them a half loaf of bread and a silver ten-kopek piece. "Thank the Lord the wheat hasn't failed this year!" he would say with a sigh. "At least we've something to give to a man of the road."

On their return journey—from the rich places back to their villages—the seasonal workers would stop again in Chevengur in order to carry out a few tasks, fill their bellies, and not squander their distant earnings on food. And so, little by little, amid empty steppe, not far from the path these travelers followed, the Chevengurians' private houses and other constructions got built.

And so there came into being a town full of slow and serious life, a town of age-old sturdiness that existed with all the dependability of nature.

And so buildings of age-old sturdiness appeared in Chevengur, befitting the people there, who were true to their feelings and interests as the sun is true to its daily path.[1]

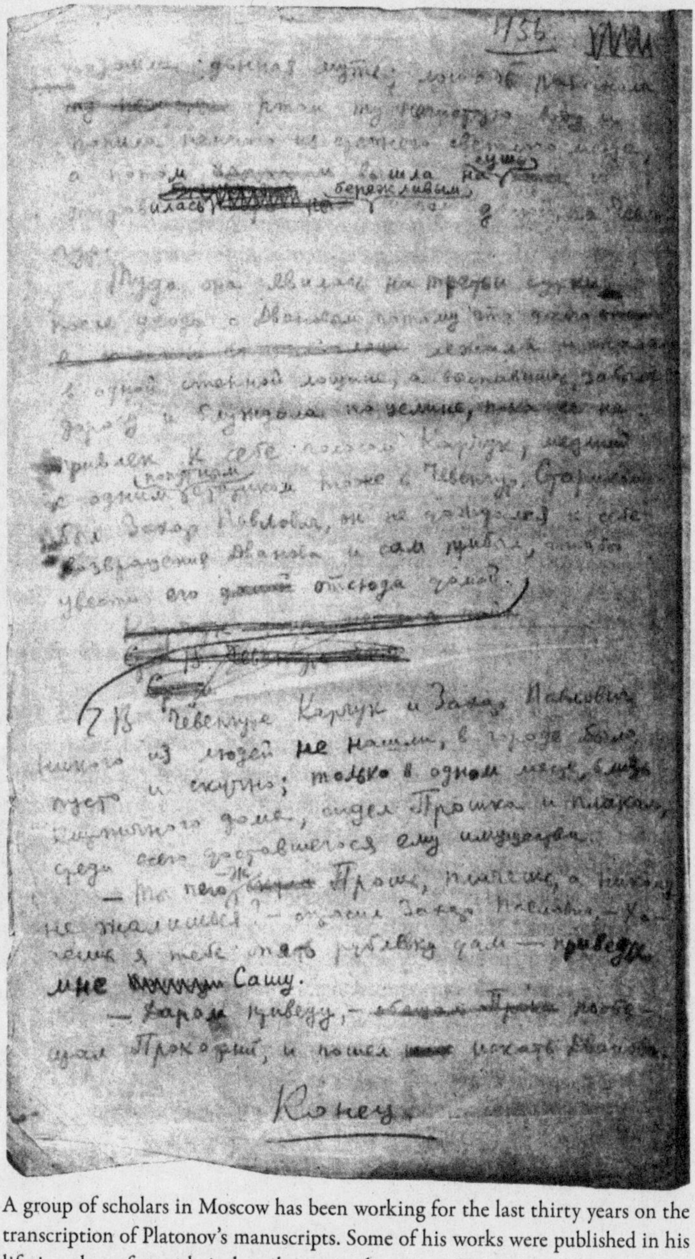

A group of scholars in Moscow has been working for the last thirty years on the transcription of Platonov's manuscripts. Some of his works were published in his lifetime, but often only in heavily censored versions. Some existed in typescript. Some existed only in penciled manuscripts, often faint and full of corrections, and sometimes using both sides of the page.

One of the 331 wells dug under Platonov's supervision while working as a land reclamation specialist during the mid-1920s.

PLATONOV'S PEOPLE

PLATONOV first came my way, if I'm not mistaken, in 1967. My father was given a barely legible typescript of *The Foundation Pit* for his birthday, and I read it there and then, at the age of fifteen. I can still remember the physical impression it made on me, perhaps because that feeling has barely changed with time. By the late 1960s, plenty of samizdat had already passed through my hands, and my loathing of Soviet power was well entrenched. Even so, it was this short book that struck me as precisely the type of final, unappealable judgment of which the authorities themselves were so fond.

I, like others, could not forgive Soviet power for many things big and small, for the millions who had been shot or driven to death in the camps, among them two-thirds of my own family, for the ubiquitous hypocrisy and mediocrity. Not to mention the sheer dreariness of Soviet rule—in fact, it was beyond me how anyone could find anything interesting about it. To me it seemed astonishingly cold, characterless, featureless, emotionless. Just a weight that crushed you and crushed you.

Then suddenly I read something by a person for whom none of this was true, for whom everything about Soviet power felt warm, everything touched him to the quick, moved him, made him suffer, who was brought to ecstasy by its slightest success. Who—this much was clear—kept faith with it for a very long time, tried to keep faith with it for even longer, and was ready to work for it day and night. I, in other words, was no match for him in any respect. Soviet power was his flesh and blood (or he yearned madly for it to become such) and now here he was delivering his judgment, the like of which I had never encountered, never having read a more terrifying, more anti-Soviet manuscript.

Here, I will try to take a more systematic approach to the impression Platonov's prose has made on me, although for me personally it's enough to know that I have long viewed the first half of the Russian twentieth century entirely through Platonov, and whatever I understand of it is thanks first and foremost to him.

On the whole, it seems to me that from the very beginning there were two easily distinguishable perspectives toward the Revolution, and I don't mean that some people were in complete sympathy with it while others loathed it. It's just that one perspective was external, alien, detached. Among good writers this gaze was very precise, very harsh and sharp; after all, many things are clearer and easier to understand when seen from the outside. But the external perspective is always drawn to what is most powerful and most vivid: the eye instantly picks out contrasts. This view is romantic through and through, seeing in revolution the beginning of one thing and the end of another. The whole vastly complex spiderweb of civilization, with all its rules, conventions, and etiquette, collapses just like that, and in a flash the world passes into the hands of primal heroes, returning to a state of savagery, barbarism, and bravado.

This viewpoint was very common, because most writers had grown up inside the old culture, which they loved and valued. Now that it had been destroyed, they were trying as honestly as they could to grasp what would take its place, but they found this very hard. Platonov, as I see it, was perhaps the only writer, or one of the very few, who saw, and knew, and understood the Revolution from within. And from within everything was different.

It was obvious to Platonov, I think, that the revolutionary understanding of the world was bound up with an eschatological tradition that was originally Christian but had long been specifically Russian; that it was tied to the various sects that had been so numerous in late nineteenth-century and early twentieth-century Russia. The members of those sects were also expecting the end of the old world at any moment; they believed in it and tried to hurry it along, bring it nearer.

They were waiting for Christ to come and the new world to begin. And for them this beginning was tied not just to the rejection of the old life, but also to the rejection of the body, the flesh—the main custodians of filth, sin, and lust, the chief tempters that prevented people from mending their ways and living righteously in accordance with the divine covenants.

The sectarians, following their various doctrines, did all they could to mortify their flesh, so that spirit, purity, and sanctity would increase in them, while flesh—those chains dragging man into sin, into the depths, into hell—would diminish. This is the path followed by Platonov's characters whether in *Soul* (*Dzhan*), *Chevengur*, or *The Foundation Pit*, and by all of Russia during the Revolution and Civil War. While strong, fearless heroes, the Whites, do battle with strong, fearless heroes, the Reds, sparing no thought for their own lives or anyone else's, the quantity of spirit in the rest of Russia grows immeasurably day by day; it can be seen through the wispy flesh of people who are on the point of dying of hunger, typhus, cholera.

These people, if we are to speak of their flesh, are infinitely weak, they are constantly wavering, languishing, and cannot decide whether to live or die. Two radiant kingdoms that are almost identical (hence the difficulty of the choice) are beckoning to them: the regular one, heaven, and the one promised here on earth: communism. Actually it's all the same to them, and they don't really mind whether they will be resurrected only in the spirit or in the flesh as well, because they have already walked most of the path toward renunciation of the flesh, of their own body, and they recall without the slightest fondness the time when it was precisely their bodies that ruled them.

It seems to me that for a vast part of Russia this purification through suffering, through many years of the cruelest hunger, of forced fasting, may have seemed, and did seem, to be the very thing for which people had been praying for centuries, aware that salvation was impossible without it. And this is how Platonov writes his characters.

When I read him I have the constant, purely physical sensation that he fears picking them up or touching them for this same reason: their flesh is so thin, so decrepit, and they themselves so weak that you could all too easily damage them, wound them.

And there's another sensation, one of inconceivable embarrassment and shame, because the same human soul that in ordinary times is concealed beneath a thick, solid layer of flesh is now almost laid bare, and you are embarrassed to look at this, embarrassed to see it. You can't understand whether you even have the right to look, because you always thought that only the Almighty can see this, know it, judge it, and even then only when the person has already died and the soul has flown off to God and come before His judgment.

There is in all this a violation of the natural course of life, its rules, its laws, its entire order. A man who has come from the old life discovers that all the skills he gained there are of no use here. This is clearly a country of people entirely prepared for death, who do not fear it in the least and do not value life. And it will take a very long time to persuade them to live. Or at least to give life a go.

Of life they know that it is suffering and anguish. Death, on the other hand, is rest and deliverance. They are hungry but rarely think of food, because by now they are used to the fact that either there is no food or only the most wretched crumbs. In Platonov's writing the place of food is taken by warmth. Warmth is something they still value. And this makes sense: their flesh is sparse, translucent, and they are always freezing. But even the warmth usually comes not from food but from the dying, from the people burning up right next to you with typhoid fever.

Those "prophets" who try to win over this country so ready for death, who try to persuade it to live, are filled with faith, and in the end the country will follow them. But we, who were born later, know in our turn that the country will be deceived by them.

Here, perhaps, a brief historical observation is in order. A great many people in Russia still insist that the Bolshevik victory of 1917 came out of nowhere, that it was a conspiracy or freak event, a demonic hallucination, a supernatural occurrence—something, in other words, impervious to any rational explanation. That's not how I see it. In my view the Revolution was passionately anticipated by an enormous quantity of people, parties, and religious groups of all stripes. These forces often knew nothing about one another and took no interest in each other, but on the most important questions they were close enough, and in February 1917 their joint efforts toppled the monarchy with relative ease. All of them saw the regime and the life they themselves were living as an evil without end, the kingdom of the Antichrist, which had to be overthrown, however many the victims.

Who were they and where did all these ideas and moods come from? Why did the country turn so easily and abruptly from its previous path? Let's begin with some general, even oblique thoughts about those who constituted what can justly be called "Platonov's people."

There's a remarkable discipline known as toponymy, the science of geographical names, from which it follows that the names of cities and rivers, mountains and even countries, often live on for many hundreds, even thousands, of years, while the people who bestowed those names, who plowed and defended the land, who put up houses on it and laid down roads, the people who, above all, loved in that land, gave birth to children there, contemplated Creation and prayed to God—of them, nothing remains. It's only archaeologists who, by turning over ton upon ton of earth, find some meager proof that those were not phantoms, not mirages, but people who actually lived there at some point in the past. On this topic, two gloomy maxims come to mind. The first: "After victory the battlefield belongs to the looters." The second: "Hangmen are the heirs of their victims."

Literary criticism is—and always will be—the science of what writers have in common. Just as, in an anatomical theater, the doctor scarcely needs to cut open the corpse in order to reveal how astonishingly similar we all are in our internal structure, so in textbooks we become assortments of one and the same genres, devices, techniques, and styles. In reality, of course, we all understand that the only interesting thing about authors, the only thing that makes them worth studying, is the dissimilarity of the worlds they create to those of their fellow writers; consequently, it's not primers we need to be reading, but books. Books are living things, and it's precisely life, with all it contains, that makes us different from each other. A true writer is a one-off, irreplaceable by any other. If you remove him from literature, as happened to Andrey Platonov, if you don't publish his manuscripts—or worse, lock him up or just kill him—the place that should have been occupied by his books (his poems, his prose) will remain vacant.

I say all this because, as history has shown, even those who appear to stand most firmly on their own two feet turn out to be astonishingly fragile. They easily drift away, abandoning the land on which they grew up, and perish and die more easily still, while new people move into their homes: in *Chevengur* these are "the *others*," who neither know nor want to know anything about the people who lived there before them. As a result, not a trace remains in anybody's memory. A good prose writer can save a whole tribe from oblivion; Platonov, in *Soul*, saves an entire people, dozens, even hundreds of human beings—not types or characters, not vaguely conventional and less than comprehensible figures, personifications of this or that, but living souls. Stories, novellas, novels, these are always a kind of "Synodicon of the Disgraced":[1] all writers commemorate those they loved and knew, and in their wake readers commemorate them too, thanks to which the departed remain alive; they do not disappear or dissolve in nonbeing.

In his novellas and novels Platonov sometimes portrays those who do not belong, "the *others*," those who, like the nomads of ancient times, have come from—and will soon return to—no one knows where (his prose contains many tramps and wanderers). Far more often, though, his characters are locals through and through. This is where they were born, all their roots are in this earth, and they have never seen or known anything else. Then one day something happens in their heads, in their souls, and they begin to see the world in a completely different way. And that is enough for the world itself to become different all at once, for everything in it to change just like that. Often, to change so radically that good suddenly begins to resemble evil, and vice versa.

The people on the pages of Platonov's books behave accordingly.

But the point here is not whether the author does or does not take their side, and it's irrelevant how strong they are, how much faith they have in their own rightness; rather, Platonov chooses only those who bear the expression known by doctors as the Hippocratic face, the mask of death. As if the author knows that their understanding of the world and they themselves will soon perish, or at best dissolve without trace among what remains of their people, and Platonov weeps; he weeps both for them and for those they killed in the name of their truth. He weeps over all the grief that they brought and that they suffered themselves, for the trust they placed in the future, for their hopes and delusions.

If we are to talk of the origin, the genealogy of the people of Platonov, then we should probably begin like this. In any country's history, but in Russia's especially, the contrast between the worldly life and life in God is stark. Although there is no insuperable wall between them (they are more like connecting vessels), they are inhabited by two utterly different peoples, though among both, of course, there are many waverers. Dreadful calamities—catastrophic events, famines, hostile invasions—drive them with astonishing force out of their ordinary life (which collapses there and then with all its culture, its rules and customs) into the midst of the people that is turned toward the End, toward the last days and the Last Judgment. The people that has lived from the beginning of time in such a way as to be ready at any moment to come before the Lord. Periods of long and stable calm, on the other hand, bring nearly everyone back to the life that we are used to considering normal. In 1917, in a country ravaged by the First World War, one people went over to the other, assuring the Bolsheviks of their victory. In general, for all those we might call "the people of faith" (the people that interests Platonov), reality is a small, restless float bobbing on the surface of the water, when it should be clear to all that what really matters is the fish that has just swum up to the bait and has either already taken it and swallowed the hook, or is still sizing it up.

An example: in the history we are used to, Peter the Great—the most important character in Platonov's story "The Locks of Epifan"—stands for victories on land and sea, the reform of the machinery of state, the Treaty of Nystad; and in this roll call of momentous events the shaving of beards is just a trivial episode in the struggle with traditional Russian backwardness. For "the people of faith" it's all the other way around: in their world, Peter's decree means that humankind, which was created in the image and likeness of God, is now severing all ties with the Almighty and doing all it can to resemble Satan. The same goes for the Russo-Japanese War, with which our catastrophic twentieth century began. For the "people of faith" it's not so important who exactly the Japanese are, where they live and how. It knows almost nothing about the sinking of the *Varyag* or the surrender of Port Arthur, but what it does understand, clearly and precisely, is that the Orthodox kingdom is suffering defeat, which means that the Lord has turned His back on His chosen people and the Antichrist is already here, on the threshold. In other words, completely different events and details matter to Platonov's characters, and this is the case whatever he happens to be writing, be it in the genre of tragedy or the absurd.

In September 2004 I took part in a conference devoted to Andrey Platonov, and predominantly to *Chevengur*. What I heard there, along with what I read in the new collected works (which included Platonov's journalism of the 1920s, with detailed and expert commentary) and in the corresponding issue of the journal *Strana filosofov* ("Country of Philosophers") combined unexpectedly easily with ideas about Russian history that had been brewing in my mind some twenty years earlier, when I was still a historian by profession.[2] A great deal was filled out and completed, and it began to seem that a coherent explanation of both the personal fate of Andrey Platonov and the fate of his people had now become possible.

The root of the people of Andrey Platonov is truly ancient. It's no secret that Christianity, in the form in which it entered our world, was a religion of the End. The first generations of Christians, seeing that the cup of human sins had long been running over, believed that

Christ would set foot on earth for a second time during their own lifetimes, that they themselves would witness the Last Judgment and the triumph of the righteous. Then, over centuries, although most people resigned themselves little by little to the fact that nobody was granted knowledge of the hour of His next appearance—the Lord moves in mysterious ways—this original faith, having been driven below ground, kept bursting forth, not least in Russia.

The fifteenth century witnessed several events of importance to our story, above all Moscow's refusal to ratify the union of the Catholic and Orthodox churches that had been proclaimed at the Council of Ferrara-Florence in 1439 and supported by Isidore, Metropolitan of Kyiv and all Rus. Then came the taking of Constantinople, capital of Orthodoxy, by the Turks, and the liberation of Muscovy from the Tatar-Mongol yoke. Under the influence of these events, Rus reconsidered the entire spectrum of its relations with the world. Church writers saw in them clear and certain evidence that Christ really had turned His face toward the descendants of Adam, who were drowning in sin and suffering. With ever greater insistence they told the Muscovite princes that it was they, the princes, who were destined to lead the crusade of the forces of good, to play the main role in saving and spreading the true faith.

On the one hand, this was a gaze manifestly turned toward the End. On the other, it exalted to the very heavens, to the Lord's own throne, both the Russian land—the new Holy Land—and the Russian people, the only independent people to have retained the true faith, the new people of God. It also exalted the Russian tsars, His deputies on earth.

The country accepted this readily and instantly, perhaps because, lost among the forests and marshes of the enormous East European Plain and virtually cut off under the Tatars from the rest of the world, Rus itself felt like a monk living apart from his brethren. The doctrine known as "Moscow, the Third Rome," with its insistence that this Rome was the last, that with it all earthly life would also end, derived from a sense of abandonment and loneliness; from the fact that no compromises with the surrounding world were needed; and from the conviction that there was and could be no other world, or at least no world that was right and pleasing to God.[3]

This understanding of itself and its mission allowed the country to live in relative harmony for almost a century and a half, and to restore the tsardom more or less unscathed after the Time of Troubles. But in the mid-seventeenth century, due to the liturgical innovations of Patriarch Nikon, the Russian church broke in two, and this schism, as it became known, was soon followed by the schism of the entire Russian social order.

In its depth and consequences this trauma proved more terrible than even the Tatar yoke. In the years that followed attempts were made on both sides to heal the wound, but there was either a lack of patience and tolerance on the part of Nikonians and Old Believers alike, or else they had grown too far apart in their understanding of the world—either way, the rupture could no longer be repaired. Worse still, the official church proclaimed the Old Believers heretics and schismatics, while among Old Believers themselves the conviction began to spread ever more widely that neither the realm nor the church enjoyed the Lord's blessing and that Rus, the Holy Land, was being ruled by the Antichrist himself under the guise of a divinely chosen tsar. (The Antichrist, after all, is meant to seize power during the last days, just before the coming of the Savior, and to seduce a great many and lead them astray.)

Trying to save themselves and their loved ones from sin, the Old Believers went off into the forests or fled to the remotest peripheries, or even, if they had to, beyond the borders of the state. When Power caught up with them all the same and they saw that evil was everywhere and no help would come their way, these heterodox people would often set fire to themselves and turn their huts into coffins, determined as they were to come before the Lord unstained and clothed in white. Entire villages, from elderly men to newborn infants, went up in flames to the greater glory of God.

It's happened often in our history that even for ordinary people who usually followed the tsar, the burdens imposed by the demands of endless new wars became too much to bear and they, too, began to think that under a true tsar life on earth could not be so unjust and so awful. And then the number of those who had given up waiting for the Kingdom of God multiplied beyond measure, and civil wars set in. They rarely lasted long but they were cruel and bloody to the point of insanity (the rebellions and uprisings led by Razin, Bulavin, Pugachov).

Until 1917, it was always the tsar, and those loyal to him, who eventually came out on top.

Returning to the shared life of the two peoples, we should note that even in relatively calm years the relations and internal boundaries between them were extremely unstable, uneasy, and fluid. That they feared each other and did not understand each other is beyond question. At times the country was as tense as the Holy Land on the eve of the Savior's coming. The most vehement proponents of the other, radiant kingdom were either put to death by Power or forced out to the peripheries, where they gradually put down roots. They became quiet and secretive, but their refuges, which they called ships—the arks on which the righteous saved their souls—were steered as expertly as any modern squadron. Later on, all this would be repeated by the revolutionary cells of the People's Will and of the Social Democratic Labor Party.

Up until the middle of the nineteenth century, when Russia definitively came out of the shadows and saw the big world in all its complexity, it was still possible to believe that everything around her, beyond her borders, was an illusion, a phantom. Far more terrible, though, was the shock of seeing that other nations were not at all prepared to acknowledge her as their leader and teacher. The military failures that soon followed—first and foremost, the Crimean War—merely confirmed that the sense of rightfulness, before oneself and before God, which had been granted to the people three centuries earlier was on the wane. In this crisis the Slavophiles blamed Peter, who had razed traditional culture to the ground almost wholesale and who had indiscriminately imported a slew of Western novelties, the sole legacy of which, for ordinary Russians, was an inferiority complex. But whomever you blamed, the basic reality remained the same.

The philosopher Nikolai Fyodorov, who, just like Andrey Platonov, lived for many years in the town of Voronezh, began writing soon after the Crimean War, when society was trying to make sense of what had just happened. He was among the first to grasp that the old foundation of the Russian state order had cracked and could no longer bear the load. The splitting of the Holy People, the different ways in which it understood where the country ought to go and how, were too far advanced and its energy was lost. It was then that Fyodorov, by supplying a new commentary, as it were, to the Gospels of Christ, succeeded, if only on paper, in overcoming this schism and knitting the two hostile factions—imperial and popular-sectarian—back together. It was his *Common Task* that joined them.

By not just preserving but radically strengthening both interpretations of Moscow as the Third Rome, Fyodorov found the point at which they finally converged. He showed Supreme Power the path by which it could find, reclaim, and reaffirm its right to exist—namely, its unbreakable bond with the Lord. Showed it the path by which, in a matter of years, it would annihilate its external enemies and haters one by one, including even the worst schemer of all—England. In other words, the most important thing would come to pass: the entire earth would become the appanage of the Russian tsar and thus be transformed, in the blink of an eye, into an indivisible Holy Land, just as it was before the Fall and the expulsion of Adam from paradise. Fyodorov also indicated the means to achieve this.

Fyodorov, who undoubtedly exerted an immense influence on Andrey Platonov, saw that Power was weary beyond measure, that it was barely coping with its own independent and permanently disgruntled servitors, with a countryside ready to rise up at a moment's notice, with the muffled dissatisfaction of the townsfolk; that it had been worn down by constant resistance from the peripheries—whether in Poland, Finland, or the recently annexed Turkestan. Its strength had been sapped by life's complexity, by the futility of its attempts to find some way of harmonizing and reconciling the interests of its subjects, so incorrigibly unalike. It was this and not the discharging of its fundamental mission—the conquest of chunk after chunk of secular land and its transformation into Holy Land—that consumed Power's energy and resources.

Fyodorov was ready, in one fell swoop, to help Power deal with all its woes. All that was needed, he said, was to turn everybody, without exception—regardless of rank, title, and status; of social origin, creed, and blood; of education and disposition—into soldier-plowmen.[4] To give them the same clothes and shoes, the same orders, which would be carried out in the same way, to the letter, and then this numberless host would vanquish any conceivable adversary. Even the devil, even human sin, would give way to it, and equality and justice would reign on earth once more, just as the Lord had commanded.

He offered no less to the peasants, the empire's innumerable soldiers of the future. He told them that droughts and poor harvests, hunger and epidemics, had nothing to do with bad luck, that the root of all misfortune lay far deeper: in the imperfection of the world that God had made and bequeathed to humankind. His words served, among other things, to exonerate the human race, to cleanse it of sin. For the earth to be made viable for life, radical reconstruction was needed. This Fyodorovan idea, which might well have occurred to Platonov in any case, was affirmed and borne out for him by his own work in land reclamation in the provinces and by his despair in the face of the famines and droughts that recurred every four years, with machinelike regularity, in the Black Earth and Volga regions.

Equally essential, Fyodorov continued, was the just repartitioning of everything. Isn't it obvious that if a man looks at a high, majestic mountain and sees, at its foot, boggy lowland teeming with vermin, and if he knows that both the mountain and the bog are the handiwork of one and the same Being, he will think it inevitable that the world contains some important, highly placed people and others who, like himself, belong to the class of the lowly and the "base"? Not even those living in neighboring log huts are equal: some have children you can't take your eyes off—strong, clever, beautiful—while others have weedy runts and fools. How could anyone think of describing the created world as orderly and rational when even the rivers flow whichever way they fancy: east for a bit, then, a few hundred versts later, a sudden turn to the south, not to mention their constant meandering. And then there's the water itself: after the spring floods it rises above your roof, while in summer, when the earth is parched and cracked, it barely reaches your knee and you can get across wherever you like.

So Fyodorov said: How can nature be corrected—and not just any old how, but properly, scientifically? His answer: raze mountains to the ground and use the extra rock to fill in ravines, hollows, and swamps so that the entire earth becomes one single, flat, easily tilled field. And so that every plot of land receives the same amount of moisture as every other, the rivers should be transformed into a regular grid of canals covering countries and continents. If, after all this, water is still lacking, the army should be ordered to direct round after round of cannon fire at the sky. Not, as some fools might think, to frighten the Lord, but for strictly scientific reasons. Back in the time of the Napoleonic Wars, many had noticed that after big battles, when cannons had thundered all day and all night, you could always count on rain.

Above all, of course, Fyodorov was addressing those who had been waiting for the Savior and His Kingdom for so long that they had no strength left. He told them—and verily these were glad tidings—that there was no longer any need to try to hurry anything or anybody up: humankind could and should build the Kingdom of God on its own. And not in the sky, but in the middle of this ocean of sin; in other words, right here on earth. Humankind really was capable of this. It had been granted not just the ability to correct the life it was living, it had also received the blessing of the One Who had gone to the cross for all our sakes to resurrect every person who had lived on earth since the time of Adam.

Platonov fully aligned himself with the hopes that Fyodorov had placed in humanity, but the view he took of them was far more tragic. Fyodorov's plan for the salvation of man by man is mild and almost painless. Platonov's experience, on the other hand—revolution, War Communism, civil war—left him with little reason to expect salvation without suffering and pain. Without death and the Last Judgment that man also passes on man. "We will surrender our own selves to the world," Platonov writes of eternal life, "for it to tear us asunder in the name of its aims. And its aims (this is clear now) are the creation of an immortal humanity with a marvelous single rational soul and, through humanity, the creation of a new, omniscient being that is still unknown but will be even mightier than man."[5]

Where should man begin? Above all, Fyodorov thought, by renouncing the family and, for that matter, all sexual intercourse with women. And not even because of lust or the suffering, pain, and torment with which the Lord punished our foremother Eve and all Eve's daughters. It was simply the fact that woman, by giving birth to a child, gives birth to a new sinner and, by multiplying sin, leads the human race farther and farther from God. This road had to be abandoned once and for all. It was time to choose the good, to turn back and finally begin walking once more not away from the Lord but toward Him.

Fyodorov's solution was a stroke of genius that managed to combine God and earthly human life. This released a sea of energy, an astonishing surge of enthusiasm by which the country lived and nourished itself for almost a century. Fyodorov is the magic key by which we can understand both the life that Russia had already lived and the fate that lay before it. Perhaps no one has ever set out the totality of Russia's conceptions of itself more clearly and more fully than Fyodorov in his *Philosophy of the Common Task*: conceptions of its history, the paths it should follow, and—above all—the destiny, the mission, that had been imposed on it. Before continuing, though, we should note that there were never actually many true, "all-out" Fyodorovans. But those who counted him among their teachers included some of the standard-bearers of Russian culture: Tolstoy, Dostoevsky, Soloviov, Bogdanov, Khlebnikov, Mayakovsky, Filonov, Tsiolkovsky, and others. There's no doubt that through them Fyodorov's ideas spread far and wide.

We will never understand the victory of the Bolsheviks unless we take into account the belief, from one end of the country to the other, that the old life had to be done away with once and for all, it was just too terrible. That human beings could and should destroy the previous world themselves, that it was up to them to clear the rubble and begin the creation of a new world. The belief that it was possible—soon, right here on earth—to establish full justice and equality, to build heaven and lengthen life so much that it became eternal and the dead would be resurrected. That people could be educated in such a way that they would all become true geniuses, thereby accelerating the march of progress. That the climate could be entirely changed to humanity's maximal benefit. (It was with this in mind, for example, that Andrey Platonov proposed that humans themselves alter the direction of the wind in Eastern Siberia, so as to warm the land there and render it suitable for farming.) That in future wars no human blood would be spilled; instead, we would rout the enemy with the help of ultrasound signals or even hypnosis.

The Russian understanding of the purpose of life, derived from the fifteenth century, was renewed and strengthened in equal parts by the teaching of Fyodorov, who said that the reunited Holy People could save the entire human race without Christ's help, and by communism, with its notion of a global proletarian state and the building of heaven on earth. That is to say, in a country entirely founded on the faith that the ordinary, earthly life of humankind was just about to end (this was unavoidable, good, and right), on a readiness to beg the Lord day and night not to prolong this life, and on a willingness to accept with joy any suffering, any torment—in such a country, revolution could not fail to happen. Maybe sooner, maybe later, but happen it would. Its unconditional necessity was written into the very statutes of the Russian state order.

After 1917, it took Russia almost another decade to decide once and for all on the path it would follow. In general, though, no magnifying glass is needed to discern the eschatological character of the communism that triumphed in the Civil War. It is present in the beliefs in a beautiful world without evil, and above all in the conviction of the first generation of Communist leaders that a Soviet republic surrounded by hostile capitalist states would not survive. Hence Trotsky's "permanent revolution." This idea more or less suggested itself: after all, nobody could imagine two neighboring kingdoms—one of goodness and happiness, the other of evil and sin—living at peace.

Nor, two decades before Trotsky, could Fyodorov. Permanent war that would last until the definitive triumph of the kingdom of good (Russia) is one of the key ideas of his *Common Task*. Astonishing parallels with the first years of Bolshevik rule—for example, War Communism (both as it actually occurred and as it was dreamed of by philosophers close to the Communist Party such as Bogdanov and Gastev)—can also be found in many of Fyodorov's conceptions of a radiant kingdom: the almost total militarization of the population, the brutal attempts to level it out (the requisitioning of food, ration cards, the shooting on the spot of black marketeers) and, flying in the face of all Marxist principles, the decline and dying out of towns, the closure of factories and manufacturing plants, and the return of workers, townspeople, and bureaucrats to the countryside, to take up farming and horticulture. And, alongside all this, ecstatic debate about the vital questions of Being: what the new Soviet person should be like and what kind of education would be needed to achieve this; how the soil and climate should be corrected so as to make the entire planet fit for human habitation. What needed to be done not just to prolong human life, but also to rid us of death. How to resurrect those who had died before the triumph of communism.

There's no doubt that Fyodorov sincerely considered himself an Orthodox Christian. But even the Communists' policies toward the church all but followed from his teachings. True, in Fyodorov we find that God (and God's help) is rejected in the name of God, but even so, this is the start of the removal of the Lord from our world, when even the resurrection of the dead is withdrawn from His jurisdiction. The energetic, optimistic atheism of the Bolsheviks, therefore, can be traced not only to Marx but also, with equal justification, to Fyodorov's *Philosophy of the Common Task*. After all, if there's no longer any need to wait for Christ, if God has already given us everything we need for the salvation of the human race—the rest we can and should do ourselves, with our own hands—then why bother going to church at all, why keep on begging for this or that? We must work, day and night, and not wait for favors, whether from God or nature.

The first generation of Communist leaders was a generation of doctrinaires and dogmatists. They had spent the greater part of their lives writing articles and debating the tenets of Marxism. To admit in public that the Revolution had, in Marxist terms, taken place in the wrong place and at the wrong time, and that it was heading in the wrong direction, would have been to condemn themselves as "revisionists"—a terrible accusation in their milieu. The hopelessness with which they took to their graves one by one can be explained precisely by their loss of a sense of rightfulness. The end that awaited them was the fate of the apostles of Platonov's *Chevengur*: having killed all the unrighteous, and then their families, they saw that, though the world had been cleansed, the kingdom of God had not arrived, so now they allowed themselves, too, to be killed. True, in 1930 Platonov still thought that they wouldn't give up just like that, without a fight, but in the end Lenin's brothers-in-arms, like the tsar before them and Gorbachev's Politburo much later, simply threw up their hands and Power fell out of them, all on its own.

There's one last thing to add, especially in relation to Andrey Platonov. As a young man, I heard plenty of stories about the Stalin era, and I was always struck by the frequency with which the words *jolly* and *happy* appeared in them. I couldn't understand how people who had lived back then could speak, as if echoing Platonov's characters, about their faith, their fervor, sincerity, enthusiasm. After all, almost every family could count at least one person who had been repressed, and every fifth storyteller had probably experienced the same fate themselves. They'd be talking about the fear that no one could escape, about their own fear of arrest and how it kept them out of bed until dawn, and then, in the next sentence, they would speak about joy and lives lived to the full. And there was something else I couldn't get my head around: How did a people that had lost millions of lives on the front lines of the First World War—a people so exhausted by the trenches that in 1917 it couldn't take any more and, abandoning its positions, fled in droves to the rear, to its home—how did it suddenly find the strength to fight a savage civil war, to survive collectivization and the famine in Ukraine? And then, despite the endless executions and imprisonments, to find the will to build thousands of plants, factories, power stations, to defeat Nazi Germany and then not just restore the country but place a good half of the globe under its control in one form or another?

This enthusiasm, of course, might have been no more than a life buoy, a mask that shouted for all to hear: "I'm one of you, I can be trusted, I'll fight our corner to my dying breath"—but I think it was genuine. And it came from Fyodorov. From the faith that he had restored to Russian life that we were going where we were meant to be going. It was a priceless feeling, one that nobody was prepared to renounce. People accepted any quantity of victims, any quantity of innocent people killed right next to them, joyously agreed to know nothing about them, to hear nothing, just so long as they did not lose that faith again.

The fate of Fyodorov's gift, the last traces of which coincided with my own lifetime, is a tragic and desperate story. In my view, the main addressees of Fyodorov's *Philosophy of the Common Task* were precisely the people who became Andrey Platonov's characters; it was they who became the mycelium, the incubator of all this joy, enthusiasm, strength. They lived by this faith in the radiant kingdom until Stalin managed to seize everything they had nurtured and brought into the world. Soon they were slaughtered almost wholesale, but he grafted their faith and joy onto the tree of the Russian empire and used them, as if they were his own, for almost another three decades, primarily for evil purposes.

The anthropology of the people of Andrey Platonov cannot, of course, be reduced to Fyodorov's influence alone. Yes, the reasons for which this people suffers and languishes, for which it goes without a second thought to its own death, have their roots largely in Russian history and in holy scripture, but there is a great deal else that must be mentioned, at least in outline. In the nineteenth and early twentieth centuries in Russia, even the better restaurants would serve so-called *vzvar* in the mornings. After the establishment closed for the day, the leftovers of all the meat dishes would be tipped out of drip pans and frying pans, gravy boats, saucepans, and sometimes even plates, into a single pot, which would be shoved into the stove for the night. The resulting brew could put you back on your feet even after the most punishing drinking bout. The country described by Andrey Platonov reproduces this recipe unswervingly. We find in the pot a vast quantity of the most varied faiths and meanings, ideas and conceptions of truth, the universe, the essence and purpose of human life—everything, in other words, that people had thought about for the previous two thousand years. In this brew, heated to boiling point, the terrifying tension of the approaching end shatters the sturdiest barriers, taboos, and partitions: nobody knows any more what's theirs and what isn't, everything copulates shamelessly with everything else, and the thing that eventually emerges from this womb is often so horrifying that you can't help shivering.

As with any people in its last days, Platonov's characters reject ever more decisively the usual mode of prolonging themselves and their kin. This is no longer a country of children—it takes too long to bring them to term and bring them up, they die far too easily from hunger, cold, sickness—but a country of ideas. Correspondingly, the place of children is taken by the thousand-strong crowds of disciples who have left the home where they were born, grown up, abandoned their families, and, free of all doubts, are following their prophets and teachers.

It is a country of philosophers and dreamers who teach that, as in the first days of Creation, there is no difference between man and beast: all suffer the same agonies and pain. (In *The Foundation Pit* Mikhail Medvedev is a proletarian bear, a blacksmith's striker who possesses a bestial ability to sniff out class and unerringly exposes all the kulaks in the village.) What is more, this is a country that thinks of both the earth and machines as living creatures, and feels and understands them as such. (See Platonov's story "In the Beautiful and Savage World.") A world, in short, where everything is kin. Not only that: following Vladimir Vernadsky and his doctrine of the noosphere, the people of Platonov is convinced that, from the top layer of the earth to all that lies on the earth, and even to the air above the earth, we are a single organism.

It is a country of science and communism, where work will be an entirely voluntary activity and only the sun will labor on behalf of human beings (*Chevengur*), where not only people but also animals will live in eternity, which is why their most easily frayed and worn-out parts are replaced with metal substitutes. The main thing, though, is that this people, which only recently had been unable (and even, as John the Apostle says, could not hope) to distinguish the Savior from the Antichrist and, for that reason, was ready to be burned alive to preserve its soul, has seen the light and finally gained the truth.

But the happiness of Platonov's heroes rarely lasts long, because this endlessly attractive, just, and rational brotherhood, and the very possibility of humans themselves resurrecting other human beings, suddenly begin to teem with terrible consequences.

If evil is reversible and death is not eternal, then to kill those who are stopping us from building an earthly paradise for the people, in the quickest and easiest way possible, is no sin; and later, nothing will stop us restoring what we took away—by resurrecting the dead for life together in pastures green. Something similar applies to the noosphere as well. Here, too, the murder of man by man is no sin: we are, after all, part of a single universal organism in which cells that are harmful and sick are killed and consumed for the common good by those that are healthy and useful. In 1920 Platonov evidently considered the creation of this universal organism to be the Revolution's most pressing task. "The task of the Social Communist Revolution," he writes in one of his articles, "is to destroy the individual and to beget by its death a new living and powerful creature—society, the collective, one united organism of the earth's surface, one fighter, one fist against nature."[6]

Needless to say, the survival of this creature, like that of any other, depends on the most ruthless specialization: it's hard to run with the same cells that you use for breathing, or to digest your food with the cells you need to look at the world. In Platonov's articles of the early

1920s this theme crops up time and again. He writes (in the vein of Alexei Gastev and H. G. Wells):

> The creation through appropriate education of strictly defined types of workers.
>
> From their first breath two children should live in the different conditions that correspond to the aims for which society intends them. If one child will grow up to be a civil engineer, and the other to be an aircraft mechanic, then their education should also correspond to these aims, so that the mechanic among his engines feels as happy in his own specific labor production process as in a well-fitting shirt. So that, in other words, he can maintain his own organic norm and be in psychophysiological harmony with his external environment. Therefore, the solution to the question of the labor normalization of society's members lies in their purposive education, in the artificial alteration of characters in accordance with the production aims of society.[7]

I should mention at this point that in his many articles, unlike in his fiction, Platonov is of course both a Fyodorovist and an ultra-Communist. He is honest in both genres; it's just that in his journalism he had no need to negotiate with his characters. In good prose fiction, after all, the author is never in charge—only the people he writes into his books have a say there. The truth of life is on their side alone, and authors who are not prepared to admit this—who think they have the right to dictate what their characters should think and do, how they should understand the life around them and their own fate—will never write a truthful book.

The language of Platonov's prose is probably the sincerest and most impartial witness of the kind of revolution he was waiting for and that he joined with such joy. From the outside it often seems that authors exert absolute power not only over their characters but also over all the words in the language, of which they can freely avail themselves without asking anybody's permission. The reality, however, is that here, too, we are kept firmly in line almost from our swaddling days. From our first year at school, under threat of low grades and parental summons, people teach us the rules of grammar and the many restrictions associated with the various literary styles, with the fact that the spoken word is far from equal to the written. It's hammered into us that just because some people are allowed to say certain things, it doesn't mean everybody can, and the things that can be said in some circumstances will hardly be suitable in all. Having myself been punished a thousand times for neglecting these rules when at school and during my attempt to enter university, I am perfectly aware of how effective and cruel such taboos can be.

Some were described and formalized a long time ago, ended up in textbooks and became their foundation; others are still wandering at large. Even so, when one word ends up next to another, we can usually judge whether the effect is seemly. That is, language consists of a multitude of intersecting dictionaries, and when we think, talk, and write, we can only use words from a single one of them, and certainly not from the entire language. Because of these constraints, the quantity of words available to us in any given instance is reduced many times over; and for speech to sound fresh, talent or even genius is required. We commit these well-assembled words to memory and repeat them to each other with joy. Literary and linguistic norms also change, of course, but on the whole they are far more conservative than life. In any society they are a bulwark of stability.

It goes without saying that the Bolsheviks, like any new elite, sought to shore up their rights and privileges. To do so, they not only had to seize bridges, banks, and the telegraph exchange, they also had to create a distinct language—the first external border between themselves and the rest of the world. This was how, before the introduction of any credentials, certificates, or permits, you could identify who was with you and who was against you. In this new language, born just yesterday, words had not yet been rolled smooth. No one had managed to put any makeup on them, to touch them up with the suffixes, prefixes, and endings needed for them to resemble, however distantly, the Russian everyone knew. Nobody had had the chance to explain to these newcomers that it would be a good idea, if only as a matter of courtesy, for them to doff their caps to the old indigenous words. And so, having ended up in someone else's home, the newcomers, not through malice but through their ignorance of the house rules and their inability to adapt and fit in, start breaking and smashing all conventions and norms.

It's generally thought that it is precisely the widespread use of these uncut, alien-sounding words that makes Platonov's prose so unlike that of his contemporaries. It seems to me, though, that two other things play a larger role here. First, Platonov fearlessly joins together words from very distant dictionaries. It's all still Russian—there's no hint of Newspeak—it's just that we aren't accustomed to using one and the same words to describe both the subtlest, most ephemeral matters, the sufferings of the human soul, and things as coarse and material as the functioning of various machines and mechanisms. At the root of the very possibility and naturalness of such speech is Platonov's conviction that no boundary exists between man and beast, or between the animate and the inanimate: everything that moves and labors is alive and can turn to the Lord with confidence.

But the main thing that rips grammar apart in Platonov's texts is, in my view, the year 1917—a time of meanings and faiths. Their pressure, their density, are what produced Platonov's phrases. Meanings did not just trample each other underfoot, they destroyed the etiquette that had previously been observed among words. The sheer concentration of meaning was such that, without even noticing, almost en passant, it annihilated literature as a refined art, destroyed the rules and laws by which that literature had lived. If anything, Platonov's prose is closer to homily, and not ordinary sermons, but the kind that are preached in the last days. Which, incidentally, is why his characters are so chaste, so ascetic. Ordinary prose requires gaps and air, or else the words themselves will suffocate, but a sentence by Platonov is entirely made up of hope and expectancy, it is literally choking on them, because the wait is very nearly over and there are still so many important, decisive things that must be said in order to help all those who can still be saved to save themselves.

I read *The Foundation Pit* while I was still at school, but both then and now, forty years later, I doubt there is a single book, other than *Chevengur*, that testifies with such clarity to the fact that communism, even in its purest, most childlike, and naive guise, leads to evil. Power understood this no worse than I did, and only at its last gasp, having lost all interest in life, did it sanction the publication of both works.

At the same time, whenever I reread Platonov, I can't get away from the thought that he was—and I don't know how else to put it—either the prophet of this massive wave bringing a new understanding of the world, an understanding of what is good and what is bad, and how one should live in this world in order to please God, or the first authentic person of that new world.

At times his biography can seem almost fake: you could not find a more precise illustration of what the ideal Soviet person and the ideal proletarian writer were meant to be. Background: working class, son of a railway mechanic. Interests and occupations, aside from literary work (following the typical 1920s view that an actress should spend the first half of the day at the loom and go off to perform only in the evening): railway depot worker, irrigation engineer (digging wells, but also inventing new ways of boring holes into the earth), land-reclamation specialist, developer of new hydraulic and steam turbines. It's as if Platonov were a sort of sanction for the existence of the entire Soviet order, made it possible and lawful. He had a gift, a magic wand, that justified every Soviet absurdity, such as the trains stuffed to the gills with writers that, on the party's instructions, hurtled now to Siberia, now to various Komsomol building projects. Platonov also traveled on these trains (in Central Asia), with the result that he alone produced a book of genius (*Soul*) instead of the expected hackwork.[8]

It seems that inside the entire popular movement that overthrew the monarchy in 1917 lay enormous reserves of inner justice and truth ("The Revolution was conceived in dreams and carried out in order to fulfill those things that, more than any other, had never been realized").[9] Then, under the Bolsheviks, these reserves began to be squandered with pitiless speed, and the moment when Platonov and Soviet power separated was, in my view, the moment when whatever truth remained in Soviet power ran out.

As we know, Power took this "divorce" in its stride, but for Platonov it was an inconceivable tragedy, and for a long time he carried on trying to persuade and deceive himself that the truth was still there, that it hadn't all vanished: "I am so desperate to write artistically, with clarity, feeling, and class loyalty!"[10]

The denouement, both for Platonov and for the people of Platonov, was despair. Soviet power's last dregs of justice and truth were long gone, and a broken Platonov concluded:

> Imagine if my brother Mitya or Nadya, twenty-one years after their deaths, were to come out of their graves as adolescents, as they were when they died—and look at me. What's happened to me? I've become a monstrosity, mutilated inside and out.
>
> "Andriusha, is that really you?"
>
> "It's me: I've lived a life."[11]

—Vladimir Sharov

translated from the Russian by Oliver Ready

TRANSLATING PLATONOV

THE LAST few hundred years have seen two great Russian revolutions, two revolts against Russia's seemingly fated role of being a backward despotism. The first began with Patriarch Nikon's church reforms (1653–66) and was continued in the following century by Peter the Great. Saint Petersburg was the symbol of this revolution and Pushkin was its bard. Pushkin, however, does not merely celebrate Petersburg; he also lays bare its paradox: it is a city not only of light and harmony but also of darkness and tyranny, a city founded on marshland subject to terrible flooding and therefore fated to crush the lives of its inhabitants. As Pushkin makes clear, Peter the Great was a man of immense and perverse will; no one less willful would have dreamed of building a capital on such an unsuitable site.

Pushkin's ambivalence about Petersburg reflects an important truth about the revolution it symbolizes: that in their zeal to modernize, Nikon and Peter created a schism in the national psyche. Everyone who opposed Nikon's reforms was anathematized; the enormity of this trauma is hard to imagine. A huge number of people were left permanently alienated from both church and state; it seems likely that, by the early twentieth century, as much as one-fifth of the Russian population may have been Old Believers. As a result of this alienation, the apparatus of the state became still more repressive, thus further reinforcing the country's general backwardness.

All this led to a second Russian revolution, which climaxed in October 1917 and can best be seen as a vast, spontaneous popular uprising that the Bolsheviks, perhaps somewhat surprisingly, managed to hijack. It was a revolt of those who had been dispossessed not only of power and property but even of their religion and their national myth. It was an assertion of suppressed Russianness, an attempt by only slightly remodeled Old Believers to establish a kingdom of heaven on earth. And just as Pushkin was the bard of aristocratic Petersburg, so Platonov became the unacknowledged bard of the workers and peasants of Central Russia.

Scholars have proposed many different explanations for Platonov's choice of the name "Chevengur" ("Cheh-ven-*goor*"—with the stress falling on the final syllable). One of the most plausible is that—in Russian, at least—it closely echoes the name "Petersburg" in both vowel sounds and rhythm. Andrey Bely had evoked the 1905 revolution in his novel *Petersburg*. *Chevengur*, an evocation of the 1917 revolution in the remote steppe, can be seen as a counterpart to Bely's novel. Elena Tolstaya—one of the most perceptive of Platonov scholars—writes, "Chevengur is the absolute ideological antipode of Petersburg: an anticity, an antistate, the victory of the element of formlessness, the Asiatic element on which 'rational,' 'European,' 'historical' Petersburg tried to impose its will. And the sound-image *Chevengur* is as if cast from *Petersburg*—a replica of the name in Turkish, Asiatic sound matter."[1] It is also significant—as Eric Naiman has pointed out—that Platonov would probably have known that *gur* is the Farsi word for "grave."[2]

Pushkin sought balance and clarity; Platonov seems to have reveled in exposing the absurdities of the language of his time. Pushkin established a language that is clear and sophisticated, yet close to colloquial speech; Platonov reflects the chaos of his times by creating a language that is an incongruous blend of opposites: of the metaphysical and the absurdly concrete, of the religious and the political, of the colloquial and the bureaucratic. Platonov's characters are not at home in language. They repeatedly stumble, caught between the down-to-earth speech of the Russian village and the Sovietspeak being imposed on them through newspapers, political meetings, and incomprehensible party directives.

Platonov's world is a world without boundaries. In *Chevengur*, boundaries have collapsed because the world of the past has been turned upside down; in works written during the apparently more stable mid-1930s they have collapsed because every area of human existence has come to be informed by the same ideology. In both cases, this dissolution of boundaries is embodied in the syntax of almost every sentence.

Throughout much of the novel, there is little distinction between the narrator's thoughts and the thoughts of the individual characters. The Russian scholar Yevgeny Yablokov writes, "The element of free indirect speech is so powerful that the narrator appears ready to agree with any point of view, ready to assimilate anyone's words and make them his own."[3] This makes it hard for readers to sense where Platonov stands in relation to a particular political or philosophical issue, or to a conflict between his characters. Sometimes Platonov evokes both the beauty and the horror of the Communist dream in a single sentence, not allowing either to outweigh the other. The late Mikhail Geller described one of the most memorable scenes in *Chevengur*, the account of the execution of the bourgeoisie, as "a nightmarish spectacle of a Last Judgment, where the writer feels himself to be both executioner and victim, the killer and the killed."[4]

For all Platonov's vivid evocation of sensory detail, there is much in the novel that is elusive and dreamlike. In the first paragraph of one chapter we read, "The Revolution had won dreams for the district of Chevengur, and the main profession there was now the soul." It is unclear whether the Revolution has won people their heartfelt desires, or whether it is a mirage, and the inhabitants of Chevengur, deprived of food and work, will soon be mere disembodied souls. The word *dream* has itself cast off any clear meaning—as has the word *communism*, which the protagonists understand in a huge number of different and contradictory ways.

There is a similar elusiveness at the level of syntax. In the first chapter, for example, we are told that the loner had been waiting all his life "for something finally to emerge from the world's turmoil, so he could begin to act after a general calming and clarification." Platonov leaves it open whether this "calming and clarification" might occur spontaneously or whether it might be brought about by people's conscious activity. Reproducing this ambiguity in English proved difficult. Our first version was "after the world had calmed down and cleared up"—but this sounds, all too definitely, as if the world is changing of its own accord, not as a result of human intervention.

Platonov's characteristic ambiguities are especially pronounced in the novel's last chapters. A cavalry detachment referred to as a "machinelike enemy" attacks Chevengur. The Chevengurians refer to these cavalrymen as "brigands," "Cossacks," and "Cadets," but they may be refusing to acknowledge an unpalatable truth: The Civil War is over. There is no longer a White Army and there are no longer Cossacks fighting for their independence. The enemy may well be a Red Army detachment dispatched from the provincial capital in response to Serbinov's critical report about Chevengur.

After the destruction of Chevengur, Sasha rides to Lake Mutevo. Platonov tells us that "without farewell, continuing his own life, Sasha got down from the saddle and into the water—in search of the path along which his father had once passed in inquisitiveness of death." Here, the crucial words are "continuing his own life." Does this mean that Sasha is continuing along a suicidal path he has been treading since childhood, following his father's example? Or is it that the fertile depths of Lake Mutevo will allow Sasha some kind of literal or metaphorical resurrection?

Neither of these last two instances are particularly difficult to translate. One need only understand that Platonov means what he writes and that it is not a translator's job to normalize or water down his often-startling perceptions. Many other passages, however, are more problematic.

Platonov's linguistic creativity is as remarkable as that of Mandelstam or Tsvetaeva or any other of the great poets who were his contemporaries. Generalizations about how best to translate his brilliant wordplay and powerful rhythmic effects are of little value; as with all true creativity, each instance is unique and must be considered on its own terms. All I can say is that it is important to reproduce his strangeness boldly, to make it clear to the reader that the strangeness is deliberate. Often, it is the smallest words that demand the most attention. Much of the uniqueness of Platonov's style lies in a disconcerting tendency to misalign words, to misuse words we often barely notice: prepositions, conjunctions, possessive adjectives. A particularly troublesome word for a translator is the preposition *ot*—meaning "because of"; "due to"; "from." Through unexpected use of this preposition, Platonov often insists on causality—or else appears to take it entirely for granted—where it is either inappropriate or absurdly tautological. In *The Foundation Pit*, a small girl asks her mother "Why are you dying, Mama? Is it because you're a bourgeois, or is it from [*ot*] death?"[5]

A memorable example of Platonov's genius is in the third chapter of *Chevengur*. The orphaned Sasha has been thrown out by his foster parents because there is not enough food. On his way past the cemetery he stops by his birth father's grave and says, "Father, they've made me go out begging. Soon I'll be dead with you—you must be lonely there on your own, and I'm lonely too." This is moving—but it does not live up to the original. The second sentence is composed of six short, everyday words that no other writer could have put together: *Ya teper' skoro umru k tebe*—"Soon I will die to/toward you." Sasha uses the word *die* as if it is a verb of motion; he talks of his own death as casually as if he were telling his father that he means to drop in on him the next day. But a literal translation fails, largely because of interference from idiomatic meanings of the English "die to."

Sasha infringes grammatical norms, but he speaks with a childlike directness that is entirely natural; there is no clearer way he could have said what he wanted to say. For all the subtle puns and allusions, Platonov's language does not—like the language of Joyce or Nabokov—give the impression of being self-consciously refined and elaborated. It has, rather, the power of an elemental force—a friend once described it as "the language that might be spoken by the roots of trees." Ordinary words and images, even clichés, are forced into extraordinary combinations by an intense pressure of experience. In this respect, the nearest English or American equivalent may be the poetry of Emily Dickinson.

Russians often say that Platonov is untranslatable. Obviously, I do not believe this to be the case. I would even say that Platonov's genius is so overwhelming that it is possible for an Anglophone reader to sense it immediately, after reading only a few sentences in translation. Here is a passage—translated entirely literally—from "Takyr" (1934), a short story set in Central Asia:

> Zarrin-Tadzh sat on one of the plane tree's roots. [...] and noticed that stones were growing high on the trunk. During its spring floods the river must have flung mountain stones at the very heart of the plane, but the tree had consumed these vast stones into its body, encircled them with patient bark, made them something it could live with, endured them into its own self, and gone on growing further, meekly lifting up as it grew taller what should have destroyed it.

It is unlikely that Platonov intended it as such, but this plane tree now seems like a perfect image for Platonov himself—for his tenacity as a writer and for the lasting vitality of his work. Our aim as translators is to reproduce both the life force of the tree (the energy of Platonov's thoughts, images, and rhythms) and the brute otherness of the stones (the euphemisms, the Sovietspeak, the horrors flung at Platonov and his contemporaries by Russian life during the first half of the twentieth century). Platonov's courage and endurance were unimaginable. And like the plane tree, his work was able to absorb the stones and emerge not weaker but stronger.

It is worth adding that when I read these last lines at a poetry reading, having clearly stated that they were from a prose story, at least five people thanked me for reading such a beautiful *poem*. Like a great many of the finest twentieth-century Russian prose writers—Andrey Bely, Ivan Bunin, Vladimir Nabokov, Boris Pasternak, Varlam Shalamov, Nadezhda Teffi, among others—Platonov began his writing career as a poet. Whatever he was writing—plays, critical articles, short stories, novels, or film scripts—he remained a poet throughout his life.

—Robert Chandler

November 2022

NOTES ON RUSSIAN NAMES AND THE RUSSIAN PEASANT HUT

RUSSIAN NAMES

A RUSSIAN has three names: a Christian name, a patronymic (derived from the Christian name of the father), and a family name. Thus, Mavra Fetisovna is the daughter of a man whose first name is Fetis, and Prokhor Abramovich Dvanov is the son of a man called Abram. The first name and patronymic, used together, are the usual polite way of addressing someone or referring to that person; the family name is used less often. Close friends or relatives usually address each other by one of the many diminutive, or affectionate, forms of their first names. Sonia, for example, is a diminutive of Sofia. Less obviously, Sasha is a diminutive of Alexander. Masha, Mashenka, and Marusya are all diminutives of Marya. Sometimes, two different Christian names can have the same diminutive—or diminutives; Prosha and Proshka are diminutives not only of Prokhor, but also of Prokofy.

THE RUSSIAN PEASANT HUT

In Northern and Central Russia, where wood is plentiful, the *izba*, or peasant hut, was built of logs (in the south it was of brick.) Usually it was one story high, with its floor raised two or three feet above ground level; this allowed space for a cellar beneath the hut. The hut was often surrounded by an earth ledge—heaped earth, sometimes held in by boards; this protected the hut from the wind and served as a bench during the summer.

Between the outer door or porch and the habitable room or rooms was an unheated entrance room (*seni*). This provided further insulation from the cold and could be used for storing tools and firewood or for housing animals.

Winters were long and cold; effective heating was important. A Russian stove was a large brick or clay structure taking up between one-fifth and one-quarter of the room it stood in. It was used for heating the house, for heating water, for baking bread and for all the cooking, for drying linen and foodstuffs, for conserving grain and plants, for protecting small farm animals (holes were made in its walls for them), and sometimes for taking a steam bath: when the fire had burned out a person could climb right inside the stove's mouth.

Loaves or pies to be baked were placed deep inside the stove after the fuel had burned out or been raked to the side. Soup was cooked in a large cast-iron pot.

Beds as such were rare, but several sleeping places were arranged in relation to the stove. A sleeping bench might be attached to one side of it to share its warmth; a wide shelf extended under the ceiling above it and could be slept on; and people often slept directly on the warm brick surface of the stove itself; this might be a few feet above the ground or as high as a person.

—R.C.

FURTHER READING

OTHER WORKS BY PLATONOV AVAILABLE IN ENGLISH

Robert Chandler, *Russian Magic Tales from Pushkin to Platonov* (New York: Penguin Classics, 2012). This includes Platonov's versions of six well-known Russian folktales.

Andrey Platonov, *The Foundation Pit*, trans. Robert and Elizabeth Chandler with Olga Meerson (New York: NYRB Classics, 2009).

———, *Fourteen Little Red Huts and Other Plays*, trans. Robert Chandler, Jesse Irwin, and Susan Larsen (New York: Columbia University Press, 2016).

———, *Happy Moscow*, trans. Robert and Elizabeth Chandler and others (New York: NYRB Classics, 2012).

———, *The Return and Other Stories*, trans. Robert and Elizabeth Chandler with Angela Livingstone (London: Harvill Press, 1999).

———, *The Russian Revolution Poems of Andrei Platonov*, ed. Adam Halbur and Dmitri Manin (complete original text, translation, and discussion of the poems Platonov wrote 1914–22), https://www.academia.edu/37060986/Blue_Depths?email_work_card=view-paper.

———, *Soul and Other Stories*, trans. Robert and Elizabeth Chandler with Olga Meerson et al. (New York: NYRB Classics, 2007).

RUSSIAN EDITIONS OF PLATONOV'S WORK

Arkhiv A. P. Platonova (Moscow: IMLI RAN, 2009). Material from Platonov's personal archive, including letters to his wife and early drafts of a number of works.

Arkhiv A. P. Platonova (Moscow: IMLI RAN, 2019). All the material from Platonov's archive relating to *Chevengur*. The "dynamic transcription" of the novel's complete text indicates all Platonov's changes, additions, and deletions.

Sobranie sochinenii (Moscow: Vremya, 2011). These eight volumes constitute the most complete and readily available edition of Platonov's work to date.

Sochineniia (Moscow: IMLI RAN, 2004–). A superb and scrupulously edited scholarly edition. So far, only the first four volumes have been published, covering all Platonov's work up to the early 1930s.

Ya prozhil zhizn': Pis'ma, 1920–50 (Moscow: AST, 2019). A well-edited edition of Platonov's complete letters.

Zapisnye knizhki (Moscow: Nasledie, 2000). A carefully annotated transcription of the huge quantity of disparate, often enigmatic material in Platonov's personal notebooks.

BACKGROUND READING, IN ENGLISH

Philip Bullock, *The Feminine in the Prose of Andrey Platonov* (Oxford: Legenda, 2005).

Sheila Fitzpatrick, *Stalin's Peasants* (New York: Oxford University Press, 1996).

Katharine Holt, ed., *Andrei Platonov: Style, Context, Meaning, Ulbandus: The Slavic Review of Columbia University* 14 (special issue, 2011/2012).

Tora Lane, *Andrey Platonov: The Forgotten Dream of the Revolution* (Landham, MD: Lexington, 2020).

Angela Livingstone, ed. *Essays in Poetics* 26, 27 (autumn 2001, autumn 2002), Andrei Platonov special issue.

Alexander Nakhimovsky, *The Language of Russian Peasants in the Twentieth Century* (Landham, MD: Lexington, 2019). No other book affords us such a deep understanding of the life and language of the Russian peasantry under the Soviet regime.

Thomas Seifrid, *Andrei Platonov: Uncertainties of Spirit* (New York: Cambridge University Press, 2008).

BACKGROUND READING, IN RUSSIAN AND OTHER LANGUAGES

The seven volumes of *Strana Filosofov* (Moscow: IMLI RAN, 1994 and ongoing) contain essays on all aspects of Platonov's work, as do the four volumes of *Tvorchestvo Andreya Platonova* (Saint Petersburg: Nauka, 1995–2008). I have read only a small portion of this vast amount of material. Of what I have read, I particularly recommend all articles by Ben Dhooge, Maria Dmitrovskaya, Natalia Duzhina, Robert Hodel, Nina Malygina, Valery Vyugin, and Yevgeny Yablokov.

Mikhail Geller, *Andrey Platonov v poiskakh shchastia* (Paris: YMCA Press, 1982; also Moscow: MIK, 1999).

Hans Günther, *Andrej Platonov* (Berlin, 2016). An excellent short book about Platonov's life and work, unfortunately available only in German.

Robert Hodel, *Andrey Platonov: Rodina i elektrichestva* (Moscow: Polimedia, 2021).

L. V. Karasiov, *Dvizhenie po sklonu* (Moscow: RGGU, 2002).

E. A. Kolesnikova, *Malaya proza Andreya Platonova* (Saint Petersburg: SPGUTD, 2013).

Lasunsky, *Zhitel' rodnogo goroda* (Voronezh: VGU, 1999). A reliable account of Platonov's childhood and adolescence.

N. M. Malygina, *Andrey Platonov: poetika vozvrashecheniya* (Moscow: TEIS, 2005).

Olga Meerson, *Apokalipsis v bytu* (Moscow: Praktika, 2016).

——, *Svobodnaia Veshch'* (Novosibirsk: Nauka, 2001). Both Meerson's books are full of subtle insights into the psychological and philosophical subtleties of Platonov's unusual language.

M. Mikheev, *Andrey Platonov i drugie* (Moscow: Yask, 2015).

Evgenii Romanov, *Bogucharskii kommunizm Andreya Platonova* (Voronezh: VGU, 2017). Platonov's land-reclamation work in the mid-1920s, with photographs of some of the wells and small power stations he built in the province of Voronezh.

E. A. Rozhentseva, *A. P. Platonov v zhizni i tvorchestve* (Moscow: Russkoe slovo, 2014). A clear introduction to Platonov and his work.

Elena Tolstaya, *Mirposlekontsa* (Moscow: RGGU, 2002). Includes six essays devoted to Platonov.

Tvorchestvo Andreya Platonova. 4 vols. (Saint Petersburg: Nauka, 1995–2008).

V. Yu. Vyugin, *Andrey Platonov: poetika zagadki* (Saint Petersburg: Izdatel'stvo. Russkogo. Kristianskogo. Gumanitarnogo. Instituta., 2004).

E. A. Yablokov, *Deti i vzroslye v mire Andreya Platonova* (Moscow: 2016).

———, *Na beregu neba: roman Andreya Platonova "Chevengur"* (Saint Petersburg: 2001).

———, *Putevoditel' po romanu A. P. Platonova "Chevengur"* (Moscow: 2012).

———, All Yablokov's many articles about Platonov are well worth reading. Some can be accessed at http://eajablokov.ru/index.html.

NOTES

INTRODUCTION

1. Andrey Platonov, *Vzyskanie pogibshikh* (Moscow: Shkola Press, 1995), 630.
2. Platonov, *Sochineniia* (Moscow: IMLI RAN, 2004), 1:456–57.
3. Platonov, *Ya prozhil zhizn': Pis'ma* (1920–1950) (Moscow: AST, 2019), 194.
4. Platonov, 220.
5. April 7, 1834.
6. Platonov, *Ya prozhil zhizn'*, 210.
7. Platonov, 227.
8. E. A. Rozhentseva, *A. P. Platonov v zhizni i tvorchestve* (Moscow: Russkoye slovo, 2014), 35.
9. Andrey Platonov, *Zapisnye knizhki* (Moscow: Nasledie, 2000), 353–54n58.
10. Platonov, *Sochineniia*, 3:245, 3:706.
11. E.A. Yablokov, *Putevoditel' po romanu A. P. Platonova "Chevengur"* (Moscow University Press, 2012), 10.
12. Yablokov, 16.
13. Yablokov, 23.
14. Yablokov, 23.
15. Yablokov, 23.
16. Reprinted in Pier Paolo Pasolini, *Descrizioni di descrizioni* (Milan: Garzanti Libri, 2016).

CHEVENGUR

Chapter One

1. Harvest failures were all too frequent. From the late 1880s it was common for men to leave their villages in search of work, often for as long as six months. During one of the most serious famines, in the autumn of 1891,

about half a million people set off south from the province of Voronezh, mostly to the Northern Caucasus or to Luhansk and other coal-mining centers in the Donbas (the Donets Basin). Platonov's grandfather, Firs Klimentov, worked at times as a miner and died in a mining accident. As for Kyiv, it is the location of the Pechersk Lavra, a cave monastery that was one of the most important pilgrimage sites of Russian Orthodoxy.

2. In "Builders of the Country" (see the introduction), this episode is presented somewhat differently. After several days without eating at all, the narrator's younger brother and sister die from accidental mushroom poisoning. This tragedy inspires the narrator and his companion with determination to create a better world: "They stood over the grave of Dvanov's brother, who had died at the age of two. [. . .] Dvanov and Gratov decided to revenge themselves on nature for the children's death and to realize a tender dream of eternal memory. The friends were young and angry; the victory of the Revolution inspired them toward more mighty deeds." (*Sochineniia*, 3:436.) Platonov himself had suffered a similar tragedy. During the catastrophic 1921 famine, his fourteen-year-old sister and twelve-year-old brother both died of mushroom poisoning. Platonov did not forget them. In a notebook entry in 1942 he wrote:

> What if my brother Mitya or Nadya, twenty-one years after their deaths, were to come out of their graves, the young people they were when they died, and look at me now? What has happened to me? I've become a monstrosity, mutilated inside and out.
>
> "Andriusha, is that really you?"
>
> "Yes, it's me: I've lived through life." (*Zapisnye knizhki*, 237)

3. Among the meanings of the noun *mut'* are sediment, sludge, murk, and turbidity. The scholar Leonid Karasiov writes, "Clean, transparent water is linked in Platonov's work to thought, to mind and light. [. . .] Turbid water is the water of birth, the water of life in its strictly natural and corporeal dimension. It is clear from the lake's name that its water is turbid; that it is a mixture of earth and water, a kind of primal, colloidal mix, a life-creating emulsion." The lake's name also evokes the Russian equivalent of "to fish in troubled waters." (E. A. Yablokov, *Na beregu neba: roman Andreya Platonova "Chevengur"* [Saint Petersburg: 2001], 190.)

4. The motif of another world, parallel to ours and perhaps lying underwater, is central to *Chevengur*. Throughout the novel, Platonov alludes to the holy city of Kitezh, located at the bottom of Lake Svetloiar in Central Russia. According to legend, the citizens of Kitezh neither submit-

ted nor defended themselves when attacked in the thirteenth century by the Mongols. Instead they simply prayed to God—and Kitezh sank into the lake.

Kitezh is sometimes seen as a city of perfect justice, where the unjust are not admitted; if you stand by the edge of the water, you may hear the sound of its church bells. In Vladimir Korolenko's story "Svetloiar," an old man recounts how he has seen the city—churches, palaces, and wonderful monasteries—and is determined to find his way back to this paradise. He then disappears for a long time "as if he had vanished into the water." Performances in the spring of 1926, in both Moscow and Leningrad, of Rimsky-Korsakov's opera *The Legend of the Invisible City of Kitezh* aroused controversy. Some feared that the opera might reawaken religious feelings, but it was defended by Anatoly Lunacharsky, the commissar of enlightenment. (E. A. Yablokov, *Putevoditel'*, 105.)

5. A standard Russian unit of measurement before the Revolution, slightly longer than a kilometer.
6. An allusion to a prayer, composed by Saint Andrew of Crete, which includes the phrase "helper and protector" (*Pomoshchnik i pokrovitel'*).
7. Church bells were heard as the voice of God, marking the division between sacred time and cyclical, worldly time.

Chapter Two

1. This sounds almost liturgical, reminiscent of Christ dipping his bread in oil during the Last Supper. The words about leaving one's wife echo several passages from the Gospels, most notably: "He that loveth father or mother more than me is not worthy of me: and he that loveth son or daughter more than me is not worthy of me. And he that taketh not his cross, and followeth after me, is not worthy of me." (Matthew 10:37–39. This and all other biblical quotations are taken from the King James Version.)

Chapter Three

1. "Prosha" is the short form of "Prokhor." See the Note on Russian Names.
2. The Transfiguration. Celebrated—according to the old Julian calendar—on August 16, this was one of the Twelve Great Feasts of the Orthodox Church. The second of the Three Feasts of the Savior in August, it was popularly known as Nut Savior's Day or Bread Savior's Day; it was the first day when bread was baked from the wheat grown that year.

Chapter Four

1. In Russian, it is not unusual to describe people as going dark, or black, because of hunger. The skin of starving people can indeed darken, especially on the hands. And compare "Our skin was black like an oven because of the terrible famine" (Lamentations 5:10).
2. The moon getting washed (i.e., the new moon) was thought to bring rain.
3. A bad omen. According to folk medicine, the placenta and umbilical cord should have been buried under the floor or in some other "clean" place. Any infringement of this rule endangered the mother. (Yablokov, *Na beregu*, 242.)

Chapter Six

1. Throughout his work, Platonov is preoccupied with the nature of time. Are the repetitions of cyclical time inevitable—or is it possible to bring about a new world and put an end to world history? In *The Foundation Pit* he writes: "Leaning his back against the coffins, Voshchev was gazing up from the cart at the gathering of stars and the dead, murky mass of the Milky Way. He was waiting: When would a resolution be passed there to curtail the eternity of time and redeem the wearisomeness of life?"

   Elena Tolstaya puts the issue well, though she fails to consider whether Platonov's views may differ from those of his characters: "In accord with the tradition of Russian Symbolist literature, Platonov declares war against the stupefaction of natural life and the 'irrevocability' of time [...] Platonov's Apocalypse springs from his obsession with Fyodorov's ideas about the immorality of progress, which sanctifies the succession of generations and the consignment of the fathers to oblivion. [...] For Platonov, participation in progress is something shameful. In Platonov's system, time is equated with such facts of nature as animals devouring one another and love for a woman. The way out for Platonov lies in the cessation of time." (Quoted in Yablokov, *Na beregu*, 214.)
2. Evidently, this is now 1913. The tercentenary of the establishment of the Romanov dynasty was celebrated with great pomp throughout the country, from February 1913 until the autumn of that year. Zakhar Pavlovich, characteristically, shows little interest in such matters.

Chapter Seven

1. Sasha is the diminutive of Alexander; the relationship between a Rus-

sian Christian name and its diminutive, or affectionate, form is not always obvious. Usually, an adult would use a diminutive when addressing a child. (See the Note on Russian Names.)

Chapter Eight

1. This tells us that Sasha Dvanov would have been born between 1898 and 1900 and was much the same age as Platonov himself, who was born on August 28, 1899.
2. Platonov and his characters often reverse the usual meanings of such words as *fool* and *clever*. Thus Foma Pukhov, the perceptive and resourceful hero of "The Innermost Man," says of himself, "I'm a fool by nature" (*prirodnyi durak*) (Yablokov, *Na beregu*, 81). And in "Builders of the Country," Platonov writes, "Fools are those who consider life in general to be smarter than their own head" (*Sochineniia*, 3:453).
3. The foreman may not intend this himself, but Platonov certainly means to evoke the widespread contemporary discussion of the need to create "a new man." In "A Few Words about the Education of Man" (1927), Trotsky wrote, "And can you really not improve man? Yes, we can! The production of a new 'improved edition' of man is the farthermost task of communism." (Yablokov, *Putevoditel'*, 17.)

Chapter Nine

1. Introduced in 1912, the series Shch. locomotives were considerably more powerful than any preceding design.
2. The spontaneous popular uprising that erupted in February 1917 and culminated in the abdication of Tsar Nicholas II on March 2, 1917.
3. The former Governor's House in Voronezh had by then been converted to the "House of People's Organizations."
4. These two parties are probably the Mensheviks and the Socialist Revolutionaries.
5. The first Sunday in Lent, a commemoration of Byzantine Orthodoxy's final victory, in AD 843, over the iconoclasts (i.e., the faction opposed to the use of icons).
6. The Communist Party's official title was "The Russian Social-Democratic Party of Bolsheviks."
7. One of Platonov's provisional titles for the novel was "Journey with an Empty Heart." Several of his early articles emphasize the value of emptiness. In 1921 he wrote, "It is best to be no one, because then everything

can flow through you. Emptiness possesses no resistance, and the entire universe exists in emptiness" (*Sochineniia*, 3:615).

8. A kind of coarse tobacco, widely used in Russia throughout most of the last century.
9. This marks the end of the novel's opening section, first published in 1929 as a self-contained work titled "Origin of a Master." There is no general agreement as to whom this title refers to. Some scholars argue that it refers to Zakhar Pavlovich; others that it refers to Sasha Dvanov—or even to Platonov himself.

Chapter Ten

1. Urochev is a fictional name. In drafts, Platonov had written "Novokhopiorsk," the real name of a town to which he himself was sent in June 1919 (see the introduction, page viii).
2. That is, the Revolutionary Committee—one of the many abbreviations and acronyms that characterized the world of Soviet bureaucracy.
3. Platonov may well have composed these slogans himself—not only for this novel, but also in historical reality. From May to July 1920 he worked for the newspaper *Red Village* (*Krasnaia derevnia*) and was responsible for such slogans as "Who treasures the blood of workers and peasants will not abandon the Red Army at a difficult moment," and "A Red Army soldier unable to become a leader and victor is no Red Army soldier." (*Sochineniia*, 3:618.)
4. Another allusion to the drowned city of Kitezh. (See chapter 1, note 4.)
5. "Builders of the Country," narrated in the first person, includes a longer version of this passage. This appears to be a direct statement of Platonov's own thoughts and feelings—something rare in his fictional work:

   > In anguish, I hurried to the station. In those days I had a vivid and sad sense of our perilous time and inevitable early death. I felt sorry for the shelterless people who had been rushing about in turmoil and were now united in abandonment, on behalf of whom a band, rather than their own mothers, was now suffering, and whose names were now vanishing in mass graves beneath anonymous grass. I did not believe that struggle was people's eternal calling; being young, I dreamed of another, peaceful fate—about a deep human consciousness that saw the world's events before their appearance, about the richness of the universe, enough to satisfy ev-

ery greed of life, and I had an absolutely sincere sense of faith in the meaning of mankind, as the conqueror and savior of future nature.

I had thought all this through many times—what interested me now was the transformation of thoughts into an event. My old mother, my brothers and sisters, who had died, my father, who had worn himself out in work—they all demanded a justification of their tedious and tormenting lives; they had, after all, been born.

At the station, I sensed the sucking pull of space. Like everyone, I was attracted by the earth's distant parts, as if everything distant and invisible were missing me and calling to me. Probably man truly does belong to the same family as all the forgotten things scattered about a world overgrown with expanses of space. (*Sochineniia*, 3:350)

6. A Russian translation of this collection of articles about art by the German Romantics Wilhelm Vakenroder and Ludwig Tieck was published in 1826; a facsimile edition was published in 1914.
7. Dzhankar is a major railway junction in the north of the Crimean peninsula. The inscription alludes to these verses of Saint Paul: "That [...] we might have a strong consolation, who have fled for refuge to lay hold upon the hope set before us: Which hope we have as an anchor of the soul, both sure and steadfast" (Hebrews 6:18–19).
8. The Red Army at this time had no officers. Its commanders were referred to as ***kombat*** (battalion commander), ***komdiv*** (divisional commander), ***komarm*** (army commander), and so forth. Each unit also had its political commissar, whose role was to strengthen the soldiers' political awareness.
9. "The hard earth wants to take Sasha's life even though the moment she takes it, she will lose it, and she seems almost to know this" (Alexander Nakhimovsky, personal email, June 3, 2022). Paradoxically, the earth is seen as Sasha's child. It is she who is in danger of being orphaned.
10. The longer version of this passage in "Builders of the Country" may well be autobiographically true:

    Avoiding Razguliay station in case I were stopped there, I disappeared. For a long time I continued to hear the whistle of steam from the locomotive and the long melody of alarm sirens. Had I perished or vanished in that steppe emptiness, society would never have remembered me. Only my mother would have counted the days, waited for a letter, and wept. I was standing then at a psychological

> crossroads—of history and personal life. I was nearly nineteen years old, and so was the twentieth century. I was born the same age as my century, which was growing at the same pace as human beings. Within me was youth and the sharpness of personal fate—and out in the world, at this same time, was revolution. (*Sochineniia*, 3:358)

Chapter Eleven

1. During the Civil War, at least thirty thousand—perhaps even sixty thousand—Chinese fought in the Red Army. Their claim to "love death" may have been a defiant response to the knowledge that they faced certain death if taken prisoner; General Denikin had ordered that any captured non-Russian soldiers—Chinese, Latvians, or others—were to be shot immediately. The fish soup is no random detail; throughout the novel fish are associated with death. Sasha's fisherman father saw them as "a special being that most probably knew the secret of death."
2. After World War I and during the Russian Civil War, an epidemic of louse-born typhus caused between two and three million deaths. In 1919, at a meeting held to discuss the epidemic, Lenin said, "All attention to this problem, comrades. Either lice will conquer socialism, or socialism will conquer lice." (Cited by K. K. Vasil'ev, "*Rol' pervykh vserossiskikh s'ezdov bacteriologov i epidemiologov v bor'be s epidemiyami parazitarnykh tifov*," *Zhurnal mikrobiologii, epidemiologii, i immunobiologii* [April 1981], 106–7.) Sasha's recovery after nine months of illness suggests that he is reborn after a second period in the womb.
3. Strange though it may seem to us, advance preparation of a coffin was a standard practice among the Russian peasantry.
4. Sonia's teacher may be unconsciously imagining himself as a modern Saint Paul, half remembering his words about leaven:

   > Know ye not that a little leaven leaveneth the whole lump? Purge out therefore the old leaven, that ye may be a new lump, as ye are unleavened. For even Christ our Passover is sacrificed for us: Therefore let us keep the feast, not with old leaven, neither with the leaven of malice and wickedness; but with the unleavened bread of sincerity and truth. (1 Corinthians, 5:6–8)
5. In an article first published in 1923 Platonov proposed diverting warm rivers to Siberia and cold Siberian rivers to the Gobi Desert. He concluded, "Siberia freed from frost! A warm country on the shore of the

Arctic Ocean! This should be the slogan of the Soviet Union." (*Sochineniia*, 3:623)

Chapter Twelve

1. That is, "Provincial Executive Committee."
2. The young Platonov saw the dawn of communism as imminent. In "The New Gospel" he wrote, "The drought will bring forward the advent of communism. The drought, in the end, will strengthen people and make them into brothers, since the prelude to organization is always catastrophe" (*Sochineniia*, 3:624).

Chapter Thirteen

1. In "Water Is the Foundation of a Socialist Economy" (1923), Platonov wrote, "Other fuels will be replaced by hydroelectric energy, which can provide the necessary foundation of power both for a Communist society's industry and for its agriculture. Water is the foundation of socialism." (*Sochineniia*, 3:626).
2. Belief in the possibility of establishing the kingdom of heaven on earth is an important part of the philosophical background to *Chevengur*. Many Russian sectarians believed that men could become godlike, and many early Bolsheviks inherited these beliefs. Such beliefs were perhaps articulated most clearly of all in the first decades of the Reformation. The German theologian Thomas Müntzer (1489–1525) wrote, "We, earthly people made from flesh, will become gods by virtue of the incarnation of Christ and we will become students of God, and he will teach us and we will become godlike. Yes, we will transform ourselves into Him and earthly life will become heavenly life." (See *Putevoditel'*, 131.)

   Platonov well understood that reason and science could not answer all people's psychological needs. He addressed this question repeatedly. In "About Love" (1927), he wrote:

   > If we want to destroy religion and are conscious that this has to be done, since communism and religion are incompatible, then, in place of religion we must give the people not less than religion but more than religion. Many of us think that it is possible to take faith away without giving people anything better. The soul of contemporary man is organized in such a way that if faith is removed from it, it will be completely overturned. (*Sochineniia*, 2:432)

   In "Builders of the Country," he further develops these thoughts:

All over Russia, that evening, people were hunting for bread. The louse had turned into a hefty wild beast, devouring the whole country. Ordinary people whose souls had remained intact were gripped by a deep anguish. Did God exist—or were the Bolsheviks right and God was nowhere to be found? If he existed, then everything was good and peaceful—your mood would improve and you'd beat your wife less often. But if there were no God, then you'd have to stand on your own feet. You'd have to think up the entire meaning of the universe for yourself and refashion the whole unwieldy business all over again.

Wandering about the steppes where the Civil War was being fought, I realized that people were suffering from a double hunger. They hungered for rye, and for their souls. The Bolsheviks had poisoned people's hearts with doubt. A fierce sun of arid knowledge had risen over their feelings. They were no longer in touch with the rhythm of their hearts; they were hurt and angry; they were suffering. Instead of the mysterious night of religion, there now shone an empty pinpoint of science, illuminating the world's emptiness. People were scared and despairing. As I see it, two different things—heart and head—had been confused. The Bolsheviks had wanted to replace the heart with the head—but while the head may be curious to know that the world is filled with ether, the heart feels otherwise. For it, the ethereal world, too, is empty and hopeless—even to the point of suicide. (*Sochineniia*, 3:369–70)

3. In 1917, to undermine the Provisional Government, the Bolsheviks had encouraged the peasants to rise up against their landlords and seize their land. The Bolsheviks then found themselves having to fight a prolonged war in order to reassert the authority of central government. The peasants resisted "grain requisitioning"—the Bolshevik policy of forcibly confiscating grain from the peasants to feed the cities—and peasant revolts continued on a massive scale until as late as 1924.

Chapter Fourteen

1. In "The River Voronezh—Its Present and Future" (1923), Platonov wrote, "A once powerful, full-bodied river has grown decrepit. It has exhausted itself and become little more than a foul puddle. And to a considerable degree, this is because of the hand of man. We do not, as a rule, value healthy water. We think of a river simply as something that

will always be there—whereas, in reality, water is as necessary and as precious as bread" (*Sochineniia*, 3:628).

2. "Little Apple" ("Yablochko") was one of the most popular songs from the time of the Civil War. There were both pro-Soviet and anti-Soviet versions, and the lyrics were constantly evolving. In *Memories*, Teffi recalls someone singing,

    Sweet little apple,
    stay where you belong.
    Don't let the Cheka
    silence your song!

3. Socialists and anarchists had been arguing for several decades. Georgy Plekhanov, one of the founders of Russian Marxism, wrote in "Anarchism and Socialism" (1894), "How is one to decide where a 'comrade' ends and a 'brigand' begins? Often even the anarchists themselves can't tell the difference. [...] In the name of revolution anarchists serve the cause of reaction; in the name of morality they approve the most immoral acts; in the name of individual freedom they trample underfoot the rights of their neighbors" (Yablokov, *Na beregu*, 258). Platonov, however, was sympathetic toward anarchism, certainly as a young man and perhaps also later. In 1919 he published a poem and an article in the official journal of the All-Russian Federation of Anarchist Youth, and in "Anarchists and Communists" (1920), he wrote, "We are not talking about the people wandering about villages and forests, murdering and plundering and calling themselves anarchists. They are not anarchists; they are simply plunderers and murderers. True anarchy is the understanding that all power and authority on earth is unnecessary and harmful, that people do not need to be led" (*Sochineniia*, 3:629).

4. Dvanov is quoting—or rather, slightly misquoting—the French philosopher Pierre-Joseph Proudhon (1809–65), best known for his slogan "Property Is Theft." In "The Solution of the Social Problem" (1848), Proudhon wrote, "The Republic is positive anarchy. [...] It is mutual freedom [...]; freedom is the mother, not the daughter, of order!"

5. Mrachinsky is modeled on a real figure, Sergey Mrachkovsky. As a member of the Trotskyist Opposition, he was expelled from the Communist Party in September 1927.

6. The Wandering Jew—sometimes known as Agasfer or Ahasfer—was punished with immortality for taunting Christ and refusing to allow him to rest on his way to Calvary. In "Builders of the Country" Platonov wrote,

"It turned out that Mrachinsky had been writing books and articles for fifteen years and had then fallen in love with one of his heroes—a contemporary Agasfer—and had determined to relive his fate. [. . .] Mrachinsky decided that it would be only slightly more difficult to fulfill Agasfer's dream of finding the house of God than to write about it" (*Sochineniia*, 3:631). Agasfer appears in several of Platonov's works, from his juvenilia to *Noah's Ark*, the play he was working on during his last months.

7. In Platonov's story "For Future Use" (*Vprok*, 1929–30), the narrator writes, "But for such occurrences, we would never organize humanity and come to feel our humanness, since the new man seems laughable to us, as Robinson did to the ape." Both this narrator and Dvanov are conflating Robinson Crusoe with a passage from Friedrich Nietzsche's *Thus Spake Zarathustra*: "What is the ape to man? A laughingstock or a painful embarrassment. And man shall be just that for the overman: a laughingstock or a painful embarrassment" (New York: Modern Library, 1995, 12). Characteristically, Platonov reverses Nietzsche's hierarchy. In Nietzsche, the higher being looks with condescending amusement at the lower being; in both passages of Platonov, it is the lower being who, due to his lack of understanding, is amused by the higher being. See Jason Cieply, "The 'Strangely Apolitical' Politics of Tora Lane's Platonov," review of *Andrey Platonov: The Forgotten Dream of the Revolution*, by Tora Lane, *Stasis* 10, no. 2 (2020): 230–51, and Platonov, *Sobranie sochinenii* (Moscow: Vremya, 2011), 2:294.

Chapter Fifteen

1. Sonia's experiences reflect those of Platonov's wife, Maria Kashintseva, who worked as a village teacher in Voloshino from the summer of 1921 until the spring of 1922, under the auspices of a major official campaign to "liquidate illiteracy."
2. An allusion not only to Soviet censorship but also to Nikolay Gogol's *The Inspector General*. Gogol's postmaster regularly reads other people's letters, saying, "I do this not as a precaution but more out of curiosity. I really love to know what's new in the world. I can tell you that this makes for extraordinarily interesting reading" (*Sochineniia*, 3:632).
3. Platonov would have known about the Boguchar Regiment, "a family army" numbering about 3,500 men that took part in battles against the Cossacks during the Civil War.

   The women and children followed in a long transport convoy. [. . .]

In the fighting around Bobrov in July 1918, the women took part in the regiment's attacks on the town. During lulls in the fighting there were occasions when a son would replace a father, a nephew replace an uncle, or a brother replace a brother. Wherever the Boguchar Regiment fought, it impressed the Red Army units with its excellent morale. Their morale did not weaken even when they sustained losses. (*Sochineniia*, 3:631)

4. Rosa Luxemburg (1871–1919), a Polish Jew, played a central role in the revolutionary movements of Poland, Russia, and Germany. In 1915, she and Karl Liebknecht founded the antiwar Spartacist League, which evolved into the German Communist Party. During the January 1919 Spartacist uprising in Berlin, she and Liebknecht were executed by government-sponsored paramilitaries. Both have been revered as Communist martyrs. Bertolt Brecht's "Epitaph 1919" reads:

   Red Rosa now has vanished too,
   And where she lies is hid from view.
   She told the poor what life's about,
   And so the rich have rubbed her out.
   May she rest in peace.
   (*Poems, 1913–1956*, ed. John Willett and Ralph Manheim)

   The name Luxemburg means "city of light," but Rosa's importance to both Kopionkin and Platonov stems, above all, from the clarity of her criticisms of Lenin's authoritarianism. In "The Russian Revolution," composed during one of her spells in prison during the First World War, she wrote, "Freedom only for the supporters of the government, only for the members of one party—however numerous they may be—is no freedom at all. Freedom is always and exclusively freedom for the one who thinks differently."

   Rosa is also a reincarnation of the Virgin Mary, and Kopionkin—as well as being a modern Don Quixote—is a caricature of the poor crusader, devoted to the Virgin Mary, who is the subject of one of Pushkin's best-known ballads. This crusader's battle cry is "Lumen coelum, sancta Rosa!" (Light of heaven, holy Rose!)

5. The British, in fact, played no part in Rosa Luxemburg's murder. Anglo-Soviet relations, however, were particularly bad in 1926 and 1927, and this is reflected in several of Platonov's works from those years.

6. Such phrases as "the locomotive of history" and "the locomotive of revolution" were a common part of the political language of the time. In

1921, during a meeting held in Voronezh, the Bolshevik politician Grigory Zinoviev said that the Revolution was moving forward "with a speed resembling the movement of a locomotive heading a passenger train." And in a brief "autobiography," Platonov described an experience of his own from the Civil War: "Even though I had not yet completed technical school, I was hurriedly put on a locomotive to help the driver. The remark about the Revolution being the locomotive of history was transformed inside me into a feeling that was strange and good: remembering this sentence, I worked very diligently on the locomotive..." (Alexey Varlamov, *Andrey Platonov*, 15). The sentence Platonov remembers is from Karl Marx: "Revolutions are the locomotives of history" ("The Class Struggles in France, 1848 to 1850" in Marx and Engels, *Selected Works* [Moscow: 1962], 1:217). In "The Innermost Man" Platonov writes, more ambiguously, "During those years, history was hurtling forward like a locomotive hauling uphill the world's burden of poverty, despair, and submissive inertness" (*Sochineniia*, 3:635).

7. The next chapters, up to "In the morning they left the hut on the edge of the forest" in chapter 19, are probably presented as seen by this eunuch. Sasha, in these scenes, is almost a sleepwalker.

Chapter Sixteen

1. During the Civil War there were many such traders, most of them using the railways. They were, essentially, black marketeers, facing constant harassment from the authorities, but it was often unclear how much flour, salt, and so forth someone could legitimately be transporting for personal use. The word *trader* is our translation of *meshochnik*—literally, "a sack person."
2. Perhaps an allusion to the Seven Sleepers of Ephesus, a legend about a group of young Christians who hid in a cave outside Ephesus to escape Roman persecution and emerged some three hundred years later. A slightly different version of the legend appears in the Koran.

Chapter Seventeen

1. This description of Kopionkin's horse is in keeping with descriptions of warriors' horses in the orally transmitted short epics known as *byliny*.
2. The Bitiug, a tributary of the Don, flows south through the province of Voronezh. *Bitiug* is also a common noun meaning "dray horse" or "cart horse."

3. Compare this sentence from *Don Quixote*, chapter 3:

   Then he came to a place where the road divided into four, and he remembered the crossroads where knights errant would ponder which road to follow; and to imitate them, he paused quietly for a while. Having duly deliberated, he let go of the reins, leaving it to Rocinante to choose the route, and the horse stuck to his original plan, which was to make for the stable.

Chapter Nineteen

1. During the Civil War, the White armies made effective use of powerful radio transmitters.
2. An allusion to the Gadarene swine of the Gospels—and also one of many allusions in *Chevengur* to Dostoevsky, who uses Saint Luke's account of the swine as an epigraph for *The Demons*: "And there was there an herd of many swine feeding on the mountain: and they besought him that he would suffer them to enter into them. And he suffered them. Then went the devils out of the man, and entered into the swine: and the herd ran violently down a steep place into the lake, and were choked" (Luke 8:32–33). The Russian-Canadian scholar and translator Maria Bloshteyn understands *Chevengur* as Platonov's rejoinder to *The Demons*. Dostoevsky sees the revolutionary movement as a foreign import—Holy Russia in danger of being possessed by evil forces from Western Europe. Platonov sees the Revolution as being informed by a characteristically Russian religious fervor; Platonov's revolutionaries are not Western demons but Russian saints and holy fools.
3. *Moshonka* means "scrotum."
4. Franz Mehring (1846–1919) was a German Marxist, another co-founder of the Spartacus League. The word *merin*, however, is the Russian for "gelded horse." Renaming oneself after a revered political figure was common practice in the 1920s. There was a vogue for newly coined names, such as Marlen—an amalgam of Marx and Lenin. People also took, or were given, the names of major writers. The formalist critic and scholar Viktor Shklovsky (1893–1984) has described how, in 1925, in the province of Voronezh, he and Platonov visited a large orphanage: "400 orphans, three in a bed. They are sick, with malaria and hospitalism. The absence of a personal fate—something a child needs. These children have new surnames: Turgenev, Dostoevsky" (Viktor Shklovsky, *Third Factory*, trans. Richard Sheldon [Chicago: Dalkey Archive Press, 2002], 80).

5. After fasting in the desert for forty days and nights, Christ was tempted by Satan. First, Satan suggested that Christ should make bread out of stone. Christ replied, "Man shall not live by bread alone, but by every word that proceedeth out of the mouth of God" (Matthew 4:4). Dostoevsky alludes to this temptation in *The Brothers Karamazov*, in the chapter known as "The Legend of the Grand Inquisitor." Platonov's attitude toward Dostoevsky is complex. Often, he argues with him; here, though, he may be using Dostoevsky to make fun of the naive dreams of such figures as this RevCom plenipotentiary.
6. During the Civil War both Reds and Whites regularly requisitioned the peasants' horses, making it all but impossible for them to plow their fields.
7. There were three categories of peasants: *kulaks* (the supposedly wealthy and exploitative—mostly deported by the end of the 1920s); "middle peasants" (*sredniaki*—treated with suspicion by the authorities); and "poor peasants" (*bedninaki*—looked on with approval by the authorities).
8. The first of many allusions to Dostoevsky's parable, in book 5, chapter 5, of *The Brothers Karamazov*, about the Grand Inquisitor. The Inquisitor refers to humanity as "unfinished trial beings, created in mockery"; his word for "unfinished" (*nedodelannye*) is the word here translated as "half-baked."

Chapter Twenty

1. Nikolay Arsakov is modeled on Konstantin Aksakov (1817–60), one of the social thinkers known as Slavophiles. A believer in gradual change, Aksakov was critical of Peter the Great's Westernizing reforms, which he saw as an attempt to force the country to follow a spiritually alien path.
2. Since this is a formal document, Kopionkin uses the full form of his patronymic. Elsewhere, this is shortened to the more colloquial Yefimych.

Chapter Twenty-One

1. In the early 1920s many communes bore similar names. Among the newly formed communes in the province of Voronezh were Fraternal Labor, New Life, The Awakening of the Ploughman, The Path of Socialism, The Invisible Ship, The Commune of Karl Marx, and The Commune in the Name of Trotsky.

2. In his article "A New Gospel" (1921), Platonov writes, "Man will soon deliver his Last Judgment over the universe, to condemn it to death" (*Putevoditel'*, 149).
3. Kopionkin's noble ideal impels him to an act of extreme violence. Platonov's understanding of this paradox may have been inspired by a passage from *The Meaning of Love* (1893), by the poet and religious philosopher Vladimir Soloviov:

> Mediaeval love was, of course, linked to a hunger for great deeds. But these destructive feats of arms bore no relation to the ideal that had inspired them and could not lead to its realization. Even the poor knight who entirely devoted himself to a revelation of heavenly beauty did not link it to earthly phenomena and was inspired by it only to acts that served more to harm others than to promote the good and glory of the "eternal feminine." (*Putevoditel'*, 150)

Chapter Twenty-Two

1. Rudimentary fences were often put up on fields so that snow would drift against them instead of being blown away by the wind. This helped to protect the winter crops against extremes of cold.
2. Kronstadt was a large Russian naval base near Petrograd. In 1917, the Kronstadt garrison and the crews of the ships based there were among the Bolsheviks' staunchest supporters, but in March 1921 approximately eighteen thousand soldiers and sailors rebelled, demanding greater political and economic freedom for both workers and peasants. The Red Army's brutal suppression of this left-wing rebellion disillusioned many of the Bolsheviks' supporters, both in Russia and elsewhere. In "Builders of the Country," Sasha Dvanov tells Sonia:

> If Kronstadt had been an ordinary White Guards affair, Lenin would not have introduced this new policy [i.e., the NEP]... I heard conversations in trains—I didn't believe everything, but now I can understand for myself. And I saw many things in the villages. Another six months would have been the end of us. Even the very meekest people would have begun to strangle us. And there we were, stupidly calling them White Guards. (*Sochineniia*, 3:652)

The intended meaning of the newspaper slogan is something like this: "If we use the snow to protect the winter crops, we will enjoy a better harvest. And better living conditions will decrease the likelihood of future rebellions against the Soviet regime" (*Putevoditel'*, 58). Platonov may also be hinting at a more magical, or mythical understanding—that an activity as apparently senseless as plowing snow, or churning the ocean, can bring about the creation of a new and better world. (*Na beregu*, 268.)

3. Many anarchist thinkers, including Mikhail Bakunin, looked on the intelligentsia with suspicion. Daniil Novomirsky (1882–193?) saw the intelligentsia's "monopoly of knowledge" as one of the three most dangerous enemies of human freedom, along with private property and the state itself (*Putevoditel'*, 151). In chapter 23 of Platonov's *A Story About Many Interesting Things* (1923), the engineer Ivan Kopchikov, says, "People trade knowledge like goods. [...] Formerly, one person oppressed others by means of property of all kinds, but now he oppresses through knowledge. Knowledge has become property, a kind of goods. He who possesses it can trade it and grow rich."
4. This sculpture alludes not only to the Three Graces but also to these lines from Pushkin's *Eugene Onegin*:

   I to this day would love a ball.
   I love the youthfulness and madness,
   The crush, the glitter and the gladness,
   The care with which the women dress;
   I love their little feet, yet guess
   You'd be unlikely to discover
   Three shapely pairs of women's feet
   In all of Russia.

   (*Eugene Onegin*, trans. Stanley Mitchell, 1:xxx)
5. Dvanov sees Pashintsev as a contemporary Don Quixote—or as a pretender to this role.
6. Pashintsev is a semimythological being, modeled on Polyphemus, a one-eyed giant whom Odysseus encounters in *The Odyssey*. Like Polyphemus, he lives in a world of his own, underground and apart from society. His basement is a womb and, at one point, seems close to becoming a tomb. The brass plate on a column outside bears an inscription of cosmic significance.
7. There are striking images in an early, longer draft of this passage:

   Dvanov knew that the Revolution was struggling not only against the class enemy, but also within itself and against itself; it was trying, simultaneously, to overcome both itself and an external enemy. Dvanov understood Pashintsev and his sincere despair—he knew that Pashintsev was doomed. He could see that Pashintsev had been enchanted once and for all by the first months after the October 1917 Revolution—those months when the most impassioned Communist enthusiasm had gripped the dying, despairing masses of Russia's workers and soldiers. It had seemed then that the warm day of a life of universal friendship was close at hand. But that faith had soon become folk legend—and in Pashintsev it had turned to avid superstition. The years of Civil War had compressed the Revolution and made it into a merciless fighting force. There was more now in the Revolution by way of sturdy sinews and less of the unstable moisture of inspiration.

The Revolution was moving on, like a comet, rendered incandescent by the opposition of the future and leaving behind it a fading tail of slag from conquered events and spent people. But Pashintsev was not slag from the Revolution; something was continuing to burn in him—but it was burning tormentedly, apart from the general blaze.

Dvanov did not understand everything. Pashintsev sensed that Kopionkin was a man like himself, an orphan of the earthly globe, and he begged him with heartfelt words to stay with him forever.

(*Sochineniia*, 3:577–78)

8. November 1927 was the tenth anniversary of the October Revolution. The preceding months saw much public debate as to how this should be celebrated. Platonov's contribution to this debate was a satirical sketch titled "Appropriate Measures" (*Nadlezhashchiye Meropriyatiya*). Among the "measures" proposed are a traveling mausoleum and the establishment of ten "Revolutionary Reserves" where "the great events' attributes and living participants would be gathered together [. . .] and can exist in intact and naturally heroic rest." There is also a proposal for exploiting "the energy of Crimean and other earthquakes for immediate electrification of the regions concerned" (*Sochineniia*, 3:565–66, 3:649–50).

Chapter Twenty-Three

1. Half-serious, half-joking references to the physical resurrection of the dead are common throughout Platonov's work. One of the main intellectual influences on Platonov was the work of Nikolai Fyodorov (1829–1903), an ascetic Moscow librarian and visionary philosopher admired not only by Leo Tolstoy, Fyodor Dostoevsky, Boris Pasternak, Nikolay

Zabolotsky, and many other writers, but also by Konstantin Tsiolkovsky (1857–1935), one of the founding fathers of modern rocketry and so of the Soviet space program. Fyodorov's writings were gathered after his death by his disciples in Moscow and published as *The Philosophy of the Common Task* (or *Common Cause*). His ideas have been well summarized by Irina Paperno:

> In brief: fusing Christian mysticism with the positivistic trust in science, Fyodorov urged his fellow citizens to devote their collective energy to the "project" (his word) of resurrecting the past in its totality by means ranging from science and cosmic exploration to art and archival preservation. He actually hoped to reassemble the bodies of ancestors from material particles that bear traces of an individual. (Paperno, *Stories of the Soviet Experience* [Ithaca, NY: Cornell University Press, 2009], 44)

Fyodorov's influence on Platonov has been studied by Ayleen Teskey (*Platonov and Fyodorov: The Influence of Christian Philosophy on a Soviet Writer*, 1982); and Fyodorov himself is a protagonist of Sharov's novel *Before & During*. As a young man, Platonov hoped that the Revolution might realize Fyodorov's utopian ideas. Many of these ideas remained important to Platonov throughout his life. Even if he ceased to believe in them literally, he continued either to argue with them or to use them as metaphors.

2. October 1920 saw a major peasant uprising, centered on Chornaya Kalitva, in response to grain requisitioning. By November, the rebels numbered ten thousand, most of them mounted, and they remained active until May 1921. There were similar uprisings elsewhere in the province of Voronezh, and a still larger uprising in the neighboring province of Tambov. Platonov's Timofey Plotnikov is clearly modeled on Ivan Kolesnikov, the leader of the Chornaya Kalitva uprising. The name Ispodny Khutor could be translated as "The Inside-Out Little Village" (*Putevoditel'*, 155, and *Sochineniia*, 3:658).
3. The rebels enjoyed the support of almost all the peasantry, but they were neither brigands nor in any way sympathetic to the Whites. One of their slogans was "Against Plundering and Hunger!"
4. The historical Ivan Kolesnikov was a member of the Red Dragon sect, which identified Soviet power with the Dragon of the Apocalypse. Kolesnikov declared himself a prince of the angelic forces (*Putevoditel'*, 155).

5. This surname is derived from the adjective *Soty*, meaning "one-hundredth."
6. During the first years after the Revolution, a great deal of cultural work was purportedly being carried out in the provinces. According to a June 1919 report:

   VORONEZH PROVINCE: Huge organizational-cultural work has begun in all the villages. Performances, concerts, and lectures are being arranged. Clubs and Houses of the People are being opened. Consumer societies and credit agencies are eagerly cooperating with these cultural initiatives in the villages, assigning large sums of money to enlightenment work.

   The confusion shown by the peasant speaking to Dvanov is testimony to the gap between the reality of village life and official accounts of it (*Sochineniia*, 3:660).
7. In the spring and summer of 1921, several newspapers reported meetings between Lenin and delegations of peasants. Lenin was said to have listened attentively to the peasants' complaints about grain requisitioning and to have been swayed by their arguments (*Sochineniia*, 3:661).

Chapter Twenty-Four

1. An oblique allusion to an official euphemism from tsarist times. An escaped prisoner was referred to as "Ivan who does not remember his family" (*Ivan ne pomniashchii rodstva*).
2. Frequent hiccups were thought to indicate that someone was thinking of you.

Chapter Twenty-Five

1. Throughout the period known as War Communism (1918–21) the entire economy was under central control and there was an almost total ban on private trade. Severe food shortages led to all kinds of substances being sold as "millet" and "beef." The helpers are wanting to make it clear that what is for sale in this shop is *real* millet and *real* veal. On March 21, 1921, War Communism was replaced by the somewhat more liberal NEP (New Economic Policy), which allowed a measure of private trade. Many idealistic Communists saw the NEP as a capitulation, a return to capitalism, but it was welcomed by the population as a whole. The NEP continued until 1928.

Chapter Twenty-Six

1. In 1920 Platonov was accepted as a candidate member of the Communist Party. In October 1921, however, he was excluded as "an unreliable and inconsistent element, an undisciplined party member." He was reported as having refused to attend party meetings, saying, "I already know everything." In February 1924, he unsuccessfully applied to rejoin the party. Platonov's own account is different; he stated that he resigned of his own accord, out of impatience with long discussions at party meetings when there was more important work, such as electrification, to be carried out. He went on to say that he regretted "this childish act" and that he "had made a mistake but would not make such mistakes again" (*Na beregu*, 282). It is possible that the true reason for his resignation was his opposition to the NEP.
2. There is no doubt of Platonov's own views on the destruction of forests. In "Man and Desert" (*Chelovek i pustynia*, 1924), he wrote, "Felling forests on slopes, disturbing the steppe turf, man allows the spring and other floodwaters to flow freely over the earth's surface. These waters remove beneficial substances from plowed steppe and carry them away into rivers, and then to the sea" (Platonov, *Gosudarstenny zhitel'* [Moscow: 1988], 543).
3. The first Soviet military decoration, the Order of the Red Banner was established in September 1918, during the Russian Civil War. It remained the highest Soviet award until the establishment in 1930 of the Order of Lenin.
4. Bast fiber, from the inner bark of a birch tree, was used to make a variety of everyday items, including sandals, baskets, food containers, and sponges. *The Primary Chronicle* (the first history of the early Eastern Slav state known as Kyivan Rus'), includes a legend about the creation of mankind: while in the bathhouse, God wiped the sweat off his body with some old rags and threw these rags down to earth. God and Satan then argued about which of them would create Man from these rags. In the end, Satan created Man—and God gave him a soul (*Na beregu*, 284). To this day, Russians sometimes use a bast sponge to scrub themselves in a bathhouse; they also often beat themselves, or one another, with birch twigs.
5. A Red Corner was a special room in a Soviet hostel, factory, or other institution, stocked with educational literature and reserved for reading and recreation. Before the Revolution, however, the term was used differently, referring to the corner of the room in a private house where the

icons were kept. The Russian word for "red" (*krasny*) originally also meant "beautiful"—a connection independent of communism.

6. Another allusion to Dostoevsky's Grand Inquisitor, who asserted that "freedom and enough bread for all are inconceivable together." In "Pushkin and Gorky" (1937), Platonov writes, "The people, according to Dostoevsky's Inquisitor, are like an animal, needing only bread and peace; as if universal happiness can be glued together with the bread paste of basic need."
7. Here Gopner voices the thoughts of the young Platonov. In "The New Gospel" (1921) Platonov had written, "Only great trouble can sow communism in a man's heart, for, when I am happy, I don't need anyone—but when I am unhappy and close to death, I need everyone" (*Sochineniia*, 3:663).
8. Gopner evidently has in mind the Marxist thesis that at a time of revolution the proletariat becomes the subject—the active agent—of the historical process.
9. The Tenth Voronezh Province Party Conference, dedicated to discussion of the transition to the NEP, took place in September 1921 (*Na beregu*, 285).

Chapter Twenty-Seven

1. "The tsarist war" was a common way of referring to the First World War, but it is possible that it refers here to the Russo-Japanese War (1904–5) and that this man's nickname alludes not only to his looks but also to his having taken part in this war (*Sochineniia*, 3:667).
2. In his article "Piotr Chaadaev" (1915), Osip Mandelstam writes:

> There is a great Slav dream about the cessation of history in the Western sense of the word. [. . .] It is a dream of a universal spiritual disarmament, after which something called "peace" will set in. Not long ago, Tolstoy himself appealed to humanity to call an end to the deceitful and unnecessary comedy of history and begin to live "simply." [. . .] Seen as unnecessary, all earthly and heavenly hierarchies are annulled forever. The church, the state, and the law disappear from consciousness, seen as absurd chimeras with which man—out of stupidity and from having nothing better to do—has populated the "simple," "godly," world. Free of tedious intermediaries, man and the universe are at last left alone with each other.
>
> (*Sochineniia*, 3:667; see also chapter six, note 1)

3. Another allusion to Kitezh. See chapter 1, note 4, and chapter 10, note 4.
4. For the name *Chevengur*, see the first part of "Translating Platonov" in the present work. The name also calls to mind such real place-names in the provinces of Tambov and Voronezh as Kachagury, Karachan, Chagory, Karachun, Karabut. The town may be modeled on Boguchar, a town in the south of Voronezh Province where Platonov spent several months in late 1924, building wells and a small power station that is still standing. The last part of the novel is set in this area, and Boguchar lies on the Bogucharka River just as Chevengur lies on the Chevengurka. Boguchar was the home of the Fyodorovans, an ascetic sect whose adherents lived in imminent expectation of the Second Coming. (Note: This sect was named after its leader, Fyodor Rybalkin, and has nothing to do with Nikolai Fyodorov, the philosopher so important to Platonov—see chapter 23, note 1.) Two communes founded soon after the Revolution were also located in the area.
5. The name Chepurny hints at two dialect words: *chapurit'sya* ("to be self-important") and *chapurny* ("punctilious," "petty," "capricious"). There are probably at least three reasons for Chepurny's nickname: that his face looks Asiatic; that Chevengur, the city of the sun, is associated with Japan, the land of the rising sun; and that one of the most widespread folk legends about a faraway land of justice and peace is the legend of "White Water" (*Belovodye*), an archipelago believed to be close to Japan. Platonov refers to White Water in his 1926 story "Ivan Zhokh" (*Na beregu*, 123).

Chapter Twenty-Eight

1. A *pood* is a pre-Revolution measure of weight, equivalent to approximately forty pounds.
2. Several of Platonov's characters follow in the footsteps of *Don Quixote*. This exchange recalls an episode from the second chapter of Don Quixote: "The innkeeper asked if he had any money with him. Don Quixote replied that he did not have so much as a farthing, since he had never, in any history of wandering knights, read of a knight carrying money. 'Nowhere did knights ever pay for a night's lodging, or for anything else.'"
3. One million roubles was not an exorbitant sum. War Communism had wrecked the economy and led to hyperinflation.

Chapter Twenty-Nine

1. The name Drabanov occurs in Platonov's story "In the Fierce and Beautiful World" (1937) and Platonov also once used it as a pseudonym, signing a book review (1940) as "I. Drabanov." It is an invented name, derived from *drabant*, an obsolete term for a bodyguard. This is the only moment in the novel when the horse's sex is spelled out; Russian grammar allows this to be left unclear. Here, however, the peasants use the masculine *Ivanych* rather than the feminine *Ivanovna*—and a peasant would certainly be able to tell a mare from a stallion (Chandler, "*Pol zhivotnykh v povesti A. Platonova 'Dzhan'*" in *Baltiiskii filologicheskii kur'er* [Kaliningrad, 2003], 71).
2. It is clear from the general context that it is the economic benefits of NEP that have caused the "brigands" to grow quieter—but Kopionkin does not realize this.
3. On March 25, 1921, Lenin did indeed sign a decree purportedly granting more power to local organs of government "with the aim of decreasing bureaucracy" (*Sochineniia*, 3:670).
4. The summer of 1918 saw discussion of a large-scale project for "monumental propaganda." A list of fifty cultural and political figures to be commemorated was published on August 2. Among them were Spartak, Marx, Engels, Robespierre, and Stepan Razin; Tolstoy, Dostoevsky, Lermontov, Pushkin, Belinsky, and Chernyshevsky; Lomonosov and Mendeleyev; Rubliov and Vrubel; Mussorgsky and Scriabin. The spring of 1919 saw the publication of plans for monuments to Rosa Luxemburg and Karl Liebknecht, in both Moscow and Petrograd (*Sochineniia*, 3:671).

Chapter Thirty

1. Platonov's paternal grandfather was called Firs. The hero of "The Macedonian Officer" is also named Firs; the hero of "The River Potudan" is Nikita Firsov; and Platonov published several literary-critical articles under the pseudonym Firsov.
2. This episode is irrelevant to the plot but important symbolically. Firs is a positive figure and the dense, muddy water he so loves is a source of life and creativity, like Lake Mutevo. See chapter 1, note 3.
3. The mission of this Moscow daily newspaper was to reinforce the supposed union between the peasantry and the industrial workers. It supported the co-operative movement, which was established in Russia in

the 1860s and remained important until 1928, when Stalin introduced his first Five-Year Plan and began the enforced collectivization of agriculture.

4. Nikolay the Miracle Worker (270–343), also known as Saint Nicholas of Myra and Nicholas of Bari, was an early Christian bishop and martyr. In Russia, he was seen as a meek pilgrim and wanderer, a healer and defender of the poor—a counterpart to the frightening Elijah the Thunderer. The gentle Alexey Alexeyevich has much in common with Nikolay.
5. The threatening, potentially vengeful face of the Old Testament God, leader of "the heavenly hosts."
6. As well as the Orthodox Church and the Old Believers, there were many other breakaway sects in Russia. It was in central southern Russia—the provinces of Tambov, Oriol, and Voronezh—that these sects were most influential. In 1928 there were probably around ten to fifteen thousand sectarians in Voronezh Province alone. Contemporary Soviet newspaper reports are obviously untrustworthy, but many of these reports sound strikingly like passages of Platonov. For example, "In 1927, in the village of Novy Liman in Voronezh Province, Fyodor Rybalkin, the leader of the 'Fyodorovans,' tried to fly into the sky. One of his followers, a poor-peasant widow by the name of Koroleva, damaged her leg while trying to fly into the sky." And also: "The 'Fyodorovans' scheduled the Second Coming for January 1, 1926" (*Na beregu*, 217; see also chapter 23, note 4, and chapter 27, note 4).
7. The maiden name of Platonov's mother was Maria Vasilievna Lobochikhina.
8. Lenin was commonly believed to have said, "Any cook can manage the state." In reality, he said, "We are not utopians. We know that managing the state is not, at present, within the ability of every manual worker and every cook." The epigraph to Platonov's early article "Instruction in Government" reads "Our task is to instruct every cook in the management of the state." Platonov goes on to say, "When we are all truly equal and honest in all areas of life [...], then it will not be only the 'best,' chosen people who manage the state, but all of us, taking it in turn" (*Sochineniia*, 3:675).
9. The *zemstvo* was an organ of local government. Established in 1864, three years after the emancipation of the serfs, these democratically elected councils were responsible for building schools, hospitals, roads,

and so forth. They were central to the liberal movement during the last fifty years of tsarism but were closed down soon after the October Revolution.

Chapter Thirty-One

1. The Soviet tradition of *Subbotniki*—Saturdays during which people "volunteered" to work on a variety of social projects—dates back to May 1, 1920, when Lenin himself took part in the first "All-Russian Subbotnik," helping to clear building rubble from the Kremlin. Participation in Subbotniki soon ceased to be voluntary—if ever it was.
2. This name hints at the dialect *piukha* or *piuka*, meaning "drunkard" (*Na beregu*, 295).
3. To the young Platonov, the idea of the sun as a laborer and ally of the proletariat was more than a poetic image. In "Light and Socialism" (July 1922), Platonov wrote:

> Socialism needs a physical force equivalent to it, in order to become a solid thing and to assert its worldwide dominance. [...] The name of this force is light, the ordinary scattered daily light of the sun, but also the light of the moon and the stars. We want to harness this force to drive our machine tools. [...] Let us remember that the basis of the world of plants is light. Let us make light the basis of the world of man too. [...] Phototechnology must construct the mechanism that will transform sunlight into ordinary working electric current, to power our electric motors. Such a machine has already been half constructed. It is called a photoelectric resonator-transformer. [...] Socialist production must be founded on light—otherwise socialism will never come into being, there will be only an eternal "transitional epoch." Socialism will come only when light has been harnessed as a motor of production. Only then will the production of light give rise to a socialist society; to a new man—a being full of consciousness, wonder, and love; and to the universal sculpture and planetary architecture that will be Communist art. Only then will humanity be united into a single physical being.
>
> (*Sochineniia*, 1(2):218–20)

In "The Struggle against the Desert" (December 1924), Platonov wrote:

> The restitution of the losses brought about by transformations of the elemental productive forces of the soil must be carried out at the expense of the sun. [...] The earth must be whole and virgin,

> while all the splendid life of humanity runs its course at the expense of the sun. (*Sochineniia*, 1(2):276)

And in 1926, in "Solar Motors," he wrote:

> The telegram in the newspapers about the projected solar energy station in Tashkent, the first in the Soviet Union, tells us about a fact of great power. The direct exploitation of the rays of the sun as a source of mechanical energy is one of the paths that the technology of the future must inevitably follow in countries where there is a lot of sun and little fuel. (*Sochineniia*, 3:678)

4. The Soviet security service, founded on December 5, 1917, was renamed many times; the most important of its names and acronyms, in chronological order, are the Cheka, the OGPU, the NKVD, and the KGB. The word *Cheka* is itself an acronym, formed from the initial letters of the Russian words for "Extraordinary Committee."
5. Surprising though it may seem, there was nothing unusual at this time about a soviet being located in a church. All church buildings and other property had been appropriated by the state, and people were exhorted to use churches just as they might use any other large building (*Sochineniia*, 3:679).
6. Words spoken by Christ in the Gospel according to Saint Matthew, 11:28.
7. The Socialist Revolutionaries (the SRs) were an agrarian socialist party with broad support among the Russian peasantry. In 1917–18 they were the Bolsheviks' main rivals, but they were soon marginalized. The first major trial of SRs took place in Moscow in the summer of 1922; twelve SR leaders were sentenced to death, though the sentence was not immediately carried out (*Sochineniia*, 3:679).
8. The ambo (or ambon) is the platform from which the deacon reads the Gospel. It is considered part of the sanctuary, and only the clergy and those about to receive the Eucharist go up onto it.
9. This textbook by Vasily Yevtushevsky was republished many times in the early twentieth century.
10. Chepurny and Prokofy are in some respects modeled on Moses and Aaron. When God chooses him to lead the Israelites out of Egypt, Moses is initially reluctant: "And Moses said unto the Lord, O my Lord, I am not eloquent [...] but I am slow of speech, and of a slow tongue." Eventually the Lord agreed to allow Aaron to be Moses's spokesman:

> Is not Aaron the Levite thy brother? I know that he can speak well. [...] And thou shalt speak unto him, and put words in his mouth:

> and I will be with thy mouth, and with his mouth, and will teach you what ye shall do. And he shall be thy spokesman unto the people: and he shall be, even he shall be to thee instead of a mouth, and thou shalt be to him instead of God. (Exodus 4:10–16)

11. During the 1920s and 1930s, Russians usually referred to the First World War as "the German war" or "the tsarist war."
12. An allusion to "On the New Russian Idealism," a critique by the religious philosopher Nikolay Berdiaev of contemporary philosophical systems that, in his view, ignored the living variety and richness of the real world: "Idealism and pessimism join touchingly together, amounting in the end to one and the same thing: a philosophy of a subject without a predicate" (*Na beregu*, 298).
13. The sun's cultural symbolism is inexhaustible, but one of Platonov's allusions may be to *The City of the Sun*, a fictional account by the Dominican philosopher Tommaso Campanella (1568–1639) of a utopian city where everyone works equal hours and all work is accorded equal dignity. There are no servants and no personal possessions; everything —food, houses, women, children—is held in common.

Chapter Thirty-Two

1. Several of Platonov's characters profess a similar faith in the joy and benefit of movement. The hero of "Ethereal Tract" (1926), writes in a letter:

> Only wandering over the earth, under the sun's various rays and over the earth's various hidden depths, am I able to think. [. . .] External forces are needed to awaken thoughts. These forces are scattered about the roads of the earth; it is necessary to seek them out and place one's head and body beneath them, as if beneath a downpour. You know what I am doing and searching for—the root of the world, the soil from which the universe has grown. [. . .] Apart from that, you know my living muscles. They need tension and exhaustion—otherwise I would wear myself down and kill myself. [. . .] Perhaps this is an illness, an unfortunate inheritance from ancestors who were vagabonds and wanderers, making pilgrimages to Kyiv. (*Sochineniia*, 2:84)

2. The early Bolsheviks mostly believed that true socialism could be established only through world revolution. In 1924, however, Stalin put forward the view that socialism could be achieved in a single country. Prokofy's proposal accords with this revision of Bolshevik doctrine.

3. The Whites had been defeated long ago and this area was entirely under Communist control. Kopionkin cannot conceive of the Revolution being threatened by any force other than the Whites.

Chapter Thirty-Three

1. These words mark the beginning of a flashback. The events described in this chapter seem to take place in 1919, two years before Kopionkin's first appearance in Chevengur.
2. One of Chevengur's historical prototypes is the German city of Münster, which was ruled by radical Anabaptists from February 1534 until June 1535. The Anabaptist leader Jan Matthys ordered all "nonbelievers" to be executed, but the mayor then ordered them merely to be exiled.
3. At least two of these surnames occur in other works by Platonov: Komiagin in *Happy Moscow*, and Zavyn-Duvailo in "Appropriate Measures" (*Nadlezhashchiye meropriyatiya*, 1927). A historical Siusiukalov was a member of the Voronezh Revolutionary Tribunal and was responsible for the execution of participants in the Kalitva 1921 uprising; with characteristic irony, Platonov subjects a real executioner to a fictional execution (*Na beregu*, 302).
4. A folk belief to which Platonov often refers. Interestingly, in an article about translating the Bible, the scholar and translator Robert Alter writes of the important Hebrew term *nephesh*:

> There is no Hebrew concept of a soul distinct from the body. The term itself is explicitly rooted in the body—its primary meaning is "life-breath." From there it branches out in several directions to mean also the life of the individual person, [...] and, by metonymy, "throat" or "neck" (the passageway of the life-breath). [...]
>
> At the beginning of Psalm 63 we have "God, my God, for You I search. / My soul thirsts for You, // my flesh yearns for you / in a land waste and parched, with no water." All the translations I have looked at use "soul" for *nephesh* here. "My soul thirsts for You" is beautiful, but in all likelihood wrong. If you consider the immediate context of a land waste and parched, with no water, and the poetic parallelism of "flesh," the compelling sense is "throat." Now, "My throat thirsts for You" is not as beautiful as "My soul thirsts for You," but it has its own poetic power. (Robert Alter, "Putting Words in His Mouth," review of *On the Translation of the Bible*, by John Barton, *Times Literary Supplement*, December 16, 2022)

5. Members of the Constitutional Democrats, an important moderate political party in early twentieth-century Russia, were nicknamed the Cadets—after the initial letters, *C* and *D*, of the party's name. In 1917, Red Army soldiers and others often confused this with other meanings of the word: for example, young aristocratic "cadets" in military academies.

Chapter Thirty-Four

1. Fish are associated with Christ. In both Orthodox Christianity and folk religious belief, they are associated with spiritual truth more generally. This image of a fish being caught yet returned to the water may suggest that truth is often ignored, even after being found.
2. In 1926 Dziga Vertov directed a silent film titled *A Sixth Part of the World*, a travelogue emphasizing the wealth and variety of the Soviet land and peoples. The belief that the Soviet Union covered a sixth of the earth's surface then became a generally accepted part of Soviet mythology.
3. Sasha misremembers the story. In the standard version, the threesome go out to chop wood. They need to cross a river. The bast sandal tells the straw to stretch itself across the river to make a bridge. The straw breaks as the bast sandal walks along it. The bubble then laughs and laughs, till it bursts. Sasha's positive take on the story may be an indication of his overoptimistic understanding of the world.

Chapter Thirty-Five

1. A refreshing drink, lightly alcoholic, usually made from stale bread.
2. This phrase first occurs in Isaiah 61:1–2: "The Spirit of the Lord God is upon me; because the Lord hath anointed me to preach good tidings. [...] To proclaim the acceptable year of the Lord, and the day of vengeance of our God; to comfort all that mourn." Christ quotes the words "the acceptable year of the Lord" in Luke 4:19.
3. In "Che-Che-O" (1928), a short sketch told in the first person, Platonov writes, "I wandered about the town, read signboards, and thought about the unpaved hell bottom along which the Revolution was now walking barefoot." The similar wording highlights Platonov's awareness of the similarities between the Bolsheviks and the apocalyptic sects that were so influential in Central Russia.
4. Later these eleven men will be joined by a twelfth, with the biblical name Simon. These twelve Bolsheviks parallel Christ's twelve apostles.

5. A common style of Italian dessert wine. One of several possible explanations for its name is that a similar wine was produced in the Greek island of Santorini. This was exported to Russia and adopted by the Orthodox Church as its main Communion wine. It was also widely drunk by the laity; being both sweet and strong, it could be kept for a long time, even after being opened.

Chapter Thirty-Six

1. See "The History of Chevengur," p. 481 in the present work, for a longer, draft version of this account of the town's history.
2. After seizing power in Münster in February 1534 (see chapter 33, note 2), the Anabaptists distributed pamphlets throughout northern Germany, calling the poor to join them in their New Jerusalem and share in the city's wealth.
3. A kind of open carriage. Drawn by one or two horses, a phaeton had a lightly sprung body and large wheels. It was fast and dangerous—which is why it was named after Phaeton, who nearly set the earth on fire while trying to drive the chariot of the sun.
4. In *Diary of My Meetings*, the artist Yury Annenkov comments on how well some of the leading Bolsheviks lived during "the hungry years of the Revolution." He singles out Grigory Zinoviev, who apparently returned to Russia "as thin as a rake" and then put on so much weight that he became known as "Rum Baba" (Annenkov, *Dnevnik moikh vstrech* [Leningrad: Iskusstvo, 1991], p. 32).
5. That is, the Comintern or Communist International. This worldwide organization held seven congresses in Moscow between 1919 and 1935. After Stalin abandoned the goal of world revolution, it gradually lost its importance and was finally dissolved in 1943.
6. His surname means "ancient" or "agelong."
7. The woman's "touching voice" and her dream of being a fish suggest that she may be a *rusalka*, a water spirit much like a mermaid. This episode as a whole can be read as a reworking of a classic folktale motif: In the standard versions, a young woman is locked in a barrel along with her son or brother and cast into the sea; miraculously, the two end up in some other land, where they set up a new and happier kingdom. Platonov's darker version serves, among other things, to illustrate the fate of art and artists under the murderous rule of Chepurny and Prokofy.

The barrel symbolizes an egg, but the Chevengur Bolsheviks do not allow anything to develop from it.

8. A breed of hens developed in the United States in the mid-nineteenth century. They are large, colorful, and productive.
9. The island in the sea may be a reference to *Utopia* (1516), a partly satirical account by Thomas More of the political system of an island state.
10. This quatrain can be read as a summary of the entire novel.

Chapter Thirty-Seven

1. Many characters throughout Platonov's works refer to themselves as "nobody" or "nothing." In *The Foundation Pit*, when an orphaned girl is first brought to the worksite, a worker asks her who she is—and she replies, "I'm nobody." This blankness can be understood as a closeness to death or, more positively, as an emptiness allowing room for infinite possibilities. The Chevengur Bolsheviks look on the *others* as the seed of a new humanity, perhaps remembering a line from the "Internationale": "*Nous ne sommes rien, soyons tout!*" ("We have been nothing, let us be everything!") (*Na beregu*, 151–52).
2. Chepurny ends his speech with allusions to two famous Communist texts. First, he quotes, with one significant change, another line from the "Internationale": "We will destroy the whole world of violence." Then he quotes the conclusion of "The Communist Manifesto" (1848): "proletarians of all lands, unite!"
3. An almost exact quotation from Lenin's article "The Routine Tasks of Soviet Power" (April 1918). This ends, "We need the measured tread of iron battalions of the proletariat" (*Sochineniia*, 3:690).
4. "A Great Beginning" is the title of the article in which Lenin first proposed the organization of Communist *Subbotniki* (i.e., voluntary working Saturdays; see chapter 31, note 1).
5. The chronology of *Chevengur* is far from straightforward; the various episodes are not told in chronological order. The reader first encounters Chepurny in chapter 25, at a party conference in the provincial capital. Chepurny is evidently now on his way to attend this same party conference.

Chapter Thirty-Eight

1. During the 1921 famine, people were driven to cannibalism; instances

in the Boguchar District were reported in the press. The boy's nightmare may hint at this.

2. The tragic death of a child is a repeated theme in Platonov's work. In the unfinished story "Lobskaya Hill," he writes, "The child cried a little and stopped: it had died after living a short while, perhaps two hours; it was as if it had merely half opened the door into the world, and then not gone in, because it had made a mistake and come to the wrong place" (Andrey Platonov, *The Return* [London: Harvill, 1999]). In *The Foundation Pit*, as in *Chevengur*, a child's death symbolizes the failure of a utopian project. A workers' collective adopts a small girl who embodies their hope for a better world. Her death from fever throws them into despair.
3. Bast is not a good protection against the cold. Felt is warmer.
4. The Red Star was introduced in the spring and summer of 1918 as the emblem of the Red Army. The gold hammer and sickle at its center symbolized the union of the industrial workers and peasantry; the color red symbolized Mars—the god of war—and the Revolution itself.

Chapter Thirty-Nine

1. See chapter 31, note 8.
2. This was made from boiled wheat or other grains and sweetened with raisins and honey. It was a traditional Christmas food and also a standard part of a funeral feast.
3. In *Thus Spoke Zarathustra*, in the section "On Love of One's Neighbor," Nietzsche wrote, "I do not exhort you to love your neighbor: I exhort you to love of the most distant."
4. *Yakov* is the Russian for *Jacob*, and Yakov Titych is modeled in part on the biblical Jacob, the father of the twelve tribes of Israel. Jacob dreams of angels climbing up and down a ladder leading to heaven; on another occasion he wrestles with God, who has taken the form of an angel. The story of Jacob and the angel is a recurrent theme in Platonov's work. The hero of "A Clay House in a Small-Town Garden" is also a blacksmith called Yakov—and he imagines that a boy knocking on his window may be an angel. (See *Na beregu*, 155–57.) Linked to this theme is the image of flying or falling upward. In an early story titled "Notes" (*Zametki*), Platonov wrote, "I was walking along a deep gully. [. . .] If one looks at a star intently, horror enters one's soul. One can weep from hopelessness and ineffable torment—so very distant is this star. One can think about

infinity—that is easy enough—but now I'm seeing it, reaching it and hearing its silence. To me it seems that I'm flying and there is only the light of the unreachable bottom of the well and the walls of the abyss are not moving in spite of my flight" (*Sochineniia*, 1[1]:184).

5. Here Prokofy almost paraphrases the thoughts of Dostoevsky's Grand Inquisitor. The Inquisitor considers humanity unable to cope with the freedom granted it by Jesus. By granting humanity freedom of choice, Jesus has doomed it to suffering.
6. In book 3, chapter 3 of *The Brothers Karamazov*, Dmitry Karamazov says, "Yes, man is broad, too broad, indeed. I'd have him narrower." And in *The Demons*, Piotr Verkhovensky puts forward a program that will lead to "Total obedience. Total impersonality."
7. Here too Platonov reproduces the thoughts of the Grand Inquisitor: "The most painful secrets of their conscience, all, all they will bring to us, and we shall have an answer for all. And they will be glad to believe our answer, for it will save them from the great anxiety and terrible agony they endure at present in making a free decision for themselves. And all will be happy, all the millions of creatures except the hundred thousand who rule over them. For only we, we who guard the mystery, shall be unhappy. There will be thousands of millions of happy babes, and a hundred thousand sufferers who have taken upon themselves the curse of the knowledge of good and evil." (Translation by Constance Garnett.)

Chapter Forty

1. The London–Calcutta telegraph line functioned from 1870 until 1931.
2. This geographical error is probably intentional on Platonov's part—though not, of course, on Sasha's. Solitude Island is located in the Arctic. Sasha may be thinking of the Society Islands in French Polynesia. The confusion between "solitude" and "society" is pointed.
3. Platonov may be alluding to Captain Lebiadkin, a minor character in Dostoevsky's *The Demons*. Lebiadkin is a drunk, a thief, a blackmailer, and the author of several absurd poems, one of which is about a cockroach.
4. For locomotives, see chapter 15, note 6. It is significant that Nazar Chagataev, the hero of *Soul* (1935), chooses to descend from his train and cover a long distance on foot, as if aware that there can be no quick and easy journey to a new world.

5. The Chevengurians may have taken this man for the Messiah. The image of God among the clouds appears several times in the Bible; e.g., "And then shall appear the sign of the Son of man in heaven: and then shall all the tribes of the earth mourn, and they shall see the Son of man coming in the clouds of heaven with power and great glory" (Matthew 24:30); "Behold, he cometh with clouds; and every eye shall see him, and they also which pierced him: and all kindreds of the earth shall wail because of him. Even so, Amen" (Revelations 1:7).

   This may also be a reference to Agasfer, the Wandering Jew, described in chapter 14 as "a man living alone, right on the line of the horizon." (See chapter 14, note 6.) In "The Impossible" (1921), a story about a visionary scientist and inventor, Platonov wrote:

   > Not long ago, this undying Agasfer appeared on the roads of our world and disappeared forever, having done nothing—having been sent here to do everything, to set on fire or blow up this great bulk of a universe that has turned to stone, and to throw open the doors of mysteries leading to free expanses of power and miracle. Among us who are dead and sleeping, he alone was alive and anxious. And through his disappearance, through his death, he proved to us that there is another universe. And all people must follow his path. [...] A melancholy and affectionate wanderer, Agasfer passed by and showed the way, showing nothing and saying nothing. We must see the world through his clouded and yearning eyes (*Sochineniia*, 1[1]:193)

6. A millrhynd is the metal arch that supports the millstone and around which the millstone pivots. (See, for example, "Millstones from England," Center for Medieval Studies, Pennsylvania State University, https://www.engr.psu.edu/MTAH/photos/photos_millstones.htm.)
7. In 1921–22, Platonov was himself doing similar work. (*Sochineniia*, 3:698.)
8. The Roma woman is twisting a Russian saying ("*Khleb vmeste, a tabachok popolam*") meaning that bread is shared communally while tobacco is to be enjoyed privately—i.e., that there are some things that even friends do not share. In this woman's version, both bread and love are to be enjoyed communally.
9. The woman's last words echo Christ's words to his disciples: "Verily, verily, I say unto you, He that heareth my word, and believeth on him that

sent me, hath everlasting life, and shall not come into condemnation; but is passed from death unto life" (John 5:24).

10. A quotation, slightly adapted, from Gogol's "Notebook 1846–51."

Chapter Forty-One

1. Gleb Uspensky (1843–1902) was a populist writer and journalist. Much of his work is devoted to the living conditions of the Russian peasantry. Platonov's account in the first pages of *Chevengur* of the life and death of the loner is in the spirit of such passages of Uspensky as the following: "For a man living in immediate contact with the natural world, life and death are almost fused into one" (*Sochineniia*, 3:577).
2. Another allusion to *The Brothers Karamazov*. In book 2, chapter 4, Zosima recounts how a doctor once said to him:

   The more I love humanity in general, the less I love man in particular. In my dreams [...] I have often come to making enthusiastic schemes for the service of humanity. And yet [...] I become hostile to people the moment they come close to me. But it has always happened that the more I detest men individually the more ardent becomes my love for humanity. (Translation by Constance Garnett.)
3. In 1925, there was indeed 20 percent less land under cultivation than there was before the First World War.
4. A type of educational institution, existing from 1919 until the mid-1930s, that prepared Soviet workers and peasants for institutes of higher education.
5. Abortion was a dangerous operation. Poor women, especially among the peasantry, often chose to go through with the pregnancy and then kill or abandon the newborn baby.
6. There is a hint of irony in the words "coupled himself to the Bolsheviks." At the same time as representing the more skeptical Platonov of the late 1920s, Serbinov is modeled on Viktor Shklovsky, who spent several weeks traveling around Voronezh Province in 1925 (see chapter 19, note 4). Platonov would have known that Shklovsky had been an active member of the Socialist Revolutionary Party (see chapter 42, note 5). As such, he was threatened with arrest and possible execution, and in 1922 he escaped to Berlin. After appealing to the Soviet authorities, he was allowed to return to the Soviet Union in late 1923. (A. Yu. Galushkin, "K istorii lichnykh i tvorcheskikh otnoshenii A. P. Platonova i V. B.

Shklovskogo," in N. V. Kornienko and E. D. Shubina, *Andrey Platonov: Vospominaniya Sovremennikov* [Moscow: Sov. pisatel', 1994], 182. See also Viktor Shklovsky, *Third Factory*, trans. Richard Shelton [Chicago: Dalkey Archive Press, 2002], 80.)

7. Serbinov is parodying a passage from the Psalms: "I am troubled; I am bowed down greatly; I go mourning all the day long. / For my loins are filled with a loathsome disease; and there is no soundness in my flesh" (Psalms 38:6-7).
8. An important daily newspaper, published 1922–32. By 1927, it had a circulation of three hundred thousand.
9. For typhus, see chapter 11, note 2.
10. There is disagreement about when Platonov's mother died, but it was certainly between 1927 and 1929, while Platonov was working on *Chevengur*. Her death is reflected not only here but also in Kopionkin's dream of his dead mother (chapter 24). In his account of "the first day of communism," in the left-hand margin opposite the words "Chepurny lay down on the straw" (chapter 35), Platonov wrote, "Help me, Mama, to remember and to keep living" (*Arkhiv A. P. Platonova* [Moscow: IMLI RAN, 2019], 2:366). Natalia Kornienko comments, "In Platonov's artistic world, the dead are the chief advisers to his heroes." She goes on to quote two passages from his notebooks: the sentence "Only the dead, of course, can nourish the living in all senses," and a fragment of dialogue: "'The dead will give you advice.' 'Why?' 'Because they are impartial.'" ("Akademicheskii Platonov," in *Andrey Platonov i khudozhestvennye iskaniya 20–ogo veka*, ed. T. A. Nikonova [Voronezh: VGU, 2019], 85.)

Chapter Forty-Two

1. In his early articles, Platonov wrote about electricity with religious fervor:

   > Electricity is a revolution in technology that has the same significance as the revolution of October 1917. [...] The path of the coal from mine to furnace is the road to Calvary; during this journey the most precious red blood of life is eaten by the sufferings of resistance. [...] Communism fights not only against Capital but also against Nature. Electrification is our best long-range artillery in our struggle against this Nature. [...] Electricity is a light, elusive spirit of love; it comes out of everything and goes into everything where there is energy." ("Electrification," in *Sochineniia*, 1[2]:133-142)

Platonov, however, was far from being an impractical visionary. During 1923 and 1924, for example, he managed, in chaotic conditions and with minimal funding, to plan and construct two hydroelectric power stations and one small turf-fired power station. In his proposal for the latter he wrote, "This power station will illuminate 300 peasant huts (assuming one 25-candlepower bulb in each hut). During the day it will power a mill and help to irrigate the communal vegetable garden, thus insuring the population of the village of Bobiakovo against drought" (*Strana Filosofov*, [Moscow: IMLI RAN, 2000], 4:764).

2. Sasha's thoughts are close to those of the young Platonov. In "Electrification" (see previous note), Platonov writes:

> What does the proletariat live by, spiritually speaking? It lives by labor. [...] By labor—insofar as man loses himself in labor, forgetting that he needs a life with meaning, with an aim, with goodness and joy, etc. Labor swallows up life and frees man from life. [...] Labor is like sleep. Until now, mankind has slept in the sleep of labor, and thanks to labor it has stayed whole. [...] The electrification of the world is a step toward our awakening from the sleep of labor, the beginning of our liberation from labor, the transfer of production to the machine, the beginning of a truly new form of life that no one until now has foreseen. (*Sochineniia*, 1[2]:142)

3. From 1920 to 1922 Platonov himself tried to develop such a machine: "a photo-electric resonator-transformer." He mentions this in several early stories and articles, and he included "the transformation of light into ordinary working electric current" in a list of projects to be undertaken in a laboratory he was setting up for the Voronezh provincial government (*Sochineniia*, 1[1]581–82; and 3:704). Platonov may have been inspired by a passage about a similar invention in Émile Zola's utopian novel *Labor* (*Travail*, 1901). See also chapter 31, note 3.
4. See chapter 29, note 4. At this time, monuments to important revolutionary figures were often made of clay and other cheap materials. Those judged successful might then be cast in bronze. Such monuments were often criticized in the Soviet press—as poor likenesses and for failing to convey the right revolutionary spirit. (*Sochineniia*, 3:705.)
5. The literary historian A. Yu. Galushkin points out that the words "clever, ambiguous, hostile, and mocking" aptly describe Shklovsky's *Third Factory* as a whole. (*Andrey Platonov: Vospominaniya Sovremennikov*, 182.) Platonov seems to have been consistently hostile to Shklovsky, perhaps

irritated by his breezy wit and seeing him as a city intellectual removed from the real world and with little capacity for emotional empathy. In "Literature Factory" (1926), he parodies Shklovsky's theories about "Left Art." In an ironical inscription to a book given to him by Shklovsky in 1927, Platonov refers to him as "the greatly respected maestro of life and cinematography" and "the inventor of formalism, the bureaucratism of literature." And in the short story "Among Animals and Plants," he mocks Shklovsky's penchant for montage. (See my introduction to Andrey Platonov, *Soul and Other Stories* [New York: NYRB Classics, 2007], xxv–xxvi.) Shklovsky, on the other hand, greatly admired Platonov. In *Third Factory* he shows a genuine appreciation of the importance of Platonov's work in land reclamation. A central theme of this largely autobiographical book is Shklovsky's difficulty in finding a place for himself in the new Soviet world. Most of the other writers he encounters seem to be similarly disorientated. Platonov, by contrast, is in the right place at the right time—supervising the digging of wells and ponds, clearing silted-up rivers, doing what he can to combat rural poverty. (*Andrey Platonov: Vospominaniya Sovremennikov*, 183.)

Paradoxically, Serbinov is also another of Platonov's self-portraits. Sasha Dvanov represents the young, idealistic Platonov of the years immediately after the Revolution; Serbinov represents the mature, somewhat disillusioned Platonov of the late 1920s.

Chapter Forty-Three

1. Another allusion to Kitezh. See chapter 1, note 4; chapter 10, note 4; and chapter 27, note 3.
2. A "Bolshevik foxtrot" is an oxymoron. In the early 1920s the Bolsheviks considered the foxtrot decadent, bourgeois, and potentially corrupting. For "Little Apple," see chapter 14, note 2.
3. Prokofy is quoting from "Whirlwinds of Danger" (*Varshavianka*) a revolutionary song composed in Poland between 1879 and 1883. It was adopted as an anthem by Polish revolutionaries in 1905 and later, with altered lyrics, by Russian revolutionaries. An English version by Douglas Robson begins

   Whirlwinds of danger are raging around us,
   O'erwhelming forces of darkness assail,
   Still in the fight see advancing before us,
   Red flag of liberty that yet shall prevail.

4. Here we have smoothed over a minor inconsistency in the original. On his first appearance in chapter 22, Pashintsev is addressed as Maxim Stepanych; at this point in the Russian text, he is addressed as Vasya.
5. A seminomadic Turkic people from Central Asia.
6. Under the rule of Prokofy and Chepurny, there was no place for art; when a woman with "a touching voice" was heard singing inside a barrel, Zheyev said, "We need fellow feeling, not art," and the barrel was allowed to crash to the bottom of a ravine. In Sasha Dvanov's kinder and more comradely Chevengur, however, art is accorded high value. The Chevengurians' new understanding is perhaps best conveyed in a sentence from Platonov's sketch "Che-Che-O" (1928): "Art is the most precious of things, it draws one person closer to another—and nothing is more difficult and necessary than that."
7. Prosha is, in fact, younger than Sasha. Sasha was first sent out begging when he was eleven years old and Prosha was seven.
8. Perhaps an ironic allusion to a 1927 painting by M. G. Sokolov, *V. I. Lenin at the All-Russian Subbotnik in the Kremlin on May 1, 1920*. (See chapter 31, note 1, and chapter 37, note 4.)

Chapter Forty-Four

1. The Bolsheviks saw the Cossacks and the Cadets as the two most dangerous defenders of the old order. (For Cadets, see chapter 33, note 5.)

Chapter Forty-Five

1. In his preface to his first published book, the poetry collection *The Blue Depth*, Platonov wrote, "The bell of the Chugunka church was the settlement's only music. During quiet summer evenings, the beggars, the old women, and I myself listened to it with deep feeling." And in a later unfinished story, "The Gift of Life," he wrote:

   > Like an eternal time, childhood remains in someone's memories without moving. Later time—the time of youth and maturity—flows, passes by, and expends itself in oblivion, but childhood remains like a lake in the windless country of our memory, and its image is preserved unchanging inside a person until the very end.

2. See chapter 33, note 4. This image of the skeleton fish on a hook may repeat the suggestion that truth, even when found, is often ignored.
3. The tone of this last episode is uncertain. Sasha may simply be committing suicide, thrown into despair by the destruction of Chevengur and

the death of Kopionkin. Or he may, in some metaphorical and more positive sense, be "continuing his own life." Leonid Karasiov writes: "As he dies, Dvanov resurrects the life-creating meaning of water, transforming a lake-tomb into a lake-womb. [. . .] He is united not only with his father [. . .] but also with his mother. He returns to the womb of the mother-earth [Lake Mutevo—see chapter 1, note 3] from which he himself, his father, and all other people first emerged into the world" (*Na beregu*, 73).

THE HISTORY OF CHEVENGUR

1. *Sochineniia*, 3:571-73.

PLATONOV'S PEOPLE

1. A reference to "The Synodicon of Those Who Fell into Disgrace under Tsar Ivan the Terrible." In the novel *Before & During*, Sharov's narrator says of this historical document:

   > For thirty years a human being [Tsar Ivan] murders other human beings without compunction and now, on his deathbed, he begins to recall them and to set aside a certain amount of money for prayers in their memory. Some he recalls himself, others are recalled by his accomplices, but there are many, needless to say, they can't recall: they didn't even know their names when they killed them. And so, Ivan leaves money for monks to remember even those whom, as he writes, "You know Yourself, Lord." (Vladimir Sharov, *Before & During*, trans. Oliver Ready [Sawtry, UK: Dedalus Books, 2014], 16)

2. In 1984 Sharov defended his "candidate's dissertation" (roughly equivalent to a PhD) on the studies of late sixteenth- and early seventeenth-century Russia written by the historian Sergey Platonov (1860–1933; no relation of Andrey Platonov). In the late 1970s and mid-1980s, Sharov also spent six years working at the All-Russian Scientific and Research Institute for Records and Archives Management (VNIIDAD). The conference Sharov mentions took place in Moscow, and the proceedings appeared in the sixth issue of *Strana filosofov* (Moscow: IMLI RAN, 2005).
3. The notion that after the fall of Constantinople (the "second" Rome), Rus might accede to the role of guardian of Orthodoxy was articulated most famously by Filofey (Philotheus), a monk from Pskov, who wrote in the early sixteenth century that "two Romes have fallen, but a third stands, and a fourth there shall not be."

4. Attempts to combine military and agricultural life had already been made in Russia under Alexander I, who, taking a cue from his minister of war, Alexander Arakcheyev, had established military settlements where soldiers could own property and practice the latest agricultural methods. The settlements proved extremely unpopular.
5. From Platonov's 1920 article "Vechnaya zhizn'" ["Life Eternal"], *Sochineniia*, 1(2):66–68.
6. "Normalizovannyi rabotnik" ["The Normalized Worker"], *Sochineniia*, 1(2):132.
7. *Sochineniia*, 1(2):132
8. These last two sentences have been added from a shorter version of this essay, published in Vladimir Sharov's *Iskushenie revolyutsiei (russkaya verkhovnaya vlast')* [Temptation by Revolution (Russian Supreme Power)] (Moscow: ArsisBooks, 2009), 65.
9. Andrey Platonov, *Zapisnye knizhki. Materialy k biografii* [Notebooks: Materials toward a Biography] (Moscow: IMLI RAN "Nasledie," 2000), 171.
10. Platonov, 64.
11. Platonov, 229.

TRANSLATING PLATONOV

1. E. A. Yablokov, *Na beregu neba: roman Andreya Platonova "Chevengur"* (Saint Petersburg: 2001), 201.
2. Eric Naiman, "The Thematic Mythology of Andrej Platonov," *Russian Literature* 21, no. 2 (February 1987): 210, https://doi.org/10.1016/0304-3479(87)90038-X.
3. Yevgeny Yablokov, "Khudozhestvennaya filosofiya prirody," in *Vestnik Moskovskogo universiteta*, series 9, *Filologiya*, no. 6 (1988): 57.
4. Mikhail Geller, *Andrey Platonov v poiskakh shchastia* (Paris: YMCA Press, 1982), 222.
5. "Mama, a otchego ty umiraesh'—ottogo, chto burzhuika, ili ot smerti?" (Andrey Platonov, *Kotlovan* [Saint Petersburg: Nauka, 2000], 52).

Discover more in **VINTAGE CLASSICS** red spine

Brave New World	Aldous Huxley
To Kill a Mockingbird	Harper Lee
Catch-22	Joseph Heller
Native Son	Richard Wright
The Handmaid's Tale	Margaret Atwood
The Gulag Archipelago	Aleksandr Solzhenitsyn
The Master and Margarita	Mikhail Bulgakov
Beloved	Toni Morrison
Stoner	John Williams
The Sailor Who Fell from Grace with the Sea	Yukio Mishima
The Savage Detectives	Roberto Bolaño
The Joy Luck Club	Amy Tan
Autobiography of Red	Anne Carson
I Who Have Never Known Men	Jacqueline Harpman
Oranges Are Not the Only Fruit	Jeanette Winterson
Disgrace	J. M. Coetzee
My Left Foot	Christy Brown
Sugar	Bernice L. McFadden
Death and the Penguin	Andrey Kurkov
Persepolis	Marjane Satrapi